"Historically accurate and deftly told, *Without Warning* is a riveting saga of Union leadership at the Battle of Gettysburg. The challenges General George Meade faced upon taking command of the Army of the Potomac three days before the battle, and how he inspired his subordinates to a remarkable victory over the undefeated Robert E. Lee, make for a gripping and illuminating story of character under great pressure—every bit as timely today as it was fateful in Meade's time. Superb!"

—Lieutenant General Christopher Miller, USAF, retired, Former Deputy Chief of Staff for Strategic Plans and Programs, HQ USAF, and President, Air Force Historical Foundation

"Fighting men and women want leaders of character…it's a central, unchanging aspect of the Profession of Arms. In this brilliant historical novel, Terry Pierce extracts from the chaotic tapestry of Gettysburg the moral character of General George Gordon Meade, an individual who reluctantly took command of the Potomac army and led it to victory over the forces of the vaunted General Robert E. Lee some six days later. In the process, he replaced the Napoleonic frontal attacks learned at West Point with the dominance of tactical defense. Most importantly, he demonstrated that camaraderie and combat effectiveness are forged by character, not charisma and popularity. This lesson continues today."

—Lieutenant General Erv Rokke, USAF, retired, former Dean of the United States Air Force Academy, President of Moravian College, Defense Attaché in the former Soviet Union, Director of Intelligence, the U.S. European Command in Europe

*Tom —
Great book
Check out page 734 —
a first for me.
Bro Tom Dick*

*July 2020*

# WITHOUT WARNING:
## THE SAGA OF GETTYSBURG,
### A RELUCTANT UNION HERO, AND THE MEN HE INSPIRED

# TERRY C. PIERCE

Heart Ally Books
Camano Island, Washington

Cover design: Deranged Doctor Designs
Cover art: *Expecting a Battle* by Dale Gallon
www.gallon.com

Maps created by: Aaron "Taldoz" Matney

Published by:
Heart Ally Books
26910 92nd Ave NW C5-406, Stanwood, WA 98292
Published on Camano Island, WA, USA
www.heartallybooks.com

ISBN-13: (epub) 978-1-63107-026-6
ISBN-13: (paperback) 978-1-63107-028-0
ISBN-13: (hardcover) 978-1-63107-027-3
Library of Congress Control Number: 2020935531
12 11 10 9 8 7 6 5 4 3

# Dedication

For Fred Rainbow, a quiet leader of character who mentored two generations of Navy officers and whose great-grandfather, Frederick Lee Rainbow, earned a battlefield commission serving in Sickles's Third Corps on the second day of fighting at Gettysburg. Thank you, Fred, for your unwavering enthusiasm and support for this novel and throughout my 28-year naval career. You are truly the best of the best!

General George Meade

# Friends and Foes Comment on General George Meade

"Meade, in my judgment, had the greatest ability. I feared him more than any man I ever met upon the field of battle."[1]

—from a letter of Robert E. Lee

"My idea is that Meade was the most skillful general in the Federal army. General Lee once said to me that he could understand the movements of all the generals in the Federal army easier than those of General Meade."[2]

—Confederate President Jefferson Davis

"You [Meade] handled your troops in that [Gettysburg] battle as well, if not better, than any general had handled his army during the war. You brought all your forces into action at the right time and place, which no commander of the Army of the Potomac has done before. You may well be proud of that battle."[3]

—from a letter of General-in-Chief Henry Halleck

"I esteem him [Meade] highly, and second only to Sherman, and but for his quick temper he would have no superior; and yet with that quick temper goes his quick perception of what is required on the field of battle.... He seldom makes mistakes."[4]

—General Ulysses S. Grant

---

1  Cortlandt Parker quoting from a letter written by General Lee after the war, Isaac Pennypacker, *General Meade*, New York D. Appleton and Company, 1910, p. 5

2  Cortlandt Parker quoting Jefferson Davis, Isaac Pennypacker, *General Meade*, p. 5

3  General-in-Chief Halleck letter to General George Meade, *The War of the Rebellion: Official Records of the Union and Confederate Armies*, Volume 27, Series 1: 16, 104

4  Pennypacker, p. 4

"Thanks of Congress: For the skill and heroic valor which at Gettysburg repulsed, defeated, and drove back, broken and dispirited, beyond the Rappahannock, the veteran arm of the rebellion."

—Act of Congress, January 28, 1864

"A few days having passed I am now profoundly grateful for what was done, without criticism for what was not done. General Meade has my confidence as a brave and skillful officer and a true man."

—Abraham Lincoln, Executive Mansion, Washington, July 21, 1863

"For Meade, this was the particular moment of truth when all within him, particularly his moral courage, had to bear tough and strong on the problem ahead. No council of war could be called. No delay for leisurely study would be permitted by Lee. The decision had to be made. And the decision was solely Meade's responsibility. As he turned his horse, he is quoted as saying, almost to himself: 'We may fight it out here as well as anywhere else.' Then he quietly rode away to issue the orders that would make his decision operative. In all this, there is neither visible drama nor glamour; only the loneliness of one man on whose mind weighed the fate of ninety thousand comrades and the Republic they served. Meade's claim to greatness in that moment may very well be best evidenced by the total absence of the theatrical. When thousands of lives were at stake there was no time for postures or declamations."[5]

—President Dwight D. Eisenhower

---

5  Dwight D. Eisenhower, *At Ease: Stories I Tell to Friends*, (New York: East Acorn Press, 1967), pp. 45-46; Quoted in *The Gettysburg Magazine*, Issue 28, pp. 38-39.

# Table of Contents

# ❧ List of Maps and Illustrations ❧

All photographs in this list are in the public domain.
The link below each entry will take you to a reliable source.
Maps copyright Terry C. Pierce.

Gouverneur K. Warren, William H. French, George G. Meade,
Henry J. Hunt, Andrew A. Humphreys, and George Sykes
in September 1863

# ᔒᕀᕲ Preface ᕳᕲᖇ

This story of Gettysburg begins four days before the battle and ends on July 3, 1863. It is told from the viewpoints of George Gordon Meade and the Union men who fought, and won, there. On the eve of one of the most important battles in US history, Meade is ensconced as commander of the Union's Fifth Corps. Early in the morning on June 28, he is awakened by President Abraham Lincoln's messenger. Caught off guard and thinking he is being arrested, Meade explodes, espousing his innocence. But the messenger is there for another reason. He hands Meade a secret order from the president. Meade is to relieve General Joseph Hooker and assume command of the Army of the Potomac.

Michael Shaara's Pulitzer Prize–winning novel, *The Killer Angels,* tells the story of the Battle of Gettysburg primarily from the Confederate viewpoints of Robert E. Lee and James Longstreet. In Shaara's book, Meade is a minor character. He is painted as "vain and bad-tempered, balding, full of self-pity.... No decision he makes at Gettysburg will be decisive, except perhaps the last."[6]

This book tells the other side.

The genesis of this Union story at Gettysburg began when I was a Navy officer attending Marine Corps Command and Staff College. Before the students visited Gettysburg, we read *The Killer Angels.* The guided tours of the battlefield mostly covered the terrain, officers, and men in Shaara's book and focused primarily on the Confederate actions. The visit was a great experience, in part because I learned more about my great-grandfather, Private Thomas E. Pierce, Company K, Sixth Louisiana Infantry, who fought for the Confederates and was wounded at Gettysburg.

---

6  Shaara, Michael, *The Killer Angels*, Modern Library Edition, imprint of The Random House, New York, 2004, p. xx

My knowledge of the Union actions at Gettysburg, however, was limited. Though Shaara's book covered General John Buford's cavalry defending the high ground and Colonel Joshua Chamberlain's Twentieth Maine defending Little Round Top, I was under the impression that Meade played little part in the Union victory. It was not until my command tour of USS *Whidbey Island* (LSD-41) that I began to wonder about the Union victors at the Battle of Gettysburg—Meade and the men he commanded.

As commanding officer of a large warship, I had the opportunity to get to know my officers, sailors, and embarked Marines for several months before we joined the Atlantic Fleet in real-world operations. Meade was not so fortunate. He was ordered to take command of a 94,000-man army with 372 artillery guns three days before the battle, and somehow he won. From a commanding officer's viewpoint, this was an astonishing feat. After my retirement from the Navy, I started researching Meade and his generals and other Union leaders in an attempt to unravel the mystery of the Gettysburg conflict.

Meade, as commander of the army, and his accomplishments are quite different from those suggested by Shaara. Although he lived up to his nickname, Snapping Turtle, the cautious and competent Meade demonstrated effective and remarkable leadership of the Union forces. As Stephen Sears, the acclaimed author of *Gettysburg*, writes, "The fact of the matter is that George G. Meade, unexpectedly and against all odds, thoroughly outgeneraled Robert E. Lee at Gettysburg."[7]

Meade was the fourth commander of the Army of the Potomac in just eight months. Having lost their last two major engagements, many Union soldiers were indifferent to his surprising promotion. Meade reluctantly assumed command, protesting vigorously that General John Reynolds was more qualified. When Meade took over from Hooker, he felt like a condemned man at the gallows. He knew that if he lost the battle, Lincoln would fire him. To make matters worse, and

---

7  Sears, Stephen, *Gettysburg*, A Mariner Book, Houghton Mifflin Company, Boston & New York, p. 506

unbeknownst to Meade, Hooker had no plan to thwart the Rebel invasion of the North and did not know with accuracy the whereabouts of Lee's forces. Upon learning this, Meade felt it just a matter of time before the gallows' trap door opened.

*Without Warning* describes what it was like to be with Meade and his key subordinates as they faced their trials, including Meade's volatile temper, which often erupted without notice and could be aimed at anyone, including himself. It also tells the story of Meade's conduct during the battle: his thoughts and feelings about the enemy as well as his subordinates; his commitment to duty and his deep doubts about his qualifications to lead the Army of the Potomac; his savage distaste for politicians and reporters; his modesty and restraint; his devotion to planning; and his instinctive ability to function brilliantly without a plan—even when the unthinkable descended on him without warning.

In the context of Meade's actions, new names appear, including General George S. Greene, who with just one brigade successfully defended Culp's Hill against an entire Rebel infantry division; the controversial General Daniel Sickles, the former congressman who killed his wife's lover and was the first person to beat a murder charge using the temporary insanity defense; Chief of Staff General Daniel Butterfield, whose loyalties lay with the dismissed Hooker; General Winfield Hancock, the gallant and charismatic corps commander, who, with a few of his personal staff, arrived at Gettysburg, rallied the retreating Union soldiers on Cemetary Hill, and successfully repulsed the swarming enemy; General Gouverneur Warren, the savior of Little Round Top; Brigadier General John Gibbon, the division commander occupying the angle during Pickett's Charge; General Alexander Webb and Lieutenant Frank Haskell, who led the final repulse of Pickett's charge; Colonel William Colvill from the First Minnesota regiment, who led one of the most dramatic charges in military history; his Sergeant James Wright, whose good nature and strong character made him a natural-born leader; and First Minnesota Medal of Honor winners Private

Marshall Sherman and Corporal Henry O'Brien, who helped to repulse Pickett's Charge.

These soldiers' stories provide readers a greater appreciation of the bitter controversies and the gallant heroics of the Union soldiers, new insights into Meade and his lieutenants, what it was like to be fighting on the Union side, and why they made the decisions they did. No facts have been knowingly altered. When possible, key characters' written accounts of their experiences have been paraphrased. As a result, the story is not a work of narrative nonfiction, but a novel of biographical and historical fiction that strives to accurately portray what happened to Meade and the men he led into battle at Gettysburg between June 27 and July 3, 1863.

No American has received a more important call to duty, nor resisted the challenge with greater zeal, than did Meade. This is the story of one of the United States' greatest reluctant heroes, who, in displaying brilliant generalship, survived Sickles's blatant disobedience and Lee's devastating attacks. The United States owes a great deal to this flawed, seemingly uncharismatic man who saved the Republic.

—*Terry C. Pierce*

# Key Characters

June 1863

## The Armies

**General Joseph Hooker** commanded the Army of the Potomac, which recently had suffered a crushing defeat at Chancellorsville, Virginia. The army consisted of seven infantry corps numbering 94,000 men.

**General George Meade** was the Fifth Corps Commander. Early on the morning of June 28, 1863, he was ordered by President Lincoln to assume command of the Army of the Potomac.

**General Robert E. Lee** commanded the Army of Northern Virginia, which numbered 78,000 men. Fresh from his victory at Chancellorsville, Lee invaded the North in hopes of drawing out the Union army, crushing it, and ending the war.

# The Men

## These men wore Union blue:

### ———— Army Commander ————

*Joseph Hooker*, Major General, 47; West Point 1837
*George Gordon Meade*, Major General, 47; West Point 1835

### ———— Army Headquarters Staff Officers ————

*Daniel Butterfield*, Major General, 32; Union College;
   Chief of Staff
*Gouverneur Kemble Warren*, Brigadier General, 33; West Point
   1850; Chief Engineer
*Seth Williams*, Brigadier General, 41; West Point 1842;
   Adjutant General
*Rufus Ingalls*, Brigadier General, 44; West Point 1843;
   Quartermaster General
*George Sharpe*, Colonel, 35; Yale Law School 1849;
   Chief of the Bureau of Military Intelligence
*Marsena Patrick*, Brigadier General, 52; West Point 1835;
   Provost Marshal

### ———— Infantry Corps Commanders ————

*John Reynolds*, Major General, 42; West Point 1841;
   First Corps
*John Newton*, Major General, 40; West Point 1842;
   First Corps
*Winfield Scott Hancock*, Major General, 39; West Point 1850;
   Second Corps
*Daniel Sickles*, Major General, 42; New York University;
   Congressman; Third Corps
*George Meade*, Major General, 47; West Point 1835;
   Fifth Corps
*George Sykes*, Major General, 41; West Point 1842; Fifth Corps

*John Sedgwick*, Major General, 50; West Point 1837;
   Sixth Corps
*Oliver Howard*, Major General, 33; West Point 1854;
   Eleventh Corps
*Henry Slocum*, Major General, 36; West Point 1852;
   Twelfth Corps

### Cavalry Corps Commander

*Alfred Pleasonton*, Major General, 29; West Point 1844

### Cavalry Commanders

*John Buford*, Brigadier General, 37; West Point 1848;
   First Division
*George Custer*, Brigadier General, 24; West Point 1861;
   Second Brigade, Third Division

### Artillery Commander

*Henry Hunt*, Brigadier General, 44; West Point 1839

### Artillery Battery Commanders

*Alonzo Cushing*, Lieutenant, 22; West Point 1861;
   4th US Artillery, Battery A
*Evan Thomas*, Lieutenant, 20; West Point 1861;
   4th US Artillery, Battery C
*Charles E. Hazlett*, Lieutenant, 25; West Point 1861;
   5th US Artillery, Battery D

## Division, Brigade, Regimental Commanders,
### Aides de Camp

*Francis Barlow*, Brigadier General, 29; Harvard College;
   First Division, Eleventh Corps
*James Biddle*, Major, 27; University of Pennsylvania;
   Aide de Camp, General George Meade
*David Birney*, Major General, 38; Andover Academy;
   First Division, Third Corps
*Joshua Chamberlain*, Colonel, 34; Bowdoin College;
   20th Maine

*George Custer*, Brigadier General, 23; West Point 1861;
    Second Cavalry Brigade, Third Division

*Rufus Dawes*, Lieutenant Colonel, 24; Marietta College;
    6th Wisconsin

*John Geary*, Brigadier General, 44; Jefferson College;
    Second Division, Twelfth Corps

*John Gibbon*, Brigadier General, 36; West Point 1847;
    Second Division, Second Corps

*George Greene*, Brigadier General, 62; West Point 1823;
    Third Brigade, Second Division, Twelfth Corps

*Andrew Humphreys*, Brigadier General, 42; West Point 1831;
    Second Division, Third Corps

*Frank Haskell*, Lieutenant, 34; Dartmouth;
    aide to Brigadier General John Gibbon

*David Ireland*, Colonel, 31; 137th New York

*Henry Lockwood*, Brigadier General, 49; West Point 1836;
    Second Brigade, First Division, Twelfth Corps

*George Gordon Meade, Jr.*, Captain, 20; West Point entered
    1860, left 1862; Aide-de-Camp

*Charles Morgan*, Lieutenant Colonel, 29; West Point 1857;
    Chief of Staff, Second Corps

*Patrick O'Rorke*, Colonel, 26; West Point 1861;
    140th New York Commander

*Carl Schurz*, Major General, 34; University of Bonn 1848;
    Third Division, Eleventh Corps

*George Stannard*, Brigadier General, 42; Farmer,
    Third Brigade, Third Division, First Corps

*Strong Vincent*, Colonel, 26; Harvard College;
    Third Brigade, First Division, Fifth Corps

*Alexander Webb*, Brigadier General, 28; West Point 1855;
    Second Brigade, Second Division, Second Corps

## First Minnesota

*Charles Adams*, Lieutenant Colonel, 32; Physician;
    Executive Officer

*Daniel Bond*, Private, 21; Company F

*William Colvill*, Colonel, 33; Buffalo Law School;
    Regimental Commander

*Phillip Hamlin*, Sergeant, 22; Company F
*Christopher Heffelfinger*, First Lieutenant, 29;
    Commanding Company D
*William Lochren*, Second Lieutenant, 31;
    Acting Regimental Adjutant
*Nathan Messick*, Captain, 36; Cobbler;
    Commander of Company G
*Henry O'Brien*, Corporal, 20; Company E,
    Congressional Medal of Honor Recipient
*Ellet Perkins*, Sergeant Color Guard, 27; Company D
*Marshall Sherman*, Private, 30; Company C,
    Congressional Medal of Honor Recipient
*Patrick Henry Taylor*, Private, 22; Company E
*Isaac Lyman Taylor*, Private, 20; Company E
*James Wright*, First Sergeant, 22; Hamline University;
    Company F

## President Lincoln's White House Staff

*James Hardie*, Colonel, 40; West Point, 1843;
    Assistant Adjutant General

# These men wore Confederate gray:

## Army Commander

*Robert E. Lee*, Lieutenant General, 57; West Point 1829

## Corps Commanders

*James Longstreet*, Lieutenant General, 42; West Point 1842
*Richard Ewell*, Lieutenant General, 46; West Point 1840
*A.P. Hill*, Lieutenant General, 37; West Point 1847

## Cavalry Commander

*J.E.B. Stuart*, Lieutenant General, 30; West Point 1854

## Division Commanders

*Edward Johnson*, Major General, 38; West Point 1845
*George Pickett*, Major General, 42; West Point 1846

# Overview
## June 1863

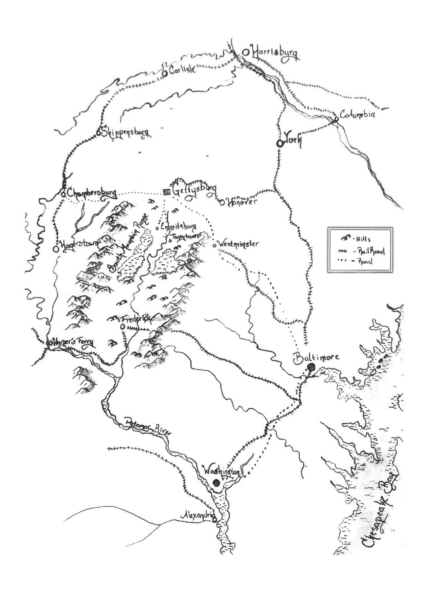

# Saturday

June 27, 1863

*General Robert E. Lee, Commander*
Army of Northern Virginia
Commanding for One Year

*General Joseph Hooker, Commander*
Army of the Potomac
Commanding for Three Months

*General George G. Meade, Commander*
Fifth Corps
Commanding for Three Months

# 1

## The Messenger — Saturday, June 27

*7:37 p.m. (dusk)*
*The White House porch and lawn*

The messenger walked out of the front door of the White House into the inky twilight and paused on the edge of the columned porch. He reached into the satchel on his hip and fished for the two envelopes, his fingers brushing over their wax sealings. One contained a note from the General-in-Chief of the four major Union armies, General Henry Halleck, and the other an order from President Abraham Lincoln. Leaving the envelopes in the satchel, he closed the leather flap and fastened the clasp. Dread gripped his insides. The Northern newspapers were screaming the Union was in grave danger, reporting the Rebel army was prowling somewhere in Pennsylvania like a ravenous, red-eyed beast, unopposed. He frowned. After he delivered Lincoln's order this evening, the nation would be in far greater danger than the reporters could ever imagine.

"My God..." He shook his head. "Sheer madness."

The messenger turned toward the open-spaced lawn of Lafayette Square, where his horse, Fancy, patiently waited. Three soldiers huddled in the gateway, chatting and smoking pipes. One of them, in a wrinkled jacket, held Fancy's reins.

The messenger strode toward them. His blue double-breasted jacket was adorned with two silver-eagle shoulder straps and fastened down the front with fourteen gold buttons. He did not disagree with Lincoln's order, per se. Six weeks ago it would have been the right move, after the terrible defeat at the Battle of Chancellorsville. But the tardiness of tonight's order could nullify its intended purpose. His throat tightened as he swallowed down a surging dread.

The soldiers moved out of the shadows and straightened their uniforms. The messenger angled toward them, his body leaning forward as if battling an invisible headwind. With luck, the special train would arrive at army headquarters in Frederick before midnight.

Heavy, clopping footsteps approached from behind. "Colonel Hardie. Sir! Colonel Hardie, please wait," yelled a voice.

He paused and turned around. "What now?" A servant chased after him, waving a hat.

"Colonel Hardie. Here you go," the old servant yelled, his breath rasping. "The president's messenger should have his hat."

"Unbelievable," Hardie muttered, muffling the profanity hanging on his tongue. He had departed the White House without his cover. Could this night get any worse?

The colonel donned his staff officer's cover, thanked the servant, turned, and walked toward the soldiers.

His face partially obscured by a drooping slouch hat and full, bushy sideburns, his damp, stringy hair nearly touching his shoulders, Hardie wiped his coat sleeve across his chin.

"Damn fool politicians. Damn fool decision."

This was the third time this year the president had charged him with delivering the same orders. *Three times this year!* Only the names were different—and the fact that this time, he'd been instructed to memorize the order in case he had to destroy it. In case Rebel raiders roaming the countryside threatened to capture him. But the orders were far more than a few sentences with the president's signature on a piece of paper. They were a grisly instrument designed to lop off the head of the Army of the Potomac with the speed and efficiency of a French guillotine. This staff job had turned him into Lincoln's notorious executioner of the army's senior generals. God, he hated this duty.

Squish! His right boot sloshed into a thick, oozy pile. He stopped and glared down. His face stiffened with crackling heat.

"What the hell?" His freshly shined boot was drenched, ankle deep in thick, sucking horse manure. The outrage that had been building now threatened to erupt. He scraped the bottom and sides of his boot against tall grass, then covered the remaining ground between himself and Fancy in quick, decisive steps.

Hardie pulled his watch out of his pocket and grumbled to the soldiers. "Hello, boys."

They saluted. "Good evening, sir."

He returned a half-hearted salute.

"It may be evening," Hardie said. "Not sure how good it is."

The brassy sergeant holding the reins winked. "Colonel, we had Fancy bedded down for the evening. We were surprised you needed her tonight."

"You're surprised?" Hardie muttered caustically. "The last thing I thought I'd be doing tonight was making a Paul Revere midnight ride across Maryland."

"Are the Redcoats coming?" the sergeant said, cracking a smile. "If they are, it will give old Henry Longfellow a chance to write another poem about a messenger changing history."

"No folklore is brewing tonight," Hardie said. "Remember, the British captured Revere between Lexington and Concord."

Hardie strapped the knapsack filled with a change of clothes across the saddle's cantle. Ideas for different routes on the fastest and safest way to the Baltimore & Ohio Rail Station near the Capitol Building swirled around his mind. But whatever route Hardie chose to ride tonight, the train better be ready to go when he arrived or there was going to be hell to pay. He mounted his horse.

"Will you be returning this evening, Colonel?" asked the sergeant.

"No," said Hardie.

"When, sir?"

"Never, if I'm lucky. Probably tomorrow night, if I'm not."

The sergeant gaped with visible shock, and the barest hesitation preceded his baffled reply. "Where will you be if you don't return?"

"In a Confederate prison or dead."

Hardie took a last look at the White House. Its shaded windows flickered with yellow light. He pictured Lincoln pacing inside with the anxiety of war taking its toll. He also pictured the

White House's two henchmen, Halleck and Secretary of War Edwin Stanton, hovering close by the president like vultures, ready to prey on the bones of more generals.

Dread settled around him with the darkening night as the president's last words filtered through his head, disturbing and hopeful. "Urgency, Colonel, urgency. You cannot fail tonight."

*7:45 p.m.*

He flicked the reins and nudged Fancy through the White House gate toward the railroad depot. "Well, Fancy," he sighed, "I know one certainty. Not even Napoleon could step in at the last moment and win this one."

Taking a risk, Hardie chose to take a shortcut through Murder Bay. His breath quickened. He knew that soldiers riding alone were moving gun targets in this section of the city at night. But tonight seemed different. The streets were empty and house doors normally open were shut. Reports of Confederate cavalry lurking to the northwest had left the city besieged by fear.

Only the faint lights of a few lanterns outside the closed brothels pushed back the darkness. Hardie smiled a little as Fancy trotted faster. There was little activity in the seedy enclave typically overflowing with the prostitutes of more than a hundred brothels.

"A slow night, Fancy, for General Hooker's whores," he whispered. Now that was going to put the Army of the Potomac in a dreadful mood. But he was sure Hooker had his own special delight waiting for him tonight.

Ever cautious, Hardie turned his head side to side, scanning for trouble. Even a daytime ride through Murder Bay was perilous: cutthroats, pimps, and prostitutes all killed, with little fear of the law. Hardie read about these daily murders in the newspapers. Men vanished routinely while riding through this section of the city, their bodies later discovered floating in the local canal. Normally, a soldier on duty would not be traveling these streets alone at night, especially not a brevet colonel. But this wasn't a normal night. Time, measured in hours, not days, mattered for the new commander.

Hardie wiped his forehead with the edge of his hand. He wasn't sure the new commander would have time to reorganize headquarters staff. Guessing that the new commander would have to find a replacement for General Daniel Butterfield, serving as Hooker's chief of staff, Hardie cringed. Butterfield was one of Hooker's two most poisonous vipers. The other bootlicker was General Daniel Sickles, commanding Third Corps. Both generals needed to be flushed out of the army like turds down the crapper.

Hardie squeezed the reins tighter. The streets were eerily quiet.

"Fancy, stay alert," Hardie warned. "This doesn't feel right."

He reached down and unsnapped the holster housing his Colt revolver. He rode peering straight ahead; the darkened streets seemed hardly wider than a narrow goat track winding along the side of a steep mountain. Despite the blistering humidity, his skin and muscles had tightened, and goose bumps popped up like the standing hairs of a threatened dog.

*Crack.* A bullet whickered overhead. Hardie ducked, blood pounding in his ears. Snapping the reins, he jabbed his spurs into Fancy's flanks.

"Come on, girl," he shouted.

Fancy fired forward into a full gallop. As Hardie raced toward the train station, he reached up again, adjusting the satchel strap looped across his chest, a weight more moral than physical. Hooker was beloved by the soldiers of the Army of the Potomac. Tonight, Hardie was delivering an order that shattered the invisible bond between the army's commanding officer and his soldiers. Without that undefinable spirit, an army could not win. Making matters worse, the new army commander would have no time to forge such a bond with his men before the battle.

It was a bad fix. Relieving the army commander on the eve of a pending battle was idiocy. Lincoln's ill-timed decision tonight had effectively ensured victory for Robert E. Lee's army in the upcoming battle.

Fancy's nostrils roared like a high-pitched whistle. "Hang on, we're almost there."

He licked his lips, tasting a tangy saltiness. The half-built Capitol Building was within eyeshot, hanging above the rooftops. The *New York Times* wondered if all the construction effort would be worth it.

In this morning's newspapers, Hardie had read that fear was growing among Northerners. They depended on Lincoln's generals and the Army of the Potomac to protect them. The people's confidence had crumbled to an all-time low. Six weeks earlier, the Union army had been defeated at Chancellorsville, and most Northerners thought its commander, Hooker, was a blockhead after New York reporters published blistering indictments of his performance.

Hardie had heard the president say how astounded he was by the ineptitude of his army, especially its string of charismatic commanders, McDowell, McClellan, Burnside, and now Hooker. These incompetent commanders had suffered one defeat after another. Inexplicably, Lincoln had left Hooker in command, notwithstanding his miserable performance and despite Stanton and Halleck's cries for his removal. The president said he was not willing to throw away a gun because it misfired once. He would reload and try again.

Hardie spotted the Baltimore & Ohio railroad clock tower and pushed Fancy into the darkness. The telegraph wires above his head were quiet. J. E. B. Stuart's Confederate cavalry had cut the lines somewhere between Baltimore and Frederick. But even if this new form of communication were available, Lincoln still would have sent him to deliver these vital dispatches. Lincoln insisted these sorts of things were better done in person.

*8:00 p.m.*

Hardie galloped into the rail yard, into the glinting light of the train depot. He dismounted and removed the knapsack. An anxious young captain waited with a squad of riflemen. The locomotive, poised and bridled with its steam up, hissed from the pistons, ready for its journey.

The captain saluted. "Colonel Hardie, the train is ready to depart."

"Good. First, I need to change," Hardie replied.

The captain looked confused, probably wondering why a colonel would change out of his uniform. Hardie had also been mystified, but bullet-headed Stanton wanted him in civilian clothes.

The captain pointed toward the terminal. "You can change in the station, sir."

Hardie nodded, handed the reins to the captain and sprinted to the terminal. Arriving in the locker room, he slipped on a flannel shirt, gray vest, and baggy wool pants. Damn Stanton; he'd ordered him to travel alone as an unarmed civilian, without an armed escort, believing posing as a reporter was his best chance to avoid capture by Rebel cavalry if they stopped the train. Traveling alone seemed pretty damned suspicious, as the Rebels could easily mistake him for a dignitary and take him prisoner, or worse yet, mistake him for a spy and shoot his ass.

Hanging his uniform in a locker, he removed the twenty-dollar gold certificates from the leather satchel that Stanton had given him and put them in his pants pocket. Stanton had told him to use the money as necessary when he arrived in Frederick to deliver the order.

Maybe posing as a reporter might work? If stopped, he'd say he was traveling to the front to report on a certain Rebel victory for the Northern newspapers. Yes, that story would work; Stuart's cavalry warriors were perhaps the most arrogant bunch of rapscallions within Lee's army, and they loved to read about their own exploits in the newspapers.

He ran back to the train. The captain was waiting for him. Hardie handed him his revolver and holster. "Hold these until I return."

The captain nodded. "Colonel Hardie, we just received a dispatch from Baltimore. Several reports of Rebel cavalry in Maryland this evening, creating havoc in Gaithersburg and Columbia. Another report has an enemy cavalry unit riding hard toward Finksburg. The engineer said the train ride may be slower than usual because of the enemy guerillas raiding the countryside."

Hardie frowned. His heart thumped against his ribs.

"God almighty," he muttered, "what a fiasco."

The captain kept his gaze steady.

"What are you staring at?" Hardie asked.

"Sir," the captain said. "Your civilian attire. You look like a…"

"Like what?" said Hardie.

The captain swallowed. "Like a spy, Colonel. And spies get shot."

"A spy? I was hoping to pass as a reporter."

"Wearing spectacles might help," replied the captain, shaking his head. "All the reporters I've seen wear glasses."

"I have a pair of reading glasses. I'll wear them if stopped by the enemy," Hardie said.

"We'll hold your horse here at the station until you return," the captain said. "You're traveling into a Rebel hornets' nest, sir. Be careful, Colonel."

Hardie smirked. "Well, hornets don't fire bullets and I'm mad as hell, so I plan on blazing right through them."

* * *

*8:10 p.m.*

*On the special train carrying Hardie to Frederick, Maryland*

Hardie boarded the passenger car from the rear, the satchel dangling from his hip. The captain signaled to the locomotive engineer. The engineer waved and looked down the tracks, releasing the engine brakes and slowly opening the throttle. Without the usual piercing whistle of the steam trumpet, the train lurched forward through a cloud of smoke and steam.

Hardie stood on the rear platform, swaying gently as the train gathered speed, looking back at the vanishing station lights. Lightning streaked the sky. Thunder rumbled overhead. A storm gust belted his face. The train was heading due north, following the Baltimore & Ohio iron highway to Baltimore, where it would jump onto the westward B&O main line, cutting across enemy-infested Maryland toward Frederick. With the train moving at full speed and no stops along the way, it would ordinarily be a three-hour trip. Given the captain's news about guerilla raids, tonight it would be longer. Damn, this was a cursed mission. How many more things could possibly go wrong?

Yet there was nothing for it but to keep plodding ahead. Disembarking at Frederick, he would visit army headquarters and establish the reign of yet another new army commander. Lincoln's order was a rash riverboat gamble, wagering the Republic's survival on a last-minute blind bet. The president was calling up an unheralded, stodgy general with a hair-trigger temper to lead a demoralized army against a seemingly unbeatable enemy. This couldn't possibly end well.

Hardie wished he were back commanding troops, not assigned to a desk job in the capital. A swelling dread crept down his spine. Tonight he felt more like an assassin than a herald.

He lurched hard to his left, banging his shoulder against a metal awning support as the train sped through a sharp curve. "Damn it, conductor, just get me there alive," he shouted, though he was the only person there to hear it. Holding tightly to the metal support, he held his breath as the front of the train cleared the curve and hit a straightaway, righting itself.

From the front of the car a loud chorus of vulgarisms erupted. Hardie's breath caught in his throat; he was supposed to be the sole passenger.

"Son of a bitch!" he growled. "Who in the hell else is on this train?"

# 2
# Meade — Saturday, June 27

*3:00 p.m.*
*5 hours earlier*
*Approaching Ballinger's Creek, Maryland*

George Gordon Meade rode uphill in the sweltering afternoon heat, leading a seemingly endless blue ribbon of 11,000 infantry soldiers stretching four miles behind on the narrow road. His Fifth Infantry Corps had been marching since sunup, and tonight's bivouac was about an hour's march in the northerly direction of Frederick.

He turned to Major James Biddle, his twenty-seven-year-old aide-de-camp and his senior and most trusted personal aide, riding alongside. Biddle supervised Meade's seven other personal aides, including the general's son, Captain George Meade, Jr., and nephew, Captain Francis Bache.

"Damn it, James. The *Baltimore Sun* is reporting that Harrisburg is gripped by a perfect panic. The capital of Pennsylvania is being evacuated for fear of falling into Confederate hands. What the devil is going on?"

"Does General Hooker have a plan for responding to this threat?" Biddle said.

"If he does he has not shared it with me," Meade replied. "I'm damned if I know why Hooker refuses to share his plans for fighting Lee's army with me."

Biddle cracked a smile. "You don't call our daily marches from bivouac to bivouac each day a plan?"

Meade scowled, his face burning like a brimstone cloud. "Hell, no. That's just executing orders. I learned Hooker told Lincoln a week ago he may never discover the whereabouts of the enemy or his intentions so long as Lee fills the country with a cloud of cavalry."

"Maybe Hooker's staff should subscribe to the daily newspapers," said Biddle. "The Northern reporters seem to have a nose for finding Lee's army."

Meade frowned as the beating of brigade drums rattled up the hill. "I want more than orders, which a goddamn drunk monkey can follow. I want to know how each day's marching ties in with Hooker's plan for dealing with the Confederates. I want to know where all the enemy forces are. Is that too much to ask from Fighting Joe?"

Biddle nodded, tight-lipped.

---

*3:30 p.m.*

Meade fished out his watch. Half past three. "I will give Hooker credit for the commendable job he did in reorganizing the army and raising morale after he assumed command after the horrible defeat at Fredericksburg. But at Chancellorsville, Fighting Joe was paralyzed by fear and could not make timely decisions. Despite having a huge numerical advantage, he retreated instead of counterattacking. I swear it was as if both his feet were stuck in the mud. Damn it, we could have won that battle."

Near the crest Meade pulled on Baldy's reins and moved off the road, lingering, peering through his thick glasses. The tall, thin-faced general sported a hawkish nose and a grizzled beard sprinkled with gray, looking more like a frumpy professor than a corps commander. His slouched hat had a conical crown and a turned-down rim. Biddle reined up.

Meade removed his glasses, blew on them, and wiped them with a handkerchief, squinting at the horizon. The rumors of him replacing Hooker as army commander were flying thick. Pure hogwash. But he couldn't quell the misinformation. The clatter of hooves echoed over the crest as the rest of his personal staff arrived.

His pulse rate climbed. Only a charismatic leader beloved by his men could defeat another charismatic commander and an idolized general such as Robert E. Lee. That person was John Reynolds. Hell, both Reynolds and Lee were former superintendents of West Point. They should be squaring off. Not Hooker and Lee or Meade and Lee.

Meade shook his head as he put his glasses back on and stuffed the handkerchief in his coat pocket. He was not a suitable opponent for Lee. He was neither charismatic nor beloved, and he had a quick temper. But there was no doubt that he made a good corps commander. He clutched his chest as a burning pain like a barbed hook ripped through his lung. The Minié ball wound in his chest from a year ago was acting up. The wound had made him less than whole, reminding him he had a fragile lung that seemed to act up when he was riddled with self-doubt. The rumors of him replacing Hooker conjured up plenty of self-doubt.

He reached up and jerked the brim of his hat down over his thick eyebrows. The black slouch hat had an insignia sewn on the front of the crown, adorned with two gold stars sitting close together—the hat of a corps commander. He gripped his binoculars and scanned the countryside. The Fifth Corps soldiers flowed through it like a glittering, blue mountain stream.

"It's a stunning sight," Biddle said.

Meade grimaced. His gut cramped as if he had swallowed a bucket of broken glass. He removed a flask of quinine from his jacket, took a swig, and spat. "Bthaa!" Gripping his canteen, he gulped down warm water, letting it slop down his beard.

"Maybe Hooker doesn't have any plans he can share with you," Biddle said.

Meade paused, scratching his chin. "If that is the case, Hooker is dumber than I thought." Meade shook his head. Even having a bad plan was better than no plan at all.

"Hooker isn't even bright enough to wipe the bullshit from his lips," Meade said. "Even that asshole Sickles knows to ride to the sound of the guns."

Meade's brain was hissing like a lit fuse. "I'm also galled with that bootlicker Butterfield. That Little Napoleon is worse than a meddlesome mother-in-law. I can't imagine a worse chief of staff. Neither Hooker nor Butterfield seem interested in locking horns with the Rebels."

His pulse stalled as he sucked air between his teeth. Then a blinding flash of clarity struck. *My God. Hooker really is afraid of Lee and doesn't believe he can beat him. That's why there's no plan.* He turned in his saddle toward Biddle and waved his arm forward. They trotted across the sprawling summit.

"Where in the devil is the Rebel cavalry?" Meade said. "Newspaper reports have Stuart's horsemen roaming nearby, and if that's true that means Lee's army is right on his heels."

"That would be my bet, sir. But what if Lee's cavalry wing is not screening the main force? What if his cavalry is conducting raids?"

"Lee is too smart for that," Meade said. "He's going to keep Stuart's cavalry close at hand. He has to. A surprise engagement north of the Potomac would catch him flat-footed."

"Hooker would tell us if Lee's army was marching toward us, wouldn't he?"

"Maybe, under normal conditions," Meade said. "But nothing is normal with Hooker. I'm worried that Lee is going to waltz into the capital."

Meade paused, wiping his brow with the back of his gloved hand as he glared at Biddle.

"What the hell is Hooker thinking?" Meade ranted. "Why haven't we heard from him? Not even a note from that idiot chief of staff of his. I can't make sense out of it."

Biddle shook his head. "Maybe we'll hear something this evening. Tonight's bivouac will be just a few miles from army headquarters."

Meade shot a sharp glance. "Don't blow smoke up my ass, James. The only person visiting me from headquarters will be Hooker's provost marshal with an arrest warrant."

Biddle frowned, shaking his head. "You haven't done anything wrong, except tell the truth about Hooker's poor performance at Chancellorsville…and that's not a crime. It was the truth."

"I should have kept my mouth shut when Governor Curtin asked me why Hooker lost the battle," Meade said. "But my damn temper flashed and I told Curtin that at the critical moment, Hooker lacked the nerve to deliver."

14

"That's true," Biddle said. "But it's not your fault Curtin blabbed to Lincoln about your supposedly private conversation."

Meade raised an eyebrow. "Well, he did, and now I'm at open war with Hooker because he believes the rumors of a generals' revolt. And the idiot believes I'm leading the coup, just like he did against Burnside." He mulled that thought over for a minute. "Hooker isn't smart enough to realize it's too late in the campaign for Lincoln to replace him," Meade said. "Instead of focusing on Lee, who is getting ready to hand him his ass again, he's more interested in revenge against potential rivals in the General ranks. What a damn, whoring fool."

Biddle shook his head.

"Did I ever tell you that after Chancellorsville Hooker told me he didn't want to command anymore and was willing to turn it over to me?" Meade said.

"I didn't know that," Biddle said. "No wonder Hooker is spreading rumors about your possible arrest."

"Hooker looks and speaks the part. But he froze. He missed a wonderful chance to end the war."

"Did Hooker ever discuss the Curtin incident with you?"

"Yep. Hooker summoned me to army headquarters and accused me of maneuvering for his job. I assured Hooker that I have no friends in government and wanted nothing to do with politics. I just wanted to command Fifth Corps."

"Did he believe you?"

"Apparently not. The rumors persist." Meade smirked. "After the Curtin episode, I reached some important conclusions: One, there is no privacy in proximity to politics. Two, Butterfield and Sickles are Hooker's cronies, and for that reason alone are no friends of mine. And all three—Hooker, Butterfield, and Sickles—are political scorpions."

"Isn't Sickles still on convalescent leave, with General Birney commanding Third Corps in his absence?" Biddle said.

"Yes. Birney is commanding Third Corps, and if we're lucky, Sickles won't return." Meade furrowed his brow and continued. "By the way, have we heard anything from our scouts?"

"Not yet. They departed at seven this morning. Bache rode southeast toward D.C. and Mitchell headed east toward Baltimore, following the B&O railroad."

"Let me know as soon as they return. I told them to report to me immediately." Meade pushed his glasses back on his hawklike nose. "Without intelligence flowing from Hooker's headquarters, it's damn hard to set up the defenses for each night's encampment." Meade paused, his throat tightening as if a hand had squeezed around his windpipe. "How am I supposed to command Fifth Corps wearing a blindfold? I'd be completely in the dark if it wasn't for the Northern newspapers reporting enemy movements. As for Hooker…*Va te faire foutre.*"

Biddle grinned. "Since I've been around you, sir, my translation of French swear words is improving. Didn't you just say 'Hooker should go screw himself'?"

"That's close, but my version is a bit more vulgar." He furrowed his brow. "Damn you, Hooker, you mindless devil," Meade cursed, spitting spray on Baldy's neck. He hated stupidity and those who failed to do their duty.

Biddle reached into his jacket pocket, plucked out a cigar, and handed it to Meade, smiling. "General Meade, here you go."

Meade nodded a thanks and took the cigar. James was trying to cool his temper. Normally, curbing his rage was like trying to plug an Icelandic geyser, and it would take more than a relaxing smoke. He lit his cigar and blew several smoke rings, watching them float away and collide.

At heart, Meade was a topographical engineer who loved designing and building things. He puffed out his chest. Those spiral lighthouses he designed and built off the coast of Florida as a lieutenant were still standing, all weathering those one-eyed monsters. But he was not bad at commanding an infantry corps, either, where grit, hard work, and blunt truthfulness could carry you a long way. You didn't need charm to lead an infantry corps. But you sure as hell had to be charismatic to command an army! He had no choice but to refuse General Henry Slocum and General Darius Couch's petition to Lincoln requesting that he replace Hooker. Charismatic generals like Hooker and Lee drew

16

men to them like moths to a flame. For guys like him, it wasn't so easy.

A courier rode up next to Meade, handing him a leather pouch. "Compliments from General George Sykes, sir."

"Please give my compliments to General Sykes and thank him."

Meade opened the pouch; inside was a New York newspaper. His face brightened with a warm glow. Good. He'd read it tonight. Hopefully, it had some updates on enemy activity. Maybe they'd even printed Hooker's plan—if he had one.

"James," Meade said. "What Hooker doesn't understand is that I want no part of a generals' revolt that wants me commanding the army. Yes, Hooker needs to be replaced —but not by me."

"Who should replace him?" Biddle said.

"We need a smart, inspirational leader to match Lee—a magnificent leader who is willing to take measured risks but always acts like a perfect gentleman and looks sharp in his uniform, like a Wellington. Someone the men can be proud of and cheer when he rides by. Hell, we had one in McClellan."

"But Lincoln fired him," said Biddle.

"That was a mistake. But Reynolds fits the bill and that's Lincoln's best choice." Meade pointed. "C'mon, Biddledee, let's ride a ways in front of the column." He flicked the reins and Baldy trotted forward.

---

*3:45 p.m.*

Biddle rode even with Meade. Warmth flooded Meade's chest. The boys had covered a lot of ground against a blistering sun. But spirits were high. The men were marching smartly in perfect step to the fife and drum corps.

"It's hot, but the troops look better than I thought they would by now. They might have a good amount of fight in them even though we've been marching them hard."

"After we bivouac this evening, haven't they earned a swim in Ballinger's Creek?" Biddle asked.

"Yes."

17

They rode in silence for several moments. Meade stubbed out his cigar in the palm of his leather-gloved hand and started chewing on it in frustration. He shook his head as rage started simmering again. How could that conniving Hooker replace Burnside as commanding general? If he was that good at plotting, why in the hell couldn't he lead? Meade shook his head and swore an oath. Did he think he could do a better job than Fighting Joe? Hell, yes. But Reynolds was the person who should replace Hooker.

Meade spat out his cigar with a wracking choke. His chest heaved and a deep cough racked his ribs as if something was clawing at his scarred lung.

"Sir, are you all right?" Biddle asked.

Meade squeezed his eyes, held his breath, the burning searing through his chest like a branding iron. He jerked back on the reins, holding Baldy as still as possible. After a few moments, the coughing eased. He reached up with his gloved hand and rubbed the bullet scar on the side of his chest.

"Yeah, give me a mo—." A throaty hack chopped his voice. *Damn Glendale battle wound.* He pursed his lips tightly and breathed shallowly through his nose. Using his legs, he gently nudged Baldy into a slow walk.

He held his side as he rode, his mouth twitching. He gazed up the road, where the countryside turned hilly, the rolling summits providing a view in every direction. Sunset would come in a few hours over the South Mountain range, some fifteen miles to the west, extending northward from the Blue Ridge Mountains into Pennsylvania.

Biddle pointed. "Look, General. The church spirals of Frederick are visible ahead. See…they're clustered together like cornstalks."

Meade adjusted his glasses. Nearly blind without them, he always kept a spare pair in his saddlebag. Frederick was charmingly picturesque and peaceful, a sanctuary in a war-torn country. A pang of urgency seized him. The Union army was vulnerable. Lee would never make such a mistake.

"Well, James, I hope it holds the answers. For starters, where are the other six infantry corps of Union forces located? My fear is that Hooker has spread the army across the whole of Maryland."

—————— • ——————

*4:00 p.m.*

He spurred Baldy into a gallop. Cocking his head back, he yelled, "Keep up with the old man, if you and the boys can."

Meade broke off from the advance party and raced out into the open countryside, pulling away from his cavalry escort. Old Baldy splashed across Ballinger's Creek, some three miles south of Frederick, and raced up the long slope on the north side of the creek. He leaned forward, creating his own breeze.

Splashing sounds echoed from the shallow creek. Turning his head briefly, Meade spotted Biddle in the lead, spurring his horse. The rest of his personal staff and security dragoons thundered through the shallow creek and fanned out behind the aide-de-camp. Meade peered ahead again, focusing on the large hill, much closer now. He spotted the white Victorian mansion that rested on top, surrounded by groves of trees.

"Arcadia Manor," he muttered.

Major Biddle pulled alongside Meade, sweating profusely. "General, sir. Begging your pardon, but is something wrong?" he asked. "What's so important to get you running away from your escorts?"

Meade, who had yanked back on the reins, looked up. His face was fiery hot. He needed to draw up tonight's plan and distribute it to the division commanders. An army could fight without plans, but not coordinated or well.

He gritted his teeth. "I'm thinking about riding into Frederick this evening after we survey the terrain for positioning the corps for tonight's bivouac," Meade said. "I'm tired of being in the dratted dark. How do you think Hooker and Butterfield would react to an uninvited guest?"

"You'd be breaking protocol, that's for sure." Biddle said.

"To hell with protocol," Meade said. "For all I know, the reason I don't know a damned thing is the rumors are true. Hooker is planning to have me relieved of my command."

Biddle wiped his face and frowned. "That could be what Hooker wants. Sir, don't feed into his plot by arriving uninvited. You'll give him a reason to fire you."

"You're probably right, but dammit, enough is enough. Restraint is not serving us well. I'm still thinking about riding over to visit him."

Meade stewed, his stomach knotting tighter as his uncertainty grew. For all the pestering he had done at army headquarters for information, apparently Hooker was keeping his strategy close to his chest—assuming he had a strategy. But Hooker lacked nerve, and his approach was too ad lib. Simply reacting to Lee's movements would let Lee drive events, as he had done six weeks earlier at Chancellorsville. Using surprise and boldness, Lee would force the Army of the Potomac to react from a weak ground position.

*4:15 p.m.*
*Ballinger's Creek, Maryland*

On the crest near the manor, Biddle's horse drew even with Meade's. The general dismounted and stood quietly, stroking Baldy's head, letting the nickering warhorse catch his breath while the rest of Meade's personal staff caught up. His own lung problems, for the moment, had subsided. The rattling snare drums crackled, the steady beat of thousands of marching men, moving in step with the precision of a well-oiled machine—Meade's machine.

The security troops crested the hill, fanned out, and deployed in a loose perimeter. The staff wheeled up moments later, dismounting quickly from their lathered mounts. The aides were chatting, chiding Captain George Meade, the general's son, who arrived last on the summit. There was not an ounce of fat on the wiry frame of the younger Meade, and no wonder: he was the spitting image of his father but without, thankfully, the old man's fiery temper.

"For Christ's sake, James," Meade complained, "where are the maps?"

"They're coming, sir."

An orderly opened his saddlebag and fetched the maps, handing them to the general.

"About time," Meade grumbled.

He knelt and spread the maps out on the ground. He would decide tonight's bivouac positions after riding the defensive line. He loved using hills and ridges to create a defense.

Meade turned to Biddle. "After I issue tonight's bivouac orders, I'm riding over to Frederick."

"Beg pardon, General," Biddle said with a hint of surprise. "Apparently, I didn't win the protocol argument. Do you want me to ride with you to army headquarters, sir?"

"No, I'll take Captain Meade with me."

*4:30 p.m.*

Meade mounted Baldy. Captain Frederick Rosenkrantz was sitting astride his horse, waiting, his long fingers holding his drawing pad and pencil. The Swede was a bull of a man and the best artist on Meade's personal staff. "Come on, Rosie," said Meade, "let's ride the perimeter."

They turned and rode around the perimeter as Rosie sketched the line. Meade told him where he wanted the divisions and batteries placed. When they had finished, Meade stopped.

"Rosie, let me look at your sketch." The captain handed it over. Meade studied it, nodded his approval, handed it back. "Your sketches are getting better. Have you been practicing?"

"Every night, sir."

Meade and Rosie rode back up to the crest and dismounted. Meade walked toward Biddle and the cluster of his staff officers, wincing. His butt ached. "I'm getting too old for this crap."

*5:00 p.m.*

Meade spotted Captains Bache and Mitchell sitting on a log, eating a bowl of beans. Fury flared in his gut and burned his cheeks. He lurched toward the two captains, flashing his fangs like a cottonmouth snake settling a score.

"I told you idiots to report to me as soon as you got back. And here you are lingering about, feeding your damn faces. What the hell?"

Bache and Mitchell stopped chewing and snapped to attention, stammering incoherently. Bache gulped down a swallow and said, "Sir, Major Biddle said you and Rosie were riding the perimeter and surveying the terrain for tonight's bivouac, and we didn't want to disturb you, sir."

Meade said, "Are you half-wits playing me for a fool? If I told you to report to me when you got back that means you damn well better report to me immediately. Not after you've stuffed yourselves. Now what in the hell did you discover? Where's Lee?"

Bache stuttered. "Sir, I rode southeast toward D.C. and did not find Lee or any signs of Rebel cavalry."

"Sir," Mitchell added, "I rode east toward Baltimore following the B&O railroad and we located a large Rebel cavalry unit operating near Westminster. The force appeared to be about three brigades."

Meade's fists clenched. He shouted, "You don't think that's important information to give to me as soon as you returned here to headquarters? Were they screening the Rebel infantry or raiding?"

"No sir, we did not spot any infantry." Mitchell said. He walked over to the map table and pointed. "My scouting party rode northeast to Manchester and then rode west to Taneytown and then south to the Frederick area. We didn't see any Rebel infantry."

Meade stiffened and plunged forward a step, pressing his chest against Mitchell. The captain leaned back as the general loomed over him, eye to eye. Meade glared, his eyes squeezed into thin slits.

"Impossible," he said. "If there is a large cavalry force roaming around, then the infantry can't be far behind. How could you have missed them? You know, they're dressed in gray and there are about a hundred thousand of them. Lee would never have a large cavalry unit out joyriding around. Never."

Mitchell shrugged slightly and stared down at the ground in front of Meade's boots.

"Lee doesn't make mistakes like that," Meade shouted. "A Rebel cavalry unit of that size is screening for Rebel infantry on the move. You muddled-headed numbskulls somehow missed his infantry. Damn!"

Mitchell glanced at Bache, wordlessly. Meade said, "Don't look to Bache for answers for your blundering. Look at me, you prickish fool."

Mitchell peered into Meade's face, trembling.

Meade pursed his lips and forced his rage down into the pit of his stomach. He turned to Rosie. "Captain Rosenkrantz, let me see the sketch. Based upon Mitchell's half-assed discovery of a large Rebel cavalry force operating northeast of our bivouac tonight, I need to shift the artillery batteries and sentries."

"What about the roaming enemy cavalry threat?" Rosenkrantz asked.

"I want two regiments from each division posted as an extra screening effort." Meade ordered. "I want one of the regiments posted a quarter mile from the division bivouac and the other a half mile, creating a layered defense."

"That's really a tough assignment for these six regiments after an all-day march in this blistering heat," Biddle began.

"Damn it, James, with Mitchell's discovery of an enemy cavalry brigade operating nearby, I have no choice. I sure as hell don't trust Hooker to provide cavalry protection for Fifth Corps. This is the problem when the army commander doesn't have a plan. Or if he has one and doesn't share it with his corps commanders. Without a plan, there is no way for the different corps to create interlocking defenses and support each other. Hell, I don't even know where the six corps are bivouacking tonight."

Rosie handed the sketch to Meade and the general pointed to three new positions for the batteries, the sentries, the six regiments. Rosie nodded and re-drew them on the sketch. Meade gritted his teeth and suppressed the anger coursing through his veins. Then he turned back to Bache and Mitchell with a withering stare. Mitchell pulled himself together, wiping his filling eyes.

"Listen, you two river rats," Meade snapped. "Before any roosters are crowing tomorrow morning, I want both your sorry asses in the saddle, riding northeast. You damn well better find the infantry that the enemy cavalry is screening for or I'm going to skin you both alive. Now get the hell out of my sight."

The flustered captains scurried away like a couple of yellow-bellied skedaddlers.

Meade moved over next to Biddle and stared at the map. "Rosie," he instructed, "draw positions on the big map."

Rosie placed the sketch on the ground and began drawing the bivouac positions. Meade shook his head. *Damn it, watch yourself. Being known as a hard-nosed soldier is a fine thing, but being a prickly old man who explodes without warning and pitches into the poor devil closest isn't professional.* He needed to work on that. He rubbed his hand over his chest scar.

*That's why you'll never be the commander of this army. An uninspiring commander with a volcanic temper could never defeat a charismatic military genius like Lee. To hell with it. You never wanted to be a lickfinger political general with an eye on Lincoln's presidency like a lot of these damn scoundrels.* He took a deep breath and let it out slow. *No thanks. Not getting my ass handed to me by Lee will do me just fine.*

He turned to Biddle. "Send for my division commanders."

"Yes, sir."

Meade pulled out his small notebook and began drafting orders for the night's bivouac.

---

*5:20 p.m.*

Several moments later, a cavalcade of horses rode up the crest. Meade raised his head, spotting a flagbearer flying the Second Division pennant. Sykes arrived and dismounted. The general stood bowlegged and unsteady from being in the saddle most of the day, but he regained his balance.

Meade dropped his head and finished writing and then handed the notebook to Biddle. He glanced at Sykes, his best

24

division commander, who might someday gain command of a corps of his own—hopefully replacing the inept Sickles. Concern draped over Sykes's face as he saluted smartly. Meade returned the salute.

"Long ride?" Meade greeted him.

"Yes, sir, but we made good time," Sykes replied. "Last night's pickets had a pretty tough time keeping up, so I let them fall back, making their way the best they could. I sent a couple of aides back and they arrived safely."

Meade nodded. "Good."

"Do you have any idea of what General Hooker is planning?" Sykes said.

Meade's eyes narrowed. "No. I have no idea what is going on at that damnable headquarters. Unlike McClellan, a competent leader who worked with his corps commanders, Hooker never tells us a damn thing until the last minute, if at all. Lincoln never should have fired McClellan."

Sykes nodded. "Given a chance, Little Mac could have easily whipped Bobby Lee."

"What does the president know about fighting wars, anyway?" Meade said. "Not a Goddamned thing. I'll tell you this. Successful military operations take a lot of planning."

Sykes frowned, shaking his head. He knocked the dust off his field hat on his trouser leg without dropping his eyes from Meade's glare.

"I'm riding into Frederick to visit Hooker's headquarters," Meade said. "We've been floundering around for days while Lee's army is gallivanting around Pennsylvania. I refuse to stand by and let Hooker feed this army piecemeal into Lee's meat grinder."

"Would you like to join me for a bite to eat before you ride over to visit Hooker?"

"No," Meade growled. "The only thing I'm hungry for is a piece of Hooker."

"The newspapers say the people of the North are weary of a war that already has cost thousands of lives and millions of dollars."

"Hooker doesn't seem to realize a Rebel victory in Pennsylvania would add to this, perhaps even convince Britain and France to recognize the Confederacy," Meade said. He paused, scanning the crest. The din from Ballinger's Creek grew into one long roar of joy as blue-clad figures splashed in the cool summer runoff.

Meade's skin prickled. Fifth Corps had arrived. He extracted two cigars and handed one to Sykes. They stood in comfortable silence, engulfed in cigar smoke swirling around them, as the troops set up tents and campfires. Meade nodded. Sykes was one of the few generals who had a calming effect on him.

He turned to Lieutenant Colonel Joseph Dickinson, the senior aide supervising the orderlies delivering messages to the division commanders. "I don't want the men lingering too long around the creek," he said. "They need to deploy into their positions before nightfall."

Dickinson nodded. "Do you want me to shoo them out of the creek now?"

"Oh, no," Meade said. "The boys marched hard today. They deserve some splash time. Let them linger as long as possible."

His two other division commanders, General Samuel Crawford and General Romeyn Ayres, arrived together. They joined Meade and Sykes, and Meade discussed the night orders with instructions and sketch maps, guiding their units into the defensive encampment. They all protested against supplying two extra regiments for tonight's bivouac. Meade explained he had no choice, based upon the three enemy cavalry brigades roaming about and the lack of support from Hooker's cavalry corps. He told them he was visiting Hooker's headquarters this evening and if he learned anything he would share it with them. The division commanders departed.

---

*6:30 p.m.*
*(Dusk is 7:37 p.m.)*

Meade mounted Baldy and turned to Dickinson. "Joseph, I'm riding to Frederick to visit with Hooker. I'm taking Captain Meade with me. If I learn anything I'll let you know."

"I'll have supper waiting for you," Dickinson said.

"If Hooker places me under arrest, I will send George back to inform you and pack up my personal things. My guess is Butterfield would get his old Fifth Corps back and I'll be on my way to the capital to face a court-martial."

Meade reined Baldy hard to the right. If Hooker relieved him, at least he wouldn't have to watch his corps get chewed up by Lee again. Lee…where the hell was he? As for Hooker…*Va te faire foutre*.

# 3

# Hardie — Saturday, June 27

*8:14 p.m.*
*On the special train carrying Hardie to Frederick, Maryland*

Hardie stood on the train car's rear platform, rubbing his bruised shoulder, his face flush to the door. His stomach hitched and his heart pounded in his ears. Who was swearing in a high-pitched voice inside the car? He held his breath and his muscles tightened. He pulled on the handle and opened the door. Ducking low, almost in a crouched stance, he crept into the passenger car. A thick cloud of blue cigar smoke filled the air.

Apprehension turned to fear. Were they Rebels? He reached for his revolver. He was unarmed. "Damn," he whispered.

He inched his way forward, gripping each seat back for balance as the train rocked. Through the smoke he spotted two passengers near the front, sitting across from each other. Even in the poorly lit car there was enough light to see the insignias on their blue uniforms.

Hardie was only slightly relieved by the identification. Union officers. Why were they on this train? The captain at the station had not mentioned other passengers boarding. The president's instructions had no mention of other passengers on this mission. He clenched his fist, drew a deep breath, and held it as if jumping from a burning building. If the officers were senior generals, there was a good chance he knew them. Despite the smoke clouds shrouding his presence, he couldn't ride unnoticed for over four hours.

The train banked around a tight curve and Hardie slammed against an empty seat, striking his shin bone. He let out a muffled growl and rubbed his hurt leg.

The high-pitched voice said, "Did you hear that? It sounds like we have a visitor."

A younger voice said, "Or a tramp who is train-hopping. Or it could be a Rebel spy."

Hardie gripped the wooden seat back and stood up, regaining his balance. *Well, they know I'm here. Now it's time to figure out who they are.* He walked forward, his eyes darting back and forth in the smoke, glancing at the ghostly figures. He eyed a familiar face. "Holy shit!" he whispered. He stiffened and forced a tight-lipped smile, peering at the worst of all the possibilities: General Daniel Sickles.

Sickles was pointing his revolver at him.

The general called out, "Come on down here. Show us your hands."

Hardie walked forward a few steps and paused, his hands raised.

"Keep on moving forward," Sickles shouted.

Hardie moved forward, emerging from the smoke. Turning as if on a swivel chair, Sickles faced him like a hawk eyeing its prey and gazed at Hardie with curious delight.

"Looks like we have a vagrant riding the rails," he said to his traveling companion.

Hardie stared into Sickles's eyes. "Beg your pardon, General, do you mind if I sit with you?"

Sickles said nothing as he kept the gun pointed at Hardie, studying the president's messenger.

Dread gripped Hardie by the throat.

Suddenly, a devilish mischief crossed Sickles's face. "Colonel James Hardie," he said. "My, my, what a surprise and splendid pleasure to have Secretary Stanton's adjutant traveling with us. To what do we owe this great honor?"

Sickles's face beamed as he lowered his revolver and slid over toward the window, with some sizeable effort, pointing to the now-vacant aisle seat kitty-corner from him.

"Please sit and join us, Colonel," Sickles said.

"Thank you, General." Hardie lowered himself into the straight-back seat, clutching the satchel to his chest.

Sickles grinned. "Would you like a cigar?"

Hardie shook his head. "No, thank you."

"I recall you smoking one of my Cubans during my last visit to the White House," Sickles smirked.

"That's true," Hardie said. "But remember we were drinking Old Crow. I like whiskey with my Cubans, General."

"Old Crow," the general snickered. "I happen to have some of that right here." He reached into his coat pocket, produced a silver flask, and handed it to Hardie.

"Oh, no, sir," Hardie said. "I'm on duty tonight." *Damn it, be careful.*

"So you're on duty tonight but you're wearing civilian clothes. That's odd." Sickles twisted the cap off the flask and took two long swigs.

Hardie fought to control the shiver scurrying down his back. As a gifted orator, former lawyer, and congressman, Sickles was a fiendish rhetorician, a master word acrobat, possessing the ability to simultaneously convince and deceive. He used words like a carving knife, gutting opponents who then spilled out information. His best chance for concealing the mission was to take control of the conversation and guide it in a neutral direction.

Sickles stared at him. "So what is your mission, Colonel?"

"I'm taking a quick trip to army headquarters to confer with the commanding general of the Army of the Potomac. I rather thought it might be an inconspicuous visit." Hardie had answered in a steady voice. *Good.* He studied Sickles, a close friend with Hooker, waiting for him to start probing for weaknesses in the story.

Surprisingly, Sickles merely nodded. Hardie spoke deliberately, carefully weighing each word. "I'm most pleased to see you recovered from your wound at Chancellorsville. The president will be pleased to hear you're returning to take command of Third Corps."

"By the grace of God, I didn't die," Sickles said. "The enemy shell fragment almost crushed my chest. I thought I was a goner."

Hardie chuckled inwardly, knowing the rumors about the general's injury. Many of Sickles's critics said the fall from his horse hit harder than the shell fragment.

"Tell me more about your mission tonight," Sickles said.

"Stuart's cavalry continues to play mischief with the telegraph wires, cutting them as soon as we can fix them," Hardie said. "You know Secretary Stanton doesn't like being out of touch with his field commanders. Not sure how long the wires will be down."

Hardie halted, wrinkling his nose at the acrid cigar smoke blowing in his face. "Tonight, I'm the president's eyes and ears, sir. I'm supposed to find out from Hooker the whereabouts of Lee's army. The second Rebel invasion north of the Potomac is causing a great deal of anxiety. A report from General Hooker will calm everyone down, especially the president."

There was confidence in Hardie's voice, but he was not sure how long he could keep up the charade. Sickles eyed Hardie, slowly bobbing his head, staring at him with beady eyes like a fanged bat.

Hardie's jaw tightened. Damn it, no one was supposed to be riding with him tonight, especially Hooker's friend Sickles. The Third Corps commander was a glory hound whose vanity rivaled Narcissus. Hardie struggled to appear matter-of-fact and not overplay his hand. It was difficult hiding the truth from Sickles. Like most corrupt politicians, he was familiar with the smell of deceit.

Sickles blew smoke out of his mouth as he talked excitedly. "Indeed, I heard the reports of Stuart's Cavalry riding north of Washington and west of Baltimore."

"Yes, yes," Hardie said while nodding. "But what are they after? Lincoln wants to know."

---

## Sickles
*8:45 p.m.*

Sickles raised his eyebrows, vaguely disappointed, wishing for the opportunity to mix it up with Stuart's boys. "Maybe Stuart's boys are just joyriding around, trying to piss off the president."

"Lee wouldn't approve of joyrides," Hardie said.

Sickles chomped on the cigar, blowing wobbly smoke rings past his thick walrus mustache. The blue smoke shrouded the face of a young artillery captain sitting across from him on the train's single car. Sickles peered at Hardie. The general sat cross-legged, tapping his foot in the air, his eyes protruding beneath his heavy lizard-like eyelids as the train rumbled over the steel rails, the flanged wheels ringing a clickety-clack.

Sickles cocked his head toward the third traveler. "Allow me to introduce my companion, Captain James Smith, commander of the Fourth New York Independent Battery."

"Delighted to meet you, Captain," Hardie said. Smith smirked and nodded.

Sickles eyed Hardie. He couldn't stop himself from guessing why a colonel dressed in civilian clothes would be traveling to army headquarters. Hardie's story seemed a bit farfetched. Even though the telegraph wires were cut, Hooker still had a regiment of couriers capable of delivering rapid dispatches and updates to the president, day and night. Why the need for a midnight trip to Frederick on a special train? Something else was up.

"My boys at Chancellorsville fought like badgers," Sickles said, in a nasally squeal. "They did a great job executing my midnight attack plan—a stroke of genius if I say so myself. Those laggards Meade and Howard sat cozily around their campfires shooting the shit while I'm attacking the Rebels. You got to be aggressive, my boy, and do the unexpected, chase down the enemy and catch him by surprise, just like that bastard Lee."

Sickles paused momentarily, taking several puffs on his cigar and exhaling, filling the car with a dense fog of smoke. *I love being a general. And I'm damn good at it.*

"Opportunities don't linger for the gutless," he continued. "They favor the daring and gallant who chase after them."

Hardie nodded.

Sickles raised his arms as if conducting a symphony. "I'm sure my Third Corps boys are anxious for the return of their heroic general. We've been separated long enough. But that convalescent leave after Chancellorsville did me a great deal of good. Surprising I healed as fast as I did and so said my doctors. My boys and General Hooker all want me back for the upcoming battle."

Hardie ran his fingers over the clasps of his satchel.

Sickles clapped his hands, a gleefulness bubbling inside. "That midnight attack I led against Stonewall Jackson's corps was a fierce victory, my boy," he said, his pitched voice ricocheting off the cabin bulkheads. "We recaptured the cannons Howard's corps lost earlier when the cowards retreated. Howard's disgraceful skedaddle led to the crumbling of the Union right flank. He cost us, my boy. Howard is a bullet-head just like Meade, two peas in a pod. Scourges of the army." Sickles paused, retrieved a cigar, and lit it.

## Hardie
### 9:30 p.m.

As the train rattled along, Hardie chattered about minutiae, staying on the offense and controlling the discussion. He was gifted at exchanging pleasantries while not providing privileged information, but his instincts warned him that Sickles was not entirely sold on his story. Luckily the general's arrogance made him an easy mark, readily distracted and seduced by flattery.

Sickles had made a decent showing at Chancellorsville, his first real test of combat leadership, but by most generals' standards he was an amateur. One decision particularly bothered the professional officers: the midnight attack against Jackson's corps. They questioned Sickles's aggressive temperament, the charge seemingly contrary to sound military judgment—lots of risk for an uncertain reward.

But Sickles bragged that the attack was a huge success, telling the president during a White House dinner that he was his only aggressive corps commander. Incredibly, Lincoln bought into the bravado, even though Sickles had bagged only one Rebel cannon and recovered only part of a Union supply train the Rebels had captured. Many said it was reckless. Others called it idiocy. Regardless, the impromptu offensive had cost several hundred Union casualties.

Hardie grounded his teeth together as a plan emerged that would kill time. He leaned slightly forward, giving Sickles an encouraging audience.

"General, I've heard President Lincoln talk about your gallant midnight attack at Chancellorsville and your serious injury. If you don't mind, tell me more about your attack against Jackson's corps. Some are calling it brilliant."

The captain rolled his eyes and moaned.

---

## Sickles
*10:00 p.m.*

Sickles slapped his leg and licked his lips as he puffed several smoke rings, each chasing the one before. His face blossomed with a mischievous sparkle, like a child sneaking a cookie.

"By God, if Howard and Meade had supported me, I would have carried the day." Sickles hand-gestured as if he was sword fighting.

"I don't think Meade's corps ever really joined the fight. He did what he does best—sit back, fret, and plan for retreat. You can't expect backing from the likes of those two."

Sickles gained steam, his words booming. "Meade is a prickly son of a bitch. You can't win battles with commanders like him. He is an overly cautious, backstabbing weasel, always looking for the opportunity to flee. No one else had the courage to lead a midnight attack. In fact, besides General Sedgwick's attack against Marye's Heights, I'm the only one who made a successful attack during the three-day battle. Can you believe that? Those West Point officers couldn't fight their way out of a women's prayer group."

Sickles paused, wiping the wetness from his brow. "Let me tell you something, Colonel, I led the Third Corps charge into that forest, saber flashing, pointing them ahead like a modern-day Napoleon. Every man in the long infantry lines behind me marched confidently, knowing he had a lion for a commander leading them to victory. That lion, my boy, has a name, and it's Daniel E. Sickles! I can still hear the bugles as the first infantry line stormed into the abyss, screaming madly. What a magnificent sight!"

Sickles leaned back, trying to taste again the adrenaline, the thrill of fighting.

Hardie's eyes widened. "What happened next?"

"I was riding at the vanguard, drawn into battle. We ran into a line of Rebel skirmishers, and a wave of musket fire erupted, bullets ripping through the tree branches and skimming over the infantry lines. I remember a butternut soldier rushed forward, his bayonet pointed at my chest, but by God I thrust my saber forward just in the nick of time to parry the strike. I swear, bright white sparks flew everywhere. After I deflected the bayonet, I rocked forward in the saddle, sliced my sword across the lad's face and then drove it into his side."

Sickles slid forward to the edge of the seat, his face hot.

"Then, suddenly, the night lit up with thousands of pops and bursts of yellow flame snaking toward us. I could hear the bullets zipping by my head, the thud of Minié balls smashing into flesh. Death was everywhere, my boy; bodies covered the ground. My boys were slaughtering the enemy. Riding ahead, I crested a reverse slope and pell-melled into an enemy brigade. The smoke of battle hung static and burned our eyes. We rushed toward the Rebels, and it didn't take long for them to recognize me as a two-star general leading the attack. They fired volleys at close range, trying to take me down. But, by God, I raised my pistol in one smooth motion, blowing the head off a Rebel trying to bayonet me. I dropped him right there! With my other hand gripping my saber, I slashed another Rebel fiend."

Hardie said, "So, General…you were in the front lines, leading the attack?"

"Damn right. I love hand-to-hand combat! A moment later there came a jarring explosion, followed by the hideous sounds of thousands of sharp metal shards cartwheeling through the air. Yet, I felt no fear. I charged forward until a shell fragment crashed into my chest. The blow knocked me from my horse, twisting me to the ground. I thought I had caught a cannonball right to the chest!"

Sickles paused, taking several puffs on his cigar.

"It didn't hurt at first. I lay paralyzed on my back and dully conscious until I grew numb and began shivering. There was a moment of vacancy, as I waited to see if the wound was mortal." He paused as if reliving the moment.

"But then there was an empty darkness. I later learned my boys carried me to the rear, praying I would live. I can only imagine their worry at losing their beloved commander. When I awoke, my coat was shredded and covered with blood. The surgeon said I had been struck by a shell fragment. He recommended several weeks of convalescence. I wanted to stay in command of Third Corps, but General Hooker ordered me, his most gallant of generals, to rest for the next big fight."

Sickles paused and puffed.

"I reluctantly gave over my command to General Birney. And now, finally, I'm riding back to the front to resume command. I know my boys will be relieved to have me back. And Hooker, too—who else does Hooker have that can take on Lee and his boys?"

Sickles paused to reflect on his soliloquy, a noble knight's tale of harrowing adventure. *I was born to lead men in battle. The battlefield is where I belong. And then, after I win this war, perhaps the White House.*

Warmth flowed through his veins. He had performed like a Shakespearean actor delivering a well-rehearsed monologue to a grateful audience. Being a heroic general was one small step from becoming a heroic president. The corners of his eyes crinkled.

---

# Hardie

*10:45 p.m.*

Hardie's head bobbed rhythmically, encouraging Sickles's persistent chatter. The general's boasting removed the immediate pressure of answering probing questions about his mission. Hardie, like most other West Point graduates, detested this man, having no faith in his character. Sickles was stout, with a drooping moustache and full lips locked around his Cuban cigar. Most of the West Point officers said he was unsuited as a commissioned officer, let alone for command of an infantry corps. General Henry Halleck, General-in-Chief of the Union Armies, had little use for Sickles, believing he was a drunkard. Halleck had once said, "It seems but little better than murder to give important commands to such men as Sickles."

Hardie uttered a deep sigh. Behind Sickles's back, the West Point generals referred to the former congressman as a "political general," a mocking moniker for those earning rank through their connections. But Sickles was more than just one of Lincoln's amateur generals. He was the most senior Union officer without formal military experience, now in command of nearly 11,000 men. His connection was Lincoln; the president championed Sickles for the rank of general because he believed it would appease important blocks of Northern Democratic voters. Whether Sickles actually could command a corps was not the president's main concern.

At last, Sickles paused. He reached inside his jacket and produced a silver flask, took a long swig of whiskey, and then offered it to Hardie. Hardie declined once again. Then Sickles turned toward Captain Smith and asked him about his unit during the battle. Smith reluctantly began relating the actions of the Fourth New York Battery at Chancellorsville.

Grateful that Sickles had stopped talking, Hardie let his mind drift, thinking about his West Point days, remembering the academy's focus on developing leaders of character whose allegiance was to duty, honor, and country. Sickles had none of those characteristics.

Sickles reached over to his satchel and extracted another cigar, his third since Hardie had arrived. Bored with Smith's talk of the Fourth New York Battery, he resumed his monologue, but his mood had become irritable. He ranted, extolling the brilliance of Hooker and General Butterfield.

"If Hooker's other corps commanders fought like Third Corps at Chancellorsville, we would've whipped Lee," he shouted. He slid forward to the edge of the seat, placing his face a few inches from Hardie. "Howard and Meade should be court-martialed!"

Hardie froze, his chest tightening. He leaned back at his waist, away from Sickles. He wiped the whiskey spittle from his face, stunned by the general's sudden outburst. Sickles continued berating the West Point generals, especially the ones defecting and fighting for the Confederacy and the incompetent ones serving in Hooker's army.

"Colonel Hardie," Sickles said, "Do you know what Benedict Arnold and Robert Lee have in common?"

Hardie shook his head no.

"They both are former commanders of West Point, and both are traitors like Judas."

"General Sickles, Benedict Arnold commanded the West Point fort in 1790, twelve years prior to the establishment of the military academy."

"No matter," Sickles said. "The only West Point commander worth his salt was Captain Partridge, who tried to convince Congress to close that loathsome breeding ground for military aristocrats and traitors."

"Well, General Sickles, you might take solace knowing the current corps of West Point cadets will all end up fighting for the Union, if the war lasts that long." Hardie smirked. *Indeed, they'll all end up as generals to replace the ones Lincoln fired.*

"Rebel traitors," Sickles shouted. "Bobby Lee, James Longstreet, Richard Ewell. They should all be shot! And look at what we're left with, the dregs of West Point, like George Meade, a damned old goggle-eyed snapping turtle, who always is popping off at somebody. He couldn't lead a funeral detail, let alone an infantry corps."

Hardie nodded, concealing his growing disgust. Did Sickles remember that he had graduated from West Point? Doubtful. The stories about Sickles before the war started to make sense: ballot tampering, embezzlement, even murder.

The newspapers had provided a graphic report of Congressman Sickles shooting his wife's lover—Philip Barton Key—son of Francis Scott Key—in cold blood, in the middle of the day, in Lafayette Square. Hardie remembered the stories. Sickles had returned home and seen Philip Key leaving. He chased the man down, shooting him in the groin and chest at close range. Keys died within a few minutes.

During the trial, Sickles employed a team of eight high-powered lawyers, including future Secretary of War Edwin Stanton. His lawyers claimed Sickles suffered from "mental unsoundness sufficient to cause deadly violence." *Mental unsoundness sufficient to cause deadly violence.* It was a new defense, but it worked, making Sickles infamous—the first American acquitted of murder by pleading temporary insanity. Hardie shuddered at the thought of such a man—in possession of so little control over his own faculties —in a position of so much authority over thousands of lives. And Lincoln—championing a temporarily insane man to command a Union Corps! Maybe the whole country was temporarily insane. At least, Hardie hoped it was temporary.

Sickles was gesturing again, sweat pouring from his brow, swearing loudly. "George Pickett, Lewis Armstead, and A.P. Hill all are West Point traitors too! They will burn in hell."

Sickles glanced at Hardie and stopped abruptly. When he resumed speaking, his voice was calm and warm. "I feel a great battle brewing, and I'm going to be in the middle of it." He chatted on, but now amiable and friendly.

Hardie was dumbfounded by the general's rapid mood swings and his turbulent emotions. In one moment, Sickles appeared mentally unsound; in the next moment, he seemed sane, almost self-effacing. It was unsettling. But he had to keep feigning interest in Sickles's ranting, as his strategy for controlling the discussion was working. For the time being, Sickles was more interested in promoting himself than extracting information from Lincoln's messenger.

Sickles paused, sat back, crossed his legs, and puffed on his cigar, blowing smoke rings that chased one another. After a few moments of silence, he reached out, slapped Hardie's knee, and smiled.

"My compliments to you, Colonel Hardie," Sickles said triumphantly. "You've done a marvelous job keeping me at bay, but I've figured out your unfortunate mission."

Hardie caught his breath, taken aback by how quickly Sickles had turned the conversation on him. Sickles's eyes narrowed, enjoying his moment. Hardie's cheeks burned.

"As the great armies of the Union and the Confederacy drift toward this great collision, my heart tells me something. You, Colonel Hardie, are the dark angel tonight, delivering the death blow to a general's career."

Hardie's heart sank. Sickles had guessed right.

"Rumors are swirling that Hooker requested Lincoln to relieve George Meade as corps commander. My guess," Sickles said, "is that I'm riding the executioner's special train and the Secretary of War's adjutant is charged tonight with beheading Meade."

Hardie's mouth opened slightly. Sickles had not been fooled by his story about visiting army headquarters to gather news on the current situation.

"During Hooker's evening council of war at Chancellorsville, Meade voted not to attack the next morning," Sickles said. "I was there, Colonel Hardie. I was an eyewitness, hearing Meade refusing to attack; and then afterward lying about his decision, blaming Hooker for retreating."

"My guess," Sickles brightened, bobbing his head with delight "is that Meade is soon to be arrested."

Hardie stared wordlessly.

"Meade and his West Point henchmen started rumors of a generals' revolt to replace Hooker, purposely orchestrating an avalanche of lies, deceit, and innuendo to assassinate Hooker's character so Meade could take his place," Sickles roared. "I know for a fact that Slocum and Couch started a petition to have Meade replace Hooker. If I were to guess, Meade has political ambitions. He has his eye on the White House."

Hardie remained stone-faced, but the accusations against Meade left a nagging ache in his core. Hardie's skin prickled. Meade was the most apolitical corps commander in the army. Sickles had completely misread Meade's trajectory.

Bluntly, Sickles demanded, "Colonel Hardie, are you traveling to the front to arrest Meade for insubordination against

Hooker?" His eyes bored directly into Hardie's. "Remember, Colonel, you are addressing a senior officer. I want the truth!"

Hardie stared at him, his breath tripping in his throat. He heard again the president saying, "Do not disclose your mission to anyone other than the officers whose names appear on this order."

Hardie responded slowly, ensuring he did not misspeak. "The fact is, General Sickles, my mission this evening is to gain a better understanding of the whereabouts of Lee's army and to learn how the Army of the Potomac plans to deal with the Rebel invasion. It is a most anxious time for the president and his administration." Hardie had told the truth, if not quite the whole truth.

"Hmmm," Sickles murmured as he studied Hardie for any signs of dishonesty. "By God, I think you may be telling the truth, Colonel Hardie, but not all of it. There's something you're not telling me."

Hardie sat motionless, sensing that Sickles truly believed he had an arrest warrant for Meade.

***

## Sickles
*11:20 p.m.*

Sickles was smug, delighted with himself. He had largely figured out Hardie's untold mission of cutting off Meade's head. He smirked. Meade and the other cliquish, cautious West Point officers disrespected ambitious officers like himself. Luckily, they had a president who understood the value of promoting non–West Pointers to senior ranks in the army. *Don't mess with friends of the president.*

Sickles turned to Smith, who had remained silent throughout the discussions, and started retelling the well-worn story of how he was called to the service of his country. He loved revealing how Lincoln had pleaded for him, a Northern Democrat, to become an officer. Sickles claimed he volunteered for frontline fighting as an enlisted recruit, but the president had assured him he did not want Sickles serving as a private.

Tears welled up in Sickles's eyes, as though he and the president had shared a mystical moment.

Reciting his own script, Sickles quoted the words Lincoln had said to him. "I believe in pushing the Democrats who want to fight right up to the head, where everybody can take a lesson from their example."

---

## Hardie

*Sunday, June 28*
*12:55 a.m.*

Hardie sat back against the wooden seat. Sickles was an incredible actor, transfiguring instantly from one emotional character into another. But the real Sickles story had no heroes, just flawed characters motivated by vice, anger, and revenge, seeking status and prestige. Hardie closed his eyes and pretended to sleep.

The forward passenger door banged open. Hardie snapped alert and rubbed his eyes. Then he remembered. *Be careful.*

The conductor entered the car and walked over to Hardie, ignoring Sickles. "Sir, the train is nearing Frederick. We should arrive in five minutes."

Hardie nodded. "Thank you."

Sickles clamped down on his cigar, glaring. "I'm the senior officer here. You're just a colonel, dressed in civilian clothes. Fool conductor. What is his problem?"

Hardie's eyebrows rose. "General," he said diplomatically, "may I give your compliments to General Hooker when I visit with him?"

Sickles paused, nodded. "Yes, please give my compliments to the Commanding General. Tell him his gallant hero has returned this evening and will resume command of Third Corps."

---

*1:12 a.m.*
*Frederick, Maryland, train station*

The train ground to a halt at Frederick. Hardie stood and bowed his head slightly. "With your permission, General Sickles, I will take my leave."

Sickles puffed up like a peacock. "Indeed, Colonel Hardie, you have my permission."

Thankful he was getting away, Hardie bade him farewell. "Sir, may good fortune be your friend tonight and in the coming days."

Nodding to Smith, he exited the coach, stepping off onto the station platform, clutching the satchel. Hardie checked his watch: a quarter past one in the morning. Sickles was right about one thing: someone would be fired today.

# 4
# Haskell — Saturday, June 27

Lieutenant Frank Haskell sat on his horse, scanning the horizon through his binoculars, waiting for General John Gibbon to arrive. Gibbon's trim, thirty-four-year-old aide-de-camp squinted westward across the rolling farmlands, shading his eyes from the red glare as the setting sun dropped behind Sugarloaf Mountain, an isolated, rocky hill near Frederick. This evening Sugarloaf stood like a lone sentinel over the hamlet of Barnesville, watching over Hancock's 11,000 Second Corps soldiers striking tents, lighting campfires, and stacking arms. High-pitched fiddle melodies drifted across the open pastures.

Keeping an ear for roaming Rebel cavalry, Haskell's gaze fixed on a pair of bald eagles circling gracefully, hunting. A touch of envy welled up, and he wished he could ride currents like an eagle, spotting enemy movements. He scowled. No word from Hooker on how he was doing in locating the enemy, although the more likely story was how well Lee was doing hunting Hooker. Lee's cavalry was searching for Hooker's army like the two predators flying overhead, scouring the area for exposed prey. Suddenly, the raptors tucked their wings and swooped downward in a steep dive toward their unsuspecting victims, most likely rabbits. He shuddered. *That's how swift and deadly Lee's attack will be when the Rebel cavalry locates us, if we don't find them first. Damn Hooker.*

A thundering clap echoed from Barnesville. He spotted a lone rider wearing a black Hardee hat looped up on one side, galloping toward him down the narrow, rutted road. He straightened up, wiping his face with a handkerchief, watching Gibbon approach.

The former commander of the Black Hat Brigade rode up and dismounted, as did Haskell. They exchanged salutes.

"Have you heard anything from corps or army headquarters?" Haskell asked.

Gibbon frowned, shaking his head. "Nut'n."

Haskell grimaced. "Damn. I'm worried Lee's cavalry is going to pop out of nowhere and slice up our boys."

"Speaking of slicing," Gibbon said, "Hancock heard that Meade's head is on the chopping block."

"Do you believe the rumors?" Haskell asked.

Gibbon removed his hat with just a hint of a wry smile and scratched his head. He lilted back into his native North Carolina drawl. "Now, just 'tween you'n and the gatepost, if there is lots of smoke, then there's probably a fire burning somewhere."

"Who is stoking the rumor fire?"

Gibbon's face twisted. "Butterfield. He wants Meade's corps back. Also, Hooker believes Meade is leading a generals' revolt against him."

"What? Is Meade maneuvering for Hooker's job?"

"Hell, no! Meade hates politics and despises politicians as much as priests despise Satan. It takes those Washington devils to orchestrate a coup like Hooker did. Christ almighty, I doubt if Meade knows if Lincoln's a Democrat or a Republican."

"Well, if the rumor flames continue to leap, about all we can do is watch things burn and wait for the ash to settle," Haskell said. "Hopefully, Lee won't attack in the interim!"

"Well, there is nothing we can do about it, anyway, but stay ready," Gibbon said. "Lincoln is the judge and jury in the Hooker-Meade squabble. In my opinion, Lincoln favors Fighting Joe, who couldn't win a fight to save his life…or the Union's. Meade might be better—Lord knows he's meaner than a venomous snake. But who knows for sure? God, I wish Lincoln would re-appoint McClellan to command the army."

Heat flared in Haskell's face. "McClellan isn't the answer. He's not an aggressive enough commander because he is an anti-emancipation Democrat—"

"Damn it, Frank. I don't want to debate the *Cause*," Gibbon said, his mouth tightening.

Haskell stroked his mustache like a criminal judge rendering a verdict. He had to wait for the right moment to broach the subject with his boss. Gibbon moved in front of his horse, lit his pipe, and puffed large pillows of smoke. Haskell stood by, studying the compact, ruddy-faced general. His face was a contradiction, much like the man himself, with sharp cheekbones, brown hair, reddish mustache, and deep-set eyes. He was intelligent, blunt in speech, and unshakeable during a battle. But he didn't look the part.

When Gibbon assumed command of the only all-Western brigade in the Army of the Potomac as a new brigadier general, he had chosen Haskell as his aide-de-camp and outfitted the brigade with black Hardee hats—hence their name, the Black Hat Brigade.

Gibbon frowned. "If Hooker remains in command, I'm afraid Lee will destroy this army and this country."

"Lincoln reached low in the barrel when he pulled out Hooker," Haskell nodded.

"Generalship is not a game for the slow or unimaginative," Gibbon continued. "Leaders of character are the heart of the military, leaders capable of taking the fight to the enemy. Hooker is neither a fighter nor a man of character. We need McClellan."

"Yes, McClellan wants to restore the Union," Haskell rushed on, trying to keep his fists from clenching with frustration. "But the Republicans believe he is not willing to take the necessary risk to cleanse our nation from the foul blot of slavery."

Gibbon barked with a rare touch of harshness. "I disagree. McClellan is the right general to lead this army. The army loves Little Mac, and he is every bit the equal to Bobby Lee. As for his views, I'm a believer in McClellan's politics that stand for the idea of bringing the Southern states back into the Union as quickly and easily as possible and leaving the slavery question out of the picture entirely."

Haskell kept his gaze steady as he swallowed his surging rage. *Watch your tongue. Don't be insubordinate.*

Gibbon continued, "I'm fighting for the North to save the Union, and it has nothing to do with slavery. If I could save the Union without freeing a single slave, I would do it. I'm a strong Union man, but I am not willing to shed one drop of blood to fight slavery up or down."

Haskell's rage erupted. "Restoring the Union without ending slavery would be a hollow accomplishment," he snapped. "No democracy worth its name can continue to drag the burden of slavery around after it. What is freedom, where all are not free?"

Gibbon grunted and shook his head. He raised his boot and tapped his pipe against his heel, emptying the bowl. He narrowed his eyes and stared at Haskell. "You're a radical Republican bent on destroying slavery. I'm a McClellanite, and I'm a pro-slavery man trying to reunite the Union with the least amount of bloodshed. We view the world differently. Perhaps we should leave it at that."

Haskell paused, tight-lipped, glaring at Gibbon. After a few moments he said, "I think we can agree on one thing. Neither my goal of fighting to free the slaves nor McClellan's goal of fighting to restore the Union is possible without the triumph of the Union army."

Gibbon shot up an eyebrow and nodded. "Yes, we can agree on that. We first have to defeat the enemy to accomplish our different goals. So let's focus on that."

Haskell let out a breath he hadn't even realized he was holding. "Well, if Lincoln reached low in the barrel when he pulled up Hooker, maybe he should reach low again and replace Hooker with a Southern West Point grad. Maybe one from North Carolina who has three brothers serving in the Confederacy and one in Lee's army as a surgeon."

Gibbon's lips parted slightly. Using an exaggerated southern drawl, he said, "I'm not sure Stanton would approve of a Southern Democrat leading the Army of the Potomac. He and his radical Republicans have a great distrust of Southern West Point graduates. He believes that had there been no West Point Military Academy there would have been no rebellion."

Haskell curled a grin. "What if this person was one of the best-known generals on either side, having written *The Artillerist's Manual*—known as the 'The Book' by Rebel and Union artillerists?"

"Well, if you put it that way, Lincoln just might ask me to take command from Hooker. But if asked, I would have to turn down the promotion, just as Reynolds did. My excuse is that it would take too long for headquarters staff to learn to understand my southern drawl."

Haskell's eyebrows shot up in mock shock. "I had no problem learning it."

"As I recall, you're an Ivy-school Dartmouth grad, which makes you a fast learner for a Yankee," Gibbon said. "That's why I've kept you close by ever since I formed the Iron Brigade. I needed a translator to decipher for those Badger, Hoosier, and Wolverine boys."

"That Black Hat Brigade is still the best in army, and the Rebels are scared to death of those fighters," Haskell replied.

"The fact is," Gibbon said, "all our soldiers are just as good as the Rebels. But Hooker is not. They have General Bobby Lee. That old warhorse has faith in his army, and the army has faith in him. They have confidence, knowing their commander can defeat any of the Union commanders. Lee follows a simple principle, one worth considering for our army as well. After a battle, he removes the incompetent officers discreetly and promotes capable officers publicly. He always is making his army better—and it wasn't ever bad."

Haskell nodded. "That's why Lincoln should consider you for commanding the army. As army commander you could turn the entire army into a fierce fighting machine like the Iron Brigade."

Gibbon reached inside his jacket and grabbed his tobacco pouch. He filled the bowl, tamped a fresh pack, lit his pipe, and puffed on it for a few minutes.

"I tell you, Frank, our army is different from others," he mused. "The Rebels are mostly Anglo-Saxon Protestants of Old English ancestry, glorifying a past age. Our men are diverse—Catholics and Protestants, Irish and Scottish…fiercely independent, rugged men who display initiative, thought, and action." Gibbon puffed on his pipe. "It makes them potentially the best soldiers in the world. But these qualities also can be explosive under the adverse conditions of combat if the commander does not have the respect of his men. Just look at General Oliver Howard in the Eleventh Corps. Hancock says Howard is wracked by self-doubt and has a hard time leading his German immigrants."

Haskell raised an eyebrow. "But Howard is tactically sound. He graduated near the top of his West Point class."

"The fact is," Gibbon added, "the ability to lead men in battle depends less on tactical ability and more on the commander's character, his reputation, and the feeling the men hold for him. It's called leadership."

Haskell looked toward the darkened South Mountain. The air was thick but the heat was retreating somewhat, chased upward by a fast-moving wedge of cold air. The growing coolness portended the arrival of thunderheads, dangling high in the sky like black cotton balls. He spotted the first lightning flash heralding the approaching storm.

Gibbon continued, "The feeling a winning army has for a commander is not about popularity. Hooker is popular with the men, especially Hooker's Murder Bay division, but his generals do not respect him. The deficiencies exhibited by the Army of the Potomac at Chancellorsville fall squarely in Hooker's lap—his failure as a commander."

"We need a commander who will take the fight to the enemy," Haskell interjected.

———— * ————

*7:10 p.m.*

They remounted their horses, trotting back to Second Corps headquarters. Haskell's mind was spinning. It would be idiocy to replace Hooker at this late stage of the campaign, but it was certain that leaving him would mean defeat. Damn it, it was

Reynolds's duty to accept Lincoln's offer to relieve Hooker. He would ask Hancock why Reynolds turned down command of the army.

Haskell and Gibbon rode silently during the remaining leg of the ride, arriving at Hancock's camp in an orchard just south of Barnesville. The large sergeant standing guard in front of Hancock's headquarters tent recognized Gibbon and Haskell and said he would let the commander know they were there. They dismounted, waiting, Gibbon perched on a stool next to a makeshift table supported by two flour barrels, staring at a map of Maryland. Haskell stood, his fingers drumming on the map table.

Gibbon's finger traced the two passes, traversing the range. "Look here, Frank. My bet is that Lee's army will move east, crossing the range through Cashtown Pass, the narrow road leading to Cashtown and Gettysburg ten miles beyond. That's what I would do. Or perhaps they will cross at Monterey Pass just above the Mason-Dixon Line, the road leading to Fairfield, with Gettysburg lying some eight miles northeast and Emmitsburg nine miles southeast."

"Yes, sir, I agree," said Haskell. "I've talked to the Pennsylvania troops in Webb's Second Brigade, and those mountain passes can be easily defended by the Rebels. At key chokepoints, roads are dug out of the mountainside, sloping at angles of thirty degrees, with one side being a steep embankment and the other side a deep abyss."

"Hooker should have occupied those passes as soon as Lee's army moved north across the Potomac," Gibbon said. "He should have ordered a few hundred men from Harper's Ferry or from the Union cavalry to block those passes. Twenty-five sharpshooters would do the trick. In some places the passes are just wide enough for four horses to walk abreast. Can't Hooker or Butterfield read a map? Don't they have any instincts?"

"Yes, they have an abundance of basic instincts." Haskell's lips pulled up into a devilish smirk. "Unfortunately, they're mostly of the carnal variety."

Gibbon's mouth twitched. "Well done, Frank. A nicely played witticism from the most humorless Dartmouth Yankee I know."

Haskell suppressed a grin, quietly accepting a rare Gibbon compliment. *Remember, you're not a pithy guy. Let's not press your luck with wisecracks.*

———————————— • ————————————

*7:44 p.m.*
*(Sunset was 7:37 p.m.)*
*Outside of Hancock's tent*

Hancock walked out of his tent. Gibbon stood up, saluted. Haskell saluted, holding it until the Second Corps commander returned the salute.

"Gentlemen." Hancock removed a cigar from his jacket and lit it. He walked over to the table and stared at the map.

Haskell studied the handsome General Winfield Scott Hancock. He was a magnificent leader, the thunderbolt of the Army of the Potomac. He was wearing a black felt slouch hat stiff enough for the brim and crown to hold their shapes. He was a picturesque officer, standing at six feet, two inches, towering over his two subordinate officers, looking, as always, dignified, gentlemanly, and commanding. Unlike many of the general officers who sported full beards, Hancock wore a mustache and a tuft of hair on his chin.

"How are you, gentlemen?"

Gibbon frowned. "I'm doing well. But I feel we are stumbling toward a slaughter, drawn unwittingly toward our demise."

"How so?" Hancock asked.

"Well." Gibbon paused, removed his black Hardee hat, and scratched his head, stalling.

"Damn it, John, stop hemming and hawing," Hancock said. "Spit it out."

Gibbon unleashed a spirited retort. "We look for orders and swift action from Hooker. And what do we get? Nothing. Lee paralyzed him at Chancellorsville. Since McClellan, we are plagued with army commanders whose problem is slowness." He paused for a moment, raising his brows. "Butterfield, Hooker's chief of staff, is villainous."

51

Haskell's jaw tensed. *And McClellan is the epitome of slowness.*

Hancock's eyes hardened into a darkened stare. "Go on."

"If Hooker remains in command, Lee will crush us," Gibbon said. "This army is laboring under a stroke of paralysis."

Hancock turned to Haskell. "What are your thoughts on this, Lieutenant?"

Haskell cleared his throat. "Hooker is a disaster. Everyone knows it, including Lincoln. And everyone knows the president offered the command to Reynolds, and he turned it down. Replacing Hooker now at this late stage of the campaign would be idiotic. But leaving him in command means certain defeat. It makes me sick to my stomach knowing the army is in such a pickle. Why in the hell did Reynolds turn down command?"

"For the same damn reason I turned down the command when Lincoln asked me," Hancock said.

Haskell's face froze. His cheeks burned. "General Hancock. I'm…appalled, sir. Why did both you and Reynolds turn down command?"

Hancock paused, his eyes tightened, his nostrils flared.

"Lieutenant Haskell," Gibbon interjected, "you're out of bounds and teetering on being insolent and insubordinate."

Hancock glared at Haskell, scrunching his eyebrows together into furrows over his nose. "General Gibbon," he said, "I asked Lieutenant Haskell to give me his opinion."

Haskell, staring wide-eyed, gasped in a half breath, bracing for another Hancock swearing fit.

"Lieutenant Haskell," Hancock continued in a frighteningly cold voice, "since Lincoln sacked McClellan, this army has been wallowing in the dark, overburdened with second-rate commanders. But Reynolds and I are not the answer. I told Lincoln that he needs to re-appoint Little Mac. And when he does, he must have unlimited and unfettered powers to command the army."

"Yes," Gibbon said. "McClellan's name is on everyone's tongue. Lincoln's puppets will not win this war."

"I don't believe the president will re-appoint McClellan," Haskell ventured. "Lincoln and the Republicans believe Little

Mac favors colluding with his Southern West Point classmates to end the war immediately and let the Confederates preserve slavery."

Hancock pointed his finger at Haskell as if scolding a child. "That's pure crap! And those radical Republicans are shitbirds. They're the reason why Reynolds and I will not take command. Hell, after every battle they hold an inquiry and then sacrifice the commanding general on their political altar. I refuse to be Lincoln's little puppet and under Halleck's thumb."

"The Republicans didn't hold an inquiry after Hooker's defeat at Chancellorsville, sir," Haskell replied.

"Of course not," Hancock said. "Hooker despises McClellan, and that is the type of commander they care to support. I'm not going to be sacrificed like McClellan. I agree with Reynolds that interference from Washington is to blame for McClellan's woes and the next two commanders of the Army of the Potomac. Lincoln can't get it through his thick skull that the army commander shouldn't have to consult with Stanton and Halleck before he takes a crap."

"Our prospects are dark unless we get stronger minds and clearer heads to lead 'em, like McClellan," Gibbon added. "Jealousies and political intrigue are just as great enemies to the Union as the Rebel Bobby Lee."

Hancock turned to Gibbon. "McClellan's removal was wrong. Both Reynolds and I are McClellanites, and we do not want to be Halleck or Lincoln's boy. Hell, Hooker, who is anti-McClellanite and who has the support of the Committee on the Conduct of the War, has the same complaints that McClellan, Reynolds, and I have. Hooker's remedy is the Union needs a military dictator. Naturally he thinks he's that dictator."

Haskell scowled as he stood with his hands clasped behind his back.

Hancock stepped in front of him, staring down into the lieutenant's face. "You got anything more to say, Mr. Haskell? Have I answered your questions?"

"Sir. I'm frustrated. You and General Reynolds turned down command and now we are left with Hooker, who can't win. And it's too late for you or Reynolds or anyone else to relieve Hooker and win this next battle. With all due respect, sir, I don't see a way off this dunghill."

"Go on?" Hancock nudged.

"For the life of me, wasn't it your duty, General Hancock, to accept command when the president offered it to you?" Haskell said. "You're one of our best, sir. And, there is no higher calling than to command the Union's largest army. Duty is what gives us a temper of will. Isn't duty our guidepost?"

Hancock snarled, jaw agape. "Damn you Haskell, don't lecture me on duty. Damn right I believe in duty. And country. And honor, damn it! It might seem *appalling* to you, but I did do my duty by refusing Lincoln's offer to command this army. If I had accepted the offer, I believe I would have been fired just like McClellan. I believe I'm doing my duty by commanding a corps. Hell, I've only been in command of Second Corps for six weeks and I've never led it during a battle. Jumping from division command at Chancellorsville to army command six weeks later without ever commanding a corps is absurd."

Haskell stared down at the map table.

"There's just one person and that's Meade," Hancock said. "I told the president that he should appoint Meade to replace Hooker."

Haskell straightened a bit, surprised. He had no idea Hancock thought so highly of Meade.

"But it's too late to replace Hooker with Meade," Gibbon added, "so we are going to support the commanding general the best we can. He just has to give us a fighting chance. And at the moment he is not."

*8:10 p.m.*

A yellow flash streaked the darkened sky. Then suddenly it came, first the low, distant thunder, then bolts of lightning, the bright flashes leaping several miles between thunderheads, the wind swinging to the north. Another crack of thunder popped over their heads and the night burst with a cold, pouring rain. They moved under the awning of Hancock's large tent, seeking shelter from the sheets of rain and the flashes of lightning, the fury of the storm catching them all by surprise.

At that moment a courier rode up. The thin-faced lieutenant dismounted, wiped the mixture of sweat and rain from his brow, and saluted briskly.

"General Hancock, sir, General Caldwell sends his respects and wishes to inform you that his division has placed pickets five miles beyond the Second Corps and is standing by for marching orders for tomorrow."

Hancock returned the salute. "My compliments to the general," he said sharply. Turning to Gibbon and Haskell, he added, "At least we can agree on one thing tonight, gentlemen."

Hancock turned back to the courier, "Tell General Caldwell that I will send him marching orders as soon as I talk with Hooker."

Hancock puffed on his cigar and turned to Gibbon and Haskell. "I'm worried that unless God directly guides Hooker, our army is in grave danger. Good evening, gentlemen." He excused himself and entered his tent.

Haskell and Gibbon walked toward their horses. Haskell wrestled silently with the evening's conversation. He disagreed vehemently with Hancock and Reynolds's decisions. Both had declined a duty to take command of the army. The Union had a chance to beat Lee's army with one of those two commanding. He touched his mouth, tasting disgust. How could they refuse to do their duty and expect others to do theirs? Apparently, duty and honor and country weren't guideposts for the custodians of the nation's defense. No, it was just lip service, an empty ideal that both the Southern and Northern West Point grads chose to honor when it was convenient. For pity's sake, Hooker matched up against Lee again in battle? It was madness. *We are doomed.*

*I probably won't survive to ever see the slaves freed.*

## ⁓ 5 ⁓
# Meade — Saturday, June 27

*6:37 p.m.*
*About one-and-one-half hours earlier*
*(Sunset is 7:37)*
*Riding to Hooker's headquarters*

Meade spurred Old Baldy, galloping toward Frederick with Captain Meade. His stomach clenched in knots; tension crawled up his spine.

"Damn you, Hooker," he muttered.

Only an hour left before sunset. When they reached an open clearing, the white, glittering buildings in Frederick were visible in the light of the fading sun. Meade reigned up Baldy, speaking to his son. "George, have you written your mother recently?"

"Not lately, sir," the young Meade replied.

"She would appreciate a letter from you," Meade said.

George nodded, saying he would. Meade had worried about his middle son during his first year at West Point. George had earned the maximum 200 demerits through after-hours escapades, sneaking away from the Academy, pursuing some of the local girls, putting his graduation and his commission in jeopardy. When Meade found out, he sent young George a pointed letter that ended his shenanigans. The general's son earned good marks during his second year at West Point, then left in 1862 to join the Eighth Pennsylvania Volunteer Infantry. He was turning into a fine officer.

---

*7:10 p.m.*
*At General Hooker's camp*

They rode in silence until they reached Hooker's camp, located in a dense copse of trees just south of Frederick. Ahead, up a long grey slope rising into the sunlit emptiness of an ebbing dusk, four armed sentries blocked the road, pointing bayoneted rifles. Meade pulled slightly back on the reins, slowing Baldy to a walk. As they approached the picket line, a clean-shaven lieutenant slid between the sentries, his right hand on his holstered pistol, poised to strike like a big cat. He stepped a few paces forward, peering at Meade.

Abruptly, the lieutenant ripped his hand from his holster and saluted smartly. "General, may I help you, sir?"

"Where is General Hooker's tent?" Meade demanded, returning his salute.

The lieutenant pointed. "General Hooker's headquarters is in Prospect Hall."

Meade fought to contain the anger he felt rising in his throat. Even in the dusk, the building was imposing, standing on the highest point in the city. "Do you think the commanding general could have found a bigger castle?" he hissed.

"It's the largest home in Frederick, sir," the lieutenant replied.

"I don't give a goddamn hell how big his headquarters is!" Meade shouted. *So much for restraint.*

The lieutenant's face flushed red as he dropped his gaze.

Meade turned his horse toward Prospect Hall, its grand marble catching enough light to outline the Grecian architecture, pediment, and eight classic columns on the entry portico.

As they rode closer, George said, "I can see silhouettes moving inside."

Meade gritted his teeth. "I'm not sure this is grand enough for Hooker. My guess is that's probably filled with the finest French wine and French maids. What a way to fight a war!"

---

*7:20 p.m.*
*At Hooker's headquarters*

Off to the side of the manor stood a large, imposing tent, open side flaps revealing the forms of two senior officers. Meade's heart lightened in the warmth of recognition. General Gouverneur Warren, chief of engineers, was examining a map with General Henry Hunt, chief of artillery. Warren was a marvelous officer, a close colleague from their time as topographical engineers.

Meade dismounted and stepped into the tent, removing his slouch hat. Dressed in a dusty blue blouse, corduroy pants tucked into his high jack boots, his gaunt, grizzled appearance reflected his fatigue and irritation.

"Gentlemen."

An automatic exchange of salutes ensued. Warren beamed.

"General," Warren said with true affection. "It's good to see you, sir." He paused. "Are you here to see General Hooker?"

Meade shot a glance at Hunt, an unfamiliar officer. Then he peered grimly at Warren, his eyes narrowed. "No, I'm here for the party with the French whores. Of course I'm here to see Hooker! Is he in his tent or in that obscene marble palace?"

Hunt said nothing, staring.

"No, General, Hooker has not arrived from his visit to Harper's Ferry," Warren said, almost apologetically. Hunt shifted his feet.

"Incredible," Meade said shaking his head. "What about Butterfield?"

"The chief of staff is still in Poolesville, waiting for Hooker's return," Warren said.

Meade spewed out several expletives, faced with the probability he would not see Hooker tonight. It was past sunset, and all through the camp soldiers were talking, cooking, and milling about, smoking cigars. No sense of urgency. No battle rhythm. No discipline. The only real activity was from the fireflies.

In an icy tone, he asked, "Does headquarters have any verbal orders for Fifth Corps?"

"No, sir," said Warren, with some hesitation.

Meade glared at Warren as frustration hobbled his tongue. "Damn it! Does Hooker even have a plan? Does he know where Lee's army is located? Does he know what the hell is going on?"

Hunt hedged. "I've heard nothing about Hooker's strategy. Colonel George Sharp's intelligence unit believes Lee's entire army is operating in Pennsylvania."

"Son of a bitch!" Meade railed, raking his hand through his hair. "How can that be? My scouts today located a large Rebel cavalry force operating in Maryland. Lee would not leave his infantry wandering around Pennsylvania unprotected by his cavalry."

"We're not sure why Stuart's cavalry is operating separately," Warren offered. "It's mystifying."

"God Almighty! You think so?" Meade exploded. The situation was worse than he thought. "Hooker's yawing back and forth without purpose will result in a devastating Union defeat on Northern soil. Someone needs to chart a course to find, fix, and fight Lee's army. Do you have any Pennsylvania maps we can examine?"

Warren said worriedly, "No. Hooker hasn't asked for any maps beyond Maryland."

Hunt shrugged, shaking his head.

"I'm sorry, sir," Warren said, as he tucked his hands behind his back. "We expect Hooker to arrive later this evening. As soon as he does, I will tell him you came to report, and that you're expecting orders."

Lightning bolts lit the skies in jagged streaks, followed by cracking thunder. Meade shook his head, aware his voice had risen, and that he was shooting the messenger. He paused, his mouth perilously dry. His instincts toggled between restraint and tenacity. He needed to hold his temper, save his rage for Hooker, and not unleash it on these men.

Warren grabbed Meade by the elbow and guided him away from Hunt. "You should know, sir," he whispered, "General Butterfield continues to pass rumors among the headquarters staff that you might be removed as corps commander."

Meade stood stoically and looked into the night, his eyes fixed, a tightness gripping his chest. He paused, letting an awkward silence linger. Turning, he noticed a group of people strolling toward him, laughing and flirting. Several young officers were escorting salaciously dressed and overly made-up women—Murder Bay residents.

"Good Lord!" Meade raged. "Look at this place! Hooker isn't running an army headquarters—he's got a first-class brothel."

He scrunched his eyebrows together, creating two vertical furrows between his narrowed eyes. Hunt and Warren did not move. "Sickness has infected this headquarters," Meade growled. "Butterfield and Sickles are the disgrace of this army. Hooker loves flattery, and Sickles and Butterfield are blowing it up his ass."

Meade caught himself. All his military life he had followed army protocol: praise in public and rebuke in private.

"Forget I said that," Meade said.

Hunt took a deep breath, and then nodded. Warren nodded, too.

Meade turned away, struck by a premonition of sorts: The uncertainty that had plagued him today was warranted. Lee would outmaneuver Hooker, likely defeat the Union army, and end the Republic.

He turned back to face Hunt and Warren. Here were two competent professional warriors. It wasn't their fault, and he shouldn't blame them. Reynolds must replace Hooker. Butterfield must be fired. Sickles must be relieved for cause.

If only it were that easy.

Meade clasped his hands in front, letting them hang below his belt, looking each man in the eye. "You're fine men, both of you—gallant and professional soldiers. I have the greatest respect for you." He put his hat back on. "These are trying times. If you learn of anything that would be of value to Fifth Corps, please let me know. From one soldier to another, that would be greatly appreciated."

Meade extended a hand, shaking first with Hunt and then with Warren. "Good night, gentlemen. May God help us."

---

## Warren
*9:00 p.m.*

Still somewhat unsettled from the evening's unexpected visit, Warren waved as Meade left Hooker's headquarters bivouac to head back to Fifth Corps. When darkness had engulfed the departing general, Warren walked back to the map table, standing across from Hunt.

He studied the map and traced his finger over the myriad of roads leading to Gettysburg.

"The roads leading to Gettysburg look like the strands of a giant spider web."

"By the time Hooker moves that far north, the Rebels will be occupying the high ground around Gettysburg and waiting for the Union army to become entangled in Lee's web," Hunt said grimly.

"Then Hooker is going to order the army to attack Lee's prepared defensive positions. It will be Fredericksburg all over again." Warren shook his head.

"Meade was pretty pissed off at Hooker tonight," Hunt said. "Do you think he is going to survive as Fifth Corps commander?"

"Not sure. But I think we will find out tomorrow. Meade seems hell-bent about forcing the rumor issue. Arriving unannounced again in the morning could seal his fate."

"Maybe that's what he wants," Hunt mused. "I can't imagine him controlling his temper when he visits with Hooker. He'll blow at the slightest provocation." He rubbed his beard, pondering. "Meade doesn't play the political game well. I think Hooker might bait him into being insubordinate."

"You may be right. But one thing is for sure," said Warren. "Meade has had it with both Hooker and Butterfield playing their rumor games. Those two gossip whores are worse than a women's quilting bee."

They said good night and moved into their own tents. As he did most nights, Warren fell into an uneasy slumber, racked by a recurring nightmare of an event that had occurred during the Plains Indian Wars. He was exploring the North Platte River as a topographical engineer when his unit encountered a tribe of Sioux Indians. They killed the Sioux men in battle, then slaughtered their unarmed families along the river. Scarcely a night had passed since that he had not awakened covered in sweat, remembering himself carrying a small boy to the bloody water to bathe his saber wounds.

# Meade

## 10:00 p.m.
## Fifth Corps' camp

Meade and George mounted their horses and rode back toward Fifth Corps. Arriving at the Fifth Corps picket line, Meade glanced at his watch. It was ten at night. A waiting escort of cavalrymen fell in quietly around the general and his son, turning off Buckneytown Pike and moving to the entrance to Arcadia Manor, the well-lit porch silhouetting the sentries, dark figures entering and departing, waiting for the return of their commander.

Meade dismounted and walked hurriedly toward his tent. He had left orders not to impose his late arrival on the Arcadia host, preferring to sleep like his men in the camp's bivouac shelters. The night air was still stuffy, and small beads of sweat slid down his face. He halted and coughed up his damaged lung, afterwards gasping for a breath. He rubbed his chest until the burning stopped.

Meade's nose caught a whiff of roasting chicken. His stomach gurgled, and he licked his lips. He caught Biddle's eye.

"Good evening, sir," said Biddle. "I've got a plate of food coming. Trust your trip to General Hooker's headquarters went well?"

"Hooker was not in his camp," Meade said. "Butterfield also was absent."

Biddle shook his head. "I assume that if Hooker and Butterfield were not in camp that a senior staff officer at headquarters would have orders for Fifth Corps," Biddle said.

Meade couldn't help himself. "Remember, this is Hooker and Butterfield. They take a certain pride in keeping secrets within their little cabal. I didn't receive any written or verbal orders."

He stared across the dale of Ballinger's Creek, the dying campfires of Fifth Corps flickering like thousands of stars in a distant galaxy. He was losing hope. The Union army needed to be saved—but by whom?

"Lincoln is a fool for keeping Hooker in command," Meade bellowed to no one in particular. "Everyone knows it, except for him." His heart shredded into tiny pieces. The army needed

Reynolds to take command, but it was too late to change now, with the two armies maneuvering toward each other.

"Here you go, General," Meade's cook called out.

His cook brought him a plate of roasted chicken and a mug of hot coffee. Meade's stomach growled. Was breakfast the last time he had eaten?

Meade accepted the plate and mug. "Thank you." He turned to Biddle. "James, would you like to join me? It's too warm to eat inside my tent."

"Yes, sir," said Biddle. "Let me refill my coffee cup." The cook overheard Biddle's request and walked over and refilled his cup.

"If Lee's army is operating in Pennsylvania, Hooker needs to move this army quickly to the north," Meade said. "General Darius Couch is in Harrisburg. The danger with Couch is he is commanding five thousand elderly militia." Meade frowned. "My guess is half of them fought in the Revolutionary War, probably for the British."

Biddle chuckled. "Well, at least Couch will fight the Rebels."

*11:00 p.m.*

After Meade finished his dinner, Biddle saluted, then moved to his tent, located next to Meade's. Meade stood for a moment alone, staring at the sky. How could the corps commanders trust Hooker, Butterfield, and Sickles? Those jackals were trying to advance their careers at the expense of the Republic.

Meade yawned. *Need some sleep.* He entered his tent and sat at his small writing table. He adjusted the wooden candle holder. The yellow flame flickered, providing light for some last-minute paperwork and a quick scan of the New York newspaper.

Then he stretched out on his cot and closed his eyes, letting his mind wrap around the uncertainties he faced. He had no choice. He was tired of bending with the rumor winds. He would ride back tomorrow morning and visit headquarters—again uninvited. *If Hooker is going to fire me, I want to get it over with bright and early. There will be no more rumor-mongering about my status tomorrow. But Hooker needs to know we spotted Lee's cavalry roaming around near Winchester, and that means Rebel infantry are on the move, possibly southward toward D.C.*

He yawned again and muttered, "*Va te faire foutre*, Hooker." He fell asleep.

# Sunday

June 28, 1863

### *General Robert E. Lee, Commander*
Northern Army of Virginia
Commanding for One Year

### *General George G. Meade, Commander*
Army of the Potomac
Commanding for One Day

### *General George Sykes, Commander*
Fifth Corps
Commanding for One Day

## 6

# The Messenger — Sunday, June 28

### *Hardie*
*1:07 a.m.*
*Frederick, Maryland*

Hardie walked toward Frederick's cluster of church cupolas, counting five spires in the moonlit skyline. A gunshot whizzed over the spires, followed by yelling and screaming coming from the direction of the town square. His shoulders tightened. Rebel cavalry? He reached for his pistol, forgetting he was unarmed. *Damn it.* Slinking around a corner, he paused, masked by the shadows. His first glimpse of the ruckus sent him reeling, and his stomach recoiled. Scores of prostitutes and rowdy soldiers swarmed over each other like crazed ants, passing a bottle of whiskey from mouth to mouth. *How could this be?* Army headquarters was bivouacked here. *Who is in charge?*

Hardie proceeded down the street, eyes wide, sweat pouring down his brow. Ahead, a soldier lunged from a gaggle of blue-clad ruffians, naked to the waist, with a gash over his brow and blood running down his face. He staggered back into a saloon, waving a pistol. Two gunshots rang out. A moment later, a fully clothed soldier tumbled out of the bar into the street. A dead drunk.

A fracas of savage screams, bellowing growls, and cracking bones rent the night. Up the street, an all-out drunken brawl burst out among blue-clad soldiers. A soldier grabbed a man by the hair and rammed his fist into the man's crotch, lifting him up and slamming him to the ground.

Why were the provost marshal troops allowing this donnybrook at army headquarters? Hell, maybe these drunken vandals *were* the provost marshal. Hardie hastened toward the town

66

center, scouring the throngs of drunk and boisterous soldiers roaming the streets, looking for someone sober enough to guide him to Fifth Corps headquarters.

Near the town center he spied an ancient, grizzled figure standing and watching the mayhem. Hardie approached him. "Where is the Frederick provost marshal?"

"There are no provost marshal troops, son," the old man raised his voice above the din. "The mayor asked General Hooker about it, but his staff must still be *studyin'* the situation."

"God damn it," Hardie muttered.

"When we were fighting in 1812, our militia never behaved this badly, especially when the British were roaming nearby," the old man said. "Old Hickory would have never tolerated it. In fact, he would have shot these thugs himself."

Hardie moved on, spying a major flirting with three camp prostitutes. The officer took a long pull from a whisky bottle, wiped his shirtsleeve over his lips, and passed the bottle to the hookers.

"Major," Hardie asked, nostrils flaring, "do you know the whereabouts of Fifth Corps headquarters?"

The major turned and took a menacing step toward Hardie, his right hand resting on his holstered revolver. Hardie shifted his stance into a shallow squat with his lead foot ahead of his rear one, his hands open, belt high, ready to strike. The major leaned forward, pushing his nose inches from Hardie's face. Hardie gagged on the whiskey breath blowing past the major's wet lips.

"Damned if some civilian coward needs to know where Fifth Corps headquarters is," the major snarled. He reached out with both hands to grab Hardie's coat collar. Hardie parried the attack, blocking his arms. He grabbed the man's jacket and butted his brow into his nose. The major screamed, stunned and bloodied. He tried to paw Hardie with a right, but Hardie launched a powerful left jab to his head. The major grunted and clattered backward to the ground. Hardie fell on him and snatched the revolver, jamming it hard against the officer's chest.

The major stared wide-eyed at his own gun in Hardie's hand. The hookers screeched and fled toward a gaggle of soldiers belting out a verse of an Irish folksong.

"I'll ask you again, Major," Hardie said. "Where is Fifth Corps headquarters?"

The major lifted his arm, pointed to a road heading south, and whimpered, "It's a few miles up that way. On the left."

⸻ • ⸻

*2:30 a.m.*

*Frederick town center*

Hardie stood up, keeping the gun. He spotted a buggy parked outside a house and walked over and banged on the door, offering to pay for a ride to General George Meade's headquarters. At the sight of Hardie's gold certificate, the astonished but sleepy occupant agreed and rushed to hitch up his horse. Hardie jumped up onto the single wooden bench and checked his watch. Two thirty in the morning. Next to him, the driver snapped his whip and the buggy lurched forward, skirting past straggling parties of soldiers and a long, disorganized line of supply wagons.

"Hurry! As fast as you can!" Hardie shouted over the clamor in the street and the clatter of horse hooves.

The driver snapped the reins and his horse burst into a trot.

The night was clear, heavy with humidity. Campfires licking at wet logs hissed like frightened cats. The trees and road were wet from the fierce thunderstorm that had passed through a few hours prior. Hardie swayed as the buggy plowed its way down the muddy road, holding tightly to the siderail with one hand and gripping the leather satchel holding Lincoln's orders with the other.

Hardie recalled previous fiery encounters with the Fifth Corps commander. Meade's volcanic temper was legendary and frightening, erupting without warning. Waking up the unsuspecting Meade was going to be harrowing; Lincoln's messenger shuddered with an unwelcome chill. God, he hoped this was the last time he had to deliver an order like this.

"How much further?" he asked.

"About a mile." A dim glow emerged ahead. "Fifth Corps is just beyond Ballinger's Creek, around this bend." The driver snapped his whip and the buggy picked up speed, bouncing from side to side. Barely three nights shy of a full moon, there was just enough light in the lurching buggy for Hardie to check his watch. Almost three.

*2:50 a.m.*
*Meade's Fifth Corps camp*

The camp was dotted with several thousand smoldering campfires, many still flickering. Sentries blocked the road. The messenger had reached the picket line. "Halt!" a young lieutenant yelled. "Why in the hell are two civilians trying to cross the picket lines at this hour?"

The sentries held their rifles ready, their index fingers curved around the triggers.

"Please lower your rifles, Lieutenant," Hardie said. "I'm Colonel Hardie from the War Department, and I'm acting as President Lincoln's courier. I'm carrying an urgent dispatch for General Meade. Here are my orders."

Hardie showed the officer his papers. The lieutenant held a lantern, reading the papers twice. His face tightened and he saluted Hardie. The officer motioned for the buggy to pass. The sentries lowered their rifles and stepped aside, watching the "civilians" with an incredulous stare. The carriage lurched forward, passing through the outer perimeter of the Fifth Corps. Hardie told the driver to head toward the Fifth Corps command flag, a red Maltese cross on a white background inscribed with the number 5.

Hardie fidgeted and his eyes narrowed. Meade did not need to know he was Lincoln's third pick, and he certainly wouldn't hear it from the president's messenger. The buggy stopped near Meade's tent and Hardie jumped out, gripping the leather satchel. He handed the major's revolver to the driver. "Here you go, sir. This ought to help if you run into drunken soldiers on your way back to Frederick."

The driver took the revolver. With eyes wide, he muttered, "Thank you, sir, and God bless."

<hr />

*3:00 a.m.*

Hardie walked toward the sentries guarding Meade's tent, dreading what he had to do. Meade was about to be ambushed.

The sentries eyed Hardie curiously. The man standing before them wore mud-splashed civilian clothes but acted with authority.

"I'm Colonel Hardie from the War Department," Hardie announced. "I have urgent orders from President Lincoln for General Meade. I must speak with him immediately, alone."

A stout staff sergeant holding a rifle with a fixed bayonet across his chest took his time scanning Hardie from head to toe before speaking. "Well, fella," he snorted, "I don't think that's going to happen. I typically don't let folks in civilian clothes claiming to be a colonel waltz in to see the general at three in the morning. You're not wearing a uniform, and you don't have any authority here."

Hardie took a calculated breath and bellowed in a graduating crescendo, "I want to speak to the officer in charge, now!"

The sergeant moved a step closer. "Keep your voice down! If you wake the general, I'm going to thump your ass."

Hardie's eyes narrowed. He came nose to nose with the sentry, his hands clenching into tight fists. "Sergeant, you will take me to the officer in charge. Now!"

The startled sentry did not budge. Hardie's breath tripped in his throat. *Keep making noise. It's your only hope.* He berated the sentry at the top of his voice. The sentry blinked and tightened his grip on his rifle, his chest heaving with every breath. Hardie shouted louder. Maybe the yelling would wake up some of Meade's staff. A circle of staff officers and aides started to gather, all staring with amusement.

After a moment, Colonel Locke, Meade's chief of staff, turned out, asking in a low, agitated voice, "What the hell is going on?"

Hardie's head whipped around at the gruff voice. "Good morning, Colonel. I am Colonel James Hardie. I have urgent orders from President Lincoln to deliver to General Meade." He paused, clamping his mouth shut. Locke had to understand that he was on a critically urgent mission from the White House.

Colonel Locke scowled. "Colonel Hardie, why for God's sake are you in civilian clothes? And why are you here at this ungodly hour?"

Hardie stepped closer to Locke and whispered, "President Lincoln felt delivering this order in person to General Meade was of such importance that he directed me to wear civilian clothes in case I ran into Rebel raiders."

Locke raised an eyebrow, then shrugged and turned to the sentries. "Let Colonel Hardie enter General Meade's tent."

The sentries stepped aside. Hardie took a step forward, paused, and cocked his head, nodding a thank-you to Locke. Locke's face was pale and grim. Small wonder, Hardie thought; an unexpected 3:00 a.m. visit by the president's messenger ought to portend something ominous. He spotted other orderlies and junior staff officers arriving outside Meade's tent, joining the circle of spectators.

Turning and walking past the sentries, Hardie set his course, eyes narrowed, like a soldier charging forward into an enemy line. He slowly opened the tent flap and disappeared inside.

## George
*3:02 a.m.*

Colonel Locke turned to Captain Meade. "My God, what a nightmare! I'm so sorry, George. The rumors must be true about General Meade. It appears Colonel Hardie is arresting him for crossing swords with Hooker."

The younger Meade stood in dread silence, saying nothing, staring as Colonel Hardie disappeared behind the flap of his father's tent. The other staff officers mumbled among themselves about the fate of their beloved commander, but George could hear nothing but his heart pounding in his ears like the merciless, relentless beat of the drum on the way to the scaffold.

## Hardie

Hardie tried to be as quiet as possible, not wanting to startle Meade. A lantern was burning on a makeshift writing table near the entrance, the flame casting a dim light on the dark corners. In the back of the tent, the flicker gave a hint of a sole figure lying on a cot.

Meade was snoring, his back turned to Hardie. Hardie sighed. "General Meade, sir." He paused. "General Meade, sir, it's Colonel Hardie from the War Department. Are you awake?" Hardie watched him for a moment, scarcely daring to breathe.

## Meade

*3:02 a.m.*

Meade was dreaming of the Mexican War. It was a confusing dream. Colonel Hardie was calling his name, but Colonel Hardie did not serve with him in Mexico. Sensing someone was near, touching him on the shoulder, Meade slowly surfaced from deep sleep, still trying to sort this out.

"General Meade, sir?"

Meade rolled toward the voice. *Why is there an intruder in my tent?* He squinted, trying to focus without his thick glasses, and recognized a blurry Colonel Hardie.

He snapped awake. *Why in the hell is Lincoln's man visiting at this unearthly hour, wearing civilian clothes?* Bolting upright onto the edge of the cot, he glared at Hardie's face, backlit by the lantern flame.

"Good morning, General Meade. Sorry to startle you, sir," said Hardie as he backed away.

Meade's stomach lurched and twisted into a knot. Sons of bitches. That was why army headquarters did not send orders yesterday. Hooker knew Colonel Hardie was on his way to arrest him. Hardie stood motionless in the dark, holding the leather satchel.

"Why are you here, Colonel Hardie?" Meade demanded coldly.

The corner of Hardie's lips curled as he said, "General Meade, I have come to give you trouble."

A torrent of anger rushed over him. Meade stood erect, his head nearly touching the top of the tent roof, his hands clenched at his side.

"Damn you Hardie, if you're here to arrest me, my conscience is clear. I'm prepared to face any charges."

Hardie's face showed his surprise. He held up a hand. "Sir, I apologize for my ill-timed humor on delivering this order."

"What order? Does Hooker require Stanton's adjutant to deliver his orders now?"

"No sir! Give me a second."

Hardie moved to the writing table, opened his satchel, and removed Lincoln's order placing Meade in command of the Army of the Potomac.

He handed it to Meade. "Please read this order from President Lincoln."

His throat tightening, Meade moved over to the table, grabbed his glasses, placed them on his hawkish nose, and sat down in a chair. He opened the sealed envelope. With a steady, deadpan face, he read the order in the flickering light, studying each word, trying to understand. He searched for the words *under arrest*, but he did not see them. He continued reading in stunned silence. Only his eyes moved, darting rapidly across the page. The words echoed hollowly.

He read the order again. Uncertainty billowed like rising dark clouds. His breathing rasped, and drops of sweat burned his eyes. He gave a loud groan. The Devil be damned! President Lincoln was ordering him to assume command immediately and attack an army whose whereabouts were unknown. He shot Hardie a glance. A beat of silence. Then relief bubbled up: he was not being arrested. For one brief moment, a sigh like a spring breeze escaped him.

Meade read the order a third time. Pure fear seized him and his heart began pounding like a galloping horse racing into an icy wind. He shook his head and gulped a breath. "No. This can't be."

He turned his head, his eyes raking Hardie. "Son of a bitch, Colonel," Meade shouted. "This is a terrible, terrible mistake. Reynolds is our best commander. I know that. You know that. All the corps commanders know it. Lincoln should appoint Reynolds."

Hardie said nothing.

Meade swore again. *Keep ripping Hardie's ass until he rescinds the order.* "Damn it Hardie, I'm totally ignorant of our army's positions and where Lee's army is operating!"

Hardie stood with his hands clasped behind his back, staring calmly at the overwhelmed general.

"Common sense dictates that I must refuse this assignment for the good of the army and the Republic," Meade railed. "I'm clearly not the most qualified general to lead this army in this time of peril. I will telegraph General Halleck immediately, refusing this assignment and strongly recommending Lincoln select Reynolds to replace Hooker."

Hardie finally piped up. "General Meade, Lincoln, Stanton, and Halleck knew that would be your response. The president has great confidence you can deliver our nation from the Rebel army's invasion." Hardie paused. "With all due respect, General, this is an order you cannot refuse. Lincoln has ordered you to take command, immediately."

Meade struggled to inhale as he slowly absorbed Hardie's words. He brooded, his obstinacy beginning to wobble, his brain cluttered with conflicting thoughts. The position put him in the public eye, and he faced disgrace if he failed. *Damn it.* Everyone knew he was not charismatic and popular with the soldiers. He was a quiet person, and he did not like or seek public attention. This was bloody mindlessness. He despised vermin-pestering reporters and whore-mongering politicians. And these were the people who would comment on his every decision, his every move.

Meade took a deep breath. Being a good soldier brought with it a responsibility to obey. The idea of duty before self demanded he accept the unacceptable. He sighed—and conceded.

"Well, I have been tried and condemned," he said, setting his jaw. "I suppose I shall have to march to the execution in as dignified a manner as I can muster."

Hardie's eyes widened and glowed. The messenger reached into his satchel and pulled out the letter that had accompanied Lincoln's order.

"I have a note from General Halleck."

Meade took the letter, read it carefully:

*General Meade:*

*You will receive with this the order of the President placing you in command of the Army of the Potomac. No one has ever received a more important command. I cannot doubt that you will fully justify the confidence which the Government has reposed to you.*

*You will not be hampered by minute instructions from these headquarters. Your army is free to act as you may deem proper under the circumstances as they arise. You will, however, keep in view that the Army of the Potomac is the covering army of Washington, as well as the army of operation against the invading force of Rebels. You will therefore maneuver and fight in such a manner as to cover the Capital and also Baltimore, as far as circumstances will admit. Should General Lee move against either of these places, it is expected that you will either anticipate him or arrive with him, so as to give him battle.*

*All forces within the sphere of your operations will be held to your orders. Harper's Ferry and its garrison are under your direct orders.*

*You are authorized to remove from command and send from your army any officer or other person you may deem expedient.*

*In fine, General, you are instructed with all the power and authority which the President, the Secretary of War, or the General-in-Chief can confer on you, and you may rely on our full support. You will keep me fully informed of all your movements and the positions of your own troops and those of the enemy, so far as known.*

*I always shall be ready to advise and assist you to the utmost of my ability.*

*Very respectfully, your obedient servant,*
*H.W. Halleck, General-in-Chief*

"I will wait outside, General," Hardie interrupted. "When you are ready, we ride immediately to Frederick, where you will relieve Hooker and assume command of the army."

"Bugger the devil," Meade shouted. Bile rushed up his throat. "It is improper for me to show up at army headquarters without Hooker sending for me. You know this better than anyone, Colonel. As Lincoln's messenger initiating previous changes of command, you know that McDowell sent for McClellan. McClellan sent for Burnside. And Burnside sent for Hooker. Good Lord, this is madness. We must wait for Hooker to send for me."

Hardie was respectful but insistent. "In this exceptional circumstance, time is of utmost importance. We are to travel to Hooker's headquarters immediately. I accept all local responsibility for the protocol of our orders." Hardie had carefully emphasized the "our."

An icy chill shot down Meade's spine. "This is going to be an awkward situation for both Hooker and me. Hooker thought his position was secure because of the impending battle."

Hardie nodded, his face showing no emotion.

If there was anything Meade understood in his bones, it was duty. Even as he resisted, instinct was taking over, invoking his inherent inclination to plan. No time to worry about hurt feelings. In a few hours, he would be commanding the army. He needed to gain an awareness of the situation, the location of dispersed troops and enemy forces, immediately.

"I will ask Colonel Locke to have someone saddle your horse and prepare an additional mount for me," said Hardie. He saluted and departed the tent.

Meade reread Lincoln's order and Halleck's letter. A dark void filled his soul, the emptiness consuming everything inside. He finished dressing, blew out the lantern, and left the tent. Colonel Locke and the rest of his personal staff were waiting anxiously. Meade and Locke exchanged salutes, and Meade said quietly, "I have been ordered to report to Hooker's headquarters. I will take Captain Meade with me. That's all I can tell you now."

Locke's face was ashen; his mouth gaped. "Yes, sir," he said, staring at Meade as if Hardie were escorting him to his execution.

* * *

*4:15 a.m.*

Meade walked over to Baldy and mounted. After a glance at his staff, he turned toward Frederick. They rode together, Meade and Hardie abreast, Captain Meade trailing behind. No one spoke. Meade had heard the rumors about a generals' revolt, hoping Reynolds would be Hooker's replacement. Damn. What about McClellan? If Reynolds didn't want command, McClellan would take it. And he was everyone's first choice, except Lincoln's.

How was he going to defeat Lee? He was going from a corps command of 11,000 men that he'd had for three months to commanding an army of 100,000 men. He swallowed hard and listened. Other than chirping crickets, the blackness of early dawn was gloomily quiet. His heart pounded in his ears, keeping in step with Baldy's hoofbeats.

Two lines in Halleck's letter played in his mind: "*No one has ever received a more important command. I cannot doubt that you will fully justify the confidence which the Government has reposed in you.*"

"For God's sake, why me?" Meade muttered. The Army of the Potomac was jinxed—four commanders in one year. His side cramped as if he had sprinted a mile. He had been handed a post no one would dare to undertake. He rubbed his throbbing forehead.

Baldy snorted; Meade leaned forward and patted the horse's muscled neck, comforting and coaxing him. Fetching his handkerchief from his coat pocket, he removed his glasses, closed his eyes, and wiped the sweat from his face. In that moment, his former Fifth Corps command lurked inside like a second mind. By God, he would miss his boys.

* * *

*4:40 a.m.*
*(Sunrise: 4:48 a.m.)*
*Riding to General Hooker's headquarters*

They rode at a brisk pace, the predawn morning already warming. Meade did not know where Lee's army was, but he hoped Hooker would tell him. So his thoughts turned to likely rivals within the Army of the Potomac: Butterfield and Sickles. Meade frowned. He despised army amateurs like those two, dishonoring the profession of soldiering with their questionable military judgments and personal immoralities. How could they be trusted to win battles, which depended on a leader's character?

Sickles, the highest-ranking non–West Pointer in the Army of the Potomac, did not fit the role of general. Meade disliked Sickles's bumptious air, falsetto voice, and vulgar bravado. He also was concerned about Sickles's lack of combat experience and his rapid promotion to division command, then to corps leadership. Although Sickles had the aggressive spirit to excel as a regimental or brigade commander, Meade doubted he had the leadership skills to command a corps.

Meade cocked his head and spotted George a few yards behind at a respectful distance, looking as if he had seen a ghost.

He turned his head back around. Promotion to corps commander required a greater ability to coordinate, to maneuver larger bodies of troops, and to act independently, albeit in accordance with the commander's plan and in cooperation with the army as whole. No easy task for a political general, an amateur having never studied the military theories of Antoine-Henri Jomini or Henry Halleck's *Elements of Military Art and Science*. Sickles's greatest shortcoming was being promoted too fast. But he was Lincoln's little butt boy. And what did Lincoln know about warfighting? Not a damn thing. Commanding a corps required experience and military skills beyond tactical thought. Sickles had neither.

Lee's corps commanders, in contrast, were James Longstreet, A. P. Hill, and Jubal Ewell, all West Point grads and veterans of the Mexican War. Meade's heart plunged. Shaking his head, he turned to Hardie.

"Halleck's letter said I am authorized to remove any officer," he said. "I desire to remove Butterfield and Sickles from this army."

For a long moment Hardie pondered, then replied, "Indeed, you are authorized to remove any officer. Butterfield should be replaced. His disloyalty and contempt toward you have grown even greater since you relieved him as Fifth Corps commander following Fredericksburg."

Meade nodded approvingly.

"I would not recommend removing Sickles, however, at least not until after the impending action," Hardie added. "Lincoln would waver in his support, as would Stanton, as he was Sickles's lead lawyer when Sickles killed Philip Key. It comes to this: Sickles is a former Democratic congressman. Retaining him as corps commander has all to do with politics. Lincoln needs to develop and retain the support of Northern war Democrats, and Sickles is their darling."

Meade scowled. So much for Lincoln's assurance that he would have a free hand in commanding this army. He spat out an expletive. "I really am a lamb being led to slaughter."

Hardie nodded without a word.

Meade faced fire from two directions. In front, he expected a fight from Lee; from the rear, he feared sniping from Washington. No matter what he did, he was vulnerable. He now understood why Reynolds turned down command of the army.

"As God is my witness, I did not covet this command," he muttered.

Meade's own darkness deepened. Lee had the advantage. Changing commanders in the middle of a campaign was dangerous; just before a decisive battle was suicidal. Moments ago, Hardie had handed command of an army in movement, its units widely separated, to a corps commander with no experience leading an entire army. Meanwhile, somewhere out in the darkness waited a wily opponent with a formidable string of victories to his credit. The beloved General Lee had served as Meade's mentor at West Point. But Lee had broken his oath to the nation.

Now his new task was to break Meade.

Meade wiped his brow. He remembered the principles engraved on his conscience at West Point—his obligation to duty, to honor, to country. He believed fervently in all three. He would soon find out if holding fast to those principles was going to be enough to overcome his personal shortcomings and defeat Lee—who also once believed in them.

He straightened in the saddle, his resolve stiffening. *You've done enough bitching. It's time to take this fight to Lee.* As dawn's first fingers of light crept into the sky, he cocked his head toward Hardie.

"By God, this army is going to find and fight the Rebel invaders, and every soldier is going to give his last full measure in doing it. Now, let's hurry up and finish this tawdry business with Hooker."

Meade spurred Baldy and broke into a gallop. Hardie kept pace, with Captain Meade riding close behind. As the senior Meade bounced in his saddle, a new realization dawned, kindling his resolve. *I do have one advantage over Lee: he doesn't know there is a new commander of the Army of the Potomac. A flaming son of a bitch who is going to maneuver this army faster than this army has ever moved.*

## 7
# Warren — Sunday, June 28

*5:00 a.m.*
*Hooker's camp; Warren's tent*

Five in the morning. Warren awoke, his heart thumping. A distant voice was calling.

"Gouv, are you awake?"

Warren opened his eyes, his pillow soaked around his head. In the dim light of a lantern, he eyed the face of a thin, whiskered man wearing glasses on his large beaked nose. "I'm awake," he said, though it was only partly true, as his muddled mind rang a warning.

"Gouv, it's me. George Meade."

Warren rubbed his eyes. "What the hell?" he muttered.

He stared up. Meade stood still, his crumpled uniform unkempt, making him look more like a bedraggled wagon master than the commander of Fifth Corps. Something was dreadfully wrong.

Meade took a step back. "Gouv, are you alright?"

Warren nodded, the nightmare growing faint. Meade was not a casual visitor—this had to be serious. He sat up on the cot, wiping the wetness from his face.

"What's wrong, George?" he heard himself say, his fuzzy brain bracing for bad news.

"I want to discuss something with you when you're wide awake," Meade said.

Warren stood, waiting for the machinery in his head to start churning. He stroked his handlebar moustache. He and Meade were kindred spirits: both were West Point engineers, and they trusted each other.

"Oh, my God," Warren said. "Were you summoned to headquarters?"

Meade placed the lantern on the map table near two chairs. "Yes, I was summoned to headquarters. But not by Hooker or Butterfield. I need you to sit down for this, Gouv."

Warren sat, staring at Meade. Meade took off his hat, his thinning hair gleaming in the lantern light.

"I wanted to see you alone before I met with General Hooker," Meade said, his eyes scrunched tight. "I'm sorry to wake you so early."

"Sir, that's fine," Warren replied, sitting forward a bit. "But what the hell is happening?"

"Colonel Hardie woke me two hours ago, giving me an order from Lincoln."

Warren's muscles tensed like bundles of tight wire. *My God, powerful forces are at work this morning. Is Hardie relieving me as well?*

"And?" Warren said, hearing a bit of irritation in his own voice.

"The order appointed me commander of the Army of the Potomac," Meade said. "Colonel Hardie is waiting outside and will escort me to Hooker's tent, per Lincoln's direction, where I will relieve him immediately."

Warren flopped back in his chair, his limp legs quaking. He squished his eyes shut and slapped his thigh, making a loud clap. Meade in command! Lincoln had a new standard bearer. Incredible, almost a suicidal risk, but brilliant…if it worked. His insides started to untwist.

"You are probably wondering why I stopped at your tent first before seeing Hooker." Meade continued. "I would like for you to replace Butterfield as my chief of staff. I need you, and the army needs you. I trust you, Gouv. I'm not sure I can beat Lee if I don't relieve Butterfield."

Warren took a deep breath, held it for several seconds. His heart nearly stumbled over itself.

"My chief of staff must be a trusted advisor, working behind the scenes, solving problems, mediating disputes, and acting as a sounding board for ideas…not to mention able to handle my occasional bouts of intemperance," Meade added with a grin.

Warren listened as Meade pitched each word carefully. *He is working hard to sway me into saying yes.*

"I'll let you stew a few moments on my offer." Meade paused, then added, "Hooker's command has been disastrous. His poor leadership has resulted in murderous carnage, wasted opportunities, and a frightened civilian population. The Union is facing a defeat from which it may not recover. I believe Butterfield holds as much responsibility for this miserable performance as Hooker."

Warren nodded. Gloom covered Meade's face as if he were preparing to give a eulogy.

"The fact is," Meade continued, "the army suffers from poor coordination and confused generalship. I can end the confusion, but winning depends on improving coordination. Our army moves against Lee as if it were trudging through mud, sinking its left foot in while the right struggles to pull itself out."

Meade paused, frowning, and rubbed his chest for a few moments.

"We move insidiously slow. I blame Butterfield for the army's poor maneuvering and fighting capabilities. He failed as Hooker's integrator, unable to seamlessly mesh all the moving parts. There is no doubt he would perform no better for me, a person he loathes."

Warren nodded and looked down, pondering. After a few moments, he looked up.

"General Meade," he said, "I'm most grateful Lincoln chose you to lead this army. In doing so, he has revived my spirit for defeating Lee. But changing the two top positions simultaneously is inviting disaster. Relieving Butterfield now would cost the army time, time we don't have, as it would take me a while to familiarize myself with my new duties."

Meade listened, his stone face unmoved.

Somewhat hesitantly, Warren went on. "Despite Butterfield's flaws, he does have the best knowledge of staff processes to execute your orders. You will have many questions that only he can answer. And this position keeps him away from the fighting, which he likes."

Warren paused, peering at Meade's contorted face blossoming with redness. *Be careful. Don't piss him off.* "I'm worried about serving as your chief of staff in addition to fulfilling my regular duties as chief engineer. I would be doing you a disservice by holding both positions simultaneously. My terrain-scouting duties frequently require me to be absent from headquarters. That will not do for a chief of staff. With all due respect, sir, I can best serve you as chief engineer, because this position still enables me to work directly for you, fighting on the front lines. With your permission, I would like to respectfully decline your offer, sir."

Meade glared. "Very well. I'm glad you're my chief engineer." Then he extended his hand. Warren gripped Meade's hand with both hands in a heartfelt double handshake.

"And you are correct," Meade said. "It would be almost impossible to serve as both chief of staff and chief engineer. Report this morning to the army headquarters tent so you can brief me—as my chief engineer."

Meade opened the tent flap and departed.

Warren closed his eyes, breathing a sigh of relief and an earnest prayer. "Thank you, God. You may have just evened the odds."

## 8

# Sickles — Sunday, June 28

*1:09 a.m.*
*Four hours earlier*
*The train station at Frederick, Maryland*

Sickles stepped off the train, lit a cigar, and gazed at Hardie making his way into town. Hardie had kept his cards close to his chest, hiding the details of tonight's covert mission. But Sickles had detected enough clues to figure out what hand Lincoln's messenger was playing. *Damn, I'm good. Hardie underestimated my shrewdness in discerning why he was being so cagey. But I deduced that he's traveling to Fifth Corps headquarters to end Meade's career.*

Hooker would be ecstatic on learning of Meade's downfall. It was time to visit Fighting Joe.

Sickles followed Hardie into town. Then he turned a corner and walked down Main Street, which was crackling with soldiers and women frolicking about, their raucous voices echoing off the buildings. *This is why Hooker is so beloved by his men. He encourages his boys to work hard and play hard. After I visit him, I should return and join them.* He licked his lips, craving a stiff shot of whiskey. *The boys always enjoy having a drink with me. I don't want to disappoint them.*

Sickles walked to Hooker's headquarters. The guards on the Prospect Hall's great columned porch saluted, and one of Hooker's aides informed Sickles that General Hooker was out inspecting some Murder Bay support troops and was not expected back until three or so in the morning. Sickles winked lewdly, stating he would return then.

At a little past three, Sickles arrived again at Prospect Hall. A young captain took him into the reception parlor. Hooker entered a few minutes later, greeting him.

Sickles saluted. "Reporting back for duty, sir."

"Mighty glad to have you back. Butterfield and I missed you." Hooker paused, chuckling. "And so did your favorite Murder Bay girls, I bet!"

"Well, as soon as we are done chatting, I will see how much they missed me. The girls back in New York are heartbroken I returned to command Third Corps."

They settled into their seats and Sickles retold his stories of visiting with Lincoln during his convalescence leave.

Then he leaned in conspiratorially. "I think I have some news that will please you. Your friend Colonel Hardie was a passenger on the train with me this evening. He was dressed in civilian clothes, which I thought odd, and hugged a satchel tightly to his chest. I probed, but he deflected all inquiries about the satchel's contents."

Hooker's jaw dropped and he groaned as if he had been gut-punched.

Sickles bobbed his head like a nippy parrot. "Hardie and I chatted at length. It seemed he had an urgent assignment from Lincoln and was making best speed to confer with you. I am convinced he has come to support you in dealing with the rumors about the generals' revolt, the uprising led by Meade. I'm surprised that he did not visit Prospect Hall immediately after the train arrived and wait for your return. I'm positive that he wanted to talk to you."

Hooker blinked, his mouth agape. "You don't know about the telegram I sent to Halleck last evening. We've been quarreling over occupying Harper's Ferry. I asked that the force there be reassigned to the Army of the Potomac. I need the men in the upcoming battle. Shit-for-brains Halleck said no."

"So what?" Sickles paused, muscles tensing, watching Hooker's frowning face. Something was wrong. "Hey, are you alright? It looks as if you're going to puke."

Hooker swallowed hard, bowed his head, and gazed downward.

"I tendered my resignation yesterday," Hooker said. "I felt the army could not comply with Halleck's orders to cover both Harper's Ferry and Washington. Of course, I knew Lincoln couldn't replace me this late in the campaign. My intent was to bully Halleck into giving me a free hand in fighting. I could no longer comply with the conditions Lincoln expected me to work under, so I requested to be relieved of this command."

"You're right," Sickles assured him. "Lincoln won't relieve you. He never mentioned anything like that, and I saw him a couple days ago."

Hooker paused, staring into the distance. "I think they may have called my bluff." It was barely a whisper.

Sickles's face tightened and a shiver darted down his back. No way would Lincoln choose Halleck over Hooker. "Preposterous! Lincoln is not going to honor your resignation. You're beloved by the army."

Hooker shook his head. "Hardie is here to relieve me of command. I'm certain." He rose shakily to his feet, and Sickles rose with him. "In a moment, I shall beg your leave to prepare for Hardie's visit, the meeting requiring that I be in my formal uniform. I'll bet he arrives soon with the new commander."

Sickles's mouth went dry. He smacked his fist into the palm of his other hand. "If it's Meade, I'll resign. Meade isn't half the commander you are." He scratched his nose. "Meade despises me because of what I said about his performance at Chancellorsville."

Hooker put a weary hand on Sickles's shoulder. "You cannot ask to be relieved on the eve of a battle. Wait until after the engagement, which the new commander will surely lose."

Hooker paused and dropped his gaze. After a moment, he glanced back at Sickles.

"Showing initiative and fighting aggressively in the upcoming battle should be enough to convince Lincoln to select you as the next commander of the army," Hooker encouraged. "Lincoln needs a hero, a willing, spirited leader, a Northern Democrat willing to act with initiative and boldness. You will be Lincoln's hero."

"Sir, I think you are overreacting. Lincoln won't call your bluff. You are the Union's only hope!"

Hooker's arm dropped listlessly to his side. "Now I must retire to my tent to prepare."

They exchanged halfhearted salutes. Hooker descended the front stairs of Prospect Hall, passing the guards and officers without a word, looking straight ahead, and entered his tent.

Sickles made his way toward Hooker's Murder Bay Division. Dismay and alarm grew while his enthusiasm about reuniting with his favorite girls waned. *God damn you, Hardie, you sly son of a bitch. Did you mislead me? Without Hooker in command, this could be my last battle as Third Corps Commander. Nah! I'm going to be as aggressive as hell. Lee is going to be totally outmatched by an aggressive Third Corps. So the next time we meet, Hardie, you will be delivering an order firing Meade and putting me in command.*

*Damn the West Pointers. None of them is worth the piss in a pot.*

# 9
# Meade — Sunday, June 28

Meade stepped out of Warren's tent and peered into the dim, windless morning. He didn't want the sentries or Butterfield's staff learning he had visited Warren before seeing Hooker. If Humphreys turned him down to be his chief of staff as Warren just had, then he would probably have to keep Butterfield for this battle. Damn, he hoped Humphreys accepted. He should give Humphreys the same discretionary offer Hardie had given him.

Meade strode toward a small grove of blossoming apple trees where his son and Hardie waited, ready to depart. The general took Old Baldy's reins from Captain Meade, stroking the warhorse's scarred white nose, a nasty wound from a Rebel shell fragment during the First Battle of Bull Run. Meade shot a somber glance at Hardie, and mounted Baldy.

The small cavalcade rode the gradual slope toward Warren, stopping a stone's throw away. Meade tipped his index finger against the brim of his hat. Warren saluted.

"I will see you soon at headquarters, Gouv." Meade paused a moment, then, with a rare touch of warmth, he added, "Don't linger here too long."

*5:35 a.m.*

The cavalcade turned and rode toward Hooker's tent. Meade's stomach stirred as a whiff of crackling bacon wafted up his nose. Shadowy figures started emerging from the long row of tents. The intoxicating effects of Maryland whiskey were replaced by regret as headquarters awoke hung over, its staff officers wobbling about with groggy faces.

Meade's jaw tightened as he rode through the camp, brooding over calling on Hooker without an invitation. Damn. This was a glaring breach of protocol, and he burned with a profound professional shame. Hooker deserved to be relieved of command. But he did not deserve to be dealt with in such a degrading manner. He took a long, deep breath. The odds were against him beating Lee. *So how long after the upcoming battle until Lincoln's messenger of death makes an unannounced visit to my headquarters for me to share Hooker's embarrassing fate? Hours? A day? Maybe two?* Lincoln's loyalty for his army commanders lasted only as long as their decisions brought victory, and victories were few and far between.

Meade rubbed his tense neck. The change of command would happen shortly. He needed to start focusing on becoming the army's commander and stop worrying about being fired. A town clock chimed in the distance. They would reach Hooker shortly.

## Hooker

*5:36 a.m.*
*Hooker's tent*

Adorned in his dress uniform, Hooker looked out through the open flap. No riders were approaching. Maybe there was hope? If there was, it was the same false hope that happened when you nicked yourself shaving, when you gasped a breath and hoped there was no bleeding. But soon the sharp stinging told you that the slice was deep and long, and then the blood gushed like a dam bursting and your breath blew out as if you'd been gut-punched.

Well, he had likely nicked his jugular by sending in his resignation letter, and there was lots of stinging, but there was no sign yet of bleeding. Maybe the letter wasn't fatal. If he could make it to noon without word from Washington, he had a chance to survive this ordeal. *Damn it, I unwittingly placed Lincoln in an awkward position.*

An idea popped into his brain—a possibility. If Washington had not responded by seven in the morning, he would telegram

Lincoln, revoking his resignation. His heart lurched with hope. *Bugger the devil.* He had figured a way out of this ordeal.

Yes, that was the answer. He would explain that he and Old Brains Halleck had quarreled. The president would support his position after learning Halleck was hindering the Army of the Potomac, taking unreasonable stands on issues far beyond his expertise, failing to give a free hand in questions of strategy. He would argue that morale had plummeted, despair and confusion sweeping over his corps commanders, upon learning he had tendered his resignation. Based on this powerful vote of confidence from his corps commanders, and with the threat of imminent battle with Lee, he in good faith could not resign.

Horse hooves clippity-clopping broke the morning silence. Blood pounded in his ears. *Please, God, let me stay in command.*

He mustered his last ounce of resolve, praying the self-inflicted wound would not be fatal. But the fear clawing his gut said it would be.

The horses halted outside his tent. Hooker pulled the tent flap aside and stepped outside as a beam of sun broke through a dark thunderhead. He froze, heart pounding. The three men dismounted. Captain Meade held the horses' reins as General Meade and Colonel Hardie headed toward Hooker.

Standing tall, Hooker clenched his hands into fists, willing himself to control his emotions. His bluffing game had failed. He had underestimated Lincoln's will and overestimated his influence. He was wrong about Stanton and Halleck being merely court jesters for Lincoln. They apparently exercised a cunning, duplicitous power over the president.

He stood blushing and his breath rasped. He was mortified, like a jilted groom at the altar. His shoulders curled over his chest, his bottom lip trembled, and his choked throat trapped his sobs. He scoffed at himself. *Fighting Joe Hooker.* He nearly had Lee at Chancellorsville. The first general to get the jump on him. All that was ancient history now.

The three officers saluted. Hooker returned their salutes and broke the silence.

"Gentlemen, I have been expecting you." True, as far as it went, but he was surprised Lincoln had picked Meade. He could not have been the president's first choice. But here he was. Hooker studied his face. No malice there. No hint of triumph. What was there squared with what Hooker knew of Meade—gloomy and resolute.

*My God, Meade must have been shocked by Hardie's visit.* Hooker blinked and swore silently. *Damn Halleck!* Meade had not been maneuvering for his job. This eased his mind somewhat. Yes, Meade was a good choice, even with that temper.

"As the president's messenger," Hardie pronounced, "I take full responsibility for arriving unannounced with General Meade."

Hooker grimaced. "I'm not sure there was a need to break protocol," he said, pausing. Resentment dribbled through his voice. "This is quite unorthodox and unprofessional, Colonel Hardie." His words were meant to sting Hardie. But Lincoln's messenger remained stone-faced.

Hooker glanced at Meade. A shiver ran through him as if there were an odd bond between them. Meade looked down and shifted his feet, his face red with embarrassment, a doleful look sketched on his mortified face. Hooker understood. Arriving at the commanding general's headquarters unannounced was not the way of gentlemen. Officers lived by honor and deserved honor's privileges in both victory and defeat.

Hardie stepped forward and stood before Hooker. He carried the leather satchel in his left hand. Clearing his throat, he announced, "General Hooker, I carry orders from President Lincoln."

Hooker nodded. "Colonel Hardie, I am prepared to receive them."

Captain Meade stepped forward to the flap of the tent, holding it open with his left hand, saluting with his right. "Please permit me, sir."

Hooker walked into the tent, followed by Hardie. General Meade stood fast. Captain Meade closed the tent flap. Inside, Hardie opened the satchel and handed the orders to Hooker.

Hooker blinked, reading the words above Lincoln's signature, slowly, silently. His heart twisted and sank. The short, simple letter transferred command authority immediately from Hooker to Meade. A wave of sorrow washed over him. He tried to swallow, but his throat had tightened as if a wire brush had scraped the skin raw. Uninvited tears slid down his cheeks.

"Sir, take a few moments to collect yourself," Hardie said softly. "This must be carried off with the appropriate amount of dignity."

"You're right," Hooker whispered. Shame coursed through him. He took a deep breath and wiped his eyes. "All right. Let's proceed."

## Meade

*5:40 a.m.*
*At Hooker's tent*

Meade stood a horse-length from the tent. His stomach churned and a cold uncertainty gripped his soul. He reached for a cigar. This part inside the tent was between Hardie and Hooker. It would be fast, like a sliding guillotine blade. He left the cigar in his coat pocket. He would have a smoke after he relieved Hooker.

Crunching boots on the gravel road approached and Meade turned. Butterfield walked up and stopped outside of Hooker's tent.

"Colonel Hardie is meeting General Hooker," Meade said. "We are to wait here until Colonel Hardie calls on us."

The chief of staff shook his head, then peered down and stared at his boots. Rage flared in Meade's throat. Working with this son of a bitch boiled his blood.

*5:50 a.m.*

Hardie opened the tent flap. "General Meade, will you please join us inside?"

For a long moment, Meade stood frozen. His face flushed red and dryness cracked his throat. He hated this cloak-and-dagger bullshit. He wanted no part of it. Yet, here he was. He had steeled himself for the task. What the hell. The deck was stacked against him for winning the next battle, triggering a repeat of this wretched scene soon with a new actor and reversed roles.

Meade turned toward the tent entrance. "Very well."

He walked in and saluted. Hooker set his jaw and returned the salute.

"Well, General Meade," Hooker said, "I regret the need to meet under these conditions and at this hour. But it is imperative we execute Lincoln's order expeditiously."

"General Hooker, sir. This order is unexpected. I was shocked to receive it in this manner." Meade paused. "But as a soldier I obey it and, to the utmost of my ability, will execute it."

An awkward pause cast a shadow on the proceedings. Bypassing the prescribed protocol for transferring power, Hardie had increased the strain between Hooker and Meade. *Better that Hardie had called first on Hooker and allowed Hooker, in turn, to send for me.* But Hardie had told him that Stanton had demanded Hardie conduct the relieving process in this way. Stanton was a flaming asshole.

All three officers sat at a table in the tent, lighted by two lanterns. Hooker extracted three cigars, offering one to Colonel Hardie and one to General Meade. Meade accepted his in grateful silence.

"George, you face some tough problems I want to discuss with you before we invite Butterfield to join us," Hooker began. He discussed his knowledge of the corps, division commanders, and various topics of the army.

Meade listened respectfully, stroking his grizzled beard, but found little value in Hooker's information. The dramatic monologue confirmed his opinion that Hooker should have been fired several weeks ago. He had already mentally retreated from fighting Lee. His devastating defeat at Chancellorsville had left him in a state of shell shock, unfit for facing the Rebel general again. Lee would have decimated Hooker's army in a battle north of the Potomac.

Hooker's rambling narrative of military dispositions, organizations, and Washington politics became increasingly tedious. The cigars were smoked out. Hooker leaned forward and made a dark observation.

"The army's Achilles' heel is its lack of West Point generals. All of Lee's corps and division commanders are Academy graduates except one VMI man. You have only fourteen West Pointers among the twenty-six generals filling these critical commands."

Meade stiffened slightly: the proportions surprised him. He'd never bothered to count the exact number, though he was aware Lee had an edge.

Hooker looked directly at him, pointing, nearly shouting. "This means that nearly half your senior officers are nonprofessionals, many being political appointees."

Meade's face grew hot as a prickly sensation crawled across his skin. *Damn it. Lincoln expects me to defeat Lee using political cronies the likes of that idiot Sickles.*

Hooker continued his alarming diatribe, warning Meade. "None of the seven corps and eighteen infantry division commanders you inherit today, with the exception of Brigadier General Andrew Humphreys, served in these vital positions at the Battle of Antietam."

*My God.* This was the second bit of information of which Meade was unaware, perhaps even more shocking than the first. He shook his head as his face tightened and his brows drew inward. Instinctively, Meade rubbed his old chest wound. Hooker held an eagle's eye view of army command, a critical experience he lacked. *Crap.* There was no time to gain this expertise before fighting Lee. Meade's stomach quivered.

Hooker rambled on as if delivering his own eulogy. Meade stopped listening, as it sounded as if Hooker was looking for empathy. *Christ Almighty, this is an impossible task.* He had performed as commander of a brigade, division, and corps. But he'd had ample time to whip his staff and key lieutenants into shape following each promotion. Not this time.

Hardie interrupted Hooker. "With your permission, General Hooker, I would like to continue the change of command with Butterfield present."

Hooker nodded.

Hardie opened the tent flap, gestured toward Butterfield. The chief of staff entered the large tent and stood near Hooker.

Meade glared at Butterfield, enjoying his baffled face. He looked like a shell-shocked soldier wandering aimlessly. If he could find Butterfield's relief this morning, he would be a casualty too, leaving with Hooker.

Hardie addressed Butterfield. "I have delivered to General Hooker and General Meade an order from President Lincoln relieving General Hooker of command. His relief will be General Meade. You will witness the turnover proceedings. The president has given Meade special powers to remove any officer and replace him with any other officer regardless of seniority. This order will be executed without delay. Do you understand?"

Butterfield nodded. "Yes, I understand."

Hardie turned to Hooker. "Please proceed, sir."

"The estimated Rebel forces number more than 100,000.[8] The Union forces are nearer to 90,000," Hooker said. "More men are departing daily as their two-year enlistments expire."

"Are you sure about this?" Meade said. "That would mean Lee's army is nearly twice as big as it was at Chancellorsville. Have you informed Halleck of the enemy numbers?"

"I told Lincoln and Halleck about this dire situation repeatedly, but they have failed to stem the exodus. Since the battle of Chancellorsville six weeks ago, the army has discharged 58 regiments, or 25,000 effectives. They've been partly replaced by five brigades numbering fewer than 12,000 greenhorns, untested in battle."

Meade groaned inwardly. *Must send a telegram to Halleck about the Union's depleted ranks.*

"Now do you understand my quarrel with Halleck over Harper's Ferry?" Hooker droned on. "The garrison is vulnerable

---

8  The actual Confederate force numbers were closer to 80,000. But Hooker thought the numbers were over 100,000.

to Lee's roaming forces, and I needed the extra infantry to fight Lee. But Halleck refused to abandon the stronghold."

Meade interrupted, not caring about Hooker's dispute with Old Brains Halleck. "Can you point to the location of each of the Union corps?"

"The entire Union army reached Maryland last evening, June 27. I received word at midnight that we occupy all the bridges crossing the Potomac. I chose Frederick as army headquarters because it has good roads, a railroad, and a canal to connect with the main base of supplies at Washington, forty-five miles away."

Hooker stood, pointed to the map table, and traced out with his finger the Army's natural defenses. "The Potomac River protects the army's left flank and South Mountain its front."

Meade choked down the rage burning his throat. In a measured voice, he said, "You've chosen a perfect natural defense with one major flaw. The Rebels are not operating in Maryland. Lee is more likely two to three days north of us in Pennsylvania, threatening Harrisburg or even Philadelphia."

Hooker straightened up, put his hands behind his back, and started pacing. His head wobbled as if he were suffering from a shaking palsy.

Meade stood, leaning forward, ready to pounce. His temper flared but he gritted his teeth and pursed his lips. His revulsion over Hooker's strategic ineptitude boiled in a mix of unstated vulgarity and military aphorisms.

Before the argument could erupt, Hardie retorted, "Generals, we have orders. We build with what we have, and it will require all the cooperation we can give in the service of our country. We have a Union to save. Let's continue."

Hooker took a deep breath and sat down. He gestured toward Meade. "Please sit down, General." For a moment, Meade remained standing, his hot face fuming.

Hardie whispered, "Please, General Meade."

Meade fought to gain control. *Don't be a fool, George. The Union is at stake.* He sat down.

Hooker began again. "All seven infantry corps, three cavalry divisions, and the artillery reserve are east of the South Mountain passes." He turned to the situation map, pointing with his finger, showing units widely scattered over a vast area ranging from Manchester to Frederick, a distance of thirty-eight miles.

Meade's mouth fell open. "Damn it! The corps are all scattered! You dispersed the corps that far apart with all of those gaps?"

"Hold your tongue, General! By God, I'm still the commander of this army, if only for another couple of minutes. I remind you of your place, sir!"

Meade's nostrils flared as he pounded his fist on the map table. "General Hooker, what fool plan are you trying to execute? Scattering the corps like this is absurd. It's an invitation to Lee to find and destroy the separate corps in detail!"

Hooker blasted back in kind, defending his force disposition on the grounds of territory protected while shielding Washington, D.C.

They ranted and quarreled, ripping at each other with slicing verbal jabs, ignoring Hardie and Butterfield. Minutes later, both generals stopped. Meade's ears burned white hot, astounded at the caustic words he had lobbed at Hooker, the senior officer. *Damn it. I've got to master my temper.*

Hardie started to speak, but Hooker interrupted, directing his words to Meade. "General Meade, I moved this army north, conforming to the pattern set by Lee and yet trying to maintain a track to the inside. Lincoln required me to keep between Lee and the capital. I found this order irksome, and it was always my plan to improvise and develop our strategy according to Lee's movements."

Meade shook his head. Either Hooker was playing him for the fool or he was trying to gain his sympathy. Either way, it infuriated him. Hooker's strategy was based on "ifs." A strategy without a plan: Goddamn absurdity. There was no consideration given to how the corps would fight—only their placement. The Union army simply was not safe in its current scattered locations.

Meade turned to Hardie, stood erect, and said, "I have no more questions for General Hooker and consider his responsibilities completed in this matter."

Hardie nodded his approval. Meade fumed. He had obtained little information about the condition of the troops or the position of the enemy, let alone Hooker's plan. *Hell, the little bugger didn't have a damn plan.* He turned to face Hooker and snapped to attention. Hooker stood up.

Meade saluted. "I am ready to relieve you, sir."

Hooker returned the salute. "I am ready to be relieved."

Meade paused and glanced at Hardie, who nodded. He turned back to Hooker. "General, in accordance with the orders of the president, I relieve you of command of the Army of the Potomac."

Hooker, his voice trembling, replied, "I stand relieved as commander of the Army of the Potomac."

They both turned and faced Colonel Hardie.

Hooker saluted with stately courtesy. "Sir, I stand relieved."

Colonel Hardie, as Lincoln's representative, returned the salute. "Very well."

Meade saluted and said, "In compliance with the orders of the president, I have properly relieved General Hooker. I have assumed full command and responsibility for the Army of the Potomac."

Colonel Hardie replied. "Very well."

Hooker bowed his head, reached down, detached his saber from its supports, and laid it on the map table.

Meade's stomach clenched. A dark shadow covered Hooker's face like a death mask. The cruel relieving words echoed in Meade's brain, already hearing the faint whispering in Washington. *Hooker's been fired!*

Hardie pulled a small journal from his shirt pocket, looked at his watch, and scribbled. Morning light seeped through the tent flap.

Meade gritted his teeth. The Grand Army of the Potomac now had its fourth commander in a year. Hooker grudgingly joined the ranks of past commanders, ghosts Meade had imagined lurking within the commander's tent. He rocked in place, his eyes darting, his mind racing with thousands of questions and waiting tasks. He swore an oath. He had a million things to do all at once, including learning the location of the Rebel army, promoting his successor as commander of Fifth Corps, finding a replacement for Butterfield, developing a plan, and issuing movement orders. *What a devil's storm. And still no loyal chief of staff.*

Meade's throat thickened and he swallowed with difficulty. Uncertainty welled up. *Oh, my God.* For the first time in his military career, there was no senior commander on the field to turn to for mentorship or friendship. A frosty chill enveloped him. He was alone.

He was now accountable for nearly 94,000 soldiers, for intercepting the Confederates, for fighting a critical battle, and for driving Lee's invading army back across the Potomac, all the while ensuring the safety of Washington and Baltimore. *Son of a bitch. What have you got yourself into?*

Hardie's voice cut through his musings. "I will have General Williams draw up the conditions of the relieving papers that the generals will sign later in the afternoon." Hardie excused himself, with Meade's—not Hooker's—permission.

Meade eyed Hooker and offered graciously, "Please stay in your headquarters tent until you are ready to depart. I will use Butterfield's tent. I will remain a guest in *your* camp until you depart."

Hooker whispered, "Thank you."

⚬━━◆━━ • ━━◆━━⚬

*6:50 a.m.*

General Meade emerged from the tent and walked over to Captain Meade, looking grave.

"Well, George," he said, eyeing his son solemnly. "I am the new commander of the Army of the Potomac."

"Sir?" Captain Meade said, looking perplexed. "Sir, you're the new commander?"

"Yes, George. I'm the new commander."

"Congratulations, Dad—uh, I mean General." Captain Meade's face lit up like an exploding shell. "I was convinced that Hooker was having you arrested. And now you're the army commander."

"I'm not sure congratulations are in order, George."

"Well, I'm very proud of you, General."

"Please ride back to Fifth Corps headquarters and have all my aides join me at headquarters and also have my personal effects brought over."

Captain Meade puffed out his chest and saluted. "Yes, sir, General."

*7:00 a.m.*

Meade sent a telegram to Halleck:

> *The order placing me in command of this Army is received. As a soldier I obey it, and to the utmost of my ability will execute it. Totally unexpected as it has been, and in ignorance of the exact condition of the troops and position of the enemy, I can only now say that it appears to me I must move toward the Susquehanna, or if he turns toward Baltimore, to give him battle.*

Meade then issued General Order, Number 67, to his army:

> *By direction of the President of the United States, I hereby assume command of the Army of the Potomac. As a soldier, in obeying this order—an order unexpected and unsolicited—I have no promises or pledges to make.... But I rely upon the hearty support of my companions in arms to assist me in the discharge of the duties of the important trust which has been confided to me.*

## ❧ 10 ❧
# Meade — Sunday, June 28

*7:15 a.m.*
*Butterfield's tent*

In headquarters' camp, a furtive sun slipped into the eastern sky. Meade stood outside Butterfield's tent at a map table, chin on his chest, his finger moving across Maryland, tracing road arterials and rail lines. The humid air was buzzing with chirping crickets and crackling with breakfast fires. Nearby, low voices were murmuring. A chill blew through him, winnowing out the insignificant and leaving cold reality in its wake. None of his personal staff had arrived from Fifth Corps. He was alone in Hooker's headquarters as if stranded in the middle of a blinding blizzard. A muscle tightened in his jaw. A great deal rode on the decisions he would make in the next few hours. How could he make decisions without having enemy intelligence, without having a trusted chief of staff, and without knowing the key members of headquarters staff?

He sucked in a deep breath and puffed it out as if extinguishing a match. After every losing battle, he had been promoted, and now he was the army commander. *In Lincoln's army, cream keeps rising until it sours, and then the president scraps it.* Meade's chest tightened. Being the army commander required instinctive skills that he didn't possess. If they were going to beat Lee's army, they would need a charismatic leader who could motivate the men. Why hadn't Lincoln chosen Reynolds? *His* cream was still rising.

Meade mustered his resolve, trying not to wallow in self-pity. Nothing he could do about not being a dashing field marshal like Reynolds. But by God, he refused to stumble awkwardly about like Hooker. Relying on his tightly stretched nerves and his fiery temper, he would spur the Union army forward against Lee and fight him tooth and nail like an attacking badger.

He stared out across the sea of white tents comprising army headquarters and shook his head. How many in the army knew he was the new commander? There had been no announcement. Unlike previous changes of command he had attended, this one lacked any military pageantry serving as a visible symbol of the orderly passing of authority and responsibility from one officer to another. Barking erupted behind him. He turned and glanced toward the cooking tent. A dog was sounding off at a suspended cauldron spewing smoke. Meade let out a rueful chuckle. The dog was the only one trumpeting him as the new commander.

But no one else cared, nor would they in a few days if he lost the upcoming battle and Lincoln fired him. Making matters worse, he had inherited Hooker's philandering staff, including Butterfield. Would any of them be loyal to him? Could they be? His mouth went dry. He was struck with doubt, mixed with a commingling of dread, humility, and wonder. He alone commanded an army of almost 100,000 men and was responsible for these soldiers' lives, deaths, and everything else the army did or failed to do. The realization twisted his stomach and locked up his chest with the same harrowing fright he'd had at age twelve when his father died. *Calm yourself. You need a clear head.*

"General Meade?" said a Hooker aide.

Meade jerked his head up. "What?"

The aide jumped back. "Would you like a cup of coffee, sir?" The aide replied, his voice quivering like a fiddle string.

Meade glared at the lieutenant holding a steaming tin cup. "Sure. Hurry up." Meade forced a snarly smile.

The lieutenant sat the cup on the edge of the map table and scurried away.

Meade gripped the cup and whiffed the earthy aroma. He closed his eyes and took a slow, warming sip. *At least Hooker's staff knows how to deliver decent coffee.* Hell, that was the most heed he had received from these yellow sheep-killing dogs in two weeks.

Meade peered over toward Hooker's tent. His breath quickened. Hooker was outside talking with several senior staff members, gesturing toward Meade. The staff officers were nodding, lips pressed, arms crossed over their chests. Meade twisted his wedding ring as if spinning a top. *If this gets any looser it's going to fall off.*

Damn it! It was torture having Hooker lurking about at headquarters. It was as if his in-laws were chaperoning his honeymoon. Grating, like sandpaper on skin. He drank deeply of the coffee, counting slowly to five. It wasn't Hooker's fault he had to wait around until the relieving letter was signed by both men. Hell, Hooker was probably more uncomfortable lingering here than he was.

Meade turned his head toward a cluster of Hooker's frightened aides—now his aides, if he so chose—standing over a campfire nearby, nervously chatting in hushed tones. Colonel Hardie had insisted that all but one of Hooker's personal aides support Meade until his own staff arrived from Fifth Corps. Eyeing them with his scolding stare, his heart rate slowed and his breathing deepened as he took some delight in their discomfort. He would not keep any of them.

Meade spied a passing aide and beckoned. The aide approached and saluted. "Yes, sir, General Meade."

"I request the presence of General Williams," Meade said.

The aide saluted and went immediately to Williams's tent.

Williams arrived and saluted with a welcoming smile. "Well, congratulations on your new command, General Meade!"

"Good to see you, Seth." Meade returned the salute. "I'm not sure congratulations are in order, as it appears I'm the poor bastard forced to hold this hot potato. Somehow, Reynolds talked his way out of the assignment."

Meade stepped closer to Williams. "Send a message to Sykes, ordering him to replace me as commander of Fifth Corps. Also, order General Ayres to replace Sykes as commander of Second Division."

"Sir, with all due respect, don't you have to ask Halleck's permission to make spot promotions?"

Meade squared his shoulders. "No. Halleck has given me special powers for this upcoming battle to promote and demote without regards to seniority. He will rubberstamp my decisions."

Williams shot up an eyebrow. "Very well. I will issue these orders immediately."

*7:45 a.m.*

Thundering horses rumbled into camp. Meade looked up and flashed a wide grin. The lead rider was Biddle, approaching at a near gallop. Hooker's aides watched, wide-eyed. Trailing beyond Biddle was the rest of Meade's personal staff, including Captain Meade. The soldiers rode up like warriors returning from a great victory. Biddle dismounted, striding proudly to Meade, saluting smartly. He was beaming, the corners of his mouth curled into a devilish smile.

"General Meade, congratulations on your promotion!" Biddle said. "President Lincoln made the right choice."

Meade's eyes widened and he slapped Biddle on the back. "Thank you, James."

"But, on my honor, sir, we were frozen with fear learning of Colonel Hardie's visit, knowing he carried grave news from Lincoln. We feared the worst. I've never seen Colonel Locke so heavy with doubt and misgiving, pacing back and forth in front of your tent like a condemned prisoner. But we all gave three cheers when Captain Meade returned to tell us Lincoln had made you commander of the army."

"Thank you for the cheers. But we have a lot of work ahead."

"General, what tent are you going to use?"

"I'm going to use Butterfield's tent as my headquarters until Hooker departs. I assumed command at seven, and General Williams is now drawing up the formal relieving papers. They should be ready sometime this afternoon. Once General Hooker and I sign the papers, he will depart, along with Colonel Hardie."

A Hooker aide approached and saluted. "Colonel Sharpe sends his respects and wishes to inform you he will give you an enemy intelligence update this morning."

"Very well," Meade said.

Meade turned to Biddle. "Make clear to my personal staff that we are guests in Hooker's camp until he departs. Then I will occupy Hooker's tent."

Biddle dipped a quick nod. The remaining aides clustered around General Meade, the gaggle looking like a dark-maned lion surrounded by his pride. He gave them their moment, letting them revel in the big part they had played in his promotion. He thanked them for doing their duty, acknowledging that staff duty was no easy berth. He reminded them of the hazards of being a general's aide, recalling two excellent young aides, Hamilton Kuhn from Philadelphia, and Arthur Dehon from Boston, who had both been killed in action. He chatted amiably with his staff for a few more minutes. Their huge, flashing grins brightened his spirits as warmth coursed through his body, and the pressure that had been mounting in his head dissipated like a morning mist.

Meade turned to Biddle and pointed to the map, where a circle labeled Sixth Corps was drawn around Poolesville. "We need to pull in the distant units of the army so we can begin a general advance toward Pennsylvania."

He paused, shooting a venomous look at Hooker's boys milling nearby, glancing at him with dread plowed across their brows. Damn it, they doubted his leadership. *Well, they haven't heard me issue any orders yet. I'll fix that.*

Meade cleared his throat. "Major Biddle!" he roared as heads snapped in his direction.

Biddle snapped to attention. "Yes, sir!"

Meade pointed to the map table and paused. With several of Hooker's aides staring, he erupted with a sharp roar and smacked the map table with an open hand.

"I want General Sedgwick to move Sixth Corps straight north to New Market using the main road to Baltimore," he bellowed. "He should arrive this evening at New Market and bivouac, putting his corps about six or seven miles east of Frederick."

"Yes sir, right away sir," Biddle shouted. He saluted smartly, like a military cadet, and darted off toward General Williams's tent.

Meade turned toward Hooker's boys, his eyes scalding as if dunked in molten iron. The aides' tongues stopped wagging and they stood up straighter, bracing for another outburst.

Satisfaction bubbled in Meade's veins. He had just issued his first marching order as the commander of the Army of the Potomac, and he had delivered it with absolute authority. Headquarters staff, both generals and officers, had just gotten their first taste of his temper and, hopefully, his grit.

*Almost 8:00 a.m.*

Everyone was up in camp, bustling and talking. Hooker's trusted officers continued to gather in small pods, speaking in hushed, excited tones. They were a bunch of scalawags. Meade ignored the chatter. He had to form a plan. He removed his spectacles, wiping sweat from his brow. The morning air was hot and still. Today was going to be a scorcher.

He turned to Captain Meade. "George, ride back to General Warren's tent and request that Gouv visit with me as soon as possible. Tell him to bring his maps. I want to review the topography with him."

Captain Meade saluted and departed. Meade continued to work outside Butterfield's tent under the large awning. He was not interested in making major changes in the staff, with the exception of Butterfield. As the morning passed, headquarters began to assume some shape, a rhythm of urgency emerging as the staff officers started sensing and anticipating Meade's untiring inquiries.

He scowled, unable to devise a plan. His typically clear head was clouded and every muscle was rigid as if frozen. Lack of sleep, damn it. The president also had shackled him, confining his movements to those areas between the capital and Baltimore and Lee's army. His head wagged back and forth. He didn't like being tethered like a dog on a leash.

Meade dropped his clenched fists to his sides. He had no fear of Lee's army. His fear was time. He lacked the time to forge his army into an efficient fighting machine. Lee would soon learn that he had replaced Hooker. When Lee learned he was fighting another greenhorn general, he would probably write a note to Lincoln, thanking him. Lee would attack at the first opportunity.

He glanced up just as General Williams arrived. "Seth, let's move inside the tent," Meade said. "I want to speak with you privately."

Williams followed him through the tent flap and they sat down at a table, where Meade took out two cigars. Williams accepted, and smoke gathered above their heads like a morning fog.

"Are you making progress drawing up the relieving papers?" Meade asked. "I would like to get them signed as soon as you can make it happen. It's distracting having Hooker hanging around. These men won't become *my* officers until he leaves." He paused, gritting his teeth for control. Would they ever be *his* officers?

"Yes, sir. I'm making good progress," Williams said. "This is the fourth time I've had to draw them up."

"Well, I hope I'm the last damn commander you have to train," Meade said, his voice laced with bitterness. After pausing for a moment, he said, with a touch of apology, "Seth, that was ill-tempered of me. I hope to make this your last labor with that set of papers."

Williams nodded. "That's my hope, too. General Meade, you are a fiery commander, willing to fight anyone, anywhere, anytime. I would follow you into the fires of hell. It's refreshing having an intelligent, bold commander making quick decisions, even if you do detonate occasionally."

Meade shrugged. "Well maybe just a bit more than occasionally."

"The verbal explosions will keep the staff sharp and focused," Williams said. "I just hope this change isn't too late."

They continued to smoke, enjoying the moment. Meade studied his friend. Competent. Hardworking. Selfless. These were rare qualities among senior army leaders. Williams, a West Point graduate, was the workhorse of the staff. His job was managing the vast sea of paperwork that ran the army: messages to and from Meade, promotions, leave, all passed through Williams and his staff. He was the glue holding the headquarters staff together, working tirelessly, having the unique ability to get along with everybody. He had faithfully served each of the previous three commanders, starting with McClellan.

"Just curious, sir," Williams asked. "What was your first thought when Colonel Hardie woke you?"

"I thought Hooker was having me arrested," Meade chuckled. "Then it turned out to be worse than being arrested. Hardie told me I was the new commander. In an icy second, I flashed from fear to rage. After erupting for a few minutes, hoping Hardie would change his mind, I shivered with fear and accepted my fate. How could anyone beat Lee after being in command for a few days?"

Williams nodded.

"Then I visited Warren unannounced and woke him. He, too, thought at first that something was terribly wrong." Meade paused and puffed on his cigar as he studied Williams.

"Seth, I asked to see you in private for the same reason I visited with Warren. I must replace Butterfield immediately. I thought you might consider double duty, acting as my chief of staff and my adjutant general."

Williams leaned back in his chair, his eyes wide. "Sir, I'm deeply honored you would request me to be your chief of staff. My guess is Warren turned you down, arguing he could serve you best as the Army's engineer. He is right. Despite Butterfield's considerable shortcomings, he is adept at performing his current duties. You will work well together."

An aide walked into the tent, handed Meade a message from Halleck, and departed. Meade glanced at the message. "Son of a bitch. I've been in command a little over an hour and Halleck wants to know what my plans are for pursuing Lee? My first plan is to get Hooker out of here. Sorry, Seth; go ahead."

"Butterfield is merely the reins and you're the general riding the beast," Williams said. "It is his job to drive the army according to your plans and orders. Butterfield can be quite effective if harnessed properly, and I am confident you will do just that."

Meade clenched his jaw and shot him a glance.

Williams grimaced. "That said, he needs a shorter rein than most chiefs of staff for whom I have worked. We are going to be fighting a decisive battle in a few days. You are better served keeping Butterfield for the time being. Then afterward, you could pick a suitable replacement."

Meade puzzled over his dilemma, his head wagging side to side as he stared at Williams, trying to decide if he was right about keeping Butterfield. The mousey Butterfield was the most despicable officer ever born. Sickles didn't count because he was a corrupt congressman—like most politicians. A wave of misery washed over him as he tried to stomach the necessity of keeping both Sickles and Butterfield.

Williams continued, "Replacing both Hooker and Butterfield would do more harm than good at this point in time."

"Perhaps," Meade replied. *Crap.* Williams was being truthful and could be trusted, but his was not the answer he wanted. *What good are my special powers if I can't use them?* He puffed on his cigar. He would ask Humphreys to serve as chief of staff. If Humphreys declined, he would keep Butterfield.

"I want Hooker's 'Special Division' out of this camp," Meade suddenly snapped, his voice sharp like a razor. "If I find one prostitute loitering near my headquarters tonight I will start cutting off heads myself, and I will probably start with Butterfield's. Do you understand?"

Williams nodded approvingly. "Yes, sir, I understand."

*9:00 a.m.*

As Williams was leaving, Butterfield and Colonel George Sharpe, the head of Hooker's recently established Bureau of Military Intelligence, entered Meade's tent and saluted. Meade glared at Butterfield. What a vainglory asshole. Butterfield stood shifting his stance.

Meade went to the map. "Colonel Sharpe, before hurtling the army forward, what is your best estimate of enemy locations and a clear story of Lee's intentions?"

Sharpe pointed to Gettysburg. "Spies and scouts operating there said Gordon's Rebel brigade had passed through town two days before. There was a strong Rebel presence idling due north near Carlisle. I believe a large contingent, perhaps one or two

Rebel corps, is loitering on the western side of South Mountain near Chambersburg. Contacts in York spotted Rebel infantry a day's ride to the west, moving eastward at a reasonable clip."

Meade swore. "That's it? Where is Lee's cavalry? Why are Rebel infantry marching without cavalry in Pennsylvania? That makes no sense. Lee is up to something. If we are not vigilant, his cavalry is going to start grinding us into mincemeat."

"I believe Stuart's cavalry is operating independently of Lee's army," Sharpe replied. "I have no explanation for his movements. But Stuart cannot provide direct support to Lee's infantry as long as he is operating to the northeast of us."

"Interesting. What is Lee's troop strength?

"I estimate about 110,000 men."

"I'm struggling to imagine an enemy force that large running unchecked over Maryland and Pennsylvania, and this army could not pinpoint them on a map," Meade said. "That's damn frightening. Is Lee that brilliant? Or is your intelligence outfit that bad?"

Sharpe furrowed his brow. "I have a few intelligence folks embedded in the cavalry reconnaissance units, including Buford's cavalry force, moving toward Gettysburg. I'm hoping to provide a better enemy update this evening."

"I need to get this army off its heels." Meade growled. "Colonel, what do you think about striking northeast early tomorrow morning, pointing the army's vanguard toward Harrisburg? If Lee's army is scattered as much as you're asserting, I want to catch his eastern army corps lollygagging, before it crosses the Susquehanna River."

"Yes, sir," Sharpe said. "I concur; you should move rapidly toward the enemy. It could provide the break we need. You can't let Lee hatch his plan as he desires. Moving will force Lee's troops to react, and my forward assets will sense this."

"Good. That's the plan. We will rush the army forward like a thrusting sword."

"General," Sharpe said, "I will refocus my efforts in the Susquehanna area. As soon as we detect Lee reacting to our movements, I will inform you." Sharpe saluted and departed.

Warren entered Meade's tent. "Gouv," Meade greeted him, "glad you're here." He pointed to the map. "Even though the enemy outnumbers us, we must shift to the offensive and speed forward. This means hard, forced marches. In this brutal heat, we'll suffer casualties, but we have no choice. If our lead elements can threaten the enemy's soft underbelly, he will have to turn and concentrate. If he does not rapidly mass, we will chop him up."

"Lee is operating in alien territory," Warren replied. "So he has a logistics problem and we do not. He cannot linger too long maneuvering if he is being pressed. If he does linger, he will run out of supplies. He either has to fight or retreat westward behind South Mountain and then back to Virginia."

Meade leaned forward over the map table. His fingertips began to tingle. "Gouv, if I can check Lee's forward momentum into Pennsylvania's heartland and make him turn toward us, I can fortify the Army of the Potomac behind breastworks of my choosing and entice the Rebels into conducting an infantry attack, right into our bayonets."

"We are going to have to find a suitable defensive line," Warren replied.

"Yes," Meade agreed. "The Pipe's Creek area may be that line." He pointed to the spot.

"General Meade," Butterfield said, "what makes you think Lee will charge strongly defended positions? Won't Lee play his typical game of waiting for Lincoln's patience to run out, like he did with Hooker, and force you to attack? I'm familiar with the way Lincoln thinks."

Meade snapped his head toward Butterfield. His breath quickened and his lungs burned. "If you were so damn familiar with the way Lincoln thinks, your old boss would still be in command. I am not playing Lee's game or Lincoln's. I am the commander of this army, not Lincoln, and I will attack when I'm damn ready."

Butterfield clasped his arms behind his back and looked down, shaking his head.

"If I can force Lee to attack, I will do that," Meade said. "Let me make this clear…when I do fight, either offensively or defensively, I plan on being victorious. Or die trying. We will not run away as *you* encouraged us to do at Chancellorsville."

"With all due respect, sir, you do not understand Washington politics," Butterfield said. "In a few hours you will receive the second of several telegrams from Old Brains Halleck. You will be nagged and harassed by Lincoln and his cronies like a henpecked husband."

"I did not ask for this command!" Meade shouted. "Lincoln ordered me to put my head in the guillotine. So if he wants to cut off my head, he can, whenever he wants. But I am telling you this: while I am in command and still have my head, I will do it my way! Do you understand?"

Meade shuddered as he glared at Butterfield. Something caustic and foul gurgled in his stomach.

"Come, gentlemen," Warren said. "Let's focus on the Confederates." He turned to Meade. "How long do you plan on keeping the army widely dispersed?"

Meade snapped, "I've already ordered the concentration of the army. By nightfall, all seven infantry corps should be within a ten-mile radius of army headquarters. After we have concentrated tonight, I'm going straight at the enemy in the morning. Lee and I face the same challenge. How do we supply and move our armies while maintaining security against an unlocated enemy?"

Butterfield's forehead furrowed.

"Logistics is the devil's right hand," Meade continued. "It takes little skill to imagine where you would like your army to be and then move it by pointing on a map. But it takes considerable skill, and old-fashioned, hard marching, to actually place your forces and know how long you can leave them there. Logistics will determine how Lee fights north of the Potomac, and for how long."

"We are no longer in Virginia, where Lee had short logistics lines and sat behind breastworks, waiting for us to attack," Warren said.

"You're right, Gouv," Meade said. "Lee is now operating north of the Potomac, where the Union army has shorter logistics lines. This means we can wait until the cows crow for Lee to attack us. We can win either by defeating Lee or when Lee leaves the North without a fight. Lee wins only if he fights. He doesn't win by retreating across the Potomac."

Meade pointed to the map. "Lee's fatal weakness is his inability to maintain his army logistically in Pennsylvania. As Napoleon noted, an army marches on its stomach, and for the moment, Lee is living off the fat Pennsylvania countryside. That's going to change. I am going to race toward him like a big cat and threaten his resupply routes, forcing him to fight on my terms, my conditions, and my battlefield."

He turned to Warren. "Gouv, I want you to start plotting the northward movement of the seven infantry corps using the main and auxiliary roads. Most of the roads north converge on Gettysburg. Use it as a compass objective."

*11:00 a.m.*

Warren and Butterfield departed. A bevy of horses clattered to a stop outside his tent. Meade emerged and moved quickly to his son George, who was riding a wagon carrying Meade's personal belongings.

"George, ride to Third Corps and request General Humphreys join me soonest."

Meade moved over to Biddle. "Leave my personal belongings in the wagon and unhitch the horses. After General Hooker departs, you can put them in *my* tent."

General Alfred Pleasonton rode up on his light-colored charger, wearing white gloves, a smart blue uniform, straw hat tilted rakishly on his head, and sporting a finely trimmed, waxed moustache. Meade stifled a laugh. Pleasonton looked like a primping peacock. But now was not the time to throw barbs at his cavalry commander. Pleasonton dismounted and saluted.

"Alfred, Hooker made a smart move appointing you to command the cavalry last month," Meade said. "But I'm not pleased with the efficiency of your command, especially several of your brigade commanders. Do you have any recommendations on who we should promote?"

"I have three superb young captains who can ride hard and fight fiercely: Captains Elon Farnsworth, Wesley Merritt, and George Custer," Pleasanton replied.

"I've heard of Custer," Meade said. "Isn't he that pretty-boy officer whose long curly hair rivals that of Confederate General Pickett?"

"Yes. That's him."

"Alright. I propose we jump-promote these three young officers to brigadier general—today."

"General, I wholeheartedly agree," Pleasonton answered. "But we can't promote junior officers over senior ones."

Meade removed his glasses. wiped his sweaty brow, and stated, "Yes, we can. Halleck has given me special powers to promote junior officers over senior officers as I see fit. I will inform General Williams to draw up the orders promoting these captains."

Pleasonton nodded, owl-eyed.

Meade glared. He was not a great admirer of the high-styling, flashy cavalry officers, but the scouting, screening, and harassing functions they performed were critical to the army's success. The cavalry acted as his eyes and ears.

"I want you to pin stars on Farnsworth, Merritt, and Custer by noon. Do you understand?"

"Yes, sir."

"I will inform Halleck by telegram, requesting that he formally approve the promotions."

Pleasonton saluted and walked toward Williams's tent.

*11:55 a.m.*

Meade glanced at his watch. Almost noon.

A majestic black horse and a handsome rider rode toward him, followed by an aide streaming a large corps flag. Meade's breath caught. Reynolds rode up, dismounted, and saluted. Meade paused, nerves humming, stomach clenching. He should be saluting Reynolds.

"Congratulations, General Meade, on your promotion. I give you my undivided, unfailing support," Reynolds said. Reverence trickled through his voice.

"Thank you for riding over to visit, John." Relief washed through Meade. "I relieved General Hooker this morning. He is still here, waiting to sign the formal relieving papers. Then he will depart. Also, Colonel James Hardie is here representing President Lincoln. He will leave with Hooker."

Reynolds cracked a slight smile.

Meade lowered his gaze to the ground and shifted his boots. His stomach rolled. Reynolds had worn his dress uniform. Standing in front of the former superintendent of West Point in his three-in-the-morning thrown-together uniform, Meade winced.

"John, my friend, you should be in command of this army," Meade said. "I protested vehemently this morning when Colonel Hardie ordered me to take command. I argued strongly that you were the better qualified. I consider myself a quiet but effective corps commander. I'm not, however, the charismatic would-be hero exalted by Lincoln, Stanton, and Halleck."

Reynolds reached out and patted Meade on the back.

Meade shook his head. "I'm not the guy. What we need is you. Only you can inspire the men and beat Lee."

"You're right," Reynolds said.

"What?"

"You're not what we need if we are looking for an inspiring leader. But—Lee beat the last three guys we needed. George, you're not only fighting Lee, you're fighting Lincoln and his controlling henchmen. So it's down to you. You're our only hope. Use that damn temper of yours and figure it out!" Reynolds smiled. "You have my support. You can do this."

Meade swallowed hard.

"Lincoln made the right choice. I promise you, George. Myself and the rest of the other corps commanders are in total agreement that you should command the army."

Meade's heart leaped. He wanted the support from the other corps commanders. But he had not expected such a vote of confidence.

"Custom dictates you should appoint a new chief of staff. Are you going to replace Butterfield?" Reynolds paused. "I think you should."

"Yes. I'm trying," Meade said. "But I've been unsuccessful thus far. I've asked Warren and Williams, and both declined, saying the chief-of-staff duties, on top of their normal duties, would overburden them. I will ask Humphreys when he arrives today. If he declines, I may have to stick with Butterfield."

"Butterfield is not to be trusted," Reynolds replied. "But he is a good administrator, and changing out both Hooker and Butterfield this near to a decisive battle might not be wise. Think on that."

"Well, Butterfield sure as hell didn't help Hooker form any plan."

"What are your plans?" Reynolds asked.

"My instincts tell me to mass the army. We don't know the location of Lee's three infantry corps. Colonel Sharpe's intelligence group is reporting that the Confederates are all spread out and operating in Pennsylvania, but I'm not sure they are all east of South Mountain."

"If that is true, Lee is vulnerable and you can take advantage of his scattered army."

"Agreed. But I'm more worried about where Stuart's cavalry is. Lee's cavalry commander roaming about willy-nilly makes no sense. Lee would never permit that. So I don't know what the hell Lee is up to."

Reynolds nodded.

"So here's what I plan to do. I'm going to concentrate the army immediately around Frederick and then go after Lee the following day. You're going to command the western group composed of First Corps, Sickles's Third Corps, and Howard's Eleventh Corps, with Buford's First Calvary Division providing forward screening."

"Good."

"I'm pushing your First Corps tomorrow, well in advance of the army, north toward Emmitsburg. I'm assigning Buford's cavalry division to you in direct support of the western group command. I want you to send him further north of Emmitsburg, extending his scouting area to Fairfield, Gettysburg, and Cashtown. If Lee has large forces west of South Mountain, he will come east using either the Monterey Pass leading to Fairfield or the Cashtown pass leading to Gettysburg."

Meade and Reynolds bent over the map table outside Butterfield's tent. Meade indicated the positions, pointing to the penciled circles showing the scattered locations of the seven Union infantry corps.

Reynolds chuckled. "I guess Old Fighting Joe didn't want General Lee skirting around the army undetected," Reynolds said. "Maybe Hooker was still thinking about Chancellorsville, where Jackson's corps managed to circle around, getting the jump on him."

"You may be right about Hooker detecting a Rebel flanking movement. But I'm not sure Hooker could have detected Lee's army if it had waltzed right up the middle against him."

Reynolds turned and looked away in the direction of Hooker, who was chatting with some staff officers. He turned back, snapped to attention, and saluted. "General Meade, I request your leave to pay my respects to General Hooker and then to Colonel Hardie."

Meade returned the salute, his face blushing with heat. "Permission granted."

"Again, George. You are a thorough soldier and a mighty clear-headed man. This army and this nation need your fiery grit and unbridled passion if we are to defeat Lee's army. You have my total support."

"Thank you, John."

The two men shook hands, and Reynolds moved off.

Meade's stomach unclenched. A rare joy shivered through him, as if he had pleased a proud father. Two battles ago he was a division commander in Reynolds's corps, and now he was commanding Reynolds. He shook his head.

*1:00 p.m.*

One in the afternoon and no breeze.

Meade sat under the tent's awning, the large canvas square providing some protection from the scorching sun. The air was heavy and humid, and he had to nearly gasp to get a proper breath. Sitting at a portable desk, sweat dripping from his brow, Meade scanned a topographical map for terrain surfaces and gaps, determining what he and the enemy could easily exploit or defend. He stood up, walked around to the north side of the map, looking at topography from Lee's perspective. He calculated the distance from Lee's supply beachhead just north of the Potomac at Williamsport to the dispersed Confederate forces operating in Pennsylvania.

His calculations confirmed Lee was operating well beyond easy reach of his supply base. Lee would have to fight with the men and ammunition he had on hand, unable to linger much longer in his current location. Time was running out. Lee had to force a fight or retreat back to Virginia. *That's good.* The vise grip around his chest eased.

Meade took off his hat and scratched his bald spot. He hated Lincoln's order to cover both Baltimore and Washington. It limited his freedom to maneuver, forcing him to fight a defensive battle. But, before he could focus on choosing defensible terrain, he had to halt Lee before he could depart York, cross the Susquehanna, and occupy Harrisburg. If Harrisburg were to be captured, the Republic could fall.

He started to map out a tactical maneuver plan to engage Lee. He would move the army aggressively forward on a main line from Frederick to Harrisburg. In doing so, he would extend his wings on both sides of that line as far as he could, mindful that he must be capable of rapidly massing his forces. His first goal was to halt Lee's forward advance into Pennsylvania. He would move north until he either met the enemy or Lee learned of his advance and turned, meeting him in battle at some point on ground of Meade's choosing.

Meade whiffed the aroma of simmering stew and his stomach growled. He turned and saw Sergeant Brown stirring a large kettle suspended from a triangle over an open campfire. He had skipped breakfast and lunch. He walked toward the kettle. Brown looked up, stopped stirring, and ladled hot coffee into a metal cup. Meade grabbed the cup handle with his right hand and used his left to steady the hot coffee, the heat burning into his palm.

* * *

*2:00 p.m.*

As Meade sipped the coffee, Sickles and Humphreys rode up. Meade's chest swelled with fury as he glared at Sickles's florid face. Should he fire Sickles and promote Humphreys to Third Corps commander? Not a bad idea, but he needed Humphreys as his chief of staff, and Lincoln wanted Sickles as a Democratic political general.

"General Meade, my compliments, sir." A smirk twisted Sickles's lips. "I congratulate you on your new command."

The haughty tone in Sickles's hiss made Meade's jaw clench. He eyed the man up and down. *Charlatan. What a murderous, conspiring little toad. Did Lincoln not consider the consequences of appointing a corrupt congressman to a senior position in the army? Was the blood price worth the gain in political capital? Damn politicians.*

"General Sickles," Meade shot back, "I am pleased to see you recovered from your *severe* wound at Chancellorsville."

Sickles's face reddened like a glowing ember.

"I've issued marching orders for your corps to arrive eight miles north of Frederick by evening," Meade continued. "Early tomorrow morning you will start your march for the Pennsylvania border. This maneuver will require close scrutiny and your personal oversight. I expect your full attention in the execution of these orders."

Sickles nodded, chomping on his unlit, fat cigar. Meade simply glared. Sickles frowned, looking a bit unhinged, as if he wanted to depart. Meade enjoyed the pause, a perfect *schadenfreude* moment. Sickles now reported to *him*.

120

"Third Corps will be under the direct command of General Reynolds, who will be acting as the western group commander," Meade said.

Sickles nodded. His face flamed and his eyes narrowed.

"Thank you for paying your respects, General Sickles. I want you to ensure your corps is ready to march. You are to personally inspect your logistics trains this evening to ensure they are ready for tomorrow's march and send a courier letting me know you're ready." Meade paused, then added, "General Sickles, you are dismissed. I need to speak with General Humphreys, alone."

Glowering, Sickles saluted formally and rode off. Meade crossed his arms and nodded a satisfied smirk. What a great payback of sorts for the nasty articles Sickles had printed in the New York papers about him after the Battle of Chancellorsville.

Andrew Humphreys waved his gloved hand. He wore a spotless white paper dickey under his shirt collar, as always. How did Humphreys manage to maintain a constant supply? If only the army's logistics trains were as efficient as Humphreys's supply of dickeys.

Humphreys dismounted and Meade extended a hand. "Howdy, Andrew. I am glad to see you."

"Congratulations on your promotion. Well deserved!"

"Thank you. I wish I felt the same way." Meade struck a match, lighted a cigar. "Let's talk under the awning."

"I rode in on the turn of the tide," Humphreys said. "But I'll tell you one thing. We can't blame that devil whore Joe Hooker anymore, can we?"

Meade nodded, puffing on his cigar. He studied Humphreys. Like Warren, he was a West Point topographical engineer. He was a tall, thin, dark-haired, grizzled gentleman, sporting a sweeping gunfighter's mustache. He loved to fight. He led his men into battle from the front. He thought of himself as a modern-day Spartan warrior. They had served together in the Seminole War.

"I would like for you to consider replacing Butterfield as my chief of staff."

"I guessed you would ask me to undertake this duty, and it is a great honor," Humphreys replied. "I have been thinking about my answer. Would you consider allowing me to command my division for this upcoming battle? After that, I would be most honored if you allowed me to serve you as your chief of staff."

Meade winced, his old lung pain flaring through his chest. "Well, if you stayed in command of one of Sickles's two divisions, I would feel comfortable knowing you could watch him. I will leave you in command for this fight. Afterward, I will request you join me at army headquarters."

Humphreys flashed relief. "Thank you, sir!" He saluted and mounted his horse.

Meade wiped his brow as Humphreys galloped down the road. A growl rumbled deep in the pit of his stomach. He turned to Biddle. "James, see if you can fetch some food and some more hot coffee."

Biddle strode toward the mess cooks. Meade spotted George and motioned. George darted over to the map table and saluted.

"George, I'm going to be studying the different maps until Hardie calls for me to sign the relieving order. I don't want to talk to any of the headquarters staff or visitors until I've signed the order and Hooker has departed."

"Yes, General. I understand."

---

*6:00 p.m.*

Hardie approached, requesting that Meade join him in Hooker's tent. They walked together in silence. Once inside, Hardie asked Meade to peruse the relieving order he had written in collaboration with Hooker and Williams. Meade scanned the document, having determined beforehand he would not make any changes. He had an army to command, and no time to squabble over incidentals. Whether he defeated Lee or not, no one would read the document. Both Hooker and Meade signed the formal relieving order.

"Headquarters tent is yours," Hooker whispered. "Hardie and I leave now for Baltimore." Hooker turned and walked outside. He announced loudly to the staff, "General Meade has formally signed the relieving letter. I bid you all farewell. It has been my great honor to serve as your general." He walked along the line of staff officers, tears on his cheeks, shaking each officer's hand.

"God bless you, General," each officer responded.

<hr />

*6:10 p.m.*
*(Sunset is 7:44 p.m.)*

Hooker boarded a spring wagon and a throng of officers surrounded him. When he and Hardie were ready to depart, Meade approached the wagon. A chill crept down his spine. He removed his slouch hat. The throng of men drew back. Meade extended his hand, shaking Hooker's hand with a heartfelt grip.

"General, I did not covet your command or seek it behind your back," he whispered. "Please forgive me, for I dishonored you this morning by showing up unannounced. You should have called for me."

Hooker's voice waivered. "I do not hold you responsible for the conduct of this change of command. I wish you the best of luck. And for the sake of the Republic, my prayers are that you destroy Lee's army. I caution you about Lincoln and Halleck. They will cut off your head if it is politically prudent. Never forget, my friend, you are but a pawn in Lincoln's chess game."

Meade nodded.

"Remember the West Point lectures about the ancient Greek hedgehog-and-fox parable?" asked Hooker.

"I do," replied Meade.

"As you remember, the fox knows many things and is always trying to eat the hedgehog. The hedgehog knows one big thing and that is how to defend himself. The hedgehog responds to the fox's attacks by rolling up into a perfect little ball with its sharp spikes pointing out in all directions."

Hooker wiped his brow, then continued. "Lee is a sly and cunning fox. He is flexible and able to devise a myriad of varied strategies for sneak attacks upon the hedgehog. George, you're like a hedgehog with your focus and tenacity. You love to plan and execute those plans. So when the fox is bounding toward the hedgehog, he sees the sphere defense with its sharp spikes threatening him and he calls off the attack and continues his journey. Despite the cunning of the fox, the hedgehog always wins."

"So you think Lee also believes I'm a hedgehog?"

"Yes, I do. He believes you will act cautiously, waiting for the opportunity to hunker down in a ball. That's where you can take advantage of your reputation. Lee will never predict a hedgehog would maneuver and attack him."

Meade nodded. "Goodbye, General Hooker. God bless you." Meade backed up a few steps. The wagon moved off with Hooker and Hardie across from each other. Meade walked into the tent just vacated by his predecessor: headquarters for the commanding officer of the Army of the Potomac. Biddle had moved his map table to his new tent.

Back at the map table, Meade stared at the open land beyond Frederick—a vast sea teeming with the enemy. As commander of the Army of the Potomac, he had total accountability and responsibility for its performance. He had no one to turn to in setting its heading, just his own moral character and the cornerstones grounding his heart: duty, honor, country. An unsureness welled up and lodged in his throat. He was alone, with all his strengths and terrible flaws. He prayed silently. *God, please guide my thoughts.*

*Now, let's finalize the all-important plan.*

# 11

# First Minnesota — Sunday, June 28

## Colvill

*6:00 p.m.*
*First Minnesota on their way to bivouac near Frederick, Maryland*

Colonel William Colvill rode at the front of the First Minnesota. He wiped sweat from his face; the early evening air was thick and muggy. The staccato beating of snare drums resonated along the regiment's lines. Throughout today's grueling march, the sun had beaten down on the rugged Minnesotans. High, puffy clouds had appeared but left without dropping any rain. Colvill coughed. Choking yellowish dust had thickened along the dirt road. Hancock's 11,000 marching soldiers were creating a monstrous dust storm.

Colvill cocked his head back toward the Old First. Blue forage caps draped over bent faces covered with white handkerchiefs. He chuckled; the regiment looked like a band of robbers. But he knew his men: those hardened frontiersmen were fierce fighters, and they loved brawling, never hesitant to settle things with their fists. This mindset had no element of vanity or presumed superiority. It was simply who they were—mostly descendents of the Vikings, the legendary seaborne warriors of Scandinavia. He breathed in air heavy with humidity and warmth and let his expanded chest hold it for a few moments. He had every confidence in his men. Despite what he had put them through the past two days, not one of them had broken. But even Vikings had limits.

Still, he worried, his stomach twisting like knotted eels. What about the Minnesota pickets? Would they survive this grueling march? Several of his boys had marched twenty miles yesterday, and then, after stopping to bivouac, they moved a quarter mile in front of Second Corps and stood picket duty the rest of the

125

night. They'd marched another twenty-five miles today. A murderous detail. These boys needed water, but the regiment had drained their canteens hours ago. They must be near exhaustion. Thank God none had dropped dead from heat stroke. They just had to hang on for one more hour. The evening's bivouac lay a few miles ahead on the banks of the Monocacy River, just below Frederick.

The dust was thickening. Colvill closed his eyes, saying a quick prayer. Wiping his brow with his gloved hand, he turned and glanced at Second Lieutenant William Lochren from Company K, riding next to him. Lochren was thirty-one, an Irish immigrant with a short, rounded beard, shaven cheeks, and full chevron mustache. He was a Minneapolis attorney and a gifted writer and now was Colvill's regimental historian.

"William, have Sergeant Wright come up to the front."

Lochren saluted and rode back down the line.

Up ahead through the yellow dust cloud, approaching horse hooves clattered like a pelting rain. A rider was flying down the road at a full gallop. Colvill gripped the binoculars hanging around his neck and peered through them. The rider was a husky man with a dark, bushy mustache and a full tag of hair hanging down from his chin—his showboat executive officer, Lieutenant Colonel Charles Adams. *I'll be damned. This better be good.* Adams was a tough man and a good fighter, but too ambitious in seeking promotions. Several of the Minnesotans had told Colvill that Adams had set his sights on becoming commander of the First Minnesota.

Adams's horse flared to a stop, kicking up dirt and whirling up dust. Colvill grunted. *What the hell, Adams?*

Adams bellowed, "There is a rumor that a couple soldiers from Webb's brigade have died of sunstroke."

"Keep your voice down, Charlie," Colvill warned.

Adams's jaw tightened. "I thought you would want to know."

"Don't bring me rumors," Colvill replied. "Bring me facts."

Colvill frowned as heat licked his face. Son of a bitch, the damage was done. The men marching at the front of the regiment turned their heads and began whispering. Adams had riled up the troops unnecessarily; his gossip was spreading through the regiment like a rushing torrent. *Son of a bitch. What a damn fool thing to blurt out within earshot of the men.*

Colvill turned to Adams and glared without blinking. "You're dismissed."

Adams shrugged, saluted, and moved to the back of the regiment.

The regiment continued to trudge on slowly. Colvill's nostrils flared. If the rumors about Webb's brigade were true, his picket men were in grave danger. Lochren rode back up, keeping pace with Colvill.

Colvill turned to Lochren. "William, I'm debating if I should order the pickets to fall out along the road and let them rest for a bit."

"They will refuse, Colonel, preferring to die walking in the heat than to embarrass themselves by lingering under a shade tree as the rest of Hancock's corps marches by."

"I agree," Colvill said. "But this is madness. These boys have bullheaded pride." There was something about being the youngest state in the Union that was in play here, as if they had something to prove to the older states.

"Saint Augustine said it was pride that changed angels into devils," Lochren replied.

"Hell, I will take arrogant devils as long as they are alive and can fire a rifle."

"We're a small regiment with a mighty heart," Lochren said. "We might be the youngest state, but I'm proud Minnesota was the first to offer 1,000 men to defend and preserve the Republic. The Old First will never falter."

"Well, this is a tough business," Colvill replied. "These boys may falter, dropping dead in their tracks from sunstroke if we don't get them some water and rest soon. I'm in no mood to write obituary letters to their relatives. It's bad enough when they fall in combat, but for marching?"

Scampering feet and a gentle whoosh of air came from behind. Face flushed, First Sergeant Wright arrived and walked next to Colvill's horse. He saluted and said windily, "Colonel Bill, reporting as ordered, sir."

Colvill insisted everyone call him Colonel Bill, including Hancock and Gibbon. He returned the salute and peered, letting Wright catch his breath. Colvill cherished this man. Wright was a twenty-three-year-old student at Hamline University when the war began. He was a tough, stout man with a high forehead, curly hair, and no sideburns. He was exceptionally bright, a superb writer, and a destructive tempest in battle. The little red-haired sergeant from F Company was the great-great-grandson of William Hooper, one of North Carolina's signers of the Declaration of Independence.

"How are the pickets doing?"

"They are as bullheaded as hell, sir, refusing to drop out of line and take a rest. They are cramping up and dizzy. Some are complaining of nausea. But they are hanging in there."

"Make sure the pickets use their handkerchiefs to cover up their heads under their hats. Also, make sure they have the first opportunity to cool in the river when we bivouac. I'm guessing the regiment should arrive at the Monocacy River within the half hour."

"They won't pull any extra duties for quite some time, either," Wright said.

"Good. After bivouacking, I will stop by to check on them," Colvill added. "That's all."

Wright saluted and moved back to the struggling pickets.

Lochren pointed ahead, dropping his binoculars to his chest. "I spy a single rider wearing the black Hardee hat of the famous Iron Brigade."

Colvill grinned. "It's probably Lieutenant Haskell."

Haskell rode up, saluted. "Colonel Bill. General Gibbon sends his compliments and requests the honor of joining you this evening for dinner."

Colvill's eyebrow shot up; something *big* must be up. "The Old First would be delighted to have you and General Gibbon join us this evening for dinner. Thank you."

Haskell saluted and rode back up the road.

"What's going on?" Lochren asked.

"Maybe Gibbon wants to check on the condition of the Minnesota pickets. I can't think of another reason why he would want to have dinner with the Old First."

"Well, whatever the reason, we need to inform the Brigade commander."

"Yes, we do. But that can wait until we've bivouacked."

Colvill spotted Lieutenant Colonel Charles Morgan, the inspector general for Second Corps, riding down the line. Morgan pulled up next to Colvill and saluted.

"Colonel Bill, Second Corps scouts report the Monocacy River is a half a mile ahead."

"Good. I think my picket boys are going to make it."

"That's good news, Colonel. I will inform General Hancock." Morgan unfastened three water canteens strapped to his saddle horn and handed them to Colvill. "General Hancock's scouts filled these for your pickets when they rode to Monocacy River." Morgan saluted and continued to ride down line.

"I think General Hancock and General Gibbon are worried about the Minnesota pickets," Lochren said.

"Yes, William. I agree. Ride back and give the canisters to Sergeant Wright."

---

## Wright

*6:30 p.m.*

Wright handed the water canisters to the pickets. "Don't gulp down the water. Take small swigs and wet your cracked lips."

Each picket took a small swig and passed the canister to the others.

One picket said, "Please tell Colonel Bill we are most grateful for his generosity."

"I will," said Wright. A wave of warmth washed over him. Colonel Bill was the perfect commander for the Old First. He was a man of iron nerve and will. He had the ability to remain calm under the most horrific battlefield conditions, facing danger with the greatest show of indifference of any man in the regiment. And he always took care of his men.

"You can make it. We are only a half mile from tonight's bivouac," Sergeant Wright encouraged the pickets.

The pickets nodded, tight-lipped, and handed the canteens to Wright. He shook them; they sounded about half full. Wright moved among the men, giving each one a drink. When the canisters emptied, he took his place, walking alongside the regiment.

Squinting through the dusty gloom toward the front of the regiment, he spotted Colvill's silhouette. The colonel looked like a giant riding a pony. Wright smiled. Colvill could dwarf any beast he rode. He was a big, burly man, standing halfway between six and seven feet, with a heavy neckbeard like a Mennonite. His height made him an easy target. A memory of the Battle of Glendale flashed through his mind. Wright had been standing next to Captain Colvill, who was commanding Company F. A yellow sheet of fire erupted from the enemy line. Colvill grunted, but he did not yell out or fall to the ground. Instead, he said in a calm voice, "Sergeant Wright, I need to visit the field hospital." Colvill turned over command to his lieutenant and walked to the field hospital.

Wright learned later that a doctor told Colvill that a Minié ball had entered his chest two inches below the left collarbone. It was a dangerous wound. When the surgeon told Colvill to stay behind at the field hospital as the regiment was marching out, he refused. Major Morgan came by looking for Colvill, offering to let the Captain ride his horse. Again Colvill refused. Instead, he took a firm grip of the horse's tail and let Morgan pull him along until they arrived at the division hospital at Malvern Hill.

Pride shot through Wright. Was there a better regimental commander in the army? Hell, no. His Minnesota boys came first. The regiment respected Colvill's silent courage, his insistence on leading from the front, and his ability to repress the pain and never complain. All these qualities set him apart.

Wright coughed, snapping him back to the moment. His feet moved in a mechanical rhythm, one foot in front of the other, lumbering along. No one talked. He started visualizing the Monocacy River just ahead, hoping it was as sparkling as the Mississippi waters near his home of Red Wing.

Private Marshall Sherman yelped and tumbled toward him. Wright grabbed the back of Sherman's jacket as the private regained his balance.

"Thanks, Sergeant Wright. I twisted my ankle on a rock."

"Are you going to be alright?" Wright said.

"Yea, I think so."

Wright let go of Sherman. But his right hand flamed as if burned by a fireball. He rubbed the two crooked fingers on his right hand. The scorching pain was a constant reminder of being struck by lightning as a young boy. The electrifying bolt had hit the house, tearing off the roof, setting it ablaze. His oldest sister and a younger brother were killed. Life in the rugged Northwest Territory was harsh and unforgiving.

He stepped off the road, glancing at the soldiers. They were about as cheerful as a rained-on rooster on a back fence, but none of the bronzed faces had fallen out. Many of the men were practically barefoot, and some feet were badly bruised and blistered. The new leather shoes issued twelve days ago in Virginia were shredded from miles of marching on roads of mud, sand, and sharp stones.

Although they were close to exhaustion, they marched. They fought like thunderbolts, with great courage and heroic sacrifice, a force of nature average men admired. Like their Viking ancestors, they placed honor above death. At the Battle of Fredericksburg, they earned the acclaim "the First Minnesota never runs." Two years prior, the regiment had fought at the First Battle of Bull Run with nearly a thousand men. Now they numbered around three hundred.

Colvill yelled, "Halt." A great cheer erupted from the regiment. Tonight's bivouac was a few hundred yards away near the Monocacy River. Colvill rode ahead toward the river.

Wright motioned to last night's pickets, shouting, "Follow me," and led them toward Colvill.

"I'm mighty proud of you men," Colonel Bill said. "You've earned the privilege of being the first to cool off in the river."

The pickets cheered and headed toward the river. Bluffs and trees lined the riverbanks, occasionally giving way to beautiful vistas of farmland and distant wooded ridges. To the north, Frederick was engulfed by a sea of white tents housing army headquarters.

Wright walked up to Colvill and saluted smartly.

Colvill returned the salute. "Sergeant, General Gibbon requests the honor of joining Old First this evening for dinner. Let's make sure we use the good china."

Wright flashed a grin. "Of course, sir. With your permission, I'll ride into Frederick and ask Hooker if he can loan us his."

Colvill guffawed. "You have my permission. Give my regards to Hooker."

"The men did well today marching in the sweltering heat. None of them fell out," Wright reported. "But several of the boys in the Eighty-second New York wilted like mown grass. Some of the men from the Fifteenth Massachusetts were falling as if struck by lightning."

"God forbid," Colvill said. He cocked his enormous head toward the men stacking arms, starting fires, and cooking coffee, soaked in sweat like workhorses. Colvill scratched his arms as he sizzled in his wool uniform in the brutally humid Maryland weather. These uniforms saved lives when the First Minnesota wounded lay freezing on the Fredericksburg battlefield, but they killed in this scorching heat.

"I noticed several men marching along with blood trickling into their shoes," Wright added. "A few of them limped in on badly bruised, blistered fleet."

"Make sure the rest of the regiment gets a chance to cool off in the river," Colvill said with concern in his voice.

Wright saluted and off he moved.

---

## Colvill

*7:00 p.m*
*(Sunset is 7:44 p.m.)*
*First Minnesota's bivouac*

Softly thanking God for the pickets' safe arrival at the river, Colvill felt the tension ebb from his body. He walked toward the river, passing Corporal Josias King, who greeted him in the sweet Southern drawl of his native Virginia. "Good evening, Colonel Bill."

Colvill nodded. It seemed ironic that some of the fiercest fighters for the Union were Southern-born men like Corporal King and General Gibbon. How many Yankee traitors were fighting for the South? Very few, if any.

Clattering horse hooves trotted toward him. He turned his head. Two of his best officers stopped, dismounted, saluted—Captain Nathan Messick of Company G, a thirty-six-year-old cobbler from Faribault, Minnesota, and Lochren. Messick reported on the day's events.

Messick finished the update then launched into a tirade on the reporting of the *St. Paul Pioneer*. "Members of the regiment have been sending missives to the *St. Paul Pioneer*, or to Minnesota Senator Morton Wilkerson or Governor Ramsey, who send them on to the *Pioneer*, and the damn newspaper prints them, typically reporting wrong information," he complained. "I would like to cuff each idiot whose letter ends up in print. The Rebels read the *Pioneer* just like we do. Doesn't the army have rules about this?"

Colvill did not respond, and Messick, his rant finished, departed.

"How is the regiment faring this evening, Loch?" Colvill asked.

"Pretty used up from today's march, but morale is high," Lochren said. "I seem to be caught up on most of my paperwork. Butterfield keeps issuing ridiculous deadlines to the corps commander historians, who in turn pass it down the chain of command, where it ends up in my hands. I swear I spend most of my time doing Butterfield's paperwork. He seems more interested in recording how we lose every battle than worrying about winning one."

Colvill pursed his lips. He didn't know Butterfield. But General Gibbon despised the army's chief of staff.

"Butterfield wants us to update our June regimental histories by the first of July," Lochren continued. "Doesn't he know a storm is brewing? He doesn't have a clue about what is important in this army."

"And Hooker doesn't have a clue about how to fight Lee," Colvill added. "Hooker and Butterfield are a pair of very low cards. Not ones with which I'd care to bet."

Lochren left to work on the regimental history. Colvill looked down the road and spotted a division flag heading his way. It was Gibbon, with Haskell riding alongside and a small group of aides trailing in the rear. The general and Haskell rode up and dismounted. Colvill saluted, put out a hand.

"Welcome to First Minnesota's fine dining, perhaps the best food in the entire division. Although the menu has not changed since the last time you visited. That is something on which we need to work."

Gibbon smiled and said, "Good evening, Colonel Bill. How are the Minnesota boys who pulled picket duty last night doing?"

Colvill said, "They all made it and are cooling off in the river."

"Good, that's very good. I was damn worried about them." Gibbon fished for his pipe and lit it. "Army headquarters provided General Hancock an update on Lee's army locations in Pennsylvania. They also passed on information on the Union corps."

Colvill stared at Gibbon.

"It seems headquarters has a renewed interest in finding and fighting the enemy," Gibbon said.

Colvill raised his chin. "What? You have reliable knowledge about the location of the Union corps?" Something had changed.

"We've had a swap of commanders early this morning. Meade has relieved Hooker."

Colvill rubbed his hands together and a rumbling laugh broke from his chest. "So that's why you know the position of the Union corps. That's good news."

"It is good news," Gibbon said.

"But the men have become so accustomed to the change of commanders they will probably care little about who is in charge," Colvill said.

Gibbon replied, "I agree. Most of the men outside of Fifth Corps don't know much about Meade. That's fine. They will grow to hate him in the next few days. He is going after Lee, and he hopes to find and fix a portion of his dispersed army and destroy it."

"Lee now faces a credible opponent," Haskell added. "That will be a new wrinkle for him."

"Haskell and I have been discussing an interesting point," Gibbon interjected. "Explain your idea, Frank."

Haskell began, "I believe the Rebels' fighting morale will ebb in Pennsylvania. One of the central beliefs among Southerners was that the Confederacy was fighting against the Yankee invaders. They were fighting on their own soil against an invading army." Haskell paused.

Colvill rubbed his chin. "Please go on."

"This Rebel excursion north of the Potomac places them in a dilemma. Crossing the Potomac enables Lee to feed his army and perhaps win a battle on Northern soil, which would start the process for other countries to recognize the Confederacy as a new country. But achieving this goal puts them in the position of fighting as the invading army."

Gibbon interrupted. "Here is the key point."

Haskell continued, "Crossing the Potomac diminished their moral status. North of the Potomac they are not fighting for their homes. This has nothing to do with Lee's leadership. People fight harder when they are defending their own homes, as the Rebels will soon find out."

"I agree," Colvill said. "I expect the Army of the Potomac to fight harder now that they are defending their own territory."

"I have another, simpler reason why Confederate morale will be impaired," Haskell continued. "Threadbare shoes. In Virginia, the roads are soft dirt. In this invasion of the North, they have made long marches, many over the hard stone roads of Maryland and Pennsylvania. Their shoes have been destroyed by now. We've seen the way our roads have worn out so many Union men and boots."

"I can believe that," Colvill said. "Many of the men of the First Minnesota are footsore this evening, and their shoes are worn out. Speaking of shoes, Lieutenant Haskell, my regiment needs new shoes now, if possible."

Haskell pulled a piece of paper and pencil from his jacket and wrote a note. "I'll try."

"You may have a point about Rebel morale," Colvill said, "but I can guarantee they still will aim true and squeeze their triggers hard, and their Minié balls and artillery shells will still do the same damage to our boys."

Haskell grimaced and acknowledged a concession.

Colvill raised his glass. "Let's celebrate our new commander, General Meade."

Colvill leaned back and sipped on his drink. Meade, eh? A fine corps commander, but did he have the talent to lead the Army of the Potomac against one of the finest generals West Point ever produced? *Lord, I hope so.* He took another long draw on his drink.

# 12
# Meade — Sunday, June 28

The moon hung orange in the dust clouds above the horizon. Meade paced outside Hooker's vacated tent, now his tent, wearing a droopy black hat pulled over his brow. His nerves were stretched tight; fear stiffened his neck. He kicked a rock and wiped his sweaty palms on his trousers. *For Christ's sake—where in the hell is the enemy?* Without some notion of the whereabouts of Lee's forces, he couldn't complete the plan. Hooker's hedgehog analogy popped into his head. Maybe he was a hedgehog, because he liked to operate within a plan, a coherent framework that he could use for making decisions. So without the *plan,* he couldn't issue the marching orders for tomorrow.

He lifted his head and scoured headquarters camp. Several lanterns were burning, but there was no sign of personal aides. *Crap.* Most of the day, they had lurked within eyeshot outside his tent, where he smoked cigars and studied maps and snarled like a blustering badger. As his fiery ranting became more explosive, his inner circle of aides had migrated away. Now they were slinking about in the shadows. Only a gaggle of predator reporters huddled near a small fire, sniffing around for a story.

"Christ almighty, Biddle," he shouted, "I need some more coffee. Do I really need to yell at you every time it's empty?"

Biddle emerged from the darkness toward him, holding a tin coffee pot by its handle. He refilled Meade's coffee cup and retreated back to the campfire.

Meade bristled. He was the damn commander of the Union's largest army and he would like to think his personal staff could anticipate when he needed coffee.

Meade held the coffee cup, took a sip, closed his eyes, breathed deeply, and took another. What a horrific day, the hours dragging by like a slow-moving coal train. He'd been in command since seven this morning and he still didn't have a good feel for what the enemy was doing. He opened his eyes. The thickening darkness was a haunting doom closing in about him.

Warren walked up to the map table. "How's the plan coming, General?"

"Not worth a damn."

"What's the problem?"

"Poor enemy intelligence. I'm literally in the dark, no pun intended."

"Colonel Sharpe hasn't given you an update on the Confederate positions?"

"No. I'll tell you something, Gouv. Sharpe's boys haven't impressed me today."

"I think Sharpe will come through for you. He's impressed me the last couple of weeks."

"Well, I need results. How in the hell am I supposed to create a coordinated plan, moving seven big infantry corps toward the enemy, without knowing where the Confederates are? That's just as risky as Hooker's idea of staying put and letting Lee find us and hand us our ass."

Meade paused and pointed. "See those sons of bitch newspaper reporters standing over there?"

"Yes, I do," Warren observed.

"Those scavenger vultures better stay clear. They have been lurking around headquarters all day, drinking my damn coffee, betting my demise is near and hoping they would be able to pluck ripe stories from the scraps of my career."

"George, be careful. They can hurt you."

"Not if I kill them first."

"You can't kill all of them. They are rats. They come in a ravenous swarm and keep scrapping and biting until they get a piece."

"Goddamn it. I swear by God's blood it's a dreadful distraction knowing I'm under their constant scrutiny, as if I'm on trial and the damn reporters are the jury. Not only do I have to defeat

Lee and put up with Lincoln's political idiots, I have to deal with those gallery rats."

"George, I know this is your first experience in dealing with war correspondents, but they can be as lethal as the Rebels."

"Hooker advised me to be watchful. In fact, Fighting Joe Hooker told me that a few days ago the *New York Herald* had printed the exact locations of all seven of his infantry corps and the cavalry commands. I didn't see the newspaper article, but I sure as hell wished Hooker had shared that information with me and the other corps commanders. I'd at least have known where they were!"

Meade bristled as he ran a hand down his beard.

"The enemy knew where *they* were before I did. I should form a Reporter's Intelligence Regiment and put them on the front lines. If the newspapermen can't tell me where the enemy is, they can at least engage them and die honorably."

"Sir, again," Warren sighed, "please be careful with them."

*9:00 p.m.*

Meade placed both his hands on the map table, eyes staring at the outdated terrain map, fingers drumming a faint staccato beat. His hair was matted with perspiration. Last night he had gone to bed as the Fifth Corps commander, ignorant about the enemy's movements and the location of the other Union infantry corps. Now, seventeen hours later, he was commander of the Union's largest army, knowing his infantry corps were foolishly spread all over the countryside and Lee's army was slithering around unimpeded somewhere.

What was Lee up to? Without intelligence, Meade had no way of knowing when and where the enemy's fangs would strike against his army. He owed his corps commanders orders by midnight. *Damn.* Knowing enemy positions and likely movements was key in creating an effective plan. Meade looked up. Many of the headquarters staff were standing outside their tents with their lieutenants, talking in low voices, staring at him. He had to go after Lee at the greatest possible speed, but he would be moving blindly toward enemy forces. Where was the Rebel cavalry?

*9:15 p.m.*

Williams arrived out of the darkness, sipping hot coffee from a tin cup. He stood next to Warren, studying Meade for a moment. "Have you figured out tomorrow's marches?"

"Still working out the damn plan," Meade snapped. "But I can tell you one thing. We are not going to grope our way along like Hooker had us doing."

"Yes, sir," Williams said. "We will need to get the orders out by midnight if you expect the northernmost corps to be marching by four in the morning."

He banged his fist on the table. "Damn it! Do you think I'm a bullet-headed idiot? I know what I have to do. Something this blasted staff didn't do for the past four weeks. Devise a plan."

Williams's eyes widened and his face grew pale. He put his hands behind his back.

"General Meade," Warren said, "if I may, what are your instincts telling you to do?"

"Well, I'm still settling on the direction of the march. But I'm leaning toward a northeast vector focused on York or Harrisburg. That's where my knotted gut is telling me to find Lee."

"I concur with your instincts," Warren said.

Meade glared at Warren and bawled, "A lot of help you are! Are you going to be another of Hooker's blasted yes men?"

Warren shifted beneath his stare and shook his head.

Meade turned and looked down. *Damn it, George. Warren is your friend and a good soldier. Don't unleash on him like that. Or you're not going to have any friends.*

Biddle arrived. "General Meade. Hooker's former cook has prepared a roast stew for you."

"Good. I'm starved."

"Well, there is something else."

"What?"

"Hooker's cook was hopeful he could remain as your cook for you and your personal staff. And he is really quite good, sir."

"I don't care." He grunted. "Hmm." *One of Hooker's personal staff wants to serve me. That's interesting.* "It's your decision to make, but I want to taste that stew. You've got my mouth watering and I'm hungry as hell."

Biddle smiled and left to speak with the cook. Meade motioned for Warren and Williams to join him over the map. He moved his finger across the map from South Mountain to Gettysburg and then to Harrisburg.

"Hooker was reacting slowly to Lee's northward movement, and Lee has been imposing his will on the Army of the Potomac for too long. I need to employ a new tactic to preempt Lee's initiative. We need to maneuver rapidly and surprise Lee with our speed of march. I want to threaten or cut Lee's long, exposed supply lines, forcing him to react to us for a change."

Uncertainty coated Meade's tone. He searched the map for a decisive point to attack Lee's critical vulnerability—his supply lines—a vulnerability that, if exploited, would cause Lee significant damage. It would at least dictate that Lee do something he had not planned on doing. Meade focused over each town north of his army: Emmitsburg, Taneytown, Chambersburg, Gettysburg, and York. His index finger traced each river, stream, and creek: Susquehanna, Monocacy, Patapsco, Deer Creek, Big Pipe Creek, Rock Creek, Willoughby's Run, Plum Run, and Alloway Creek. "Hmm." They were all too far away at this point.

He then turned his attention to South Mountain, his finger running along the Chambersburg and Monterey Passes. His face flushed hot as he jabbed a finger at Warren's chest.

"Son of bitch, Gouv, why in the hell didn't Hooker have our cavalry secure these two narrow passes? It won't take more than a few cavalry companies to hold them."

"Hooker did not believe Lee's army would march that far north," Warren said.

Meade shook his head; his stomach churned with rage. He looked down at the map and studied the geography of the Catoctin Mountain and Braddock Heights, directly west of Frederick. He examined key terrain southeast of his Frederick position, including Parr's Ridge, bisecting Baltimore and Washington, studying how it screened his logistics head at Westminster. The time-distance factor and the fact the Confederates hadn't engaged yet could only mean they were heading farther north.

"Gentlemen, we need to extend our front twenty or so miles to the northeast like a fan to control the main road from Baltimore, running west through Westminster. It is a wide front, but Halleck's orders are clear. We have to cover Baltimore and Washington at all times."

Warren smirked. "So much for the freedom to maneuver."

"I agree, Gouv. Okay, here is the challenge. If we march the army directly north, massing it against Lee's center, we risk Lee scooting around our eastern flank, threatening Baltimore. If we march forward on a sharp northeast vector, we risk uncovering Lee's western flank, allowing him to simply swing around us and gain a clear shot at the capital."

Biddle arrived, setting the stew and coffee on the edge of the map table. Meade bent down and took a whiff of roasted beef and cooked carrots and freshly baked bread. *Damn, that smells good.* The cook followed a short distance behind Biddle, looking hopeful.

Meade spooned a heaping portion of the thick stew. *Oh my God. Mouthwatering.* He looked up at the cook. "This is delicious. With Major Biddle's concurrence, I would be most pleased to have you as my cook."

The cook cracked a huge grin. "Thank you, General Meade." He departed with Biddle.

Meade and Warren gulped the stew, shoveling in several spoonfuls in rapid succession. Meade's gut swelled, the emptiness finally dissipating. Finishing, they lit cigars and sipped the coffee, studying the map some more. Meade gazed down at the key roads, frowning, dark eyes shifting from each key town to the arteries supplying them.

"Gouv, I must protect against flank attacks as the army moves forward toward the enemy. But I'm running out of time."

He paused and stood up straight, his heart rattling.

"Well, a half-baked plan is better than no plan. I've decided: Using speed as a weapon, I'm thrusting the army north, hoping to catch Lee before he can concentrate his forces and wheel to the east. We are going to march the Union army faster and longer than ever before. Lee will not expect the Army of the Potomac to pull off such a maneuver."

Warren drew a breath. "I concur. Lee will not be expecting it."

"Gouv, let's work on the start times for each corps. Several will be using the same roads so we'll have to stagger the starts."

Warren pulled out a pencil and started writing on the map.

"Gouv, we need to use as many side and frontage roads as possible. But Hooker's maps don't accurately show minor road routes and the lay of the land, including terrain features such as slope and elevation. I know from marching the past few days that several of the main roads are in miserable shape. Jesus, how could Hooker make such an elementary mistake as not using the right kind of maps? No wonder Lee kicked his butt."

"I agree, sir. As soon as I know we've located the maps I will inform you."

*10:00 p.m.*

Meade moved off into the field behind his tent. He stopped, looking at the stars, so many twinkling dots in the sky. No point in pondering anymore. A plan had formed based on rapid movement and the need to block Lee. Was there a better course of action? He paused, closing his eyes, puffing on his cigar. No, there wasn't. He would employ a fan-shaped advance, extending the flanks as far as possible while still permitting the rapid massing of the army. The army would force-march along the main line from Frederick to Harrisburg, spreading out from Frederick. The advance would protect the flanks and prevent Lee from swinging around the army...he hoped.

Biddle approached across the field at a fast gait. Meade gestured toward Butterfield's tent. "Summon General Butterfield. I have decided on a plan."

Meade walked back to his tent. Butterfield arrived and Meade described his plan for moving the army into Pennsylvania. He explained the order and starting times of the march: four in the morning for most of the infantry corps. Butterfield wrinkled his forehead and rubbed the back of his neck.

143

"Sir, do you have any further orders?" he queried.

"No," Meade said. "But I want you to get these night orders written and delivered before midnight to all the corps commanders."

"Yes, sir. Also, I've sent out couriers to all the corps commanders requesting updates on their supplies. I'm tracking the arrival of logistics supplies and replacement horses at the Westminster railhead." Butterfield departed.

Meade watched Butterfield cross back toward his tent. There was a slight difference in Butterfield's voice now; the snippiness was gone. There was no bitterness. Perhaps he had resigned to supporting Meade as chief of staff for this battle. This was a good omen, he hoped. Maybe Butterfield did possess some professionalism. *We'll see.*

---

*11:00 p.m.*

Meade sat in a chair outside his tent. Two lanterns on a portable table provided enough light to read dispatches from his corps commanders. So many things he needed to do, and there wasn't enough time to mold his headquarters staff before the impending battle, figuring out what needed to be changed and what didn't. This was all such rubbish—unprofessional as hell. Well, one thing for sure, Butterfield needed to go at the first opportunity. He rocked in his chair and gaped at the sea of white headquarter tents. So many unfamiliar faces. He pulled on his beard. His brain was as addled as if he had been drinking whiskey.

He took off his glasses, rubbing his closed eyes hard enough to see sharp blue points of light. He needed sleep, but his overwrought mind kept churning. Tomorrow's plan called for the longest forced march of the war. Most would consider it sheer folly that some of the corps would be marching eighteen to twenty hours. Some men would probably drop dead from heat stroke.

Biddle was back, holding dispatches from corps commanders. He also delivered fresh coffee, setting it on a table next to Meade. Meade sipped the coffee. The muggy heat was departing slowly, like an unwelcome guest. Good.

As the army moved forward, he needed to identify gaps where Lee was vulnerable. He needed to pit his strengths against Lee's weaknesses, especially against Lee's logistics train west of South Mountain. *I bet those trains are vulnerable.*

*11:30 p.m.*

Warren came out of the dark, his face beaming.

"General, good evening," he began. "My aides have located some excellent Maryland and Pennsylvania topographical maps in Baltimore. They should arrive in the early morning."

"Good. Very good." Meade yawned. "I'm going to try to catch a few winks. Please wake me as soon as the maps arrive."

He stood up and moved into the tent, removing his boots, collapsing on the cot, falling asleep instantly. A short while later, a distant voice called him. Meade lay motionless, hoping it would vanish.

*Monday, June 29*
*2:00 a.m.*

The distant voice called again. "General Meade, sir."

Meade struggled to focus.

"General Meade." He felt a hand touching his arm. "General Meade, wake up, sir. It's me, Gouv. You wanted to be informed when General French's garrison had departed Harper's Ferry. General French has sent a note saying the Union troops have left Harper's Ferry."

Meade shook his head, trying to wake up. On impulse, he sat up, rolling his legs off the cot. He reached for his glasses on the small stool next to the cot.

He swallowed hard and said grumpily, "What time is it, Gouv?"

"It's two in the morning."

"Thank you."

Warren waited for a moment, then he departed.

Meade stifled a cringe. He had slept for two hours. He coughed and clutched his chest, rubbing the sharp pain from the Minié-ball wound. More sleep and the pain would ebb, but there was no time for sleep. An aide brought a cup of black coffee. Meade held it under his nose and the steam filled his lungs. He closed his eyes until the throbbing pain was manageable.

Where was Lee's cavalry? Lee would never operate this far north without Stuart's cavalry screening his movements. But Colonel Sharpe said Stuart was not with Lee. How could that be? He had no confidence in Sharpe's so-called intelligence outfit. He wracked his brain. Why can't I figure it out? Why can't Sharpe find Stuart's cavalry? Lee had consistently demonstrated the ability to move and concentrate effortlessly and with impunity. What was he scheming?

Meade's legs wobbled as if he were walking on rickety stilts. He spotted Hooker's rocking chair in the corner of the tent, pulled it over to the map table, and slumped into it, rocking slowly back and forth. What the hell was up with Stuart's cavalry? His mind switched on, remembering he owed Halleck an update. He sighed. He composed a short, situational update. He called for an aide, gave him the message. Would the march today be successful? Was he marching into a trap?

Warren walked into the tent. "How are you doing, sir?"

"Lovely. My chest throbs. My feet are sore. I feel like I've been standing all last night."

"You should try sleeping again for a few hours."

Meade shook his head. "I can't sleep. We have a chance to surprise Lee if we move quickly today, marching unexpectedly toward him."

"Sir, the marching orders have been sent to the corps commanders for a four in the morning departure. You should try to get a couple hours' rest until then."

"I'm worried about this morning's corps movements," Meade admitted. "A few of the corps are traveling on the same roads, but at different times. We've never executed such a large synchronized march like this on so few roads. These movements must be executed with precision. No one can miss the orders."

Warren said, "I received word Stuart's boys tore up the Baltimore & Ohio rail line leading to Frederick. It happened around midnight. But General Herman Haupt sent word he

146

would have a new supply line in operation by midday over the Western Railroad from Baltimore to Westminster."

Meade nodded. Stanton's appointment of Haupt, a West Point civil engineer, to be the chief of construction for the U.S. Military Railroads had been a brilliant decision. McClellan had said that Haupt had built a railroad bridge of cornstalks and beanpoles a hundred feet long and a hundred feet high across the Potomac that loaded trains passed on every hour. An incredible engineering feat.

Meade asked, "Have you sent your pioneer parties out in advance of today's marches?"

"They departed around midnight, moving north on the main roads, bridging streams and removing obstructions," Warren said.

Meade nodded approvingly. "I appreciate the update." He laid his head back against the tall back of the rocking chair and closed his eyes.

Warren departed.

*2:20 a.m.*

Meade rocked in the big chair. *General McClellan was our best commanding general and he was a man of charisma. When "Little Mac" rode along the Union lines during the Peninsula Campaign, the boys in blue threw up their caps and cheered. Will the boys ever cheer me as army commander? Probably not. I'm not McClellan.* Meade faced an inadequacy he could not remedy: he lacked the charisma and warm rapport to inspire the troops' emotions.

*But charisma doesn't help coordinate the movements of seven big corps marching independently over a few bad roads. Charisma doesn't monitor movements, preventing a snarl of corps colliding into each other, delaying the march by hours. If charisma were the key to leadership, McClellan would still be the army commander. So would the next two army commanders.*

*Damn.* He was worrying too much. But he had well-founded reasons for his distress. He had to synchronize the marching of nearly 94,000 soldiers in seven corps, each with its own batteries, wagon trains, a cavalry corps, and Hunt's artillery reserve of more than one hundred guns. It was his responsibility to ensure each corps' logistics trains did not cause traffic jams. His brain did the calculus: seven corps, with men marching four abreast, each created a column two to three miles long, without wagons, artillery. Two to three miles per corps was a closed-up formation. But if each corps spread out using an open marching formation, including two hundred logistics trains, several ambulances, and artillery pieces with limbers and caissons, the marching columns would extend between ten and eighteen miles.

⦅ • ⦆

*2:30 a.m.*

Colonel Sharpe entered his tent. "Beg your pardon, sir. We know the whereabouts of Lee's forces."

Meade bolted upright. With a hint of disbelief, he demanded, "You're sure?"

Sharpe replied with enthusiasm. "Yes. The main body of Lee's infantry is west of South Mountain in the Cumberland Valley. They have departed Hagerstown and are moving leisurely north to Chambersburg. A.P. Hill's Second Corps is the vanguard, and Longstreet's First Corps is trailing, protecting the rear guard. Early's division of Ewell's Third Corps has moved through Gettysburg toward Hanover Junction and is threatening York. Ewell's remaining two divisions are operating closer to Carlisle, north of Gettysburg."

"Yes," Meade snapped as his soggy brain cleared. "But where is Stuart's cavalry? Stuart's entire cavalry can't be operating between us and Baltimore. Lee would never permit his eyes to be running around the countryside freelancing that far from the Rebel main body."

"Sir, Stuart's entire cavalry, with the exception of a small force screening Rebel logistics moving north from Williamsport, is operating to the east of our army, detached from Lee and not capable of providing support to the Rebel main body," Sharpe insisted.

"Impossible," Meade growled. "How did you come by such crappy intel?"

Sharpe said, "I'm positive, sir. My men saw them with their own eyes."

His heart fluttered as a bolt of energy shot through his chest. Was fate touching him with hope?

"Let's look at the map." Meade studied it. "Well, I'll be damned, Colonel Sharpe. Lee's army is more dispersed than ours. Tomorrow's maneuver northward may indeed threaten Early's dispersed division operating near York and the Susquehanna River. Without follow-on support, Early's isolated division will have to pull back toward Carlisle or risk being cut off and chopped up by our rapidly advancing forces."

"I agree, sir. Tomorrow's march toward Early's division is like pointing a knife at Lee's jugular. Early will have to fall back westward or risk having his throat slashed."

Meade traced his finger through the Chambersburg pass that A.P. Hill's and Longstreet's corps would have to use to support Early's divisions in Carlisle and York. Meade's pulse raced. Both Hill and Longstreet's corps would have to use the same narrow road cutting through South Mountain.

"What a stroke of luck!" Meade shouted. His whole body started to tingle. "This means Lee's two other corps cannot arrive simultaneously."

Meade slapped Sharpe on the back. "Great job, Colonel. Well done."

Sharpe departed. Meade lit a cigar. Finally, some good news!

---

*2:45 a.m.*

Butterfield entered Meade's tent. "Excuse me, sir!"

Meade kept his finger moving over different road routes and streams on the map. He did not look up. *What the hell does Butterfield want?* He continued searching, trying to find a good natural defensive line that the army could fall back to if necessary. He had not found one yet, which was bothersome.

"General," Butterfield said, "I need to speak to you about the marching orders today."

Meade's head snapped up. His hands remained on the map table, his blue eyes narrowed, and his brow furrowed. He stared at Butterfield, glaring for several moments. Butterfield shifted his stance slightly, appearing uncomfortable.

"What?"

Butterfield took a deep breath. "Sir, marching the men twice as far as normal in this Maryland heat will cause heat stroke and kill many of the men. This is stupidity…sir!"

Butterfield's tone was stinging and challenging.

Meade exploded, shouting, "Don't you get it? Lincoln fired Hooker. I'm in command now. You got that?"

Meade took a step forward, standing nose to nose with Butterfield. For a long moment their eyes locked. Meade's nostrils flared. Butterfield broke eye contact and lowered his head slightly.

"Keep your comments to yourself," Meade ordered. "If you would have backed me with Hooker at Chancellorsville to counterattack Lee, we wouldn't be worried about men dying today from heat stroke in Pennsylvania."

"Yes, sir," Butterfield replied, his shoulders slumped forward like a skulking weasel.

"I want you to watch the movements of the seven infantry corps and artillery corps like a hawk," Meade said. "Whenever possible, I want the troops marching in the fields next to the roads. I want the artillery and supply trains doubled up in the roadway. We cannot afford to have each corps column strung out over eighteen miles when a second corps needs to use the same road. I want you to send aides to monitor each corps' movement."

"Yes, sir."

"Butterfield—this is important. We've got a chance to catch Lee with his pants down. But urgency and attention to detail are required."

Meade glared at Butterfield for a few more counts. "You're dismissed."

*3:00 a.m.*

Butterfield departed the tent. Fiery rage rippled through Meade. He should have fired Butterfield for insubordination, or stupidity, he couldn't decide which. He didn't object to his advice. It would be right if the situation were different. But he objected to his insolent tone.

Meade's heart hammered louder, pounding against his ribs. He took a deep breath, letting it gently waft out. Sharpe's intelligence report was a blessing from heaven. *If Lee knew where the Union army spent last evening, he would be shocked at how much distance the Union forces cover today. With luck, at day's end, we will have seized the initiative from Lee, hopefully preventing Early's force from crossing the Susquehanna.* A spike of anxiety knifed through his chest, causing his skin to prickle. Long, grueling marches was the blood price he would have to pay today for seizing the initiative. But he had to get the jump on Lee.

Meade turned his attention to his own logistics challenges. Now that he knew the location of Lee's dispersed forces, he studied the map again. Effective logistics, in and of itself, did not guarantee victory. But it did make an essential contribution to victory by sustaining the forces conducting military operations. Logistics set the outward limit on what was operationally possible. Logistics was like a long rope secured to a dog's collar. It didn't determine where the dog would go, but it did set the limit on how far it could reach.

At West Point, Professor Dennis Mahan had taught them that plunder was an unsatisfactory method of feeding a large army. Meade had read in a French textbook André de Roginat's accounts of Napoleon. Roginat, a French officer in Napoleon's army, had argued that Napoleon's ultimate failure had been the result of inattention to supplying his army with food and ammunition. Meade had sworn at West Point he would not make the same mistake.

---

*4:00 a.m.*

Meade grimaced. Kick-off time for the seven infantry corps to begin marching. Biddle rushed into Meade's tent, his face ragged. He was followed by General Warren. Meade choked down his flaring temper. He disliked being interrupted so often. He glared but checked himself, as his senior aide was loyal and competent.

Biddle saluted. "General, sir."

Meade sat down slowly, sensing something was amiss. "What?" His voice pulsed with anger.

"Sir," Biddle said urgently, "Rebel cavalry have again cut the telegraph wires between us and Washington. With Stuart's boys running amok it's going to take a while before the wires can be repaired. It could be as long as late tomorrow."

Biddle's gaze shifted to the floor as he made a whimpering noise in his throat.

Meade frowned, digesting the news. "Annoying," he said. "Most inconvenient."

Wide-eyed, Biddle said, "General Williams was sending your latest message to Halleck when the lines were cut. He wanted me to let you know. Do you have guidance for Williams?"

Warren interrupted, "This may be a blessing in disguise."

Meade's face tingled.

"General, you now have a good excuse for not responding to the hourly suggestions flowing from the armchair generals in Washington," Warren explained. "You also don't have to hear hundreds of idle rumors rippling over the wires that would have distracted you. This is a chance for you to operate for a while untethered from our helpful friends in Washington."

Meade brightened. Exactly what he was thinking. Most of the Washington crowd didn't understand anything about war. He smiled at Warren and turned to Biddle. "Tell General Williams to send my messages again after the telegraph wires are repaired."

Biddle and Warren grinned.

"If life were only that simple." Meade stroked his beard. "Knowing damn Halleck, he will turn the army's cavalry force into his own Pony Express and start hand-delivering his hastily contrived missives."

"Halleck's Pony Express," Warren said. "I hope Old Brains gives you credit for naming it that."

"Well, gentlemen, I hope this day is not as shockingly crazy as yesterday's. Now let's move this army forward."

Biddle and Warren started to depart.

"Oh, by the way…"

Biddle and Warren halted and turned toward Meade.

Meade chuckled, making a rare joke. "If you spot Colonel Hardie returning to camp, be sure and let me know. Lincoln seems to enjoy beheading generals commanding the Army of the Potomac. I just want to have time to sharpen the executioner's axe so it will take only one clean cut to chop off my head. I'm not fond of excessive pain."

Warren winked. "I'm pretty sure Hardie won't return to headquarters for at least a day. He needs his beauty rest just like the rest of us."

Warren and Biddle departed. Meade rubbed his stomach. *Some breakfast vittles would be nice right about now. I can't keep on surviving on coffee. Logistics: an army marches on its stomach. I can make the Rebels fight on empty stomachs if I can sever their supply chain. Will the opportunity present itself?*

*God, I hope so.*

General Daniel Sickles

# ❧ Monday ❧

June 29, 1863

**General Robert E. Lee, Commander**
Army of Northern Virginia
Commanding for One Year

**General George G. Meade, Commander**
Army of the Potomac
Commanding for Two Days

**General George Sykes, Commander**
Fifth Corps
Commanding for Two Days

## 13

# Haskell — Monday, June 29

*On the road to Hancock's Second Corps headquarters*

Haskell and Gibbon rode along the road toward Second Corps headquarters, slogging through muddy roads as the sun continued to climb in the sultry morning sky above the scattered rain clouds. A slight wind carrying cock-a-doodle-doos from opinionated roosters ruffled the tall grasses of the meadows. The brims of the officers' black Hardee hats were pulled low, preventing the warm rain from hitting their weathered faces. Haskell squeezed his eyes shut, leaned his head back, fully extended his jaw, and yawned, his eardrums stretching for several seconds until they popped. He'd been a night owl last evening, staying up all night waiting for marching orders from Hancock's headquarters. Nothing had arrived.

"Did you get any sleep last night?" Gibbon asked.

"Nope."

"Well, hang on, Frank, I believe this is going to be a long, murderous day."

Haskell lifted a hand. "I'm fine." But his groggy brain wanted to shut down. He hesitated, then shook his head, managing the smallest of nods.

A thundercloud cracked overhead and a soaking rain started pouring down in sheets. Haskell reached up and pulled the brim of his hat further down on his face. Everything about this situation left him uneasy. Hancock's chief of staff, Lieutenant Colonel Morgan, the howling madman, frowned on impromptu visits to corps headquarters. But to hell with protocol. The situation was galling. Hancock had not provided Gibbon's division today's marching orders. Something was wrong.

156

"Are you damn sure we did not miss the marching orders?" Gibbon asked.

"I'm sure. I was up all night waiting for them. That's why I'm dog-tired and yawning every ten minutes. Nothing came."

"Son of a bitch. I don't like this. Meade designs marching orders with the precision of a Swiss watchmaker."

"So he would have issued orders before midnight," Haskell said.

"Absolutely. And once issued, Meade is a stickler for executing orders *on time*, just like a cruel martinet."

"My guess is that Sykes's Fifth Corps to the south is supposed to follow Hancock's Second Corps today, marching on the same roads."

"I agree," Gibbon said. "So a tardy start by Hancock would delay the departure of Sykes."

"Well," Haskell said, "if Meade was commanding, he would have issued orders. So do you think Meade is still acting commander? Or Lincoln had a change of heart, appointed Reynolds or someone else in Meade's place?"

"Hell, I don't know. Anything is possible with those idiots Stanton and Halleck whispering in Lincoln's ear. But this is pure cussedness, and we need to get to the bottom of it soon. Even though we have not been invited to Hancock's headquarters."

Haskell narrowed his eyes, and through a belt of trees the white shapes of Hancock's headquarter tents emerged like church steeples. A few phantomlike figures hovered about the morning campfires. He held his hand over the brim of his Hardee hat, trying to shield his eyes from the pounding rain. "There doesn't appear to be much activity."

Gibbon shook his head. "Bugger the devil. Something is amiss."

---

*6:00 a.m.*

*Hancock's headquarters*

They rode past the sentries and dismounted outside Hancock's tent flying the Second Corps flag. Haskell pulled out his watch.

"It's nearly six."

Gibbon grunted.

Haskell flipped the watch over in his palm and rolled it back and forth like a steel ball. The tents stood erect in a whitish gloom like rows of tombstones. A stabbing pang lingered in his chest; the inactivity was nothing short of stupefying.

"I don't get it," said Haskell. "This lack of urgency is baffling. It looks like a sea of the dead."

"Good Lord, headquarters is still asleep," Gibbon declared, dumbfounded.

A terrifying cry tore through the camp, a horrified bleat like a lamb at slaughter. Haskell flinched, his heart heaving. Was that the wailing shriek of a man or an animal? While the question tumbled in Haskell's mind, Colonel Morgan bolted out of his tent without his hat, his face deathly pale as if in deep shock. Haskell leaped back a step as Morgan brushed passed him, nostrils flared, clutching a piece of paper as he dashed into Hancock's tent. Haskell blinked rapidly. *What the hell?* Morgan was a tough taskmaster, with zero tolerance for screw-ups. But that wasn't a reason to try to knock someone over. Was he witnessing a major screw-up unfold for which someone would pay dearly? With any luck it would be that asshole Morgan.

A moment later, wicked cursing erupted from Hancock's tent. Hancock ripped open the tent cover and emerged, snorting like a bull. Halting a few yards from Haskell, he looked at the staff tents and detonated a blast of profanity that sent shock waves throughout his headquarters. Tent flaps flew open and several staff officers emerged half dressed.

Hancock yelled, "We're moving out now! I mean now! Sons of bitches, we should have departed at four!" Hancock stood ready to pounce, his swearing discharging like lightning strikes.

Haskell's lungs seized and a chill cut down his spine. If Hancock's scowl turned any darker, it would strike his staff dead, including Haskell.

Hancock turned on Morgan. "You're the chief of staff. How did we miss Meade's marching order?"

Morgan started stammering. "Sir, Meade's order was delivered to our duty sergeant late last night."

"So Meade sent it last night, right?"

"Yes sir. Sergeant Brown received the order," Morgan said. "But at the time he was busy requisitioning a logistics chit and left the order on his desk."

"God damn it. This is fricking madness," Hancock yelled. "Brown thinks a Goddamn logistics chit is more important than a marching order delivered from Meade's headquarters? Are you shitting me?"

"Sir, Sergeant Brown was planning to read it after he completed filling out the supply requisition. He forgot about it. He read it this morning and informed me immediately. I will see he is punished as soon—"

Hancock pursed his lips and raised his hand toward Morgan's chest. "Stop your Goddamn babbling. If you can't do your job, I will find someone who can! Someone who can deliver a simple order to me."

Morgan stood at attention, staring straight ahead, jaw clenched.

Haskell's heart raced; he barely dared breathe. He had never seen Hancock so unhinged. Was he going to relieve Morgan as chief of staff? Or strike him dead?

"Have the sergeant report to me immediately," Hancock shouted.

Morgan scurried off and returned with a half-dressed Sergeant Brown. The sergeant marched forward, saluted, and remained at attention.

"Sergeant Brown, your failure to read Meade's marching order last night constitutes dereliction of duty."

Brown stiffened. "Sir, can I explain?"

"Shut up."

Brown's jaw tightened.

"Your bullshit excuses may have carried some weight when we were under Hooker's command, but not now."

Haskell shifted his stance. He wasn't sure he should be witnessing this bloody debacle.

"Meade sent this order last night," Hancock said, waving the order in the sergeant's face.

159

"But General Hancock, Colonel Morgan told me to finish the logistics order before."

Hancock stepped forward and pushed his finger into Brown's chest. "Shut your Goddamn mouth, soldier. I'll deal with Colonel Morgan separately." Hancock craned his neck and pushed his nose forward, nearly touching Brown's nose, and glared.

Hancock cocked his head. "Lieutenant Colonel Morgan, get this corps up and on the march immediately. Then report back to me posthaste."

Colonel Morgan moved off, yelling and waving his arms at his aides.

Haskell studied Brown, standing at attention. The sergeant's fingers were twitching. Why was he being argumentative? What was the matter with him? Hancock was likely to shoot his ass. Haskell gulped and glanced at Hancock's waist. Good, no weapons dangling from his belt.

Hancock turned back to face Brown and shouted, red-faced, "Second Corps was to commence marching at four this morning. Your negligence, Sergeant Brown, has also delayed Fifth Corps' march using the same road. You have caused more than 22,000 soldiers a late start. To make up for the lost time, I'm going to force-march Second Corps thirty miles today. Men may well die from heat stroke because of your blunder. I am busting you to corporal and placing you under arrest for further punishment as deemed necessary. You're dismissed!"

The punishment was swift and brutal. *Holy crap*! Haskell's chest tightened. There was a silent moment of alarm, then the former sergeant saluted, about-faced, and marched off, crestfallen.

Hancock turned toward Morgan's tent, where his mortified chief of staff was opening the tent flap to another adjutant.

"Get back here, Morgan!" he shouted.

Morgan ran back and stood at attention, looking sloppy with his suspenders dangling at his sides.

"Lieutenant Colonel Morgan, you're responsible for this miserable affair," Hancock yelled. "Another failure, and I will relieve you for cause. Second Corps will not stop marching today until it has covered thirty miles. Do you understand?"

"Yes, sir."

"Now execute the damn marching order immediately. You're dismissed."

Morgan saluted and scampered away, shuddering like a leaf. Hancock hurried over to Gibbon and Haskell, who stood at attention, holding their salutes until Hancock saluted.

"I've been in command of Second Corps for six weeks and this is my first cock-up and it occurred on Meade's watch on his second day in command," Hancock said. "Damn it. This is a hell of a way to impress a new commanding officer, especially one who has such a low tolerance for negligence. In fact, he has no tolerance for screw-ups."

Gibbon said, "My guess is that Meade will erupt at this."

"Yes and Meade's explosion will make the Mount Vesuvius eruption look minor in comparison." Hancock unleashed a fury of unholy oaths.

Haskell's cheeks flushed. He always was amazed by Hancock's harsh swearing. Gibbon claimed it was a leftover from the old regular army, the army that fought in the Mexican War. Haskell was not so sure. Hancock seemed born to swear, loving it more than a salty sailor. As far as he could tell, swearing was Hancock's single vice, a blemish on one of the most brilliant combat records in the federal army.

Hancock glared at Gibbon, "What the hell do you want?"

"When are we going to start today's march?"

"Immediately. I want you to push your boys hard today, John. I plan on marching thirty miles. I'll probably be in hot water with Meade this morning, but by tonight I plan on being where we are supposed to be. Use the bayonet to keep them moving if you have to. This is going to be a forced march. Harsh, by any standards. There will be no excuses for failure."

Gibbon blinked, nodded.

Hancock reached into his jacket pocket and extracted a piece of paper. He said Meade had told his corps commanders to share today's marching orders with their division commanders. Hancock discussed the marching order as well as Meade's best

161

guess where the enemy was located. Meade planned to camp that night at Middleburg, Maryland.

Haskell's heart danced. A new thing, news of the Union's movements and those of the enemy. Yes, Hooker was no longer in command.

Gibbon asked, "Do you think we will run into enemy cavalry today?"

"No, I don't, based upon the intelligence that Meade has shared with us," Hancock said.

"Good."

"Enough talk," Hancock said. "You need to get your division ready to move soonest."

Gibbon and Haskell saluted, mounted their horses, and departed.

---

*6:30 a.m.*

The two trotted along the road to Gibbon's division headquarters. "This morning's screw-up reminds me of Professor Mahan's warfighting lectures at West Point," Gibbon mused.

"Why is that?"

"He said we are dealing with countless factors that make war difficult."

"Where are you going with this, General?"

"Well, Mahan said warfare was governed by unforeseen events, which include human errors."

"But what happened this morning is more than an error."

"Yes, this morning was an enormous blunder. Meade planned today's marches in detail, with delayed starts to maximize use of the few roads available to move the army north. But between plans and execution rage 'the winds of war,' as Mahan called them. These are the forces of unforeseen happenings that affect the execution of plans. In practice, war is governed by Mahan's idea that even easy things can be difficult."

"I accept there will be mistakes," Haskell said. "What I don't accept is mistakes caused by stupidity, laziness, and a lack of attention to detail, causing our division to be four Goddamn hours late marching this morning."

"I guess the point is that just because Meade issues an order doesn't mean a corps commander is going to execute it on time, if at all," Gibbon said. "Meade can issue all the orders he wants. But if he doesn't have an effective staff, those orders won't be executed."

"I agree," Haskell said. "But Butterfield serving as Meade's chief of staff is like having your mortal enemy at your wedding, acting as your best man."

"That's the pretty pickle Meade faces," Gibbon replied. "He doesn't have time to replace Butterfield and break in his staff. He also doesn't know his corps commanders. Meade doesn't know his staff well enough to know if they are monitoring the execution of his orders and providing timely feedback. In time, Meade's staff may be a well-oiled machine and perform as Meade desires. But this will probably not be the case for this upcoming battle."

"So what are you saying?" Haskell said. "We should anticipate screw-ups and be on our toes to fix 'em?"

"Yes. Morgan knew Meade was issuing orders last night for today's march. Morgan should have been alerted to something going awry when he didn't receive any orders by two or three in the morning. Instead, he slept through the night, unaware that orders did not arrive. That's dereliction of duty."

---

*7:00 a.m.*
*At Gibbon's division headquarters*

Gibbon and Haskell returned to division headquarters and were met by Gibbon's chief of staff. The division was packed up and ready to march. The men were lying comfortably off the side of the road, rifles stacked, awaiting orders to move out.

Gibbon explained to his chief of staff that a sergeant had failed to deliver Meade's marching orders to Hancock. Second Corps should have departed three hours ago, at four in the morning.

Gibbon turned to a courier. "Inform the brigade commanders the division is moving out immediately. We are the lead division of the corps. We will be followed by Hays' First Division and Caldwell's Third Division. Also tell the brigade commanders this is going to be a long day's march. Our destination is northeast toward Frizzelburg, which is more than thirty miles. No stragglers."

The courier moved off. Haskell turned and nodded to the command sergeant major, who bellowed out the order to move out. Drums began beating the long roll, bugles sounded the assembly, bringing swarms of blue-clad men to their feet, fetching their knapsacks and stacked rifles, falling into line at the sharp commands of their senior enlisted officers.

Watching the soldiers form in the road and swell into an endless blue line, Gibbon turned to Haskell. "Today's order is just what I expected. Meade is determined not to let the grass grow under his feet. And his nerves are going to be frayed when he learns Hancock missed the order."

"I have never seen Hancock that upset," Haskell said. "I suggest we move out quickly so Morgan can chew on Hays and Caldwell instead of us."

*7:35 a.m.*

*Second Corps' march north*

In a few minutes, the division was up and moving, marching to the quick beat of snare drums. The rain continued to drizzle, and the sun grew hotter throughout the day. Gibbon and Haskell rode at the front of the long column that stretched several miles. The logistics trains for all three of Hancock's divisions were in the rear, looking like an armada of white sails.

Haskell turned to Gibbon. "The Union newspapers reported that a large of part of Lee's army had moved through the South Mountain passes, through Chambersburg, heading northeast and threatening York and Harrisburg."

"Maybe the newspapers are right for once."

*3:00 p.m.*

Hancock's 11,000 soldiers and 28 field guns and caissons had been marching for several hours at a brutal pace. Haskell received hourly reports on the number of soldiers who had straggled from the ranks. Some had dropped by the roadside, dead before they hit the ground. Others who could not walk remained off the roadside, waiting to catch a ride in the ambulances bringing up the rear.

Haskell spotted Morgan riding up and down Second Division columns, waving his sword, hitting men's backs with the flat side of steel, pressing them forward. He was without pity, his threatening face scouring the line for his next target. "Morgan is in rare form today, apparently looking for every opportunity to redeem himself."

"I will tell you one thing," Gibbon replied. "His verbal chastisements and sword slaps are keeping the men moving at a good clip."

"Well, we just might march thirty miles today. I didn't think it possible without losing half the division to sunstroke."

Haskell twisted in his saddle and spotted a civilian trotting toward the front of Second Division. He peered through his binoculars. It was Charles Coffin, the *Boston Journal*'s war correspondent. Haskell warmed at the familiar face. Coffin was always a fun visitor. He was a tough, honest man but still possessed the heart of a rollicking farm boy. Though lacking a college education, he was the most erudite man Haskell knew. Coffin drew up next to Gibbon and Haskell.

"So how is the knight of the truth?" Haskell greeted him.

"Still trying to keep the *Boston Journal* at the front," Coffin replied. "But this begs the question of why I'm riding with the two of you. I should probably be riding with Sickles and his boys. You never know when the general will have another insanity attack and murder someone. Now that would be headline news."

Both officers laughed. "You should have been at Hancock's headquarters this morning," Haskell said. "He almost shot Colonel Morgan for failing to deliver Meade's marching order. We could have sold tickets to that shooting and made a barrel of money."

"I would have paid a week's wages," Coffin said. "Morgan and his wretched provost guards have quite the reputation."

Haskell smiled. Coffin was a welcome sight, capable of making him forget his weariness.

Coffin added, "I wrote an article on June 26 from Baltimore that the *Boston Journal* is going to publish today. As I've done previously on some articles, I wanted to give you an advance copy. This one is a bit more predictive in nature. If you agree with me, I think both General Gibbon and General Hancock would be interested in reading it. Naturally, I don't know what Meade's plans are, but at the pace he's moving the Union army northward, I see a great battle occurring in Pennsylvania in the next few days." He reached into his leather pouch, extracted an envelope, and gave it to Haskell. Haskell read the article:

*If Lee advances with nearly all his forces into Pennsylvania, there must be a collision of the two armies not many miles west of Gettysburg, probably among the rolling hills near the State line, on the headwaters of the Monocacy.... I believe Washington and Baltimore will not be harmed. I expect to see Adams, Franklin, Cumberland, and York counties run over somewhat by the Rebels, and I also expect to see Lee defeated in his plans. His army may not be annihilated. Hooker may not achieve a great, decisive victory. But I fully believe Lee will gain nothing by this move.*

Haskell finished reading the article, handed it to Gibbon, and turned to Coffin.

"Most interesting. You could not know this when you wrote the article, but Meade now wears the mantle of command. This is fortunate because there is now an opportunity for a great victory. Meade personifies the old army principle: commanding generals exist to conquer. Unlike his predecessors, he realizes that he remains a commanding general only as long as he moves rapidly against the enemy and throws them back across the Potomac."

Coffin rode along silently, listening as the two officers chatted, then Gibbon turned to him.

"I would like to send the article to Hancock, with your permission. I think he would find your Gettysburg theory most remarkable."

"That's fine with me," Coffin replied.

Gibbon summoned a courier, who took the article and rode off.

Morgan rode up, spattering mud. He said abruptly, "Hancock is determined to reach Frizzelburg, the day's objective."

Haskell stared at him, saying nothing. Gibbon shook his head.

Morgan continued, "The provost guards reported the civilians along the road have been selling whiskey. The guards caught several drunken soldiers in General Caldwell's First Division. I had the drunks tied to the rear of an artillery battery to ensure they kept up. I directed the provost guards to ride ahead as we approach each village and empty all the liquor in the taverns and shops. I'm removing the evil."

Morgan saluted, rode off.

Gibbon turned to Haskell. "This is going to be a long, miserable night."

"Well, I'm pretty confident about a couple things," Haskell said. "Hancock is going to push his corps until it covers thirty miles. Also, if Coffin is right about the big battle being near Gettysburg, Meade has us marching in the right direction. And Bobby Lee is going to be very surprised when we arrive there first."

"Anything else?"

"Yes. Morgan won't miss any more orders, and if he does and Hancock doesn't shoot the bastard, I will."

Gibbon cracked a smile. "Oh, I see. You are secretly gunning for Morgan's job as Hancock's chief of staff."

Haskell smiled. "Yes, that's exactly my goal. But until Morgan disappears, I'm most honored to serve as your adjutant."

---

*6:30 p.m.*

They marched for three more hours without a break. Morgan galloped to the front of Second Division and paused next to Gibbon and Haskell.

"General Gibbon," he shouted, "keep pushing your men. Second Division is doing better than Hays and Caldwell's divisions. I will not tolerate stragglers. I've ordered the provost guards to tie stragglers by their thumbs to wagons to force them to keep pace. So far I haven't had to do that with any of your men. But by God I will if I find them straggling. There will be hell to pay." Morgan saluted and sped back toward Hay's Division.

"Morgan enjoys being a brutal asshole," Haskell growled. "He acts like a whip-master aboard a Roman galley."

"These soldiers don't need to be whipped and prodded to march great distances and fight," Gibbon said. "They just need competent officers to execute orders on time. Meade could prove to be a great general, but if his lieutenants continue to fail to execute orders, we have little chance in defeating Lee."

Haskell nodded. "My fear is that if Meade loses the upcoming battle, Lincoln's stealthy hatchet man, Colonel Hardie, will arrive and Meade will lose his head. This merry-go-round of commanding officers has to stop. We have to win."

## ❧ 14 ❧
# First Minnesota — Monday, June 29

*Wright*
*7:20 a.m.*
*11 hours earlier*
*First Minnesota's march north*

Stomach clenching, Sergeant Wright fidgeted with a handful of priming caps as he walked among the men resting beside the road, waiting to start today's march. A fierce June sun was rising in the east, glinting off the metal of stacked Minnesota rifles. A lone fiddler played "Lorena," the beautiful ballad about a lost love. Wright's cheeks heated as he touched his breast pocket that held an ambrotype of his Hamline University classmate. *Must write her a letter tonight after we bivouac.*

Nearly half past seven.

No orders. *Christ almighty. No one knows what the hell is going on.* He had rousted the regiment three hours earlier, expecting a sunrise marching order. But the dawn rooster calls had come and gone as the boys sat lingering beside the road, packed up and ready to march on a moment's notice. Now some of the soldiers were sitting on their knapsacks, and others were using the knapsacks as pillows, hats pulled down over their eyes, dozing. He gazed at the orderlies, holding horses for officers who stood off to the side, chatting among themselves, and spied his best friend, Sergeant Phillip Hamlin, walking up to him.

"The boys are eager to get moving," Hamlin observed.

"So am I."

"What's the word?"

"There is a rumor floating about that some idiot at Hancock's headquarters failed to deliver Meade's marching order to Hancock last night." Wright grimaced, a chill pricking his bones. "If that rumor is true, it fries my ass."

169

"I had hoped that today's march would end before sunset. But that's wishful thinking. Today's march will go well into the evening."

"Look at those rain clouds rolling toward us," Wright said. "Son of a bitch. We can't catch a break. We are either getting our asses fried off by the blistering sun or mucking through ankle-high sludge."

---

*7:30 a.m.*

Major Downie rode up. "Sergeant Wright, order the regiment to prepare to march."

Wright's heart leapt. Finally. He assembled the men, who fell rapidly into a marching formation. The officers mounted their horses. In a few moments, the march began at a comfortable pace. The sultry air hinted at what was sure to become a withering heat.

---

*8:30 a.m.*

A snorting horse rumbled toward Wright's back. He turned and the speeding horse brushed his arm, splattering dirt on his uniform. *Son of a bitch, that horse almost ran me over.* The rider galloped to the head of the column and pulled back hard on the reins next to Colvill, rearing the horse up on its hind legs with its forelegs rotating off the ground as if dog-paddling. When the horse landed on all fours, he spotted the rider—Colonel Morgan, Hancock's chief of staff. Morgan was a dastardly devil. The fiend never missed an opportunity to mistreat enlisted men and dress down junior officers in front of their subordinates.

"Colonel Colvill, close up the column and move faster," Morgan shouted. Then he turned and rode toward the next regiment, the Fifteenth Massachusetts, and resumed shouting.

Wright moved out of formation and walked down the line, encouraging the boys to close the ranks. Several minutes later,

Morgan thundered past the First Minnesota. As he raced by, Morgan's stirrups clipped Wright's jacket vents.

"Damn it, watch it, Colonel," Wright shouted.

Wright moved off to the side of the road. Morgan galloped to the front and stopped on the side of the road. The columns of Minnesotans marched up the road and approached Morgan, who was sitting on his horse, yelling, "Lengthen the steps; quicken the time!"

Wright bristled with bubbling anger as he marched by Morgan. What a flaming prick.

"What's Morgan's problem?" Hamlin said.

"He is probably the asshole that failed to deliver Meade's marching order to Hancock."

"Well, he sure seems anxious to make up for his screw-up by pushing the men as hard as he can."

"Yes and the horrible road conditions are just adding to everyone's misery. Someone is going to break an ankle on these road ruts made by the damn artillery and logistics trains."

"A number of men are marching barefoot this morning. Their feet are badly bruised and blistered from yesterday's long march." Hamlin pointed toward Private Chester Durfee, his chafed shins rubbed raw and bleeding. "Since the tall marching began, no fewer than seventy men of Second Corps have fallen dead."

"Thankfully, none were from the First Minnesota," Wright said. "If it's true what they say, that everyone must eat a peck of dirt during his lifetime, then surely this wretched march accounts for a fair share."

Colvill turned his horse off the road and stopped. As the men marched by, Colvill yelled encouragement. "Sergeant Wright, you're doing a great job keeping the boys moving. I'm proud of you and our Minnesota boys."

Wright flashed a toothy smile. The boys believed in Colonel Bill. They wouldn't let him down.

*10:30 a.m.*

The regiment moved north at a steady clip. Morgan authorized very few breaks as they shuffled through the pitiless heat, the high humidity and bouts of drenching rain causing enormous misery. The men were becoming weary and sluggish. Wright turned to Sergeant Sonderman, the unofficial company singer. "George, belt out a song for us!"

Sonderman's beautiful tenor voice burst out with "The Battle Cry of Freedom": "Yes, we'll rally round the flag, boys, we'll rally once again, shouting the battle cry of freedom!"

Faces lifted and hearts stirred. A deep joy coursed through Wright. The singing had temporarily washed away the gloom. Strange how a short piece of music could suddenly fill him with energy. He didn't know how it happened and he didn't care. Instead, he let himself glide along the waves of Sonderman's soothing voice.

## Colvill

*12:15 p.m.*

The morning passed. The misting rain gave way to a burning sun, with rising clouds of dust marking the progress of Hancock's corps. Colvill rode at the head of the regiment as the First Minnesota rounded a bend. Dead ahead was Linganore Creek, a knee-deep, twenty-foot-wide tributary of the Monocacy River. A clamorous ruckus reached Colvill's ears. Something was wrong. He squinted and saw that the marching line was folding back on itself like the bellows of an accordion.

"Halt!" Colvill shouted.

He gripped his binoculars and peered through them. A huge logjam of soldiers was bunched up at the creek like a large herd of cattle packed into a pen. Several soldiers were splashing about in the creek while others were being pushed into it. What the hell was going on?

He turned and beckoned for Lieutenant William Lochren to come forward. Colvill bellowed, "William, move forward and find out what the hell is going on here."

Lochren hustled toward the creek. Wright moved up. "What's the problem, Colonel Bill?"

"I'm not sure, but I sent Lieutenant Lochren into that mess to find out."

Lochren emerged from the fracas and hustled back. "Colonel Bill, Webb's brigade has caused the backup. Apparently, they didn't relish the thought of wading through the creek and soaking their shoes and socks and then marching several more miles with wet leather and wool socks grating the bottoms of their bloody feet."

Colvill said, "So is Webb's brigade refusing to cross the creek?"

"No, sir. They placed two logs across the creek. Each log was split in two and hewn to create small footbridges. So they are crossing, but a bottleneck formed as regiments from Webb's brigade queued up in two lines to cross on the logs."

"That makes sense," Colvill said.

"But as I was watching, Colonel Morgan arrived and started ranting and raving at the men standing in the long lines," Lochren said. "He ripped his sword from his scabbard and started brandishing it as if leading a cavalry charge. He screamed at Webb's regimental commanders. 'I'm ordering your men to march, close order, straight through the creek! You're impeding the march.' Webb's commanders blinked in disbelief."

Wright said, "That's crap."

Lochren said, "Webb's commanders marched their men into the water with the soldiers swearing loudly."

"Morgan is an idiot," Colvill said. "Sergeant Wright, let's move forward."

Colvill led the First Minnesota up to the creek. Morgan was waiting at the water's edge.

"Colonel Colvill," Morgan shouted, "order your men to march through the water."

Colvill's stomach turned over, rumbling with rage. He set his jaw and glared at Morgan with pursed lips.

"Colonel Colvill," Morgan yelled. "Now march your men through the creek."

*12:25 p.m.*

Colvill turned on his horse and yelled, "Close order, march!" The regiment closed up and forged ahead into the water, swearing up a storm as they waded through the water.

Morgan shouted, "Colonel Colvill, I'm riding back to check on the Fifteenth Massachusetts. But I will be back to monitor the creek crossing." Morgan turned and rode back toward the column.

Fresh anger erupted within Colvill. His throat tightened. He turned in his saddle and scowled as Morgan disappeared around the bend. *What a flaming idiot. He doesn't give a crap about the water tearing up the soldiers' feet.*

Colvill turned back around and spotted Lochren dashing toward the nearest log and scampering across it. He landed safely on the opposite bank. Lochren turned and motioned to Lieutenant Heffelfinger, who darted across the log after him. Corporal Henry O'Brien and Private Marshall Sherman broke from the regiment and sprinted forward, racing across the two logs. Colvill smiled; pride flooded his lungs.

*My two natural-born leaders—both farm boys and Viking warriors.* The rest of the regiment cheered jubilantly and raced pell-mell across the logs and then resumed the normal marching order. Within a few minutes they were out of sight of the creek.

Colvill motioned to his chief of staff, Major Downie. Downie rode up and halted. "Mark, take Lieutenant Pellar and cross the creek. When you get to the other side, ride to the front of the regiment and lead it on in the march. I'm going to stay behind for a bit before joining you."

Downie saluted and departed. Colvill sat on his horse, letting it water in the creek. The Fifteenth Massachusetts regiment approached the creek and halted. One of Morgan's majors shouted in a wheezy voice for the them to ford the creek, marching close order. Colvill grinned. This ought to be interesting. The Boston Boys yelled loudly, many disregarding the order, breaking for the two logs and scampering across the creek.

Morgan galloped up, waving his saber. He yelled, "God damn it. What the hell is going on? I told you sons of bitches to wade across the creek."

The Fifteenth Massachusetts erupted into a chorus of boos, hisses, and taunts as they waved their middle fingers at him. Morgan turned and rode toward Colvill. Colvill's heart floated into the sky, sunning itself on puffy clouds of delight. He enjoyed witnessing Hancock's runt enforcer being belittled. Morgan was a cold, heartless asshole and deserved the scorn.

Morgan shrieked in a high-pitched voice. "What the devil? I ordered your men to wade across the creek. This is a flagrant disobedience of orders in allowing your men to cross across the logs and create a logjam."

Colvill towered over the red-faced Morgan. "Colonel Morgan, these are not my men," he said, his voice sharpened to a razor's edge. "The First Minnesota already forded the creek and is a few miles up the road."

"You will pay for this, Colvill," Morgan yelled, glaring at Colvill with open hostility. He turned and rode toward the soldiers running across the logs, brandishing his sword.

*12:45 p.m.*

Colvill glowered his concern for the men. Morgan was clearly unhinged. Enough watering; it was time to depart. Colvill turned his horse north and rode several yards upstream, and then crossed the creek, catching up with this regiment a few miles up the road. Downie and Pellar saluted. Colvill told them about Fifteenth Massachusetts and the log crossing, giving them a good laugh.

Colvill turned to Downie. "Have you seen Lieutenant Colonel Adams?"

"Not since one of Morgan's provost marshals rode up and told Adams that Morgan requested his presence, sir."

"That's strange," Colvill said. "Do you know why Morgan wanted him?"

"Not sure. But the damnable thing is that Adams seemed eager to depart—like a groveling puppy. I found that strange."

Colvill nodded. He removed his hat and raked a hand through his hair. His skin prickled. Something was up. Both Morgan and Adams were sharp-fanged creatures.

*1:15 p.m.*

A short time later, an aide of First Brigade Commander General Harrow arrived, accompanied by Adams.

Harrow's aide saluted and stated formally, "Colonel Colvill, General Harrow has placed you under arrest for violating a direct order from Lieutenant Colonel Morgan."

"What the hell are you talking about?"

"Morgan stated that you allowed your men to cross the river on logs when the order was to wade across, and that you permitted your men to be insubordinate and disrespectful of a commissioned officer. Sir, Lieutenant Colonel Adams will relieve you immediately and assume command of the First Minnesota. You are ordered to ride at the back of your regiment."

Colvill inhaled sharply and gawked at the lanky aide. Heat licked his skin and his nostrils flared as he clenched his fists, his nails digging into his palms. *Morgan is dead meat.* His chest tightened and his mouth set in a grim line as he whirled around toward Adams.

"You can't be serious!"

Adams yelled, "I relieve Colonel Colvill and assume command of the First Minnesota."

The words pierced Colvill like a hissing spear, blood scorching through his veins. He took a menacing step closer to Adams as he blinked back bitter tears. Adams took a step backwards, his lower lip twitching. Colvill glared, concentrating with every fiber of his body not to thrash Adams. *Damn you Adams, you gloating son of a bitch. What role did you have in my arrest? You've been angling to command this regiment for some time.* He tightened his jaw and glared at Adams as his stomach roiled. Slowly he backed off, moving to the rear of the regiment, under arrest.

176

The First Minnesotans erupted into frenzied shouting. "Mar his vision with a boot heel!" "Let's shoot that sniveling boot-licker Morgan!"

The men's comments were becoming bolder and more seditious—close to mutinous.

"Colonel Colvill is disgraced because of our actions," Wright shouted. "Let's quiet down or the colonel will be in more trouble."

With blistering tempers, the men continued to unleash the most unholy oaths on Morgan. The regiment wanted blood. Colvill fretted. His boys were going to kill Morgan. Wright went back to Colvill.

"For God's sake, tell them to drop it for my sake," Colvill said.

Wright made his way forward along the marching columns and told the men that Colonel Bill wanted them to calm down. The men promptly complied but still mumbled among themselves for some time. By early evening, they marched in dogged silence under the scorching heat.

Colvill's head throbbed and his chest pulsed with a hollow ache. Unbelievable. He was under arrest and forced to ride at the back of the regiment in shame.

Wright returned. "Colonel Bill, I'm worried about the boys. They won't simmer down, and they are talking about a mutiny. They won't fight for Adams. They love you leading them, and they don't want Adams leading them into battle."

"Damn it, this is not about Adams and Morgan. This is about defeating the enemy and restoring the Union. Now, I'm holding you personally responsible that the regiment won't mutiny and will follow Adams. Do you understand me?"

"Yes, sir. I understand, but the boys aren't going to like it." Wright saluted and moved forward into the regiment.

*10:00 p.m.*

Colvill's stomach clenched into a tight ball, and a frosty chill shivered down his back. Mortified, he rode, tight-lipped, at the back of the regiment. His heart pounded, slamming into his ribs. His darting eyes spotted Adams riding at the front of the regiment. Adams led the First Minnesota for the remainder of the march, arriving just past Uniontown a few hours before midnight. Colvill shook his head. Hancock had done the impossible. He marched his corps farther than any corps had ever marched. They were seven miles from the Pennsylvania border.

Colvill dismounted and remained in the darkness behind the regiment as they prepared the bivouac. How could he be reinstated as commanding officer? Timing. He would wait for the right time to visit the brigade commander and request his command back. But how long would that be? Hell, the battle could start tomorrow. *Damn you, Morgan.*

## 15
# Meade — Monday, June 29

Geneal Meade," Biddle said, "it's five a.m."

Meade woke for a fleeting moment, the voice lingering as part of a fading dream. He couldn't move his body. A hand gripped his shoulder and shook. "General Meade, it's time to wake up."

*Biddle.* Meade snapped his eyes open.

"James, I'm awake," Meade said. "What time is it?"

"Five a.m."

Meade yawned loudly, unable to stifle the wolf howl. "Summon the Quartermaster General."

Biddle departed.

A lantern hanging in the corner glowed, casting dancing light. He didn't remember dozing off in Hooker's large pine rocking chair. There was a numb prickling in his aching butt. He reached over to the small stand and grabbed his thick glasses. What a God-awful night. The interruptions had been relentless, lasting until early morning.

Most of the army should have departed an hour ago. Good. His jaw stretched open again, letting loose another monstrous yawn. Only two hours' sleep in the past twenty-six hours. And today was going to be just as long. He shook his head and shuddered. *Forget about getting sleep and stop stewing like a broody hen!* He had a rare opportunity. Lee's army was spread out and vulnerable. Lee also believed Hooker was keeping his army dammed up well south of the Confederates and restricting the flow of the Union army toward him. He had just busted the dam. The Union army rushing north would hopefully strike Lee unprepared, like a flash flood, surging and spreading without warning.

Meade rocked. Biddle entered the tent, bearing coffee. "I have some pick-me-up goodness for you," he said, handing the cup to Meade.

"Perfect timing," Meade said, accepting the coffee gratefully.

"Also, General Rufus Ingalls will be right over. He was writing out some supply orders."

Meade took two quick sips of his brewed coffee. "Thanks." His heart pounded as a bolt of energy surged through him. He rocked back and forth.

"I see you like the Harrisburg widow's blanket," Biddle said.

Meade looked down and smiled. He was draped with a cozy red, white, and blue knitted blanket. It was a gift he'd received yesterday from an elderly widow whose husband had fought in the war of 1812.

"Yes, I like it, and I'm going to keep it. But why did she make it, and how did she get it to me with Early's Rebels roaming nearby?"

"I was told she made it for the commanding general, hoping it would bring him comfort and strength. She gave the blanket to a Harrisburg man and asked him to ride south until he met up with a Union cavalry patrol and ask that they deliver the blanket to the commanding general."

"Hell," Meade said. "I want to enlist that Harrisburg man as a scout...he didn't have any problems finding our cavalry patrols. I sure as hell hope the enemy is not as skillful at finding us as he was."

"Rumor has it the Harrisburg man fought alongside the widow's husband in the war of 1812," Biddle said.

Meade smiled. "Well, after only one night, I've grown attached to the blanket. Find out her name so I can write her a thank-you note." He pointed to the maps. "Let's set them up outside on the table. I will be right out."

Biddle rolled up the maps and took them outside. Meade finished his coffee alone. Finally, the cobwebs had cleared, and his mind was racing. He stood up, testing his legs. Still a bit wobbly and tingling, but not asleep. He lifted the suspender straps

180

over his shoulders and donned his two-star general's jacket and black slop hat.

⋯⋯◦⋯◦⋯

*5:15 a.m.*

Meade moved outside the large tent into the blackness. It was sprinkled with lanterns glowing like molten rock. He set his tin coffee cup on the map table. Out of the dark, General Rufus Ingalls emerged.

"Damn, Rufus, that was a short night," Meade grumbled. "It seems like just a few minutes ago that you departed my tent and here we are again. Did you get any sleep?"

Ingalls said, "No, but I got answers to most of your supply questions."

Meade cracked a smile. "Hell, Rufus, if you keep up the good work, I just might keep you as my chief logician."

"The long marches you ordered for the next couple days are going to stretch our logistics lines right to the breaking point," Ingalls said, "But I believe I can do it for three continuous days."

"Three? That's it?"

"Yes, three days if you march in a northerly vector toward Fairfield and Gettysburg. But if you march the army on a northeast vector toward York and cover the Baltimore and Harrisburg road, I can draw supplies from Philadelphia and Baltimore, and you can march for four continuous days. That's it."

"Devil be damned, Rufus. I want five days of supplies. Logistics support should enable, not limit, my maneuver. My plan is to find Lee's army and throw him back across the Potomac. It shouldn't matter if Lee is as far north as Canada. I expect you to extend your logistics limits and support my damn plans."

"General Meade, I can do that, but you won't like your tooth-to-tail ratio. Instead of the Army of the Potomac, you'll have the Army of Logistics supported by an Infantry Corps of security. The Union troop strength I'm tracking and supporting each day is 142,098. That number includes your fighting forces of nearly 100,000. The remaining 40,000 soldiers, including cavalry escorts, teamsters, and railroad men, are being used to supply your army—for finding the enemy and fighting them for three days."

181

Meade glared. "Go on."

"The three- and four-day numbers I gave you are not arbitrary," Ingalls said. "They are the culminating points of me being able to support your advance and for you to effectively conduct an attack with the Army of the Potomac. Beyond the three and four days, you will be susceptible to counterattack and defeat."

"I swear, Rufus. I know logistics is part and parcel of any effort to maneuver an army. But I'm aimed at rapidly making toward Lee's soft underbelly. I expect you to be able to support my operational plans, whatever the hell they are. I'd rather give your 40,000 logistics boys rifles. That would give me four additional infantry corps. Those numbers would surprise the crap out of Lee."

"I'd love to, sir," Ingalls said. "But I can't with the sustainability numbers you gave me. Per your guidance, I've planned for giving each Union soldier a daily pound of hardtack, a pound of meat, plus coffee, sugar, desiccated vegetables, and bread. Although each soldier may not receive these full rations during these upcoming long marches, I still plan on those amounts."

"So how many tons on food are you moving forward each day?"

"Just over 200 tons—218 to be exact," Ingalls said. "Add to this the 53,000 horses held by the Army of the Potomac. I plan on the animals foraging 563 tons daily."

Meade whistled. "So roughly your daily requirement for human and animal subsistence is almost 800 tons. That's a gargantuan amount."

"Yes, sir. The physical needs of this army require about 800 tons of logistics, daily."

"By the love of God." Meade shook his head.

"My two forward logistics heads are Frederick and Westminster," Ingalls said. "Supplying these forward supply bases will be the major depots at Baltimore and Alexandria. I will use the railroads and teamster wagons."

Meade nodded.

"A question, sir—what's your logistics priority for resupplying the army if you get into a major scrap with the enemy in the next couple days?"

"Ammunition, rifles, and horses for the cavalry, of course. When I think we are getting close to fighting a big engagement, I want each man to have three days of food rations on his person. Hell, I'm not so worried about them starving to death, I'm more worried about them having enough ammo to kill the enemy."

Butterfield and George walked up and placed their coffee cups on the side of the map table.

"You're just in time, Daniel," Meade said. "Rufus is going to provide us an update on Lee's logistics situation."

"Gentlemen," said Ingalls. "Lee's main supply base is Richmond. His forward supply railhead from Richmond is Staunton. When the Rebels captured Winchester fifty miles to the north on June 15, that became Lee's forward supply base. But there is no rail link between Staunton and Winchester. So all supplies from Staunton to Winchester are brought forward on slow-moving wagon trains. And all supplies brought forward from Winchester across the Potomac at Williamsport and to Chambersburg are also on slow-moving trains."

"What about Lee's foraging?" Meade asked.

"Lee's army is sustaining itself primarily on local foraging. That's why it's so spread out." Ingalls put his finger on Chambersburg and traced an arc on the map through Gettysburg to York."

Fire from Meade's gut flared up, heating his face. Lee was grazing his army on half of Pennsylvania.

"How successful have their foraging efforts been?" asked Butterfield.

"Damn it, Daniel, our scouting parties are reporting the Rebels are feasting off the land and raping it bare. Pennsylvania is the richest pickings of the war for them."

Butterfield shrugged.

Meade gestured to the map table. "Rufus has just pointed out that because of our interior lines and the nearness of the Union army to our supply bases and railroad links, we have a huge advantage. Lee's critical vulnerability is his long logistics tail."

Meade glared at Butterfield. "As long as Hooker dawdled about in Maryland, Lee was able to feast off the land. My guess is that once he has fattened up his army, foraging in Pennsylvania and stealing vital supplies like shoes, he plans on slipping back across the Potomac unhindered."

"General Meade, your plan to move rapidly against Lee's soft underbelly will force him to either mass and fight or retreat back across the Potomac," Ingalls said.

"You're right, Rufus. If Lee chooses to remain spread out and continues his foraging, I will chop him up like mincemeat. If he fights, he can only sustain himself for a few days before he has to resupply with ammunition and artillery shells."

Ingalls departed. Meade beckoned to Biddle. "James, I need an intelligence update from Sharpe as soon as possible."

Biddle darted away into the darkness. Meade stared at Butterfield. "Have any of the corps reported the status of their marches?"

"No reports yet," said Butterfield.

"That's odd," Meade said. "Inform me immediately when the reports start arriving."

Meade turned toward his son, who was standing on the far side of the map table.

"George, I've developed a fierce thirst for information. I need to know what is happening. Hell, how am I supposed to command without information?" Panic and terror rumbled through him.

George said, "I'm sure couriers will start arriving soon with updates on their corps' movements."

"I sense a big battle coming, George. Probably not today, but soon," Meade said. "It will take a few days for the armies to concentrate. Success depends on arriving first and massing the army on good ground. Damn it. I need Warren's updated maps."

Sharpe arrived. "What's the latest update on the enemy's movements?" Meade said.

"The Gettysburg citizens reported Rebel infantry passed through town two days ago," Sharpe said. "Those were Early's boys. They were headed toward Harrisburg. Ewell is still lingering around Carlisle. Longstreet and A.P. Hill remain west of South Mountain. Stuart continues to conduct raids east of us. But he is causing little damage."

"I need to know what Stuart is up to. Also, Halleck is on my ass about Stuart's boys, so I had Pleasonton detach two cavalry brigades and a battery of Gregg's division to go after Stuart."

"I will keep you posted on any new intelligence developments." Sharpe moved toward Butterfield's tent.

*6:00 a.m.*

In the quiet morning darkness, Meade extracted a cigar. Sharpe was growing on him, had impressed him yesterday, providing the general location of the enemy force. That in itself had eased his mind somewhat. Unlike prickly Butterfield, Williams and Sharpe had a relaxed manner that suppressed his own fiery temper. Everything Butterfield said was cause for offence, always rubbing him the wrong way. Meade frowned. He should have made Humphreys take the chief of staff job.

Nothing to do now but wait for couriers to arrive with updates on the corps movements. He desperately wanted to meet with his corps commanders, but Hooker had spread them across the state of Maryland like dandelion seeds in the wind. He hated not having a council meeting yet. Creating a plan was one thing; having his subordinates executing it, of one mind with their commander, was another. But today it was more important to have the army surge forward like a ravaging mountain lion.

Meade watched headquarters come alive as the morning broke. Cooks were lighting fires, cauldrons steamed, bacon hissed. There could be no blunders this morning. He worried about exposing his foot soldiers to Rebel cavalry ambushes. A Stuart flanking attack could decimate long infantry columns stretched out over the long, snaking roads. Meade finished his cigar. He went back into the tent, the knot in his stomach tightening.

Biddle appeared with Williams, carrying a fresh cup of coffee.

185

Williams said, "We've heard from all the corps commanders with the exception of Hancock's Second Corps and Sykes Fifth Corps. Those we've heard from departed on time."

Meade said, "That's strange you haven't heard from Hancock and Sykes. Sykes's corps is following Hancock's corps on the same roads. We should hear from Hancock before Sykes. But I'm not worried. Hancock is typically punctual."

Biddle departed. Meade removed his glasses, pressed his hands to his eyes. There was so much to do and so much to worry about.

Meade continued. "Seth, look at how Lincoln's change-of-command order has had a huge ripple effect. Each subordinate command vacancy has to be filled. Probably something Lincoln did not consider. With me relieving Hooker as army commander, my old Fifth Corps was filled by the division commander, General George Sykes. Sykes's division command was filled by brigade commander General Romeyn Ayres. Ayres's brigade command was filled by regimental commander Colonel Hannibal Day. Day's regimental command was filled by Captain Levi Bootes. It's a long chain of dominoes."

"I have great confidence in Sykes's abilities to command a corps. We were in the same West Point graduation class." Williams laughed. "His nickname was *Tardy George*. But he was a good classmate and friend. You will have a hard time finding a better officer."

"I've been impressed with Sykes," said Meade. "He is honest, simple, and thorough—he is a tough fighter. He knows little of politics and could care less about it. In battle, he is one of the coolest men I have ever seen."

"I'm not that familiar with General Ayres," Williams replied, "except that he now commands the division of the most professional soldiers in the Army of the Potomac."

"I like Ayres. He is a stubborn fighter. With that massive beard he sports, he looks like a frontiersman. He is a classmate of General Gibbon and Confederate General A.P. Hill. Commanding a division is much different from commanding a brigade, so I will keep an eye on him. But I think he will do well."

"I was a bit surprised you replaced Ayres with Colonel Hannibal Day," said Williams. "He is a fossil. Hell, he graduated from West Point in 1823. His classmate General George Greene commands the Third Brigade in Slocum's Twelfth Corps. Greene is the oldest general in both armies, making Day the second-oldest general. Not to mention, this upcoming battle will be Day's first combat of the war."

"I know. I'm taking a chance promoting Day." Meade chuckled. "With Day's snow-white hair, mustache, and beard, he looks older than Moses."

"Sometimes Day gives me the shivers with his *old army* stare of disapproval," said Williams.

"Maybe his stare will wither the Rebels into surrendering," said Meade.

Williams winked.

"On a positive note," Meade said, "I'm confident in Captain Bootes's ability to command the regiment vacated by Day. Bootes is another West Point grad and a hardnosed fighter. He received promotions after the Battle of Malvern Hill and the Battle of Fredericksburg for gallant and meritorious service."

Biddle appeared. "General Meade, breakfast is being served, and I encourage you to join us."

"Let's go," Meade said.

*7:00 a.m.*

Meade moved outside the tent and past the men of headquarters staff idling about the embers of their bivouac fires, chatting and eating breakfast. He sniffed flapjacks, maple syrup, and frying bacon. He spotted his new cook, smiling and eyeing him. He thought a little food would do him good, although he didn't feel hungry. He told Biddle he would try to eat a few bites. While waiting for breakfast, he looked around at the sea of white tents and logistics trains. Amazing. Headquarters was at least the size of a small village.

He turned to Biddle. "I need to speak with Butterfield."

Meade's cook brought him a feast on a tin plate, enough for two people. Meade thanked him. He picked up a piece of crisp bacon, mindlessly chewing on it, knowing he wouldn't be able to eat anything else. After a few moments, he moved the plate away and went back into his tent. How could he change a command culture in a few hours? What bothered him most was the secrecy, both in planning and behavior, of Hooker's headquarters. Hooker and Butterfield had kept the corps commanders in the dark. *My ability to command and to beat Lee depends largely on receiving and relaying information rapidly to subordinates.*

Butterfield needed to understand his approach to commanding and how Butterfield could best support him. He should have had this talk several hours ago, but instead had plunged ahead without talking alone with his chief of staff. Perhaps that was a mistake. He should have made time. He would make time now.

The chief of staff entered the tent. Meade was in Hooker's old rocking chair. Butterfield sighed, drew himself up, saluted, and sat down next to Meade, yawning widely without covering his mouth. "I'm dog-tired," he mumbled through the yawn.

"Well, headquarters has had a couple tumultuous days," Meade acknowledged.

"I agree. But I think we've weathered the storm."

"That remains to be seen. For now, I want you to send couriers to all the corps commanders throughout the day to provide progress on their marches to me. I want a constant flow of information."

Butterfield nodded and wiped his brow. Meade studied his chief of staff's face. The man appeared to be trying to do his best under challenging circumstances. Must protect that. It was too late to replace him. He couldn't beat Lee without an adequate chief of staff. And yet, how much can you depend on a man who lacks integrity? Would Butterfield do the right thing regardless of the situation? Impossible to predict.

Meade added, "If you need to increase the number of couriers to transmit and relay information, make it happen."

"Yes, sir," Butterfield said.

"One way or another, finding and fighting Lee is about information. Your job as chief of staff is to integrate that information.

I want you to ensure I'm getting timely updates and you are sharing it with others."

"Yes, sir. I understand."

"Headquarters' ability to exploit a fleeting opportunity depends on our ability to share plans, intent, and events," Meade continued. "This staff must be able to direct and coordinate actions along the entire battlefield front. I cannot be everywhere at once observing, deciding, and directing the action. As you remember, at Fredericksburg, the Union assault line was more than five miles long. What matters is how we react to the changing situation."

Butterfield sat listening.

"When headquarters issues an order, the courier should be able to provide insights into how the subordinate commander's actions fit into the larger situation. Couriers must understand and convey my intent rapidly, efficiently, to the corps and division commanders."

Meade paused.

"I don't care what time of day or night it is, if you have something I need to know, I want you to inform me immediately. If I'm dozing, wake me. Your default should be to tell me. Never withhold information from me. If you do, I will replace you instantly."

Meade studied Butterfield in the dim light of the tent. Butterfield stared him in the eyes, listening attentively. *Perhaps Butterfield can be a team player.*

Meade changed the subject. "The army has way too many skulkers. Hooker failed to deal with these miserable wretches, hiding and deserting their units in battle. Most stragglers are probably skulkers. We have to nip this in the bud, now."

Butterfield said, "What do you plan to do?"

"Write an order authorizing corps commanders to shoot any stragglers today on the spot," Meade said.

Butterfield peered at Meade, his jaw dropping open. Meade met Butterfield's stare and pressed his lips together, glaring. Fury rushed through him, roaring in his ears. *The damn weasel is questioning me, already!*

"Damn it! Issue the order," Meade shouted. "If you don't think a corps commander can carry out this order, let me know and I will replace him with someone who can. You're dismissed!"

Butterfield departed the tent.

Meade took a deep breath, his eyebrows squeezed together. He despised Butterfield. How was this going to work?

*7:30 a.m.*

He plumped down in the rocking chair and closed his eyes. *God, help me.* Was his prayer going to fall on deaf ears? Lee probably was echoing the same prayer, and, based on his string of victories, God likely was listening to the wily fox. As he rocked, a murky bleakness flooded his brain. Before blackness fell, he mumbled, "Voltaire was right." Every player must accept the cards life deals, but then each alone decides how to play the cards to win the game. He had to figure out how to play Butterfield. No answer. Complete darkness.

Someone was shaking his shoulder. "General Meade, it's me, George."

Meade opened his eyes. The darkness ebbed. "I'm awake, George. What is it?"

"General Reynolds's courier arrived, saying First, Third, and Eleventh Corps are marching," George said.

"That's good, George," Meade said. "I'll be right out."

Meade stepped outside his tent to watch the activity. He saw Butterfield providing final instructions to mounted couriers preparing to depart for the seven infantry corps to observe and report the progress of their lengthy marches.

A host of senior staff officers began to arrive to visit with Meade. Each asked questions, seeking advice, requesting he choose between different courses of action. Sometimes two or three would join him simultaneously, some chatting, some listening.

He turned to Pleasonton. "I want the cavalry to guard the right and left infantry flanks and the rear infantry units like badgers. I also want the forward cavalry units probing aggressively for enemy movement. Any detected movement is to be reported immediately to headquarters."

"General John Buford, commanding two brigades of cavalry, is providing timely updates as he trails Lee's army near Chambersburg," said Pleasonton.

"That's good news," said Meade.

"Buford will be the first to detect if Rebel Generals Longstreet and Hill's corps crossed South Mountain to head east toward Cashtown and Gettysburg," said Pleasonton.

*8:00 a.m.*

Meade sat on Baldy, turned in his saddle to watch the headquarters' column form. General Williams was barking orders, wagon masters were hitching up horses, and staff officers were mounting. Meade's cavalry screening element had departed, leading the advance headquarters' party for the twelve-mile trip north to Middleburg. His cavalry escort commanded by Captain Carpenter and his company of cavalry lancers waited several yards up the road with Major Biddle and his personal staff, including the junior Meade.

Meade snapped the reins and Baldy moved forward at a trot. He rode ahead, a slight breeze brushing his face. His pulse accelerated like a racing horse as he bounced in the saddle. The army he commanded was in motion, moving ahead with a plan. He was going straight at the enemy to settle this thing one way or another.

Biddle rode up. "General Meade. Your headquarters staff is quite happy to be moving out."

"So am I," Meade said.

Meade's giddy personal staff was trailing close behind, chattering like a women's church group. *That will soon pass.*

As Meade rode, unforeseen challenges sure to erupt while he was finding, fixing, and fighting Lee bounced around in his brain. He fretted over how each corps commander should be handled, knowing he alone would bear responsibility for how each reacted to the strain of battle. In war, the greatest unknown is the human element, a man's moral and mental character. As a brigade, division, and corps commander, Meade had known that each of his subordinates required a different method of handling. How the corps commanders reacted in battle and how he should lead them depended on their personal traits, such as grit, boldness, and daring. Commanding was a skill acquired over considerable time through judgment and experience. The challenge was that he had never interacted with his fellow corps officers as their commander. At Fredericksburg, Reynolds was his corps commander, and Gibbon and Doubleday were division commanders like himself. Butterfield and Slocum were corps commanders and senior to him.

*Damn.* He didn't have time to learn how each man should be handled. Lincoln didn't give him time and Lee sure wouldn't. Lee knew this was a critical vulnerability, and Lee would exploit it in the upcoming battle, attacking with a vengeance at his first opportunity. If he were Lee, he would do the same.

Meade turned. "George, have General Williams report to me."

George saluted and rode back in the column. In a few minutes, Williams pulled up next to Meade. Meade slowed Baldy to a walk.

"Seth," he began, "it seems there are three different types of corps and division officers. The first type wants to do everything himself. He does not want specific, detailed orders. He wants to be assigned a mission, not told how it must be accomplished. They always do well with minimum guidance. Who reminds you of this type of officer?"

"Generals Reynolds and Hancock, sir."

"Yes, I agree."

"Generals Humphreys and Warren also seem to be officers who execute with little direction and a great amount of initiative."

Meade nodded. "Reynolds, Hancock, Warren, and Humphreys are capable of taking whatever steps they deem necessary based on the situation. All have demonstrated initiative that permits them to adapt their actions to the situation."

Williams said, "The trick, then, is for you to provide the proper guidance about what you are trying to accomplish, but without dictating specific actions."

Meade nodded. "The second type of officer executes every order but lacks initiative in reacting to changing situations. He requires detailed orders for every movement and engagement. These commanders need to be observed constantly. Who reminds you of this type of officer?"

Williams replied flatly, "General Howard."

Meade said, "Yes. Hooker failed to provide him detailed orders at Chancellorsville and Howard's corps performed dreadfully. I would add Butterfield to this group. I think I would also add Doubleday, who seems to act with abundant caution. At Fredericksburg, when Doubleday, Gibbon, and I were division commanders in Reynolds's First Corps, Doubleday's performance was mediocre. I was not impressed with his initiative."

"I would also put Slocum in this category," Williams added.

"I agree. He is cautious, but once committed, he is one of the hardest and toughest fighters." Meade paused. "The third type of officer opposes everything he is told and wants to do the contrary."

Williams paused for a moment. "I'm not sure any corps commanders fall into this group."

Meade said, "I'm not sure either, although I believe Sickles's First Division Commander, General Birney, might, and maybe even Sickles himself. Birney's performance at Fredericksburg was damn near insubordinate. He was ordered to support Reynolds's corps. I ordered Birney three times to support my division, and he failed to do so. I was so furious I rode to the rear and chewed his butt. Birney told me he was not authorized to accept orders from me, only Reynolds."

Williams said, "Everyone knows you're not a big supporter of Birney."

"The jury is still out for Sickles, Sykes, and Sedgwick," Meade mused. "I know Sickles's and Sedgwick's battlefield performance as corps commanders only by reputation. My guess is they fall somewhere between the first and second type of officer. I know

193

Sykes's battlefield performance as my division commander when I commanded Fifth Corps, and once committed, he is a hard fighter. But I'm not sure what kind of corps commander Sykes will be. There is a big difference between commanding a division and a corps. Not all hard-charging division commanders make good corps commanders. More to think about...and more to lose."

"I'm most concerned with Sickles," Williams said. "In my opinion he appears to be a loose cannon."

Meade said, "Well, let's keep a close watch on him and make sure we put him where he can't hurt the army."

---

*10:00 a.m.*

Meade looked at his watch. The headquarters column was making good, steady time. Meade trotted, pulling slowly away in front of the column. A red-cheeked lieutenant, acting as a courier, rode by him, saluting.

Meade was reminded of his new station; he was unsettled by the salute. He was the senior officer on the field: the commander. *Everyone* saluted him. Although aware of the formal protocol, he was not prepared for it. Yes, he was the commander, carrying an invisible burden that only the commander would understand. In time, maybe he would get used to it, if he remained in command that long. For now, he wanted to arrive in Middleburg by midafternoon to receive vital updates.

Biddle rode up next to Meade. Meade turned, pulling back on the reins to slow Baldy. "You caught my mind wandering around."

Biddle grinned. "I have a telegram from General Burnside, sir." Biddle handed it to him.

Meade adjusted his thick glasses and read the message.

*Cincinnati, Ohio*

*Major General Meade, Headquarters, Army of the Potomac:*
*I am sure that you are equal to the position you are called to fill. You are regarded by all who know you as an honest, skillful, and unselfish officer and a true patriot.*

*I will not congratulate you, because I know it is no subject of congratulation to assume such a responsibility at such a time, but I earnestly pray for your success.*
*A. E. Burnside, Major General*

A fistful of warmth grabbed his heart and held tight. He had been brewing with anger at the fix Lincoln had put him in, but Burnside's kind letter arrived at the right moment. Only a former commander of the Army of the Potomac, whose ghost was living in his tent, would know what to say at such a precarious time. Burnside's letter had reforged his cracked confidence. Meade was grateful. He put the letter into his breast pocket.

Biddle said, "I also have a second letter I received from Hancock regarding an article published today in a Boston newspaper. It was written by Charles Coffin, the reliable *Boston Journal* correspondent who is traveling with Hancock's Second Corps today."

Meade shot Biddle a glance. "A reliable reporter?"

Biddle said, "I also have a request from a news correspondent who wants to interview you after we arrive in Middleburg."

Anger seared Meade's brain. He despised newspapermen, believing they lied constantly, misreporting most of the time. "If we don't shoot any stragglers today, perhaps we should shoot a news correspondent," he quipped. "I bet the request for interviews and reported movements of our army would drop significantly." He stroked his beard. A good idea whose time had not yet arrived.

"I'm not talking to any reporters," he said bluntly. "They are a bunch of bullet-headed idiots." He added, only half-jokingly, "If I see one near my headquarters this evening I will shoot him myself, or I'll shoot you."

"Yes, sir!"

"Where's the letter from Hancock?"

Biddle passed the letter to him. Hancock had demonstrated his ability to make quick, bold decisions aligned with Meade's thinking. Hancock wouldn't waste his time sending him a newspaper article unless he thought it important. Meade read Coffin's prediction:

*If Lee advances with nearly all his forces into Pennsylvania, there must be a collision of the two armies not many miles west of Gettysburg.*

"Gettysburg," Meade said. He cocked his head to one side. Then he looked at Biddle. "Coffin claims the battle will be near *Gettysburg?* Interesting."

Meade asked Biddle to summon Warren, who rode to him in a few minutes. Meade and Warren discussed Coffin's prediction. "If we fight near Gettysburg, Lee has the defensive advantage of using the South Mountain range as a walled castle," Meade said.

Warren said, "Lee's forces could cross the South Mountain range near Fairfield using Monterey Pass. The pass road is steep, narrow, and winding, with many sharp turns. A small size Rebel force could hold off an entire Union division from penetrating Monterey Pass. The other is Cashtown Pass that leads west to Chambersburg in the Cumberland Valley. It also has a steep incline and is easily defended."

"We need to find our own strong natural defense to fight Lee," Meade said. "We need to maneuver him away from the Gettysburg area toward a place of our choosing."

"I agree," Warren said.

Meade added, "After we arrive at Middleburg, let's look at the new maps and see if we can find a suitable place to fight Lee."

---

*10:45 a.m.*

Meade spurred Baldy, moving forward at a comfortable trot. He owed a message to Halleck. He would write it when he reached Middleburg. With luck, he would learn soon if his rapid thrust forward was disrupting Lee's plans to advance across the Susquehanna. That would determine the marching orders for tomorrow.

Since assuming command yesterday, Meade had focused inward on fixing the war machine. But today he was focused on the enemy, conducting an offensive operation, a movement to contact, against a fuzzy picture of enemy dispositions. This posed a major problem. He desperately needed reliable intelligence to disrupt Lee's plans and shatter a portion of his force.

Sharpe rode to Meade and saluted. "General, Sergeant Cline, one of my soldier scouts, has been in contact with Ewell's Confederates moving near York," Sharpe reported.

Meade said, "Cline is one of your *spies?*"

"Yes, sir. He reported a large Rebel wagon train that had departed York and headed east for the Susquehanna River and Harrisburg had turned around and was headed west, back to York."

"Interesting," Meade said. "Have you heard of any Rebel activity in Gettysburg?"

"I have not heard recently from our Gettysburg spy network," Sharpe reported. "David McConaughy, who owns the Gettysburg Cemetery and is a leader in local politics, heads the Gettysburg spy group. As soon as we hear from him I will let you know."

"A correspondent named Coffin authored a column, published today in a Boston newspaper, predicting a great battle near Gettysburg," Meade said. "He also predicted we would win," Meade chuckled. "Too bad he didn't publish his winning prediction a few days ago. Hooker might have had a chance then."

Sharpe nodded and departed.

*10:55 a.m.*

A Second Corps courier rode toward Meade at a full gallop and pulled up next to him, spooking Baldy. Meade scratched Baldy's neck, glaring at the courier. The courier raised the brim of his hat and mopped grimy sweat from his brow before saluting.

"General Hancock wishes to report that he failed to execute the marching order at four this morning," he informed Meade. "The order was received last night, but it was misplaced and not discovered until six this morning. Second Corps was marching by seven thirty."

Meade's lungs seized, suddenly paralyzed. "Son of a bitch!" Meade shouted. Just what he thought might happen. A grave blunder. Success hinged on corps commanders executing his orders precisely. Despite his best efforts, a failure to execute had occurred. His worst fear had been realized: a corps commander failed to receive the marching order. In a harsh tone, he said, "I trust General Hancock punished the culprit?"

"Hancock relieved and arrested the clerk," the courier said. "Hancock said he would force-march his corps at the point of bayonet until they reach its ordered destination."

Meade nodded. The clerk was lucky Hancock didn't shoot him. Hancock would make his ordered destination. But Sykes's Fifth Corps following Hancock would not. He couldn't blame this screw-up on Butterfield.

---

*1:00 p.m.*

*At Meade's headquarters in Middleburg*

Meade arrived in Middleburg. Biddle had his headquarters tent set. Meade dismounted and lit a cigar. Couriers continued to arrive frequently, delivering messages from his corps commanders to Meade. Butterfield had performed well, keeping close tabs on the movements, pushing the corps commanders forward in a rapid march. He reminded himself to compliment his chief of staff for a good job, at least for today.

---

*6:00 p.m.*

Sharpe arrived at Meade's headquarters. "I just received a report from McConaughy with information from his group at Gettysburg. He reports that Ewell's corps turned away from the Susquehanna River at noon and appears to be marching west toward Carlisle. McConaughy also reports that Hill and Longstreet's men are operating near Chambersburg."

Meade's heart leaped. "Well, I tell you, Colonel Sharp, if Ewell has begun moving west, we've achieved the first major goal of the campaign—to diminish the threat to Harrisburg. That's great news."

"My folks will continue to monitor Ewell's movements to confirm he is moving west," Sharpe said proudly.

---

*7:00 p.m.*

Williams was chatting with Meade and Warren, both examining the old maps. A courier from Slocum's Twelfth Corps rode to headquarters. He saluted Meade and said, with considerable angst, "General Slocum sends his respects and wishes to report that Sickles's slow-moving trains will prevent his corps from reaching its objective."

Meade's mouth went dry and his heart rattled off his ribs. "Damn it," he shouted. A moment later, a courier from Sickles's Third Corps rode up to Biddle, delivering a note. Biddle gave the note to Meade, who quickly scanned it. Meade kicked a stone and swore, loudly.

"My God! General Sickles has made just twelve miles today."

"The trains standing still at Middleburg are part of Sickles's rear column," Williams noted.

"Send a dispatch to Sickles ordering him to give his immediate and personal attention to keeping those trains moving," Meade said, with a hissing tone. "I misread Sickles. In fact, I was afraid the former congressman would march his corps right past Taneytown into Pennsylvania. But Sickles covering only half that distance is a piss-poor showing."

"This is a surprising development," Williams said. "Sickles may be a lot of things, but he isn't complacent."

While relieved they had achieved most of the marching objectives today, Meade was still peeved over Sickles's sluggishness. He clenched his teeth and choked down his anger. *Think on it later.* For now, he knew he must talk with Warren about finding a defensive position. He walked toward Warren's tent, found him sitting on the ground in front of a campfire, eating supper.

Warren stood up as Meade approached.

"The general advance of the army was about twenty miles," Meade said. "I just heard from Hancock's courier, and they will cover nearly thirty miles today. Sickles managed to eke out twelve damn miles."

"I think I found a good defensive position along Pipe's Creek," Warren said.

"That's very good." He wasn't so sure about the correspondent's prediction about Gettysburg. Looked like maybe the reporter was wrong.

Meade entered his tent and sank into his rocking chair. Removing his glasses and rubbing his sore eyes, he let his mind wander into a dreamlike darkness. Within that darkness his wife appeared, smiling, her eyes crinkled. *Margaretta.* Meade always firmly disciplined his thoughts on the eve of battle, rarely allowing them to drift toward home. But tonight he found himself helpless to resist answering her gentle smile with his own. *Must write her a quick note.* He perched his glasses back on his nose, tugged his rocking chair over to the table, and began writing.

> *We are marching as fast as we can to relieve Harrisburg, but have to keep a sharp lookout that the Rebels don't get in our rear. They have a cavalry force in our rear, destroying railroads, etc., with the view of getting me to turn back, but I shall not do it. I am going straight at them and will settle this thing one way or another.*

# ❧ Tuesday ❧

June 30, 1863

### *General Robert E. Lee, Commander*
Army of Northern Virginia
Commanding for One Year

### *General George G. Meade, Commander*
Army of the Potomac
Commanding for Three Days

### *General George Sykes, Commander*
Fifth Corps
Commanding for Three Days

General Gouverneur Warren

# 16

# Sickles — Tuesday, June 30

*9:00 a.m.*
*On Third Corps' march toward Taneytown, Maryland*

Sickles rode toward Taneytown at a lumbering gait, leading Third Corps like a courtly knight, smoking a Havana. Great cherry trees in grassy meadows bent under the weight of their fruit, begging to be harvested. No field workers were in sight. The midmorning heat was threatening to turn the afternoon into a scorching barnburner. Sickles's blouse was already soaked with sweat. He wiped his brow with the back of his glove. His chest was rising and falling in stuttered bursts as he rasped with each gulp of air. *Damn you, Meade, you goggle-eyed snapping turtle. What in the hell are you doing?* He refused to push his men beyond their physical limits as Meade had ordered. *You're not killing my boys with your damned forced marches.*

Sickles's butt ached, a numbing tingle of prickly pins and stabbing needles. His five-week convalescent leave had caught up with him. "Damn," he whispered. "You're soft." *Don't let the men see you're hurting.* He spat dryly. His saddle-sore ass throbbed; his wool pants provided no padding. He winced. These long rides for the past two days had chafed his inner thighs as the saddle friction acted like gritty sandpaper, grinding his skin raw. *Damn you, Meade.*

Sickles shook his head. Meade was a prickly asswipe and possessed no natural abilities for leading soldiers. Sickles's brain flashed to Meade's pitiful face during the war council meeting at Chancellorsville. Now this wormwood was the commanding general and Sickles was no longer in the inner circle. He could not shake the jittering gloom of being rejected, again, this time by Meade and his cabal of West Pointers. *Meade rejects me because he fears me—as he should. The president is my close friend, and the newspapers are begging me to take command of the army. It's only a matter of time.* He would deal with Meade later. At the right time.

Crackling snare drums whirled past. Despite the whiskey headache pounding against Sickles's skull, warmth rose in his chest. His professional life had been brought back from the brink of ruin. Before he became a general, his reputation had been despicable—the scum of the earth. His congressional colleagues had shunned him. Now the New York papers had called for him to be Hooker's long-term replacement. Sickles smirked. That was a far cry from several years earlier, when the same papers were calling for his head following the shooting of that scoundrel Philip Barton Key. Everyone seemed to forget he was found innocent of killing his wife's dastardly lover.

A cavalcade of clattering horses rode toward the front. Sickles turned astride in his saddle. It was Major Henry Tremain, his senior aide, coming up the road on a dusty horse, trailed by a small string of staff officers.

Tremain saluted. "Sir, the corps is stretched out for several miles, but the boys are in an upbeat mood. This is a good foot-slogging pace for a long march. Lots of bands playing and drums beating."

"Good."

"The boys are excited you're back in command of Third Corps."

Sickles beamed, puffing on his fat cigar. "I'm damn glad to be back. But with Meade running the damn show, I'm not sure we have much of a chance of beating Lee."

"I'm sure President Lincoln is glad to have you back with the army," Tremain said. "He needs your battlefield aggressiveness and hopes you repeat your Chancellorsville performance. If you do, maybe you can pull out a win for us. If not a win, I bet Lincoln will replace Meade with you."

"You're right. I will need to take the initiative again. As sure as hell our West Point generals won't. All that goggle-eyed snapping turtle learned to do at the Point was build lighthouses."

He examined Tremain, a trusted agent. The medium-built, clean-shaven Tremain had been a fledgling New York attorney. He had served Sickles faithfully since McClellan's Peninsula Campaign. Tremain had been captured at the battle of Second Bull Run and sent to Libby Prison.

Using his skills as a lawyer, Sickles quickly negotiated a special exchange, and Tremain was paroled and rejoined Sickles's staff. *Meade wouldn't have done that. The bastard would have court-martialed Tremain for missing morning muster.*

"Both division commanders reported no significant problems," Tremain said. "I saw a mule kicking up a storm, knocked down a couple mule drivers. Other than that, nothing extraordinary to report."

"Good," Sickles said. "Again, don't push the men. Meade doesn't know what the hell he's doing."

Sickles grunted; his head was still pounding. Although he had a tremendous capacity for alcohol, he had overdone it last night celebrating his return to Third Corps. It was a full-fledged bender, never to be repeated. At least, not until after the next battle. Sickles was sure that if he was aggressive again during the next great battle, Lincoln would fire the cautious Meade and appoint *him* as army commander. Well, if he were Lincoln, that's certainly what he would do.

A band struck up "When Johnny Comes Marching Home," inciting a burst of sentimental pride. God, he loved his boys, and they loved him. He was proving to be a superb commander. It was like falling out of bed and hitting the floor. You either had the talent to lead men in battle or you didn't. It was something with which you were born. *Damn, you've found your calling. You're America's Andrew Jackson, on the road to the Presidency.*

During yesterday's march, great cheers had swelled along the lines as he rode by, the conquering hero. Leading from the front, he had been under fire and wounded at Chancellorsville, commanding Third Corps, proving his mettle and showing decisive leadership during the horrific ordeal. His actions had saved the Union from a rout, plugging the holes in Hooker's right flank. His men were calling him a hero. Late last evening, whiskey had flowed freely during the impromptu celebration at his headquarters. Now he was paying the price. God, his head was a clanging bell.

He gulped down some water from his canteen.

Sickles turned to Tremain. "Henry, I wish Hooker was still in command rather than Meade," he burst out. "I enjoyed moseying on over to his headquarters and chewing the fat with him and Butterfield. Frankly, I don't feel welcome at Meade's headquarters, and I'm sure not going over there unannounced to get put down by that West Point tin soldier."

---

*10:00 a.m.*

Sickles eased forward in his saddle and put all his weight in the stirrups as he tried to adjust his burning butt, raw from riding deep in the saddle. He rode toward a large red farmhouse where a hub of soldiers surrounded a lovely mother and her daughters by an arched gateway blooming with roses. Pulling up under some shade trees across the way, followed by a large collection of personal aides, he dismounted, forgetting about Meade momentarily. He shivered, lit a cigar, and drank in the beauty of being a general. There was something heartening about having a big group of followers around him.

The mother had loaves of hot bread in baskets and some of the girls held jars of apple butter. Her other daughters cut great slices of bread, spreading them with the deep brown sauce, giving the tasty treats to the soldiers. Sickles stood next to a soldier holding the Third Corps flagstaff, the large flag rippling gently in the soft breeze. The mother looked up and Sickles waved. He wanted to express his gratitude; perhaps the wife's husband was a soldier serving in Third Corps. The mother waved back and bowed her head.

"The locals are truly grateful to you," Tremain remarked.

Sickles touched his cap, joining in the three cheers shouted by the appreciative soldiers.

"Henry, let the men linger awhile, enjoying the food," Sickles said. "I do not want to press them in this blistering heat. My job is to ensure they arrive safely on the battlefield and do not die on the way."

Besides, his legs were growing stiff and his butt was numb. He rubbed his chest unconsciously, his breastbone still throbbing from the shrapnel hit. He waited for several minutes, watching, smoking his cigar. One of the daughters walked over, bringing Sickles and his group the bread treats. His mouth watered as the sugary-sweet aroma of the apple butter reached his nostrils. He wolfed down the bread in two gulps. It was delicious.

In the shade of the trees, his head stopped pounding and the hot blood slowly ebbed from his chest. He mounted and rode to the front of the column. Once a famed politician; now a famed soldier. He led a corps of nearly 11,000 fine soldiers. He was born to command.

Humphreys, the Second Division commander, rode up, his blue eyes flaring.

"What's the word?" Humphreys asked. "Are we still bivouacking at Taneytown?

"As far as I know, yes," Sickles said.

Sickles eyed Humphreys with equal measures of contempt and distrust, trying to figure out how he always managed to have a bright white paper dickey. As one of Meade's closest confidants and slithering snakes, Humphreys could not be trusted. Surprising that Meade had not appointed Humphreys, the only West Point general in Third Corps, to replace Butterfield as chief of staff. *How I would love to get rid of Humphreys. Meade's devilish spy.*

———————————————

*11:00 a.m.*

Humphreys departed. Sickles steered his horse up a long road to the top of a large hill. The eyeshot view to the north displayed rolling green terrain with a few steep, short hills. Third Corps should make good time for the next few hours. Yes, indeed. It should be an easy march to Taneytown.

Twisting in his saddle, he gazed back at the coiling columns of blue-clad soldiers stretching back over the horizon, the muffled clanking of gear echoing up the mound. What a grand sight. He clucked his tongue. He was Napoleon, riding at head of a large marching column. The Devil be damned. His lips twisted in a crooked grin. He had reinvented himself. All those backbiting political hacks in Congress now envied him. He was the people's hero, and his soldiers loved him. Who was the goat now? That cussed Meade!

A headquarters courier riding a large brown mare pulled up. Sickles reined his horse to the side of the road. The courier saluted smartly. "General Sickles. General Meade sends his respects and requests you provide army headquarters frequent updates of Third Corps' marching progress."

Sickles said nothing as his face flushed with heat. The courier departed. Sickles turned to Tremain and swore loudly, "Dammit, Henry, I refuse to be henpecked. Meade is a controlling bastard. Hooker never treated me this way."

"Meade is jealous of your accomplishments in the last battle," Tremain said. "You were the lone hero of Chancellorsville."

Sickles frowned. His stomach flinched, as if a fist had pelted him. *Meade has made up his mind against me, but there's nothing to do about it now. He can not be trusted to have my best interests at heart.*

*But I am a survivor.*

A messenger came in from Butterfield with a reminder to keep headquarters posted of Third Corps' progress. Sickles sent his compliments, said he would provide timely updates. The throb in his head sharpened. He growled deep in his throat, wanting to pitch into someone. *Son of a bitch.* He rode for the next several minutes, tight-lipped, his skull pounding to the beat of his horse's hooves. Sickles pulled hard on the reins, stopping his horse off the road. He unbuckled his "spare" canteen from the saddle and drank a long swig of whiskey, the burning, sweet liquid rushing to his gut. The pulsing pain eased.

Major Tremain rode up from the column. "Have you heard anything from Meade's staff today?"

"Not a thing, except for a couple couriers reminding me to keep army headquarters informed of our progress," Sickles hissed. "Meade's probably more concerned when he can hold his first staff uniform inspection. What a poor excuse for a commanding general. He has the personality of a dead toad. Lincoln really made a terrible mistake."

Sickles gulped another swig from his canteen.

God, he loved being in command. He could not curb his instincts for war any more than his lust for prostitutes. War and sex were more emotional than thoughtful, which was why he was such a heroic combat leader. With his charisma, he could build and lead an unstoppable band of brothers.

But the Pointers had their own special club led by Old Brains Halleck. The Pointers despised non-Pointers. Sickles was sure the cunning Halleck had swayed Lincoln into picking Meade. What a nest of weasels. Meade was the worst, having campaigned to replace Hooker. Now, he was sucking the life out of army headquarters.

After Chancellorsville, the New York newspapers promoted Sickles as a gifted, natural-born leader like Julius Caesar and George Washington. It was clear to the newspapers he was destined for glory. The *New York Herald* had urged Lincoln to fire Hooker and replace him with the aggressive Sickles—the newspapers called him the Union Blue Dragon. The *Herald* argued that because Sickles was not a West Pointer, he was not tainted by the traitorous influences of that military institution. The best Pointers had defected from the Union and fought for Lee. The *Herald* reminded readers that Sickles, Caesar, and Washington had not attended military academies but were all winning generals. Sickles agreed with the newspapers. The Union's West Point generals lacked the will to fight their Rebel classmates.

Sickles smirked. All his life he had hoped for the chance to prove his greatness. He had thought it would be as a politician, but now he believed his calling was as a soldier. He rarely prayed for himself. Now he did.

"God, give me the chance, the opportunity, to save the day," he whispered. Honor was at stake.

"Damn it, Henry," Sickles said, "I'm still pissed about Meade's dispatch last evening, rebuking me for the slow speed of our logistics train. I was pushing the men as hard as I saw fit."

"It seems to me," Tremain replied, "that Meade is riding your ass."

A courier interrupted their conversation to deliver another message from Meade:

> *The Commanding General noticed with regret the very slow movement of your corps yesterday. It is presumed you marched at an early hour, and up to 6 p.m. the rear of your column had not passed Middleburg, distant from your camp of the night before some 12 miles only. This, considering the good condition of road and the favorable state of weather, was far from meeting the expectation of the Commanding General, and delayed to a very late hour the arrival of troops and trains in your rear. The Second Corps in the same space of time made a march nearly double your own. Situated as this Army is, the Commanding General looks for rapid movements of the troops.*

"Read this, Henry," Sickles shouted. "It's all payback from Meade's dithering at Chancellorsville. He is out to get me. I can feel it. But it doesn't matter. I won't destroy the combat effectiveness of my troops just to meet his timetable."

Clapping hooves blossomed from behind as a horse approached at a fast gallop. He cocked his head. It was Birney, Sickles's First Division commander.

Birney stopped by Sickles and saluted.

Sickles shouted, "Meade is out to destroy me and my troops. Read this!"

He handed the message to Birney, who had acted as Third Corps commander during Sickles's month-long convalescence absence. Sickles watched him read the message. Everything about Birney was puritanical except his smile, and it was the same devilish one he wore at last night's whiskey celebration. His pale face was almost ghostly, his dark eyes cold.

"I think Meade is having a bad day," Birney said.

"Why does Meade enjoy being so prickly?" Sickles said.

"Meade doesn't like either one of us," Birney replied. "We're not West Pointers."

"There is more," Sickles explained. "Meade despises me because when he asked the other corps commanders to share their recollections of the Chancellorsville war counsel, I refused. Instead, I spent a few hours with Lincoln sharing my views about Meade's underwhelming performance. I made it clear to the president that Meade wanted to retreat. I also said Meade was an indecisive, cautious leader who was not respected by his men and the other corps commanders."

"I agree." Birney said. "But it appears we misread Meade's rising star in the capital. Stanton and Halleck love Meade."

"If only I could have spoken with Lincoln alone, I'd be the commanding general," Sickles lamented. "I had no inkling the president would relieve Hooker on the eve of battle."

"My guess is that neither did Meade," Birney said.

---

*1:00 p.m.*
*On Third Corps' diverted march northwest to Emmitsburg*

Third Corps slithered along the narrow road like an endless snake, the high sun beating down relentlessly on their heads. Sickles approached Taneytown expecting to bivouac for the evening, but he abruptly received orders to leave his logistics trains and march hastily northwest nine miles to Emmitsburg.

He swore an oath. How could they fight Lee with such an incompetent leader? Third Corps continued marching, passing through Taneytown, snaking along under Sickles's weary eye.

Messages from Meade continued to arrive as they marched toward Emmitsburg. Sickles learned that Meade had appointed Reynolds his western wing commander, in charge of Reynolds's First Corps, Sickles's Third Corps, and Howard's Eleventh Corps. Damn Meade was acting like a beheaded chicken, running in a circle, spraying the corps commanders with senseless dispatches.

The army needed a hero. The Confederates had Lee. And after Lee defeated Meade in the upcoming battle, Lincoln would pick a new commander. There was every reason to believe he was next in line. So he had to be aggressive again. Just as he was at Chancellorsville.

He was a man of destiny. His rightful place was among history's heroes. He alone possessed the vision, the courage, and the brave impulses to restore the Union. He understood the strategy of Napoleon and the importance of executing the grand infantry charge. If he performed courageously in battle, command of the army would be his. He puffed out his chest. He could redeem himself in battle, live or die. Dying perhaps would lead to greater glory. *Be aggressive, Daniel! Remember the newspapers—you are the Blue Dragon!*

## 17

# Warren — Tuesday, June 30

*4:19 a.m.*
*Almost 9 hours earlier*
*(Sunrise is 4:49 a.m.)*
*Meade's camp at Middleburg*

Warren walked toward Meade's mess cook, who was standing over a tripod, brewing coffee. Reddish light peeked over the eastern horizon. Sunrise in half an hour. The beardless chief engineer with the drooping black mustache asked for coffee, his first of the day. He took a small sip and winced as the bitter brew singed the back of his throat. He took another sip and gazed out over the sea of white tents. Meade's headquarters was awake—blue figures moving about, cooks working over fires, grooms feeding horses—but it was still very quiet.

Warren walked toward Meade, who was standing outside his tent. An early riser, Meade was already fretting, talking in a pitched voice with Butterfield. Warren joined the other senior staff officers gathered a short distance away, chatting in hushed tones, trying to gauge the commander's mood. He sipped the hot brew and set the tin cup on a tree stump.

Meade's crumpled blue uniform was coated with a thin layer of dust. He was pointing a finger at Butterfield, who was standing motionless and already looking frazzled. Warren cringed. Meade was starting the morning where he left off last night, fuming over Sickles's marching performance yesterday, his corps moving only half the distance ordered.

Rumors had flown yesterday evening that today Meade would fire Butterfield as his chief of staff. Warren had dismissed them as probably not true, although most everyone at headquarters, including himself, thought Butterfield contemptible. Warren looked at his watch; it was a few minutes after five. His

213

heart started galloping as Meade's snarling grew louder, like a coiled rattlesnake rattling its tail. *Hang back until he calls for you.*

Meade moved to a map sitting on top of the cover of an ammunition chest supported by two flour barrels. Hanging above the table was a lantern, casting a gray shadow over Pennsylvania. Meade studied the map for a few minutes and then looked up and spotted Warren and motioned for him to come over. Warren complied, edging around the other senior staff officers. Pleasonton, the pompous cavalry commander, scratched himself and spit on the ground as Warren passed. Pleasonton was being his typical arrogant self, a reputation he proudly cultivated. Warren choked down a sharp reply. What an asshole.

As he approached Meade, Warren saw with vague delight that Butterfield was terribly uncomfortable and unsure of himself. Warren saluted, stood with his hands behind his back, waiting for Meade to finish his browbeating.

Butterfield stood tight-lipped.

"Sickles's marching effort yesterday was wretched," Meade shouted, glaring at Butterfield. "Absolutely pathetic." He made a conscious effort to ratchet it down from a shout to a mere bark. "General Butterfield, did General Sickles provide you an update on why his corps covered just twelve miles?"

"I've heard nothing from General Sickles, sir," Butterfield said, head bowed.

"I expected Sickles to provide some justification for his poor performance. Nothing. Not even a note or a courier. Hancock sent a messenger immediately to explain his late start and several couriers after that to provide updates on his progress. And then he marched nearly twice the distance as Sickles."

Butterfield shook his head.

"General Williams," Meade addressed the waiting officer, "send Sickles another dispatch. Ensure he understands the inadequacy of his progress and my profound disappointment. Remind him to oversee all movements of Third Corps with due diligence."

Williams saluted, glanced momentarily toward Butterfield, then departed.

*5:30 a.m.*

Couriers rode into headquarters. Their arrival created a flurry of activity near Butterfield's tent as grooms rushed forward to hold the reins. Someone was yelling, "General Butterfield, couriers!"

Butterfield hurried toward his tent.

Warren watched Meade struggling to maintain control. No one moved. Warren expected an outburst, but Meade turned and began addressing his senior staff.

"Except for Sickles, I was quite pleased with yesterday's corps movements," Meade said. "I don't recall the army ever moving that far in one day. Good job, everyone."

The group nodded. Warmth pulsed in Warren's chest and his skin flushed with heat. It was a rare attaboy from Meade. Warren was comfortable with Meade's style. He encouraged and valued inputs from officers he respected. He preferred listening and forming his decisions as the group talked freely.

"Gouv, please stand next to me as we study the map," Meade said. Warren moved over next to Meade.

"I'm slowing down our three-prong thrust today," Meade said. "Don't get my intent wrong. I'm not timid about engaging Lee. My goal is to find and fix a portion of his dispersed force and destroy it and then turn on his remaining force and beat it in detail. Without updated intelligence, however, we are groping blindly. The telegraph wires are still down between Harrisburg and Washington. Our best guess is that Ewell is operating northeast of us near York, and Hill and Longstreet are loitering northwest of us behind South Mountain near Chambersburg. Stuart's cavalry also is probably northeast of the army. Gouv, when are the damn topographical maps arriving?"

"Today, sir," Warren said.

"My hope is our rapid advance yesterday will stir some reaction from Lee and make him act in a way he did not plan on doing," Meade continued. "Best case is that we disrupted his schemes. Worst case is that we are marching into a buzz saw. If we can catch Lee before he masses, we can do some damage, but if he catches us dispersed, he can hurt us terribly. We must watch for a bold scheme like Jackson's flanking attack at

215

Chancellorsville. We also must keep a sharp lookout for the Rebel cavalry force operating in our rear. I believe Lee's intent is to catch us in the open or loitering in place so he can swing around behind, find some high ground, and force us to attack."

Meade's expression became belligerent. "But we will continue to move steadily northward," he said.

"Are you going to continue the twenty-five-to-thirty-mile forced marches?" Warren said. "That's a deadly pace."

Meade shook his head and pointed to the map. "Look here. Our troops are fanned out over a twenty-five-mile front between Emmitsburg and Manchester. I will move our front forward at a responsible pace but cover a shorter distance. I will deploy our cavalry at a greater distance to screen the infantry as a blind man uses his cane. It's the best marching speed I can justify with our forces fanned out so widely and the present information on enemy positions."

"What if you tightened the distances among the forces as you move forward?" Warren said.

"If I tighten the army's position, mass our forces, and march headlong toward Lee's center, we run the risk of Lee skirting past us on our right flank and striking Baltimore or slipping by our left flank and heading unimpeded to Washington. With a good chance that two of Lee's three corps are near Chambersburg and moving eastward toward Gettysburg, I'm weighting our force's advance northwesterly toward Gettysburg."

Warren studied Meade. He was visibly edgy over the scattered condition of his forces, particularly in view of Lee's mysterious ability to concentrate and seemingly appear from nowhere with a devastating attack.

Sharpe shrugged and said, "We have a unique opportunity here in Pennsylvania. As our two armies close, we should have an intelligence advantage—the locals can inform us of Lee's movements. The tables are turned on Lee, who is used to having Virginians inform him of our movements. He is now the invader."

Meade nodded. "I'm depending on you and your Northern spy network to provide us with the critical information we need to defeat Lee," he told Sharpe. Then he turned to Pleasonton. "I want you to push your cavalry out in all directions to feel for the enemy. Keep your men in the saddle until dark. It's critical we find them before they find us."

Pleasonton responded quickly. "I've ordered Buford's cavalry brigades to Gettysburg today and, after clearing it, to ride west toward Chambersburg as far as they can, finding, but not engaging, the Rebels. I've ordered Kilpatrick to ride northeast to Hanover and Gregg to ride eastwardly to Manchester."

"Good," Meade said. "Let's not get caught napping. I want constant updates throughout the day of where our cavalry is, what they are finding, and any sign of trouble. I feel we are going to run into some Rebels today."

Meade turned to Warren. "Gouv, we need to find a strong redoubt, a natural defensive line where we can fall back easily and make a stand if Lee concentrates his forces faster than we do and attacks at a place of his choosing."

Meade pointed to the map and traced the different roads leading eastward from South Mountain.

"What are all the possible actions Lee can take?" Meade asked. "What if Lee pushes rapidly east through the mountain passes toward Gettysburg, then turns and sweeps south, attacking our dangling left flank?"

"It would be Chancellorsville all over again," Warren said.

"Consider if Ewell crossed the Susquehanna and captured Harrisburg? What if Ewell turned south and moved rapidly toward Baltimore? And while en route to Baltimore, changed his mind and swept west and smashed the Union's exposed right flank?" Meade clenched his fist and hit the map table.

"You have no control over when and where the armies will meet," Warren said. "We are on a collision course, being drawn together like magnets."

"There is not much time, Gouv," Meade said. "We cannot extend our flanks any further without jeopardizing our ability to concentrate the army. With luck, we could survive a flanking attack from either York or Gettysburg. It all depends who has the best ground."

"You still have to cover Baltimore and Washington," Warren said.

"I disagree with Lincoln on this. Baltimore and Washington mean nothing to Lee. Lee's goal is the same as mine: find and defeat the other's army, not occupy his cities. Lincoln's scheme of protecting cities first and then fighting Lee has forced us into defensive thinking and planning, but orders are orders."

"Well, there is nothing defensive about plowing ahead and hoping to compel Lee to react," Warren said.

"I know the risk I'm taking by moving forward without having a strong reserve line to fall back onto." Meade shook his head. "It's critical, Warren, that you locate a strong defensive line south of the army by day's end."

Hunt, the chief of artillery, joined the group.

"It seems Lee is bent on repeating his fix-and-flank maneuver, using his dispersed infantry forces and cavalry as a nutcracker," Meade said. "If he is able to execute successfully, he will crush a portion of our army between two or more independent actions. Our dilemma is figuring out which flank Lee will attack and having supporting corps close enough to reinforce before Lee destroys it.

Warren said, "Isn't Lee dispersed over a wide area?"

"Yes, and that is forcing us to spread the army more than we would like to cover all contingencies and comply with my orders to cover Baltimore and Washington. But Lee may choose to mass his forces rapidly today for an attack."

Meade paused for a long moment, his fingers pulling on the end of his beard. Warren waited for Meade to speak. He was used to Hooker, who did not share his thoughts. Meade was like an open book; all thoughts, good and bad, came forth unfiltered.

Meade and Warren continued to stare at the map table for several more moments.

"I have to make a decision," Meade said. "What will Lee do?" Sweat beaded on his forehead and fell to the map. Meade wiped the wet spot with his hand.

"I'm betting Lee favors attacking our left flank near Emmitsburg," Warren said. "That's what I would do. It's less of a risk because South Mountain is nearby to the west to shield his supply lines."

"Agree. So I will be keeping a slightly greater part of our strength on the left wing as a precaution against a possible movement by Lee through the mountain passes leading to the Emmitsburg flank."

Meade turned to Warren.

"Gouv, ride ahead to Emmitsburg and help Reynolds select a favorable defensive position for First, Third, and Eleventh Corps. After you finish, I want you and General Hunt to conduct a terrain survey behind our lines and identify a strong defensive area near Uniontown, where all seven corps can fight a defensive battle. And if the opportunity arises, a defensive line that will enable us to launch a counter-offensive."

Warren saluted and walked over to his horse, accompanied by Hunt.

"After I visit with Reynolds at Emmitsburg," Warren said to him, "I will ride back to Taneytown and meet you."

"I will be waiting for you," Hunt assured him.

---

*6:50 a.m.*
*From Middleburg to Taneytown and Emmitsburg*

Accompanied by two aides, Warren rode out from Middleburg, moving quickly down the flat roads. They would ride first to Taneytown, a distance of seven miles, and then turn northwest and ride the eight miles to Emmitsburg.

Warren's heart lightened. There was hope. Meade refused to be intimidated by Lee. The moment had called for boldness and decisiveness, and Meade had delivered.

Warren's group caught up with Sickles's Third Corps, marching steadily toward Taneytown. Brigade drummers were tattooing a festive beat, as the most spirited corps was only a few miles from today's midafternoon bivouac.

As Warren rode toward the front of Sickles's marching corps, he saw a sea of flags, including the Stars and Stripes, swallow-tailed guidons, and battle streamers of Second Division, flying from spiked poles over the heads of Humphreys's marching men.

Sweat dripped from the soldiers' faces, backs, and legs. The dust clouds stirred by their feet seemed to muffle the clanking of metallic gear. Warren spotted Humphreys and reined alongside the division commander. Humphreys swiveled in his saddle.

Warren grinned and shook his head. How did Humphreys maintain his impeccable uniform? The contrast with Meade—perhaps the worst-dressed officer in the army—was night and day.

"Good to see you, Gouv," Humphreys greeted him.

"Likewise," said Warren. They talked for a few moments, reminiscing. Before the war, they had been together a long time, surveying the Mississippi River.

"I remember the fine ladies of New Orleans drinking a toast to both your birthday and Andrew Jackson's victory in the Battle of New Orleans," Humphreys said.

Laughing, Warren came back with "I remember you venturing into the bayous and sashaying with a gator. You're lucky you're not hobbling around on a peg leg like old Dick Ewell. He's commanding a portion of Stonewall Jackson's old Second Corps."

Humphreys said, "Ewell reminds me of a woodcock with his balding head and those beady eyes and beaked nose."

"He's bright," Warren said, "but he is no Stonewall Jackson. Since he lost his leg, he has been more tentative."

After a pause, Humphreys asked about Meade.

"Meade surprised everyone by moving the army forward incredibly fast," Warren said. "He has been snapping and barking orders. He wanted to throttle Sickles."

"How is he getting along with Butterfield?"

"Just splendidly," Warren said. "They're rapidly becoming best friends."

"Praise God." They both laughed.

Both men had turned Meade down when asked to be his chief of staff, but Warren was aware that Meade had dogged Humphreys into agreeing to take the job after the upcoming battle. Warren said his goodbye, continuing his ride toward Emmitsburg.

*9:00 a.m.*
*Emmitsburg*

Nine in the morning and already scorching hot.

Warren saw a cupola just ahead, marking the town of Emmitsburg. The large cross adorning the top of the landmark belonged to Mount Saint Mary's, the nation's second-oldest Catholic seminary. The cupola appeared to be floating atop the forest of trees blanketing South Mountain. The mountain jutted up more than a thousand feet, providing a scenic backdrop for the cupola and a signal station for Reynolds's First Corps.

As he and his two aides approached the small town, his nostrils flared; he whiffed a smoldering burnt odor. Then he saw the burned-out hulks in the town square. Muscles in his throat pulsed and his skin crawled. Was this a random act of violence? Hell, no.

Three days earlier, Brigadier General George Custer's Michigan Cavalry had camped near The Mount, as the locals called the seminary. Custer scouted the area and reported back to army headquarters that someone had torched Emmitsburg two weeks earlier, burning down the town square and several other buildings along Main Street. The Rebels had passed through Emmitsburg at the same time as the fire.

Rage and disgust surged through Warren's veins. Was this a new Rebel tactic, to target civilians and their will to sustain the war? Maybe the burning was an anti-Catholic attack? He did not believe Union forces would ever direct the war against Rebel cities and civilians. Or would they? War was changing. What if targeting civilian populations was now a part of it? If the Rebels burned Emmitsburg, war was sliding toward absolute. Total war would mean annihilation, destroying the enemy's army, cities, and ability to wage conflict.

*9:10 a.m.*

Warren and his aides galloped through the town, heading north. He spied a beautiful sight, a sea of tents like ocean whitecaps—First Corps. Twelve thousand men bivouacked across the rolling hills. He rode up to Reynolds's headquarters and dismounted. The general emerged from his tent and greeted Warren with a friendly handshake. Reynolds looked picture-perfect: handsome, six feet tall, narrow-waisted, neatly groomed beard—a gentleman's gentleman.

"Good to see you, Gouv. How is General Meade doing?"

"He has everyone hopping, especially Butterfield, who is as skittish as a cat in a roomful of rocking chairs. General Meade asked me to visit and help you select a good defensive position near Emmitsburg. Meade is worried the Rebels will descend on you from Gettysburg or through South Mountain."

"Let's take a ride," Reynolds said. Once they were on their way, Reynolds asked, "How is Meade handling the political interference from Washington?"

"Well, so far," Warren said. "Rebel cavalry cut the telegraph wires connecting army headquarters to Washington. Meade misses getting timely reports of Ewell operating near the Susquehanna River, scaring the bejesus out of the Pennsylvanians. But he does not miss hearing the carping from Washington every hour."

"Meade is the best qualified to deal with all the pestering," Reynolds assured him.

*9:20 a.m.*

They rode to Indian Lookout, the highest point in the Emmitsburg area, behind Mount Saint Mary's College. The army's signal corps had a six-soldier detachment operating there, looking through powerful thirty-inch brass-tube telescopes mounted on top of oak tripods.

"Take a look, Gouv."

Warren peered through the brass glasses. He could plainly see Gettysburg ten miles away. He discerned a good deal at first glance: the Lutheran Seminary tower just to the west of Gettysburg, the land west of the seminary rolling out in a series of low ridges running north and south like smooth ocean swells with broad, shallow troughs in between. A dirt road ran westward from the seminary, riding over the swells and troughs toward the South Mountain gap called Cashtown Pass. To the east of town was a cleared hill with a two-story red-bricked archway, sitting on the south slope—the Cemetery Gatehouse—and just beyond was a higher, wooded hill with two peaks and a saddle connecting them.

Warren had a clear view of the fields south of Gettysburg, with their white and red barns. A prominent ridge ran nearly two miles south through the fields from the flat, cleared hill beyond the town. The ridge ended at the southern end of the fields, where he spotted two round tops, one big and one little, jutting upward like the turreted ruins of medieval castles. These were the two highest hills of the area: the one nearest town was the lower of the two, rugged and strewn with large boulders on the westerly slope and thick woods on the south and easterly slopes. A saddle connected the lower hill to the higher summit, which was heavily wooded.

Warren nodded. "This is an ideal lookout station."

"When First Corps arrives in Gettysburg tomorrow," Reynolds said, "I will establish a signal station on the big round top to communicate with the signal station here on Indian Lookout."

Warren pointed. "Look, on the Emmitsburg road leading into Gettysburg. It's cavalry, riding fast."

Reynolds looked through the brass telescope. "It's Buford and his two cavalry brigades, over four thousand men," he reported. "Thank God for John. He is the finest cavalryman in both armies."

"Buford is one of the toughest officers Meade has, and he likes to fight," said Warren.

"I heard Buford hung a Southern guerilla and left the corpse dangling from a tree limb for three days," Reynolds said.

Warren added, "I heard he left a sign under the corpse saying, 'This man to hang three days; he who cuts him down before shall hang the remaining time.'"

Warren and Reynolds surveyed the Emmitsburg terrain from Indian Lookout for several more moments, discussing the best defensive positions. They were most concerned about a Rebel flanking attack from Fairfield, six miles west of Emmitsburg, and they agreed the best defensive position was just north of town. From there they could thwart attacks from Fairfield and Gettysburg.

*10:00 a.m.*
*On the road south toward Howard's Eleventh Corps*

Leaving Reynolds on Indian Lookout studying the Gettysburg terrain, Warren and his aides rode to Mount Saint Mary's College, where General Howard, commander of Eleventh Corps, had made temporary headquarters. Howard was the youngest corps commander and had been crushed by Stonewall's corps at Chancellorsville.

Warren dismounted. He greeted Howard, whose empty right sleeve was attached to the bottom of his blue coat. Howard had been shot twice in his right arm during the Battle of Seven Pines in McClellan's Peninsula Campaign and had to have his arm amputated. They talked for a few moments. Howard asked about Meade and if Butterfield remained as chief of staff. Warren explained the situation.

*11:00 a.m.*
*On the way to Taneytown*

Warren and his small cavalcade mounted their horses and departed. Commanding Eleventh Corps was a tough assignment, as it was composed largely of German immigrants, many of whom spoke no English. The Germans had a reputation for breaking and running. They were resentful that their German commander, Franz Sigel, had been replaced by Howard. Warren thought Howard would perform well as long as he was reporting directly to Reynolds, whom Meade had designated as commander of the western wing of the army. But Meade did not have confidence in Howard's ability to operate independently.

*12:00 p.m.*

Warren rode several miles toward Taneytown before he spotted pickets from Meade's advance headquarters party. A tall, thin, freckled youth with perfect white teeth stood erect with a bayoneted rifle slung over his left shoulder, his curly brown hair escaping from beneath his blue cocked cap. He saluted and said in a piping voice, "Good afternoon, General Warren."

Warren returned the salute smartly. "Has General Meade arrived?"

"No," the picket answered cheerily. "But Generals Williams and Hunt arrived an hour ago with the advance party, and they are setting up Meade's headquarters just up yonder around the bend in the road."

Warren thanked him, rode past the picket line toward the bend, and arrived at Meade's new camp, in a farm just north of Tancytown. Meade's advance party was setting up headquarters in a two-story white house on the Shunk Farm. Warren rode up to Hunt and halted. Hunt waved, mounted his horse, and, together with Warren's aides, they headed south toward Pipe Creek.

*12:15 p.m.*

Warren and Hunt galloped toward Middleburg with the Blue Ridge Mountains in the distance and the sun directly overhead. The dirt road wound through vast green fields and rolling woodland hills. The air was thick and wet, and white, fluffy clouds hung in the pale blue sky like giant heads of cauliflower.

After riding hard for half an hour, Warren pointed and said, "That's a church spiral from Middleburg."

"I see it," said Hunt, "and there's the bridge crossing Big Pipe Creek."

Warren said, "Let's pull off and ride through the creek. I want to get a feel for the depth and current."

*12:45 p.m.*
*Pipe Creek*

They departed from the road and rode through a thicket of trees toward Pipe Creek, where they stopped. A mist lingered beyond a bank of untidy, spindly trees, as if from a Grimm's fairy tale. It was a trickster event, momentarily blurring Warren's vision, as though devilish creatures lived within the haze. Then it cleared suddenly, sunlight shimmering off the greenish creek.

"Did you see that mist?" Warren asked.

"Very weird," Hunt replied. "Like a scene from *Macbeth*."

"Let's let the horses water in the creek," Warren suggested.

They rode into the shallow rivulet, stopping in midstream. The horses, steam rising off their flanks, dipped their mouths into the water and started drinking. The stream was fifteen yards wide and ankle deep. Pipe Creek would not be much of a barrier for charging infantry, who would run through it without breaking stride. More of an obstacle were the groves of trees anchoring both banks. After a few minutes, they crossed the creek to the south side, rode through the clustered tree line, and emerged in an immense, emerald field. A half mile beyond jutted a ridgeline rising one hundred feet.

"The ridgeline looks as formidable as Hadrian's Wall," said Hunt.

They rode up a gradually sloping hill that crested about a hundred feet above the creek and stopped. Warren looked through his binoculars down the hill and retraced the path they had just ridden. Then he followed the creek eastward. "It looks like the ridgeline runs parallel to Pipe Creek as far as the eye can see."

"If we anchor this end of the ridge with an infantry corps and heavy artillery," Hunt calculated, "Meade should be able to hold this part of the line."

---

*1:30 p.m.*

They rode eastward along the ridgeline toward Union Mills as Warren's two aides traced a defensive line. The further east they rode, the steeper the sloping hill rose, cresting nearly 500 feet. As they neared Manchester, the Pipe Creek ridge collided with Parr's ridge and Dug Hill and the two ridges and hills twisted together like a pretzel rising 1,000 feet above the creek. They stopped on the meeting place between Dug Hill and Parr's Ridge and Warren handed Hunt a cigar. They lit them and surveyed the terrain through their binoculars.

"My God," Warren declared, "Parrs Ridge is like an impregnable castle wall. The entire Pipe Creek line reminds me of the Hogback ridges in the Black Hills of the Dakotas."

"As we rode eastward from Middleburg, the front of the ridge facing north gradually grew steeper, like sea cliffs," Hunt said.

"Yes, and behind the ridgeline the terrain remains elevated and flat. It looks like the plateau runs four to ten miles back and would make the perfect defensive place for an occupying army."

"Parr Ridge is the perfect natural defense to anchor the right flank of Meade's army," Hunt agreed. "This must have been the view Lee had of us charging up Marye's Heights at Fredericksburg."

Warren nodded. "It was a suicide charge. Now it's our turn to return the favor. We'll see how well Rebels charge heavily defended heights."

"These heights can easily accommodate all seven Union infantry corps," Hunt said. "What's impressive is the road network in the rear. This will give Meade an opportunity to maneuver quickly and fight either offensively or defensively."

"Entrenched on this high ground," Warren said, "the army would have positions almost impossible to storm in frontal attacks or to turn, so that it could effectively cover the approaches to Baltimore and Washington. The line would also be close to the main supply base at Westminster. Should the army fall back to the line, the Sixth Corps, the largest of the army, would already be in position, and the Second and Third Corps would have but a short march to reach it."

"Enemy full-scale offensive attacks against the eastern half of the line would be suicidal, like Fredericksburg," Hunt pondered. "In the vicinity of Taneytown to Middleburg, the topography changes and becomes broader, and the hills not as steep. Meade will have to bolster up the left flank of the Pipe Creek defensive line."

"This is the perfect defensive line Meade was looking for," said Warren. "Let's pay him a visit."

"Meade will be pleased," said Hunt. "Getting Lee to attack such a formidable natural defense is another matter."

# Pipe Creek Line
## June 30, 1863

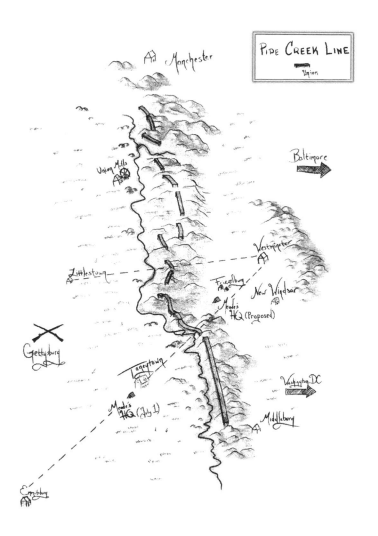

Manchester

PIPE CREEK LINE
Union

Baltimore

Union Mills

Westminster

Littlestown

Frizellburg

New Windsor

Meade's HQ (Proposed)

Gettysburg

Taneytown

Washington DC

Meade's HQ (July 1)

Middleburg

Emmitsburg

## 18

# Meade — Tuesday, June 30

*9:00 a.m.*
*Four and a half hours earlier*
*Meade's headquarters at Middleburg*

Beneath the awning outside his tent, a disheveled Meade stood scowling under his large, floppy hat. The midmorning Middleburg air was warm and humid, the rain clouds low and gray. He was bent over the makeshift table, studying the outdated map. He drank coffee alone, bristling with anger, like a hornet trapped in a glass bottle. Where were the new maps Warren promised? With any luck, they would arrive from Baltimore before he departed for Taneytown. Out of the corner of his eye he spotted someone moving toward his table—Biddle, carrying dispatches. After reading each message, Meade scribbled his initials, *G. G. M.*, in the upper right corner and returned them to Biddle. He scribbled an answer to Sedgwick's message, telling the Sixth Corps commander about the possible Pipe Creek plan; noting that Sedgwick would be in position along this line on the right flank by late this afternoon.

A breeze fluttered his beard. The rain was coming down in sheets, beating an ever-faster tattoo on the canvas awning. *Damn.* The muddy roads were growing deeper and thicker, threatening to bog down today's marches.

He lit a cigar and stared at the map. *What are you planning to do, Lee?* If he were Lee, he would be concentrating his force, knowing his leisurely days of foraging were over. If Lee was massing, Meade needed to do so as well. But this required a plan. For developing tomorrow's plan, he first needed the new terrain maps and Warren's report of the suitability of the Pipe Creek line. Armies didn't perform well without a plan. And neither did Meade. Departing off-script from Hooker's halfhearted pursuit

229

of Lee and surging northward would hopefully produce an un-expected opportunity. But moving rapidly toward the enemy was not a plan. It was a purely tactical move to get Lee to react. Then what? It was like throwing rocks at a big cat without knowing what to do when the beast turns on you.

Before Lee turned on him, Meade needed a plan, one based on favorable geography that would give him the best offensive and defensive opportunities. He gripped the edge of the map table and glared down. The map stared back, its towns begging to be protected. No town deserved to be pillaged by the enemy or burned like Emmitsburg. Meade slapped the map table. His tin cup exploded into the air like an artillery shell, coffee splashing everywhere.

"Damn it," Meade muttered. He mopped up the coffee with his handkerchief. He drummed his fingers on the table, watching the dark clouds move by, dropping more rain on the already-soaked ground.

Biddle walked up, saluting.

"Any word yet from Warren's boys about the new maps?" Meade asked. "I've just drenched this one."

"Nothing yet. Warren's adjutant said he expects them to arrive midday."

Biddle grabbed the wet handkerchief and departed.

As he puffed on his cigar, Meade watched thin tendrils of smoke rising from a black kettle hanging over a nearby fire. Minutes ticked by. His heart pounded, sending tingles up his arms. He loved planning, and he was good at it. But a workable plan depended on understanding the terrain—the high and low ground and the flowing ridges that connected them. He needed the contour maps for that. Not having the most current maps was not his gravest problem, however. Deep down, he carried a lingering doubt about his suitability for this command. The ab-sence of a senior field commander nearby providing mentorship was eerie, like cold wind whistling through a night graveyard.

Did he have the gift for command? His heart stumbled. He was, at best, a fledgling greenhorn, relying on his quiet hedgehog approach of active restraint and vigilant caution to solve difficult challenges. Lee had had more than a year to hone his heroic command style. Meade would have perhaps three days. Without the time to forge his staff into a well-oiled machine, he had to depend on his instincts, hoping his gut would lead him to the right decisions.

*9:45 a.m.*

*Damn it, instincts don't win battles; well-executed plans do.* Meade's ruminating was cut short by the sound of couriers riding into headquarters camp. Were these Warren's boys bringing the maps? They dismounted, and Butterfield's aide came out to meet them. No maps. *Son of a bitch.* He owed a message to Halleck, but that could wait.

Biddle appeared, holding a refilled cup of coffee and a clean handkerchief.

"Are you heading for Taneytown around noon?" Biddle asked.

Meade nodded and Biddle departed.

Meade's challenge was maneuvering an entire army while maintaining suitable momentum. This hinged on a new skill he had practiced for two days—a skill Lee had demonstrated time and time again: the ability to focus his efforts at the right time and place and to do so in a way that established mutual support among seven independent infantry corps and one cavalry corps, an artillery reserve, and more than a hundred thousand soldiers. It was the secret to Napoleon's success, and Lee had mastered it. Devil be damned. He had to be better than Lee at maneuvering.

Meade frowned and his gaze darkened. There was nothing more to do but wait for reports and the maps. He lumbered over to a tree where Baldy was tethered. He rubbed the flank of the beautiful horse.

"We make a good team, Baldy," Meade said. "You're calm, poised, and gentle, and I'm anxious, temperamental, and harsh."

Baldy neighed softly.

More couriers arrived, dripping with rain and sweat. They gave their dispatches to Butterfield's officers, then walked their horses over to the trees.

Meade stared. Perhaps there was a message from Buford telling him he had arrived at Gettysburg. Buford was the best cavalry general in the Army of the Potomac. He was full of good common sense and could always be relied on in an emergency.

---

*10:00 a.m.*

Colonel Sharpe walked up and saluted. "My intelligence officers embedded with Buford's cavalry forces and my civilian spies in Gettysburg are providing us reliable updates on Rebel movements," Sharpe said. "Unless Buford gets into a scrap today, I don't think we will see much fighting. Tomorrow, however, will be a much different story."

Meade nodded. "All right. I need updates on Ewell's forces operating near York. I need to know if they are moving west toward Carlisle."

"Yes, sir."

"Threatening Lee and bringing him to battle in a place of my choosing," Meade said, "are not objectives that necessarily support one another. I have positioned Buford at Gettysburg to react to Lee's movements, maybe surprise or even threaten Lee. If Buford seizes Gettysburg first, he could perhaps disrupt or delay Lee's ability to converge on Gettysburg, the Rebels using it as a foothold to strike south against us."

"Gettysburg is a point of strategic importance," Sharpe said, "with as many as ten roads culminating there, making it easy for both armies to concentrate at that place."

"Beyond this spoiling objective of occupying Gettysburg with Buford's force," Meade said, "I'm unsure if I should take the initiative and start the battle at Gettysburg. I do not know if the Gettysburg terrain supports a major engagement. If possible, I want to control the precise conditions under which I would accept battle."

"Lee, of course, wants to do the same." Sharpe departed.

Meade shook his head. He hated loitering in Middleburg and begging for scraps of information like a dog slinking around the dinner table. Maybe he should ride now to Taneytown. Leave Butterfield here and have him forward the dispatches.

*10:15 a.m.*

Williams approached and gave several papers to him to read and sign. Meade pored over the paperwork for an hour.

*11:15 a.m.*

Biddle and Sharpe appeared. "What have you got?" Meade demanded.

"Reynolds reports Buford ran into a couple Confederate regiments at Fairfield this morning," Sharpe said. "Fairfield was fogged in. A few shots were fired. Buford decided not to start a fight, fearing it would disrupt your strategic plans. He turned away, hustled out of the area, riding toward Emmitsburg, where he talked briefly with Reynolds. And then he traveled from there to Gettysburg."

"Did Buford see Confederate cavalry?" Meade asked, alarm in his voice.

"No," Sharpe said quickly, "just infantry."

"Damn, Colonel! If we have a couple Rebel infantry units loitering on our left flank I need to learn this a lot damn faster. We can't depend on Buford's boys to provide all our intelligence. Your intelligence boys need to pick up their game."

Sharpe nodded and departed.

Water dripped from the brim of Meade's slouch hat. He turned to Biddle. "I need Butterfield."

Butterfield appeared a few moments later.

"Send a courier to Sickles telling him to move Third Corps to Emmitsburg as fast as possible," Meade said. "I want Sickles positioned to prevent a Rebel flanking attack from Fairfield, and to support Reynolds's First Corps and Howard's Eleventh Corps as Buford heads toward Gettysburg."

Meade turned to Biddle as Butterfield left. "With Sickles's marching record so far, it will probably take him until midnight to get to Emmitsburg."

"With your permission," Biddle said, "I'll ride ahead to Taneytown to ensure the advance party has everything ready for your arrival."

Meade nodded, then turned and walked briskly back to the beehive of activity engulfing headquarters. He started playing the frightening *what if* game. What if Lee overwhelmed Buford's forces at Gettysburg and marched south, striking Meade before he had massed? What if Lee hit him with a left flanking attack from Fairfield? What if Ewell's corps and Stuart's cavalry struck his right flank? He had to do something. He spotted Colonel Sharpe and walked over to him.

"I have an update of Lee's estimated forces operating in Pennsylvania," Sharpe announced.

Meade's heart skipped several pulsing beats. His engineering mind loved numbers. "What are the estimates?"

"Approximate Confederate infantry is 92,000 men accompanied by 270 cannons. I estimate Jeb Stuart's cavalry around 7,000 men accompanied by 20 or so guns."

Meade sighed audibly. "Damn. Lee's forces number about the same as mine." He looked at his watch; it was after eleven in the morning.

Meade turned and motioned for George. "I need to speak with Butterfield."

Butterfield appeared shortly, having not ventured too far from the commander's tent.

"I'm going to depart for Taneytown," Meade said. "Between now and then, have the couriers who are reporting to you ride to Taneytown and also report to me. Williams and Pleasonton will ride with me to Taneytown."

Butterfield nodded, "Yes, sir."

"After I arrive in Taneytown, inform all the couriers to report to me directly, and then you join me."

*1:00 p.m.*
*Meade's Taneytown headquarters—Shunk House*

Meade mounted Baldy and rode north toward Pennsylvania. The rain clouds had vanished. His cavalcade rode several miles before reaching the northern edge of Taneytown in midafternoon. Meade dismounted, stared at the compact, two-story Shunk Farm house his personal staff had selected for use as his headquarters. A large army command flag hung from the awning, draping a good portion of the porch. A second headquarters flag hung from a mast extending twenty feet upward from Meade's personal logistics wagon that had arrived a few hours earlier, along with most of his personal staff.

Meade and Williams stepped into the house. Biddle had made a map table and desk for Meade in the great room, next to an open fireplace made of river stone, with a large wooden mantel. Bracketing the ceiling-high fireplace were two long and narrow wood-mullioned windows. Williams's work area was in a converted first-floor bedroom, next to the kitchen.

"Good job, Biddle-le-dee," Meade said. "The Shunk house is a cozy headquarters."

"The headquarters house is located almost midway along the Pipe Creek defensive line that Warren and Hunt are scouting and in the middle of the army's twenty-mile-wide front," Biddle said.

"Good," Meade said. "This is as far north as I will move head-quarters until I get a good feel for what Lee's up to and the terrain surrounding Gettysburg."

"Gettysburg is thirteen miles north of Taneytown," Biddle said.

"We've achieved a small accomplishment in establishing headquarters at Taneytown before Lee has had a chance to con-centrate his forces near Gettysburg," Meade said.

Williams walked over to Meade with an afternoon update message he had drafted for Halleck. Meade provided his personal thoughts on the current situation and how he felt a major battle was imminent. Williams made some notes and returned to his new office. Meade was growing used to Williams's calm, unflap-pable demeanor and his soft, soothing voice and was enjoying having him nearby. The man was an exceptional administrator.

*1:30 p.m.*

Biddle entered the great room, escorting a man yakking away. Meade looked up and growled.

"A war correspondent from the *New York Times*," said Biddle. "Henry Raymond is the founder and editor of the newspaper and says he got permission from Lincoln to have him interview you about the upcoming battle," Biddle said.

Meade scowled as if an artillery projectile had exploded in his gut. The idiocy of the request and Lincoln's approval shocked him. He shouted, "Lincoln wants me to talk with a reporter on the eve of battle so Lee can read what I'm planning? I have a better idea. Why don't I have Colonel Sharpe ride over to Lee and tell him where my forces are and what I plan to do with them in the next few days. This is a damn fool request. Now get the hell out of here before I shoot your damn ass."

Meade took a threatening step forward. The startled reporter departed briskly, with Biddle at his shoulder.

Composed and unruffled, Williams addressed Meade in a low voice. "General, we must be more careful in how we treat reporters, especially ones whose editors are friends with Lincoln. They can be useful at times, and we don't want them turning against your headquarters and writing anything they want. Destroying you."

"I'm not worried about being destroyed by the press," Meade snapped back, his voice jarringly dissonant to Williams's controlled tone. "I'm worried about being destroyed by Lee and his boys. Besides," he snarled, "reporters are like parasites, infiltrating headquarters, not caring if their news hurts this army. I'm not fighting Lee in the papers. I'm fighting him on a field of battle where men die and blood runs freely."

Williams stepped quietly back into his office.

Meade stomped outside. A rider galloped up the Taneytown road, throwing dust high like a towering wind devil. He recognized the officer from Warren's staff. Meade's chest heaved and his heart banged against his ribs. The officer raced into the headquarters yard and reined the horse into a sliding twenty-foot stop. Both horse and officer were coated in a froth of sweat. The man dismounted quickly and scurried toward Meade, carrying a two-foot leather tube, saluted Meade, and handed him the tube, gulping air.

"These are the topographical maps Warren sent me to retrieve in Baltimore," he said breathlessly.

Meade grinned. "About goddamned time!"

He carried the leather map case into the house, removed the detailed maps, and spread them out on a table, examining them with mathematical precision. His eyes focused on the thinly spaced lines along Pipe Creek. His finger traced the possible Pipe Creek defensive line, stretching some twenty miles from Middleburg to Manchester. The map clearly marked prominent ridges on the eastern flank that created a formidable natural barrier, rising nearly a thousand feet, with a four-to-five-mile-wide plateau anchoring the rear of the defensive line.

Sharpe entered the great room. "General Meade, Ewell is concentrating his three divisions of infantry eight miles north of Gettysburg at Carlisle. Ewell should accomplish the massing of his corps around noon tomorrow. Lee's two other corps of Longstreet and Hill are occupying the country from Chambersburg to Carlisle, pointed at Gettysburg."

Meade said, "So you're convinced Lee has abandoned all designs on the Susquehanna?"

"Yes, sir."

"Do you think Lee is holding the South Mountain Cashtown Gap to prevent our entrance or to enable his advance against us at Gettysburg or Emmitsburg?" Meade asked.

"I believe Lee intends to cross South Mountain and advance toward Gettysburg."

"I've ordered Sickles to march to Emmitsburg to protect the army's left flank," Meade said. "Reynolds and Howard will support Buford at Gettysburg. Slocum and Hancock are covering the middle of my front. Sedgwick, commanding a corps of 15,000 infantry troops, is at Manchester, thirty-four miles southeast from Gettysburg, preventing a right flank attack. But if Warren and Hunt confirm the value of the Pipe Creek line, Sedgwick already would be in position occupying the eastern portion of the defensive position."

"I should be getting a report soon from my intelligence officer riding with Buford in Gettysburg," Sharpe said.

"Good."

Sharpe moved off.

*3:00 p.m.*

Captain George Meade appeared in the great room and gave his father a dispatch. He turned away and was out of sight in a second. Meade was starting to see a pattern. When George delivered a message, it was from Halleck. This was ridiculous. Halleck had said he would leave him practically free in maneuvering the army. But Meade had received two messages since arriving in Taneytown expressing excessive alarm for the safety of Washington. Halleck was worse than a cow mothering its calf.

Meade read the message. Halleck said his tactical movements were good, but strategically he was too far east. Halleck wanted Meade to move his army in a way that a straight line could always be drawn from Lee's headquarters through the center of the Army of the Potomac to the White House. Halleck worried there was a grave danger of Lee maneuvering around Meade's left flank, trampling Frederick, razing a path to Washington, D.C. He instructed Meade to guard against this imaginary peril.

Meade crumpled up the dispatch and flung it into the fireplace. He lit a match and watched the message burn, waiting for the flame to go out. Meade turned around as everyone scurried about the great room, and his gaze darted to the window. "You're a son of a bitch, Halleck."

Now he understood why Reynolds had turned down command. He wished he could send a note to Jeb Stuart and have him cut the telegraph wires again. Or perhaps he should have Pleasanton's boys cut the wires and blame it on Stuart.

Biddle appeared again. "Warren and Hunt have just returned."

"Good."

Williams came into the great room, frowning. "We just heard that General Halleck had General Hooker arrested today."

"What the devil?" Meade asked.

"Apparently, Halleck told Hooker to wait at Baltimore after you relieved him of command. Hooker remained at Baltimore for two days, but he heard nothing from Halleck. So today he traveled to Washington," Williams said. "When Halleck heard he had arrived in the nation's capital, Halleck ordered Hooker's arrest because he had not obtained permission to depart Baltimore."

"Christ almighty, that's going to stir up outrage," Meade said. "If Halleck fires me, I'm going to request he send me to Philadelphia, where I will stay put with my family until the war is over."

Meade returned with grim determination to studying the new maps. Footsteps echoed off the wood floors. He glanced up to see Warren and Hunt walking into the great room. "We just got back from scouting the Pipe Creek line, sir," said Warren.

Meade held his breath. He stared hard into Warren's eyes and then Hunt's. Both registered hope they could barely contain.

"Well?" he said.

"Beautiful. It's beautiful," Warren said, his voice resonating excitement.

A great weight lifted from Meade's shoulders. "That's great news."

"We marked the locations of the corps positions for the defensive line," Warren said, pointing with his finger, "and General Hunt marked the best locations for the artillery."

Hunt said, "If Lee is defeated attacking the impregnable positions of the Pipe Creek line, you can easily move our army west through the wide valley using interior lines and intercept Lee seeking to cross the Potomac. But if we fight Lee at Gettysburg and defeat him, you will have a longer march, either a day or two, to intercept Lee before he crosses the Potomac."

Meade's face flushed. He gripped his eyeglasses, removed them from his nose, wiped the large lenses with a handkerchief from his pants pocket, repositioned his glasses. Warren and Hunt were glowing.

"Have General Williams join us," Meade instructed Biddle. He was done grappling with what to do if Reynolds was outnumbered and had to fall back. He watched as Warren and Hunt examined the map, pointing out the route they had taken along the Pipe Creek defensive line.

Williams came out of his office. "Good to see you, Gouv, Henry."

"Seth," Meade said, "I now have the final piece for my campaign. Warren and Hunt reported the Pipe Creek line is a perfect natural defense. Now we are set for both offensive and defensive operations."

"You couldn't have designed a more perfect theater, General," Williams said, examining the map.

"Let's draft a circular telling the corps commanders of the possible defensive line at Pipe Creek," Meade said. "I want the circular to describe the specific conditions that would trigger the forward units at Gettysburg to fall back and occupy the line. The key is that once any Gettysburg corps commander feels the pressure to fall back to the defensive line I want all the corps to fall back."

"So you want to fall back behind the Pipe Creek Line and fight a defensive battle?" Williams said.

"No," Meade said. "I'm not ruling out that developments tomorrow may enable us to take the offensive from our forward positions at Gettysburg. But I want the option of falling back in an orderly way to a very strong defensive line if we have to do so."

Meade looked at Williams, who nodded. Williams turned to his aides and said, "Let's start drafting the circular and get it to all the corps commanders before midnight."

<hr>

*6:00 p.m.*
*(Sunset is 7:44 p.m.)*

Meade's shoulders relaxed and he sighed loudly. His engineer's eye was drawn to the high ridge beyond Pipe Creek: It was as strong as thick castle walls. Things were starting to fall into place. If Lee decided to attack the Pipe Creek line it would be Fredericksburg in reverse. But would Lee assault the line? If his plan worked, he would.

Meade's eyes followed the line of the Taneytown road north to Gettysburg. Hmm, lots of thinly-spaced lines there, too, around the high ground in the southerly part of Gettysburg. Not a bad option, perhaps, for a defensive position.

# ❧ Wednesday ❧

July 1, 1863

### General Robert E. Lee, Commander
Army of Northern Virginia
Commanding for One Year

### General George Meade, Commander
The Army of the Potomac
Commanding for Four Days

### General George Sykes, Commander
Fifth Corps
Commanding for Four Days

# Buford's Defenses
## July 1, 1863

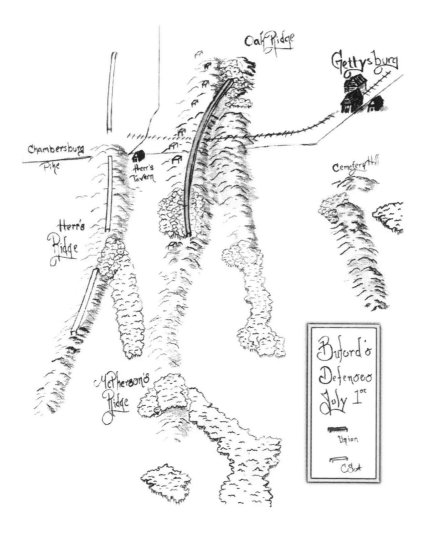

Oak Ridge

Gettysburg

Chambersburg Pike

Herr's Tavern

Cemetery Hill

Herr's Ridge

McPherson's Ridge

Buford's
Defenses
July 1st

Union

CSA

# 19

# Meade — Wednesday, July 1

*5:00 a.m.*
*(Sunrise is 4:48 a.m.)*
*Army of the Potomac headquarters, Shunk House, Taneytown*

Meade had worked through most of the night, falling asleep at two, and waking at five, courtesy of a nearby rooster. As light broke, he walked onto the four-pillar covered porch, having his first cigar and watching dim threads of reddish sun poking through a blanket of softly falling rain. He scoured the yard for the damn rooster that was nearly as irritating as Butterfield. The Shunk House was still home to several farm animals, as neither Rebel raiding parties nor Union infantry units had as yet ventured through, stripping the hamlet of livestock as they moved northward. But that might change today. Hancock's Second Corps was arriving in Taneytown around noon, and perhaps they could press the rooster into service as the main ingredient of stew.

Meade's grizzled face sported dark raccoon rings behind his thick glasses. Headquarters staff was moving about with purpose. He was no longer in awe of the vast sea of tents cobwebbed around the farmhouse. He was starting to learn some of the junior officers' names. A growing warmth was settling in; a knot loosened behind his breastbone. He wagged his head back and forth, blowing a huge smoke ring.

Things were coming together. The arrival of the new topographical maps helped. Miraculously, Sharpe's intelligence network seemed to be working, enabling him to begin to grasp what Lee was thinking. Beginning its fourth day under Meade's command, the army was at last moving to a well-designed plan—the Pipe Creek Circular. He puffed on his cigar, blue

243

smoke billowing upward. Shards of relief dissolved the tension gripping his stomach.

Biddle emerged from the house with a steaming cup of coffee. Meade sipped from the tin cup, the heat sizzling his lips as the brew warmed the rest of him. "All the corps commanders should have received the Pipe Creek Circular around midnight last night," Biddle said.

"Good. Buford's two cavalry brigades should have occupied Gettysburg by midafternoon yesterday. I'm not sure if Lee is planning to move toward the town. But if Buford runs into trouble today with the forward elements of Lee's army, he will have support from Reynolds's First Corps, which should be arriving sometime midmorning."

"What will Reynolds do when he arrives at Gettysburg?" Biddle asked.

"Having read the Pipe Creek Circular, Reynolds will assess whether Gettysburg is good defensive ground. Occupying the high ground is the key to determining if he stays or falls back to the Pipe Creek defensive line."

---

*5:20 a.m.*

Meade extinguished his cigar and moved back into the house. He plopped down in his rocking chair, the wooden floor creaking as the curved rockers glided back and forth. Faint squeaking and shuffling echoed throughout the house. He glanced around the room. Somehow his staff had all managed to disappear, like mice hunkered down in dark cracks.

"I need a drink of water," Meade shouted into the silence, his voice like a croaking frog.

Time was short. The enemy was near, lurking to the north, spread out in a crescent moon stretching from South Mountain to Carlisle and then to York. The two great armies were probing toward each other, looking for the first chance to strike, like a gray wolf and black bear circling a recent kill.

"Here you go, General," Biddle said, handing Meade a cup of water.

Meade nodded and gulped down the water.

Sharpe arrived, saluting. "Buford has occupied the westward and northern approaches to Gettysburg. His two brigades are dismounted and occupying the high ground. His patrols are out in force, scouting. My intelligence officer embedded with Buford believes one of A.P. Hill's infantry divisions will move eastward down the Chambersburg road and clash with Buford's boys early this morning."

"Has Reynolds's First Corps started moving to Gettysburg?" Meade grunted.

"Yes. They should arrive midmorning. We should be hearing around noon if Reynolds wants to stay and fight or fall back to Pipe Creek."

"Sounds good," Meade replied. Buford reaching Gettysburg first was a scythe-like stroke.

Meade rocked, steeling himself for the upcoming ordeal. All he could do was wait for Reynolds to arrive at Gettysburg and make a determination to fight there or fall back. He shook his head. If he failed to halt Lee today, the Union would fracture and sink into the abyss of a new Dark Age.

<hr />

*5:30 a.m.*

Meade twisted out of the rocker and stood for a moment by the map table, using it for support as he gazed over at the large open-hearth fireplace, its embers faintly glowing red. They seemed alive, pulsing as a slight draft slipped under the front door. He turned and stared out the large-paned windows at the view of the empty Taneytown road snaking northward over the rolling hills toward Gettysburg.

One of Butterfield's aides entered the room. "Sir, I wish to inform you that the chief of staff is now issuing the circular to the couriers, and the messengers will depart at any moment to deliver it to each of the corps commanders."

Meade gasped, horrified. Fear, fury, and foreboding all collided together in a gnarly knot inside his stomach. He erupted into a towering rage. "What? The plan should have been in the corps commanders' hands by now! Damn that dawdling Butterfield!"

The aide said, "Butterfield's staff worked nonstop drafting copies of the Pipe Creek Circular, sir, but the night passed with lightning speed."

"Son of a bitch! I want to see General Butterfield immediately." The aide departed. Meade glared, alternately growling to himself and cursing loudly to anyone within earshot while he paced furiously back and forth by the hearth. Shards of white pain ricocheted up from his toes to his ankles.

Butterfield walked into the living room. "Sir, you wanted to see me?"

"Damn it, Daniel!" Meade thundered. "I told you I wanted all the corps commanders to receive the Pipe Creek plan by midnight. What the hell happened?"

"General Meade, we worked tirelessly through the night drafting seven copies of the order."

"So Reynolds did not receive the plan before he marched to Gettysburg?"

"No, sir."

Meade slammed his fist onto the table. "The crux of the phased plan depended on the corps commanders knowing the tripwires that triggered when to stay and fight and when to retreat to Pipe Creek. Not knowing the tripwires will scuttle everything."

Butterfield looked down. "You're dismissed," Meade shouted.

He was seething. A splitting maul cleaved his chest, unleashing Hell's brimstone fires. As long as Butterfield remained chief of staff, Hooker still had a grip on this army. Where was everyone? He hated staff screw-ups, especially tardiness in issuing orders. *Soldiers die needlessly when headquarters' orders are delayed. God help the poor devils marching into the teeth of Lee's army without knowing they can fall back, dig in their heels in a strong defensive position at Pipe Creek.*

"Major Biddle!" Meade bawled.

His mind chattered on like a dozen gibbering monkeys. What a frightful danger. He was responsible for creating and executing the plan. *Hooker didn't have a plan, but if you have one and can't execute it, you're no better than Fighting Joe.* His chest tightened and the muscles in his arms and legs twitched. He should have forced Warren or Humphreys to replace Butterfield as chief of staff. *God damn you, Butterfield.*

Biddle arrived. "I want to talk with Warren," Meade shouted, and Biddle turned on his heel and went immediately to fetch the general.

Meade took a deep a breath, and a voice echoed in his head. *You will maneuver and fight in such a manner to always cover the capital and Baltimore.* The twenty-mile-long row of hills along the south side of Pipe Creek was perfect. It sat squarely across the major routes Lee would use to approach Washington and Baltimore. That was good as long they executed the Pipe Creek Circular. But now the plan was in serious doubt. The front door creaked and Meade glanced up to see Warren.

*6:00 a.m.*

Meade gestured and Warren approached the map table.

"I just heard Reynolds did not receive the Pipe Creek plan before he departed for Gettysburg," Warren said.

"This is the devil's absurdity," Meade shouted. "Reynolds is supposed to be executing the army's movement to contact. But without knowing the plan, the army is just drifting forward right into Lee's hornets' nest."

"What do you think Lee is planning?" Warren said.

"Last night around midnight, a telegrapher from Frederick arrived with news from General Couch in Harrisburg," Meade said. "General Couch said Lee is falling back suddenly from the vicinity of Harrisburg and is concentrating all his forces at or near Chambersburg. This is good news, because this means Lee's forces are still operating west of South Mountain, about twenty-five miles from Gettysburg."

Meade stopped and walked around the map table. "Well," he said, pointing toward Gettysburg, "I am thankful I ordered Reynolds to advance the army's left wing to Gettysburg. That movement order is not contingent on Reynolds having read the Pipe Creek Circular. Damn, I hope Reynolds gets the circular before he arrives at Gettysburg."

"Reynolds is the right commander to meet Lee's forces emerging from South Mountain's Cashtown pass," Warren said. "Lee's boys will be bunched up marching over this solitary road, the Chambersburg Pike, toward Gettysburg."

"If Reynolds receives the Pipe Creek plan this morning before Lee's forces arrive, it will give him the flexibility to initiate an orderly withdrawal down the Taneytown Road toward us if he feels the conditions at Gettysburg do not support a strong defensive stance."

Meade paused momentarily. Warren glanced at the map, then back at Meade. "The Pipe Creek line is very strong," Warren said. "I can't imagine Gettysburg having the same defensive terrain as the Pipe Creek line."

"I spoke to Reynolds about this possible plan when he visited me the day I assumed command," Meade replied. "He supports and understands the plan and my conditions for staying and fighting at Gettysburg or executing a general retrograde movement to a stronger defensive position. What Reynolds doesn't know is that I've chosen Pipe Creek as the defensive position and how formidable the natural defensive line is. An enemy attack against the Pipe Creek line would be uphill over open ground; beautiful fields of fire. The enemy would be crushed."

"What if Lee doesn't pursue Reynolds as he retreats toward Pipe Creek?" Warren said.

Meade raised his eyebrows and his mouth hung with lips slightly parted. "Lee only has three choices. He must either fight us at Gettysburg, pursue us and attack us at Pipe Creek, or retreat through the South Mountain passes and cross back across the Potomac into Virginia. After Lee masses his army east of South Mountain, he cannot sustain himself logistically for very long. That's his critical vulnerability—supplies."

"With our shorter supply lines and nearby railheads, we can stay forever at Pipe Creek," Warren said. "If Lee chooses to stay east of the South Mountain and not attack us, we will maneuver forces up the Potomac and cut off his escape into Virginia from Sharpsburg to Williamsport. Then Lee is forced to attack us on ground of our choosing or he surrenders. He has no other choices.

"I hope we can execute the Pipe Creek plan," Warren concluded. "It is a much stronger position than the Marye's Heights Ridge the Confederates defended at Fredericksburg."

An aide came in carrying messages; Meade read them. "Gouv," he admitted, "I'm fearful circumstances and speed of events will outpace my ability to control the action."

*6:15 a.m.*

Major Biddle entered. "Pipe Creek Circular has been sent and corps commanders are receiving it," he reported.

Meade replied, "Very well. Did Reynolds receive it?"

Biddle grimaced. "No. First Corps departed early this morning from Emmitsburg. Reynolds should have arrived in Gettysburg about an hour ago. Butterfield's courier will ride to Gettysburg to deliver the plan."

Meade was stunned. His largest corps was nearly thirty miles away, useless today if called on. If Reynolds chose to stay and fight, only the three corps for which he had tactical command would be available to fight at Gettysburg. Hancock's Second Corps, Sykes's Fifth Corps, Sedgwick's Sixth Corps, and Slocum's Twelfth Corps were too far away to support a Gettysburg fight. This could be a colossal disaster, as Lee had the ability to have almost his entire army arriving at Gettysburg today if he so chose.

Meade said, "If Reynolds did not see the Pipe Creek Circular, I assume he did not receive my follow-on message requesting him to provide me advice as to whether Gettysburg is a suitable place to fight a general engagement with the entire army." He shook his head in disbelief. *Can this be happening?*

How could such a carefully constructed plan go so terribly wrong? Meade grumbled to himself, tugging at the ends of his scraggly beard. He had done all within his power to set the stage for a victory. The battle would soon erupt, in Gettysburg or Pipe Creek or somewhere else, and it would decide Meade's career as commanding general, as well as the fates of the Army of the Potomac and the young Republic.

Meade stared at Warren's new maps as though they were a crystal ball that would eventually reveal the future. Typically, army headquarters would have a better understanding of the enemy's movements than just the reports of a lone corps commander operating forward as the vanguard wing. But Meade had set it up this way, betting all or nothing on Reynolds acting as wing commander to determine what Lee was doing in the Chambersburg-Gettysburg area. What if Lee's forces were concentrating rapidly at Gettysburg? What would Buford do? What would Reynolds do, not having the Pipe Creek Circular?

Meade stormed outside the house and stood on the porch. A sea of white tents covered the yard. He swore an oath. "For God's sake, can't this headquarters issue orders in a timely manner?" He stepped toward Old Baldy, tethered to a large oak. The blackness of dawn had given way to a blackness of a different sort: a darkening shadow creeping across the Shunk House. He stroked Baldy's neck and whispered, "Undelivered plans are as useless as no plans. I fear for Reynolds."

Biddle approached quietly. "General, would you like your eggs fried as usual this morning?"

"No," Meade snarled, with a catch in his voice. "Scrambled."

*Nearly 11:00 a.m.*

Meade gestured toward Biddle. "Ride to Manchester and give General Sedgwick an update on Reynolds moving toward Gettysburg. Update him on the Pipe Creek plan. If we execute the Pipe Creek plan, he is already nearly in position. But there is a strong possibility Reynolds will not receive the plan in time. Since Sedgwick is the farthest from Gettysburg, tell him to get ready to move forward toward Gettysburg, as he may be required to march at a moment's notice."

Biddle saluted and departed.

Meade lit a cigar. He owed an update to Halleck in Washington.

Hancock walked into the living room and saluted splendidly. "General Meade," Hancock trumpeted. "Your Second Corps commander presents his compliments and reports the Second Corps is bivouacked about a mile away."

A shiver sliced though Meade as he walked up to meet the general, reaching out a welcoming hand while patting Hancock on the back. "It is great to see you, Winfield!" Warmth echoed through his voice.

A look of surprise covered Hancock's face. "General? I would like to apologize."

"Sure, Winfield. About what?"

"A mindless devil failed to deliver your June 29 marching order when he received it. I take responsibility for this. I swear to you, General, it won't happen again."

Meade shook his head decisively. "I'm sure it won't, Winfield. You sure did march your boys that day. Mighty impressive. One of the longest marches made by any infantry unit I can recall."

Meade offered Hancock a cigar. He liked Hancock, always reliable, especially when the fighting was hot. There was something special about Hancock's leadership ability—foxlike and brilliant. He had the rare ability, an instinct, to inspire incredible moments among his men, infusing his own force and fire into them during the heaviest fighting.

"I received your Pipe Creek Circular," Hancock said. "My corps rode over portions of it yesterday. The range of hills comprising the line makes it a perfect natural defense."

"I agree," Meade said, "But Reynolds did not receive the circular before he departed for Gettysburg."

Hancock rubbed his chin, looking anxious. Meade said, "There will be a scrap today."

Hancock nodded. "I assume Reynolds will try to seize Gettysburg, deploying and concentrating his different columns on favorable ground."

"I learned early this morning that Buford's cavalry brigades occupied the western fields of Gettysburg last night," Meade said. "Buford has with him about 2,800 mounted cavalry and one six-gun battery. Indications are he will hold Gettysburg and the approaches from the west and north until Reynolds arrives midmorning."

Meade pointed to the map. "It seems every road in southern Pennsylvania and northern Maryland, some ten or twelve at least, concentrate at Gettysburg, making it a point of strategic importance. Reminds me of Sharpsburg. Every time Lee comes north, we seem to have an engagement at a rural market town, at the hub of a spider web of roads."

"Antietam was the bloodiest single day of the war," Hancock said. "A quarter of our army became casualties that day, charging over Antietam Creek."

Grimly, Meade said, "Those types of losses are to be expected when we launch attacks against Lee's infantry, dug in and fighting from strong defensive positions. But now I've found my own area I can fortify behind and Lee can make the charge."

"The tables have turned," said Hancock.

Meade looked at the map table. "With Buford holding Gettysburg, and Reynolds arriving any moment, the army can converge, or Reynolds and the left wing could easily diverge from this point and march into their Pipe Creek Line position."

Hancock nodded, wide-eyed.

"Buford won't get caught napping," Meade added. "He will deploy his forces smartly and enable Reynolds's infantry to arrive. But after that, I'm worried."

Meade puffed on his cigar. *Damn Butterfield.* He prided himself on giving exact instructions, and he expected they would be followed precisely. "Reynolds may be waltzing into Gettysburg not knowing he is supposed to be the bait that lures Lee into the trap at Pipe Creek. Sedgwick has the largest corps and he is sitting thirty miles from Gettysburg, anchoring the far right of the Pipe Creek line. Lee's entire army of 100,000 is within ten miles of Gettysburg and massing."

Meade paused. Stone-cold fear coursed through him, turning his muscles into jelly. Lee was beating him. He would destroy Reynolds and then flow south, smashing his fragmented Army of the Potomac. "How is Reynolds supposed to execute the plan if he doesn't have it? Tell me, Winfield. By failing to deliver orders in a timely fashion, we may have surrendered the initiative to Lee."

Winfield hedged. "The circular also mentioned that developments may cause the commanding general to assume the offensive from present positions."

"Yes, if the ground at Gettysburg supports such an initiative," Meade said. "But it's hard to imagine better ground than the Pipe Creek Line. That's why I devoted nearly the entire circular to defense. I want to be able to fight defensively when it comes time to fight, on ground of our choosing. My hope is that Lee will attack us as we defend the high ground of the ridge overlooking Pipe Creek. If Gettysburg offers that same natural defense, then we can fight there."

Hancock remained tight-lipped.

Meade said, "I'm willing to fight Lee at any time and any place as long as it is to our advantage to do so."

"That's a key advantage we have by having you in command," Hancock said. "Lee has been used to fighting commanders who lack your grit."

Meade nodded. "In the message I sent to Reynolds I told him I would not be able to decide whether to move the rest of the army until I heard something more definite about where Lee was concentrating. I also said I had insufficient information on the nature of the country to judge whether it would be a good offensive or defensive position. I asked Reynolds for his views on fighting at Gettysburg."

Meade removed his glasses and rubbed his eyes. He glanced down at his dirty boots. "Are you familiar with Gettysburg?"

"Vaguely," Hancock replied, "I seem to recall a couple large hills southeast of Gettysburg and a cemetery that sits on a ridgeline overlooking town."

A smoldering surge of dread accelerated through Meade. No information. No couriers. Meade and Hancock walked outside the headquarters house. A moment later, a messenger came flying down Taneytown Road at a full gallop. It was Captain Stephen Weld, Reynolds's aide-de-camp, arriving from Gettysburg. Weld's horse was frothing, having run flat out the thirteen-mile trip.

Weld dismounted, raced toward Meade and Hancock, and saluted. "General Reynolds sends his compliments, sir."

"Well?" Meade said ominously. His heart thumped against his ribs.

"General Reynolds told me to ride at my utmost speed. He said the enemy is advancing in strong force from the west along the Cashtown Road, and he fears they will get to the heights on the eastern side beyond Gettysburg before he can."

Meade's chest heaved and locked up as he shuddered with alarm. He couldn't find his breath. His plans were collapsing.

"If the enemy gets Gettysburg, we are lost!" Meade said. "If Lee were to defeat Reynolds, occupy Gettysburg, and control the roads, he could prevent Reynolds from using the Taneytown Road to join the remaining Army of the Potomac assembling along Pipe Creek."

"General Reynolds said he would fight them inch by inch, and if driven into the town, would barricade the streets and hold them back as long as possible," Weld said.

"Good! That is just like Reynolds." His breath hitched. "Did General Reynolds receive the Pipe Creek Circular?"

"Sir, we know nothing of any Pipe Creek Circular."

Meade exploded, hurling fiery clots into the air. "The plan is now useless." Meade turned, pointing toward Butterfield's room. "Damn it, Butterfield! Damn you to hell." Butterfield remained upstairs, laying low.

Weld wiped his face and shifted his stance.

Meade turned, squinting at Weld. "Tell me again, Captain Weld, exactly what Reynolds said."

Weld repeated Reynolds's message slowly, word for word. "Reynolds wants to hold Gettysburg until you can reinforce him. If you cannot reinforce him, Reynolds will fall back to Emmitsburg."

Meade shook his head. *Son of a bitch.* "Reynolds must be acting on yesterday's orders. Falling back by the Emmitsburg Road now would leave a large gap in the middle of army, which Lee could easily exploit. If Reynolds is going to fall back, I want him to use the Taneytown Road so he can plug that gap." Meade paced. Could he salvage his plan for mounting a defense behind Pipe Creek? "Is Reynolds fighting a temporary holding action at Gettysburg or is he committing his forces to try and beat the enemy to the high ground at Gettysburg?"

"I believe it is General Reynolds's intent to hold the high ground until you can decide whether you want to fight a general engagement at Gettysburg," Weld replied. "He does not plan to withdraw until ordered to do so."

Meade nodded.

"General Reynolds and several of his staff left the infantry column and rode ahead to Gettysburg," Weld said. "Up the Emmitsburg Road, the ground south of Gettysburg has strong defensive possibilities. About two miles south are two large round hills—known locally as Big Round Top and Little Round Top—that anchor the bottom of a ridgeline that runs northward to Cemetery Hill, which lies at the southern tip of Gettysburg."[9]

"It appears on the map that these two hills control the Emmitsburg Road and Taneytown Road southern approaches," Meade said.

"Yes they do," Weld said. "A short distance southwest of Cemetery Hill is another large round hill with a shallow swale in the middle connecting the two rounded peaks, like a crescent moon. This hill controls the Baltimore Pike easterly approach to Gettysburg. These hills and ridgelines form a fish hook of about three miles in distance from which an Army could easily defend."

Meade nodded, showing nothing. Reynolds may have spotted a natural defensive line at Gettysburg. Was the ground good enough to hold off Lee's entire army until the dispersed Union forces could arrive? Sedgwick was thirty miles from Gettysburg.

"Tell General Reynolds if he is forced to fall back from Gettysburg, I want him to use the Taneytown Road as spelled out in the Pipe Creek Circular," Meade said. "The key contingency of the Pipe Creek plan is for Reynolds to hold the enemy

---

9 The Union soldiers called Big Round Top and Little Round Top by other names during the battle. I used their common names we call them today for ease of telling the story for the reader.

in check long enough at Gettysburg to bait Lee into following. As Reynolds retreats down the Taneytown Road he will cross Pipe Creek and assume the middle position of the army that is waiting for him."

Weld nodded.

"Let Reynolds know I will remain for now at Taneytown. If I decide to execute the Pipe Creek defensive line, this central location is the best place to coordinate the assembling forces."

Weld saluted and left, riding on a fresh horse.

*12:00 p.m.*

Meade shook his head. The Pipe Creek plan was in jeopardy. He guessed Reynolds had ordered Howard and Sickles's corps to join First Corps at Gettysburg. One of those corps should be arriving at Gettysburg right about now. Meade said a silent prayer.

A messenger from Buford rode up, bringing Meade a dispatch. Written by Buford at ten in the morning, it read:

> *General Meade: A.P. Hill's enemy force is advancing on me and driving my pickets and skirmishers very rapidly. There is a larger force at Heidlersburg that is driving my pickets from that direction. General Reynolds is advancing, and is within three miles of this point, with his leading division. I am positive the whole of A.P. Hill's force is advancing. John Buford.*

"Winfield," Meade said grimly, "Buford reports he is tangling with the whole of A.P. Hill's corps advancing from the west over the Chambersburg Pike. There are also Rebel forces to the north driving back his pickets. Reynolds is advancing and is within three miles with his leading division."

Hancock asked, "Does Buford mention Howard or Sickles?"

Meade shook his head no. "I'm still hopeful of executing the Pipe Creek line. But I want you to advance Second Corps up the Taneytown Road to fill the gap in the middle of our forces."

Hancock nodded, departed. Meade shook his head. Oh my God, they might suffer a decisive defeat today. Had he moved forward too fast over the past few days, outrunning his support wings?

Meade walked out onto the porch.

Reynolds not knowing about the Pipe Creek Circular left Meade in a quandary. He was not enthusiastic about fighting at Gettysburg. He wanted to control where the fight would be, and that was at Pipe Creek. But Reynolds seemed to be committing the army to a fight at Gettysburg. He had complete faith in Reynolds and trusted he would make the right decisions. What did Reynolds know about Gettysburg that he didn't?

Meade's cook walked out on the porch with a bowl of steaming beef stew. Meade inhaled the comforting odor. For a moment, his mind turned off and he focused on the simple task of eating. Momentarily appeased, he walked back into the house and settled into his chair.

*1:00 p.m.*

A First Corps staff officer entered the house, saluted. His eyes were filled with tears. Something was terribly wrong.

"I apologize for the interruption," Major William Riddle said. He paused, took a deep breath and announced, his voice breaking, "General Reynolds is dead. He was killed this morning." Tears rolled down his face, pelting his blue jacket.

Meade jerked, his muscles seizing. Riddle's words ripped through him like a saw. *Oh my God! This can't be true*, he cried out, or thought he had cried out. His face turned icy cold.

He stood up slowly, unsteadily, stared out the window toward Gettysburg, unable to speak. Grief pierced him like a backstabbing knife. The reality was overwhelming. He had seen plenty of death and dying, but it had never before been such a dear friend.

Riddle stood frozen. Neither officer said anything.

Meade's sadness was so profound it sickened him. His knees buckled, threatening to give way. He leaned against the map table. Reynolds was dead. Reynolds would no longer be a source of wisdom, providing advice and guiding him past his fears. Meade's skin prickled as Lee's army coiled around Gettysburg, striking against his cavalry brigade and his outnumbered, vulnerable infantry corps.

"Who is commanding the forces at Gettysburg? Meade asked.

"General Howard, sir."

Meade swore silently. Howard was not an instinctive man. His corps had performed poorly at Chancellorsville. He was not the right commander for this situation.

Meade turned away, masking a breaking heart and a black distress. His grief turned jagged, shredding the insides of his roiling stomach. He sat down at the map table.

His mind traveled back to the battle at Fredericksburg. Reynolds commanded First Corps, with Doubleday, Gibbon, and Meade as his division commanders. Meade's division was assaulting the Rebels and breaking through. He looked up at Reynolds on a superb black horse, sitting tall in the saddle, his head thrown back, black eyes flashing. He was the classical gallant general, appearing fearlessly everywhere on the field, seeing all things, giving commands in person. Soldiering was natural to him. He did it with high honor, courage, and commitment. His untimely death was a disaster for both Meade and the army. Meade did not quite accept it, but he knew it was true.

"How did it happen?" he asked softly.

"First Corps was arriving west of Gettysburg where the fighting was galling hot," Riddle explained. "General Reynolds was placing the Wisconsin regiment of the Iron Brigade on a slope leading to a ridge crest near some thick woods to halt the advancing attack from General Archer's Rebel brigade. Recognizing the Rebels might break through the Union line, Reynolds shouted from his horse, 'Forward men, forward for God's sake, and drive those fellows out of the woods.' The Badgers leaped forward, loading and firing as they ran down the slope through the trees. Reynolds looked back to urge on reinforcements. Suddenly, he lurched in his saddle, falling to the ground. We thought at first he was just stunned, but in fact, he had been hit at the base of his skull by a Minié ball. General Reynolds was dead. Private Veil, Captain Mitchell, and Captain Baird carried the general toward the rear of our lines."

"Did he say anything before he died?

Riddle shook his head, "No, sir."

"Where is he now?"

"General Doubleday ordered Captain Rosengarten to transport the body to Taneytown and then on to the railhead at Westminster."

"Alright," Meade whispered. "Thank you for the update."

Death had taken his friend, the army's top general, the only general on the field with the instinctive vision to manage the battle. Neither Howard nor Sickles had the instincts to fill Reynolds's shoes. Meade had even less confidence in Abner Doubleday, Reynolds's senior division commander.

He had never expected Reynolds would be killed. Fear gripped him; now Howard was forced to stave off Lee's attacking forces.

Meade bowed his head. His options seemed bleak. A voice deep within said, *Get hold of yourself.* For the good of the army, he had to get past Reynolds's death. *You are in command. You must act like a commander.*

He stood up, almost running into Major Riddle. "Let's visit General Hancock," he said urgently.

*1:20 p.m.*
*Hancock's headquarters, one mile south of Meade's Taneytown headquarters*

Meade, Butterfield, and Riddle galloped the mile to Hancock's Second Corps headquarters, just south of Taneytown. Hancock was waiting outside his tent.

Meade dismounted, steadied himself for a moment, then said softly, "General Reynolds is dead."

Hancock bowed his head. "Damn Rebels. Damn them to hell."

"I'm ordering you to the front, where you will take command of First and Eleventh Corps forces at Gettysburg and Third Corps forces at Emmitsburg," Meade directed. "I want you to advise me if Gettysburg is a good place to fight under the existing circumstances. If so, I will order all troops there. If not, our forces will occupy the Pipe Creek line."

Hancock stared, shaking his head.

"I'm staying at Taneytown, where I'm better positioned to manage the defense of the Pipe Creek line," Meade continued. "Only two infantry corps are at Gettysburg; the remaining bulk of them are closer to Taneytown. I haven't given up hope that the general engagement will be along Pipe Creek. If, however, you determine the ground at Gettysburg can be defended, we will depart immediately for the front."

There was a second of silence.

Almost apologetically, Hancock said, "Howard is senior to me. He will not relinquish command to me."

"Well," Meade said icily, "I don't know Howard well, and I'm not sure how he will react, but I assume he did not receive the Pipe Creek Circular. I must have a commander I can trust and who knows my intent."

Hancock nodded.

"I appreciate your apprehension. But General Halleck granted me the power to appoint officers to command based on ability and not seniority. I'm choosing to exercise this power by appointing you to replace Reynolds as overall commander of the forces at Gettysburg."

Hancock stared tight-lipped.

"Depart now for Gettysburg," Meade said. "As you ride, look for positions the army might concentrate and defend. I'm appointing Gibbon to assume command of Second Corps, even though he is not the senior division commander, and ordering him to begin marching toward Gettysburg.

"Godspeed," he added. "I eagerly await your assessment of the situation at Gettysburg."

## 20

# Hancock — Wednesday, July 1

*1:30 p.m.*
*Hancock's Second Corps headquarters at Taneytown*

In Second Corps' encampment, Hancock and his personal staff gathered around the Moses ambulance wagon, preparing to depart for Gettysburg. Hancock turned away, walked a few steps, and stopped and closed his eyes. God-awful shivers ripped through his chest. It was unbelievable that Reynolds was dead. Images of Reynolds riding with perfect form on his black horse bounced around his mind as if he were still alive. His nerves fidgeted like a frightened hare. His mentor and friend gone, forever.

Hancock turned back and walked toward his staff, collecting his resolve. He stopped before Morgan. "Send a courier to have the other two division commanders come to headquarters. I want to talk with them before I depart." Morgan started immediately toward the couriers standing next to their horses.

Hancock shook his head. Meade had ordered him to ride forward and assume command of the army's left wing forces and Gibbon to assume command of Second Corps. This was an unbelievable stroke of providence for Hancock. He loved the thrill of leading men in battle. His growing excitement sounded like a creek burbling in his ears.

It was an hour and a half past high noon, hot and muggy.

Hancock cocked his head toward a bright-cheeked lieutenant and jerked a nod. Lieutenant William Mitchell, Hancock's aide-de-camp, strode over to him.

"William, ride ahead to General Howard and tell him General Meade has ordered me to take command of all forces at Gettysburg," Hancock said. "Howard will be pissed. Do not argue with him. Tell him that I will be arriving shortly, but I wanted to give him a heads-up about Meade's orders so he is not blindsided by my arrival."

"I understand," Mitchell said.

"As soon as you speak with Howard, ride back down the Taneytown Road, where we will meet. I should be only a few miles from Gettysburg by then."

Mitchell nodded, waiting.

Hancock reached out and grabbed William's shoulder. After a momentary pause, he said, "Godspeed. Please be careful. I can't lose you and Reynolds in the same day." He released his grip.

Mitchell saluted smartly, mounted a splendid chestnut horse, and galloped up the Taneytown Road toward Gettysburg.

"Stay safe," Hancock whispered.

As he watched Mitchell crest the hill, an inescapable excitement swelled Hancock's chest. A hellish battle was waiting for him to command.

He turned to Gibbon. "I'm not sure what I'm going to find at Gettysburg, but I think it's prudent that Second Corps be ready to move. My instincts tell me that Meade will want you to move forward to Gettysburg or back to the Pipe Creek line."

Gibbon shook his head. "It's disturbing that Meade is not following rank and precedence in promoting generals for command. General Caldwell outranks me and should assume command of Second Corps."

Hancock gestured for Gibbon to walk with him past the circle of bystanders. Away from others, Hancock paused.

"I know you're unsettled by this rank thing," Hancock said. "I was as well, but Meade showed me the letter from Secretary Stanton authorizing him to make any changes he deemed necessary, without regard to rank, and the president would support these decisions."

Gibbon nodded. Hancock said nothing. He kicked a rock. Abruptly, without warning, he was unable to curb his swelling emotions. His grief erupted like a dam bursting, releasing a flood of tears, streaming down his cheeks. A feeling like choking rose in his throat, and he coughed.

"Reynolds is gone." Hancock choked. "He was such a fine man, nearly flawless."

Hancock closed his eyes tightly, letting the tears fall onto the ground like a hard rain. It was like entering a vivid and nightmarish dream. Reynolds had been the stabilizing element in an army that swapped out commanders after every battle. The consummate professional, the rock everyone depended on, was gone. After several moments, Hancock opened his eyes and mopped them with a handkerchief.

Gibbon stood silently, watching.

Hancock set his jaw and patted Gibbon on the shoulder.

"Meade could easily have appointed Howard to command the forces at Gettysburg," Hancock said, his eyes distant and unfocused, trying to make sense of it all. "That would have been the safe thing to do. No one would have criticized him for following the army's seniority rules for promoting officers." He came back to himself, his eyes focusing clearly on Gibbon. "But Meade believes we could lose again with Howard commanding. He took a huge risk promoting us." He drew a deep breath. "Let's not let him down."

Gibbon listened with a stolid face. After a long pause, he murmured, "They will crucify Meade if we fail."

"He believes you and I are the right officers to lead us to victory. That's why he promoted us over those more senior officers. Meade is depending on us to take the fight to the enemy and make the hard decisions."

Gibbon's lips tightened and his forehead wrinkled. Finally, with a resigned voice, he said, "Yes, sir."

"In a few moments, you will be at the head of Second Corps. You will be riding alone, John, just as Reynolds was at Gettysburg."

Gibbon smiled, slightly.

Hancock's two other division commanders arrived together. Generals Hays and Caldwell dismounted and saluted.

"I regret to inform you that General Reynolds was killed this morning at Gettysburg," Hancock announced gravely. He paused, letting the words take hold. Both men looked stunned.

"General Meade ordered me to ride to Gettysburg and take command of the forces fighting there. He also ordered Gibbon to take command of Second Corps."

Caldwell sidled up to Hancock. In a low, conspiratorial tone he whispered, "Sir, I'm senior to Gibbon. Military protocol states that I should command Second Corps."

"God damn it, I'm well versed in military protocol, General." Hancock's face flared red-hot. "President Lincoln gave General Meade permission to appoint juniors over seniors as he sees fit for this battle. So I'm not going to quibble with you about this. Do you understand?"

Hancock stared at Caldwell until the First Division commander looked down.

"Good," Hancock said. "Now get your divisions ready to move out on a moment's notice."

Hays saluted and departed. Caldwell, apparently bruised by the rebuke, broke with military tradition by departing without the customary salute. Hancock let the slight go; he had more important things to do.

He turned to Gibbon. "You will make the right choices, John, just as Reynolds did. I have the utmost confidence in you. Now let's get busy and ensure Reynolds's death was not in vain."

Hancock extended his hand. Gibbon gripped it firmly, shaking it. They exchanged salutes and Hancock smiled. "I'd better ride forward to Gettysburg."

Hancock walked toward the large Moses ambulance wagon. It was framed with light wood, with a canvas roof stretched over the top and down the flanks. Inside it held fourteen portable seats. Hancock's staff had raised the seats on one side, locking them into an upright position. They had removed the seat back cushions and laid them on the wooden floor to create a single bed. They left the seats on the other side rigged so Hancock and his aides could sit, using the bed as a map table.

Hancock climbed up the two steps in the rear and into the ambulance, snaking sideways down the row of chairs and wriggling into one across from the makeshift map table. Waiting for him inside were Colonel Morgan and Major Riddle from Reynolds's staff.

"Everyone is aboard," Morgan shouted. "Let's move out."

The ambulance driver snapped the reins and the wagon lurched forward, bouncing toward Gettysburg, thirteen miles away. Hancock's personal staff, including his guidon, rode behind, leading three riderless horses.

Hancock looked out the back and spotted Gibbon. Hancock waved his large-brimmed hat. Gibbon saluted smartly.

In the ambulance, Hancock pointed back toward Taneytown's scattered houses. "My grandfather visited this same village during the Revolutionary War in 1777 to pick up prisoners following the British surrender at the Battle of Saratoga," he mused. Hancock continued to look back, his mind in a different time, remembering a glorious past.

Then he remembered Meade's order, plucked it from his jacket, and opened it for Morgan:

*Headquarters, Army of the Potomac: July 1, 1863 — 1:10 p.m.*

*The Commanding General has just been informed General Reynolds has been killed. He directs that you turn over command of your corps to General Gibbon; and that you proceed to the front, and by virtue of this order, in case of the truth of General Reynolds's death, you assume command of the corps there assembled, Eleventh, First, and Third, at Emmitsburg. If you think the ground and position there a better one to fight a battle under existing circumstances, you will so advise General Meade, and he will order up all the troops. You know the general's views, and General Warren, who is fully aware of them, has gone out to see General Reynolds.[10]*

10 Shortly before Meade gave this order to Hancock, Meade ordered Warren to ride from Taneytown to Emmitsburg and then ride up the Emmitsburg Road to Gettysburg. In traveling this route, Warren would learn where Sickles's Third Corps was along the Emmitsburg Road.

Meade instructed Warren to meet with General Reynolds if he was still alive. If Reynolds was dead, Warren was to support Hancock when he arrived at Gettysburg. Warren was not riding to Gettysburg to view Reynolds's body or his funeral possession, as the order seems to indicate.

Hancock lighted a cigar. This was a great moment of truth for Meade. No one doubted his physical courage. But appointing him over Howard was a display of moral courage not seen before in the commanding general of the Army of the Potomac. Meade called no council of war. He alone made the decision. Howard and Sickles, both senior to Hancock, would object strenuously to him assuming command while they were on the battlefield. Gibbon was right. If he failed at Gettysburg, Meade would face unholy hell that would destroy him.

Hancock blew a smoke ring and turned back to the makeshift map table, scooting to the edge of the chair. He stared closely at the Taneytown Road as it snaked toward Gettysburg. Using his finger, he traced its path, looking for natural defensive lines that could be easily defended if he had to order the army's retreat. He then studied the approaches the Rebels would use to mass at Gettysburg. They would be swarming over two narrow roads, destroying everything in their path. From the West they would be moving along Cashtown Road; from the North they would be moving down Carlisle Road.

* * *

*1:45 p.m.*
*From Taneytown, Maryland, to Gettysburg, Pennsylvania, about 13 miles*

The driver was pushing the horses hard, snapping the whip freely. The passengers could barely carry on a conversation. The wagon bounced and bobbed side to side, creaking and moaning like a wooden frigate cresting through white water. Suddenly the wagon lurched hard left, spilling the officers out of their seats.

"Christ almighty," Hancock said, "can't that muleskinner drive a steady course?"

He glanced up the Taneytown Road. He was growing weary of the ambulance's rough ride and slow pace. He had to get to Gettysburg fast, but before riding forward, he needed to understand the lay of the land and what had happened so far.

"Major Riddle," Hancock shouted, "Tell me about the scrap Buford and Reynolds fought this morning at Gettysburg."

Riddle nodded, sucked his bottom lip and leaned forward over the map table. He pointed to the Chambersburg Pike west of Gettysburg.

"Most of the fighting this morning took place west of Gettysburg. There is a great deal of open country to the west and south of the town. With few exceptions, the dominant features are north-south ridgelines. The three dominant ridgelines west of town are Seminary Ridge, McPherson's Ridge, and Herr's Ridge."

Riddle traced each ridge with his finger.

"Seminary Ridge is roughly three-quarters of a mile from town. It is well-wooded, and a Luthcran Theological Seminary sits on the ridge, just south of the Chambersburg Pike. About a half mile further west is McPherson Ridge, consisting of patches of woods on rolling hills. Herr's Ridge is two miles from Gettysburg."

Hancock nodded.

"Buford deployed his two small cavalry brigades in a battle line the night before along McPherson Ridge," Riddle continued. "He positioned pickets near Herr's Ridge. The Rebels were camped in his immediate front to the west of Cashtown. Just about sunrise, lead Rebel elements of General Henry Heth began marching toward Gettysburg."

"Is Heth still a division commander in General A.P. Hill's corps?" Hancock said.

"Yes. Heth was the lead element of A.P. Hill's corps rolling down the road."

"Good old Harry Heth," Hancock said. "Dead last in his class at West Point just like his class clown cousin George Pickett. What a pair of knuckleheads."

"Buford's advance pickets engaged Heth's forces, warning Buford the Rebels were approaching. Buford realized he was heavily outnumbered, but if he could keep the massive Rebel columns bunched up on Chambersburg Road, he might delay them until Reynolds arrived. Buford's forces made a stubborn fight, slowing the Rebel advance and costing them dearly, and then retreating slowly to the next ridge."

Riddle pointed to McPherson Ridge.

"What time was this?" Hancock asked.

"Around nine in the morning."

"Continue."

"About this same time, Reynolds's advance party was about half the distance between Moritz Tavern and Gettysburg. At 4:00 a.m. Reynolds had received Meade's orders to advance to Gettysburg."

"Did Reynolds receive the Pipe Creek Circular?"

"No, he did not."

Hancock shook his head.

"We departed Moritz Tavern at 8:00 a.m. and traveled the Emmitsburg Road. Reynolds and his staff rode at the head of the lead infantry division. I heard Reynolds tell Colonel Wainwright, the First Corps artillery chief, that he expected a quiet day and was only moving up so as to be within supporting distance to Buford, who was going to push out farther from Gettysburg."

"When did you learn Buford was engaged with the enemy?"

"It was nearly 9:00 a.m. when we heard booming and gunfire in the distance. We were within a mile or so south of Gettysburg, moving north on the Emmitsburg Road."

Hancock listened intently, his eyes fixed on the map.

"On the Emmitsburg Road we saw a courier galloping toward us," Riddle said. "Buford had sent a note saying the Rebels were advancing east on the Chambersburg Pike toward Gettysburg. Reynolds asked how many Rebels were advancing, and the courier said heavy columns of about 4,000 infantry were approaching Buford's two brigades and the Rebels were beginning to fan out and form a long line of battle. Buford's dismounted cavalry and Lieutenant John Calef's artillery battery were fully engaged.

"Reynolds immediately galloped toward Gettysburg, his advance party following closely. He slowed at Cemetery Hill. The cemetery gatehouse is a large two-column arch structure.

"'We should put a reserve unit on this Cemetery Hill,' Reynolds said.

"Reynolds then hurried through Gettysburg, heading west on Chambersburg Pike, where he found Buford's cavalry defending

McPherson's Ridge," Riddle said. "Buford's dismounted troops were laying down a storm of lead, firing in excess of twenty rounds a minute with their magazine-fed, repeating Spencer rifles. It was a magnificent sight. I have to tell you, sir, I've never seen such a display of so much firepower by so few troops."

Hancock nodded approvingly. "What did Reynolds and Buford discuss?"

"Buford said he was mighty relieved to see Reynolds," Riddle recounted. "Buford explained he had deployed his cavalry troops as dismounted infantry and planned to yield ground stingily, falling back slowly until Reynolds had arrived. Buford had rejected the idea of holding the forward line at all cost because he couldn't create a single, strong defensive line that could withstand an attack from the Rebels, who heavily outnumbered him. So Buford placed his troops on McPherson Ridge in successive withdrawing echelons designed to absorb attacks and give ground slowly. In doing so, he could fight a strong delaying action until the infantry corps arrived. Reynolds said it was brilliant."

"Did they discuss Buford's ammo supply?" Hancock said.

"Yes, Buford said he was starting to run low on bullets and could sustain the fight for about another half hour."

Hancock nodded approvingly. He closed his eyes, visualizing the Kentuckian, the fierce Indian fighter on the Western frontier, battling with flare and tenacity. There was not a finer officer in either army.

Riddle carried on with his story. "Rebel officers moved on horseback along the line of fourteen Confederate battle flags. Then they attacked. The wailing Rebel Yell, and the firing began again, spreading all down the line."

"Had Reynolds's corps arrived yet?"

"Not yet. Just the Black Hat Brigade. Reynolds told Buford to hold the Rebels in check as long as possible, to keep them from getting into town. Buford said he'd do his best. Reynolds then told his aide, Captain Weld, to ride to General Meade with all speed and tell him the Confederates were coming on in strong force, and that they might get to the heights on Cemetery

Hill before he could. But he said he would fight the Rebels all through the town and keep them back as long as possible."

Riddle's voice lowered. "Smoke hung over McPherson's ridge, reducing visibility. Bullets zipped overhead, but surprisingly, very few Rebel artillery shells. Reynolds's officers and aides bunched near him, receiving rapid-fire orders. Reynolds was inspirational and in full command. He told an aide to tell General Wadsworth he needed him to move his division at best speed to the ridge.

"Captain Hall, who Howard had sent ahead to get orders, arrived, and Reynolds told him to have Howard advance the Eleventh Corps to Gettysburg with all speed. He wanted Howard to place a strong reserve of infantry and artillery on Cemetery Hill, near the gate. If the Rebels were able to push us off the ridges and through the town, he was going to make a stand at Cemetery Hill."

Hancock shook his head.

"Howard was to ride ahead of Eleventh Corps. Reynolds wanted to talk with him about our right flank. He was worried about the Confederates sweeping down from the north over a ridge called Oak Hill, enveloping First Corps."

Hancock interrupted. "Show me where Reynolds wanted Howard's reserve element."

Riddle pointed to the spot on the map—Cemetery Hill.

Hancock traced the Baltimore Pike running southeast from Cemetery Hill. His finger paused on Culp's Hill. "Did Reynolds ride to Culp's Hill?"

Riddle said, "No, sir. But we saw it from Cemetery Hill. Culp's Hill is less than a half mile away. It's two rounded peaks, separated by a narrow saddle. The higher peak is heavily wooded. Culp's Hill dominates Cemetery Hill and Baltimore Pike. It's about 100 feet higher than Cemetery Hill, which sits about 100 feet above the town of Gettysburg."[11]

Hancock grinned. "Damn good ground." He just hoped Howard had put reinforcements on these hills as well.

"What about Sickles?" Hancock asked.

---

11 Cemetery Hill is 503 feet. It is 80 feet above the town center and 100 feet above Winebrenner's Run at its base. Culp's Hill is 630 feet and 530 feet.

Riddle shook his head. "Reynolds sent a courier to Sickles to bring up Third Corps from Emmitsburg. But Reynolds was not confident Sickles's corps would arrive in time to support First and Eleventh Corps."

Hancock grumbled. Sickles didn't have any business commanding a corps.

Abruptly, Hancock pitched forward, hitting his head on a side board as the ambulance swerved off the narrow road to pass a train of six-mule wagons headed for Gettysburg with ammunition and artillery shells.

"God damn it," Hancock yelled, as he rubbed his knotted head. He bit down hard to cut off the throbbing. "Lost my balance. Please continue, Major Riddle."

"After Reynolds dispatched orders to Howard's aide," Riddle said, "he and his aides rode hard back through town and down the Emmitsburg Road toward Wadsworth's division, the head column of First Corps. To save time, Reynolds ordered his aides to tear down the roadside fences on the west side of Emmitsburg Road and then ordered the divisions to depart from Emmitsburg Road where we had removed the fences and march across the open fields to McPherson Ridge. He waited until Wadsworth arrived and told him to have his division cut across the fields toward the Lutheran Seminary and bypass Gettysburg."

"What time was this?" Hancock asked.

"Around 10:40. The Confederates apparently were marching on a single road toward Gettysburg, so they were racing to put troops on the battlefield. Reynolds thought the scrap that morning was an unintended meeting, based on the disorderly fashion the enemy was engaging Buford. Buford also thought the Confederates were surprised to find his dismounted cavalry waiting for them as they moved toward Gettysburg."

Hancock turned to Morgan and shouted, "We are going to disembark in a few minutes and ride to Gettysburg." He turned to Riddle, "Go ahead."

"When the Rebels failed to push Buford off the ridge, they fanned out into a battle line and attacked again. Buford greeted them with a horrendous fire and crept slowly backward, firing steadily, giving up ground deliberately so he would not be flanked. At the moment, neither side had an advantage. Buford was controlling the key terrain west of Gettysburg and occupying the single approach road from Cashtown, but he was heavily outnumbered. Reynolds knew he would have to retreat into Gettysburg, but he thought if First Corps could move and act faster than the enemy, it could provide Buford a powerful advantage and surprise the enemy. He figured the Rebels knew they were fighting a couple of light cavalry brigades and would not be expecting an entire infantry corps."

"Show me McPherson's Ridge again," Hancock said.

Riddle pointed to the ridge.

"Reynolds told Wadsworth to march his division with all speed to McPherson's Ridge and relieve Buford's besieged troops. Wadsworth departed immediately. Leading the column was Cutler's Iron Brigade that was followed by Captain Hall's Second Maine battery. Reynolds directed traffic, encouraging the men to hurry forward. Behind him, the men could see shells bursting in the sky west of town. Artillery projectiles were shrieking overhead.

"Sickles's chief aide, Major Henry Tremain, then arrived, bringing Sickles's respects and asking if Reynolds had updated orders for Third Corps. Reynolds said he had better come up to Gettysburg immediately.

"After the Iron Brigade passed, Reynolds headed to McPherson's Ridge, where he posted Hall's battery and Cutler's brigade. When the Iron Brigade arrived, he posted them and yelled for them to drive the Rebels from the woods. He was then killed."

Hancock paused and shook his head. After a moment he asked, "How did the Iron Brigade perform?"

"Brilliantly. The Second Wisconsin regiment was first to arrive and engage the enemy. Close on their heels was the Twenty-Fourth Michigan regiment, which fired and kept advancing on the left of the Second Wisconsin into the smoke-filled woods without reloading. These two regiments were quickly joined by the Nineteenth Indiana and Seventh Wisconsin regiments. In total the Iron Brigade of about 1,500 men smashed into Archer's Brigade of equal size and swept them away. It was a beautiful sight. I heard a Rebel shout out, 'There are those damned black-hatted fellows again.' The Iron Brigade captured General Archer and about 200 Rebels."

Hancock beamed. "That's damn good. That Iron Brigade is one of toughest units in the army. What about casualties?"

"They're heavy on both sides. It's a bloodbath like Antietam."

*2:00 p.m.*

Hancock had heard enough. The terrain Reynolds had identified as Cemetery Hill was the key to this battle. Howard must hold it, and he must occupy the key terrain of Culp's Hill. He turned to Morgan, his chief of staff. "It's time to ride to Gettysburg. Call for the horses."

Morgan bellowed forward to the teamster to halt. Hancock, Morgan, and Riddle departed the wagon and mounted their horses. Hancock rode the sorrel, his quickest horse. He pulled off the road momentarily, pausing to retrieve his binoculars and scan the terrain, looking for possible natural positions the forces in Gettysburg could defend if they had to withdraw. His sword flashed in the sun as he turned in the saddle, his eyes moving rapidly over the wide, undulating plains.

Abruptly, he said, "Let's see what Lee's been up to in Gettysburg."

They moved out rapidly, Hancock in the lead. His guidon rode out to join him, carrying his command flag. Morgan and the remaining staff rode behind. They followed the serpentine Taneytown Road, weaving in and out of the long lines of Howard's logistics trains moving to the front.

A soaring exhilaration rippled across Hancock's skin, so intense it almost tingled. The order to relieve Howard was stuffed in his pocket. All his life he had felt he was destined to do something great for his country. This was it. This was the moment. His first independent command.

He lived for these life-and-death moments.

*2:30 p.m.*

The road ahead was jammed by several mounted Union officers escorting an ambulance. Hancock slowed and almost came to a stop. As he crept forward, he recognized the escort officers as Reynolds's personal staff.

"Oh my God," he muttered softly, "Reynolds is in the ambulance." The aching hollowness that had pervaded him earlier renewed tenfold, and the day around him darkened despite the afternoon sun. Reynolds's forlorn officers stopped the ambulance. They saluted Hancock.

Hancock dismounted, walked to the ambulance, and climbed aboard.

He removed the frayed blanket covering the makeshift coffin, saw Reynolds's peaceful face. But he did not see the bullet wound. Sergeant Veil, Reynolds's orderly, seemed to read his mind and turned Reynolds's head to the side, showing where the Minié ball had struck. Hancock fought back the grief, giving a silent prayer as anger simmered inside him.

There was little time to mourn. He had to get to Gettysburg. Hancock covered Reynolds with the blanket, climbed out of the ambulance, and mounted his horse, swiftly urging it to a gallop. Seeing Reynolds had stunned him. My God, the man was dead after hardly an hour on the battlefield. *Will I be dead an hour from now?* He had never thought about it before. Would his officers be as distraught and distressed as Reynolds's officers?

---

*3:10 p.m.*

He spotted Lieutenant Mitchell riding hard toward him. Mitchell approached and turned his horse around, pulling up to ride with Hancock toward Gettysburg. Hancock slowed to a trot.

"How was your visit with Howard?" Hancock asked.

"Howard was shocked and said under no circumstances would he relinquish command to you when you arrived," Mitchell said.

"Very well. That's the answer I would have given if I were in Howard's shoes," he replied. "What does the battle look like?"

Mitchell shook his head, "It's not good. Howard's Eleventh Corps has broken and is running through Gettysburg toward

Cemetery Hill. Stonewall Jackson's old Rebel corps demolished Howard's corps just like it did at Chancellorsville. Howard's retreat caused Doubleday, holding the Union left flank, to cave in and retreat as well. No one seems to be in charge."

Hancock was furious. He worried he would not arrive in time. With Howard's corps breaking, he had a sinking feeling Gettysburg could be a repeat of Chancellorsville.

"Let's go!" he cried as he spurred his horse into a gallop. Gettysburg was two miles ahead. Hancock could hear the booming thunder of artillery echoing overhead. *Please God,* he prayed silently, *give us a chance.*

# 21

# Sickles — Wednesday, July 1

*7:00 a.m.*
*Eight hours earlier*
*Third Corps' march toward Taneytown, Maryland*

Sickles rode slowly toward the green ridges of South Mountain, tapping his thumb against the saddle horn. He snarled as he scanned the terrain, the reddish dawn, the dark clouds hanging in low puffs. A chilling, irksome rain fell softly. Here and there flocks of small black birds raced from one grove of trees to another. His pulse jittered like a shivering dog.

At every opportunity, Meade had criticized his performance, complaining his corps was moving too slowly, failing to live up to Meade's ridiculous expectations. This morning would be no different. For the rest of the short march to Emmitsburg, Meade's hissing voice echoed in his brain, sharp and foul.

Sickles peered through his binoculars. *We must be getting close to Emmitsburg.* Sloshing horse hooves approached from behind. The chief of the Third Corps artillery brigade, Captain George Randolph, paused next to Sickles, riding on a mud-splattered horse.

"How are the gunners doing?" Sickles asked.

"No complaints," Randolph replied. "When we arrive at Emmitsburg, do you want me to leave the batteries mounted to the limbers and caissons or deploy them for possible action?"

"I want the batteries to remain mounted. I'm not sure how long we will remain there. It all depends on what Reynolds finds in Gettysburg."

Sickles twisted in his saddle, his eyes darting through the marching columns, nearly 11,000 men and thirty guns, snaking slowly along. The usual bantering and singing was absent. Heart rattling, he twisted back around, glowering as dark images of

276

Meade chewing his ass filled his head. His nerves were stretched tight. He had disobeyed Meade's marching orders.

He reached into his jacket pocket and quickly reread Meade's order, sent yesterday at 12:45 p.m. It directed him to march to Emmitsburg and report to Reynolds, who was the new tactical commander of the left wing, consisting of the First, Third, and Eleventh Corps. But later that afternoon, Reynolds had ordered him to bivouac five miles short of Emmitsburg. *Devil be damned!*

Sickles scratched his chin. He had never faced conflicting orders before. As much as he despised the man, he didn't want to disobey Meade and get fired. But had Meade sent orders to Reynolds to order him to bivouac short of Emmitsburg? Or was Meade issuing orders directly to him and bypassing Reynolds? *If Hooker were still in command, I would just ride over and get clarification. You don't do that with Meade. The old snapping turtle would cut off my head.*

Both men were his superiors; which one should he obey? He had even sent a written request to Williams late afternoon yesterday asking for clarification. He didn't hear back from Meade's headquarters, so he had dubiously disobeyed Meade's orders yesterday afternoon to march from Taneytown to Emmitsburg and bivouac there for the evening. Instead, he made the shaky decision to obey Reynolds, and bivouacked five miles short of Emmitsburg. After all, that was the chain of command, right? Any barefoot corporal greenhorn knew that! Meade was useless. This was the Devil's absurdity! Reynolds it was. Sickles tried to repress a shudder.

Birney rode up, and Sickles gave a hearty wave and flashed a huge grin at his trusted division commander. "I'm not sure how long we will stay at Emmitsburg. But I'm not moving until we have orders from Meade."

"It's a confusing situation," Birney agreed. "And with Meade hanging back at Taneytown, it's even more unclear."

"Agreed. Yesterday afternoon after Third Corps arrived at Taneytown, Meade ordered me to Emmitsburg, taking three days' rations in haversacks, sixty rounds of ammunition, and my ambulances. I had to leave all other trains at Taneytown until further notice. All of it! Then Meade informs me that Third Corps is now under tactical control of Reynolds, commanding the left wing—First, Third, and Eleventh Corps."

"Why did Meade put you under Reynolds's control?"

"Because Meade doesn't know a damn thing about commanding an army!" Sickles brandished his cigar like a sword. "It's hard to command forces at Gettysburg when you're 13 miles away, sitting on your fat ass."

"Why did we bivouac near Bridgeport and not Emmitsburg?" Birney asked.

"After Third Corps had been marching for a few hours toward Emmitsburg, a First Corps courier arrived. He told me that Reynolds had arrived at Moritz Tavern, about halfway between Emmitsburg and Gettysburg. Reynolds *instructed* me to stop five miles short of Emmitsburg, bivouacking at the Cattail Branch of the Monocacy River near Bridgeport."

Sickles puffed on his cigar. "I told Reynolds's courier that Meade had ordered Third Corps to Emmitsburg. I was completely baffled—*completely baffled*—so I told the courier I would obey Reynolds's orders."

"Why did Reynolds countermand Meade's orders for Third Corps to march to Emmitsburg?" Birney asked.

"Reynolds and Meade are conspiring to snare me into their trap!" Sickles leaned toward Birney and fixed him with two bloodshot eyes. "They want me to disobey orders so Meade can fire me. Meade plotted to get Hooker fired, now he is after my ass. Next will be Butterfield, you mark my word."

"This isn't the first time you've received conflicting orders since Meade assumed command," Birney mused.

Sickles's skin prickled, crawling and tingling with fear. He had disobeyed Meade. "I'm unsure if Meade's orders supersede Reynolds's instructions. Does Meade have the authority to bypass the newly appointed wing commander and give orders directly to me?"

"I'm not sure, but I would continue to follow Reynolds's instructions," Birney said, shaking his head. "Meade is proving to be completely incompetent."

"I'm also pissed off because Meade bypassed me and ordered Humphreys to examine the ground at Emmitsburg and report back to Meade on whether it could support a fight. That's a clear violation of the chain of command and sets a bad precedent."

"Meade is an idiot," Birney said. "He is unable to issue clear and decisive instructions. Lincoln made a monstrous mistake, appointing Meade to command the army."

"Unsure what to do last night," Sickles droned on, "I wrote a note to Williams asking for clarification on where to bivouac: Bridgeport or Emmitsburg? Receiving no response, I stopped five miles short of Emmitsburg." He shrugged, making a helpless gesture with his hands. "What else could I have done?"

*7:30 a.m.*

Sickles and Birney chatted for a few more minutes before Birney rode back to his division. Third Corps engineers returned from Emmitsburg, reporting they had located this morning's encampment, a mile north of the town.

Uncertainty plagued Sickles as he rode the long slope toward Emmitsburg. He had not received any orders overnight from Reynolds to move to Emmitsburg, nor had he heard from Meade this morning. Since Meade's orders yesterday were to march to Emmitsburg, Sickles guessed it was safe to march early this morning the five miles from Bridgeport. He was in great trouble if he was wrong, but he would rather face Reynolds than Meade.

Sickles rubbed the side of his head. He had awakened this morning cobwebby, his head throbbing. Sitting around the campfire last night, he had smoked fat cigars and sipped brandy, wishing Hooker were still in command. Feeling the brandy's effects and gaining confidence, he pontificated, reminding his personal staff that while living in England he had learned that Samuel Johnson, arguably the most distinguished man of letters in English history, had asserted that "a hero must drink brandy." Then he bawled, "Now pass the bottle back!" He was paying the price this morning for his overindulgence.

Tremain, his senior aide, rode up, saluting. "Emmitsburg is just ahead," he said. Tremain gestured, pointing his gloved hand forward. Sickles spotted the many steeples of Emmitsburg which were now visible above the tree line. He wiped his face; a knot loosened inside.

He was eager to stop and dismount, having been constantly in the saddle for the past three days. His chest wound pulsed, burning like hot coals. He had grown soft convalescing at home after his injury at Chancellorsville.

It had stopped raining. A murderous sun was continuing its rise in the east. The fields near Emmitsburg were littered with the clutter left by Reynolds's First Corps and Howard's Twelfth Corps. Sickles's soldiers marched slowly on the winding road around the last crown of low-rising hills. No music was playing. The soldiers halted on the far northern side of town.

Sickles looked through his binoculars northward up the Emmitsburg Road. No booming cannons echoing from Gettysburg, but he was not sure if he should remain at Emmitsburg. A huge part of him wanted to keep moving and join Reynolds and Howard. But did Reynolds want me to follow him to Gettysburg? Meade remained silent on this issue. He wasn't sure what to do.

"Tremain!" Sickles shouted.

Tremain rode up and stopped.

"Ride on to Reynolds's headquarters and ask about the positions of the other units of the left wing," Sickles said. "Tell him Third Corps has arrived at the northern part of Emmitsburg. Also, ask for the wing commander's orders for Third Corps."

Tremain saluted and galloped off.

Sickles's head pounded. But he couldn't blame Meade entirely for his headache. The brandy was partly to blame. Meade was keeping him in the dark. He sighed. *Be vigilant and protect yourself. Meade is looking to court-martial you.*

The heavy thud of clapping horse hooves echoed off the road. He spied a courier from Meade's headquarters. What now?

*8:00 a.m.*

The courier saluted and slid down from his horse. He handed Sickles the order. "General Sickles, I'm delivering the Pipe Creek Circular."

> *The Commanding General has successfully relieved Harrisburg and prevented the invasion of Philadelphia. He no longer will assume the offensive. This circular details the plan for the whole army to retire and take up the defensive on Pipe Creek.*

Sickles's cheeks heated and his heart thumped like a caged animal. Son of a bitch. Knowing the fight was coming and expecting a Union defeat at Gettysburg, Meade had designed the Pipe Creek Circular, preferring to retreat and not support Reynolds.

His eyes narrowed and a low groan rumbled from his throat. All his life he had been a decisive man, taking the fight to others. This was ridiculous. *The Union has a chance to hit first and take the fight to the Confederates and win, and Meade wants to retreat. Meade is a coward.*

Sickles rubbed his eyes. What was his role in this ruinous debacle? He read the circular again. His role was to remain at Emmitsburg to cover Reynolds's retreat and then withdraw through Mechanicsville to Middleburg, where he was to deploy his corps along Pipe Creek.

*To hell with Meade. I'm not doing anything until I hear back from Tremain.* For a short while Sickles strolled about, mumbling to himself, digesting the Pipe Creek Circular. Something dark and cold coiled in his gut. Meade did not want him involved in any of the Gettysburg action. Meade was trying to end his military career. This was payback for Chancellorsville.

---

*12:00 p.m.*

After what seemed ages, Henry Tremain arrived, skidding to a stop, sweat streaming from his face. His blue eyes were alarmed. In a throaty voice, he reported, "Reynolds moved out from his Emmitsburg bivouac early this morning, marching toward Gettysburg. About two miles from Gettysburg I heard booming and could see powder smoke drifting upward. As I moved forward, I could hear the cracking sounds of rifle fire mixing with the low thumping of artillery. I found Reynolds on the southern approach to the town."

Sickles scowled, his chest tightened.

"I overtook Robinson's division, which was last in the First Corps line of march," Tremain said. "They were closed up, coming on rapidly, almost double-timing. Reynolds was ahead at a break in the fence line, directing troops across a large open field toward a white cupola west of Gettysburg. I spotted the Black Hats of the Iron Brigade moving toward a ridge just beyond the cupola."

Sickles nodded nervously, his breath quickening.

"I asked Reynolds what orders he had for Third Corps. He said, 'Tell General Sickles I think he better come. Tell him to make best speed. Leave his logistics trains in Emmitsburg."

Tremain looked at Sickles, who said nothing. Tremain continued.

"I waited for General Reynolds to say something more. I was gravely concerned. I did not know who was fighting. But he provided no additional details. He glanced at me and said, 'Godspeed, Major Tremain. Give my regards to General Sickles.' I saluted and rode off."

Sickles briskly shook his head and licked his lips. "I don't understand. Did General Reynolds discuss the Pipe Creek Circular?"

"He did not. I don't know anything about it, either."

Sickles glared at Tremain, blood churning in his ears. He said, "The Pipe Creek Circular is a withdrawal order. A headquarters courier delivered it after you departed for Gettysburg."

Sickles paused and scratched his face. "Do you think Reynolds received the Pipe Creek withdrawal order and ignored it?"

"I don't think he received it because he never mentioned it."

Tremain excused himself. Sickles started pacing. He wanted to rush forward, but he worried about Meade. What a damnable dilemma. He had seemingly contradictory orders from Reynolds and Meade—again. And again, Sickles wished Hooker were still commanding. His panicky stomach knotted. This was his first serious action as a corps commander without Hooker providing friendly oversight, mentorship. Sickles's mind froze, going silent as if paralyzed.

General Birney and Colonel Trobriand rode up. Birney's face was glowing, his voice rigid with anticipation.

"General, do you want me to prepare First Division to march to Gettysburg?" he asked.

Sickles hesitated and shook his head. A slow-tolling death knell was beating in his skull. *Do something. Make a decision.* He cocked his head toward his staff officers, spotting Captain Alexander Moore.

Sickles yelled. "Captain Moore!"

Moore walked quickly over. "Ride swiftly to Gettysburg and ask Reynolds if he wants Third Corps to come up to Gettysburg or to stay at Emmitsburg in accordance with Meade's Pipe Creek Circular."

Moore saluted and rode off.

Sickles turned to Birney. "Third Corps will wait here until I hear back from Captain Moore."

"Yes, sir," Birney replied.

"I have three conflicting options: Rush to Reynolds's support; prepare to hold Emmitsburg; or prepare to execute the Pipe Creek Circular and move Third Corps toward Middleburg. Meade is ten miles to the east. Does he know about Reynolds's orders for me to march Third Corps up to Gettysburg?"

"Don't you think Reynolds told Meade he ordered you to Gettysburg?" Birney said.

"Not sure. It just doesn't make sense without knowing the larger plan—fight at Gettysburg or along Pipe Creek. For now, I'm staying at Emmitsburg, waiting for Captain Moore to return."

His instincts favored rashness—strike the first blow with the maddening frenzy of a wild animal. Without Hooker, he was alone and racked by self-doubt. His despondency reminded him of the days following his murder acquittal, sitting alone in the great halls of Congress, insulted and ostracized. After proving his courage at Chancellorsville, he was sure he had moved past those days. Painfully, he was wrong. Old Four Eyes hated him.

There would be no relief. Meade would goad him with humiliating rebukes, dishonoring him in front of his staff. He wanted a drink. No one was around, so he removed the flask from his jacket, taking a long swig, the brandy stinging the back of his throat. He extracted a cigar, lighted it, took another swig. His muscles began to relax.

*3:00 p.m.*

One of Reynolds's couriers found Sickles standing in front of his headquarters tent. "Sir, message from General Doubleday. He regrets to inform you that General Reynolds has been killed. He respectfully requests you move your corps to Gettysburg at once."

A cold shudder froze him to his bones, impervious even to the warming powers of brandy. Shaken, he asked, "Who is commanding?"

"General Doubleday."

Sickles gestured for Tremain to join him. As Tremain arrived, Major Charles Howard, a messenger for General Howard, rode up and dismounted, saluting. "General Sickles. General Howard has assumed command of all forces at Gettysburg following General Reynolds's death. General Howard requests you move your corps to Gettysburg immediately."

Sickles's mind raced. His gut told him to move Third Corps to Gettysburg and if his gut was right, the army was in great danger. Lee could smash through Howard's vanguard forces at Gettysburg and move quickly south to destroy the remaining part of the army. But if he departed for Gettysburg, he would leave the left flank of the army unguarded and face Meade's wrath for disobeying a written order telling him to stay put.

What bothered him most was Meade's Pipe Creek Circular—the withdrawal order. He looked up to see an eager face: Tremain.

"General Sickles," Tremain said, "behind the flat, open ground Reynolds was defending are large crested ridges anchored by prominent hills."

Tremain was passionate; his eyes were wide. "If the Rebels push Howard to the far eastern side of Gettysburg, the army can hunker down behind the natural defenses of the long ridges and high hills and make a stand there. The hills jut up like castles and the long ridges connect them like fortified walls."

"But with Howard commanding," Sickles said, "there is little chance we can survive even with good defensive ground."

"You, sir, have a chance to save the day," said Tremain. "I encourage you most earnestly to move Third Corps with all speed to Gettysburg."

Sickles brightened. His scalp hair prickled. He could be the hero of Gettysburg. He drew in a deep breath and held it. He could hear the men shouting as he arrived in time to rally Howard's men, saving the Republic. With any luck, the battle would be in the balance when he arrived to save the day. And that miserable Meade would still be in Taneytown, waiting to execute the cowardly Pipe Creek order.

Sickles called together his division and brigade commanders. "The storm has arrived. The First and Eleventh Corps are heavily engaged at Gettysburg. Reynolds is dead. They need help." Sickles paused for a long moment. He swallowed hard. What an opportunity! The officers stood in inspired silence.

Sickles sighed, "Howard has assumed command of the forward forces." The news elicited some audible groans.

***

*3:15 p.m.*

Sickles finished giving orders. Knowing he had to leave behind a reserve force, he detached one brigade from Birney's First Division and one brigade from Humphreys's Second Division and two artillery batteries. He placed them under General Graham's command, to stay behind and hold Emmitsburg. Leaving two brigades behind allowed him to comply with Meade's order to defend Emmitsburg. He told Graham to hold Emmitsburg as long as possible. If the enemy was an overwhelming force, he should fall back to Taneytown. Sickles cracked a grin. He'd thought of a way to comply with both commanders' contradicting orders.

285

"Let's march to the sound of the guns!" Sickles shouted.

"Do you want to send a messenger to find Humphreys wherever he's examining the ground around Emmitsburg, and let him know where his men are?" asked Tremain.

"Hell, no!" Sickles smirked. "Meade ordered Humphreys to conduct a survey of the terrain, and when he returns to Emmitsburg, he will learn that I've ordered his division to Gettysburg to save the nation."

Tremain nodded.

"Ride ahead and notify Howard that Third Corps is departing immediately for Gettysburg." Tremain saluted and departed.

Sickles then turned to his adjutant. "Send a note to General Meade. Tell him I received news from General Howard, who is engaging a large enemy force at Gettysburg. Howard requested me to support him. General Reynolds was killed. I am moving out immediately on two parallel roads to Gettysburg. I left General Graham in charge of two brigades at Emmitsburg."

---

*3:45 p.m.*

Within the half hour, Third Corps departed Emmitsburg, marching to the sound of distant guns. Sickles rode at the head of Birney's First Division. Nothing in his short experience commanding a corps had prepared him for receiving contradictory orders. In other circumstances, he knew exactly what to do, primarily because the Union army under Hooker moved at a snail's pace. If there were doubts about how to execute an order, there was plenty of time to ride over to Hooker's headquarters and chat with the commanding general. But Hooker was out. Old Four Eyes was commanding, and he was issuing conflicting orders, designing retreat plans, shifting the corps around the countryside willy-nilly.

Sickles swiveled in his saddle, looking back at Third Corps flowing along the Emmitsburg Road, thousands of flags fluttering from man-of-war mastheads. He sat proudly, his doubts quelled. The great river of blue stretched as far as the eye could see.

---

*4:15 p.m.*

They moved swiftly, nearly a forced march. It was the fastest marching Third Corps had ever done. They had been on the move for an hour when a courier from Meade arrived. Sickles read Meade's note. Crap. His breath rasped. Meade had just learned that Howard had ordered Sickles to Gettysburg. Meade ordered Sickles to stay in Emmitsburg. Sickles was to coordinate with Hancock, who had ridden to Gettysburg to relieve Howard and take command.

"Meade's an idiot," Sickles said. *I'm not turning back.* He had left a strong covering force at Emmitsburg, and it faced no enemy. That was sufficient. He would obey common sense and march toward the sounds of guns. He would push the bulk of Third Corps to Gettysburg where it could do the most good. He had a destiny of glory to achieve—and that was at Gettysburg.

With that decision, Sickles extracted a cigar from his jacket. How could Meade effectively command the battle at Gettysburg when he had decided to remain secured in his bunker at Taneytown, several miles from his corps commanders and several miles behind the front lines?

Sickles felt the warmth of unexpected opportunity. He was senior to Hancock. He would relieve Hancock upon arriving at Gettysburg. What an opportunity. He was soon going to be the nation's hero.

## ❦ 22 ❦
# First Minnesota — Wednesday, July 1

## *Wright*
*5:17 a.m.*
*Eleven hours earlier*
*(Sunrise was 4:47 a.m.)*

Sergeant Wright stood as the First Minnesota boys groused around their morning campfires. The boys flapped around like angry wet hens, pissed that Wright had rousted them two hours before dawn, expecting a dawn march. Sunrise had been half an hour ago. Another delayed marching day.

The regiment's mood was edgy and dark and overtly seditious. Stories circulated that Morgan at Second Corps headquarters had fouled up the marching orders again. The men were still raging mad over Morgan arresting Colonel Colvill two days earlier, and this morning several hotheads wanted Morgan's head. Others wanted to mutiny against the cocksure Adams—perhaps more despised by the regiment than Morgan.

They were bivouacked just north of the agricultural village of Uniontown, near Big Pipe Creek. Perched in the Maryland highlands, Uniontown was an isolated area of rolling farmlands hemmed in by long, thick rows of trees along Union Road and featuring barns, stables, washhouses, and smokehouses on shaded lots. Some six miles southeast of Taneytown, the area was generally pro-Union, and the locals proudly flew the stars and stripes.

Wright checked his watch. The smoldering sun burned hotter. Something was wrong at Hancock's headquarters, again. Wright desperately wanted the regiment to start marching before the rising hackles flared into something ugly. Hard marching tended to crush hot tempers.

Wright walked over to Colvill standing at the back of the regiment, whittling on a small branch.

Sergeant Wright saluted. "How you doing, Colonel?"

"I would be a lot better if I were commanding again," Colvill grumbled.

"Talk with brigade commander General Harrow and request to be reinstated," Wright suggested.

"I will," Colvill said with iron certainty. "But I can't push the issue too soon. I'll wait until we are nearer the battlefield, when we arrive at Gettysburg."

Wright grimaced, sharing Colvill's unease. "The boys are pretty pissed about you being arrested and Lieutenant Colonel Adams assuming command. They also are worked up over Little Crow murdering several of their relatives back in Minnesota."

"Keep a sharp eye on last night's hotheads. I won't tolerate mutinous talk. I'll handle Adams and my arrest," Colvill blurted. "I'm holding you accountable for squashing the mutinous talk of running back to Minnesota and killing Little Crow."

"I'll handle it," Wright said. He walked back among the regiment soldiers lingering about. The suspected mutinous hotheads were grousing around a campfire, drinking coffee. Wright moseyed over and stopped a few feet away.

"Do you boys mind if I pour me a cup?" Wright said. He spat the words out through gritted teeth. Without waiting for a response, he reached for the coffee pot and poured. Wright took a sip and steeled himself for a possible confrontation. The men remained silent, looking down at the ground.

---

*Tuesday, June 30*
*8:15 p.m.*
*Nine hours earlier*

The regiment had remained in bivouac at Uniontown, resting after trudging more than thirty-one miles the day before under a hot, scorching sun. The eleven companies had performed housekeeping duties, including making out their bimonthly muster rolls, according to which they would draw their pay. Throughout the day, the people of Uniontown had greeted the men, showering them with baskets of buttered bread and jugs of buttermilk.

Sergeant Wright had received permission from acting Regimental Commander Adams to allow the men to have swim call in the Big Pipe Creek. Some of the younger men had stripped down buck naked, hollering as they splashed in the water. Most of the regiment sat on large river rocks, dangling their bare feet in the mountain water.

After dinner, the men chatted around the glowing campfires, passing flasks, each soldier taking a pull on the thin metal container. As the Maryland whiskey flowed, so did the babbling voices, growing into a raucous roar. A recurring topic for the past few weeks had been the Sioux Uprising—also known as Little Crow's War—on the Minnesota frontier six months ago. President Lincoln said the Sioux had killed more than eight hundred Minnesotans—men, women, and children—in an attempt to drive the whites from Minnesota. Several of the soldiers in the First Minnesota had relatives or friends who were among those massacred. Ultimately, thirty-eight Sioux warriors were hanged on a single scaffold at Mankato, Minnesota, the largest mass execution in U.S. history.

But the regiment was furious that Little Crow remained at large. Many in the regiment, including Wright, were still worried that their loved ones might be massacred. Their fear was stoked by the gruesome tales told by supposed survivors and eyewitnesses to the massacre. Aided by the whiskey, the men's imaginations ran wild, telling stories of Little Crow ravaging their frontier farms and slaughtering their families.

As the night grew darker, a soldier in the shadows beyond the campfire shouted, "Why are we here fighting the Confederates instead of protecting our kinsmen back home? The Rebels aren't going to massacre our families."

"Let's mutiny against that asshole Adams, shoot his ass, and hightail it back to Minnesota," someone else shouted.

A man near the campfire bellowed, "Let's leave this damned Maryland hellhole tonight and find Little Crow and skin him alive!"

A tall man with the build of a bear stood up, took a swig from a flask, and raised his fist to the sky, belting out several obscenities against Little Crow. "Yes, let's leave tonight. We should protect our families. This army won't."

Wright worried; the rumblings were growing more rebellious. This would not be happening if Colvill had not been arrested. Wright tried to identify the speakers, but it was too dark. The distant voices were familiar but anonymous. But he had an idea about those sowing the seeds of sedition.

Abruptly, his best friend, Sergeant Hamlin, stood up and moved toward the bear of a man who was inciting the violence, stopping across the campfire from him. "The rumors about Little Crow are rubbish until we receive written word," Hamlin declared. "I call hogwash on your grizzly tales. Yes, many Minnesotans have been killed. Too many. But I'm not convinced of the truth of the atrocities you describe."

There was an awkward pause while several drunken men stood up, staring at Hamlin. Wright moved quickly to his side. Out of the darkness emerged a large, shadowy figure. Despite being under arrest, Colvill walked up behind Wright and Hamlin and stopped.

"Boys, it's time to turn in," Colvill said. "That's enough chatter for tonight."

The men stopped their rabble-rousing immediately and moved away from the dying fire to the haversacks serving as their beds. That was it. The night turned quiet. Colvill slipped back into the darkness.

---

*Wednesday, July 1*
*7:00 a.m.*
*First Minnesota's camp*

Second Lieutenant William Lochren, the acting adjutant, shouted, "Sergeant Wright, assemble the men. We are moving out."

A jolt snapped through Wright. He saluted, turned toward the regiment lying in the open field, and yelled, "First Minnesota: Form up!"

The men grabbed their knapsacks and rifles and scurried toward the Taneytown Road.

Lochren turned to Wright and said, with too much glee, "I heard from reliable sources at corps headquarters that Morgan's body servant accidently defaced the marching orders by dropping them in the wet grass. Morgan went berserk, knowing Hancock would skin him if Second Corps was late marching again. When he reported the incident, Hancock blew up. Morgan rode to Meade's headquarters and returned with orders for Second Corps to march immediately to Taneytown."

Wright smiled. "Colonel Colvill will want to hear of these developments," Wright said, pointing toward a large oak tree where a figure stood, back against the trunk. Lochren nodded, mounting his horse and heading over to tell Colvill the news.

Within a few moments, the First Minnesota departed for Taneytown.

Second Corps marched nonstop for the next five hours. When they were a quarter mile from Taneytown, Wright stepped out of line and paused, listening. For a moment, cracking rifle fire echoed like distant thunder. But when the First Minnesota arrived in town, all was quiet. They rested for an hour, boiling coffee, playing banjos, singing songs. They were in a good mood.

---

*2:00 p.m.*

Sergeant Wright bellowed for the regiment to fall in. Adams ordered the regiment to march quick time, keeping the ranks well closed up. Wright watched the men, their rifles right-shouldered, rocking slightly side to side. Soon the thousands of marching feet on the dirt road created a low-hanging cloud of dust, turning the regiment into three hundred shadowy figures.

---

*3:30 p.m.*
*At the rear of the First Minnesota regiment*

Colvill rode alone at the rear. He removed his yellow handkerchief from his neck, retying it with the chevron flap hanging from the bridge of his nose like a stagecoach robber. He peered ahead through the dust but could see only the rear guard of the regiment.

They had marched a mile northwest from Taneytown when distant thunder, booming, filled the sky—exploding artillery shells. As they approached the halfway mark to Gettysburg, the regiment crossed a higher ridge with an opening among the trees that provided an extended panoramic view of hot fighting. The sharp cracking of rifle fire reverberated over the rolling hills. Heavy, persistent artillery fire generated mountains of smoke puffing up into white clouds.

Second Corps continued to march steadily forward with rifles shouldered, colors fluttering, toward Gettysburg. No music. No beating of drums.

As he rode, Colvill's gut writhed and his thick lips were pressed tight. Adams was shouting that *his* regiment must step smartly. "*Your* regiment?" Colvill muttered to himself. He vowed to deal with that scoundrel later, with no witnesses.

Beyond the road, moving down from a distant knoll toward the regiment was what appeared to be a large, scattered herd of cattle. As the throng came into clear view, Colvill drew in a quick breath. A gaggle of blue skedaddlers, some breaking for the woods.

The regiment began to run into men staggering away from the battle. Some were camp followers, cooks, servants, civilian noncombatants. But most were German immigrants wearing the crescent moon insignia of Eleventh Corps—Howard's soldiers, escaping the fight and running toward the rear. Each of the men told a tale of carnage, defeat, a rout of the Army of the Potomac.

Colvill stiffened. His instincts said he should do something, but he was not commanding. So he bellowed, "Turn around, you cowards! Fall in behind us!" The shell-shocked soldiers blinked at Colvill, then hurried toward the rear of the marching column, not wishing to tangle with the snarling giant.

Despite Colvill's bellowing, the skedaddlers continued to stream by while the First Minnesota marched doggedly forward. Colvill ticked off one hundred of the deserters before he stopped counting.

He pulled out his binoculars, spotting long trains of baggage wagons racing to the rear by panic-stricken drivers escaping the fighting. The regiments ahead of the First Minnesota peeled off the road, enabling the wagons to pass. It appeared the fleeing wagons had no intention of giving way to the approaching Second Corps artillery and ambulances. Colvill set his jaw. This ought to be good: the mulish First Minnesota would not move. Colvill spotted Sergeant Wright moving off to the side of the road.

Wright swore loudly, waving his hands over this head. "Hey, fellas," he bawled, "tear down the fences and force them damn wagons to park in the fields."

The First Minnesota broke rank, running off the road and removing the roadside fences. Sergeant Wright moved to the middle of the road, drew his pistol, and pointed it at the lead wagon. The wagon driver pulled back hard on the reins. Second Lieutenant Lochren grabbed the harness and pulled the horses toward the downed fences, walking the wagon off the road. The next wagon in line followed the first. Wright used his pistol as a baton, steering the remaining wagons toward the fields.

Colvill spotted Adams sitting on his horse at the front of the regiment. The acting regimental commander had nothing to do with it. Colvill's boys had acted instinctively, without orders, to clear the road of baggage wagons. In doing so, the First Minnesota permitted Second Corps artillery and ambulances to travel uninterrupted while the infantry marched alongside.

Wright walked back to Colvill and saluted. "My compliments for a job well done," Colvill said.

"Thank you, sir." Wright said. He holstered his pistol and turned back to the regiment as it formed and began marching again.

"These are my Minnesota boys," Colvill whispered. *They fight for one another and for me. They are my brothers for whom I am willing to die.*

*That opportunity may come soon enough.*

Tomorrow, he would fix the Adams problem, one way or another.

# 23

# Hancock — Wednesday, July 1

*3:10 p.m.*
*Minutes earlier*
*En route to Gettysburg*

Hancock galloped up the Taneytown Road toward Gettysburg with Lieutenant Mitchell keeping pace alongside.

Trailing a few yards behind was the general's escort, flying Second Corps' blue swallowtail flag. Wiping burning sweat from his eyes, Hancock swerved to avoid civilian refugees escaping the battle.

"How far is Gettysburg?" Hancock asked.

"About three miles," Mitchell replied.

The cannonading of the big guns rumbled. Hancock's breath came faster, and his heart danced. The crucial moment was nearing. What situation would he find at Gettysburg—disaster or opportunity?

As they rode, Hancock scanned the area, inspecting the terrain on both sides of the Taneytown Road. An occasional white farmhouse and red Dutch barn dotted the open fields crested with low, rolling ridges. Offering little in the way of natural barriers, this was not great defensive ground. The enemy could flow down the road unimpeded like a surging spring flood.

As Hancock drew closer to the fighting, dark, puffy shell-bursts floated lazily in the sky over Gettysburg, and rifles popped like firecrackers. He visualized the blistering fighting, picturing what was happening and would happen if he didn't arrive soon.

He shouted to Mitchell. "Let's go."

Hancock spurred the horse into a full gallop, racing toward Gettysburg. Suddenly, up ahead, the Taneytown Road swelled like a river gorge with shattered blue men, horses, and wagons streaming pell-mell south, away from the battle. Hancock pulled hard on the reins, slowing to a trot. His mouth went dry. Many of the men's uniforms were covered with dark red blood seeping through. Was the battle already over?

He reached for his field glasses. His eyes strained at the scene—wounded men wobbling down the road. *Damn.* It had all the appearances of a slaughter.

Hancock turned to Mitchell, his voice booming like a bass drum. "Howard needs help!"

Hancock and Mitchell moved off to the side of the road, picking their way forward through the retreating soldiers. There were no gaudy flags and guidons tilting proudly into the wind. Repulses never had the same pageantry as armies marching into battle.

---

*3:25 p.m.*

Now the thundering of the great guns echoed with regularity, the pulse of battle at a fever pitch. The ground trembled and yelling filled the air, a chorus of whooping wolf-howls—the Rebel Yell. The Gray tide was advancing, signaling the coming of a monstrous collision of two armies. After colliding, the Rebels would continue charging, sensing victory, and Howard's boys would turn and flee—another devastating rout—unless something could be done to stop it.

Choking clouds of dust thickened every moment. The booming sky hurled shards of metal in a fierce hailstorm. Above the dust, blue sheets of powder smoke drifted over Gettysburg. The pungent bite of gunpowder filled Hancock's nostrils.

A mounted courier with a dispatch satchel slung over his chest galloped down the middle of the Taneytown Road, giving no quarter. Hancock jerked his horse hard off the side of the road and smashed into a fleeing soldier.

"Get out of the road, you idiot!" Hancock screamed. The skeedaddler bounced to his feet, eyes fearful. Hancock halted his horse, unsheathed his sword, and struck the soldier on the back with the flat side, knocking him to the ground again. The soldier screeched and scrambled off the road.

"You cowardly son of a bitch," Hancock shouted as he sheathed his sword.

He turned his horse and bolted forward, not caring if he crashed into retreating soldiers. But the thought had no sooner formed when a flock of soldiers appeared. Any minute now he expected to see Howard's Eleventh Corps rolling toward him like a prairie fire.

"Damn you, Howard," Hancock muttered. *Hell is breaking loose, and you're useless in curbing it.*

Hancock rode forward as fast as the dust clouds would allow, using his horse to force the wounded and the deserters from the road. To his left, two large round hills appeared. Beyond these two round tops were Howard and Eleventh Corps and Reynolds's remaining First Corps, probably commanded by General Doubleday.

"Are those two hills Big and Little Round Top?" Hancock asked.

"Yes," shouted Mitchell.

⋆⋆⟨ ∗ ⟩⋆⋆

*4:10 p.m*
*At Little Round Top*

From the base of Little Round Top, Hancock rode northward on the Taneytown Road, paralleling Cemetery Ridge to the west. The cemetery was a mile and half away from Big and Little Round Top. But Cemetery Hill seemed much closer. His heart surged. The two hills anchoring the southern end of the ridgeline and Cemetery Hill at the northern end would make superb natural defenses, almost as good as the Pipe Creek line. Meade—as any soldier—would be pleased with the terrain along Cemetery Ridge.

The far-off warble of bugles and the terrible Rebel Yell grew louder. Artillery was thundering steadily, like a pounding storm. Northwest of the town, the white cupola of the seminary protruded skyward like a castle turret. No sign of smoke from artillery fire or sounds of rifles west of town, where the map had shown McPherson's Ridge. Hancock gritted his teeth.

The Rebels must have pushed Howard's forces from the western fields of Gettysburg through town.

⊶⊷ • ⊶⊷

*4:20 p.m.*
*At Cemetery Hill*

He stopped near the end of Taneytown Road, just short of where the Emmitsburg Road cut across, a stone's throw from the crest on Cemetery Hill. He remained mounted, taking in the panoramic view of the town, the Union soldiers darting through the narrow streets like scrambling mice.

Hancock shuddered as the beaten blue troops tried to outrun the blossoming roar of gunfire. Abruptly, a new line of enemy gunfire opened up, sending many of the blue boys sprawling forward, dead before hitting the ground.

The Union divisions were wrecked. Reaching the cemetery crest, the scrambling soldiers fell to the ground, winded and weary from hard fighting since midmorning. Hancock grimaced. Was he witnessing another Chancellorsville disaster? Not if he could help it.

Hancock shouted to Mitchell. "We must pull together a defensive line. I'm not sure how much time we have before the Rebels come bursting through."

Mitchell said, "If the Rebels continue the attack beyond Gettysburg, they will drive Howard's men off Cemetery Hill within the hour."

Hancock's heart galloped. Yellow specks of gunfire from the town hissed overhead. The enemy fire was strengthening. He turned toward Cemetery Hill. An Eleventh Corps brigade deployed at the western base of the hill was anxiously waiting, ready for action. Two thousand kneeling infantry, shoulder to shoulder, rifles cocked, bayonets fixed.

A tingling of hope rose up and splayed in his chest. "It appears Howard planned ahead, anticipating the need for a reserve occupying a strong natural position."

Mitchell nodded. "That's good. I wonder if Reynolds told him to do it?"

"Not sure whose idea it was, but it was a brilliant move."

298

Hancock trotted his horse up the hill, stopping close to the brigade of soldiers. The reserve brigade wore worried faces, awaiting the flood tide of Rebels. Hancock turned and scanned the streets of Gettysburg below. The enemy would soon emerge from the town, forming in long lines, and then charge and probably overrun the brigade. The tightness around his heart increased fourfold. If he didn't take command soon, the reserve brigade would soon lie forever in the cemetery at the top of the hill.

"These boys can't be held inactive much longer—it breeds fear and doubt," Hancock said. "They need a jolt of action!"

Hancock rode slowly up a section of the long reserve line as if on a Sunday stroll, composed, staring into each man's eyes.

Someone yelled, "It's Hancock, the Superb!"

"Looking good, boys. Stay sharp. Keep focused," Hancock shouted.

The men's faces brightened as he passed, their energy building along the line like a small ground tremor. A good start.

Midway up the line, Hancock spotted Colonel Orland Smith, the brigade commander. Sitting slightly swaybacked in the saddle, Smith saluted, his face a chalky white.

"General Hancock. Mighty glad to see you, sir."

"Orland," Hancock said, "you have a fine-looking brigade."

Smith nodded. "Thank you, sir," His voice trembled.

"My corps is on the way but will not be here to help," Hancock said. "This position must be held at all cost." Hancock stared fiercely at Smith. "Colonel, can you hold it?"

Smith paused, rubbing his face. "Well, sir...maybe."

Hancock's face flushed with heat. He banged a fist on the saddle horn. "Damn it, Colonel! Will you hold it?"

Smith's face grew pale, but resolute. "I will, sir."

"If you are attacked, hold your line to the last man," Hancock said. "I will reinforce you with the units gathered at the cemetery. Your brigade's line of battle is the breakwater for the Rebel tide. Do you understand?"

"Yes, General Hancock," Smith said.

"Colonel, I want you to force the enemy to go over your position, not through it. I don't expect you to lick the whole Rebel army, but I do expect you to halt them momentarily. Just give me time to reinforce you."

"Yes, sir," Smith nodded.

Hancock turned and glanced up and down the brigade line. Smith's brigade was alone. It was a dirty detail, but not necessarily a death warrant. If he could augment these soldiers in time, they would survive. They just had to hold and not flee.

On the slope of Cemetery Hill behind the Buckeye Regiment of Smith's brigade flew the colors of the Union, floating over the imposing blue line. His pulse ratcheted up and a burst of pride pitched up his throat. Old Glory unfurled in her finest splendor. Yes, Smith's brigade would hold.

Hancock spurred his way to the hill's crest. He stopped momentarily at the cemetery gatehouse. It consisted of two two-story red brick buildings with windows, each guarding a side of the cemetery's road entrance. The brick towers were joined at the top, creating a castle-like archway. Each tower had rooms upstairs and down. He guessed the cemetery's caretaker lived in one.

A bullet whisked past his ear, prickling the hairs on his neck. *Damn, that was close.*

Down below in the town, Union troops were still retreating in confusing disorder, hotly pursued by the enemy. Hancock winced, swallowing the drear horror of scores of men shot in the back, lurching forward to the ground like clumps of willow trees in a whipping wind.

"Damn you, Howard. Can't you direct a fighting retreat?" Hancock glared, his jaw muscles working.

Mitchell pointed to the right of the town. "Look, General. More soldiers running for their lives."

Hancock turned his head. Abruptly, thousands of throats erupted into the Rebel Yell, shrieking like gray-cloaked banshees.

"Christ almighty! Soldiers are slaughtered like pigs when they turn their backs and flee pell-mell from the enemy."

"If they can make it to Smith's Brigade, they have a chance, General."

Smith's brigade was creating spaces for the fleeing soldiers to pass through the line. Hancock prayed; the brigade had to hold until he could form the retreating troops in a defensive line.

Hancock scanned the crest for Howard. He spotted him, sitting on horseback, a hundred yards away, outlined against a rising hill consisting of two rounded peaks. That must be Culp's Hill. Hancock rode at a gallop across the crest of Cemetery Hill toward the Baltimore Pike, weaving around the wounded and exhausted.

Hancock rode up, saluted grandly. Without waiting for Howard to return the salute and speak, Hancock spoke loudly, ignoring the formal pleasantries. "General Meade ordered me forward to take command of all forces at Gettysburg."

Howard frowned and raised his hand as if parrying Hancock's words like a sword blow. "You have no authority to relieve me of command. I'm the senior officer," Howard snapped with rage.

"I am aware of that, General, but I have written orders in my pocket from General Meade, which I will show you if you wish."

"No!" Howard shouted. "I do not doubt your word, General Hancock. But you can give no orders here while I am here. I'm senior and you have no damn idea of what is going on. I do."

Hancock clamped off a burst of rage pitching up his throat. No time to argue. Howard would not concede. It was a perilous situation. The defeated, disorganized Union forces were vulnerable to attack. They occupied a critical piece of terrain that could anchor a defensive system, but only if they were able to rally the retreating forces rapidly. He would let Meade deal with Howard's hurt feelings later. He was in command and would work with Howard to use him in the best way.

Hancock said sternly, "Very well, General Howard. As ordered by Meade, I'm now in command of the forces at Gettysburg and have assumed responsibility for the conduct and safety of all Gettysburg forces until General Slocum arrives."

Howard glared, his face set, quivering with anger. It looked as if he had been sucker punched, the air kicked right out of him.

"I will second any order that you have to give," Hancock continued. "But General Meade has also directed me to select a field on which to fight. Either here or at Pipe's Creek."

Hancock cast a long glance toward Culp's Hill, to Cemetery Hill, to Cemetery Ridge, and to the two round tops. The Union line was in a defensive formation resembling a fishhook: Culp's Hill serving as the barb, Cemetery Hill as the hook, and Cemetery Ridge ending at Big and Little Round Top as the shaft. His heart warmed, expanding against his rib cage. He was surprised at the powerful advantage Cemetery Hill offered as a natural defense. It towered a hundred feet above the town, its slopes to the north and west rose gradually. The eastern slope was a steep rise. The crest of Cemetery Hill was nearly half a mile long with a shallow saddle on its northeast slope that connected to Culp's Hill. Cemetery Ridge to the west provided a natural flanking defense.

Hancock said, "I think this the strongest position by nature upon which to fight a battle that I ever saw, and if it meets your approval I will select it as the battlefield."

"I think it a very strong position, General Hancock. A very strong position," Howard replied flatly.

"Very well, sir, I select this as the battlefield."

Howard said tersely, "I suggest you take the forces to the left of the Baltimore Pike on Cemetery Hill, and I arrange my forces to the right on Culp's Hill."

Hancock nodded. "Agreed."

Howard's suggestion was a good remedy to their current impasse. Hancock departed, riding to the western slope of Cemetery Hill and taking charge of the field. Swarms of fleeing blue troops sprinted wildly from Gettysburg. The cracking of enemy musketry fire was swelling. The blue lines northwest of town had given way, and the positions west and north were abandoned. Small bands of Rebel troops began appearing from the fringe of the town. They began clustering together in larger groups, suggesting the forming of a long gray line. Hancock fretted—they would be coming soon. Over on the left was growing confusion. He saw a horse coming across the ridge. No rider. Hancock halted to let the animal go by, hoping to see the rider afoot. He spotted the man clamoring after the horse, blood streaming from a slash zigzagging across his brow. He said a silent prayer for the wounded officer.

Hancock swiped unconsciously at his face as a bullet whirled by like a buzzing mosquito. In the distance he spotted Warren approaching, riding toward the gatehouse. As he approached Hancock, the musket firing and whine of bullets were mounting, becoming a steady roar. An ocean of white smoke was forming at the bottom of Cemetery Hill. Hancock wondered if he would catch a stray bullet and die like Reynolds. He moved along the crest, pausing frequently to look through field glasses at the shattered army racing through the streets.

*4:45 p.m.*

Warren reined to a stop, saluted. "I thought I might have beaten you here. You started off mighty slow in that ambulance."

Hancock returned the salute. "Good afternoon, Gouv. I'm glad to see you." Warren would make an immediate impact in saving Cemetery Hill. "I'm just as surprised as you that you didn't beat me here."

"Riding up the Emmitsburg Road to Gettysburg proved to be a good deal longer than I anticipated," Warren said. "But I did pass Sickles marching Third Corps toward Gettysburg. I would guess his lead division will arrive about six this evening."

Hancock swiveled in the saddle, looking down Emmitsburg Road.

"The Rebel army will be cooking dinner on this hill before Sickles arrives," Hancock snapped.

"Sickles is force-marching his corps," Warren said.

Hancock nodded and said, "We will rally here on the hill behind the stone walls and stop the onslaught. Then we can assess the natural defenses of Gettysburg and let Meade make his choice of where to fight."

Suddenly a shell from a faraway Rebel battery came pitching down, exploding on the back side of the hill. It caused no harm, but it made the Union soldiers jumpy, knowing other enemy shells would soon start arriving in clusters.

"Stop the stragglers, Gouv. Return them to their regiments, and reorganize the lines," Hancock said. "Push as many of the men as possible behind the stone walls that cross the forward slopes of Cemetery Hill."

Warren saluted, bolted to the far left flank of Cemetery Hill. Hancock turned toward Gettysburg. Time was running out. A great multitude of gray figures was appearing at the edge of town. Cemetery Hill was swarming with stragglers, skulkers, and retreating soldiers. A lively cannonade had broken out between a Union battery located on the crest of Cemetery Hill and Rebel artillery pieces on the edge of town.

Hancock turned to Mitchell. "Get the troops in some line of order behind those stone walls. They should have a good chance of holding until nightfall."

"Yes, sir," Mitchell said.

Hancock half expected the Rebel assault to come at any moment, but the firing and the yelling seemed to be slackening. Why were they waiting? Lee was a predator and after stalking his prey and tasting blood would rarely pass up the opportunity to press for the kill.

"Why aren't they attacking?" Hancock muttered.

As every moment passed, the Union army was gaining ground, pouring onto Cemetery Hill, a natural fortress. Lee was making a grave mistake. It was not like him. A sputter of rifle fire broke out, but it was not coordinated. Hancock ducked as a shot whickered overhead. His heart stopped and a chill shot from his brain straight to his toes.

He had to get the artillery units in place on the left and right flanks. Cemetery Hill was defensible so long as the enemy did not occupy Cemetery Ridge on the left and Culp's Hill on the right.

Hancock turned his focus to positioning the artillery units. Enough artillery, properly placed, could compensate for the lack of infantry and have a devastating effect in halting an attack. Howard had told him there were nearly forty-eight artillery guns between First and Eleventh Corps, believing only four were lost to the enemy.

Hancock spotted Captain Wiedrich's battery of four three-inch ordnance rifles at the corner of East Cemetery Hill.

Hancock rode up. "Captain, you must hold your position by all means," he said.

Wiedrich saluted. "Yes, sir."

Hancock then spied Captain Greenleaf Stevens's batteries at the top of Cemetery Hill. Hancock cupped his hands around his mouth and bawled, "You! You, the artillery battery captain."

Stevens spurred his horse and rode over. He saluted and said, "Reporting as ordered, sir."

Hancock pointed toward Culp's Hill. "Take your battery there and stop the enemy from coming up that ravine."

Stevens paused. "By whose order...*sir*?" he queried. The tone was one of extreme formality but bordered on disrespect.

"General Hancock's!" he bawled. His body shook with bristling rage. "Now move your damn battery over to that hill now. Do you understand me?" Hancock was a two-star general, and there weren't many in the Army of the Potomac. Who did this captain think he was dealing with?

Stevens saluted, wheeling his horse away, riding toward his artillery battery. He shouted, "Fifth battery, forward!"

Hancock rode back toward the arched cemetery building, still swearing. He stopped and watched as Stevens escorted his battery's sections along the Baltimore Pike until they reached the McKnight house on a knoll at the base of Culp's Hill. Stevens placed the six big guns in line on the bare knob, forming a deadly defensive position.

A cracking blast erupted from Stevens's battery like the warning thunder of a coming storm. Hancock rode back to Stevens's position. He spied a large group of Confederates in the fields next to Gettysburg, drawing up into a line of battle. Stevens's batteries opened up on the Rebels, unleashing a wicked tempest of iron, the whirring shells piercing the air through the thunderclap of explosions. The enemy scattered, leaping across their dead as the plunging shells pockmarked the ground in a fiery hailstorm. Within moments, blue sheets of low-lying smoke grew into a mist.

Hancock shouted over the roaring noise of the cannonades. "Good job, Captain Stevens, a most fearfully beautiful sight. I'm going to find you some infantry support, and I will move more artillery to this knoll. Keep a heavy curtain of artillery fire on them."

Hancock turned and galloped off. Steven's battery fire quickly turned from a ringing boom to a deafening roar. Hancock nodded. What a wonderful sound.

Hancock rode to the western side of Cemetery Hill. His heart surged. Stevens's battery was achieving devastating success. Now he had to extend that success across the entire defensive front. The earsplitting noise made it difficult to hear. He stopped as soon as he could carry on a conversation. Turning to his chief of staff, Colonel Morgan, he yelled, "Ride down the Baltimore Pike toward Twelfth Corps. Locate General Slocum and request he arrive with his corps at Gettysburg as soon as feasible."

Morgan saluted and departed.

Hancock rode to General Doubleday, acting commander of First Corps. "General Doubleday, I would like you to send Colonel Wadsworth's Iron Brigade to the west slope of Culp's Hill and provide infantry support to Stevens's battery."

Doubleday protested, a sneer splitting his lips. "Sir, my men are worn out, and they are short of ammunition. We've been fighting since ten this morning."

Hancock snapped. "General Doubleday, I do not want to hear any damn excuses. The situation is desperate!"

Doubleday hesitated. "Yes, sir." He turned, ordering Wadsworth and the Iron Brigade to Culp's Hill.

Hancock immediately assessed Doubleday as a weak reed to lean on in an emergency. Doubleday's style was the same today as it had been at West Point—extraordinarily deliberate and chronically mediocre. He reminded himself to tell Meade that Doubleday should not replace Reynolds as commander of First Corps.

Hancock rode to the left side of Cemetery Hill, counting twenty caissons of eight three-inch artillery guns and eleven twelve-pounder Napoleons. The three-inch guns contained a rifled barrel, accurately throwing a shell more than 1,800 yards, the perfect long-range weapon. The Napoleons had a smooth-bore barrel. They were the choice gun for close-in fighting, using canisters filled with metal balls packed in sawdust, which acted like a shotgun blast, the shrapnel deadly against charging infantry.

Hancock ordered Bancroft and Dilger's batteries of Napoleons loaded with canisters for firing at close range. He was pleased with the job Warren was doing shoring up this side of the hill. By this time, Colonel Wainwright, the young, talented commander of the artillery brigade of First Corps, had placed four additional batteries to support Stevens, an imposing force of twenty-three caissons of thirteen three-inch artillery pieces and ten Napoleons. Hancock had two talented officers, Warren and Wainwright, guarding the western and northeastern approaches to Cemetery Hill. *Well, General Lee. You're no longer fighting the cautious Howard. Hancock is now in command, and you're not going to brush me off this hill.*

Hancock found Warren and the two of them rode the ground together. Hancock said, "If we can hold this position until night, it would be the best place for the army to fight on if attacked in the morning."

Warren agreed.

*5:25 p.m.*

Hancock turned to Major Mitchell. "Ride to General Meade and tell him that we will hold the ground until night so that he can come forward and decide himself whether to fight here."

Mitchell saluted and departed.

Hancock ordered another aide to ride to General Gibbon, acting commander of Second Corps, approaching Gettysburg over the Taneytown Road. "Tell Gibbon to halt the corps two or three miles south of Gettysburg to cover the rear position and any flanking attack."

Hancock stopped and listened. The firing rate of Stevens and Wainwright's batteries protecting Culp's Hill was tapering off. This was a good sign. The enemy no longer was clustering and surging forward, acting more like an ebbing tide. After hitting the edge of town, they had halted, finding shelter and digging in. Now there was time to think. Hancock dismounted, pulled out his binoculars, and sat on a stone wall watching the enemy's half-hearted pursuit of General Carl Schurz's Third Division toward Cemetery Hill. Schurz's soldiers slipped easily through Smith's brigade at the bottom of the hill and scampered up toward the cemetery gate.

*5:45 p.m.*

Schurz arrived, walking. He was the last general officer to reach the hill. He was covered in dust and sweat. "I'm glad you're holding this wall, Winfield," Schurz said, relieved.

Hancock responded with pride. "I'm absolutely delighted I'm holding this wall. As of a few moments ago, it might easily have been one of our friends in gray sitting here waiting for you."

"Is Meade here?"

"No, I'm in command until Slocum arrives."

"Good choice sending you forward to take charge. I'm not sure we would have held without you."

"What happened to your horse?" Hancock said.

"My horse was shot," Schurz said, "while we were defending Oak Hill, the area northwest of Gettysburg."

Hancock nodded. Schurz looked more like a college professor than a general, with his thick spectacles, tousled brown hair, and reddish beard. But Hancock liked the German-born Schurz.

"Half my division didn't make it to Cemetery Hill," Schurz said. "They were killed, wounded, or captured."

Schurz pulled out his binoculars. They both scanned the enemy positions for several moments. Hancock extracted a flask from his jacket, handing it to Schurz, who took a long swig of whiskey, then passed it back. Hancock let the burning warmth rush through him, then put the flask away, his limbs tingling.

"Whose corps is that?" he asked.

"It's Ewell's," said Schurz.

They both watched as Ewell's boys swept the town, clearing the streets, corralling Union prisoners. Son of a bitch. Nothing he could do, given the tenuous terrain advantage they held.

"Our lines are woefully thin," Schurz said. "I'm not sure we can withstand a concentrated attack."

"I'm a bit nervous as well," Hancock said. "But I think our artillery can hold them until help comes. Both Slocum's Twelfth Corps and Sickles's Third Corps should be arriving soon."

Abruptly, Wiedrich's battery on Cemetery Hill unleashed a thunderous artillery barrage, ripping holes in Ewell's corps. It was a deadly fire. In just a few moments, several of the enemy were dead. The Confederates halted.

"The Union batteries are damn accurate," Schurz said.

"Our artillery has performed superbly this evening," Hancock said.

Hancock and Schurz begin to relax as minutes ticked by and the Rebels did not charge. Hancock lit a cigar as he reflected on the events of the past two hours. Upon his arrival at Cemetery Hill, the Union army had been on the precipice of panic. After directing, positioning, and rallying the defeated soldiers for more than an hour, things had begun to turn in his favor. A renewed belief had emerged, and the army's resolve had returned. With each passing moment, the army's collective strength was rising, its spine stiffening to fight another day.

Meade should be happy. He had taken an incredible risk in appointing a junior-ranking general to take command. But Meade gambled that, with Reynolds dead, the personality of the army at Gettysburg would align with the uncertain Howard, the senior general on the field. This was unacceptable. Meade could not risk another dismal performance. Lee would have skewered Howard and all hopes of the Union army.

Hancock moved back behind the stone wall. He prayed for darkness. There would be another hour of daylight, and the moon that night would be nearly full.

Morgan rode up, dismounted. "I spoke with General Slocum. I met him about a mile from town at a place called Powers Hill. Slocum said he did not wish to go to Cemetery Hill."

Hancock swore, loudly. "What?"

Morgan said tightly, "Slocum had seen so many Eleventh Corps stragglers that he feared Gettysburg was another

Chancellorsville. He thought it prudent to deploy his troops behind Gettysburg to check the rout. Slocum placed Geary's Second Brigade in reserve along the Baltimore Pike. He sent Geary and his two other brigades to report to you.

"I explained that you were waiting for him to arrive in Gettysburg and relieve you," Morgan continued. "Slocum objected to assuming the Gettysburg command because Meade had selected you and you are familiar with the position and terrain. Finally, he said he did not care to assume the command that might make him responsible for a condition of affairs over which he had no control."

"Son of a *bitch*," Hancock muttered.

"But I told Slocum you had things under control at Gettysburg. You had rallied the retreating soldiers and were waiting for him to take command so you could ride back and report in person to General Meade. After hearing this, Slocum said he would ride to Cemetery Hill and relieve you of command. He should arrive momentarily."

Hancock's throat tightened, his breathing becoming shallow and quick. Slocum's response was borderline dereliction of duty. In moments like this, he wished dueling were still legal.

Hancock shook his head. "Well, Slocum is living up to his name—Slow-Come."

---

*6:00 p.m.*

General Geary, commander of Slocum's Second Division, rode up to Hancock and Schurz, dismounted, and saluted. "General Slocum ordered me to report to you for further assignment."

Hancock shook Geary's hand. John Geary was a giant of a man, standing six feet six inches tall, solid build, perfect physique. He was the only general in the army with a more violent temper than Meade's. Most men feared him because of his size and his short fuse.

"Good to see you, John." Hancock said. "Where are your troops?"

"Two brigades are advancing up the Baltimore Pike. They are about half a mile from here. The Third Brigade is guarding the rear down the road a few miles at Two Taverns."

Hancock asked quickly, "Do you see the large knoll on the left?" Hancock was pointing out Little Round Top. Geary turned and saw two large knolls, the closer one a bit smaller. He turned back to Hancock, nodding.

"John, I want you to take your command over to the left of First Corps, to occupy a prolonged line along Cemetery Ridge. I want you to anchor your division on Little Round Top. That knoll is a commanding position and we must take possession of it. If we fail to hold the knoll we will have to fall back to the Pipe Creek Line."

Geary saluted and departed.

Hancock walked along the long line below the crest of Cemetery Hill. The troops waited, crouching behind the stone walls, bayonets fixed and glimmering in the fading western sun. A swelling pride filled his chest. These young men from the small farms of the North were tough. Many had visible wounds, blood caked on grimy, sweat-stained faces. A few hours ago these lines did not exist, but now they were plugging a gap Ewell could have used to ride all the way to the nation's capital.

A thumping clapping between his ears grew as he waited for Slocum's arrival. The troops could hold the lines until tomorrow morning, but he needed to talk with Meade. Meade had to make the key decision to move the rest of the army to Gettysburg or move the troops back to the Pipe Creek line. The army's largest corps, Sedgwick's Sixth Corps, was anchoring the right position of the Pipe Creek line at Manchester, some thirty miles from Gettysburg. Meade could not hold Gettysburg tomorrow without Sedgwick's corps. The Rebel force of nearly 100,000 would chop Meade's army into small pieces.

Hancock mounted his horse, trotting back up the hill to the gatehouse. The rumbling cannons filling the air had faded, and the musket fire had grown silent.

He waited, with Morgan nearby. It was twelve miles south on the Taneytown Road to visit with Meade. "Where are you, Slow-Come?"

———————— • ————————

*7:40 p.m.*

After a while, several riders came galloping up the Baltimore Pike. Hancock squinted. The second rider, the guidon, was carrying the large swallow-tailed flag with a single large red star of the Twelfth Corps commander. It was Slocum and a trail of aides. His rigid shoulders relaxed. About time.

Slocum arrived, dismounted unhurriedly, and led his horse toward Hancock, who saluted. Slocum returned the salute, but the greeting was brisk, strangely cold. Slocum appeared unsure. Will this man assume command? Hancock stared at him, trying to gauge his state of mind. He had never seen Slocum so unnerved.

"Do you think they'll try to attack again?" Slocum asked.

Hancock looked at the Rebel forces occupying the town, Seminary Ridge, and beyond Culp's Hill. He shook his head. "Truthfully, no. There was a moment when they could have devastated us. But Jackson's old corps was uncharacteristically slow in exploiting the opportunity."

Slocum nodded.

Hancock gave a quick recap of events since arriving on Cemetery Hill. He explained he was to ride immediately to Meade after Slocum had assumed command.

Hancock said sternly, "I'm ready to be relieved."

Slocum paused. He seemed seized with fear. He finally said, softly, "I relieve you."

Hancock saluted. "I stand relieved."

Hancock mounted his horse and rode swiftly down the Taneytown Road. As he rode, his face tightened.

"Damn," he muttered. Today had been a close call for the Republic. Way too close.

Sedgwick's large corps sitting some thirty miles from Gettysburg was a major problem for Meade. Although Slocum held good ground, if the Confederates attacked without

Sedgwick's corps at Gettysburg, the Army of the Potomac could be decimated. It was critical Hancock meet with Meade so the commanding general could order Sedgwick to begin marching tonight toward tomorrow's battle if he chose to fight at Gettysburg. If, however, Meade chose to fight along the Pipe Creek line, Meade needed to order Reynolds, Sickles, and Howard's corps to depart Gettysburg tonight.

Hancock shook his head. What would Meade decide?

# Cemetery Hill Defenses
## July 1, 1863

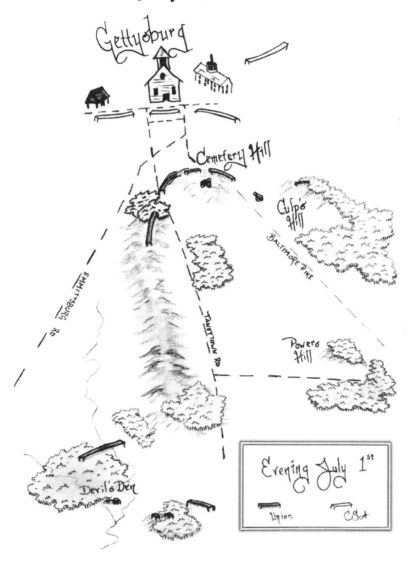

Gettysburg

Cemetery Hill

Culps Hill

BALTIMORE PIKE

EMMITTSBURG RD

TANEYTOWN RD

Powers Hill

Devil's Den

Evening July 1st

Union                CSA

# 24

# Greene — Wednesday, July 1

*12:00 p.m.*
*Almost eight hours earlier*
*On the Baltimore Pike toward Gettysburg*

General George Greene swallowed hard, his throat choking with dust as he angled off the Baltimore Pike, riding toward a copse of trees. The blistering sun was beating against his burning face, fiery red and dry. He dismounted under a broad-topped white oak, letting the shade under its large branches cool him. He gulped warm water from his canteen. Relaxing in the leafy shadows for several moments, the 62-year old's fuzzy brain began to clear up like black clouds rolling away. What would his brigade face this coming afternoon? If the rumors were accurate, the steady popping of gunfire and thumping of light artillery six miles toward Gettysburg was probably Buford's cavalry scrapping with Rebel horsemen. From this distance, it didn't sound like an infantry fight with heavy supporting artillery.

Greene removed his blue slouch hat, wiping sweat from his brow. Testifying to his advanced years, a thick mane of silver hair framed his face, which was covered by a bulky spade-shaped beard and a monstrous handlebar mustache, curling up toward his nose. His dark blue eyes were shaded by unruly white eyebrows. A throwback to the toughness of Old Hickory, Greene looked over at his New York brigade of 1,500 men, resting briefly in a grove of trees at a place called Two Taverns, southeast of Gettysburg. A voice whispered in Greene's head: *Your brain's still a bit foggy. Stay in the shade a few more moments.*

The Baltimore Pike ran northwest to Gettysburg. The scorching heat was refracting the light, rippling the air like sheets draped over a clothesline. One by one, Greene's picket patrol

315

was succumbing to sunstroke. The remaining men in the brigade were in distress, hardly able to stand. General Slocum had halted the 10,700-man Twelfth Corps for an extended period.

Suddenly, several men started pointing up the road. Greene sniffed and his stomach turned as the putrid scent of something nauseating like a rotting pork roast floated in the humid air. Probably a dead horse upwind in the hot sun. He glanced back over at his boys sitting in the shade. Many of them had tied handkerchiefs over their faces. Old Pop, as his soldiers called him, almost chuckled: The brigade looked like a gang of thugs from Manhattan's Five Points waiting for the next highway robbery.

Greene unhitched a second canteen tethered to the horse's saddle, took a long swig of water. Good. The dizziness was passing.

He looked at his watch. A quarter past noon. As the minutes wore on and the cannonading blossomed, Greene was less sure it was horsemen mixing it up. He rubbed the back of his neck and his pulse quickened. The barrages sounded too big for cavalry cannons. More like large-caliber artillery cannons, the heavy guns supporting infantry. It was beginning to sound like a large-scale engagement. Slocum needed to move Twelfth Corps toward the sound of the guns.

Captain Charles Horton, the brigade's assistant adjutant general, approached Greene and saluted. "How long do you think we will stay here, sir?"

Greene said, "No clue. But make sure the regiments are ready to move out at a moment's notice. It sounds like at least one Union corps has arrived, maybe two. This could be the beginning of the big fight."

As he stood in the shade, Greene's tight muscles started to unwind. He rubbed his sore butt. He had been in the saddle since five this morning, seven straight hours. Although he was the oldest general in the Army of the Potomac, he was physically strong and surprisingly agile. But he kept rubbing. If only his thighs would stop aching.

*12:25 p.m.*

Greene strolled slowly through the Brigade's five regiments, working out the saddle-soreness. The army would never be victorious until they had a commanding general capable of moving reserves rapidly to support and exploit successes. To date, none had been able to think on their feet, taking risk to gain victory. Perhaps Meade possessed the necessary grit. He sure had thrust the army daringly forward for the past three days, marching the hell out of the men.

Greene stopped. The roar of artillery and musket fire seemed close at hand, melding into one long rumble. The ground started shuddering under his feet.

He turned to Horton, "Captain, climb to the top of that barn and see if you can see anything happening in Gettysburg."

Horton galloped to the tall red barn and scrambled to the top. After a few minutes, he rode back to Greene.

"I can see all the way to the hills of Gettysburg and high ridges rolling beyond toward South Mountain. Clouds of smoke from cannons and little black puffs from bursting shells are hanging in the air west of Gettysburg. The spits of smoke seem to be growing in number, indicating the fighting is growing."

Greene's gut fluttered and his heart grew cold. "Approximate numbers of the opposing forces?" he asked.

Horton thought for a moment. "I'd say about sixty thousand or so. It sounds like the battle is moving closer, and I fear the Union troops are falling back."

"I'll be damned," Greene said. "So it is more than advance cavalry units tangling. We've finally found the Rebel army. Or they have found us."

"I agree, General."

"Ride to Slocum's headquarters and tell him what you've seen," Greene said.

Horton rode off.

Greene ordered shelters struck and rolled up, preparing the brigade to move out at a minute's notice. No orders came. Greene waited. Something was not right. After an hour, he rode over to his Second Division commander, General John Geary. Greene saluted. A vein in Geary's forehead throbbed.

Geary said, "I spoke with Slocum about moving up toward Gettysburg and he told me to sit tight. I asked how long we were supposed to sit while the fight was going on, and he said until he had heard from General Meade."

"Is Meade at Gettysburg?" Greene asked.

"Hell, no. Slocum said Meade was still back in Taneytown. Can you believe that? At least Hooker showed up where the fighting was happening."

Greene was tight-lipped and said nothing. Being one of few Union generals who sprinted toward the sounds of gunfire, Geary was not a big fan of his slow-moving corps commander. Greene shook his head. At the critical moment, it appeared Meade lacked the urgency to join the fight at Gettysburg. What a pisser.

---

*4:00 p.m.*
*Four in the afternoon*

A bugle blew, signaling the brigade to fall in. Old Pop heard lots of swearing from many of the soldiers hoping to stay in the shade a bit longer. But the New York infantry unit formed up, stepping off smartly to the beat of regimental drums. The duty pickets, who had been standing in the heat for nearly three hours, heard the beating drums and rushed to fall in at the rear, struggling to keep pace. Old Pop mounted and rode along the edge of the road, staring down the long column.

Colonel David Ireland, the handsome, spectacled, thirty-one-year-old Scot in command of the 137th New York Regiment, rode up to Greene, stopped, and saluted.

"Good to see you, David!" Greene greeted him.

"Delighted to be here, sir."

Ireland reminded Greene of a Scottish terrier: feisty, barrel-chested, sturdily built, with a drooping mustache. Greene's brigade was composed of five New York regiments, and Ireland commanded the largest. Greene studied his companion closely, knowing he suffered from a painful intestinal infection. Ireland was hollow-eyed and pale, looking a bit jittery.

"I see the surgeon discharged you from the hospital," Greene said.

Ireland shook his head. "The surgeon said it's chronic dysentery and told me to take castor oil in the morning, opium at night, and wrap myself in flannel bandages."

Greene shook his head, wondering whether it was worth the risk keeping Ireland in command. Dysentery was a killer, the scourge of the army. But sending him back to the surgeons could be a death sentence; the sanitary conditions of the corps hospitals were terrible. Keeping him in command under a watchful eye was the sensible approach. The Scotsman was tough, and during a fight, he was ferocious. Greene needed this Scotsman.

"Let me know how you're doing," Greene said with a concerned tone. Then he added, "I'm worried about your pickets who stood watch this afternoon. Most of them are straggling behind the brigade. Post a couple of rested men with them and make sure they make it to Gettysburg. I would rather have them arrive late than dead."

Ireland saluted, rode to the rear of the brigade.

Greene fretted about Ireland, empathy leaking out from the hardened shell enclosing his soft soul. He was fatherly toward all his regimental commanders, but particularly Ireland. As Greene moved forward, Captain Charles Piltortan, one of his staff officers, rode up.

"Captain Horton's observation from the barn may have been on the money," Piltortan said. "This sounds like more than a cavalry skirmish."

"It sounds like large infantry forces are engaging," Greene said. "My bet is we've found Lee's infantry."

Piltortan departed. Greene pulled out of line and rode down the brigade column, stopping to chat with each regimental commander from the Empire State. He wanted to check on Ireland again, bringing up the rear of the brigade. Colonel Abel Godard led the 310 men of the Sixtieth New York, mustering from Ogdensburg, New York, a small settlement guarding the St.

Lawrence River and the northern border with Canada. Greene was fond of the Sixtieth New York; the unit had been his first command. Many of the men who made up this force were loggers and builders.

The Seventy-eighth New York followed. Numbering 200 Scotsmen, it was the smallest regiment in Greene's brigade. The Highlanders were a mix of New York City companies and companies from Buffalo, Rochester, and Utica and were infamous for their love of engaging with fists. They loved brawling, with anyone, including each other. They were commanded by Colonel Herbert von Hammerstein, who had resigned his commission in the Austrian army and joined General McClellan's staff. Greene liked having him as regimental commander because of his emphasis on strict discipline. The regiment had suffered 130 casualties at Chancellorsville.

Next in line was the 102nd New York, numbering 250 men. They mustered from New York City, mostly Manhattan and Brooklyn, and were commanded by Colonel James Lane, a civil engineer.

The 149th New York was commanded by Colonel Henry Barnum, heralding from Syracuse and the hills of Onondaga County. This regiment numbered more than 300 men. Greene worried about Barnum, a tough fighter but still recovering from wounds received at the battle of Malvern Hill. The regiment had suffered 186 casualties at Chancellorsville.

Bringing up the rear was Ireland's 137th, the regiment numbering 450 men. These soldiers were mostly country boys from the Binghamton region near the northern Pennsylvania border, where the Susquehanna River crosses into New York.

Greene rode to Ireland and turned to see how the pickets were doing. They were falling back but still in sight.

He grinned at Ireland. "How are you, Colonel?"

"Fine, General. Long time no see," Ireland said in a light tone. "Just wanted to check on the pickets."

"I'm keeping a sharp eye on the pickets," Ireland replied. "I'll make sure they arrive safely."

Greene nodded and rode back to the head of the brigade. He was not completely satisfied. This march might be too fast for the pickets. And Ireland probably should be back in the hospital, but he was stubborn and he was needed.

A roaring wail echoed ahead. Greene held his breath. His heart sank. Large crowds of locals were racing to the rear, carrying household goods in carts and on their backs. Some driving cattle and horses with them. The first sign of a devastating rout—the disorderly flight of civilians.

"Those men, women, and children are running for their lives," he said to Horton.

Behind the throng of Gettysburg fugitives, a number of wounded soldiers and Rebel prisoners appeared, drudging toward Greene's brigade. When Howard's routed soldiers came alongside, they described how their command had been cut to pieces. Greene noticed with pride that the stories did not have the slightest effect on the brigade. But the New York boys did exchange some choice comments with the prisoners.

"Damn you, Lee," Greene muttered.

How odd that Bobby Lee, his favorite of all the students he had taught at West Point, was now a few miles down the road, waiting to destroy his brigade, and perhaps even a Rebel sharpshooter under his command waiting to kill him like they killed Reynolds. He did not fear his own death. He had narrowly escaped being killed at Antietam, and he was aware that in battle the risk to a general was twice that of a private. He expected to catch a bullet soon enough.

What did trouble him was that he had nurtured and supported the rebellious Lee. There were plenty of traitorous West Point students he had taught, but there was only one Robert E. Lee. How could he have known that Cadet Lee would one day break his solemn oath to protect and honor the Republic? My God, how could he have known he was mentoring a traitor? The whole Lee matter was foul and ugly, lying edgewise in Greene's brain like a rotting corpse.

Greene rode to an elevated portion of the road, stopping to look northwest through an opening in the trees, across several small ridges, at white puffs of smoke dotting the lower sky. Gettysburg. They would be there soon. He rode ahead, his thoughts drifting back to West Point.

After Greene graduated from West Point, he had served as a lieutenant of the artillery. Within a year, he was back teaching mathematics and engineering to cadets. In his final year as a professor, Green taught Lee. Lee was a particularly promising cadet, credited fourth in mathematics with a rating of 197 from a possible 200 in his first year. He was the most gifted, instinctive leader Greene had ever seen. Even the first-class cadets had the greatest respect for the plebe. Lee's ancestors were Revolutionary War heroes. His father was Light Horse Harry Lee, earning fame as cavalry officer in the Continental army and later serving as the ninth governor of Virginia.

Robert E. Lee was fun, friendly, quick-witted, and strikingly handsome. He enjoyed joking, and his eyes sparkled with a touch of mischief. But his record of conduct was impeccable. His conversations with Greene frequently focused on European warfare, especially the campaigns of Napoleon. Lee admired Napoleon's use of distributed maneuver—allowing military units to operate separately but being able to concentrate them at precisely the right moment—and his ability to see the complete picture of war, analyzing all its components and combining units into an integrated campaign plan.

Greene and Lee also discussed the Revolutionary War at length. Lee's father had served under Greene's relative, General Nathanael Greene. Although Light Horse Harry Lee had performed brilliantly in the war, Robert did not like talking about his father. The "young" Lee was sensitive about being abandoned by him when he was six years old, his father sailing off to Barbados. Greene sensed Robert's perfect conduct at West Point was driven by his own father's misspent life and lack of self-control.

When the Southern states seceded, Greene was shocked when Lee decided to fight for the Confederacy. Of all the cadets who attended West Point, no one better exemplified the school's philosophical ideals of honor, duty, country. But those West Point graduates fighting for the Confederacy were traitors, modern-day Benedict Arnolds.

As he approached Gettysburg, Greene tried to focus on Lee's flaws, something that might help him defeat his former student. A critical vulnerability was Lee's love of the Napoleonic decisive battle, the one crushing victory. But today's rifled weapons had made the frontal assault against entrenched troops obsolete. Wasn't the Union's disastrous charge at Fredericksburg against an entrenched enemy proof of that?

The brigades in front of Greene were moving slowly, as if no fighting were happening. Slocum was in no hurry to arrive on the battlefield. As Greene's brigade approached Cemetery Hill, there was a lull in the fighting, indicating the Rebels were moving into a new attack position or were done for the evening.

*5:15 p.m.*

Greene spotted Geary and halted his brigade.

Geary rode up and said, "George, Hancock ordered us to anchor the far left of the Union line." Geary pointed to two round hills about three miles south from Cemetery Hill. "Move your Brigade and bivouac next to the Little Round Top."

"Where is the end of the Union left flank now?" Greene asked.

Geary pointed. "It's Robinson's Division. They are about a fourth of a mile southwest of us, sitting between the Emmitsburg and Taneytown Roads. March your brigade toward Robinson's division and when you arrive on Cemetery Ridge, follow the ridgeline down to the two round tops," Geary said.

"Is this a temporary assignment or is this our position for the fight that's coming?" Green said.

"Early in the morning, Sickles's corps will be arriving, and his people will relieve you. Your brigade will then move back to Culp's Hill and rejoin Slocum's corps occupying the right flank."

"Has Hancock's Second Corps moved up yet?" Greene asked.

"Hancock's Second Corps is under the temporary command of Gibbon; he is marching here on the Taneytown Road. Hancock said he was riding back to visit with Meade in Taneytown and on his way, he would tell Gibbon to bivouac Second Corps east of the two round tops. So if you run into any trouble you will have 11,000 soldiers about a mile in rear."

"Good!" Greene saluted and turned and ordered the brigade to load their weapons and fix bayonets. The metallic ring of ramrods rang along the line. After loading the muskets, the brigade double-quicked through the fields along the ridgeline to Little Round Top. With the exception of Colonel Ireland's regiment, they halted in a wheat field[12] in front of the hill. Greene sent skirmishers into the peach orchard[13] next to Emmitsburg Road. Colonel Ireland's regiment camped on the lower base of the hill, acting as a reserve unit for the brigade. The sun was setting as the men settled down for the evening, their loaded muskets next to them. Greene's brigade was positioned as the far left flank of the Union line.

---

*8:00 p.m. (dusk)*
*(Sunset is 7:44. Dusk ends at 8:17 p.m.)*
*Little Round Top*

Greene turned to Captain Horton. "Charles, I don't think the Rebels are going to attack this evening. Let's ride up this Little Round Top and see what's up there."

---

12 Many Gettysburg scholars treat *Wheatfield* and *Peach Orchard* as proper names and spell *Wheatfield* as one word. But the Union soldiers did not call them by these nomenclatures. They called them the wheat field and the peach orchard. This later labeling conforms with Allen Guelzo's *Gettysburg: The Last Invasion*, (Alfred A. Knopf, New York, 2013). Guelzo is Director of the James Madison Program Initiative on Politics and Statesmanship and Senior Research Scholar in the Council of Humanities at Princeton University and was, at the time he wrote this book, the Director of Civil War Era Studies and the Henry R. Luce Professor of the Civil War Era at Gettysburg College in Gettysburg, Pennsylvania. As Guelzo's book is an important recent scholarly Gettysburg publication, I elected to go with his nomenclature of *wheat field* and *peach orchard*.

13 See footnote 12, above.

"The western slope is pretty damn steep and covered with lots of big rocks. It's a formidable defensive position. Let's check out the eastern slope." Horton said.

"I agree."

They rode around the northern end of Little Round Top, which loggers had recently forested. The eastern side was covered with trees and scattered boulders.

"It's not as steep," Horton observed.

They continued to the summit of Little Round Top, picking their way around boulders and trees, and dismounted at the top. They had a clear view of Gettysburg to the north as well as South Mountain to the West.

Greene peered toward Gettysburg through his binoculars and saw two parallel ridges running north and south about a mile apart. The most westerly ridge ran south from the Lutheran Seminary and the other ridge ran south from the Cemetery.

"Impressive," Horton said. "This summit is like a castle sitting in the sky."

"If occupied by a strong force of infantry supported by artillery, this castle is impenetrable. A magnificent natural defense," Greene said.

They walked to the south end of the summit toward Big Round Top about 400 yards away. Standing on the edge of the summit, they spotted a small spur connecting to a saddle of high ground that joined the two Round Tops.

"Interesting," said Greene. "Big Round Top is about a hundred feet higher than the summit of Little Round Top, but it's heavily wooded. I don't think it is tactically useful like this summit."

"I agree," said Horton. "The key to holding the left flank of the Union line is this Little Round Top."

They walked back to the middle of the summit, planting their boots on the edge of the western slope.

Greene looked through his binoculars; westward and beyond Little Round Top was an expanse of open fields blanketed with dark, dense trees. He saw the wheat field where most of his brigade was bivouacking for the evening. He pointed toward a large rock formation about 500 yards from the base of Little Round Top and just beyond a creek.

"Look, Charles, at those clumps of boulders," Greene said. "Some of them are at least twenty feet high. They're connected by large caves and crevices."

Horton laughed. "It looks like the home of a huge, devilish snake that worms his way through his den."

Greene chuckled. "Good name. The Devil's Den."

"Speaking of the Devil," said Horton, "look at those thousands of enemy campfires glowing like hordes of lightning bugs around most of Gettysburg."

Greene stared at the campfires. Must have been nearly seventy thousand of them blazing away. There was a certain arrogance to the flickering flames. They burned without fear an enemy shell would find them. It was a deliberate show of Rebel power.

Inside the city, the lights of Gettysburg flickered softly, like candles blowing in the wind. Greene wondered: Would the lights be there tomorrow night?

# 25

# Meade — Wednesday, July 1

*2:30 p.m.*
*Five and a half hours earlier*
*Meade's Taneytown headquarters*

**M**eade stood alone under a large chestnut tree on top of a small knoll just north of Taneytown, overlooking the army's headquarters. No reports from the battle. No idea if Hancock had arrived in Gettysburg. No information whatsoever.

Was he being mulish by staying in Taneytown? If the battle was to be at Gettysburg, then he was still thirteen miles away from it. But if he could save the Pipe Creek plan, he could easily move his command there with minimal disruption to his headquarters staff. From Pipe Creek it was only eight miles to his logistics railhead at Westminster. Occupying the Pipe Creek line satisfied Lincoln's order to keep the army between Lee and Baltimore and Washington D.C., and it was a shorter distance to cut Lee off should he try to retreat across the Potomac at Williamsport. And the long, high ridgeline would be almost impossible for Lee's forces to breach. *All* more favorable conditions for waging this battle.

But was there time to save the Pipe Creek plan?

Meade's eyes flickered across the landscape. The low-hanging branches provided some shade from the blistering early-afternoon sun. The sky was pale blue, with puffy clouds that would be gone by late afternoon. There was no wind, and the air was thick and grainy. Baldy grazed untethered close by, ready. His personal staff and General Williams's aides lingered outside, their horses tethered to a white rail fence.

Waiting for him to decide. They were chatting and stealing glances at him, standing on the knoll.

Meade put the field glasses to his eyes, sweeping the horizon for messengers arriving with news. Any news, from anyone, would be welcome. Still no sign of riders. He swallowed hard. Something was terribly wrong. His nerves stood on edge, hissing as a razor scraped over the long, raw fibers.

Grumbling under his breath, Meade paced. Although Sedgwick's infantry was sitting on the right flank of the Pipe Creek defensive line, panic gripped him. Sixth Corps was more than a hard day's march away from Gettysburg. With luck, they could arrive at Gettysburg by midday tomorrow, if they started marching in the next few hours. *No time for uncertainty.* Sweat drenched his skin, and his eyes throbbed. He had to make a decision.

"God damn it," he muttered. Lacking knowledge of the outcome of the fighting at Gettysburg, he was reluctant to order Sedgwick forward. What if Hancock had ordered the two corps at Gettysburg back to the Pipe Creek line? The stakes were high, the consequences dire—the wholesale slaughter of the Army of the Potomac, possibly the end of the Republic—if he misplayed his hand. A growing urgency as strong as a gale-force wind erupting from the battle was pressuring him to hazard everything at Gettysburg. But rushing to that unseen ground with the remainder of the army, with no plan, was pure stupidity.

He closed his eyes, plucked his glasses off his nose, wiped them clean, and then slid them back on his face. *Damn it.* He owed a message to Halleck, but that must wait until he had heard from Hancock.

"Butterfield, you son of a bitch," he muttered. Failing to give the Pipe Creek plan to Reynolds and Howard in time was disastrous. Now he was just reacting to Lee's moves, with no plan. Just like damn Hooker.

*2:45 p.m.*

A burst of shouting. A lone messenger was racing down the road, kicking up a dust storm. A shiver of hope darted down Meade's spine. Perhaps news from Hancock. The courier dismounted, disappearing into the white house. In moments, Colonel Sharpe emerged from the house and sprinted to the mound where he stood.

"My messenger passed Hancock and his cavalcade at the halfway point to Gettysburg," Sharpe said. "Two of Lee's three corps are concentrating and pounding away at Howard's and Reynolds's corps. First Corps is putting up a hell of a fight against A. P. Hill's corps advancing from the west. But our forces are greatly outnumbered and are slowly moving back toward Cemetery Ridge and Cemetery Hill."

"What about Howard's corps? Does Howard have a grip on the battle?"

"Eleventh Corps is engaged with Ewell's corps, driving down from the north. My messenger said the battle reminded him of Chancellorsville, with Howard's corps retreating like scared rabbits. No one seems to be in charge."

"Jesus Christ! This can't be happening!" Meade raged, his voice rising several notes. Had he made a tragic blunder in not riding forward? If so, the army was in mortal danger. "Do you think Hancock will arrive in time?" Meade said.

"Maybe. It will be close." Sharpe said.

"Damn, you Butterfield. Damn you to hell."

Sixth Corps needed to move *now*.

---

*3:00 p.m.*

All hell was breaking loose at Gettysburg, and he had chosen to remain at his headquarters at Taneytown. He'd kept his options open as long as possible. Despite his best efforts, this scrap at Gettysburg was becoming less like a brawl and more like an all-out engagement.

His gut screamed that it was time to commit to Gettysburg, sensing the power behind the enemy's lead forces, perhaps Lee's entire army. He'd clung stubbornly to the hope of executing the Pipe Creek line. He was an engineer. A planner. A hedgehog. Topography mattered. Pipe Creek was ideal, a perfect natural defense. Gettysburg looked good on the map, but he hadn't seen it personally. And he wasn't ready to give up the perfect in exchange for the expedient but unknown. Yet.

Meade spotted George Jr. riding up the knoll. "General Williams wanted to remind you that you owe an update to Halleck," he reported.

"Got it," Meade snarled, his tone sharp as a butcher's blade. George saluted and returned to the house.

Meade stared at the Taneytown Road, his heart shuddering at the prospect of meeting Lee without massing all seven infantry corps. *Damn you, George, stop fretting the afternoon away, trying to force the fight into a plan that was obsolete as soon as it failed to reach Reynolds and Howard and the scrapping began.*

*Trust your instincts, soldier. Order the army to Gettysburg.*

He gestured toward the staff officers standing near the house. Biddle mounted and rode to him.

"James, I want you to ride to General Gibbon and order him to start marching Second Corps toward Gettysburg."

"Are you abandoning the Pipe Creek plan?" Biddle said.

"Not quite." Meade scowled. "But I need to push Hancock's corps forward toward Gettysburg. Should the Rebels repulse Howard and gain Gettysburg, I will have Howard fall back to Emmitsburg instead of Taneytown. Pushing Second Corps up Taneytown Road will plug a possible huge gap in the middle of the Army of the Potomac."

Biddle rode off.

The afternoon dragged on. Dust from the Taneytown Road, stirred by the thousands of men from Second Corps marching to the beat of regimental drums, obscured the view of the headquarters house—a frustrating reminder that his staff was in the dark about the battle right now. Behind the troops stretched a long white ribbon of wagons.

Meade shook his head to clear it. Gettysburg or the Pipe Creek line? The longer he waited, the greater the chance Lee would destroy his forces at Gettysburg. The words of his instructor at West Point years ago rose above the clamor in his head. *Between plans and execution rage the winds of war.*

Events eventually would make the choice for him at Gettysburg if he didn't decide soon.

*4:20 p.m.*

Colonel Sharpe rode to him, jerked the horse to a fast stop, dismounted.

"What do you have?" Meade snapped.

"It's clear from the prisoners we've interrogated that Howard has been fighting elements of Hill's and Ewell's corps. We've found no indication of Longstreet's corps being engaged, which is odd. We believe his corps of about 40,000 remains west of the South Mountain near Cashtown and will not arrive until tomorrow, probably midmorning. Then Lee's force will be at full strength, nearly 100,000 troops.[14] My best guess is Lee will attack full force tomorrow in the early afternoon," Sharpe reported.

Meade chewed on the information while Sharpe waited. A new factor. An opportunity.

"Lee didn't conduct a planned, coordinated attack," Meade said, the light dawning. "So we both stumbled into an unplanned engagement."

Sharpe nodded. "Gettysburg is where the lead elements of two moving armies have unexpectedly collided."

"There's hope," Meade said. He stood straighter. "It's become a foot race. Whoever concentrates first on the best ground will have the edge."

"Yes," Sharpe said.

Meade cogitated on these revelations, stroking his beard. If he could concentrate the entire army at Gettysburg before Longstreet's corps arrived, he had a chance to defeat Lee. *Lee will never predict a hedgehog would maneuver quickly and curl up and hunker down, unfurling its protective spines before Lee's next attack.* General Hooker had left him some pearls of wisdom after all.

"This is good news, Colonel. Thank you," Meade said, a touch of power in his voice.

---

14 Colonel Sharpe and General Meade believed Lee's forces numbered nearly one hundred thousand. Actually, the Confederate force was much smaller, numbering over 70,000 men and 283 guns. The Union force was 90,000 men and 360 guns.

Sharpe added, somewhat bewildered, "Something else is odd. Jeb Stuart's cavalry boys are not present at Gettysburg. I can't make sense of this."

Meade paused for a long moment. "I can't make heads or tails of it either. No one has infantry move alone and blind in enemy country. What is Lee up to?"

*4:30 p.m.*

Meade mounted Baldy and gestured for Sharpe to follow him; both men galloped down the hill to the house. Meade found Williams inside. "Seth, order Sedgwick's Sixth Corps to begin the march from Manchester to Gettysburg, now!"

Williams hedged, staring and confused. "Are you sure? Sedgwick is in position, anchoring the far right of the Pipe Creek line."

Meade's brow furrowed. "We need to start Sedgwick marching toward Gettysburg. I can always send him back to Manchester."

Williams arched a brow, alarm painted across his face.

"I know it's a risk," Meade said. "But we have an opportunity, a small window to exploit Lee's mistake of not having Longstreet's corps and Stuart's cavalry available for the fight today. If we can mass before Lee does tomorrow then we have a good chance of beating him."

Meade glanced at his watch. Half past four. He would hold off ordering the remaining corps and Hunt's artillery reserve forward until he heard from Hancock. The Pipe Creek plan was drifting to the background—a back-up plan.

Meade turned to Sharpe. "What do you know about Gettysburg?"

"It's a rural market town, mostly brick buildings and cramped, narrow roadways. Home to about two thousand folks. There is a great deal of open country, meadows and pastures, surrounding the area. Long low-rising ridges flow across the countryside. The high ground south of Gettysburg has several large hills that could offer solid natural defenses."

Meade nodded. "Good. Very good."

Meade slipped into his rocking chair and accepted a cup of coffee from Biddle. As he sipped, General Pleasonton arrived, waxed moustache finely trimmed and a perky straw hat perched rakishly on his head. Meade pursed his lips, curtailing a sarcastic smile. Pleasanton looked more like a Rhode Island yachtsman than the commander of the cavalry corps.

Pleasonton saluted. His face was white. "I just received this disturbing dispatch from Buford timed 3:20 p.m."

Meade read the message:

> *A tremendous battle has been raging since nine and a half a.m., with varying success. At the present moment the battle is raging on the road to Cashtown, and in short cannon range of this town; the enemy's line is a semicircle on the height from north to west. General Reynolds was killed early this morning. In my opinion, there seems to be no directing person. We need help now.*

He clenched his jaw. "Christ. Buford." *We need help now.*

"Buford doesn't think Howard and Doubleday are working," Pleasonton said.

"I think he's right. Lee is concentrating faster than I."

A second messenger from Buford arrived, delivering the dispatch directly to Meade. Meade read the short note: "Send up Hancock. Everything is going at odds, and we need a controlling spirit." Meade handed the note to Williams, who read it quickly and passed it to Pleasonton.

Meade dropped his head, staring at his boots. He was picturing Howard's troops breaking, running from the battle as they had six weeks earlier at Chancellorsville.

"Damn you, Butterfield," Meade cursed. "We are losing the battle at Gettysburg."

Meade stepped outside and lit a cigar. He was playing in a high-stakes poker game but betting little, trying to be prudent and cautious. But Lee was an unshakable risk taker. Damn it, if he didn't act fast, he would be playing right into Lee's hand. He had to make an all-or-nothing bet—put everything either on Gettysburg or on Pipe Creek. He had to do what the fox did not expect.

Williams walked outside. "What do you want to do?"

Meade took a deep breath. *Enough is enough. You're either all in or all out.*

"Playing cautiously has proven to be more than crippling," he said. "It's just providing Lee a steady stream of Union troops for his meat grinder."

"If Reynolds had committed to a fight, he must have found suitable ground," Williams said. "Trust Reynolds. You can't hold anything back when fighting Lee. That has been the critical mistake of each of the past four commanders. They always held something back."

Meade's breath hitched. "Let's do it."

Without hearing from Hancock, he decided to take the ultimate risk, committing the entire 100,000-man army. *Christ Almighty.* He had just killed the Pipe Creek plan.

Meade turned to Williams. "Send orders to Third and Fifth Corps to march to Gettysburg. Have Sickles leave two or three brigades at Emmitsburg in case Longstreet swings south and tries to flank us."

"First and Eleventh Corps will soon be joined at Gettysburg by Slocum's Twelfth Corps," Williams said. "That gives us three corps at Gettysburg by late afternoon."

"Hancock's Second Corps will arrive late this evening," Meade said. "Hopefully, Sedgwick's Sixth Corps will arrive by early morning. Order Hunt's artillery reserve to Gettysburg, following behind Second Corps."

Williams saluted, moving over to his staff and barking out instructions. Headquarters grew steadily noisier. Williams was turning out to be a superb adjutant general, as calm as he was volatile. Perhaps he should have picked Williams as his chief of staff.

Meade walked about and prayed. *For the sake of the nation, please let me have made the right decision.*

---

*6:00 p.m.*

Warren's courier arrived, dusty and sweaty. "General Meade. General Warren is delighted with the southern and eastern Gettysburg defensive positions."

"By the grace of God, this might work," Meade murmured. *Focus on massing all forces. Take the defensive. Establish strong interior lines of support. Then look for an opportunity to take the offense.*

He puffed on his cigar. He still hadn't heard from Hancock, and rushing everyone to Gettysburg without a detailed plan was at best worrisome. But he trusted Reynolds's decision this morning to hold and fight. He sighed. It was reassuring knowing he was reinforcing Hancock.

Meade gestured for Biddle. "I want to send a note to Halleck."

Biddle nodded and retrieved a pen and paper. Meade sat down at the dining room table and wrote:

> *The First and Eleventh Corps have been engaged all day in front of Gettysburg. The Twelfth, Third, and Fifth have been moving up, and are I hope, by this time on the field. This leaves only the Sixth, which will move up tonight. General Reynolds was killed this morning, early in the action. I immediately sent up General Hancock to assume command. A.P. Hill and Ewell are certainly concentrating. Longstreet's whereabouts, I do not know. If he is not up tomorrow, I hope, with the force I have concentrated, to defeat Hill and Ewell; at any rate, I see no other course than to hazard a general battle. Circumstances during the night may alter this decision, of which I will try to advise you.*

Meade gave the dispatch to Biddle. "Telegram this note to General Halleck."

---

*6:10 p.m.*

Major Mitchell from Hancock's staff walked into Shunk House. Meade drew a deep breath.

"General Hancock begs to report he has checked the enemy," Mitchell reported. "He will the hold the ground until dark."

Meade slapped the map table. His heart soared. "Damn, that's good news!"

He turned to Williams. "Send messengers to Third and Sixth Corps telling them to hurry to Gettysburg. Hancock has halted the Rebel attack. We have a great opportunity."

He turned back to Mitchell. "Show me on the map how the events unfolded."

Mitchell pointed to Cemetery Hill. "General Hancock stopped here and rallied the retreating soldiers and organized a sound defensive position."

Meade nodded.

"General Hancock said the Cemetery Hill and Culp's Hill ground he was defending reminded him of Marye's Heights at Fredericksburg, except this time the Union occupied the high ground."

As Mitchell talked, a warmth began to radiate in Meade's gut. He had made the right decision, curbing his natural impulse to rush to Gettysburg and take control. By choosing Hancock to command the forward forces, he was better able to coordinate the remaining corps movements to Gettysburg from his position at army headquarters.

Mitchell wrapped up his recounting. "It is General Hancock's opinion that Gettysburg is the place to fight a general battle. He will hold it until nightfall to give you time to decide if you want to maintain this position."

"Gettysburg is the place to fight," Meade said. "Before you arrived I ordered the army to concentrate at Gettysburg."

Meade walked out of the house and mounted Baldy. Biddle followed. They rode up to the small knoll. At the crest, Meade could see the last remnants of Hancock's supply wagons in the distance, rattling toward Gettysburg. The blue columns of marching soldiers had disappeared. Calm washed over him. Hancock had saved the day. But they had been lucky. Hancock had arrived just in time to rally the troops.

"Thank you, God, for allowing him to mass the army before Lee had done so," Meade whispered.

"When do you want to depart for Gettysburg?" Biddle asked.

"I want to depart after Sedgwick arrives. I asked Sedgwick to ride ahead of his corps so we could chat at the soonest possibility. I haven't spoken with him since assuming command."

"Sedgwick may not arrive until very late this evening," Biddle said diplomatically. "He has nearly twenty miles to cover to get to Taneytown."

"You may be right," Meade conceded. "But one way or another, I'll go forward this evening. I want to arrive in Gettysburg by midnight."

Meade paused, puffing on his cigar. "Start breaking down headquarters camp. When you're finished, depart for Gettysburg with the advance party and locate a suitable place for army headquarters."

Biddle saluted and left to inform the others.

*7:30 p.m.*

Meade looked at his watch. Nearly half past seven.

A rider was coming down the Taneytown Road toward headquarters. A staff officer outside pointed him toward the knoll. Meade recognized him—Captain Parker, from Hancock's staff. Parker saluted, handed Meade a message.

*General Meade:*

> *When I arrived here an hour since, I found that our troops had given up the front of Gettysburg and the town. We have now taken up a position in the cemetery, which cannot well be taken; it is a position, however, easily turned. Slocum is now coming on the ground, and is taking position on the right, which will protect the right. But we have as yet no troops on the left, the Third Corps not having yet reported; but I suppose it is marching up. If so, Sickles's flank march will in a degree protect our left flank. In the meantime, Gibbon had best march on so as to take position on our right or left, to our rear, as may be necessary, in some commanding position. General Gibbon will see this dispatch. All is quiet now. I think we will be all right until night. I have sent all the trains back. When night comes it can be told better what had best be done. I think we can retire; if not, we can fight here, as the ground appears not unfavorable with good troops. I will communicate in a few moments with General Slocum, and transfer the command to him.*

*Howard says Doubleday's command gave way.*

*Your obedient servant,*
*Winfield S. Hancock*

Meade gestured for Captain Meade to ride to him. He arrived, saluted. Meade said hurriedly, "Have General Williams send further orders to Sedgwick urging him forward to Gettysburg with all speed. Tell Sedgwick I will wait at Taneytown to speak with him before I go to Gettysburg."

Captain Meade saluted, rode off.

It was nearly dark when Meade rode back to the house. The evening passed with no new information. Meade rebuked a couple newspaper correspondents who wanted to know if Howard had broken again at Gettysburg.

"Hardly," he said. He scolded them for never getting a story right and kicked them out of the headquarters house. God, he hated reporters. But he remembered Williams's advice to treat reporters with a bit more tolerance, as Lincoln would read and believe their stories.

---

*8:05 p.m.*
*(Sunset 7:44 p.m. Dusk ends 8:17 p.m.)*

Captain Meade returned. "I just received word Reynolds's body is coming on the Taneytown Road accompanied by two or three mounted officers. They should arrive in a few moments. They will pause for you to pay your respects."

Meade let out a long groan, recalling the brilliant image of Reynolds in his dress uniform visiting him just three days ago. Unwelcomed tears pooled in his eyes, some spilling over. He had lost his friend, his mentor.

"Thank you, George." It was barely audible.

Meade walked outside. When the death wagon arrived, a young captain saluted, turned, and removed the blanket covering Reynolds's body. Meade bowed his head, softly praying. He looked up, trying to read the body for signs of Reynolds's last moments. His friend's face was calm. He must have died instantly. He still smelled of the battlefield and of the beginning of decay. Apparently, the shadow army of embalmers, typically trailing the army, had failed to arrive.

His glance moved from Reynolds's head to his boots. Everything seemed normal, except for the stillness. It seemed too cruel that John was dead.

Meade cleared his throat and touched Reynolds's face. Cold. So cold. He stared at his friend's still chest, where a heart used to beat with emotion. *Damn it, John. I needed you. We needed you.* He turned and forced out a thank-you to the young officer for taking care of General Reynolds, then he walked back into the house.

*9:30 p.m.*

Meade slumped into his chair, closed his eyes, and rocked back and forth, wondering when Sedgwick would show. Lee's right arm was Longstreet. Meade's was Sedgwick. His soldiers called him Uncle John. A grandson of a Revolutionary War officer who served under George Washington at Valley Forge, Sedgwick was a short, thick-set, muscular officer with curly chestnut hair and a full beard. He dressed sloppily, like Meade, with minimal attention to spit and shine. And he was honest, like Meade. He had seen more combat action than any other West Point graduate, fighting at Vera Cruz, Cerro Gordo, Churubusco, and Chapultepec during the Mexican War, and winning three battlefield promotions for bravery. He also had fought the Seminoles, Cheyenne, Kiowa, and Comanche, and the Mormons in the Utah War. Unlike glory-hungry generals like Sickles, Sedgwick never campaigned for promotions, preferring to let his war record stand for itself.

Meade had great respect for Sedgwick. At the Battle of Antietam, Sedgwick was severely wounded when a bullet went through his leg and another fractured his wrist, but he refused to retire from the field. He was then hit by a third bullet, shattering his shoulder. His aides carried him from the battlefield, unconscious. Meade had hoped that, after Reynolds, Lincoln would offer command of the Army of the Potomac to Sedgwick. He prayed his loyal friend would arrive soon.

*10:00 p.m.*

An earsplitting yell. Hancock's voice. Meade opened his eyes. Hancock burst into the house and Meade's heart leaped. He had not expected Hancock to return from Gettysburg. He rose to his feet; Hancock saluted Meade smartly. Meade returned the salute and grasped his hand. Hancock looked haggard, almost asleep on his feet. His typically spotless uniform was a mess.

In a shocked tone, Meade said, "I did not expect you back tonight, Winfield."

"I wanted to report to you in person, so you could decide whether to reinforce Gettysburg or fall back to the Pipe Creek line," Hancock said.

"I've already ordered the army to fight at Gettysburg,"

Hancock looked surprised. "You already ordered the army to Gettysburg?"

"Yes, I did," Meade affirmed, nearly smiling. "Colonel Sharpe confirmed you were fighting two of Lee's three corps, and Longstreet's corps was not on the battlefield. He also said the ground south of Gettysburg provided an excellent defensive position. This presented us a great opportunity to mass our army before Lee. If we can concentrate at Gettysburg tomorrow before Lee, I want to conduct an offensive attack."

"Good. Very good," Hancock said. "Damn, I was hoping you would do that! You read my mind."

Meade continued, "Just after I ordered the army to Gettysburg, Major Mitchell arrived and gave me a detailed report of the terrain and the actions of today."

"Excellent," Hancock said. "The terrain south of Gettysburg offers a nearly perfect defensive line."

"Great. That's great," Meade said.

Hancock frowned. "I wasn't pleased with Slocum's slow arrival at Gettysburg. He seemed hesitant about coming because you had chosen me to command after Reynolds's death. Once I explained that you wanted him to relieve me he seemed motivated to take charge."

Meade shook his head. Slocum was competent, but he needed detailed orders. He typically executed them with perfection, but he moved at a snail's pace. That's why he had chosen Hancock to replace Reynolds: the youngest corps commander acted brilliantly on instinct.

Several voices were at the front door. A group of Meade's senior staff officers were walking into the house. One was covered with dust and sweat, drinking from a canteen. Warren. He had brought along Hunt and Butterfield, tagging behind like two little brothers. Warren stopped before Meade and saluted. He then turned and saluted Hancock.

Hancock grabbed Warren in a bear hug and slapped him on the back. "Great job today, Gouv!"

"Thank you, Winfield," Warren said. "You did a great job as well. That was a close one, today."

Meade said, "Good to see you, Gouv."

Meade motioned for everyone to sit at the dining room map table, showing northern Maryland and southern Pennsylvania.

Warren flashed a hello as Williams joined the group. Butterfield stood watching.

"Winfield was describing the action this afternoon at Gettysburg," Meade said. He turned to Warren. "Please join in. I'm interested in your thoughts." Warren nodded but let Hancock take the lead.

Hancock and Warren talked for almost an hour, giving the commanding general a detailed account of the situation at Gettysburg and what had transpired after their arrival. They explained the defensive line formed by nearly seven thousand infantry and cavalry, together with forty-three pieces of artillery. The Rebels initially had achieved a minor victory on July 1 by massing a superior force, but the Union troops had fought them bitterly to a stalemate. After a prolonged and savage struggle, Reynolds's First Corps had been shattered. The Union survivors had retreated to the heights beyond the town of Gettysburg. But the Rebel forces had suffered tremendous losses, both killed and wounded.

"Gibbon's former unit, the Iron Brigade, punished the Confederates severely," Hancock said with a spirited tone. "No better evidence can exist as to the discipline, bravery, and doggedness of Reynolds's corps than its ability to receive and repulse attack after attack, from ten in the morning until four in the afternoon. Only after both its flanks were enveloped by overwhelming numbers of the enemy did this heroic corps abandon its last position."

"For some strange reason," Warren said, "Ewell's corps did not advance against Cemetery and Culp's Hills when they had the chance."

Hancock opened his mouth wide and yawned for several seconds. After closing his mouth he rubbed his eyes and stared at Meade.

"Lee's army made a huge blunder today by not taking those hills," Hancock said.

Meade stood as his heartbeat sped up, pulsing like a bass drum in his ears. Hancock had saved the advanced left wing from total defeat. The Rebels may have claimed victory in today's tactical battle, but the stalemate that ensued meant they did not win the campaign—thanks to Reynolds and Hancock.

"Winfield, superb job today. Thank you," Meade said. "Why don't you rest here for a bit and join your corps in the morning. I'm going to depart in a few minutes for Gettysburg. I will speak with Gibbon along the way."

Hancock saluted and trod wearily up the stairs.

<hr />

*10:40 p.m.*

Meade turned to Warren. "Great job today, Gouv. Are you ready to ride to Gettysburg again? We need to draw out the defensive positions to take full advantage of the topography."

Warren nodded. "I'm ready." He stood, motioning to Captain Paine. "Captain Paine is a superb sketch artist; he will accompany us. He has located a young civilian guide who knows the road to Gettysburg inside and out."

"Good. Let's get to it," Meade said. "I'm anxious to arrive there as soon as possible." He turned to Captain Meade. "Let's head for Gettysburg. Ready the horses."

Captain Meade saluted and left the house.

Meade turned to Butterfield. "I want you to stay and coordinate with any couriers who may arrive in my absence. Also, I want you to meet with Sedgwick when he shows. Give him an assessment of the terrain at Gettysburg and tell him of my plans to hold Gettysburg until we can mount an offensive attack. Tell him I need his corps at Gettysburg immediately. If he has to force-march his corps to Gettysburg to arrive by morning, he must do it. You're dismissed."

Butterfield saluted and walked away.

The small group—Meade, Hunt, Warren, Captain Paine, and Captain Meade—went outside and mounted their horses. Their guide was a lean, red-haired, freckle-faced, twelve-year-old boy named Freddie, whose father owned a livery stable in Taneytown and whose best friend lived in Gettysburg.

"Freddie," Meade said. "Are you sure you know how to get to Gettysburg in the dark?"

"Yes, General Meade. I make the ride to Gettysburg and back two to three times a week. I could do this in my sleep."

"This ride, Freddie, is critical to beating back the invading Rebels. It's as important as Paul Revere's ride that fateful evening in 1775. Do you understand?"

Freddie beamed. "I understand, General Meade."

"Let's go," Meade said. "I want to get there as soon as may be."

"Yes, sir, General Meade," Freddie said.

The boy and his horse raced toward Gettysburg with incredible speed. Meade spurred Baldy, trying to keep pace.

"Jesus, this boy can fly in the dark," Meade muttered. "Keep on his tail, Baldy."

Although Freddie was riding at a blazing sprint, Baldy and Meade did not slow him down. After almost half an hour galloping at breakneck speed, they came upon a tremendous congestion caused by Hancock's wagon trains lumbering toward Gettysburg. Freddie slowed and scooted off the road, with

Meade close behind. Suddenly, Freddie's chest hit a low-hanging branch, bending it backward. It snapped back, hitting Meade and sending his glasses into the vast dark beyond the road.

"God damn it," Meade shouted.

Freddie slowed to a trot, turning in his saddle. Meade pitched into him. "Watch out for the damn branches, Freddie!"

"Sorry, General Meade," Freddie said.

Meade couldn't take time looking for the glasses. But he had a spare pair in his saddlebag. "Pick up the pace, Freddie," he shouted. "We'll be right behind you."

Freddie nodded, pressing on lickety-split. Baldy fell into a comfortable cadence a few yards off the small horse's right flank. Meade thought back three days ago to the early-morning ride with Colonel Hardie to Hooker's headquarters. It seemed a lifetime ago. Now he was riding to Gettysburg, where Lee was waiting for him. There was no turning back.

Voices shouted out ahead and Freddie's horse slowed to a stop. Meade reined in Baldy. Several men with muskets armed with bayonets appeared. They had bumped into Gibbon's rear pickets. Meade's cavalcade had arrived at Second Corps, where 11,000 men were bivouacking about three miles south of Gettysburg.

---

*11:40 p.m.*
*Gibbon's headquarters' bivouac near Big Round Top*

Meade looked across the fields at thousands of campfires sparkling in the night. A large sergeant greeted them. "Halt."

Bursting with pride, Freddie blurted out, "I'm escorting General Meade to Gettysburg."

The sergeant spotted the army headquarters command flag being carried by Captain Meade and saluted. "General Meade, we will escort you to General Gibbon's headquarters."

Meade's cavalcade stopped at Gibbon's headquarters. Meade looked at his watch and calculated they had covered eight miles in fifty-seven minutes, with a moon that was not up yet. Not bad.

"Good evening, General," Gibbon greeted him. "Hancock halted me south of town because the fighting had trailed off and there was no pressing need for his corps to be in the line."

"Have you run into any Confederate activity?"

"No. But Hancock was worried about the possibility of the Rebels slipping in behind the Union forces somewhere along the Union flank between Gettysburg and Emmitsburg. By keeping Second Corps three miles south of Gettysburg, I could easily intercept a Rebel force taking one of several crossroads connecting the Emmitsburg and Taneytown roads."

"John, I want your corps moving toward Gettysburg before first light," Meade directed.

He turned to the young boy. "Ok, Freddie. Let's go!" Meade shouted.

They were back on the road again, with Freddie leading the way.

Not long after, Meade sighted two formidable rocky hills looming in the darkness. They must be the Round Tops, the extreme left of the Federal line. Freddie led them past the hills on the road running along the top of Cemetery Ridge. The rising yellow moon revealed troops sleeping in the shadows of Little Round Top, guns lying beside haystacks, ammunition piled nearby, and rows and rows of army wagons.

*11:55 p.m.*
*Gettysburg Cemetery*

Freddie turned off the road and trotted up the gradual incline leading to the cemetery. The grassy hill was dotted with clumps of trees. At the crest, Freddie, Meade, and the rest entered the rear of the little graveyard on Cemetery Hill. It was quiet, dark, and eerie.

Baldy picked his way past broken tombstones and monuments, heading for the large, two-columned, arched gatehouse. Across the way, only a few miles beyond the cemetery gatehouse, was Lee's headquarters. He was now face to face with his mortal enemy.

Meade clutched the reins tightly and shuddered. He had less than six hours before sunup to ride the perimeter, study the terrain, establish defensive positions, and develop a plan. Would Lee attack at dawn? The Union army had to be ready if he did.

Colonel William Colvill

# ❧ Thursday ☙

July 2, 1863

**General Robert E. Lee, Commander**
Army of Northern Virginia
Commanding for One Year

**General George G. Meade, Commander**
Army of the Potomac
Commanding for Five Days

**General George Sykes, Commander**
Fifth Corps
Commanding for Five Days

**General John Newton, Commander**
First Corps
Commanding for One Day

## ❧ 26 ❧
# Meade — Thursday, July 2

*12:01 a.m.*
*Cemetery Hill*

The moon hung bright in the midnight sky as Meade and Baldy snaked their way among the grave markers on Cemetery Hill, following closely behind their twelve-year-old guide. A chorus of low moans echoed over the cemetery. Meade's heart started pounding. There was something unsettling in those cries and weeping sobs, a fatal pain behind them. Meade squinted, struggling to focus without his thick-lensed glasses fixed on his hawklike nose. His stomach was knotted as his blurry eyes navigated like a blind man following a guide dog. Hell, he had been in the dark most of the day.

His nostrils flared as he caught his first whiff of death, thick and rotten. A flood of misgiving swept over him. He shook his head. His orders to move units to Gettysburg had ravaged the living on this hill. He gasped as the putrefied stench of decaying flesh mingled in the air. He sucked in another breath, death burning his lungs. He coughed, hacking up phlegm pooling deep in his injured lung. He spat, narrowly missing a headstone.

As they climbed through the cemetery, he licked his lips, tasting the salty sweat. General Reynolds's image popped into his mind. Soon Reynolds's body would be laid to rest beneath a marbled headstone etched with his name and a few kind words. Meade grieved. How many enlisted boys also had died in the past several hours? Hopefully, somebody had written a few notable words on their wooden grave markers.

Death was the great equalizer on the battlefield. Regardless of your rank, grave markers made of marble, stone, and wood all served the same function—marking a rotting corpse.

Meade pushed Baldy as fast as he dared. Freddie was picking up speed as if sledding down a mountain slope. "Come on Baldy," Meade urged. "Stay with him."

He did not know the terrain of the high ground they were holding. Hancock and Warren had said it was suitable. He trusted their judgment, but he wanted to see for himself. Clenching his jaw, he rode on, needing to make an eyeball inspection of the natural defenses. He would do that after meeting with Slocum and Howard.

Freddie turned and yelled, "We're almost there!"

"Good. Keep pressing, Freddie," Meade said as the blurry boy slipped into the shadows, his jingling spurs marking the path forward.

Meade's shoulder muscles tightened. He was not looking forward to meeting with Howard. Howard's anger must be raging. Being relieved of command by Hancock was a point of honor, a chivalry matter resolved in the recent past by a pistol duel. Howard wanted satisfaction. He might even deserve satisfaction. He'd need to handle the man delicately.

He had last spoken with Howard during one of Hooker's council meetings. At thirty-two, the young corps commander was a gentleman, but he was neither a profound thinker nor blessed with natural ability for making war. He was a brave man and an honorable one, but not well suited to lead men in battle. Meade had witnessed the tragedy of Howard's men running at the battle of Chancellorsville.

But Howard had not received the Pipe Creek Circular and didn't have the information he would need to effectively lead in the heat of this particular battle. Howard didn't know Meade's crucial plan of retreat for the First, Third, and Eleventh Corps should they need to withdraw from Gettysburg and occupy the Pipe Creek line. In that event, without that knowledge, the carnage would have been unthinkable. He needed to make sure Howard understood that.

Heart rate quickening, Meade shook his head. *Damn.* Howard was a good man. If only he could fight. Reynolds had told him Howard had taught mathematics at West Point while studying theology, with the thought of going into the ministry. Meade swallowed. Perhaps Howard should have pursued his passion for theology.

"Freddie, slow down a bit," Meade shouted. "I can't see a damn thing."

"Will do, General Meade," Freddie said.

Moments later, Meade called out again. "I see you now, Freddie. Keep moving."

Meade spotted several freshly dug graves. It was the butcher's bill for orders he had given while safely positioned thirteen miles from the fighting. He was damn lucky Hancock had held the lines.

They weaved around gaping shell holes. Meade covered his face with his gloved hand at the pungent odor of rotting horse carcasses. There had been one hell of a fight here.

He spotted the cemetery gatehouse, the place Hancock described as the high-water mark of the Rebel assault. His breath caught. The vast number of soldiers scurrying about this modest patch of land resembled an ant colony. All around him, and down the hill below, the soft clanking of metal picks rippled the air. Soldiers were building a series of linked redoubts, fortifying Cemetery Hill as officers on horseback watched their progress.

Building a trenched defensive ring was a good plan, and having all night to dig in was fortunate. If the soldiers were firmly dug in and firing from behind protective rifle pits, they just might repulse the Rebels. The hill was superb defensive ground. Not as perfect as the Pipe Creek line, but more than adequate.

"Here he comes," a voice yelled. "It's General Meade!"

In the distance, Meade spied a bleary cluster of figures mingling. He picked up the pace, anxious for news from his corps commanders. A large group of men engulfed in a blue cigar cloud were waiting. He trotted toward them, mindful that these men had fought a savage battle and had survived, allowing his army to fight tomorrow.

He rode to the gatehouse and dismounted, handing the reins to Biddle. Hunt and Warren arrived and dismounted. Meade turned and Slocum, Howard, and Sickles saluted, watching him closely.

Meade returned their salutes and growled, "Well, Generals, what do you think? Is this the place to fight?"

"I am confident we can hold this position, General Meade," said Howard.

Slocum said, "Cemetery Hill and Culp's Hill are good for defense."

"I was able to get a glimpse of the Round Tops from the Emmitsburg Road and of Cemetery Ridge and Culp's Hill," Sickles said. "All are good places to fight, General!"

"Well, gentlemen," Meade said, "I am glad to hear you say so, for it is too late to leave it. I have ordered the other corps to concentrate here."

The three corps commanders showed surprise.

Meade turned and strode toward Baldy. He plunged a hand into his saddle bag and wriggled his fingers past a metal whiskey flask and his cigar case. "Damn it, I know they're in there," he muttered. His shoulders tensed as he hand rifled through the saddle bag. Maybe they were in the other saddle bag. As he pulled his hand out, his fingers touched the spectacle case. He released a breath he didn't know he was holding. He looped the temple frames around his ears. His blurry vision disappeared. He turned in a slow circle, scanning the hill. Thousands of blue soldiers were dug in, barricaded, rifles fixed with bayonets, waiting anxiously for enemy attackers to roll forward.

He recalled Buford's note: *In my opinion there seems to be no directing person. We need help now.* That was Buford's on-scene assessment of Howard's performance as acting commander earlier that day. Meade also remembered Howard's note saying he was shocked and disgraced by Meade's decision to place Hancock in command. This had to be addressed, but carefully. He needed Howard to remain engaged, functioning at his best for the upcoming fight. He didn't want this to become an honor issue.

Meade turned back to his corps commanders.

Slocum, the senior corps commander, moved forward. "We are most pleased you've arrived." He saluted and said, "I stand ready to be relieved."

Meade returned his salute. "General Slocum, I relieve you and assume command of all forces at Gettysburg." Both men dropped their salutes, and Slocum's face flushed with relief.

Meade eyed these three corps commanders. This was the first time he had spoken with two or more of them together. An unfamiliar warmth stole around him. There was something unexpected, even strangely comforting, about the moment. The meaning was clear. His arrival had excited them—a surprise to Meade, who was expecting a far lesser response. It was an unexpected gift, a welcome reassurance.

With unfeigned fervor, Meade said, "Thank you, gentlemen, for your good work today. We took a licking, especially the loss of General Reynolds, but the Rebels paid a heavy price for their tactical victory. As I understand the army's disposition, we saved the high ground, ready to fight again tomorrow. But this time, with the entire Army of the Potomac dug in."

He turned toward Freddie, still sitting on his horse. Meade extended his right hand, shaking the boy's hand firmly. "You did well tonight, Freddie. You have done a great service for your country."

Freddie blushed under his freckles. "Um, thank you, General Meade. It was an honor."

"Are you hungry?" Meade asked his young guide.

Freddie nodded yes.

Meade turned, spotted Biddle standing near Sickles and one of Sickles's protégés, Major Tremain. Meade's good humor faded at the sight of Sickles and his sycophant aide-de camp. He could not fire Sickles now, but after the battle he would replace him.

Meade motioned for Biddle. "Get this fine, brave young man some vittles and a place to sleep. It's the least we can do for his valiant effort."

Meade turned to the boy. "I can't thank you enough for your services, Freddie. The Union owes you a debt of gratitude far beyond what I can bestow upon you now."

"Please follow me, Freddie," said Biddle. He and Freddie walked towards Meade's aides.

Howard went up to Meade. With a formal salute, his voice tight, he said, "Good evening, General Meade."

"Good to see you, General Howard," Meade said, with a pleasant tone. Howard looked ragged and dead tired.

"General Meade, I was dismayed this afternoon when General Hancock arrived with an order from you saying he was to assume command of all forces at Gettysburg," Howard said. "Sir, I respectfully request your approval of the actions I took."

"Walk with me," said Meade.

Meade took a few steps away from the other generals and stopped. Howard followed.

Using a soft voice, Meade said, "Oliver, I assure you I imputed no blame when I ordered Hancock to take command. Hancock knew my desires to execute the Pipe Creek plan, which you did not receive before fighting at Gettysburg. That was my staff's fault."

Howard paused, tense, frowning.

"Hancock was best informed to act as my proxy to determine whether we should stay and fight at Gettysburg or fall back to the Pipe Creek defensive line," Meade said. "Nothing more."

Howard said, "General Meade, I..."

Meade held up his hand and pursed his lips, quelling a hot flame of anger that threatened to flare up. He turned his back to Howard and gestured for Slocum, Sickles, Warren, and Hunt to join him. Time was precious, and he had several decisions to make. Soothing Howard's feelings would have to wait.

After the five generals formed a semicircle around Meade, he eyed Howard and said, "Oliver, placing a reserve brigade on Cemetery Hill at the beginning of the fight was brilliant. That enabled us to hold the high ground."

Howard bowed his head and said, "Thank you, sir. It was one hell of a fight."

"Well done!" Meade said.

"General, would you like a bite to eat before you ride the lines?" Howard said. "The wife of the cemetery's caretaker, Mrs. Peter Thorn, has coffee and hot biscuits with honey prepared for you."

Meade's stomach growled. "Yes, thank you."

He followed Howard into the cemetery gatehouse with Hunt, Warren, and Sickles in trail. Mrs. Thorn, a striking woman in a white blouse and blue skirt, greeted them. As they sat at the kitchen table, Mrs. Thorn stood next to Meade and looked directly into his eyes.

"General Meade," Mrs. Thorn said, her voice cracking. She paused as she placed her right hand across her heart. "I've been praying that you and your army would save us." She wiped a tear from her cheek. "I've been terrified for the past few days with the Rebels riding in and out of town."

She dipped down and her hands skimmed his neck like the touch of an owl swooping down. She wrapped her arms around Meade, giving him a tight hug. Her long hair grazed against his jaw as he caught the sweet scent of honeysuckle.

Meade stirred in his chair, his heart pounding and his throat going dry. He returned the hug as they held each other for a few moments. Then as quickly as she had hugged him, she let go and fetched the coffee and hot biscuits with honey. Tiny sparks flicked inside him, sparks that had been buried since his last visit with his wife. For a brief moment Margaretta's sharp cry echoed in his head as her body had quaked against his.

They sat at the dining room table and Meade sipped hot coffee and gulped down a biscuit. He licked drops of honey that had dripped onto his beard. Mrs. Thorn walked over and handed him a napkin. He couldn't help blushing.

"Thank you, Mrs. Thorn," he said. "The biscuits are quite tasty."

Sickles offered cigars and the room filled with blue smoke. Howard and Sickles provided their updates on today's events, and the positions their corps now occupied. As they talked, Meade started to develop a plan for positioning the army in a fishhook disposition that traced along the hills and ridges south of Gettysburg.

Biddle walked into the dining room. "General Meade, we've located a small white house just south along the Taneytown Road and behind the ridge for your new headquarters."

"Thank you, James," Meade said. "I will depart in a few minutes."

Meade eyed Howard. "Do you think Lee will attack tonight?" Meade asked.

"No, not tonight," Howard said. "Ewell's corps had a chance to attack Cemetery Hill and Culp's Hill when First Corps and Eleventh Corps were rallying at the crest. But for some reason, Ewell decided not to tangle with us further. Instead, he just sat watching us shoring up our defenses. While Ewell was lingering below Culp's Hill, Hancock and I placed artillery batteries in the largest gaps and started firing at the Rebels. They are keeping a respectable distance for now."

Meade nodded. "Good."

"We are now all in a line of battle in a good position that will be hard to penetrate," Slocum said. "But I fear it being turned, especially our left flank. The soldiers are worn down by hard marching and want of sleep. I've received reports from my advance pickets who have probed Ewell's front on our right flank. I believe Ewell might be attacked from my far right position on Culp's Hill."

A thrill jolted through Meade, and his brows drew together. A reversal of Chancellorsville. This time the Union forces would be decimating Lee's flank.

"This may be an opportunity," Meade said. "If Longstreet is not up in the morning, I will order Slocum's Twelfth Corps and the remnants of First Corps to attack Ewell. Once they get the Rebels on the run, I will order Hancock's Second Corp to conduct a supporting attack. Sickles's Third Corps on the Union far left flank would stay in place and fix the enemy, preventing Lee from flanking him."

Sickles stared at Meade with a puzzling look. Meade ignored him.

"Who will serve as your reserve?" Slocum said.

"Sykes's Fifth Corps will remain as the reserve force ready to exploit Slocum's attack," Meade said. "We will have Lee outnumbered by 20,000 to 30,000 infantry, if Longstreet's corps doesn't move up by morning.

"If Sedgwick arrives in time, I will use him as the reserve force and order Sykes's Fifth Corps to support Slocum's attack."

Meade turned to Sickles. "Place your left flank on Little Round Top. Your right flank will connect with Hancock's corps on Cemetery Ridge when they arrive in the early morning. Hancock's corps is a few miles south of you, and these troops will be departing from their bivouac before first light."

Sickles frowned and saluted. "Yes, sir."

To Slocum, Meade said, "Reconnoiter your front and prepare to attack Ewell's corps in the morning."

Slocum saluted, "Yes, sir."

Meade went over to Mrs. Thorn and shook her hand. "Thank you for your generous hospitality. I'm worried about your safety, however. Please consider moving to a safer place at dawn, as I'm expecting another big battle today."

Mrs. Thorn said, "Thank you, General Meade. And I hope you win."

Meade glared deeply at her. "I plan on winning, Mrs. Thorn."

Meade left the gatehouse, followed by Howard, Warren, and Hunt. Outside he spotted Captain Meade, holding Baldy's reins. He took the reins and walked Baldy halfway down the gently sloped hill, stopping at the forward batteries of First and Eleventh Corps. His breath quickened. Almost lazily, thousands of Confederate campfires flickered across the fields behind Gettysburg. A tremendous display of massive power. From the direction of the Rebels, a crack and bullet whickered overhead. An eerie reminder the Confederates were eager to begin the attack. Soon a barrage of enemy shells would be howling overhead. No time to dwell. He mounted Baldy.

"I want to examine the Federal positions on the left flank."

*1:00 a.m.*

He rode southwesterly from the cemetery gatehouse, followed by Howard, Hunt, Warren, Captain Meade, and Captain Paine, Warren's topographical engineer.

As they reached Steinwehr's division of Eleventh Corps, Meade turned in his saddle. "Captain Paine, come ride next to me."

"Yes, sir." Paine pulled next to Meade.

"I want you to sketch the path we ride. This will be our defensive line. Mark the Union corps positions as I call them out," Meade said.

"If it's okay with you, sir, I also will sketch as many of the terrain features as I can," Paine said.

"Good. After we're done riding the line, I want you to copy tracings of the sketch for all the corps commanders."

Meade rode Baldy, crossing the Taneytown Road, moving down Cemetery Ridge. A tremor of excitement poured through him. He loved this part of commanding, something for which he had trained at West Point and was damn good at. His lengthy experiences as a railroad surveyor and construction engineer enabled him to discern the advantages of the ground for attack, defense, earthwork sites, and sites for a field battery. As Baldy walked, Meade painted a defensive line for Paine, using the landscape's curves and slopes.

Paine had propped a drawing board on his saddle's pommel, sketching a map of the surrounding terrain as they rode. After a few hundred yards, Meade halted. "Let me see what you've got so far."

Paine handed him the drawing pad. Meade scanned the sketch and said, "These are accurate enough for engraving. Damn, you're good."

Paine reached out and took the sketch pad. "Thank you, sir."

Meade, Paine, and the cavalcade rode south along Cemetery Ridge toward Little Round Top. Federal campfires still flickered near its base.

"Captain Paine," Meade said. "After we ride the defensive perimeter and mark all the corps positions, I will be in a much better position to determine if Slocum should launch an attack in the morning."

Paine nodded and kept sketching.

Off to the west, Meade spotted two figures sitting on horses in a field behind a long line of soldiers.

"Is that General Stannard and his Vermont Brigade?" Meade asked.

"Yes, according to Slocum," Paine said. "This is where Hancock placed Stannard's brigade. Stannard is acting as the night field officer along Cemetery Ridge."

Meade rode toward General Stannard and motioned for Hunt, Howard, and Warren to join him. Meade stopped next to General Stannard and returned Stannard's salute. Stannard was a medium-sized man, full-bearded but slightly balding. He commanded a Vermont brigade previously assigned to the defense of Washington. The last time Meade had seen Stannard was in Virginia, during the Peninsula Campaign. Hancock had credited Stannard with securing a critical bridge during the Battle of Williamsburg.

"General Stannard. When did you arrive on the battlefield?"

"We arrived yesterday from Washington at twilight," Stannard said. "I reported to General Hancock, and he assigned this section of Cemetery Ridge to me. My brigade was assigned to Doubleday's Third Division, First Corps, but we were not involved in any of yesterday's fighting."

Meade nodded. He admired Stannard; the Vermonter had a reputation for courage. Stannard was physically tough, previously operating a foundry in St. Albans near the Canadian border. His quiet but disciplined command style had earned him the respect of both his men and his superiors, including Meade.

"I'm damned glad you're holding down the left flank," Meade said. "Has there been much enemy activity in your front?"

"No, sir, just an occasional shot ringing overhead," Stannard said.

Stannard provided a detailed description of his front, including the positions of Doubleday and Robinson's battered divisions of First Corps.

"I'm concerned about the half-mile gap in the line between Sickles's forces on the left down by Little Round Top and Howard's forces on the right occupying the brow of Cemetery Hill," Stannard said.

"When Second Corps comes up this morning, they will fill the gap," Meade assured him.

Stannard nodded. Meade turned, peered west across the flat field. In the distance, perhaps a mile or so, there was another dark rise.

"Is that Seminary Ridge?" Meade said.

"Yes, sir," Stannard said.

Meade stared toward Seminary Ridge. No movement; no sound.

A rifle cracked at long range and a bullet rippled through the air. The two generals listened.

"Probably a Rebel forward picket hoping to see if a Union soldier would return fire," Stannard said.

"My guess is the Rebel is trying to figure out the end of the Union line," Meade said.

A Vermonter, several hundred yards in front and off to Meade's left, returned fire. Meade looked in that direction and could make out several large structures.

"What are those buildings over there?" Meade asked.

"That's the Codori Farm," Stannard said.

After a few moments, Meade proceeded south along Cemetery Ridge toward the bivouac of Third Corps near Little Round Top. He paused when the Codori Farm was straight across from him.

Meade turned to Hunt. "If you can place the reserve artillery batteries here along the Cemetery Ridge line, supporting the infantry, they could create a formidable rampart."

"Yes, sir."

---

*4:05 a.m.*
*(Dawn is breaking at 4:15 a.m. Sunrise is 4:48 a.m.)*
*Cemetery Ridge*

Meade and his group continued to ride the ridge. The cool early-morning air was soothing. He glanced at Paine, totally absorbed in sketching the line, his hand a blur as if sandpapering a wall. All along the ridge to Little Round Top, thousands of blue troops were sleeping. Meade's entourage arrived at the base of Little Round Top. He was met by General Greene, whose Twelfth Corps brigade was occupying the lower ridge where Cemetery Ridge fused into the lower edge of Little Round Top.

"General Greene, it's good to see you occupying this terrain."

Greene saluted, "It's good to see you, General Meade. It's a mighty great pleasure to serve under you, sir!"

Meade appreciated his oldest warhorse, commanding one of the toughest brigades in the army. They talked for a few moments. Meade learned that General John Geary's Second Division of

Twelfth Corps had two brigades, including Greene's, and two regiments supporting the Little Round Top landscape.

Greene pointed to the top slopes of Little Round Top. "Geary placed two regiments there to occupy those commanding heights. At daybreak Sickles's corps is supposed to relieve all of Geary's troops, including those occupying Little Round Top. Geary's units will go back into line at Culp's Hill with the rest of Twelfth Corps."

"Very good," Meade said. "Hancock did a good job recognizing the importance of Little Round Top and ordering Geary to occupy it. It's the perfect anchor of the southern portion of the fishhook."

Greene nodded. "The eye of the Union army's fishhook line."

"Any enemy activity in your front?" Meade said.

"No, sir."

*4:42 a.m.*

*Culp's Hill*

Meade and his party trotted northeast toward Culp's Hill. The sun was just beginning to break, casting a long shadow west toward the Confederates. They rode behind Cemetery Hill and crossed the Baltimore Pike and as far as Rock Creek, turned, then rode north following Rock Creek until they reached the far right flank of Culp's Hill. Slocum was waiting for them at Culp's Hill. Meade rode there and halted.

Slocum saluted. "Culp's Hill is the far right of the Union line."

"The hook in the fishhook defense line," Meade said.

"Yes," Slocum said. He pointed. "But I'm worried about the steady buildup of Confederates in my front."

Meade glanced at the enemy fires at the bottom of Culp's Hill.

"I'm also concerned about an unmanned gap on Culp's Hill between the right of First Corps and left of Twelfth Corps' line," Slocum said. "I fear Ewell will exploit this gap."

Meade turned to Hunt. "Can you move some artillery to cover the gap until Geary's division arrives this morning from Little Round Top and provides the permanent plug?"

"Yes, sir, we can cover the gap."

Hunt turned to an aide. "Locate Major Thomas Osborn, chief of artillery of Eleventh Corps, and have him post three artillery batteries that can cover the narrow saddle gap."

Meade's face grew hot. Why in the hell didn't Slocum plug the line himself? Was he timid? God, this lack of initiative drove him insane.

He glared at Slocum. "Geary's division will be relieved at first light by Sickles's Third Corps that is bivouacked close by Little Round Top. Geary's division will move back to Culp's Hill where you can use them to plug the gap."

"That's good," Slocum said.

With Paine beside him, Meade rode to the top of Culp's Hill. The other generals trailed close behind. The hills were heavily wooded sides, making artillery placement difficult. But the hill had to be held because it dominated Cemetery Hill and the Baltimore Pike, the road providing the Union army's supplies. Meade rode to the narrow saddle between the two mounds. Sure enough it was without a single Union soldier. Christ Almighty. The gap was so huge Ewell could have marched his entire corps through it, unmolested by any of Slocum's defenses.

Meade spent several moments on Culp's Hill scanning the campfires of Ewell's army. He turned and glanced toward the Baltimore Pike. It was a much better road than the Emmitsburg and Taneytown roads leading to Gettysburg.

"Henry. We must protect the Baltimore Pike at all cost," he said. "Hill's corps is opposite the northern portion of Cemetery Ridge. Ewell's corps is surrounding Cemetery Hill and Culp's Hill. If Longstreet's corps appears beyond the Union's far right on Culp's Hill and attacks before Sixth Corps is up, the army is doomed. Lee will blow out the right flank of the Union."

Slocum nodded.

Meade turned to Slocum and his tone was sharp. "As soon as you have plugged the gap, I want you to reexamine the terrain on the right of Culp's Hill to determine if it is suitable to launch an attack from that front. If it is, the attack would take place east of Rock Creek. Twelfth Corps would lead, supported by Fifth Corps, which is just arriving on the field, and Sixth Corps, which is marching toward Gettysburg over the Baltimore Pike."

Meade dismounted and walked over to Paine, examining the sketch laid out on the ground of the defensive line he had just ridden.

"The line really does look like a fishhook," he said, his voice full of warmth and wonder at both the plan and Paine's rendering of it. "The point and barb are on Culp's Hill, defended by Slocum; the bend is Cemetery Hill, defended by Howard and parts of First Corps; the shank running nearly two miles south is Cemetery Ridge, defended by Hancock and Sickles's corps; and Sickles's corps is the eye of the shank, anchored on Little Round Top."

Meade pointed to different parts of the fishhook, detailing where each corps should be placed. Paine marked the positions on the sketch. "What do you estimate the distances along the fishhook to be?"

Paine studied the sketch for a few moments. "The distance from Little Round Top to the edge of the curve at Cemetery Hill is about two miles. The distance from that point to the far right of the Union line at Culp's Hill is about a mile and quarter." Paine pointed to the two extremities, Culp's Hill and Little Round Top. "These two end points are about a mile and three quarters apart as the crow flies."

363

"Short interior lines," Meade said. "Excellent. What would the distance of the Confederate position be, if they occupied Seminary Ridge around to Culp's Hill?"

"About six miles," Paine answered.

"This is a huge advantage. The Union army's fishhook defense has shorter interior lines than Lee's army. A rare mistake by Lee. We can easily supply and communicate and move interior forces faster than Lee," Meade said. "This is good. When you finish making the tracings, deliver them to the corps commanders."

Meade turned to Hunt. "I want you to ride the line again, to ensure the artillery is properly placed. Make whatever changes you see fit."

Hunt saluted and moved off. Meade gestured for Howard to ride with him toward Cemetery Hill. He guessed Howard was itching to discuss the Hancock incident, again. It was time Howard got everything off his chest.

Howard began, "I want you to know, General Meade, that I'm the one who, upon arriving at Gettysburg, noticed Cemetery Hill and saw its immediate advantage as a military position."

Meade nodded.

"I placed my Second Division under General von Steinwehr and three artillery batteries under Major Osborn on Cemetery Hill as the army's reserve. It was not General Reynolds or General Hancock. I feel I performed well under the adverse conditions in which I found myself and the army."

Meade said nothing for a few moments, finding the right words. "Oliver, I was most proud of your performance yesterday. But I need you now to focus on the attack that will happen sometime this morning. We have a good chance of defeating Lee today. And you will play a big part in that victory."

"Thank you, General Meade, for your vote of confidence," Howard said.

"Good, Oliver. Now let's focus on today's battle."

Meade and his party rode up to General Carl Schurz, who was inspecting Howard's division commanders' positions on Cemetery Hill. Meade greeted him and they briefly reviewed the division placements. Then he paused, his penetrating glance sweeping across the field. "Well, Carl," he mused as if he had finally settled the matter in his mind, "we might as well fight it out here just as well as anywhere else."

He turned to Biddle. "Let's ride to the headquarters house. I'm hungry and could use a hot cup of coffee."

<hr />

*5:30 a.m.*

*Emmitsburg Road; the copse of trees*

Biddle led the small group behind Cemetery Hill, cutting across Taneytown Road, riding until they reached Emmitsburg Road, where they traveled south for a bit among the Vermont boys. Meade left the road, stopping at a copse of trees. The copse was located within a small stone wall that ran north-south along the ridge.

"This stone wall will provide a good defensive position for soldiers to kneel behind," Warren observed.

Meade nodded and looked past the copse of trees. His eyes glared at the huge gap in the Union line, seeing no approaching blue soldiers marching from the Round Tops. Meade's muscles tensed. If Lee attacked, he could exploit this large hole in the defensive line. Second Corps was marching to this very spot, and they needed to arrive soon.

He stood on Cemetery Ridge, looking through his binoculars for any clues of Confederate activity amid the trees. Morning's early light brought a chill that slid over him. Somewhere on Seminary Ridge, Longstreet's corps was coiled and fixing to strike. But he saw no enemy movement. *Where have you gone, Longstreet? Are you in front of me? Or are you on my far right, preparing to strike Slocum?* A prickly tingle bunched in his neck.

365

The morning was already turning hot. By noon it would be blistering. Meade and Biddle rode east from the copse of trees toward the small white cottage. Meade crested the ridgeline and, down below, next to the Taneytown Road, he spotted the white two-story cottage, a wee bit longer than wide.

"This is the Widow Leister's house," Biddle said. "Its central location close behind the Union lines on the reverse slope of Cemetery Ridge makes it a perfect place for headquarters."

"What happened to Mrs. Leister and her family?" Meade asked.

"Lydia Leister departed yesterday around midmorning when Reynolds was deploying the Iron Brigade on McPherson's Ridge. Her six children accompanied her. She went to stay with her sister, who is married to John Slyder, whose farm is near Big Round Top. She is not expecting much fighting near the Round Tops."

"I hope she is right," Meade said. "Make sure no one ransacks the house. It would be nice if we left it as we found it." Meade doubted that was possible.

Biddle nodded.

The porch ran the length of the front of the house. A portion of the right side of the porch was enclosed, creating what appeared to be a small bedroom. Looked at from the Taneytown Road, the slanting porch roof was connected to the house a few feet below the roof overhang. Above the porch's far left side, where the house roof peaked, protruded a brick chimney. Viewed from whatever angle, the walls and porch seemed paper thin.

"This house will provide little protection from a Minié ball. An artillery shot would rumble right through it," Meade said.

"It's in a good location, however. We don't think too many artillery shells will be flying this way," Biddle said.

"We'll see," Meade said.

Meade dismounted and walked into the house. His butt hurt, and his back was tense. A hot cup of coffee was waiting for him. He took a few sips, letting it jolt him awake.

*6:30 a.m.*

Captain Meade entered the house and announced, "General Gibbon is headed here using the Taneytown Road."

The coffee's heat flowed through Meade's veins. He set the cup down and went outside. He mounted Baldy and rode a bit down toward Little Round Top, stopping in a field on the east side of Taneytown Road. He spotted the Second Corps Flag coming on the road. A rush of relief eased his fluttering stomach.

It was seven in the morning.

Gibbon, accompanied by Major Haskell, stopped and saluted. Just behind them, Meade spotted the vanguard of Second Corps marching rapidly toward him. Thousands of bayonets shimmered in the low eastern sun, moving to the beat of the regimental drums. *Damn, what a beautiful sight!* Second Corps had arrived before Lee launched his attack.

"General Meade," Gibbon announced, "I report the presence of Second Corps on the battlefield. I respectfully request your assignment of the corps."

Meade pointed to the ridge and the copse of trees behind Gibbon and Haskell, "I'm damn glad to see you, John. Place your corps on Cemetery Ridge. Your right flank should meet with Howard's left flank. You should extend your line south toward Little Round Top. I've ordered Sickles to connect with your left flank."

Gibbon saluted and he and Haskell departed for Second Corps' line on the ridge.

Meade turned and rode back to his headquarters. Inside, the small white house was a hive of activity. Williams had arrived, transforming the house into the nerve center of the Army of the Potomac. Meade gestured for Biddle and told him he was famished. Biddle said they were cooking a hot breakfast for him. Meade smiled, turned, and moved out to the porch. "I hope to God Sedgwick arrives before Lee attacks," he muttered.

For a few moments, Meade stood, watching, and listening to thousands of Union troops marching, stopping south of Gettysburg to cover the fields and ridges like rows of blue flowers.

Captain Paine reported. "General Meade, I've completed all the sketches of the defensive line and marked where the different corps should be."

"Good. Have them delivered to all the corps commanders." Then Meade pointed to the map on the table. "Then plot the defensive line on this map. Good job, Captain Paine. Thank you."

Meade sighed. *Well, it's not the Pipe Creek Line. But it is a damn good line. Thank you, God.*

# Fishhook Defenses
## Midmorning, July 2, 1863

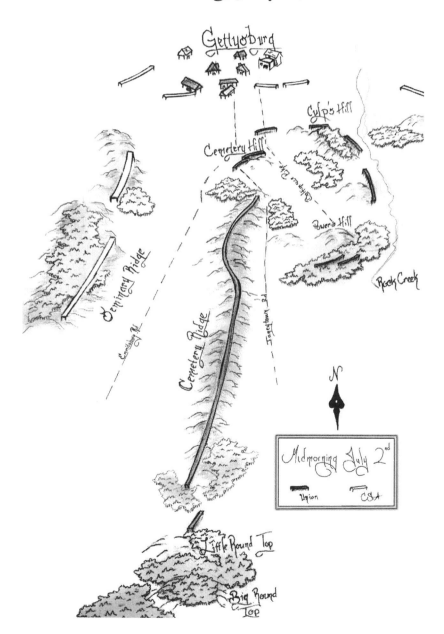

# ❧ 27 ❧
# First Minnesota — Thursday, July 2

*2:00 a.m.*
*Four and a half hours earlier*
*First Minnesota's bivouac, three miles south of Gettysburg and about one-half mile southeast of Big Round Top*

Sergeant Wright's body lay crumpled on the ground, the side of his face sunk into the damp field grass and his knees curled up like a Red Wing boy cannonballing into the Mississippi. Yellow flames like dragon's fire leaped out of rifle muzzles protruding from enemy earthworks. A Minnesotan fell and tried to rise. The flames spurted again and the body tumbled, quivering, to the ground. Bullets spat around the First Minnesota regiment like a violent hailstorm. The dying cries of the wounded shrieked over the battlefield. A familiar voice was speaking. A hand gripped his shoulder and squeezed like a vise. Captain John Ball's faint voice crept into his darkened brain.

"Sergeant Wright!"

He tried to open his eyes but they were frozen shut. The vise grip tightened as if sharp talons were clawing into his soft flesh. He opened his mouth to shout, but nothing would come.

"Sergeant Wright! Wake up, wake up now!"

Wright roused slowly, prying his eyes open. There in the moonlight, Captain Ball's face appeared above him. His heart leaped, pounding in his chest. Thank God. The recurring nightmare was over.

Ball whispered, "Sergeant Wright! Get up and wake the soldiers from the other companies and form the regiment at once!"

"Yes, sir!" Wright said, somewhat embarrassed he had been so difficult to wake.

"The First Minnesota is to march at once," Ball said. "Tell the boys to make as little noise as possible."

Wright nodded, grumbling under his breath. He checked his watch.

Two in the morning.

He stood, gathering his blanket and stuffing it into his knapsack. Nausea swirled in his stomach. The two armies were now close enough to strike like vipers. They would be fighting in a matter of hours.

The grass was wet, and the leaves on the trees and bushes showered Wright as he passed. It was taking longer than he wanted to wake the boys and make them understand they were to march at once. They groaned, annoyed at his intrusion. They had been on their feet since three the previous morning and had marched more than twenty-two miles. Three times after the sun set they had received permission to start fires and brew coffee, and three times they had been ordered to pack, fall in, and march farther. They were convinced the senior army leaders did not know what in the Sam Hill was going on, and many grumbled that the new commanding general must be a senseless idiot like the previous ones.

Wright found First Lieutenant Christopher Heffelfinger, commanding Company D, snoring like a grunting pig. Wright shook his shoulder hard, and the startled lieutenant let out a loud yelp. Wright put his hand over the lieutenant's mouth.

"Wake up, Lieutenant," Wright said. "We're moving out."

Heffelfinger nodded. Wright glanced at the other members of the regiment. The outcry had jolted most of the regiment awake. Wright's mouth split into a white-toothed grin. The loud yelp had pissed off Adams, but it made less work for the sergeant.

The exhausted soldiers of the First Minnesota formed in a column, grumbling about the early reveille, passing along rumors about why they were moving now. Their faces in the dappled darkness were tight and tense.

Roll was whispered. Wright took the head count. All were present except the early-morning picket detail, located a half mile behind them. He walked to the head of the regimental column. Flagstaffs jutted upward like aspens, the flags wrapped around the poles. No wind was stirring.

*2:15 a.m.*

Wright saluted Lieutenant Colonel Adams, acting commander. "Sir, all men are accounted for except the picket detail. Should I send some boys back and fetch them?"

"No. Leave them and have the First Minnesota join the brigade," Adams said.

"Sir, we can cannot leave them. I will go back alone and get them," Wright said.

"No," Adams said. "Follow orders and fall in."

Wright stood still and glared, his face burning like a furnace.

"I'm the commander of this regiment," Adams said. "Now move out, Sergeant."

Wright turned and formed the regiment behind the Fifteenth Massachusetts. The brigade joined the other brigades to form Gibbon's division: more than 3,500 infantry soldiers.

The division stood fast as the provost guards fixed bayonets, passing the word to each regimental commander that no one was to make any noise and that they were to muffle the clinking of mess tins. As they waited, Wright's ears picked up a chilling whisper: "This is a death march."

## Colvill

*2:25 a.m.*

Colonel Colvill, still under arrest, was sitting astride his horse at the back of the regiment. He scowled. Without bugle calls, the Minnesota pickets guarding the rear of the division would be left behind, having no way of knowing to fall in with the regiment.

Colvill's cheeks burned. "Damn you, Adams," he muttered. *You're more concerned with looking good. Failing to send a few men back to retrieve the pickets is heartless vainglory. You never leave a Minnesota boy behind.*

Colvill shook his head. Should he order the last few men in the column to fall out and warn the pickets the regiment was moving out? He took a deep breath, letting his military bearing overrule his instincts. Today's battle would be of epic proportions, and he *had* to assume command again, before the start of fighting. *Damn it.* He refused to sit in the rear as the First Minnesota went into battle. These were his boys. He had trained them, bled with them, and knew them down to their souls. As soon as the regiment was deployed at Gettysburg, he would find General Harrow and request to have his command back. There was a good chance Harrow would say yes, having witnessed his prowess in leading the regiment. He glowered. Don't play into Adam's hand and ruin your chance of regaining command by issuing illegal orders to warn the pickets.

*2:30 a.m.*

The soldiers of the First Minnesota waited for the order to march. Muffled grousing spread among the men about not being allowed to make coffee before marching. Wright promised coffee in a few hours, after arriving at Gettysburg.

After a few minutes, Wright whispered, "Let's march." The regiment started. More than 12,000 soldiers of Second Corps moved forward in silence, without the formality of reveille, the trumpeting of bugle notes, or the beating of snare drums. At first there was much stopping and starting as the corps bunched up and spread out like an accordion. But soon the spacing among Second Corps' 50 regiments became regular and the marching fell into a quick, steady pace of dull, thumping feet.

Private Alonzo Pickle, a young, good-looking lad from Company K, gestured for Wright. Wright walked over; Pickle was bubbling with excitement. Wright shook his head. What mischief was the regimental clown creating?

Pickle whispered, "It's my birthday. I'm twenty."

Wright relaxed, flashed a smile. "One thing sure, Alonzo, you will never forget your twentieth birthday. Someday, you will tell your grandchildren of this day."

Pickle's jaw dropped, and he looked away with a muddled face as if he might not live to celebrate. He turned back to Wright. "Perhaps this evening we can have Captain Searles play the banjo for us."

"Now that's a good idea," Wright said. "I will suggest it to him this morning."

Wright moved back outside the regiment, looking up and down the column. Everyone was keeping pace, and the formation was taut and straight. It was growing lighter, a pale blue appearing in the eastern sky. Today was going to be a scorcher. The humidity was thick. There was no wind. Sweat was forming on his brow. In another hour, he would be drenched.

The regiment quick-marched northward on the Taneytown road, keeping a steady stride a few paces below a double march. Wright scanned their faces. Concern covered them. It was eerie being near yesterday's battlefield. Wright's mind flashed to the First Battle of Bull Run as he was marching into battle. He had nearly been killed by a Minié ball that creased the left side of his forehead. Would he survive Gettysburg?

The painful memory of the regiment's first casualty was burned in Wright's mind. Joseph Garrison had fallen during the First Battle of Bull Run, the greater part of his forehead torn away by an artillery shell. Wright had stood motionless, with quivering lips, looking at Garrison's still form. Garrison had been a classmate at Hamline University, warm-hearted and generous. His death was a searing reminder of what was facing the First Minnesota today.

Wright gazed up the winding Taneytown Road; stretching as far as he could see was Second Corps. General Hays's Third Division would arrive at Gettysburg even as General Caldwell's First Division was just departing the bivouac four miles back. Incredible! Hard to grasp the enormous size of Second Corps.

Wright shook his head. Damn, this was going to be a big battle today. More than two hundred thousand men engaged in mortal combat. Meade was beginning his fifth day in command of the Army of the Potomac. But Lee didn't care if Meade had been in command for five hours or five years. Lee would show no quarter. Would Meade?

Silence enveloped Wright as the tension built. He checked out the regiment. Everyone seemed to have a grip on their nerves. But Wright was certain of one thing: Not a soldier in the First Minnesota doubted Meade's resolve to march them until their shoe leather was destroyed and their feet blistered. Meade had a gift for marching.

They marched the Taneytown Road, leaving behind Big and Little Round Top to their left. With the breaking light, occasional distant shots rippled up ahead, behind Cemetery Hill.

*6:00 a.m.*

The First Minnesota was passing a small white house on the left. General Meade's large command flag was flying out front. Wright spotted aides coming and going, but he did not get a glimpse of General Meade. Two burly sentry guards holding bayoneted rifles stood on either side of the front door. Tethered to the white picket fence framing the large yard, nearly fifty cavalry horses nibbled grass and witnessed the First Minnesota's passing. After marching a hundred yards past Meade's headquarters, Second Corps halted on the eastern side of Cemetery Ridge.

Lieutenant Colonel Adams shouted, "First Minnesota, left-face."

Wright turned left face. Adams shouted, "Half-step march!"

The First Minnesota marched the eastern slope of Cemetery Ridge, occupying the Federal left center of Meade's defensive line. First Minnesota and its three sister regiments of First Brigade were halted in the rear of Gibbon's division, just behind the crest of Cemetery Ridge.

Adams rode to Wright. "Gibbon designated First Brigade as the division's reserve. First Brigade is to be deployed in one long double-rank line with twenty feet spacing between each regiment."

"Yes, sir," Wright said. "Where did Third Division halt?"

Adams pointed north toward Cemetery Hill. "Hays's Third Division is butted up against First Corps in a crook at Ziegler's Grove, where Cemetery Hill meets Cemetery Ridge," Adams said.

"After we are in position, do we have permission to stack arms and light fires for coffee and breakfast?" Wright said.

"Yes."

Wright gave the orders to the First Minnesota, along with instructions to distribute extra ammunition among the soldiers. The men stacked arms and ignited fires. An unexpected awe erupted inside Wright's chest as he watched hundreds of smoke spirals rise into the cloudless blue sky. My God, why hadn't Lee launched a dawn assault against Meade's left flank before Second Corps had arrived? What a missed opportunity. Maybe lady luck was favoring the Union today.

Wright's nose flared and his stomach grumbled as the odor of roasting coffee drifted by. It was more than he could stand. Wright walked over to Private Charles Muller of Company A and requested a cup. Muller poured a steaming cup.

"Thank you, Charlie. God bless you!" Wright said with a big grin.

Wright brought the cup under his nose, sniffed the lovely aroma. He took a large gulp, then another, letting the black elixir do its magic. He scanned the ridge in front of them about a mile away and spotted no enemy movement. He brightened.

He turned and eyed the regiment. There was not much talk among the Minnesota boys. Wright turned away, looking to the east across the fields Meade had asked Gibbon's division to defend as the sun rose above another large rise, Power's Hill. To the west, directly in front of them, was a stone wall, two to three feet high, running north-south for a considerable distance each way. North about a hundred yards, Wright saw a large copse of trees nestled behind the wall. Beyond that, the stone wall jutted ninety degrees eastward for a bit, then ran north again. Gunners from Second Corps had arrived behind the wall and started unhitching the caissons and positioning the big artillery guns.

*7:00 a.m.*

On the ridgeline toward Gettysburg were thousands of tightly packed blue soldiers. Wright spotted two soldiers trundling the line wearing the black hats of the Iron Brigade. When they arrived at the First Minnesota, they talked with Lieutenant William Lochren, Corporal Henry O'Brien, and Private Marshall Sherman, three of the First Minnesota's toughest soldiers.

Wright watched the conversation, trying to suppress his curiosity. Sherman wore a sweeping gunfighter mustache and fought like a bull, wielding a razor-sharp knife in hand-to-hand combat. O'Brien's baby face barely supported a wispy, down-turned mustache, but the Irishman's fiery temper was feared by all; even Colvill was wary. Lochren was strikingly handsome, a quality earning him tons of good-natured ribbing, but no one questioned his battlefield mettle.

The two soldiers walked over to Wright. They were from First Corps, Doubleday's division. Wright learned there had been heavy fighting. The Iron Brigade finally had been brushed away by an overwhelming force, but the Confederates had suffered heavy losses. Both men were certain Lee would attack again today, with his entire army. He had been lacking Longstreet's corps and his eighty-seven cannons yesterday. Wright shrugged, glooming at the Black Hats. Today was going to be one hell of a fight.

The Black Hats moved on down the ridgeline occupied by Second Corps soldiers stretching for nearly a mile, digging in along the ridge, preparing for the Rebel attack.

"Breakfast!" someone yelled.

The odor of sizzling bacon lingered in the air; Wright licked his lips. "I smell it," he shouted. I'll be right there!"

*7:45 a.m.*

Colvill sat on his horse at the back of the regiment, his mouth dry and his heart hammering against his ribs. Time was running short to regain command. If his boys were going to fight today, he wanted to lead them. He spurred his horse, heading toward his brigade commander, rehearsing what he would say, relying upon his quiet passion to sway General Harrow.

Harrow was talking with General Gibbon and his adjutant, Major Haskell. Colvill dismounted, clenched his jaw, and walked over, his large frame casting an enormous shadow over them. He stood with his arms behind his back as huge knots formed in his stomach. He eyed Harrow. After a few minutes,

Harrow looked at him. Colvill snapped to attention and saluted. Harrow returned the salute.

Colvill said in a low voice, "I should like to have command of my regiment before today's battle." He paused, as his face grew hot. "I would be greatly obliged to you if you would relieve me from arrest."

"You're right about a battle today," Harrow said. "You're released from arrest. I need you in command today. It's looking like we are going to have one hell of a fight. I was more than pissed with Hancock's idiot adjutant, arresting two of my top regimental commanders over that foolish creek incident."

Harrow paused and wiped his forehead.

"I'm also going to release Colonel George Ward of the Fifteenth Massachusetts from arrest, placing him back in command. Proceed back to your regiment and assume command," Harrow said. He added as Colvill turned, "Colonel Colvill, I'm sorry I didn't correct this matter sooner. You're a fine commander."

Colvill saluted smartly, "Thank you, sir."

A wave of joy washed away the suspended fear hovering in his chest. He mounted his horse and rode toward the First Minnesota lines, his heart swelling with gratitude.

Arriving at the regiment, Colvill found Lieutenant Colonel Adams. He dismounted, arms at his side and fists clenched, and walked to where Adams stood. He hauled in a deep breath.

"General Harrow has released me from arrest, and I'm to take back command of the First Minnesota," Colvill said.

Adam's black eyes narrowed into slits, and he put his hand on the handle of his sheaved saber. "You will not relieve me of command without written orders from above."

Colvill glared into Adam's eyes for several moments. After a few moments, Adams blinked.

Colvill turned, mounted his horse and rode back to Harrow, explaining Adams' response. Harrow cursed, then turned to his personal aide and directed him to ride back with Colvill and tell Adams that he was relieved of command, and that Colvill was reinstated as commander of the First Minnesota.

When they found Adams, the aide remained mounted. "Lieutenant Colonel Adams. Colonel Colvill is now in command." The aide turned to Colvill. "Colonel Colvill, formally relieve Lieutenant Colonel Adams." The aide smirked at Adams.

Colvill dismounted, strode toward Adams, stopping an arm's length away. "I assume command of the First Minnesota," he said in a low, gruff voice. Touching his hat, he took a half step toward Adams, so that they were standing nearly toe to toe.

Adams swayed, his lower lip twitching, his breathing raspy, like a wheezing boy. After a long moment, he saluted.

"I stand relieved," he said. He glanced away, looking down.

"I will report to General Harrow that Colonel Colvill has assumed command," said Harrow's aide. Before riding off, he winked at Colvill and said, "Good luck, sir. Give 'em hell!"

Colvill smiled at the aide as he rode off, and then folded his arms. He turned to Adams. "Ride your damn ass back to our bivouac, find the picket detail, and have them return to the regiment."

He paused, watching Adams's face twitch. His tone was fierce. "If you ever leave a Minnesota boy behind again, I'll skin you alive."

Colvill turned and mounted his horse. Relief coursed through him. He rode toward Wright and found him eating breakfast with several other soldiers. He reined his horse next to the sergeant. Wright rose.

"I'm no longer under arrest. General Harrow reinstated me as commander of the First Minnesota."

"Colonel Colvill is our commander again!" Wright shouted.

A spontaneous cheer erupted from the First Minnesota, and at the same time, the Fifteenth Massachusetts boys began to cheer just as loudly.

"Great news, Colonel Colvill," said Wright.

"Colonel Ward is no longer under arrest either and has assumed command again," Colvill said.

The two sister regiments, numbering over five hundred men, unleashed a deafening clatter, triggering curious stares from the rest of Hancock's Second Corps.

Delight rushed up Colvill's spine. He had not expected thunderous gratitude. Moving slowly among the clusters of men, his cheeks flushed red.

"Rest, boys," he said, wishing the whooping and hollering would simmer down.

The soldiers began to quiet down, but their eyes sparkled.

A distant rifle crack. A bullet zipped by Colvill's head. Everyone hushed.

He put the field glasses to his eyes and scanned the field. No sign of the enemy. How many Rebels were nested in the tall grass, waiting to pick off a Union officer?

"All right boys, let's get back into our lines. No more celebrating. We've got a fight to win."

The soldiers dispersed, moving to their campfires. Warmth spread through Colvill from his head to his toes. He was their commander again.

*9:45 a.m.*

Colvill was scanning Seminary Ridge through his binoculars, trying to take a fix on the source of the intermittent artillery fire splashing down near his regiment. From time to time, he spotted a puff of smoke from a Rebel shell. Confederate gunners from Hill's corps were firing eastward from Seminary Ridge. Most of these cannon shells were flying well over the First Minnesota lines, hitting harmlessly in unoccupied fields, closer to Meade's headquarters than to the regiment.

He turned north toward Culp's Hill. Because of the fishhook defense, Ewell's gunners, located north of Culp's Hill, were firing south and southwest on Federal positions on Cemetery Hill and Culp's Hill, with most of their shells falling well short of the Minnesota boys.

The whistling of an enemy artillery shell fired from beyond Culp's Hill drew Colvill's gaze to the north as he tried to catch a glimpse of its trajectory. The whistling grew sharper, but the shell was as invisible as a phantom. It flew overhead, exploding fifty yards south of the regiment. Colvill stiffened; that was a little too close. As the Rebel fire intensified, undershooting projectiles from Seminary Ridge and overshooting shells from beyond Culp's Hill were crossing in midair and starting to land in the First Minnesota area. The regiment was getting the worst of it. Occasionally, a Federal artillery battery returned fire, but the First Minnesota was now vulnerable, being fired on from two different directions.

He swiveled in the saddle, spotting a shell from Seminary Ridge bursting low over the First Minnesota, hurling hot fragments. Colvill raced over to Company I and dismounted. The ground was riddled with hats, broken bayonets, and mess tins lying around on green grass, spattered with blood.

Sergeant Oscar Woodard's body, lying face up, was cut by shell fragments. Sergeant Oliver Knight lay wounded, stunned, his breathing coming in shallow bursts. Colvill's stomach spasmed. He was close to both men's families.

Colvill turned to the company commander, First Lieutenant Boyd. "George, have a couple boys carry Knight and Woodard back to the division hospital. Bury Woodard's body with a marker."

He shook his head at Lochren. "It's unnerving as hell to be shelled and not be able to defend yourself."

"Maybe we should move up or back," Lochren said. "Every shell seems to be falling on the regiment."

As if some benevolent power had heard him, the sporadic enemy bombardments stopped. The sudden quiet was eerie.

"We'll stay here for the time being," Colvill said.

He turned and looked south toward the Taneytown Road. No sign yet of the pickets arriving. *Damn you, Adams.* He shook his head; his face burned. This matter with Adams was not over. After today's fight, he would settle that score when the two of them were alone. No witnesses.

## ✖ 28 ✖

# Sickles — Thursday, July 2

*1:00 a.m.*
*Nine hours earlier*
*Cemetery Gatehouse*

Sickles stood under the arch of the Cemetery Gatehouse, glaring at Meade and his small cavalcade riding south toward Cemetery Ridge. He turned to Tremain. "Meade is a damn son of a bitch. He will run the first chance he gets. What kind of commander hangs back twelve miles from an all-day battle?"

"Someone who is afraid to fight Lee," Tremain said.

"Hell, the only reason Old Goggle Eyes rode to Gettysburg this evening is because the fighting stopped, and he was likely to not catch a bullet, like Reynolds."

"Meade appears timid and indecisive, like his mentor, General McClellan," Tremain sniffed.

"Damn right. Meade is just like all the Union West Point army commanders—sluggish, and terrified to aggressively engage Lee's army." Sickles wiped his brow. "Thank God I disobeyed Meade's order yesterday to stay put in Emmitsburg. In just three hours in the heat and dust, I force-marched Third Corps to the sound of guns at Gettysburg. I bet that's the fastest march of the war by any corps." Sickles lit a cigar.

"Howard was mighty pleased to see you!" Tremain said.

"Damn right he was. I'll never forget his greeting. 'Here you are—always reliable, always first.'" Just remembering it sent delicious shivers surging through him.

"That's a generous tribute from one general to another," Tremain said.

Sickles nodded, glowing inside.

"I'm convinced, General," Tremain said. "If Third Corps had arrived earlier at Gettysburg, you would have handed the Rebels their ass instead of Lee handing us ours."

"Perhaps you're right. But I'm damn pissed I piddled around Emmitsburg trying to figure out why Meade ordered me not to support Reynolds and Howard. That's crap. I'm not going to make that mistake again. Meade will retreat the first chance he gets and I'm not going to let him. I'm going to be aggressive and do what's right to defeat Lee."

*1:05 a.m.*

Captain George Randolph, chief of the Third Corps artillery brigade, rode to General Sickles. "Do you want me to guide you to the Weikert House, where we've established Third headquarters?"

"Yes, let's go." Sickles and Tremain mounted their horses.

"How far is the Weikert House?" Sickles said.

"It's about a mile."

"Did Humphreys's division arrive?"

"I left the Weikert House about midnight, and he had not arrived yet."

Sickles cocked his head toward Tremain. "So much for Meade's bootlicking cronies being able to arrive on time. I thought Humphreys was supposed to be this great West Point topographical engineer—the god of maps. He should have arrived several hours ago."

"Maybe he ran into the enemy around the Black Horse Tavern," Tremain said. "Buford's scouts said Rebel cavalry had been lingering around there."

"Lingering? The Rebels probably were in the bar throwing down a few," Sickles said. "Damn Humphreys. He thinks he's privileged because he is friends with Meade."

Sickles and Tremain followed Randolph as he rode down Cemetery Hill and turned onto Taneytown Road. After riding a half mile, Sickles spotted a yellow glow pulsing in the shadows of the Little Round Top. He pointed. "Look, George. Are those Third Corps' fires?"

"Yes, that's Birney's division, and they are bivouacked just south of the Weikert Farm," Randolph said. "When Humphreys's division arrives, they will bivouac just north of Weikert Farm. Your headquarters tent is located near the Weikert House."

"Good." Sickles lowered his voice. "Henry, what did you think of the meeting with Meade?"

"Meade always seems nervous and excitable, as if he is ready to pop off like a firecracker," Tremain said.

"Ha! I agree," Sickles said. "He lacks the boldness and tenacity to defeat Lee. Mark my word, Meade will skedaddle from Gettysburg at the first opportunity. Hell, I don't know why he didn't stay in Taneytown tonight and save himself the trip of riding back there with his tail between his legs at the first sign of trouble today."

The glow of the fires grew brighter. Randolph pointed off to the right. "There is the Weikert House and your headquarters tent."

Sickles glanced to his right. The Weikert House was a two-story, flat-rock house with four white pillars supporting the front porch. A large barn was adjacent to the house.

Sickles dismounted in front of his tent. He lit a cigar and said, "Henry, I sure as hell wish Humphreys would get his ass here. I don't like having half my corps lollygagging about with the enemy so near."

---

## Humphreys

*1:10 a.m.*
*Emmitsburg Road*

Humphreys spotted shadowy figures ahead, blocking the road. A Union picket line, if he was lucky. To his right were two large, rocky hills, Big and Little Round Tops, anchoring the southern end of Cemetery Ridge, according to the map he had purchased yesterday morning. He had memorized the nooks and crannies of the terrain. His studying had paid off, enabling him to recognize the key terrain features of Gettysburg in the darkness.

A large, chunky sergeant sporting whiskery lamb chops and bushy eyebrows was leading the armed picket detail. Humphreys spotted the friendly face. The sergeant's valor defending Sickles's Hazel Grove salient at Chancellorsville had earned him a nomination for the Congressional Medal of Honor.

The sergeant saluted. "General Humphreys. Good morning, sir. I've summoned Lieutenant Colonel Orson Hart. He requested that he be awakened when you arrived so he could guide your men into position."

Humphreys saluted. "Well, I *hope*," he began, his booming voice growing louder with every word, "Sickles's *assistant adjutant* general is a better guide than Sickles's *inspector* general, Lieutenant Colonel Hayden. Because *Hayden* almost got me *killed*." His volume had crescendoed to an all-out bellow.

"How's that?" the sergeant asked, unruffled.

"We were marching a few miles west of the Emmitsburg Road when we came to a fork. I wanted to go right and merge with the Emmitsburg Road. But that idiot Hayden insisted Sickles wanted me to take the left fork, past Black Horse Tavern, where we nearly blundered headlong into Rebel pickets at the Tavern. We backtracked several miles, wasting three hours marching because of that damned Hayden."

The sergeant nodded. "Well, I'm glad you made it to Gettysburg. We've been waiting for you, General."

Humphreys spotted Hart riding toward him, yawning widely. "Christ Almighty," he muttered, "I hope I didn't disturb his beauty sleep." Humphreys shook his head. Sickles's personal staff was loaded with a bunch of moronic lawyers like the contemptuous Major Tremain. *What a shitbird.*

"General," Hart said, "I'm delighted you've arrived. I was worried you might have got mixed up with some Rebels along the way. If you follow me I will show you your division's bivouac area." Hart turned his horse and started moving.

Humphreys swore and rode up even with Hart.

"Late yesterday afternoon, Sickles ordered my division to depart Emmitsburg without me," Humphreys snarled, spraying spittle into Hart's eyes like an angry cobra. Hart wiped his face. Humphreys clenched his fist. "I had not yet returned from surveying the terrain as ordered by General Meade. When I returned, I found that Sickles and the majority of Third Corps, including you, Colonel Hart, and most of my division of over 3,500 men, had departed for Gettysburg. Sickles ordered this without so much as the courtesy of letting me know. That is bullshit."

"Sir, here is the position Sickles desires your division to occupy," Hart said, rolling his eyes.

Humphreys lunged forward, angrily, his nose touching Hart's. "Don't ignore me, you little twit!"

They both froze, drawing raspy breaths, letting a couple beats pass by. Hart broke out into a cold sweat. Humphreys's forehead grew molten. Hart gestured from left to right, marking the two endpoints of Humphreys's bivouac. Humphreys noted the position was north of a wheat field, beginning about 1,000 yards north of Little Round Top, and north of a house he guessed was George Weikert's.

"At least the men will be sleeping on something softer than rocks," Humphreys growled.

Humphreys turned toward his aides, pointing out the bivouac boundaries. The tension in his neck began to ease like a passing storm.

"Where is Sickles's headquarters?" Humphreys demanded.

Hart pointed. "Just south of the Weikert House."

---

*1:30 a.m.*

Humphreys trotted into the open field and toward Third Corps headquarters. Arriving, he found Sickles outside his tent at a map table, smoking a cigar. Humphreys dismounted, giving the reins to an aide. Sickles looked his way and nodded. Tremain was standing on the far side of table, watching with a shit-eating smirk on his face.

Humphreys saluted. "General Sickles, I wish to report two of my brigades have arrived, and Lieutenant Colonel Hart has shown me the bivouac position."

"I'm glad your brigades are here," Sickles yawned. "I want you to occupy Cemetery Ridge near the Weikert House and the woods to the north until morning, when I can get a good look at the terrain assigned to us to defend."

"On the march to Gettysburg I met up with Lieutenant Colonel Hayden, who said you desired me to take a route by the Black Horse Tavern," Humphreys said. "We ran into Rebel pickets at the tavern, narrowly missed a scrape, and had to retrace our steps, causing us to march for at least a few hours more than planned. That's why my division is late arriving."

"I assure you, General Humphreys, that Hayden was mistaken," Sickles said with a half-smirk.

Humphreys bared his fangs as he stared at Sickles. "This incident just goes to show how precarious the gap is between poor planning and disaster."

Without acknowledging the comment, Sickles said, "You're dismissed, General Humphreys."

Humphreys saluted and departed, choking back the bile that was scorching his throat.

---

## Sickles
*4:30 a.m.*

Sickles stood over the map table, gripping the wooden edges, his knuckles white. A lantern hung from a tent pole, casting an eerie yellow light. His eyes scanned the key terrain features from the two Round Tops to the Emmitsburg Road. He yawned, having stayed up all night. He closed his eyes and shook his head.

He should have never left de Trobriand and Burling's brigades behind in Emmitsburg. The damn battle was in Gettysburg. But how in the hell would Meade know this, commanding from Taneytown? Sickles glanced at his watch. Two hours ago Meade had ordered the two brigades to Gettysburg. Damn, they would probably not arrive until midmorning.

---

*5:30 a.m.*

Tremain entered Sickles's tent. "A courier from army headquarters has brought orders from Meade. Meade has established his headquarters at the Leister House just behind Cemetery Ridge."

Tremain handed the orders to Sickles.

"Meade has ordered Third Corps to relieve General Geary's forces occupying positions near Little Round Top," Tremain said. "Geary's forces are to move to Culp's Hill, rejoining Twelfth Corps, occupying the right flank of the defensive line. Third Corps is to occupy Cemetery Ridge from the left of Second Corps to Little Round Top. If possible, Little Round Top is to be occupied."

"I don't have a good feel for the terrain I'm supposed to occupy," Sickles said.

"This means we will be occupying the left flank of Meade's line," Tremain said.

"Let's relieve Geary's division with Birney's division," Sickles said.

Sickles extinguished his cigar. He yawned, making a high-pitched *aaaaawaaaaawh*.

"Why don't you try to get some sleep, General?" Tremain said.

Sickles nodded. "Not a bad idea. We're going to be tangling with the enemy soon."

Tremain departed the tent.

Sickles lay down on his cot, buried his head in a down pillow, and closed his eyes as a heavy blackness overcame him.

---

## Tremain

*5:40 a.m.*

Tremain mounted a large, pale horse, riding west to the rise ahead, stopping at a small knoll in the rolling field. He found General David Birney there outside his tent, talking with his staff officers. Tremain dismounted, moving toward the tall, slim man with the cold stone face.

Tremain saluted. "General Sickles has ordered you to relieve Geary's division. You are to form a line resting its left on Little Round Top and your right thrown in a direct line along Cemetery Ridge, connecting on the right with Humphreys's division."

"Once the division is in place, does Sickles want me to begin entrenching?" Birney said.

"No. Sickles wants to inspect the terrain first," Tremain said. "He is taking a short nap and once he is up at daylight he will make the final determination for the position."

Birney turned to his staff and began issuing orders to relieve Geary's division.

*6:30 a.m.*

Tremain spotted a courier approaching from Meade's headquarters. It was one of Warren's staff.

The courier halted before Tremain. He saluted and dismounted. "I stopped at General Sickles's tent. Captain Randolph told me Sickles was sleeping and that I should deliver the map tracing to you, Major Tremain."

"Yes, that's right," Tremain said.

The staff officer handed Tremain the tracing and said, "General Warren sends his compliments to General Sickles. This is the map traced from Captain Paine's drawing early this morning during his ride with General Meade. On the map you will find where General Meade has assigned General Sickles's Third Corps."

Tremain returned to Sickles's tent and stood outside under a flickering lantern hanging from a tripod. He examined the sketch. Third Corps' position was in a general line following Cemetery Ridge, starting left of Hancock's corps, ending at Little Round Top. He shot a glance west toward Emmitsburg Road. Through the ghostly grey light, he could make out the general features of the terrain in the shadows of Little Round Top. He gripped his field glasses, spotting scattered clumps of Third Corps' pickets patrolling along the Emmitsburg Road ridgeline.

Tremain shook his head and exhaled, deflating his chest. "Third Corps is bivouacked at the bottom of a long slope," he muttered.

Tremain focused his field glasses on a two-story brick farmhouse owned by Joseph Sherfy. On his several rides yesterday back and forth between Emmitsburg and Gettysburg, Tremain had noticed the Sherfy farmhouse, a strong structure designed to withstand the harsh winters. He had plucked a peach from

Sherfy's orchard, counting it as his noon meal. He scanned the area of the peach orchard, which appeared to be about a four-acre lot. East of the peach orchard was a wheat field of several acres.

Tremain remembered certain elevation oddities. He studied the sketch. Paine failed to include on his map the ridge the Sherfy farm was sitting on that intersected the Emmitsburg Road. This ridgeline was forward of Third Corps position about a mile, extending in front of the peach orchard, running nearly parallel to the Cemetery Ridge line.

Tremain turned to Randolph, sporting scraggly, uneven whiskers, proving he was old enough to grow some facial hair.

"George, I'm going to ride forward, taking a gander at the terrain surrounding the Emmitsburg Road," Tremain said. "It appears Third Corps is sitting in a marshy swale and rocky belt unfit for artillery, and the high land in our front is unoccupied. If this is so, it's another Hazel Grove in the making."

"I still can't believe Hooker ordered us to give up the elevated Hazel Grove at Chancellorsville," Randolph said. "It was the perfect position for artillery, an open grassy ridge several hundred yards long, anchoring thirty-four artillery guns, a forward bastion from which to blast the Confederates."

Tremain shook his head. "When Hooker made us retreat, the Confederates used it as an artillery platform and blasted us mercilessly."

"This can't happen again to Third Corps," Randolph said.

"We will occupy the high ground whenever possible," Tremain said. "I told General Sickles of my concerns about Third Corps' position last night. I told him at first light I would examine the terrain more closely. If he wakes up before I get back, tell him I'm checking out the terrain and possible positions for artillery on the high ground."

---

*7:00 a.m.*

Tremain mounted his horse, rode across the rolling fields toward Emmitsburg Road. He stopped at the western edge of the peach orchard. At the bottom of a long downward slope, Third Corps sat underneath Little Round Top. He glanced toward Gettysburg. Cemetery Ridge ran south from the cemetery toward Little Round Top like one continuous wave. The grassy wave near the cemetery was higher than the marshy wave near Little Round Top. Hmm. He estimated the peach orchard ridge, eighty or a hundred feet higher than the base of Little Round Top.

Tremain's mouth tightened. The peach orchard ridge was almost exactly the same as Hazel Grove at Chancellorsville, a long, elevated position that could anchor several artillery pieces. It would be negligent for Third Corps artillery not to occupy this ridgeline, easily ranging the Confederates lurking in the woods beyond Seminary Ridge to the west.

A rifle cracked and a bullet whizzed over his head. He snapped around to the echo of the rifle, seeing a white puff of smoke, his heart pounding. The Rebel sharpshooter was firing from the direction of Seminary Ridge. Tremain had seen enough. He rode downhill toward the low, marshy ground next to the base of Little Round Top, stopping near Plum Run, a little stream flowing south.

His belly quivered. It would be impossible to occupy and hold the Plum Run line. The low ground was springy and marshy, covered thickly with stunted bushes, masked by woods. Directly in front of the Third Corps, the elevated Emmitsburg Road dominated the low ground, providing excellent covering for the Rebels to shoot at Third Corps infantry.

Tremain grimaced. On their early morning ride, Meade and Paine probably did not have a chance to get a good look at the position Third Corps was asked to occupy. Meade was a topographical engineer, for God's sake. If he'd had a good view of the terrain in daylight he would have seen the low ground he had ordered Third Corps to occupy as inadequate, a position easily commanded by the land in front. If Third Corps occupied the ground on the sketch, they would be at the mercy of the occupants of the high ground on the extreme left front, as well as being at the mercy of the possessors of the elevated land of the peach orchard.

## Meade

*7:30 a.m.*
*At Meade's Leister House headquarters*

Meade was sitting at a large table in the Leister House living room, studying a map of the Gettysburg area. He had just finished chatting with Colonel Sharpe, who had briefed him that Lee's army numbered more than 100,000. Sharpe had said Longstreet's corps would arrive on the battlefield around noon and would deploy along Seminary Ridge across from Sickles's Third Corps and Hancock's Second Corps occupying Cemetery Ridge. The front door swished open. It was a messenger from Twelfth Corps.

"Good morning, Lieutenant."

"General Slocum sends his respects and wishes to report General Geary's division has arrived at Culp's Hill and is beginning to entrench. General Geary was relieved by General Birney's First Division from Sickles's Third Corps, sir."

"Thank you for the report," Meade said. "Please inform General Slocum I would like him to ride here to army headquarters. I want to discuss with him the possibility of having Twelfth Corps conduct an attack this morning against Ewell's forces."

The lieutenant saluted and departed.

Warmth trickled through Meade's veins. Gibbon had moved Second Corps on the Taneytown Road behind Big Round Top, deploying three divisions south of the cemetery on Cemetery Ridge for about a mile. Sykes, commanding Meade's former Fifth Corps, had just reached Gettysburg with two of his divisions. Sedgwick's Sixth Corps would arrive around noon. Slocum's Twelfth Corps was deployed on Culp's Hill, along with remnants of First Corps. Howard's corps was occupying Cemetery Hill. Sickles's Third Corps was holding down the left flank of the Union line, stretching from Gibbon's Second Corps to Little Round Top.

Another lieutenant walked into the living room. "The Union Artillery Reserve left Taneytown at dawn, expecting to arrive around eleven."

"Very good," said Meade.

He turned to Williams, standing near the map table. "Situation permitting, I want to meet with all corps commanders."

Meade walked outside to the front porch, extracted a cigar, and lit it.

He shuddered with vague hope. Not since his taking command had the army been in such a good position. This morning he had achieved his first tactical victory over Lee: massing the army on better ground than the Confederates. He had maneuvered Lee into an inferior position, forcing Lee to attack or retreat beyond South Mountain. Unless he made a major blunder today, the Army of the Potomac would have the advantage.

From the side of the porch, George's voice was chattering. Meade's heart glowed. He walked to the side of the porch. His son was rubbing Baldy's neck, the horse tethered to the porch rail.

"George. I am tardy in congratulating you on your new job as aide-de-camp. Well deserved. I'm proud of you—as a general of the army and as a father."

George looked down with a touch of shyness.

With warmth in his voice, Meade continued. "Have you written lately to your mother? I've been remiss, writing only once since assuming command."

"I wrote yesterday afternoon from the Taneytown headquarters," George said. "I said we were both fine, but a little short on sleep. I did not say anything about the loss of General Reynolds."

Meade nodded. "I'm glad you wrote."

*8:00 a.m.*

"George, ride to General Sickles and explain to him where my headquarters is located, asking him if his troops are in position yet and what he has to report." Meade pointed toward Little Round Top. "Sickles's headquarters should be a bit north of that giant knoll called Little Round Top."

## George

"Yes, sir." George untethered a horse at the side of the porch and rode south along Taneytown Road. He spotted the Third Corps' command flag flying next to a tent near the Weikert House. Outside the tent stood a junior officer. George rode to the officer, Captain Randolph, and dismounted.

"General Meade requested I inform General Sickles of the location of army headquarters," George said. "It is about a mile north on the Taneytown Road in a small white farmhouse owned by the widow Lydia Leister."

Randolph nodded.

"General Meade requested I speak with General Sickles and ask him if his troops are in position yet and if he has anything to report," George said.

"General Sickles is resting," Randolph said. "I will go in and speak with him."

Randolph turned and walked into Sickles's tent, emerging after a few minutes.

"General Sickles said Third Corps is not yet in position," Randolph said. "There is some doubt as to where he should go."

George furrowed his brow. "Well, I thought, er...didn't General Sickles receive previous instructions on where to deploy? You should have received the map tracing sketched by Captain Paine."

"Yes, he did," Randolph said. "But there is some doubt about the area that General Geary occupied last night. It appeared to General Sickles that General Geary had merely bivouacked in a general area near Little Round Top and was not in defensive line. General Sickles will survey the area and determine the best position to place his corps, including the need, if any, to place any troops on top of Little Round Top."

George stared at Randolph with his mouth gaping open. The Geary bivouac comment was baffling. Sickles should have received orders, and he was merely confirming Sickles was executing them. He did not have precise knowledge of the orders his father had given to Sickles.

George mounted his horse. He rubbed his chin, perplexed at what Randolph was telling him. He was pretty sure Sickles was to place infantry on the crest of Little Round Top. That was just common sense.

"I'm unable to provide further clarification on General Meade's orders," George said. "But I will ride back to army headquarters and find out."

George mounted his horse, galloping back toward the Leister House.

## Sickles

*8:45 a.m.*

Sickles squinted as the early-morning sun slipped through the cracks in his tent. He pulled on his boots. His brain was chugging along like a train pulling a heavy load. Heart rate quickening, he lit a cigar. Meade hated him and was trying to prevent him from becoming the hero the army desperately needed.

Sickles walked out of his tent into the clear, crisp morning air. Waiting for him was Tremain.

"Did you get some rest?" Tremain said.

Sickles rubbed his eyes. "I slept a bit, but my mind is filled with cobwebs."

Tremain said, "I just rode the ground we were assigned, and we are sitting in a low, marshy swale and rocky, wooded belt unfit for artillery and a bad front for infantry. The peach orchard out ahead near the Emmitsburg Road is the perfect place for Third Corps to occupy."

"Very well," Sickles said. "Let's take a ride up to the peach orchard."

They mounted their horses and moved at a walking pace. "Henry, I'm pissed. Meade has relegated Third Corps to marking time on the far left, well away from the upcoming action. We have nothing to do but defend a big rock."

"I agree with you, General," Tremain said.

Sickles's mouth twisted into a menacing sneer. "Meade purposefully is screwing me. This is payback for Chancellorsville. Meade knows that if I perform well Lincoln will appoint me commander of the army. Reynolds is dead. Hancock is a fan of McClellan, so Lincoln will not pick him. The president will choose me, his friend and confidante."

Tremain nodded.

"Meade's job is for the taking as long as I'm aggressive on the battlefield. But there is no honor in defending a damn hill."

"I didn't ride up to Little Round Top," Tremain said.

"Don't worry about it," Sickles said. "Third Corps is not going to sit on a damn rock and watch the rest of the army fight today. I'm betting the peach orchard is like the Hazel Grove salient we occupied at Chancellorsville. No one told us to occupy the Hazel Grove position, but we did, and we nearly knocked the Confederates back to Richmond with our artillery. I should have trusted my instincts and not obeyed Hooker's order to retreat."

"If we would have stayed, we would have won that battle," Tremain said.

"I'm telling you now, we are going to occupy the peach orchard, whether we are ordered to do so or not, and this time we are not going to give it up."

Tremain smiled.

Sickles puffed on his cigar. *Lincoln made you a general because of your aggressiveness. Don't let Lincoln down. Meade probably will retreat before the opening shot. His time as commanding officer is limited. Be aggressive. Be strong. The Republic needs you.*

# 29

# Greene — Thursday, July 2

*12:30 a.m.*
*Eight hours earlier*
*In the shadow of Little Round Top*

Standing next to a smoldering fire in the early-morning darkness, Greene stared up the rugged slope of the smaller of two hills south of Cemetery Ridge. His isolated brigade anchored the left flank of the Union line. A quarter-mile north along Cemetery Ridge was Birney's division of Sickles Third Corps.

Greene winced. It was quiet, lonely, and eerie in the hazy moonlight. Too quiet. He expected Sickles's last two brigade elements to arrive soon and relieve his brigade before dawn. Then he could rejoin the rest of Slocum's Twelfth Corps, occupying Culp's Hill and the key to the right flank of the Union line. General Geary had briefed that the fight was coming, maybe at dawn. Greene clenched his jaw as he scanned westward toward Seminary Ridge. His breathing was shallow and raspy. No enemy movement—yet.

Greene turned to Captain Piltortan. "Sickles lets his boys crash willy-nilly above us on Cemetery Ridge. What a fool. Third Corps is a half-assed operation. They're not ready if the Rebels attack at dawn. Damn you, Sickles, and your ragtag staff officers."

"I rode their lines an hour after they arrived at midnight, and Sickles's gunners had failed to unlimber his batteries and post them," Piltortan said. "In fact, they are scattered about like thistle weeds, and the artillery horses are unharnessed and grazing about like mustangs on the open range."

"The rest of Sickles's troops were supposed to have arrived several hours ago," Greene said. "Where in the hell are they?"

"That's Humphreys's division, and they should be coming up Emmitsburg Road, right?" Piltortan asked.

"Yes." Greene paused, stroking his thick white beard like a preening bald eagle. "I don't like this. Something is wrong. Ride forward and find a better vantage point to view the Emmitsburg Road. That's the same road the enemy might use if conducting a flank attack." A surge of maddening fear shot through him. Something dark and deadly lingered beyond the left flank.

Piltortan galloped away toward Plum Run Creek. Greene mounted his brown horse and rode slowly westward across a large, open field with a long, rising slope, stopping near the beginning of a wheat field filled with waist-high golden stalks topped with bristly spikes. He spotted Piltortan bursting into the wheat field, heading toward the peach orchard and Emmitsburg Road.

Greene gazed southwest toward the moonlit road beyond the wheat field, unconsciously holding his breath. He imagined something in the distance, perhaps enemy skirmishers slithering unseen up the road. A dark silence covered the open fields. Except for Piltortan, nothing was moving.

After a long moment, a muffled thumping, *clunk, clunk, clunk.* Approaching troops.

Greene's breath grew sharp and uneven and his nerves went taut. The shuffling steps, clattering mess tins, and rattling bayonets grew louder. He rode a ways up the slope, plowing deeper into the wheat field. Beyond the huge, sunken boulders off to his left lay a road jammed with approaching soldiers.

Sweat prickled Greene's scalp. Panic shoved his heart against his breast bone. Son of a bitch. Were they the lead infantry elements from Longstreet's corps trying to flank them? God damn it. There had been no riders from Sickles alerting him to the arrival of Third Corps' two brigades, a professional courtesy even a political general would render. Greene turned to his aide, sitting on his horse next to him.

"Roust the brigade," Greene said. "We may have trouble brewing."

The aide galloped back toward the dark emptiness of Little Round Top, where the brigade was bivouacked in the hill's shadow.

<hr />

*Almost 1:00 a.m.*

The rumbling sound of the approaching soldiers was growing louder. Greene drew his revolver from its holster, cocking the trigger with his thumb. Where he sat he did not have a clear view of the advancing troops. He spurred his horse forward, halting midway in the dark wheat field. Southward he saw thousands of soldiers strolling forward almost aimlessly, like childhood boys moseying to their favorite fishing hole. They seemed to not care how much noise they made.

A forward picket from Greene's brigade galloped across the wheat field, skidding to a stop in front of Greene.

"General Greene. The approaching soldiers are from Sickles's Third Corps. They were guarding the far left Federal flank at Emmitsburg last night. They are coming to relieve us."

Greene nodded. "Good." A couple pounds of menacing weight lifted from his shoulders.

He uncocked his pistol and took a deep breath, letting it out like a soft sigh. *Christ Almighty.* There were thousands of blue troops bunching on the road next to the peach orchard. They turned, facing Cemetery Ridge.

The long lines moved forward like a gentle wind toward the wheat field where Greene was posted.

<hr />

*5:45 a.m.*

A young lieutenant from Sickles's headquarters rode across the fields at a gallop and reined up in front of Greene. It was the same officer who, earlier in the evening, had said he would inform him when he was relieved.

Greene snorted. His eyes narrowed as a wave of anger seized him. He disdained Sickles and his asshole aides. All a bunch of cocks.

The officer saluted. "General Sickles sends his compliments and wishes to inform you he is relieving your brigade from its currently assigned duties of anchoring Little Round Top. You may proceed and report back to your division commander for new duties."

Greene saluted. "Very well. Send my compliments to General Sickles and please inform him my brigade will move out momentarily."

Greene paused as he pointed to the hill.

"One more thing," Greene said. "Captain Piltortan will show General Sickles the position I occupied last night, including the crest of Little Round Top, which must be held. Colonel John Patrick of the Fifth Ohio occupied Little Round Top. Patrick was also in charge of the 147th Pennsylvania to help beef up the defenses on the crest of Little Round Top."

Sickles's aide shot him a cocky smirk. Sickles and his staff had become well known for their dismissive arrogance. "General Sickles will attend to your position in due time. You're relieved, sir."

Sickles's man turned and rode north along Cemetery Ridge toward Sickles's headquarters.

Greene frowned and swiveled in the saddle, spotting Piltortan's approach. Sickles's soldiers moved into the wheat field like a rising river spilling its banks, creating an enormous lake of blue. Greene's heart lightened. Now his brigade could rejoin Twelfth Corps, occupying Culp's Hill.

Piltortan arrived. "Form the brigade," Greene ordered. "We are marching back to Culp's Hill." Piltortan saluted and departed.

Greene swung his horse toward Little Round Top, riding back to the brigade's bivouac. The darkened sky was filled with wispy clouds, reminding him of his boyhood home in Warwick, Rhode Island. He loved Rhode Island, especially in late fall, with the added color along its coastlines. His ancestors had founded Rhode Island, and his famous Revolutionary cousin General Nathanael Greene was buried in Warwick.

---

*5:55 a.m.*

The New York brigade advanced in marching columns over open, grassy fields, Greene leading them, riding forward toward the barely discernable Cemetery Hill. The sixty-two-year-old Greene pushed the brigade hard, moving at a forced-march pace, expecting enemy action this morning. He wiped his brow with his gloved hand.

Greene turned to Piltortan. "Charles, keep the brigade pressing. The sooner we can arrive and entrench, the better. We are vulnerable in these open fields."

The brigade marched north along Cemetery Ridge. They arrived at a large grove of oak trees nestled southwest of the arched cemetery gatehouse, sitting on the dark hill like a fortress. Greene rode a ways into the oak grove before turning sharply right, skirting behind Cemetery Hill, moving east across the Baltimore Pike Road, arriving on the other side of East Cemetery Hill. Geary's aide met them and said he would escort them to their position on the hill. Following the aide, they marched along a small ridge leading to a massive hill, the twin peaks towering over the arched cemetery gateway. As they moved up Culp's Hill, the bright light of the climbing sun blinded them, forcing the men to pull their hats down over their eyes. Greene's stomach knotted.

"Crap. What a perfect time for the Rebels to attack." A blinding sun behind them, charging a vulnerable brigade without constructed breastworks.

Greene spurred his horse upward, stopping at the crest of Culp's Hill. He gazed south, seeing another hill about four hundred yards away. Interesting. Culp's Hill was not one giant hill, but rather two hills connected by a narrow saddle. The north hump stood about a hundred feet higher than the one south. He gripped his binoculars and scanned the terrain. Culp's Hill was rugged and rocky with heavily timbered slopes, quite steep in places. Beyond the south hump was a marshy meadow. It would be a difficult ascent.

To his left on the crest of the hill, Greene spotted the remnants of the Iron Brigade on the upper hill, positioned behind hastily constructed breastworks, facing northwest toward the town of Gettysburg. Turning in the direction of Little Round Top, he scanned the long line of thousands of blue soldiers flowing down Cemetery Ridge like a coastal seawall. What a view.

Greene turned to Piltortan. "Culp's Hill is Meade's castle tower, protecting his right flank."

"Yes, Culp's Hill is the barb of the fishhook defensive line."

Greene dismounted, gripping the reins in his left hand. He knelt down, using his gloved hand to dig the ground, easily pulling up a handful of sod. He peered down the slope. The hill was a natural fortification, covered with heavy woods and matting material. A flicker of warmth zigzagged down his back.

"Charles, this is good digging ground." He paused as he dug his gloved hand into the soft ground, letting the dirt sift through his fingers like a rainy downpour. "The boys can trench deep enough for firing from a standing position behind formidable breastworks."

Greene stood. The murderous sun rose higher in the eastern blue sky. He wiped sweat from the back of his neck. "Charles, tell the regimental commanders to ride forward and muster with me."

Greene scanned the hill. A plan started to form. The boys from the Sixtieth Regiment would take the lead in building the breastworks. Raised in the north woodland counties of St. Lawrence and Franklin, they were skilled loggers and gifted woodcraftsmen, easily capable of constructing formidable log breastworks from the readily available timber. It would take them only a few hours.

---

*6:15 a.m.*

Greene spotted General Geary, Second Division commander, Twelfth Corps, riding toward him, accompanied by an aide Greene did not recognize. He chuckled. The six-foot, six-inch Geary looked ridiculous riding his small horse, nearly as small as a pony. Geary's long legs almost scraped the ground. Geary preferred riding small horses to reduce his target size. He had the dubious distinction of being the most wounded Union general still actively commanding. Last count was eight serious wounds.

Greene squinted and his vision sharpened. Geary's aide was tall and hefty. Greene enjoyed ribbing Geary and his aides. Geary had a hard time keeping his personal aides healthy, mostly because sitting on a horse next to Geary was a surefire way to ensure the Rebels would use you as target practice. The standard joke Greene told Geary was that if Geary asked you to be his personal aide, you'd be smarter to shoot yourself in the foot immediately, because some Rebel was sure to shoot you in the head by the end of the day.

Geary arrived, his dark eyes hidden under his floppy hat, his black beard flowing down to his chest. He reminded Greene of Confederate General Longstreet: both were very big men, fully bearded, with stubborn faces, dark moods, and ferocious fighting skills. Greene could not remember the last time he had seen Geary crack a smile.

Greene saluted. "Good morning, General Geary. Where would you like me to place my division?"

"General Slocum ordered the division to extend General Wadsworth's First Corps line. I want your brigade to move into position next to the First Corps Iron Brigade troops. The division will form off your brigade. I'm going to call a conference of the brigade commanders in a few minutes. We will discuss the disposition of the brigade forces."

"I see you got a new aide," Greene said.

Geary smirked. "I recruited him before he heard your stories."

"Lucky for you." Greene smiled and saluted.

Geary rode south toward where the other brigade commanders were gathering. Greene spotted where his regimental commanders were meeting, waiting for instructions, and rode over to them.

"We have orders to deploy on the north mound of Culp's Hill. Our left will form a right angle with the right of General Wadsworth's division of First Corps. I believe the Hoosiers of the 7th Regiment are Wadsworth's far right. I want the following deployment of the regiments in this order: The 78th will butt next to the Hoosiers; next will be 60th; then the 102nd, 149th, and 137th will be the far right flank of the brigade. Go ahead and deploy. I will issue further instructions in a few minutes. We are going to build breastworks, so start thinking about who are the best loggers from your regiments."

Greene rode to where Geary was assembling with the other brigade commanders. He dismounted and stood next to General Candy, a medium-sized, squared-faced man commanding the First Brigade. General Kane, the Second Brigade commander, joined them, a small and precise-looking man full of pluck, known to carry an umbrella for sunshade while drilling his soldiers. Greene liked him. Kane was a bit persnickety, but he was one hell of a visionary, inventing skirmisher tactics: scattering under fire, pressing continually forward along whatever cover the ground offered, firing only when the target could be seen.

"Good morning, gentlemen," Geary said. "This looks like a fine place to defend. I want to deploy the brigades as follows: Greene's brigade will be on the far left on upper Culp's Hill, butting against General Wadsworth's First Corps. Kane's brigade is to file to the right of Greene's, extending the defensive line through the lower saddle and back to the crest of the lower knoll. I want Kane's brigade to cover the eastern slope of the Culp's Hill, anchoring the far right of the line at Spangler's Spring. Candy's brigade will be posted to the right rear of Greene's, acting as a ready reserve for the two forward brigades."

The three brigade commanders nodded. Geary stepped back for a look, pointing a gloved hand. He looked at Kane. "The lines don't have to be straight. They can bend forward or backward to conform to the crest of the upper and lower hills. I've already told General Greene that his line extending First Corps should be thrown back nearly at a right angle."

Kane nodded. "Yes, sir. I understand."

"I noticed the Black Hats of the Iron Brigade on Green's left have entrenched their positions on the upper hill," Geary said. "I'm opposed to building rifle pits. Honor, bravery, and courage are the key factors for winning battles. Building and fighting behind a breastwork diminishes all three of these attributes in a soldier. It's bad for morale."

Kane and Candy both nodded their heads in agreement.

Greene spoke quietly. "I don't think constructing entrenchments diminishes our boys. In fact, well-constructed rifle pits and redoubts are a lost art of war."

Geary's reply was more forceful. "Entrenching has a negative effect, making troops timid, unwilling to move beyond the protection of the breastworks and charge the enemy. I agree a solid breastwork is sometimes necessary to protect a unit from a sudden sally, but our troops are too slow in leaving their well-covered lines to assail the enemy. I'm convinced they won't leave the breastworks without the pointy end of a bayonet in their backs."

Greene's eyes narrowed and his jaw tensed. "At Chancellorsville, you said the conduct of my brigade was admirable. With the enemy outnumbering us, we held off several Rebel attacks because we were fighting behind breastworks. And when ordered to attack, the men instantly jumped over the redoubts, charging the enemy. I personally have witnessed this on the battlefield time and time again."

Greene paused, his nostrils flaring. Geary nodded silently, his dark eyes brooding.

"At Chancellorsville, after we made a forward breastwork of logs and earth, we constructed a secondary trench in the rear," Greene said. "This provided us the means to survive both frontal and flank attacks. If I have time to build them, I will ensure my men have them."

"Very well," Geary said sharply. "I will leave the decision whether to build breastworks to each brigade commander."

Greene nodded. Despite Geary's reluctance, a great deal rode on this consent. A knot loosened inside him. He saluted, mounted his horse, and rode toward the crest of the upper hill. His five regimental colonels had mustered next to where the Iron Brigade's line stopped.

<hr />

*6:30 a.m.*

He rode up to join the colonels on the upper hill and dismounted. "Geary's division is occupying the northern hill. Williams's division is occupying the southern hill, with Lockwood's brigade anchoring the right flank. Kane's brigade will butt up against the right of our brigade. Candy's brigade is the reserve behind us." Greene turned and indicated the position of Candy's brigade reserve position to the regimental commanders.

"Geary has given us permission to build breastworks," Greene went on. "We will start as soon as I trace out a line along our front and the men are positioned. As you can see, the northern slope of the upper hill is the steepest." He pointed toward the right flank of Wadsworth's Iron Brigade, holding the northern apex of the hill.

"I don't see the enemy having much success attacking the steep northern slope. But as our line travels southward toward the lower knoll of Culp's Hill, the slopes are less steep. If the Confederates are to have any success, they will focus their attack along the lower eastern slopes."

The regimental colonels listened, their faces growing anxious. The morning air was growing more tense, like a dark thunderhead forming over Culp's Hill and the enemy positions beyond Rock Creek.

"I'm not particularly concerned about the upper eastern slopes being the attack route of the enemy," Greene said. "The terrain is covered with a heavy growth of timber and large rock ledges that will provide excellent cover for our marksmen. With little undergrowth, our boys will have good visibility, a free line of sight, should the enemy storm the higher hill."

Greene glanced at the terrain left to right. He nodded. *This will work.*

"The 78th will throw its line back at a right angle with Wadsworth's men. The 78th will be followed by the 60th. The 102nd will throw their line back at nearly a right angle to follow the crest of the terrain. It will be followed by the 149th and then the 137th."

Greene paused, looking down toward the end of the line, the right flank, occupied by the 137th. "If the enemy gains the peak on the lower hill, they could continue unchecked behind the 137th, flanking the rest of the brigade line."

He turned to Ireland. "Colonel, I'm not satisfied letting your right flank hang in the open. General Geary ordered General Kane's brigade to occupy the line on the right. But I would feel more comfortable if you built a traverse at a right angle at the end of your line and the beginning of Kane's. This trench will fold back across the hill and should be about the size of a company front."

Ireland frowned. "General, with all due respect, building a traverse trench seems like a massive waste of time and a huge physical effort in building it."

Greene's brow furrowed. "I know your boys will grouse. That's why I will supervise them."

Ireland shook his head. "Yes, sir."

Greene turned and watched the Sixtieth scurrying about, laying out and examining all sorts of woodworking tools, including axes, wedges, chisels, hammers, spades, and picks. They were to be lumberjacks again for a few hours.

The soldiers waited for a sign to begin cutting and building. The Sixtieth had transformed itself from a crack infantry regiment into a band of lumberjack crews, loggers of great physical strength and unrivaled skill, readying to harvest timber.

Greene pointed to Colonel Goddard. "Abel, I need to spread the Sixtieth's building skills among the other four regiments of the brigade. Pick fifteen to twenty men from your regiment who are talented in felling trees and wood construction and assign them to the other four regiments. I think they would be very valuable in building a solid breastwork for the entire brigade."

"Good idea, sir," said Goddard. "I'll have my adjutant select the best men and have them report to the other regiments. Now, as soon as they have finished constructing the breastworks, they will be permitted to return to the Sixtieth?"

"Absolutely. They will."

"Good. Thank you, sir."

Greene motioned for the five regimental commanders to follow him as he walked the proposed defensive perimeter, tracing a line of breastworks along the brigade's front. Starting from the far left where the Sixtieth was fixed, Greene walked down the hill several feet and stopped.

"I'm placing the brigade's trench line on the military crest."

"Why not build the trench line on the crest line of the hill?" Ireland questioned.

"If we make the line of breastworks on the highest crest, we will create a dead space at the bottom of the hill that cannot be engaged by direct fire above because of the rolling, rounded slope of the hill," Greene said. "The enemy would be able to hide in this space. So we move down the hill until a rifle can hit anything at the bottom of the hill."

"Makes sense," Ireland said. "I understand."

"The military crest also minimizes our own troop's visibility by not having them silhouetted against the sky, as would happen if they were firing from the crest of the hill," Greene said. "Having our boys blend into the background of the hill will make them a more difficult target for the enemy to hit." He paused. Ireland and the other regimental commanders nodded, expressing their understanding and appreciation.

Greene walked the breastwork line for each regiment. When he finished on Ireland's far right flank, he said, "Here is where I want the transverse line."

"Yes sir," Ireland said.

As soon as Greene had designated the regiments along the military crest trace line, the soldiers began felling trees and throwing up breastworks using logs, cordwood, stones, and earth. Using his engineering eye, Greene moved up and down the defensive line, examining the measurement and angles of breastworks. The constructed works stood about chest high, providing excellent protection from the ordinary musket. After a few hours of work, the dirt and wooden ramparts were nearly shoulder high for the average soldier.

Greene turned to Captain Piltortan. "Tell the regimental commanders I want them to build head logs on top of the breastworks to protect soldiers' heads and create a three-to-four inch slit through which the soldiers can fire."

"Yes, sir." He rode off.

*11:30 a.m.*

Greene lit a cigar. The earthworks were finished. There was little chance Ewell's corps could overrun Slocum's Twelfth Corps of 8,600 Federals standing behind a solid line of breastworks. To the right of his brigade, Kane's brigade stretched several hundred yards down toward the swell between the two hills, and beyond Kane's brigade was Williams's division. Greene puffed on his cigar. The tightness in his muscles was melting.

*12:00 p.m.*

From atop the highest point of Culp's Hill, Lieutenant Colonel Rufus Dawes, commanding the Sixth Wisconsin of the Iron Brigade, studied the building of the Twelfth Corps breastworks. Although Dawes's boys had thrown up hasty breastworks on the Culp's Hill northern crest the night before, they did not compare to the ones constructed by the Twelfth Corps brigade.

Colonel Robinson, acting commander of the Iron Brigade, walked over. "How you doing, Rufus?"

"The regiment is doing fine," Dawes said. "We've rested from yesterday. Lost a lot of good men on McPherson's Ridge, including General Reynolds."

Robinson looked down and nodded. "Are you ready for the Rebels today?"

"The breastworks we constructed will do the job if the enemy attacks." Dawes pointed to Greene's breastworks. "But our construction doesn't hold a candle to that of the fellows next to us."

Robinson turned. "Those are splendid breastworks."

"Who is that old man riding along the line directing everyone?" Dawes asked.

"Oh, that's General George Greene," Robinson said. "Don't let the white beard fool you. He's one of the toughest sons of bitches in the army. He was General Lee's instructor at West Point. And we all know how Lee turned out."

Dawes stared. "That's Old Man Greene? I've heard lots about him. He's related to General Nathanael Greene."

"Rufus, wasn't your great-grandfather William Dawes, who rode with Paul Revere, warning about the arrival of the British? Wasn't he a friend of Nathanael Greene?"

"My great-grandfather was close friends with Nathanael Greene," Dawes said. "He thought the world of him. If George Greene is anything like his famous ancestor, we should be in good company defending this hill."

"Yes. I heard about Greene's New York boys at Antietam," Robinson said. "They fought like devil dogs."

---

## Greene
*12:10 p.m.*

Greene sat on his horse behind the Sixtieth, examining the lines. He swiveled in his saddle, spotted Colonel Robinson chatting with another officer he didn't recognize. He assumed it was probably a regimental commander. Greene turned and glanced toward the Confederate positions several hundred yards to the northeast. The enemy had watched and heard him all morning build the redoubts. Why had they not attacked? Lee had made a critical mistake in not assaulting Culp's Hill at the crack of dawn.

Greene smirked. *I taught you better than that, Bobby Lee. Maybe the teacher will show his old student a few new tricks today, including rifle trenches dug along the military crest, sporting protective headlogs. You haven't experienced something like this before. But today you will, and you'll pay the price.*

# 30

# Meade — Thursday, July 2

*8:05 a.m.*
*Four hours earlier*
*Leister House*

Meade stood alone, smoking a cigar on the front porch of the Leister House, his bedraggled uniform spangled with dust and dirt. Baldy was tethered nearby, batting flies with his tail. The bright blue dawn promised the day would be another barnburner. Although the porch blocked some of the blazing sun, it did little for the heat licking Meade's weathered face.

He stepped off the porch and walked into the yard. Several weatherworn aides and couriers lingered inside the fenced area, chatting in low voices. At the far edge of the yard stood Captain Castle's flagmen, snapping their flags from one fixed position to another, signaling the flagmen on the crest of Little Round Top. Meade gripped his binoculars and scanned the terrain west of the Leister House. Four hundred yards beyond the rising slope, thousands of small fires burned, creating smoke plumes as if curling up from narrow chimneys. The smoke collected into a hazy fog floating above Cemetery Ridge. The long smoke band marked the site of the Union battle line, extending continuously for a distance of two miles toward Little Round Top.

Meade untethered Baldy and rode toward Cemetery Ridge with Biddle riding next to him. He stopped near a copse of trees and studied the terrain. West of the ridge, the ground fell away gradually, crossed by the Emmitsburg Road, then rose again, forming Seminary Ridge. More than a thousand yards away, this ridge ran parallel to Cemetery Ridge, and its western side was covered with dense woods. Meade frowned. A chill sleeted through him. Had Longstreet's corps arrived? The trees were perfect for concealing enemy forces.

"If the enemy decides to occupy Seminary Ridge, the Union artillery on Cemetery Ridge will still have greater range and power than the Confederate artillery," he said to Biddle.

"If the enemy decides to attack Cemetery Ridge, they will have to advance upward," Biddle replied.

"Yes, and they will be moving slower and be under Union fire longer than if they were moving across flat terrain."

"This gives us a distinct advantage," said Biddle.

"I agree. If the enemy decides not to attack, we can stay in place for a lengthy period with a continuous flow of supplies pushed in from the nearby logistics depots."

Meade turned and rode back to the Leister House, dismounted, and moved onto the porch. He removed his floppy hat and scratched his head. A steady stream of ammunition wagons rumbled along the narrow and rutted Taneytown Road. Pack mules, whinnying, mingled among the wagon trains, bearing boxes of cartridges. Couriers galloped up and down the edges of the road, arriving with messages for headquarters and then departing with dispatches from Williams.

Meade's cook walked onto the porch and handed Meade a cup of coffee. Meade nodded a thank-you. The Leister House this morning had transformed into a mushroom town, springing up in less than a day, with the massive number of men and animals needed to support an army headquarters encampment.

Meade turned and squinted northward through his thick spectacles toward Cemetery and Culp's Hills. Would Sedgwick arrive before the Confederates attacked? Where were updates from Slocum, entrenched in front of Hill's and Ewell's corps? Meade paced. The Confederates might attack Slocum's Twelfth Corps, guarding the critical Baltimore Pike, which had to remain open at all cost. Sedgwick's Sixth Corps was marching in by this route. If he needed to fall back, the pike would be his principal line of retreat. *Damn it.* He needed enemy updates.

Meade lighted another cigar, brooding. Earlier that morning, Colonel Sharpe had informed him that Longstreet's corps would be arriving at Gettysburg sometime this morning, probably on Sickles's left flank. But what if Sharpe was wrong? If Lee placed Longstreet's corps on his right flank, attacking before Sixth Corps arrived, it would be a disaster, crushing the Union right flank, and controlling the Baltimore Pike.

He yawned and closed his eyes. A couple hours sleep early this morning was not enough. For a long moment, nothing but a dark silence. His stomach fluttered as he yawned again. Snapping flags rippled like line-drying clothes flapping in a strong breeze. He opened his eyes and gazed at the signalmen, wigwagging their flags back and forth. Had the signalmen on Little Round Top spotted the enemy moving, or were they just practicing?

Biddle came out onto the porch and handed Meade another steaming coffee. "Would you like breakfast?"

"Not yet," Meade replied. "Not sure I could keep it down. Too many butterflies fluttering around in my gut this morning."

"I will have your cook wait awhile."

"Any updates from Sharpe on enemy movements?" Meade said.

"No." Biddle turned and went back inside the house.

A sharp crack of a rifle. Then another crack, answered by two or three popping shots. Meade's head swiveled, trying to pinpoint the sounds. A few more shots rang out, answered directly by the rattling sound of rapid rifle fire near Cemetery Hill. Sounded like Ewell's and Howard's boys were starting to go at it.

Through his binoculars Meade spotted yellow flashes—rifles and muskets bursting brightly through the drifting smoke. Without warning, the skirmish intensified, clattering continuously like approaching thunder. He shuddered, recognizing the emerging pattern of fire. Heavy skirmishing usually preceded a major assault. His stomach lurched. Lee could crush him at this point in the morning. He was missing Sixth Corps, two brigades of Third Corps, and his artillery reserve. *Damn.* The thundering fire continued. He mounted Baldy and galloped toward the copse of trees. He halted a hundred yards away from Cemetery Ridge, eying Gibbon's soldiers, stopping and staring at the skirmishing, now approaching a crescendo like the roar of a locomotive.

Baldy stood motionless as Meade glanced through his binoculars. Biddle pulled up next to Baldy.

"If Lee is launching a general attack, we are in a terrible pickle," Meade said. "Longstreet's corps must have arrived during the night, tucking themselves either behind Seminary Ridge or beyond Culp's Hill. If that is true, God help us. No Sedgwick, no hope."

"What do you want me to do?" Biddle said.

"Tell General Gibbon I believe a major assault is imminent. I expect it to be against Cemetery Hill or Culp's Hill."

Looking a bit confused, Biddle asked, "Sir, if I may, why do you believe Lee will attack this morning?"

"Lee has to maintain the initiative, based upon his longer logistics lines," Meade said. "That's his critical vulnerability. To do that, he either has to maneuver or assault. Since we have found each other and established defensive lines, he no longer can engage in grand maneuver. So he must attack or retreat. And it doesn't sound like he is retreating."

Biddle nodded.

"I want Gibbon to be prepared to move his men closer up toward Cemetery Hill," Meade said. "Have him mass his corps east of the Taneytown Road facing Cemetery Hill and Culp's Hill. I want their backs facing Cemetery Ridge. They should be able to rapidly support Howard's and Slocum's forces on the right flank."

"How long do you plan on leaving the northern part of Cemetery Ridge without forces?" Biddle asked. "Longstreet could be lurking on the westward side of Seminary Ridge, waiting for us to make a mistake."

Meade made a fist and thrusted his index finger at Biddle as if shooting him. "Longstreet could be deployed behind Ewell's corps supporting an attack against Cemetery Hill or Culp's Hill! If I had the whole army massed here, I would put an entire corps on upper Cemetery Ridge. But I don't have that luxury this morning because I'm worried about Lee launching a major assault against our right."

Biddle shrugged.

Meade said, his voice calmer, "As soon as I'm convinced Lee is not preparing a general assault against Cemetery Hill, I will have Gibbon redeploy his forces along the northern part of Cemetery Ridge, facing Seminary Ridge."

Biddle saluted and rode off.

Moments later, Colonel Sharpe arrived and dismounted.

"Ewell's corps has been massing men all night across from Culp's Hill," Sharpe said. "Johnson's division is massing in the open at the end of the Union line."

"Perhaps instead of waiting for the Confederates to attack us, we should conduct a spoiling attack against them," Meade said. "That might foil Lee's attack plans. Do you still believe Longstreet's corps will position itself on our left flank?"

"Yes, I do, sir."

"Let's ride back to the Leister House."

Arriving at the house, Meade and Sharpe dismounted and went inside. General Williams was waiting for them.

"Seth," said Meade, "have Slocum come to headquarters. I want to discuss launching a possible spoiling attack from Culp's Hill against Ewell's corps."

Heavy gunfire erupted, booming in the direction of Cemetery Hill. Meade rushed to the front door of the Leister House. Blood pounded in his ears. *Please God, let Sedgwick arrive in time.* He stopped on the porch. "Colonel Sharpe. Let's ride to Cemetery Hill," Meade shouted.

Meade, Sharpe, and a cavalcade of aides rode, stopping near the arch gateway. Meade scanned the town through his binoculars. *What's going on?* Little movement from the enemy occupying Gettysburg. He took a deep breath and held it.

Biddle arrived. "General Meade, Gibbon is marching his men east of Taneytown Road and massing at the foot of Cemetery Hill."

"Good," Meade said. He turned to Sharpe. "If Lee attacks Cemetery Hill and breaks through, we will have to retreat in an orderly manner back to the Pipe Creek line." Meade paused, closed his eyes, and wiped his sweaty forehead. *Crap. How can we conduct an orderly retreat if the Taneytown Road and Baltimore*

*Pike are clogged with arriving troops, logistics wagons, and artillery cannons? A haphazard retreat would turn into a rout.* Meade opened his eyes. His core fluttered again.

"Sir," Sharpe said. "I'm not convinced this is the beginning of the general attack. Longstreet's corps is not up yet. If he is, that means he marched all night and his corps would be exhausted and not in good shape to conduct a morning attack. My best guess is that Longstreet started marching an hour or two before dawn, so that means he would arrive around noon."

"Are you sure?" Meade said.

"Yes, sir! I'm sure Longstreet did not march all night. So he is not yet on the battlefield."

"I sure as hell hope you're right," Meade said. "Without knowing it, Longstreet and Sedgwick are racing to see which one arrives first. The winner of that race will tip the battle in their army's favor."

***

*8:15 a.m.*

"Here comes General Newton, behind us," Biddle said.

Meade turned in his stirrups, spotting General John Newton riding to the cemetery gate. Usually well dressed and swaggering, the ruddy-faced, blue-eyed Newton looked haggard from riding all night. Until yesterday, he had been a division commander in Sedgwick's Sixth Corps. That was about to change.

Newton rode to Meade and saluted. "Reporting for duty, sir."

"I'm pleased to see you, John," Meade said. "You will relieve Doubleday as commander of First Corps. They are pretty battered, but you have remnants of the Iron Brigade occupying parts of Culp's Hill."

Newton's face brightened. He said with pride in his voice, "Thank you for considering me to command Reynolds's old corps. But Doubleday outranks me, sir."

"Lincoln has authorized me to promote officers regardless of rank," Meade said.

Newton shook his head. "Sir, I have never heard of such an order. But I will execute my duties to the fullest of my abilities."

"I have complete confidence in you, John. I was not impressed with Doubleday's performance yesterday. Both Howard and Buford had negative things to say."

Meade paused. "Besides serving in the Army Corps of Engineers, didn't you graduate second in your West Point class and beat out Longstreet, Sykes, and Doubleday? That should account for something." Meade winked.

"Well, yes, sure," Newton said, grinning.

"When do you think Sedgwick's corps will arrive?" Meade asked.

"I estimate around noon. Uncle John is force-marching them as fast as they can move. Spirits are high, however."

"Good. I want you to relieve Doubleday immediately," Meade said. "I've told him you are relieving him, so he shouldn't give you a hard time. Send me a note when it's completed."

Newton saluted and departed. Meade rode back to the Leister House. No sooner had he arrived than Captain Meade galloped in, his horse sliding to a stop on the grassy field in front of the porch. He dismounted and strode to his father, saluting formally.

⁕⁖⊷⊶ ⊶ ⊷⊶⊷⊰⊷

*8:45 a.m.*

"I found General Sickles's tent, and he was resting inside," George said. "I talked with Captain Randolph and asked if Third Corps was in position. Captain Randolph spoke with General Sickles inside his tent. Randolph said Third Corps was not yet in position. Also General Sickles said there was some doubt as to where he should go."

Meade's eyes narrowed into a withering stare.

Looking down, George said, "I did not have precise knowledge of your orders for General Sickles, so I was unable to give them to Captain Randolph. I told him I would ride back and speak with you to clarify the situation."

Meade's pulse rate catapulted. He swore loudly. "I've told Sickles twice now where I want his damn corps located! He is to relieve General Geary, who has troops on top of Little Round Top and at its base running northward on Cemetery Ridge.

Captain Paine gave Sickles a tracing of the map he sketched this morning where I indicated all the corps' defensive positions. Ride back and tell General Sickles I want Third Corps on the left of the Second Corps. I want the right of Third Corps to connect with the left of Second Corps. Then Third Corps is to prolong the Second Corps line toward Little Round Top and occupy the position General Geary held last night."

## George
*9:00 a.m.*

George saluted, mounted his horse, galloped back toward Third Corps. He rode to Sickles's tent as Sickles was mounting his horse. Tremain and Randolph were sitting on their horses next to Sickles, chit-chatting.

George saluted. "General Meade's orders are for you to extend Second Corps' line down Cemetery Ridge, occupying General Geary's old position, including Little Round Top."

Sickles said with a dismissive flare, "My troops are moving and will be in position shortly. But my staff and I are convinced General Geary did not occupy any position last night. Instead, Geary just massed his division on or about the Little Round Top area."

Sickles stared at him in insolent silence. "That will be all, Captain Meade. I have to survey the terrain I'm supposed to occupy."

George swallowed a sharp reply as his cheeks grew hot.

## Sickles

Sickles turned his horse and rode toward the Emmitsburg Road, followed by Tremain and his personal staff.

"So," Tremain murmured, "General Geary 'did not occupy any position last night,' he merely 'massed on or about Little Round Top?' That was a daring play."

"Too subtle for Junior to notice. That wet-behind-the-ears papa's boy will tell his useless father exactly what I want him to hear—that we are on our way to our assigned position. And so we are."

"Have you relieved that relic Greene yet?" Tremain asked.

"I sent a message. 'General Sickles sends his compliments and wishes to inform you he is relieving your brigade from its currently assigned duties of anchoring Little Round Top.' And that is the report Meade will get from Slocum."

"'Currently assigned duties?'" Tremain chuckled. "Subtle but specific. I'd have hated to have to face you in the courtroom, General."

"You would indeed."

Tremain pondered a moment while Sickles blew smoke rings and the only sound was the empty echo of horse hooves on the Emmitsburg Road. "You know there are plenty of witnesses who can vouch that Geary did indeed occupy Little Round Top last night."

"The orders said to occupy Geary's old position. If I and my staff were persuaded that he was simply massed in the general vicinity, who can say our perceptions were otherwise?"

"It's a bold move," Tremain said. "But it could come back to haunt you."

"By then, Henry," Sickles replied, urging his horse to a gallop, "I will be the conquering hero of the Battle of Gettysburg."

<hr />

## George

George turned his horse and spurred him toward army headquarters. Queasiness gripped his stomach, and his mind transported him back in time. He was ten years old. He had dutifully informed his father that his priggish schoolmarm had scolded him for failing to do all his homework. He had completed the verbal assignment but forgotten about the assignment written on the blackboard. The tongue-lashing his father had delivered could still make him tremble. No one could survive two ass-chewings in one morning from the old man. Not then and not now.

His father had made it clear where he wanted Sickles's troops. For Sickles to claim he was not sure of Geary's position was a stretch. It seemed Sickles was quibbling over the nuances of the order and had some motive in mind for not executing it. Didn't he understand how his corps' defenses along Cemetery Ridge and Little Round top fit with the army as a whole? He was sandwiched in between conflicting stories from two different generals; what was he supposed to do?

What he couldn't do was contradict General Sickles's assertion as fact that Geary's soldiers were merely massed in the area. To do so was to risk a charge of insubordination. Thank God he didn't have his father's temper. Whatever Sickles planned to do, he had to extend Hancock's line south along the ridge. That order was clear and simple. If Sickles had any doubts, he could refer to the map tracing. Even an idiot could follow Captain Paine's map.

When he arrived back at headquarters, Meade was chatting with Hancock, who had just arrived from Taneytown, and Hunt and Warren. Meade was animated, gesturing toward Cemetery Hill. Slocum arrived from Culp's Hill and joined the group surrounding Meade.

## Meade
*9:40 a.m.*

Meade spotted George and gestured for him to join the group. George walked over and joined the generals.

"Did you speak with Sickles?"

"Yes, I told him General Meade's orders were for him to extend Second Corps' line down Cemetery Ridge, occupying General Geary's old position, including Little Round Top."

"Good. What did General Sickles have to say?" Meade said.

"General Sickles said that his troops were then moving and that he was going to survey the terrain he was supposed to occupy," George said.

Meade nodded; finally, Sickles was where he was supposed to be. With that part of the line secure, he abruptly turned back to the other generals and the problem at hand—shoring up the rest of the line. "Gouv, what units of Geary's division were occupying Little Round Top when we rode by there early this morning?"

"Fifth Ohio and 147th Pennsylvania regiments of Candy's brigade."

"Two regiments. Thanks. It sounds as if the heavy skirmishing along Cemetery Hill is subsiding," Meade said. "That's a good sign. Earlier I thought it might be setting the stage for Lee to assault Cemetery Hill. We weren't yet ready for that."

Meade turned to Hancock. "I placed Gibbon in reserve below Cemetery Hill. I'm pretty confident that nothing serious is going to come of this skirmishing. When you relieve Gibbon, I want you to place Second Corps along the northern part of Cemetery Ridge. I want you to extend the line southward from the end of Eleventh Corps toward Little Round Top. I've ordered Sickles to place his corps at the end of Second Corps and extend the line southward to Little Round Top."

Hancock saluted, moved off, looking refreshed after catching a few hours' sleep.

Meade addressed Warren and Slocum. "I want you both to examine the area around Culp's Hill for the purpose of conducting an offensive spoiling attack against Ewell's forces. Maybe we can catch them off guard."

Warren and Slocum mounted their horses and rode toward Culp's Hill.

The din of horses neighing and wagon wheels creaking down the Taneytown Road was growing. Meade glanced at this important artery. Hunt's four artillery brigades and ammunition train were arriving. One hundred and eight cannons being pulled by horses, single-file, filling the road. Each cannon was hooked to a limber carrying the ammunition chest. There were three drivers for each six-horse team.

Meade's heartbeat sped, and he let out a throaty sigh. He turned to his chief artillery officer. "General Hunt, I'm damn glad to see the artillery reserve is arriving. But I'm concerned with the amount of artillery stock remaining for First and Eleventh Corps. Howard told me he had fired off much of their artillery."

Hunt shook his head. "I think we will be okay, but I first have to update you on Sickles's artillery situation. Sickles brought the Third Corps to Gettysburg without its ammunition train."

421

Meade's mouth set in a grim line, jaw tensed. "Son of a bitch. Sickles did not bother to bring his ammunition train? How in the hell does he expect to fight without ammunition? What does he plan to do, throw rocks at the Confederates?" Despite his best efforts, the volume of his voice increased with each syllable.

"Actually, I anticipated just such a contingency, so I had the Reserve Artillery train carry twenty rounds more per gun than regulations required," Hunt interjected. "I have enough extra artillery ammunition on hand to restock Third Corps, with some left over."

Meade blinked, wide-eyed. Relief knocked all the yell out of him. *Sickles, you incompetent bastard, when this is over I will see to it that you never again command anything more than a poodle. But right now, I have a battle to win.*

He reached out to grip Hunt's shoulder. "Holy hell, Henry! Thank you. I'm damned relieved you thought ahead. This could have been an unmitigated disaster." Meade released Hunt's shoulder, extending a hand.

Hunt nodded, gripped the offered hand, and moved off toward the passing artillery cannons.

While Meade was watching Hunt disappear into the tide of men and artillery flowing down the road, Captain Lemuel Norton climbed the porch. "My signal officers have established observation stations at key pieces of high ground, including Little Round Top, and are in contact with nearly all the corps commanders.

"Excellent," Meade said. "Now I can contact everyone over the three-mile fishhook line in a matter of minutes."

Meade went back into the house and sat at the dining table, turning his attention to the incoming messages. Things were settling into a smooth battle rhythm. He caught a flash of movement in the corner of his eye, a steady flow of aides and couriers coming and going. The headquarters' noise echoing about the house was lovely. At the edge of his hearing, faint chattering, discreet discussions, and muffled mutterings resonated. His chest filled with a warming glow. A well-functioning headquarters was critical to winning.

As if on cue, Biddle appeared with coffee. Meade took a sip and lowered his gaze to the map table, four fingers drumming a rhythmic tap dance. The network of roads leading to Gettysburg looked like strands of a spider web.

Sweat puddled on Meade's forehead. He wiped his brow with a handkerchief. The late-morning air was murderously hot. Biddle opened the single dining room window. "Damn," Meade muttered. "No breeze."

"Any word on Sixth Corps?" he asked Biddle.

"Not yet." Biddle extracted a watch with a long silver chain attached to his belt. "Captain Bates has been gone for almost two hours. He should be returning before 11:00 and will update us on the position and arrival of Sedgwick's corps."

"Let me know when Bates returns," Meade said. "If I'm not at the Leister House, tell him where I've gone and have him report to me." Meade shook his head. *Where is Sedgwick?* "I'm going out on the porch to take a look at Cemetery Hill. Please have breakfast ready for me when I return."

"Yes, sir."

Meade moved off. He scanned through his binoculars toward Cemetery Hill. The heavy skirmishing had subsided, but he was still convinced the Confederates would attack Cemetery Hill and Culp's Hill today. Colonel Sharpe sent regular updates about the large number of Confederates massed in front of Culp's Hill. Lee either had to attack today or retreat westward back toward South Mountain. If he decided against those two alternatives, he would soon be without food and ammunition. A rifle cracked from Cemetery Hill. *Lee will attack. His blood is hot from yesterday's victory.*

Meade took a deep breath, filling his lungs with hot, muggy air. Two alternatives churned through his head: terrain permitting, launch a spoiling attack against Ewell's forces massed in front of Culp's Hill. If that was not feasible, rectify his lines, reassigning positions as necessary, watching the enemy, and looking for soft spots in the Confederate lines. If a forced retreat was necessary, he needed to make arrangements in advance.

Meade walked back into the dining room. His breakfast was waiting for him. He wolfed down some strips of bacon, scrambled eggs, and hot biscuits. The door sprang open and Butterfield and General Marsena Patrick walked into the house. Meade shoved another biscuit into his mouth, grabbed a cloth napkin, and wiped his face and hands.

They both saluted.

"I'm damn glad you're both here," Meade said. "I need you both to prepare for the upcoming battle and plan for the various contingencies, including a possible retreat. Sedgwick has not arrived yet, and Sharpe expects Longstreet to arrive anytime. When he does, I believe Lee will launch his attack."

Butterfield hesitated, standing there, wide-eyed and frowning. "We just arrived from Taneytown," he said. "The road is packed with logistics and ammunition trains. I waited all night, but Sedgwick did not show."

"Sedgwick should arrive a little after midday," Meade said. "Newton told me when he arrived this morning that Uncle John is riding with his corps on the Baltimore Pike, which he thought would be faster than going through Taneytown."

Meade peered at Patrick. "Marsena, it's good to see you. How is my old teetotalling West Point roommate?"

"I'm fine, George," Patrick replied. "Congrats on your promotion. I'm proud I survived as your West Point classmate. It wasn't easy rooming with the cadet who *never* lost his temper."

Meade laughed. "You're right. I don't ever recall being hotheaded. On a serious note, did you bring your brigade?"

"Yes, my brigade is in a field just south of your headquarters."

"Excellent. I felt incredibly lacking without them near. Hancock and Howard collected a fair number of Confederate prisoners yesterday, and we need to establish a compound for them soon."

Meade pursed his lips, taking another sip of coffee. Patrick was Meade's provost marshal general, the army's chief law enforcement officer. He was medium-built, fully bearded, and completely bald except for the bushels of hair sprouting out on the sides of his head, just above his ears. He was a strict disciplinarian, charged with preserving good order in camp and on marches, preventing straggling and skulking, and caring for Confederate deserters and prisoners of war.

Half in jest, Meade said, "Headquarters gossip says that you are crankier than I am."

Patrick did not hesitate. "Let's be clear, George. You're the crankiest general in the army."

Butterfield spoke. "General Meade, do you have any pressing assignments you want me to complete in addition to my chief of staff duties?"

"General Butterfield," Meade replied, "I cannot tell what the results of this day's operations may be. It is our duty to be prepared for every contingency, including a general retreat to the Pipe Creek line. I wish you to send out staff officers to learn all the roads that lead from this place and ascertain the positions of the corps and their supply trains. Familiarize yourself with these details so that, in the event of a contingency, you will be, without any order, ready to meet it."

"Yes, sir," Butterfield said, his face colored an ashen white. He followed Biddle, who led him to a small bedroom that would serve as his office.

Meade turned to Patrick. "Marsena, I can't stand having the news correspondents buzzing around me like horseflies. I'm going to delegate press relations to you. I swear, if I see any of those rapscallions around headquarters trying to snare me into a conversation, I will shoot them first, then you!"

They shared a grin as the tension in Meade's muscles dissolved.

"Well, if you shoot them," Patrick replied, not without a bit of devilishness, "you definitely won't have to speak with them. I do have a problem with that second shooting, however. If not for being dead, I would enjoy being your press spokesman."

"You have the cranky disposition to deal with them," Meade said. "And you have my permission to shoot them, seriously."

Patrick's face beamed, touching his holstered revolver.

"Marsena," Meade rejoined with a wink, "I was joshing about shooting reporters."

"George, you've ruined my day. Again, congrats on your new command." Patrick took his leave.

⋯⋰⋯ • ⋯⋱⋯

*10:05 a.m.*

Warren arrived with his report. "I've completed my reconnaissance of Union right flank." He wiped sweat from his face. "The ground is unfavorable for launching an attack. The area is very rough, being the valley of a considerable stream with dams on it. The terrain is favorable to the defense, but not to the attack. Artillery can only be moved with difficulty through woods and marshy places."

Meade extracted two cigars from his pocket, giving one to Warren. "I'm calling off the attack," Meade said. "We will stay on the defensive. Twelfth Corps can continue to entrench themselves with breastworks. I'm going to shift Fifth Corps, which is just arriving on the field, from supporting Slocum's proposed attack to holding a central position near army headquarters, where they can serve as the army's reserve until Sedgwick's Sixth Corps arrives."

Warren nodded.

"Until Fifth Corps is in place and Sixth Corps has arrived, the army is still vulnerable to a Confederate attack in strength," Meade said.

"If we have to conduct a forced retreat, the Baltimore Pike will be our principal egress route," Warren said.

Meade scowled. "I think our critical vulnerability is our far right. I've been worried about it all morning."

"Lee loves attacking the Union's right flank. Right now, Lee has Hill's corps opposite the northern portion of Cemetery Ridge, and Ewell's corps occupying Gettysburg opposite Cemetery Hill and wrapping itself around our far right," Warren continued, describing the current situation on the ground so that Meade could see it as clearly as if he were standing there. "Johnson's division is massed on the far right of Culp's Hill, threatening Slocum."

"If Lee places Longstreet's corps opposite Culp's Hill, or beyond it down the Baltimore Pike, and attacks before Sixth Corps is up, we would be in a frightening predicament," Meade said.

Warren moved to the map table, using his finger to trace along the roads. Meade believed in Warren, appreciated his honesty, his professional skill and sound judgment, and his passion to succeed. With Warren around, he had someone with whom he could consult and send out to be his eyes. He was no longer alone.

"I'm glad you're here, Gouv." Meade's tone conveyed a rare but sincere warmth.

Warren nodded. "Thank you, General."

"Let's ride over to see how General Webb is doing," Meade said.

Before they could leave, Biddle approached with news. "Sickles's last two brigades under General Graham's direction that had been guarding the very far left flank at Emmitsburg have just arrived."

"Good," Meade said. "Third Corps is now at full strength."

Meade moved toward Baldy and grabbed his reins. Things were starting to fall into place. The longer Lee waited to attack, the stronger the Union defenses would be. As soon as Sixth Corps arrived, the Army of the Potomac would be at full strength, equal in number to Lee's forces.

* * *

*10:20 a.m.*

*Copse of Trees*

Meade and Warren rode southwest toward a large copse of trees about four hundred yards from army headquarters. Webb's Philadelphia brigade was on the far right of Gibbon's division, occupying Cemetery Ridge. One of Webb's regiments was occupying a position behind a low stone wall, just to the left front of an artillery battery. His three other regiments were deployed behind the forward regiment, sitting behind the low stone wall.

Meade and Warren arrived and dismounted. Webb saluted. "General Meade, General Warren, it's good to see you."

"We came to see how you are doing on your third day commanding the Philadelphia boys," Meade said.

427

"They are one tough bunch of soldiers," Webb said. "I read your order to them this morning authorizing me to shoot any man caught leaving the line of battle. In turn, I told the men to shoot me if I failed to do my duty. Initially, I heard some rumbling, but the brigade took the order in good stride, particularly the second half."

Meade's eyes widened. Webb was a tough disciplinarian—that's why Meade had promoted him to command the Philadelphia Brigade, famous for chewing up and spitting out commanding officers—but he was new to being a general. Perhaps he was a tad overzealous in trying to prove himself.

"Be careful for what you wish for," Meade warned. "The Philadelphia boys may have a different interpretation of what it means for leaders to do their duty. They might oblige you."

Webb clenched his jaw.

"Tell me about the enemy strength in your front," Meade said.

"I don't know, General," Webb said, "but I will advance the brigade and find out."

"No, no!" Meade shouted, before Webb could give the order. "A brigade is too large a force for reconnoitering the enemy. It could bring on a general engagement, which we are not yet ready to conduct. Send only a company."

Webb turned and ordered Company B of the 106th Philadelphia to conduct the scouting mission. Meade watched them form as skirmishers, an open order formation with ten- to fifteen-foot gaps between each soldier. The skirmishers departed at a slow, steady pace, moving as if expecting the unexpected, trying to present a small target. They would probe until they ran into the enemy.

Meade could not repress a shiver. Inexperienced commanders with good intentions could be dangerous because they tried to prove their value as combat leaders. Rapidly promoted commanders like Webb must learn to act independently but in cooperation with the army as a whole. Lee would interpret an entire brigade marching forward in a skirmish formation as the onset of a major assault. What was Webb thinking? Aggressiveness without time-tested combat was a surefire way for a new commander to make unsound decisions leading to an avoidable disaster.

Meade gripped his field glasses, scanning Seminary Ridge. Would Rebel skirmishers react to Webb's probe? As the army commander, he was responsible for knowing the probable re-action of his subordinate commanders. *Hell.* He didn't have personal insights into many of his commanders, and he did not have time to learn. At the corps level alone he had two new men: Newton of First Corps and Sykes of Fifth Corps. He knew Sykes better, as the man had previously served as his division commander. But how both would perform as corps commanders was still uncertain.

Meade rode over to the artillery battery in front of the copse of trees. Captain Alonzo Cushing saluted. "General Meade, sir. Captain Cushing reporting and commanding Battery A, Fourth US Artillery, of Hancock's Second Corps.

Meade returned the salute. "Good morning, Captain Cushing. You seem to occupy the middle of the Cemetery Ridge line. Is your battery ready for action?"

"Yes, sir!" Cushing said.

Meade studied the artillery battery, gauging its readiness, pleased with its look. Cushing commanded a battery of six ord-nance rifles and 126 men. The three-inch ordnance rifle could accurately throw a shell more than 1,800 yards. Meade glanced toward Seminary Ridge. He guessed it was about 2,000 yards away. Cushing's battery was great for artillery duels and firing at distant targets, but much less effective at closer ranges, when canister was the preferred ammunition.

Meade turned and said, "Do you think your guns can hit Seminary Ridge?"

Cushing said, "Yes, sir! Would you like to see a demonstration?"

Meade liked his confidence. Hancock was very high on this recent West Point graduate. "Not now. But you will get plenty of opportunity before long."

Meade glanced at Cushing. He was a clean-shaven, lanky twenty-two-year-old. He wore a twelve-button shell jacket, a popular article of clothing among artillery officers, as well as a McClellan Cap, an officer's blue kepi with a flat, sunken top and squared visor. His cavalry boots reached over his knees and his cavalry saber hung from his waist. Meade grinned on the inside. At a time when rifled firearms and artillery pieces dominated warfighting, officers, including himself, still roamed the battle-field with swords. Ridiculously absurd, but funny, serving more as a guiding instrument than a weapon.

Meade and Warren rode back toward the Leister House. Rifle fire erupted, popping off over by Culp's Hill. "Gouv, ride to Culp's Hill and take a look at the defensive lines. I'm convinced the Rebels will attack over there soon."

---

*11:00 a.m.*

*Leister House*

Warren saluted, galloped toward the far right flank. Meade arrived at headquarters and settled in at the large table in the dining room. Williams sat down with him.

"Seth, I want you to issue an order directing the corps commanders to send a sketch of their positions with a view to the roads to the front and rear. Also indicate the position and apparent strength of the enemy in their front. Assign one general staff officer from headquarters to each corps to make sure the sketches and enemy dispositions are done as rapidly as possible. If the corps commanders need help, have Captain Paine assist them."

Meade walked to the porch and lit a cigar. His hands were jittery. Too much nervous energy. *You've done all you could do in the five days since assuming command.* He was facing the Union's most fearsome opponent. Was he ready?

He reached into his pocket and fished out his large round watch. It was nearly eleven in the morning. He said a small prayer. Would Sedgwick's corps arrive on the battlefield before Longstreet's corps? Lincoln had dealt this hand, and Meade had reluctantly picked it up and played the cards. Planning, not gambling, was in his blood, and a player without a sound strategy was a sucker. But the cards he held provided him no choice but to thrust the army forward based on a gut feeling. If the Union army was not at full strength before Lee played his trump card, disaster was looming. He shuddered as the gravity of the moment swept through him. He couldn't blame Lincoln for how he played his hand. He alone was responsible for the outcome of this battle.

# 31

# Sickles — Thursday, July 2

*9:10 a.m.*
*Two hours earlier*
*Along Cemetery Ridge*

Sickles sat on his white horse, just beyond the downward slope of Cemetery Ridge. His eyes were screwed shut, his mouth open in a noisy yawn, trying to clear the cobwebs from his head. Third Corps had completed its move into position along Cemetery Ridge, extending the line south of Hancock's position to the base of Little Round Top.

"Need more sleep," Sickles muttered. He opened his eyes and scanned the Third Corps sector of the defensive line, ending at Little Round Top.

"Damn it, Henry. You're right," Sickles said, "The marshy ground along Plum Run is piss poor for artillery and maneuvering infantry. Hell, in places it's ankle-deep in mud. Let's ride forward toward the Emmitsburg Road and explore the higher ground to our front that you described."

Sickles and his cavalcade rode forward of the Third Corps lines. A large cheer erupted as Sickles rode by his soldiers. Sickles's chest swelled and his heart pounded. He touched his cap, smiling widely. *My boys idolize me.*

"Henry, the men love an aggressive general who leads from the front," Sickles said.

"Men know that you always will be leading the charge," Tremain said.

One hundred yards beyond Cemetery Ridge, Sickles halted near some of Birney's infantry division. Sickles gripped his binoculars and scanned the terrain toward Seminary Ridge.

"Damn, the Emmitsburg Road appears to float on a ridgeline several hundred yards away," Sickles said.

"Third Corps is sitting in swampy marsh like a Louisiana bayou," Tremain said.

Sickles spurred his horse and galloped forward. After covering about half a mile over upwardly sloping ground, he reined to a stop near a large white oak tree. He scanned the terrain. Across the way was the Trostle Farm, consisting of a white two-story house and a large red-bricked barn. Beyond the barn was a wheat field of roughly twenty acres, and west of the wheat field was a peach orchard.

Sickles observed, "The Trostle House would make a good place for a corps headquarters."

"I agree," Tremain said. "It's the perfect location."

Sickles dismounted, standing in the shade of the white oak. His head pounded as if he had been drinking all night. He opened his pocket watch: Nine in the morning. He rubbed the back of his neck and returned to his horse, fretting.

He turned and faced Cemetery Ridge and the two round tops. He stared at the midpoint of Cemetery Ridge slipping downward to the right with Third Corps coiled along the long descending ridge to the two hills. Little Round Top was rocky on top, and Big Round Top was heavily wooded.

Sticking his corps on the far left flank occupying the Round Tops would mean observing the fighting from afar. That was dog shit. He was Meade's most aggressive corps commander and old Goggly Eyes knew that. He obviously wanted to prevent Third Corps from attaining glory in today's fighting.

The open lowland below him was filled with sunken boulders and large rocks. His regiments were not sitting on top of the ridge crest in a line. Instead they were stretched along the declining ridge like a meandering stream. They were not covering a particular position but were merely massed in the lower portion of Cemetery Ridge, with no one occupying the road trough directly in front of Little Round Top.

Sickles turned about, facing west toward the Emmitsburg Road. The ground sloped gently upward for half a mile, ending in an elevated orchard field.

As if he were reading his mind, Tremain said, "The ground forward near the Emmitsburg Road is elevated and would be perfect for establishing our defensive line. If we occupy that ground we can protect our ammunition trains, which will be traveling on that road this morning."

"Let's ride forward to the Emmitsburg Road," Sickles said. He spurred his horse along, and his cavalcade followed. They stopped beside the Sherfy farmhouse. Behind the farmhouse was a young six-acre peach orchard. Sitting on the Emmitsburg Road was a mature four-acre peach orchard. Birney's pickets were occupying a line along the road and north of the Sherfy House. A mile to the east was Cemetery Ridge and the Round Tops.

"The terrain is exactly as you described it," Sickles said. "The Sherfy peach orchard on the east side of the road reminds me of Hazel Grove. This long, elevated position dominates Cemetery Ridge to the east and Seminary Ridge to the west."

"We should occupy it," Tremain said.

"I agree. But we first have to convince Meade," Sickles said.

They rode north along the road, reining up in the peach orchard. The high ground was bare, no troops. Sickles swallowed his fluttering butterflies back into his chest.

"I sense Rebel eyes peering toward the salient, coveting the high ground," Sickles said. "Sooner, rather than later, the enemy will move artillery into the orchard, firing hundreds of big guns downrange, showering Third Corps with exploding iron."

"Yes, I agree," Tremain said.

"Isn't Meade supposed to be a topographical engineer?" Sickles said. "Didn't he ride the lines, marking the corps and artillery positions? Didn't he notice the peach orchard salient was sixty or seventy feet higher than the swamp behind Plum Run?"

Sickles continued to scan Third Corps' front from the Emmitsburg Road. To the front from Little Round Top were the Rose Woods, a dark, dense forest, blocking the view west. Bordering the woods to the northwest was the large wheat field.

"Where am I going to post my artillery?" Sickles said. "The low ground at the end of Cemetery Ridge and the high ground on Little Round Top are unsuitable."

"The marshy ground is easily commanded by the higher ground we're standing on," Tremain said.

"What idiot would order a corps commander to defend a swamp when there is a natural defensive ridge available along the Emmitsburg Road?" Sickles said.

Sickles dismounted. He turned slowly in place, fixing the terrain in his mind.

Tremain pointed to Seminary Ridge. "I believe the enemy is massing in those trees along the ridge. I can feel it."

"Third Corps should be occupying the peach orchard salient," Sickles said. "If we allow the Confederates to occupy this elevated ground, the entire corps will be at their mercy, eating lead until Meade orders us to retreat to the Pipe Creek line."

He turned to Tremain. "Send an aide back to have more pickets move up to the Emmitsburg Road."

Sickles's breath quickened. The truth washed over him like a rushing wave. This wasn't strategy. This was personal. A vendetta. That's the only possible reason Meade would assign Third Corps to this terrible place. Sickles stared at the rocky crest of Little Round Top. Blood pounded in his ears. Meade's order to occupy it and the lower end of Cemetery Ridge was sheer stupidity.

"Meade doesn't have a plan to fight Lee," Sickles said. "The only plan I've seen is the Pipe Creek Circular, and that has us retreating. If he was serious about fighting at Gettysburg he would have Third Corps occupying terrain that is suitable for maneuvering artillery and supporting infantry operations. I refuse to occupy worthless terrain and wait for Lee to attack from superior ground."

"I agree," Tremain said.

"I need to move forward and occupy the peach orchard salient or my corps will be slaughtered," Sickles said. "I must find a way to force Meade to stay and fight."

"I think you should interpret Meade's instructions a little more broadly," Tremain said. "I doubt he would occupy Little

Round Top or the depressed valley in front of Little Round Top and Cemetery Hill. He would move his front forward."

Sickles brightened. "Yes, that's a good approach—the *right* approach. A discretionary interpretation of the orders."

Sickles turned to Captain Randolph. "To occupy the peach orchard salient, we will need to tear down all the fences running north and south, enabling our horse-drawn artillery batteries to maneuver freely," Sickles said. "Send out details to flatten the fences. And get ready to deploy your artillery batteries forward."

Randolph saluted and rode off.

---

*9:15 a.m.*

Sickles turned to Tremain. "Henry, ride to General Meade's headquarters and give him the location of the Third Corps picket lines along Emmitsburg Road. Remind General Meade there are no infantry troops on the left of the Third Corps. Explain my concern for the poor ground he has assigned us."

Tremain saluted, spurred his horse toward the Leister House.

Birney rode up to Sickles and saluted. "General Sickles, a portion of my division is occupying the area General Geary occupied last night. We formed a line with its left resting at the foot of Little Round Top, and its right is on a direct line with the cemetery and connected with Humphreys's line."

Sickles asked, "Are all your forces along Meade's line?"

"Yes," Birney said, "but I'm worried about protecting our left flank and occupying the high ground along the Emmitsburg Road. With your permission, I would like to move two regiments to the Emmitsburg Road and the peach orchard. I've deployed three more regiments forward of Meade's line, beyond Plum Run creek near a stone wall in the woods near the wheat field."

"Good," Sickles said. Another reason he could use to justify moving his troops forward. Meade couldn't argue against protecting his men. "That makes sense. I ordered Captain Randolph to deploy his batteries beyond the Rose Woods fronting Little Round Top. Staying at the bottom of Little Round Top would limit his fields of fire.

"But Randolph's forward deployment is tenable only if the Rebels do not occupy the high ground along Emmitsburg Road and the peach orchard," Birney said.

"I agree. I want you to move Graham's brigade forward about 500 yards in front of the crest of Cemetery Ridge to support Randolph's two batteries," Sickles said.

"Yes, sir." Birney said. "Do you want me to move Graham's brigade all the way forward to the Emmitsburg Road? If I don't, they could be destroyed by Confederate artillery occupying the high ground along the Road or infantry attacking from the elevated area."

"No, not at the moment," Sickles said. "I can justify to Meade you being several hundred yards in front of Cemetery Ridge. But it would be a stretch for your division to occupy the Emmitsburg Road at this moment."

Birney saluted and rode off to deploy the majority of his division several hundred yards forward of Cemetery Ridge. Sickles stared at the Emmitsburg Road. He needed to play this carefully. Sending Tremain to Meade's headquarters to begin the lobbying process to move forward was a good start.

---

## Tremain

*9:20 a.m.*
*Leister House*

Tremain rode to Meade's headquarters and dismounted. Inside the Leister House, he found Meade chatting with General Warren. Senior aides from Slocum and Howard's commands were in a queue, waiting their turns with the commanding general. Tremain listened to the reports, his stomach knotting. Meade was seemingly bewitched with the enemy activities around Culp's Hill. No one seemed interested in the happenings on the far left flank. After several nerve-wracking minutes, it was Tremain's turn. He moved forward and saluted.

"What?" Meade said, in a biting tone.

Tremain blinked, his eyes riveted on Meade's scowling face. Tremain was surprised by an icy cold shiver. He hadn't expected Meade's caustic tone.

437

Almost apologetically, he began. "General Sickles sends his respects and wishes to report he has deployed several units forward of Cemetery Ridge as pickets. Most of the Third Corps' picket duty is along the elevated front of the Emmitsburg Road and the peach orchard. General Sickles also wishes to report that there are no troops on the left of the Third Corps. This is causing him some concern."

Meade folded his arms, frowning, "Tell General Sickles not to worry. Buford's cavalry will protect the Third Corps' flank."

Tremain shook his head and licked his lips. Meade really did not care about the concerns of Third Corps.

In a cautious tone, he continued. "General Sickles is concerned with the terrain he is supposed to defend in front of Little Round Top. It is low and marshy."

"Damn it, Major. If General Sickles is having problems figuring out how to post his corps, have him request General Humphreys's assistance," Meade shouted. "Humphreys is one of the army's best topographical engineers. I trust his advice on such matters."

Tremain nodded.

"Have you observed any enemy troops massing in your front?" Meade asked.

"No, sir. Just occasional enemy picket fire," Tremain said.

"Well, damn it, I have two or three of Lee's corps circling me on my right flank from Cemetery Hill to Culp's Hill," Meade said, his voice growling. "In fact, Ewell's corps facing Culp's Hill is poised to attack. That's what I'm worried about. If the enemy is massing in Sickles's front, I want to know about it, but until then, tell General Sickles I want him to execute my orders for the placement of his corps along Cemetery Ridge to Little Round Top."

Tremain's breath rasped shallow and quick. He opened his mouth but he couldn't find the right words.

Meade glared. "You're dismissed."

*9:30 a.m.*

Tremain saluted and departed, galloping back on the Emmitsburg Road toward Third Corps lines. Meade was a son of a bitch. Tremain squinted. Ahead a large dust cloud filled the air. He blinked and his muscles tensed. Was it Rebel infantry? He pulled back on the reins and slowed to a trot. Looking through his binoculars, his heart jumped. Blue infantry. Thank God. It was de Trobriand and Burling's brigades. He glanced at his watch.

Nine thirty in the morning.

Just before he reached the peach orchard, he stopped and asked a lieutenant commanding the forward pickets the whereabouts of General Sickles. The lieutenant pointed easterly toward the Trostle farmhouse, about 600 yards away. It was now serving as General Sickles's headquarters. Tremain rode the quarter mile toward the Trostle House and found Sickles and Birney standing in the fenced yard, smoking cigars. He dismounted and walked toward them.

---

## *Sickles*
*9:45 a.m.*
*The Trostle farmhouse—Sickles's headquarters*

Sickles spotted Tremain arriving and pounced. "What did Meade say?"

"General Meade doesn't seem concerned with Third Corps' challenges in executing his placement order. He said if you are having problems figuring out what lines to occupy, you should request help from General Humphreys."

Sickles's face grew hot.

Birney turned to him. "Do you think you should have Humphreys look at the defensive lines and the peach orchard? Perhaps Meade would listen to his assessment."

Humphreys was a Meade protégé. Sickles would rather lose a limb than ask for assistance from Humphreys.

"No. I don't need one of Meade's spies pointing out obvious terrain features." Sickles mounted his horse and rode toward the peach orchard. His tongue flicked over his salty lips. *Lee won't expect any of Meade's corps commanders to show boldness and initiative. He expects them all to be tethered to Meade's short leash like wet puppies.*

The pickets cheered him again as he rode by, his fat cigar clamped between his lips, basking in their adoration. *I have found my calling: leading men in battle.*

He halted, watching Birney's soldiers creeping forward toward the peach orchard, stopping with four hundred yards to go. They needed to move all the way forward, but not now. To the north, Humphreys's division hugged Cemetery Ridge, stretching northward, meeting Hancock's Second Corps line, continuing the line to Cemetery Hill.

Sickles turned to Tremain. "It's time I paid a visit to General Meade."

---

*11:00 a.m.*
*Meade's Leister House headquarters*

Sickles and Tremain rode the Emmitsburg Road in front of Hancock's corps. Reaching the copse of trees, they turned eastward. Sickles spotted Gibbon, Haskell, and Webb watching him as they passed through Webb's brigade line along the ridge.

Meade's camp was just ahead, the headquarters house snuggled several hundred yards beyond Cemetery Ridge, protected from enemy artillery shells. Sickles smiled. Naturally, Meade would find himself the safest place on the battlefield. Almost as safe as his headquarters yesterday. Sickles spurred his horse to a full gallop. Arriving at army headquarters, he reined back hard. His horse reared on its hind legs, front hooves rotating like a pinwheel.

The staff officers near the front porch stopped and watched. Sickles chuckled. Now that was an entrance. He dismounted, strutted into the house with Tremain trailing close behind.

He found Meade standing at a map table and he and Tremain saluted.

Meade returned the salute and said sharply, "I trust your corps is in position along Cemetery Ridge."

Sickles paused as he chose the right words. *I'm moving the line forward regardless.* Getting Meade's tacit approval was the challenge.

"General Meade," he said. "I've been scouting my front this morning, and I sense the enemy is massing for an attack against Third Corps."

Meade grunted. "You *sense* the enemy is massing? Why do you think that? Have you spotted Rebel troops maneuvering in your front?"

"No," Sickles said, immediately recognizing his blunder. *I walked into that one.* He needed to shift his approach. He reached for two fat cigars, offering one to Meade. Meade cracked a half-smile. They lit cigars, smoking casually. Sickles's mind churned. *Don't wait. Use your lawyer skills. Control the pace of the dialogue. Divert Meade from your true intentions.*

Sickles lowered his voice. "I'm gravely concerned the Rebels may be using Seminary Ridge in my front to mass before striking Third Corps."

Meade shrugged and blew a smoke ring that curled lazily through the thick air.

"I'm convinced the enemy will attack Third Corps positions," Sickles said. "I've ridden the ground, and the Emmitsburg Road is a long, elevated plateau in my front that, if occupied by the enemy, will provide him the advantage the Rebels need to dominate my position and destroy our left flank."

"Didn't you report earlier to headquarters that your two brigades in Emmitsburg had arrived at Gettysburg?" Meade asked.

"Yes, they arrived about ten this morning," Sickles said.

"Were they molested by the enemy occupying Seminary Ridge?" Meade said.

"No," Sickles muttered.

"Has the enemy threatened your front this morning?"

"No."

"Have the pickets been skirmishing?"

"No. We've just had enemy sharpshooter activity."

"It would appear that the enemy is not as fully concentrated behind Seminary Ridge as you have imagined," Meade said, his tone sharp. "When you have proof they are massed in your front, report it to me. Right now, I have the enemy massed in front of Cemetery Hill and Culp's Hill. And it's not just a feeling. I can see the damn Rebel battle flags."

Sickles shifted his stance. *Must take a different tack. Ask for clarification of your position again.* "Could you review with me the position you would like for me to occupy?"

Meade made a harsh growl. "I want you to occupy the position in which General Hancock placed General Geary last night."

Sickles's heart leaped. An opportunity, an angle, emerged. "General Meade, with all due respect, sir. Geary did not have an actual position. He merely bivouacked at the southern end of the ridge, sir."

"Damn it. Follow me," Meade said. He walked out onto the porch and pointed toward Little Round Top. "I want your right flank beside Hancock, and I want you to extend Hancock's line along Cemetery Ridge, placing your left flank on Little Round Top."

Meade stormed back into the house.

Sickles shrugged, glaring at the rocky hill. His intuition was correct. *You're not going to convince Meade to allow your corps to move forward. Meade fails to grasp the serious threat developing in your front. Meade wants proof. Intuition is not proof.*

He lifted his chin. A counteroffer popped into his mind. He darted inside the house.

"General Meade," he began, "I would like to invite you to come over and examine the ground on the left flank."

"The current crisis on the right flank does not permit me to do so," Meade said.

"Then do I have discretion to post my men according to my judgment?" Sickles said.

"Certainly, within the limits of the general instructions I have given you. Any ground within those limits you choose to occupy, I leave to you."

"There are some very good artillery positions in the *vicinity* of the area you want me to occupy, and I would like to request assistance in posting my guns."

"I will have General Hunt accompany you to examine and inspect positions you think may be good for artillery."

A courier walked into the house, saluted.

"Message from General Slocum, sir."

"Yes," Meade said.

"The General says to tell you the Rebels are moving troops down to the far right of Culp's Hill, perhaps to try to flank Twelfth Corps."

Meade grunted. "General Sickles, you're dismissed. Attend to your defensive lines soonest. Inform headquarters when your corps is in position."

Sickles and Tremain saluted and walked outside. Butterfield was on the far end of the porch and fell into step with them as they walked over to their horses.

"How are you doing, Dan?" Butterfield asked. "How is the Old Snapping Turtle treating you?"

Sickles cracked a smile. He missed Butterfield. Butterfield always could make him laugh. Things were not the same without Hooker.

"Meade has been riding my ass ever since he assumed command," Sickles said.

"Well, I have some news that will get you lathered up," Butterfield said.

Sickles raised an eyebrow.

"In my hand," Butterfield continued in a low voice, "is the retreat order Meade told me to draft up this morning."

Sickles stared at the order clutched in Butterfield's hand.

"Meade told you to draft a retreat order?"

"Yes, he did. I'm certain Meade does not plan to fight here at Gettysburg."

"Dan, do I understand you to say we are going to retreat back to the Pipe Creek line?" Sickles said.

"That's correct."

"When does he plan on issuing the order?"

443

"He hasn't said yet, but I'm pretty sure it will be soon."

Sickles gazed into the middle distance, calculating. "That's why Meade didn't want to occupy the high ground in his front. He wants to retreat. Son of a bitch."

Hunt appeared on the porch and walked over to Butterfield and Sickles. "General Meade asked me to inspect your artillery positions, providing assistance in finding new positions."

"That's correct," Sickles said. His walrus mustache shrouded his sly smile. He had played Meade perfectly. The Damn Snapping Turtle wasn't going to ride over to observe the Third Corps terrain. And he sure as hell wasn't going to change his mind about Third Corps occupying Little Round Top. Using a lawyer's redirect tactic and requesting Hunt inspect the ground for artillery positions was a preemptive win. Hunt would recognize that the small, steep-sided summit of Little Round Top could support only a few artillery guns. Those big guns could not depress their barrels to fire on attackers at close range. Placing the artillery batteries at the bottom of Little Round Top near Plum Run Creek with the surrounding ground sprinkled with large boulders was ridiculous.

A rush of something resembling joy swelled his chest. Meade would listen to Hunt, and convincing the artillery general to occupy the forward Emmitsburg positions would be easy. Hell, a blind man walking from the marshy ground of Little Round Top to the elevated terrain along Emmitsburg Road would agree that was the position Sickles should occupy.

Sickles and Tremain mounted their horses and headed toward the copse of trees occupied by Webb's brigade. Hunt followed behind. The coiled tentacles squeezing Sickles's chest eased slightly. He had chosen the longer route on the Emmitsburg Road instead of the shorter Taneytown Road route behind Cemetery Ridge toward Little Round Top. By the time Hunt caught up, they had passed through Webb's brigade and were riding on the Emmitsburg Road toward the peach orchard. Hunt now rode alongside.

"So what is the problem?" Hunt said.

"I want to move my men forward to a better line," Sickles said. "By throwing the line forward, I can avoid the low, marshy ground at the southern part of Cemetery Ridge and Little Round Top. Also, I want to guard the road to ensure my artillery train will arrive unmolested from Emmitsburg."

"That makes sense," Hunt said.

"After you see the whole position of the left flank, I'm sure you will agree the best terrain supporting a defensive line is along the Emmitsburg Road," Sickles said.

He had purposely ridden along the Emmitsburg Road so Hunt would begin his reconnaissance on the elevated highland, making it easier for him to see the disadvantages of the low ground near Cemetery Ridge.

---

*11:30 a.m.*
*The peach orchard*

They continued south until they were across from the peach orchard. Sickles pointed eastward toward the high wall of trees—the Rose Woods—in front of Little Round Top and the large rocks sprinkled about. He argued that these natural obstacles complicated his task of defending this position. The peach orchard was the better position, a natural defensive salient. But Sickles only hinted at the real reason he wanted to change lines: This was where the enemy would attack. If he held the advance line he could meet their attack from an elevated defensive position, hurling them back as he had done for a considerable time at Hazel Grove. His skin prickled. He would be the hero, the savior of Gettysburg.

Sickles lit a cigar as Hunt and Tremain surveyed the terrain through binoculars. Did Hunt know Meade had made up his mind to retreat? He had to move his line forward before the scrap started.

"Little Round Top offers a natural ending of Meade's line and is the perfect salient for anchoring the left flank," Hunt said. "But I agree, the broken ground in front of the Little Round Top area and the wooded belt in front of it make the terrain unfavorable to artillery."

445

"Yes, I fear the low ground will prohibit me from freely employing my artillery batteries," Sickles said, his voice filled with eagerness. "The enemy guns deployed on the higher Emmitsburg Road will dominate my artillery positions."

Hunt nodded his head. "What new line do you propose?"

Sickles pointed to the Emmitsburg Road ridge and the peach orchard. "I want to occupy these ridges. They command all the ground in front and behind. If I don't occupy this ground, the enemy will."

"I agree that this forward salient dominates the ground to Seminary Ridge as well as to Cemetery Ridge," Hunt said. "But it does not dominate Little Round Top. Here are the problems I see. Your line along Cemetery Ridge is about a mile and half. Your proposed forward line looks to be almost three miles. I'm not sure you have enough soldiers to adequately man the forward line. To cover the new line and anchor it on the left, you will have to refuse your lines. In doing so, you will create an awkward salient at the peach orchard that will be exposed to attack from the west and south."

Sickles said nothing, although he was simmering inside.

"But the biggest problem is that your proposed new line will be about three-quarters of a mile in advance of Hancock's soldiers along Cemetery Ridge," Hunt said. "This would create a huge hole in the Union line. Also, the left flank of the Union line would not be anchored on Little Round Top, which it must be."

"What is your overall assessment?" Sickles said.

"I see some advantages to the peach orchard," Hunt said. "I like it because it could easily be converted from a defensive line to an offensive line if the opportunity for offensive action presents itself. The Little Round Top line is a strong salient, but suitable as only a defensive line. If you repulse the enemy, you will not be able to follow up and counterattack."

Sickles smiled. "Precisely."

"But the move forward would have to be coordinated with Hancock's Second Corps line, which would have to throw its left forward to eliminate any gaps between Second and Third Corps lines," Hunt said. "Before considering any move forward, you need to determine if the woods west of the Emmitsburg Road and directly in front of the proposed peach orchard salient are occupied by the enemy. If the enemy already holds these woods, it would be almost impossible to occupy and hold the peach orchard salient. You need to reconnoiter those woods before taking any action."

A cannon boomed to the far right. Hunt looked up to see. The cannon thundered again, marking the start of heavy cannonading.

Hunt said, "That's artillery fire. I have to go."

"Should I move my corps forward?" Sickles asked.

"No. Not on my authority," Hunt said. "I will report to General Meade for his instructions."

Sickles's mouth went dry and tension gripped his muscles. Rage pounded him like cannon fire. He had failed to get Hunt's approval.

"I'm terribly concerned the Rebels will occupy the peach orchard salient before we do," Sickles shouted.

"I will pass your concerns to General Meade," Hunt said. "I'm going to ride to Little Round Top and then up the Taneytown Road so I can look at your entire proposed line from a different angle." Hunt turned and rode away.

*11:40 a.m.*

Sickles turned to Tremain. "Order Birney to move a regiment forward and scout the woods in front of the peach orchard."

Tremain rode toward Birney.

# Hunt

*11:45 a.m.*
*Little Round Top, Taneytown Road*

Hunt rode to the top of Little Round Top. A squad of signalmen were waving their flags. Hunt moved to the western edge of the crest. What a striking view! Little Round Top reminded him of the many medieval castles guarding the Rhine River. It was a floating fortress in the sky. Through his binoculars he studied the peach orchard line, nearly 2,000 yards away. Tight-jawed, he shook his head. When viewed from Little Round Top, the peach orchard salient seemed much farther in front of the Cemetery Ridge line than when he had stood in the orchard. Also, if Sickles moved his corps forward to Emmitsburg Road, his left flank would be tangled among the large boulders strewn about on a small hill about eight hundred yards in front of the Little Round Top.

Hunt rode down Little Round Top and paused at the hill's northern end. Sickles would need another corps to defend the proposed line. Without Sixth Corps on the field, Fifth Corps was acting as the army's reserve, primarily for Culp's Hill. Meade would keep Fifth Corps as his reserve until Sixth Corps arrived. He would recommend to Meade that Sickles not be allowed to move forward until Sixth Corps arrived.

Hunt spied the Trostle House. *Should I ride back and tell Sickles about my additional objections?* The sounds of artillery fire were intensifying from Culp's Hill. Blood pounded in his ear. He decided no. Sickles would not move his entire corps forward unless he had permission from Meade. That would be insubordination.

He galloped back on the Taneytown Road to army headquarters. Meade and Williams had just finished lunch and were talking with a courier from Sixth Corps, the messenger reporting that Sedgwick would be arriving midafternoon.

## Meade
*12:00 p.m.*
*Leister House*

Back at army headquarters, Hunt reported to Meade. "I've examined Sickles's position. He is concerned with the elevated terrain to his front called the peach orchard, running along the edge of Emmitsburg Road. He wants to move his corps forward. It reminds him of the Hazel Grove salient, and like Hazel Grove, the peach orchard is ideal for placing artillery batteries.

"So what's your assessment?" Meade asked.

"Although the peach orchard has some advantages over the southern part of Cemetery Ridge, the disadvantages are profound,"

Hunt said. "Occupying it would require twice as many soldiers, as the forward line is twice as long as the Cemetery Ridge line. This would require pushing Fifth Corps forward to occupy the line with Sickles's Third Corps. Also, if Sickles moves his line forward and Second Corps remains in position along Cemetery Ridge, you would have a gap of a half a mile between Sickles's corps and Hancock's corps."

"What Sickles doesn't grasp is that moving forward a mile and half would negate the advantages of our interior lines. Union reinforcements would have to cover this increased distance," Meade said. He turned to Williams. "Sickles also doesn't grasp that occupying Little Round Top enables him to dominate the entire field in his front. It's a natural fortress."

"I did not give Sickles permission to move his line forward," Hunt said. "After examining the proposed line from the crest of Little Round Top, I believe it could be a viable line if Fifth Corps were to occupy the line with Third Corps. Since Sixth Corps is not up yet to act as the ready reserve, I recommend that you not approve Sickles moving forward."

"I just want Sickles to follow my damn orders," Meade said. "He has been told at least four times where I want him to be. Is the son of a bitch an idiot, insubordinate, or both?"

Hunt and Williams said nothing, shaking their heads.

Meade turned to Williams. "I can't tell if Sickles is quibbling or if he has something else on his mind. Before Lee attacks today, I would like to muster all the corps commanders at headquarters. Maybe after that I can talk with him and see what's going on."

Williams nodded.

Several booms erupted beyond Culp's Hill.

"I need to ride over to Culp's Hill to see what Slocum is facing," Hunt said. He saluted and departed.

## *Sickles*
*11:40 a.m.*
*Twenty minutes earlier, just after Hunt's refusal to approve moving Third Corps forward*
*The peach orchard*

Sickles was sitting on his horse in the peach orchard, looking through his field glasses at Seminary Ridge. He put the glasses away and rode to the Trostle farm. No one cared about his predicament. Hunt said he would return if Meade said he could move forward. No Hunt. That must mean Meade said no.

At the Trostle farm, Sickles dismounted and went inside. The odor of freshly baked biscuits wafted through the air. His stomach growled. He was ravenous, having not eaten since the previous night. Maybe if he ate, the pounding in his head would subside. Sickles sat down, wolfing hot biscuits and ham.

---

*11:45 a.m.*
*Trostle Farm*

Tremain hurried into the dining room. "You're not going to believe this. Buford's two brigades of cavalry operating south and west of Third Corps and screening its left flank have trotted off to Westminster. I asked Colonel Gamble, commanding Buford's First Brigade, what was going on. He said General Pleasonton had permission from Meade to send Buford's men to the rear to rest."

"Did Pleasonton send replacement cavalry?" Sickles shouted.
"No!"

Sickles pounded his fist on the table. "Dammit! Ride over to Meade's headquarters and find out what the hell is going on. Without cavalry on my left flank I have no clue what the enemy is doing. Maybe this is the beginning of Meade's retreat back to the Pipe Creek line."

---

## Tremain

*12:30 p.m.*
*Leister House*

Tremain galloped to army headquarters, where he found Meade alone in the small living room, studying local maps. Meade caught a glimpse of Tremain as he entered the room. Tremain looked at his watch.

Tremain waited, bewildered, as Meade refused to acknowledge his presence. Seconds ticked by. He clasped his fidgeting hands behind his back. After minutes that seemed like hours, Meade acknowledged him.

"Well, sir?" Meade said, in an inquisitive tone.

Tremain stammered, "General Sickles and General Hunt scouted the terrain that was of concern to General Sickles. General Hunt made some recommendations and said he was going to report to you. One of General Hunt's recommendations was to reconnoiter the woods west of the peach orchard salient. General Sickles ordered Colonel Berdan and his four companies of sharpshooters to conduct the scout. They are currently conducting this probing mission."

Meade nodded and said nothing. He returned to studying the map.

"General Sickles requested General Meade's orders about the Emmitsburg Road," Tremain said. "He is concerned that there is no cavalry guarding his left flank. Buford's cavalry departed without any replacements."

Meade looked up sharply. He shouted, "Pleasonton and Williams." He then turned to Tremain. "Tell General Sickles I will send cavalry to patrol the Emmitsburg Road."

Tremain nodded, tight-lipped.

"You're dismissed."

Tremain saluted, turned, and bumped into Pleasonton. He stepped aside, letting Pleasonton pass. Once outside, he headed back to the Trostle farm, disappointment and frustration dragging at him like an anvil. Meade was the most bullet-headed person he had ever dealt with.

*1:00 p.m.*

At the Trostle House, Tremain found Sickles inside, stewing. He told Sickles about his visit to army headquarters. "Meade ignored me for several minutes, giving the impression that my visit held no importance. There was no one in the room but the two of us. When he did acknowledge me, he was contemptuous.

"I failed you, sir."

<hr>

## *Sickles*

*2:00 p.m.*

Sickles walked away into a small reading room. Based upon Tremain's reception, Meade didn't believe he was fit to lead Third Corps. He sat down, closing his eyes. All the corps commanders except him possessed the high ground. He had done his best to make Meade understand his predicament, but Meade was planning on retreating.

After several moments, Tremain entered the darkened room. "General Sickles, sir. Colonel Berdan is back from his scouting mission. He is waiting in the dining room."

Sickles opened his eyes, said he would be right out. He rubbed his head. *Do what is right. It is dangerous to stay on the low ground. You don't need permission to do the right thing.* He stood and walked into the living room.

Berdan saluted.

"Please report on your scouting mission," Sickles said.

"I took a hundred First U.S. sharpshooters and an additional 200 infantrymen," Berdan said. "We moved to the far left flank of the Emmitsburg Road and set up a line running east and west. We moved forward in a northerly direction parallel to the road until we entered the woods. We soon collided with the enemy. My guess is about three regiments from a Rebel brigade, marching to Third Corps' left flank. We exchanged fire for twenty minutes or so and suffered sixty-eight casualties. Then we moved back to the east side of Emmitsburg Road."

"What outfit were you fighting?" Sickles said.

"I'm pretty sure it was the lead elements of Longstreet's corps."

"It's clear," Sickles said. "Lee is trying to deceive Meade into believing the Rebel attack is against the Union right flank. That's crap. The Confederates are moving to attack the Union left."

Sickles's breathing was harsh and shallow. He should have heard something from Hunt by now. Hunt had concurred that the peach orchard salient should be occupied by Third Corps. He could not wait any longer. He had to decide before the Confederates occupied the high ground in his front. He must act, with or without Meade's approval. He had no other choice. Meade would soon order the army to retreat.

He came out of the house into a murderous sun. Most of his staff and senior commanders waited just beyond the white picket fence. Humphreys was not present but was represented by his senior aide. Sickles moved into the cluster of officers. He steadied his breathing. *You're doing the right thing.*

"Gentlemen, Third Corps is advancing its front to the Emmitsburg Road and will occupy the peach orchard salient," Sickles said. "Look sharp. Let's move out. Now!"

The men mounted their horses and galloped away. Sickles rode to the new front, using his spurs freely. A wide grin stretched his lips. Once again, he was riding to the sound of gunfire, defying the orders of a cowardly army commander bent on retreating within the next few hours. All morning long he had anticipated the Rebels moving to attack his left flank. Sixty-eight Third Corps casualties proved he had been right.

## Haskell

*2:15 p.m.*
*At Second Corps' line*

Haskell spotted sunlight reflecting off thousands of shiny metal objects. He looked down Second Corps' line toward Little Round Top and spotted dark forms moving forward. His mouth flopped open. Hundreds of streaming battle flags floated softly above waves of infantry lines sweeping toward the Emmitsburg Road.

Haskell shouted, "Look at Third Corps! They're marching forward away from the Cemetery Ridge line."

Hancock and Gibbon turned and stared.

"Sickles's move forward is going to leave a large gap, exposing Second Corps," Haskell said.

Hancock turned to Gibbon. "Did Second Corps miss another order?

"No, sir!" Gibbon said.

Hancock swore. "Sickles is occupying the extreme left of our line. Now that he has moved forward, there is nothing between our left flank and Little Round Top. Gentlemen, although I agree Third Corps marching is quite beautiful to look at, they will not be there long."

---

## Sickles
*2:30 p.m.*
*The peach orchard*

Sickles sat on his horse at the western edge of the peach orchard, glancing down the Emmitsburg Road where Buford's cavalry had been anchoring the Union left flank.

*I did the right thing moving Third Corps forward. Without Buford occupying the left flank, my artillery ammunition train traveling from Emmitsburg would be vulnerable. Unlike Hunt, I'm not worried about having insufficient infantry to man the extended line, because the hill on the far left is too rocky for the enemy to pass through. Meade had Buford abandon the left flank to conduct screening operations for Third Corps to begin its march back to Emmitsburg and occupy the left flank of the Pipe Creek line. He plans on retreating, just as Butterfield said he would.*

*Well, he can't retreat now because we are occupying the high ground on the left flank. The only thing Meade can do now is reinforce us when Longstreet launches his attack. We will be the heroes of Gettysburg. Just wait and see.*

# Sickles's Forward Deployment
## 4:00 p.m., July 2, 1863

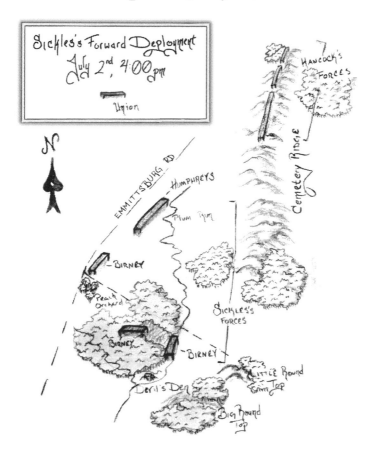

# 32

# Meade — Thursday, July 2

*12:50 p.m.*
*An hour and a half earlier*
*Leister House*

Meade burst out of the Leister House and halted on the front porch, glaring and bleary-eyed.

Stepping off the porch, he snatched the spectacles off his beaked nose and squinted as sharp sunlight seared his eyes. He fished a handkerchief from his pants pocket and wiped the lenses. Putting on the glasses, his eyes riveted on Pleasanton swaggering about like a bantam rooster. His gaggle of cavalry staff officers were milling around him about thirty yards away in the white fenced yard, smoking cigars, and indulging in idle woolgathering. *What the devil?*

"General Pleasonton," Meade shouted as he rushed toward him like an attacking barbarian.

Pleasonton turned and gawked as his lightheartedness danced away. He leaped toward Meade like a frenzied ferret and saluted. "Yes, sir!" His jaw muscles twitched and his legs tottered like a wobbling toddler's.

"Sickles's senior aide just reported that Buford's cavalry departed and was not replaced by another unit. God damn it, when I ordered you to refit Buford's division back at Westminster because his horses had been badly used up, I took it for granted that you would replace Buford's men with another cavalry force."

Pleasonton's eyebrows slanted inward into a wrinkle. His tongue clucked as if his throat was too tight. He stammered. "Sir, I was under the impression that you would provide new orders to replace Buford's division. The order I received from General Butterfield this morning directed me to have Buford collect all trains in the vicinity of Taneytown and take them down to Westminster."

"Didn't I also order you to maintain a constant guard over the army's flanks?" Meade said. "What idiot would strip his flank of its cavalry guard and leave it undefended?"

"Sorry, sir." Pleasonton's mouth dropped. "I failed to ensure Buford was replaced by another unit. We'll get a move on over there right now!"

Meade frowned, thrusting his fists behind his back into a tight clasp. His pulse beat like the wings of a hummingbird. *No wonder Sickles has been an annoying woodpecker this morning.*

"Sickles's corps is sitting out there naked as a jaybird," Meade said. "Don't take an entire cavalry division. Order a regiment to picket Sickles's left flank. Now!"

Pleasonton's lips quivered. He saluted and hurried back to his gaggle.

Meade turned and walked back into the house. *Slap!* He slammed his open hand down on the map table. "Son of a bitch." Sickles's complaint was justified. Pleasonton was derelict in not providing cavalry cover. But moving the Third Corps line forward was a different matter. Persistent badgering or vigilant wariness? Should he ride over and look at Sickles's left flank?

<hr />

1:30 p.m.

The front door whooshed open, creating a gentle breeze that fanned Meade's face. The entrant walked up, his breathing ragged.

"General Meade, I have urgent news!"

Meade stared into the flat hazel eyes of his chief signal officer. "What do you have, Captain Norton?"

"The signal officer on Little Round Top just reported seeing a large Rebel column moving to our right toward Herr's Tavern and Chambersburg Road," Norton said, panting like a dog.

"Read the signal," Meade said.

"A heavy column of enemy infantry, about 10,000 strong, is moving from opposite our extreme left toward our right."

Meade nodded, tight-lipped, and his shoulders stiffened.

"It looks as if Lee is reinforcing his troops to attack Cemetery Hill, or more likely, Culp's Hill," Norton said.

So. He had figured right. Lee planned to attack in force against his right flank. With the murderous heat, it would take at least a couple of hours before the Rebel troops were in place.

"Captain Norton," Meade said. "Good job. Update me immediately with any news from Little Round Top."

Norton departed. Butterfield walked into the living room and over to the map table. "Dan," Meade said, "tell General Slocum it looks as if Lee is reinforcing the Rebel troops in front of Culp's Hill." Butterfield turned and motioned for a courier.

Meade stroked his beard. The large infantry column must belong to Longstreet. It was the only large enemy unit that Colonel Sharpe had not been able to locate during yesterday's battle. Sharpe believed Longstreet's corps would be moving down the Chambersburg Pike and arriving at Gettysburg around midday.

Meade turned to Biddle. "There's no time to ride over to visit with Sickles. The report of the Rebels reinforcing against Slocum's right flank demands I focus on an attack against Culp's Hill."

Biddle said, "What about Sickles's concern of enemy activity in his front?

"It's clear now that only a skeleton enemy force hid among the trees along Seminary Ridge facing Third Corps." Damn Lincoln and his political generals. Sickles should never be commanding a corps. And he wouldn't be, once this was over, if he could help it.

Williams entered the room, holding messages, saying he had a note from Halleck requesting an update. Meade sent Captain Meade off to find Warren. He wanted Warren to scout Little Round Top and the southern line of Cemetery Ridge.

⸻ ◆ ⸻

*2:00 p.m.*

Biddle rushed into the dining room. "The lead elements of Sixth Corps are arriving."

"That's tremendous news!" Meade said. "With the arrival of Sedgwick's Sixth Corps, I believe our forces equal Lee's.

"Seth. Direct Fifth Corps over to the Union left, acting as the reserve force behind Second Corps and reinforcing the middle of the line. Have Sixth Corps occupy its place as the Culp's Hill strategic reserve for the right flank."

"Yes, sir," Williams said.

Meade walked out onto the front porch, glancing down the line toward Little Round Top.

A burst of yelling and cheering echoed from the direction of Culp's Hill. Meade's heart leaped. He walked out to the edge of the Taneytown Road. A senior officer approached at a gallop, with a junior officer riding alongside, flying the Sixth Corps battle flag. Meade blinked and cracked a smile. It was General John Sedgwick. Meade's skin pebbled as if it were midwinter. Sedgwick's figure grew larger and larger. Meade took a deep breath, letting it out slowly. *Thank you, God.*

He turned to Biddle. "Send a dispatch to all corps commanders requesting them to ride to army headquarters for a meeting."

At last he could meet with all the corps commanders, together. By God's bones, the first such meeting since taking command. He spotted a baseball-size rock. Taking aim, he cocked his right leg and catapulted the rock like a hard-hit ground ball. What other commander in military history met his lieutenants for the first time five days into command and a few hours before his army fought a great battle? Hell, if there were any, they were called losers. *Damn you, Lincoln, and your poisonous White House staff.*

Uncle John arrived and dismounted. His weathered face sat on top of a short, thick-set, muscular body. He walked bow-legged toward Meade as though he had been in the saddle for days. A cluster of rippling shouts rose from Meade's staff as Sedgwick and his trailing train of officers made their way to Meade. Meade's personal aides moved quickly, handing Sedgwick and the Sixth Corps junior officers coffee. A knot loosened inside Meade's gut. It was a reunion of sorts; many of Sedgwick's aides were West Point classmates of Meade's junior officers.

A wide grin split Sedgwick's grizzled beard and he saluted. "Sixth Corps is arriving on the battlefield. I'm mighty glad you waited for me before you started up with Lee's boys."

Meade turned a smile on Uncle John. Sixth Corps' grueling march to Gettysburg before Lee attacked meant a great deal—hell, the battle may have turned on it.

Meade gripped Sedgwick's hand, "Great to see you, John!" He bottled an urge to bear-hug Sedgwick and instead offered him a cigar.

"You arrived in the nick of time," Meade said. "Marching 14,000 infantry soldiers and forty-eight guns over thirty-seven miles in seventeen hours has to be one of the greatest marches in the annals of warfare."

"I'm damn proud of my boys." Sedgwick paused. "Why didn't Lee attack this morning?"

"He was waiting for Longstreet's corps to arrive. Old Pete is presently marching his corps from our left flank to our right flank. I expect him to be in position about four or so this afternoon."

"Christ Almighty, Old Bobby Lee really likes attacking our right flank." Sedgwick said. "Oh, by the way, congrats on assuming command. I supported you."

"Hell, Joe, I thought you were my friend," Meade said, smiling. "Now I know you're my sworn enemy. I'll let Colonel Hardie know that you are pining for my job."

"How is Halleck treating you?" Sedgwick asked.

"Like a goddamn hovering mother hen," Meade said. "I try to send as many updates as possible but I can't keep up with the hourly inquiries from Washington."

Sedgwick nodded. "Halleck is worse than a nagging mother-in-law."

"Agreed. I want you to place your corps close up behind Culp's Hill as the ready reserve. That will give your men some opportunity to rest."

Sedgwick saluted and was gone.

*2:45 p.m.*

Meade beamed, the tension in his muscles sliding down his bones like jelly on a hot summer day. He had caught a break, but it was a close call—too close. *You're a damn lucky bastard, George.* He savored the grateful moment, just like he had done on the surgeon's cutting table, learning he would survive the bullet piercing his lung. Over the past four days, he'd risked everything, moving directly at Lee as fast as he could, forcing him to turn and mass his troops. By the grace of God, Union infantry occupied the high ground. The Army of the Potomac, more than 100,000 strong, was massing behind a three-mile natural defensive line, with the advantage of having shorter interior lines. *Praise God.*

A voice at his side: Biddle.

"Yes," Meade said.

"Williams has sent couriers to all the corps commanders requesting they come to the Leister House for a meeting," Biddle said. "Before they arrive, you owe an update to Halleck. Perhaps you can get off a quick note before the meeting starts?"

Meade nodded. He told Biddle to round up some coffee and food for the corps commanders while he composed a message to Halleck. He sat down at the dining table and began writing.

*To Major General H.W. Halleck,*
*3 p.m. July 2, 1863*

*General-in-Chief*
    *I have concentrated my army at Gettysburg. Sixth Corps is just coming in, very much worn out, having been marching since 9 p.m. last night. The army is fatigued. I have awaited the attack of the enemy today. I have a strong position for defensive. I am not determined, as yet, on attacking him til his position is more developed. He has been moving on both my flanks, apparently, but it is difficult to tell exactly his movements. I have delayed attacking, to allow Sixth Corps and parts of other corps to reach this place and to rest the men. If not attacked, and*

*I can get any positive information of the position of the enemy which will justify me in so doing, I shall attack. I feel fully the responsibility resting upon me, but will endeavor to act with caution.*

*George G. Meade*
*Major-General*

Meade summoned Williams. The adjutant read the message, nodding his approval, then dispatched a courier to Frederick, the closest telegraph services still operating.

---

*3:05 p.m.*

"General Meade," said Biddle, "all the corps commanders have arrived except Sickles."

"I will be right out," Meade said. He moved over to the map laid out on the table and studied the positions of the different corps. There were moments, like now, when he had to think about the unthinkable. God forbid they must retreat, but he had to plan for it. He looked at the well-traveled arteries leading into Gettysburg. He studied both the large and small roads, figuring the sequence in which the corps would retreat, if necessary. He studied the path his logistics and ammunition trains would take from his supply depot at Westminster to resupply his forces at Gettysburg. He traced the Pipe Creek line running east to west across the northern portion of Carroll County, Maryland. He hoped he didn't need the Pipe Creek line, but it was a contingency defensive position he would use if he had to.

---

*3:20 p.m.*

Meade cleaned his glasses and walked out to the porch. Six of his seven infantry corps commanders awaited him. He clucked his tongue and grinned. His heart lifted as gratitude welled in his throat and hope shot through him. Depending on events, he could now attack if the opportunity emerged. Round One had been a bloodbath, ending in a stalemate with two of the seven Union infantry corps fighting two-thirds of Lee's army. But the Union held the high ground, making it a small victory. Holding the high ground again today, he had a good chance of an outright win for Round Two.

Meade faced the staff. He bottled an urge to bluster. An opportunity existed to defeat Lee's army. The air was charged with excitement. He gazed into their bright eyes; they believed in him. It was beginning to feel right commanding the army. Meade turned to Biddle. "Bring me my box of cigars." To George he said, "Ride over to Third Corps and tell General Sickles his presence is requested at once at headquarters."

The cigars arrived, and Biddle passed them out. Matches were struck, cigars lit. Warmth rushed through Meade as he basked in the camaraderie of his West Point fellow officers. Smoking together reminded him of his junior officer days, fighting in the Mexican War.

Without warning, a monstrous thunderclap cracked from the direction of Third Corps. Meade whipped his head toward Little Round Top. The corps commanders stopped chatting. The thumping cannonade mounted and the ground rumbled as if a fault line were rupturing. The artillery firing persisted for several moments as though the prelude to an attack. From the direction of the clamor, Warren came galloping toward headquarters.

He dismounted, saluting, and addressed Meade directly. "Sickles has marched his corps forward to the Emmitsburg Road." He paused for a moment to catch his breath—or from frustration, or utter disbelief. "He has created a V-shaped salient at the peach orchard nearly half a mile in front of Hancock's Second Corps line. Also, General Meade: My aides reported that Sickles did not occupy Little Round Top as you had ordered."

"I swear to God!" Sickles had disobeyed orders, moving his corps forward without permission. "Gentlemen, return to your corps. Lee's attack is beginning on our left flank."

Meade gestured to Warren and Sykes. "General Sykes, bring Fifth Corps over to the left as rapidly as possible. I will meet you there. Gouv, follow me. We're riding to Third Corps."

Sykes saluted and left immediately.

Meade strode over to where several horses were tethered and saddled. "Where is Baldy?" he asked an aide.

463

"Baldy is being groomed," The aide said. "We've saddled the gray bay for you to use." The aide pointed to the tethered horse.

"Have Baldy ready to ride when I return," Meade said.

Meade and Warren mounted their horses and started riding down the Taneytown Road. Meade spotted Sickles riding toward them. Meade spurred his horse directly at Sickles like one jousting knight charging another.

The Confederate guns continued to blast a whirling thunder like a swarm of tornadoes. Sickles and Meade met each other, stopping.

Sickles saluted.

"You need not dismount, General," Meade shouted, the words sharp and grating like the clash of steel blades. "I hear the sound of enemy cannons on your front. Return to your command. I will join you there at once."

Sickles's face flushed crimson. He turned his horse and rode at a full gallop on the Taneytown Road toward his line.

Meade gripped his binoculars, scanning Sickles's deployment of his corps.

"Oh, my God," Meade muttered as his heart pounded in his ears. He gripped the saddle pommel, steadying himself, waiting momentarily for the lightheadedness to pass. Great white clouds rose slowly from the earth near the peach orchard, and the huge artillery fire was roaring like the mighty rush of Niagara Falls.

He clenched his teeth. *Lee's forces will roll over Sickle's corps and sweep them away like swift spring runoff.* Sickles's forces were spread too thin to offer any credible resistance to the rushing gray rapids that would soon smash Third Corps into small pieces.

Meade turned to Warren and yelled, spittle flying in all directions. "How far out did Sickles move his corps from Cemetery Ridge?"

"Part of Birney's division is sitting on Emmitsburg Road near the peach orchard," Warren said. "I'm not sure Sickles has as yet placed any troops on Little Round Top."

"Christ Almighty," Meade said. "Let's follow Sickles."

Meade and Warren galloped south along the Taneytown Road. Reaching the end of Hancock's line along Cemetery Ridge,

Warren raised his hand, and they halted. None of Sickles's infantry were beyond Hancock's last soldier.

Warren pointed and said, "Beyond Hancock's anchor man, there is open space stretching all the way down Cemetery Ridge to Little Round Top."

"Son of a bitch!" Meade roared, a prickly burn cutting down his spine. "Sickles's corps has advanced nearly half a mile to the front of Hancock's corps. It's entirely disconnected from the rest of the army."

"And it's beyond supporting distance from the rest of the army," Warren said.

Meade motioned to Captain Emlen Carpenter. Emlen joined them.

"Yes, sir," Carpenter said.

"With battle about to erupt soon, I want your cavalry squadron to escort me," Meade said. "It's going to get pretty hot, pretty quick!"

"Will do, sir."

Carpenter motioned for his Sixth Pennsylvania Cavalry detachment, serving as the army's headquarters escort, to close up. Known as Rush's Lancers, they were one of the finest cavalry regiments in the Army of the Potomac, and some of the cream of Philadelphia society.

"Let's ride," Meade said.

Meade and Warren shot down the road, galloping side by side.

"I can't believe there are no troops in position on the southern part of the ridge," Meade said.

"Nearly one mile of unoccupied ridge," Warren said.

"Sickles willfully disobeyed my direct orders. I swear I will court-martial his ass when this is over. This will be the last day he serves in the army!"

The cannonading against Meade's left flank stopped. It grew eerily quiet. They rode in silence, followed by their aides and Rush's Lancers, providing escort duty. The battle was about to erupt, and damn Sickles was grossly out of position. *What a worm-ass.*

They rode past the Weikert farm and turned westerly on a small dirt road, cutting across an open field toward the Emmitsburg Road. The dirt road crawled past the wheat field and timberline, leading to Sickles's headquarters at the Trostle House. They stopped at Plum Run Creek, a small runoff acting like a shallow moat protecting Little Round Top.

*3:47 p.m.*
*Taneytown Road and wheat field road at the base of Little Round Top*

The enemy cannonading erupted again.

Meade looked through his field glasses toward the rumbling enemy artillery, estimated the thundering was coming from beyond the westward boundary of the wheat field. After examining the terrain beyond the wheat field and Rose Woods to his left, Meade turned in his saddle, staring back at Little Round Top.

"There's where the line should be," Warren said, pointing.

His words laced with anger, Meade said, "It's too damn late now. The enemy's attack has already begun."

*3:52 p.m.*
*The wheat field road and Plum Creek*

A ringing of musketry cracked from the far side of Little Round Top. Meade turned to Warren and shouted, "Gouv! I hear peppering in the direction of that hill. Ride over and see if anything serious is going on and, if so, attend to it. I'm going to ride to the peach orchard, to see if we can salvage this mess."

Warren saluted and rode toward Little Round Top.

Meade glanced at his watch; it was just about four. He scanned the area behind Little Round Top. *Where is Sykes's Fifth Corps infantry moving forward to occupy the gap in the defensive line? No one. Damn it.* Coming from the direction of Sickles's salient, distant rumbling and cracking echoed like an approaching avalanche.

Meade and his cavalcade turned and galloped westerly. As he rode, he surveyed the field, attempting to fathom Sickles's motives.

466

He saw two possible courses of action: Leave Sickles to his own peril, letting him fight his way out of his dilemma as best he could. Or move reinforcements forward to fight alongside Third Corps, trying to hold an unacceptable neutral position. *Son of a bitch.* No choice but to reinforce Sickles's screw-up. As Meade rode toward Sickles, he focused on how many reinforcements were needed, considering the risk of weakening his defensive line.

<hr />

*3:55 p.m.*

Meade spotted Sickles, Tremain, and several of his aides in the peach orchard near the Emmitsburg Road and headed for them. *Moving an entire corps beyond supporting distance of the army was idiotic.* Meade reined up, showering Sickles with dirt and grass. Sickles saluted, sitting motionless on his horse.

Meade studied Sickles's face—relaxed, as he smoked a cigar. It was almost as if he were proud that he was occupying the undefendable peach orchard salient. A jolt of reality pierced Meade's gut. *Oh, my God.* Sickles was utterly ignorant of the blunder he had committed.

"General, you are too far out," Meade said. "Your position is well beyond what I expected you to take. I'm fearful you will be attacked and will lose your artillery."

"General Meade, let me explain," Sickles said. "This ground is more elevated than the position along Cemetery Ridge. Occupying it enables me to control the enemy, who is sitting on lower ground to the west." Sickles pointed toward Seminary Ridge.

"Yes, this may be higher ground than that to the rear," Meade said. "But there is still higher ground in front of you, and if you keep advancing you will find constantly higher ground all the way to the damn mountains."

Sickles shook his head as if he was struggling to understand his point.

Bullets droned close by and missiles roared through the sky. Meade moved his horse closer, leaning over near Sickles's ear.

"Your corps is too far forward," he said. Meade pointed toward the enemy, forming in long battle lines. He quickly scanned the terrain.

"General Sickles, the Confederates can easily force you off this isolated salient."

Sickles was expressionless, like a sleepwalker, wide-eyed and dim-faced.

"I moved forward on my own initiative," Sickles said. His words came out raspy. "I stand by my decision."

Meade struggled to collect himself. Time had run out; the situation was grim and getting grimmer. His stomach clenched and a lump formed under his breastbone. He would deal with Sickles's insubordination later. Right now, he had to fix this problem. He needed more infantry to extend Sickles's defensive lines. Rebel cannonading was increasing like booming thunder on Sickles's left front.

A shell whistled overhead. Sickles said urgently, "I can hold this line, which I believe is strong. But I will need reinforcements."

Meade said sharply, "Yes, an entire corps."

Sickles said, "Say again, General. I didn't quite hear you, sir."

Meade shouted, "You've moved your damn corps too far out. I can't support you out here. If I try, I will have to abandon the rest of the line. Your line is not only disconnected from the rest of the army, but both of its flanks are exposed, and it is more than a quarter mile longer than the Cemetery Ridge line."

Sickles said, with a touch of pain, "General Meade, I was acting within the general instructions you had given me earlier at the Leister House."

Meade turned his stirrups and pointed back toward Cemetery Ridge. "The line you should have occupied is back there!" he shouted. "General Sickles, this is neutral ground. Our guns command it, as do the enemy's. The very reason you cannot hold it applies to them as well."

Sickles tilted his head to the side like an endearing dog with expectant eyes and turned-up ears. Something flickered across Sickles's face. Shock? Revelation? A *Eureka* moment? He frowned.

"I will withdraw my forces from this forward line if you desire," Sickles said.

"Yes, if you can," Meade said. "But I'm fearful the enemy will not permit you to withdraw, and I'm afraid there is no time for movement."

Sickles turned to Tremain. "Inform Birney and Humphreys to fall back to the Cemetery Ridge line."

*4:00 p.m.*
*The battlefield*

Before Tremain could depart, the air erupted with a horrific blast as enemy cannon shells rained from the sky in front and to the left of the peach orchard. Meade turned toward the enemy artillery blast. From the dense woods emerged a long grey line, dotted with several dozen blood-red stars and bars—Rebel battle flags. Meade squinted as the sunlight gleamed off of thousands of bayonets and steel blades, casting a blazing checkerboard of brilliant sunlight onto Sickles's corps.

"The infantry attack is beginning," Meade said. "Do you know who those forces are?"

"I believe the forces on our far left are Robertson and Law's brigades from Hood's Division," Sickles said.

"So we are facing Longstreet's corps," Meade said. Damn, Longstreet must have countermarched back to Sickles's front under the cover of the Seminary Ridge's thick trees.

Then that damned berserker wailing—the Rebel Yell. The Confederate attack they had waited for all day had commenced.

Another shell whizzed by Meade and Sickles.

"It's too late for you to withdraw," Meade said. "Stay put and hold the line. I will send up Fifth Corps on your left and I will have Hancock support your right. If need be, I will move some of Twelfth Corps' forces from Culp's Hill to support you."

"I request as much artillery support as you can provide," Sickles said. "Will you send General Hunt to arrange the placement of the additional artillery?"

Meade glared. "Yes. I will send you additional artillery as well as General Hunt." Rage flowed in his voice. Sickles had murdered a man in cold blood, and now he was going to be responsible for the deaths of 11,000 men. *God damn you to hell, Sickles.*

An artillery shell whickered overhead, blowing a gaping wound in the golden wheat field. Disaster loomed.

Meade turned to Biddle. "Ride to Hancock. Have him send one division here. Then ride to headquarters. Have Williams order Twelfth Corps here, but leave a brigade occupying Culp's Hill. Then ride to Slocum and tell him the order is coming and have him prepare his corps to march." To George Meade he said, "Tell Sykes to move his corps here, double-time."

Biddle paused. Meade sensed the hesitation.

"What?" Meade said.

Biddle asked, "Are you sure you want to strip Culp's Hill of most of its forces? You've been worried about the enemy attacking it all day. If the enemy attacks and carries it, we will lose control of the Baltimore Pike. We will have to retreat."

Meade's eyes narrowed and his nostrils flared. He raised his voice, ensuring he would be overheard by Sickles, "We don't have a damn choice. If we don't plug the gaps General Sickles has created, Lee will rush right through. Then it won't matter if we've held Culp's Hill. Lee will march right down the Emmitsburg Road with a clear shot at the capital."

"Yes, sir," Biddle said. He departed.

Meade glanced at Sickles. He was chomping on his cigar, seemingly oblivious to the nutcracker in which he had placed Meade's army. He would stay with Sickles a few more minutes to see how the Confederate attack developed and how Sickles's corps responded.

---

*4:02 p.m.*

A battery of four to five Rebel cannons fired a broadside of balls toward the group surrounding Meade and Sickles. The shells whooshed overhead, followed by a sudden thundering convulsion, the sound of impact shaking the air. Then the screams of the wounded. One of Meade's aides yelled for the two generals to move back. The large gaggle of officers and their staffs was drawing enemy fire. A lucky shot could kill them all. A blasting cannon boomed. A solid shot shell thundered toward him, bouncing unexploded, skidding and plowing a furrow in the ground near Tremain's horse.

The shell spooked Meade's horse, and the small bay bolted toward Cemetery Ridge. Meade leaned straight back instinctively, pulling fiercely on the reins. The harder he pulled, the faster the horse ran. *Damn, he won't slow down.* Panic leapfrogged inside his chest, ricocheting off his chest walls like a bunch of shooting marbles. Meade bounded down the small dirt road, barely missing an artillery battery riding to the front, one he would later learn was Captain John Bigelow's Ninth Massachusetts artillery battery. After what seemed an eternity, the horse eased into a canter. Meade relaxed the tension on the reins, blew out his breath. Behind him, several horses rumbled. He cocked his head. It was his aides and escort. The horse slowed, gurgling as he gasped for air.

Meade fumed. Nearly killed by a runaway horse, not an enemy bullet. He wasn't afraid of dying, but he wanted it to at least be an honorable death. His staff arrived alongside. Meade said sheepishly, "That was a close call." He spurred the horse and rode toward Little Round Top.

Sharp, burning heartburn had settled behind Meade's breastbone. He sat straight in his saddle, trying to ease the pain. Sickles's corps was going to be routed, perishing before reinforcements could arrive. In his mind's eye, he saw Sickles's boys smashed, the survivors fleeing to the safety of the ridgeline, the line Sickles should have been occupying. There was no time. *Must shift as many soldiers as possible from Culp's Hill to Sickles's salient.*

He gauged the Taneytown Road was 300 yards ahead. A deafening swoosh behind him shook the ground. He flinched. Seconds later, another shell screamed overhead, blossoming fifty yards in front, then thousands of screaming whistles as shards whizzed about. Meade turned off the connecting road toward Cemetery Hill, riding parallel to the Taneytown Road. If the enemy was bracketing and adjusting the artillery fire, and he

continued riding toward Little Round Top, the next shell should
hit right on top of him.

——————— • ———————

*4:08 p.m.*

Meade and his cavalry escort rode over Cemetery Ridge, and
then turned on the Taneytown Road, toward the Leister House.
Meade nudged the horse to an open gallop. Ahead, a large battery of nearly one hundred men and six 10-pounder Parrotts was
flying on the road toward him. He slowed slightly and turned off
the road for several yards before bending back and running along
the edge of the fence lines.

All right. Hunt was reinforcing Sickles's flank with the army's Artillery Reserve. Damn glad Hunt was at the end point
of Sickle's line directing the posting of the artillery batteries.
Although he did not know Hunt well, he was impressed by him.

——————— • ———————

*4:12 p.m.*

He spotted the stone house belonging to George Weikert
and, just beyond the farmyard, soldiers from Hancock's corps
along Cemetery Ridge. They were men from Caldwell's division,
anchoring the far left of Second Corps. The division was moving, marching by columns toward the threatened areas behind
Sickles's corps.

Meade moved over Cemetery Ridge and rode by Caldwell's
division. The men stared straight ahead, silent, their rifles right-
shouldered. Meade spotted a small break between Cross's brigade
and Zook's brigade. He cut between the two units onto a road
connecting the Taneytown and Emmitsburg Roads. He wanted
to talk with Hancock before returning to the Leister House.

Meade rode along the narrow east-west artery while his
mind chattered. *If the Rebels take control of this small but much-
traveled road, they will have direct access into the rear of the Union
army.* Meade rode into a rock-strewn field near the western base
of Cemetery Ridge and noticed one of Hunt's regular army reserve batteries limbering into position, near a knoll, protecting
the road. The battery's commanding officer was Lieutenant Evan

472

Thomas, whose father was General Lorenzo Thomas, adjutant general of the entire US Army.

* * *

*4:15 p.m.*

Meade stopped. "Lieutenant Thomas, who placed your battery here?

"General Hancock personally, sir," Thomas said.

Meade gripped his binoculars and scanned the area. At first glance, the battery seemed to be in an awful position. About one hundred yards to the west, Plum Run rippled past. Just beyond Plum Run, a rise and a knoll blocked the view southwest to the Emmitsburg Road and Trostle Farm. Due south, the roof of the Weikert House sat just above the trees. Northwest was the copse of trees occupied by Gibbon's division. Thomas's battery had a clear field of fire all the way to Cemetery Hill. Meade turned, looked back at the knoll. If the enemy occupied the rise and knoll, they could enfilade direct fire into the battery.

"You have to hold this position at all cost," Meade said. "This is a strategic position covering this road. Did General Hancock order any infantry to support you?" Meade worried that the son of the adjutant general of the US Army, a personal friend, was occupying an isolated pocket that could be easily overrun.

"Yes, sir. General Hancock ordered Colonel Colvill, commanding the First Minnesota, to support the battery," Thomas said.

Meade nodded. Good. Ordering the First Minnesota to support Thomas was a wise decision. But having one undersized regiment plug the gap left by Caldwell's division was not a long-term solution. As soon as he arrived back at headquarters, he would order Twelfth Corps from Culp's Hill to reinforce the First Minnesota.

Meade shook his head. Thomas's battery and the First Minnesota would have to fill this gap in the Union line until reinforcements could arrive. He would not have time to build a new defensive line with the support troops arriving piecemeal. The best he could do was feed them into the most vulnerable gaps as they arrived. *Must return here after seeing Hancock and Slocum, and direct the positioning of the reinforcements.*

———————— • ————————

*4:17 p.m.*

Meade raced off again, his eyes riveted on a near-giant sitting tall in his saddle, leading his regiment toward Thomas's battery. The colonel appeared to be close to seven feet tall. A powerful look of approval the size of Sickles's unoccupied ridgeline stretched across Meade's lips. There was an unmistakable toughness in the way they moved, coming very fast, rifles gleaming. Meade touched his hat, a quick commander's salute to the Minnesota regiment he expected to hold the vacated ridge. The giant colonel returned the salute.

Meade rode toward Gibbon's division, looking for Hancock. He had decided on a plan of reinforcement: A piecemeal filling of gaps in the broken battle line, success depending on how fast the troops would come. Meade rode forward to the ridge ahead, spotting Second Corps' flag flying. Hancock was on the crest directing activities, with Gibbon and Haskell sitting astride their horses next to him. Meade rode to them, jerking the borrowed horse to an awkward stop. Hancock saluted, along with Gibbon and Haskell, as Meade approached.

———————— • ————————

*4:20 p.m.*

Meade returned their salutes.

"Sickles is going to get licked, and he should lose his head for it," Hancock said.

Meade nodded agreement and said, "I've ordered Fifth Corps toward Sickles's position. I told Sykes to occupy Little Round Top. I'm going to send Slocum's corps from Culp's Hill to reinforce Sickles and to help plug the gap in your line created by the departure of Caldwell's division. I may call on you to send more troops to Sickles's aid. You're going to have to hold the center of Cemetery Ridge at all cost."

"Yes, sir, understood," Hancock said.

———————— • ————————

*4:26 p.m.*
*Leister House*

Meade turned and rode off across the open field. Moments later, he had a clear view of the Leister House, a few hundred yards ahead. He arrived and dismounted. An orderly grabbed the reins of Meade's borrowed horse.

"Have Baldy ready to ride," Meade said. He walked onto the porch where Sedgwick was standing.

"Sickles got himself into an awful spot. He did not take the position along Cemetery Ridge and Little Round Top that I assigned him. Instead he moved nearly three-quarters of a mile in advance of the Cemetery Ridge line."

"Why didn't you order Sickles back to the Cemetery Ridge line?" Sedgwick asked.

"It was too late. The enemy had opened the battle with an artillery cannonade, followed shortly thereafter with an infantry attack. Sickles's boys are fighting hard but they're being butchered. Where is your corps?"

"I halted them on the Baltimore Pike, just south of Cemetery Hill and Culp's Hill," Sedgwick reported.

Meade said, "Good. I want you to redeploy them to the left center of Cemetery Ridge behind Second Corps and Fifth Corps. Your corps will be acting as the ready reserve."

Sedgwick saluted and departed. Meade walked into the Leister House, where Williams and Sharpe and some aides from the Bureau of Military Information were looking at maps on the table. Meade joined them, studying the enemy forces drawn on the map.

"What is Lee up to, gentlemen? Do you think the attack against Sickles's front is a demonstration, and the main attack will be on our right flank?"

## 33

# Warren — Thursday, July 2

Warren galloped toward the northern base of Little Round Top, spiraling upward against the thin blue sky. Acrid smoke of spent gunpowder tainted the air. Several big guns near the Emmitsburg Road belched forth a thunderous clapping. He peered toward the crest of Little Round Top and spotted the Union signalmen waving their flags. That was good—the Union still occupied the crest. So perhaps after he reported to Meade that Little Round Top was not occupied, Sickles had sent a unit to the crest. They were probably the ones peppering the air with gunfire. Warren chuckled. Maybe Sickles had suffered an attack of penitence and decided to follow some of Meade's orders. Warren paused at the bottom of the hill, cocked his head, scanning the battlefield. Shells erupted, screaming and raining shrapnel over Sickles's exposed Third Corps, stranded a few thousand yards away from Little Round Top. His mind's eye saw the murderous slaughter like the bloody spectacle of the Chicago stockyards. Instead of hogs squealing with cut throats, blue figures shrieked and dropped to the ground as flying shards ripped through soft flesh.

He swallowed hard. But what if Sickles had failed to occupy the Round Tops? Scanning the smaller hill with his field glasses, he saw that the quickest way to ride to the top was a possible path along the northeast side.

3:56 p.m.

"General Warren, look," someone shouted. "General Sykes is approaching."

Warren turned to see Lieutenant Washington Roebling, his twenty-eight-year-old brother-in-law and aide, taking quick strides toward him on his long legs. Roebling's dark hair barely protruded below his blue cap. He wiped sweat from his clean-shaven cheeks and his thin chevron mustache and pointed.

Warren spotted the Fifth Corps flag, General Sykes, and several aides trailing behind, heading west toward the wheat field. Relief swept over him.

He rode toward them, pulling up in front of Sykes, saluting. Sykes was a small, rather thin man, sporting a full brown beard and a reddish, rough-looking face. He always looked a bit weary, and a little ill-natured. But he was one of the best generals in the army, extremely cool in the face of danger.

"Sir, General Meade has ordered me to ride to the top of Little Round Top," Warren said. "If Sickles did not occupy it with sufficient soldiers, I may call on you to provide reinforcements."

"No problem, Gouv," Sykes said. "Meade has ordered me to reinforce Sickles. I'm taking my staff forward to see where we can fill the gaps. My lead elements are just arriving on the battlefield."

The distant cannonading erupted into a furious booming. Sykes gestured toward the cracking thunder, rumbling like a violent torrent rushing down a mountainside.

"Gouv, I must ride forward and determine where to deploy my corps." Sykes spurred his horse and galloped toward the battlefield, leading eleven thousand soldiers marching close order and five horse-drawn artillery batteries consisting of twenty-six big guns.

Warren smiled slightly, eyeing General Stephen Weed leading his brigade forward, following Sykes. Weed was the same age as Roebling and looked almost identical, except Weed's clean-shaven face emphasized his more gunslinger-like mustache. Weed was a rising star and would soon receive command of an infantry division. Warren turned to Roebling.

"Washington, ride to the crest of Little Round Top to see what soldiers are up there."

Roebling spurred his horse, weaving his way up the northeast slope of Little Round Top as a billy goat would. Warren clapped his spurs against his horse's ribs and leaned into a gallop toward Weed, jerking back hard on the reins, forcing the horse into a skidding stop, and sending clods of grass flying when he reached him.

Weed saluted, his face stone cold. "What's happening, Gouv?"

Warren returned the salute. "Sickles really put us into a fix." They had been talking for a few minutes when Lieutenant Roebling returned, sweaty and breathing hard.

"Sickles did not place any soldiers on Little Round Top," he said. "The only soldiers there are from the signal corps."

Warren bristled and his heart sank. "Son of a bitch. We're going up there."

*4:00 p.m.*

Roebling headed up. Warren spurred his horse, followed by his escorts, tracing Roebling's path. He worked the northern slope, his horse slipping several times, arriving at a flat, rocky crest shaped like an oval, about fifty yards long. He swallowed hard. *Son of a bitch.* Heat blazed down the back of his neck. "Damn you, Sickles."

The summit was deserted, except for a group of signalmen. The crest was barren on top, with trees and boulders scattered below. The slope was steep on all sides, especially the western ascent facing the Rebels. He heaved a ragged sigh. At least the Rebels faced a hard climb to the western slope.

The signalmen stood on a bluff of boulders at the north end of the crest, whipping two large flags in fast, short movements, messaging the flag operators at Meade's headquarters. Warren dismounted and walked over. The soldiers' mouths dropped open. They hesitated, then snapped a smart salute. Warren returned it.

"Did I surprise you?" Warren said.

"Yes sir, you did," Captain James Hall said. "You're the first officer to visit Little Round Top since early this morning."

"So no one from Sickles's corps visited you?" Warren said.

"No sir. Troops for Geary's division manned the crest last night and left early this morning. Sickles did not replace them."

"Damn," Warren hissed. He moved to the lip of the western crest, gripping his binoculars as he scanned the terrain. Dark fear gripped him.

"What a view," Washington said, standing beside Warren.

"My God, this small hill is the cornerstone of Meade's whole position." Warren said. "It anchors the Union left and secures the Union positions along Cemetery Ridge. If it were to fall it would be disaster."

"If the Rebels occupy it and place artillery pieces on it, they could blast away the Union line along Cemetery Ridge," Washington said.

"Hell, the Rebels don't need to place artillery here," Warren said. "If they hold it with infantry, the Rebels would have access to the Union rear. The Cemetery Ridge line would have to be abandoned, forcing Meade to retreat."

"Why didn't Sickles occupy the hill?" Washington said. "Geary occupied it early this morning. Meade's sketched positions has Sickles positioning his troops on the hill."

"Whatever Sickles's reasons, it's dereliction of duty and a court-martial offense for disobeying orders, as far as I am concerned."

Warren scanned the western base of the hill through his field glasses. Big boulders lay edgewise, as if giants had played dice-rolling games with the large rocks.

Beyond the hill's base, Plum Run creek snaked north through a lush valley. About a half mile to the southwest, the large boulders of Devil's Den jutted skyward.

"I see Sickles's line ending at Devil's Den," Warren said. "Is that his left flank?"

"It appears so," Washington said.

"Christ almighty. It's dangling out there like a broken branch."

Warren shook his head. A tree-lined ridge extending north from the Devil's Den blocked his view of the wheat field and the peach orchard. Beyond the Emmitsburg Road, he scanned a tree line about a mile away marking the crest of Seminary Ridge, where thundering blasts rippled the air. Confederate artillery batteries along the tree line were dueling with Sickles's big guns in the peach orchard like two frigates exchanging close-in broadsides. Warren's stomach lurched. Were enemy infantry hiding in those woods along Seminary Ridge?

He turned south and gazed at Big Round Top. The larger hill was heavily wooded, steep, and strewn with boulders.

"The Big Round Top is not suitable for artillery," Warren said. "But I believe we can haul an artillery battery on the crest of Little Round Top."

"I think Little Round could support probably one battery," Washington said.

From Warren's position at the north end of the crest, the summit ground rose gently for forty yards, ending on a large flat knob at the center of the hill. The elevated knob screened the southern portion of the crest from view. He walked to the knob and stopped. From here the ground sloped down another hundred yards toward the big hill. Warren walked down the grade to the southern end of the crest and paused, his dusty riding boots hanging over the edge of a steep slope. About twenty yards down, a small rocky shelf jutted out like a wide stone walkway, wrapping around the hill westward toward Devil's Den and the peach orchard.

"The small shelf would be a perfect place for Union troops to occupy," Warren said.

"Agreed. The Rebels can't assault the southern part of the summit without first crossing the stone walkway," Washington said.

Warren took a step back, turned about and studied the northern side of the crest. He craned his neck but couldn't spot the signalmen. An icy chill coursed through him.

"The elevated ground along the knob blocks the signalmen's view of events at the southern end of the crest," Warren said.

"That could be a problem," Washington said.

"Not if the rocky shelf was occupied with sufficient numbers of soldiers," Warren said. "If we can get enough infantry here, this towering fortress would be impregnable."

Looking through his binoculars, Warren searched for Rebel infantry hiding along Seminary Ridge. None. His mind's eye worried otherwise, conjuring up all sorts of phantom devils lurking in the dark trees. He gestured toward Captain Hall, standing next to his small group of signalmen. Hall hurried to him.

"Are any of Sickles's soldiers below the western crest of Little Round Top?" Warren asked.

Hall shook his head. "No."

"Did any of Sickles's men scout Little Round Top?"

Hall shook his head again, "No, sir."

Warren's jaw tightened and his blood boiled in his veins.

Lieutenant Roebling pointed. "General Warren," he said, "Just beyond Devil's Den, in the wooded area, I saw the enemy massing when I was here earlier."

Warren stared at the mammoth boulders scattered around Devil's Den. A few immense flat rocks stood side by side, small openings between them like caves. These rock caves provided a shelter impervious to shot and shell, superb lurking spots for Rebel sharpshooters.

Perched atop of a few boulders in Devil's Den were two of Sickles's artillery batteries, exposed and vulnerable.

Warren said, "How in the hell did Sickles's boys get those artillery pieces on top of those boulders?"

"It was a murderous effort that took more than three hours," Hall said. "They manhandled the artillery batteries atop the rocks, pulling the guns with ropes and hand-carrying the ammunition, as the small space did not permit the use of limbers."

Warren frowned. The image of an enemy shell hitting the ammunition and blowing the nearby guns to smithereens flashed across his mind.

"The artillery placement is ludicrous and dangerous," Warren said.

"If the gunners retreat, they will leave cannons behind that could be captured," Washington said.

Warren turned to Hall. "Whose rifled battery is that in Devil's Den?"

"That's Captain James Smith's six 10-pounder Parrott's battery of the Fourth New York," Hall said. "But there's room for only four guns on the ridge."

*4:05 p.m.*

"Washington, ride to Captain Smith's battery and have him fire a shot into those woods beyond Devil's Den," Warren said. "Let's confirm your story of Rebels massing there."

Washington departed. Through his binoculars, Warren watched him ride toward Smith's battery. In a few minutes, a single artillery piece lurched backward as a long yellow flame leaped out the muzzle face. The sharp crack of cannon fire split the air as the sun glinted off the jerky movements of thousands of concealed Rebel gun barrels and bayonets sparkling like bejeweled chandeliers.

The glimmering beneath the forest foliage confirmed his worst fears. The startled Rebels were massed in the woods, poised to attack, their line of advance to Little Round Top unopposed. My God, the Rebel battle lines stretched considerably south along Emmitsburg Road, overlapping Sickles's left flank.

"Christ, Sickles. What the hell were you thinking?" Warren whispered.

Third Corps was isolated, well beyond support of the army. The Rebels would hit Sickles's uneven line with several huge assault waves, quickly surmising what they were attacking, pushing the blue defenders back like flotsam in the wake of a storm surge. They would skirt along Sickles's flanks, figuring out the blue boys were marooned on an exposed salient. With his flanks crushed, Sickles faced annihilation.

*4:10 p.m.*

Warren pulled a piece of paper from his jacket pocket, scribbled a note to Meade, asking a division be sent to defend Little Round Top immediately.

He turned to Captain Chauncey Reese, one of his aides, and said, "Give this message to General Meade. Tell him Little Round Top is undefended. Holding it is the key to defending the Union line. Tell him to send at least one division. Ride at all-out speed."

Reese mounted his horse and rode to the northeast edge of the crest. Warren walked to the edge, observing. Reese spurred his horse and plunged down the northern slope, the horse sliding on all fours the last fifty yards. At the bottom of the hill, Reese sprinted to the Taneytown Road and turned north, galloping toward the Leister House.

Warren scribbled out another note. When he finished, he gave the message to Lieutenant Mackenzie, another aide. "Give this note to General Sickles. Tell him to send Third Corps soldiers immediately to Little Round Top."

Mackenzie departed down this hill and galloped toward the Trostle House at the rear of the peach orchard.

Warren frowned. *Rebel hordes will soon be swarming the hill. I've sent out pleas for help.* What more could he do?

He walked to the western crest. Captain Smith's four artillery cannons were bombarding the Confederates hidden in the trees across from the Union's left flank. Good. Keep giving it. The massed enemy standing still was like shooting ducks in a barrel.

The enemy began returning fire against Smith's battery with alarming accuracy. Smith's men answered by increasing their rate of fire, discharging their guns more rapidly with efficiency and effectiveness. A thundering blast erupted, blowing a Rebel caisson to smithereens. Black smoke and yellow fire leaped skyward.

<hr />

*4:11 p.m.*

Abruptly, thousands of glimmering lights in the dark woods surged forward like a horde of lightning bugs. The attack was imminent. Hail started splattering against the rocks near Warren's feet. No clouds had emerged; it remained a clear day. What the hell? He glanced down the slope. A yellow flash and a rock pelted his boot. It wasn't hail. It was Minié balls. The Rebels had already worked their way through Devil's Den.

Turning, he spotted Captain Hall and his signalmen packing, preparing to scoot down the hill. Warren circled over, Minié balls careening off the nearby rocks. He did not look back, instinctively keeping his head down as he moved.

"Captain Hall! Where do you think you're going?" Warren said.

Hall, his voice filled with desperation, replied, "General Warren, those Rebel marksmen are damn good shots. It's only a matter of time before they pick us all off. I'm taking my boys down the hill so they can be deployed elsewhere."

Warren glared at Hall, who was fidgeting like a deserter facing a firing squad. "Dammit!" Warren shouted. "Keep your flags waving. I want the Rebels to think this hill is occupied by lots of Union troops. Do you understand me?"

Hall paused, his mouth gaping, staring at Warren.

"Yes, sir!" Fear rippled through Hall's voice. He turned to his signalmen. "Send a message to army headquarters: 'The enemy is getting ready to attack Little Round Top. The hill is unoccupied.' Keep sending it until I tell you to stop." Hall's signalmen began waving their flags.

A booming cannonade erupted from the enemy line, followed by a shrilling screech—the Rebel Yell. The Rebel frontal assault rushed forward.

Warren shouted, his voice brimming with panic, "Wave the damn flags faster!" The signalmen complied, grunting loudly, fear and sweat pouring from their faces. There was nothing else to do but wait for reinforcements as the enemy fire intensified, spreading like a brushfire over the summit.

He scrambled atop the highest rock on the plateau. Gripping his field glasses, he watched, horrified, as the enemy infantry started a delayed echelon attack against the Union's far left flank. The clatter of rifle fire and booming of artillery cannons grew into a pulsating roar. This was a murderous disaster. The blue-clad soldiers bent like reeds in the wind. Wave after wave of butternut soldiers charged toward Sickles's men, forcing the Union soldiers to retreat slowly back toward Plum Run Valley and Little Round Top.

A knot tightened inside him. The air filled with the thick smoke of battle, hanging in yellow-brown sheets between the sinuous lines of the two opposing armies. Mounted blue officers, swords glinting, picked their way among Sickles's retreating soldiers, urging them forward into the killing field. Warren swept the horizon, ignoring the splattering of musket fire against the hill's rocky crest. Thank God no Rebel soldiers were climbing the hill. But time was running out; the cracking rifles inched closer. Where was the reinforcement division that Captain Reese had requested from Meade? Where were Third Corps troops that Lieutenant Mackenzie had requested from Sickles? Interior lines were great, if you could move reinforcements fast enough. He stood alone on the knob of the summit. No one had come. He felt like someone had poleaxed him.

This was it. Without reinforcements, all was lost; the enemy would be taking the hill momentarily. His mind's eye saw them strolling up unopposed, digging in behind the boulders on the crest, dragging their artillery to the top. The enemy cannons would have a clear field of fire, pounding the Union troops lined up along the ridge up to Cemetery Hill. The Union boys would be ravaged from the flank fire.

The belching pitch of battle in front of Little Round Top rumbled louder, as each side began reaping the terrible harvest of death. Gray soldiers swarmed forward like angry red ants. Warren walked to the southern portion of the small plateau, looked toward Big Round Top, half expecting Rebel soldiers to be clamoring toward him. None so far. But it was only a matter of time.

*4:12 p.m.*

Warren and Roebling rode down the northeast slope toward the dirt road at the foot of the hill. At the bottom of the hill, they crossed to the northern slope. Warren had a brief glimpse all the way out across the wheat field. He pointed, the thunder of the battle deafening. They galloped that way toward a column of soldiers marching toward the peach orchard. As they neared the column, a bolt of energy like lightning hit his gut.

Was it his old brigade? As he drew closer, Warren spotted Colonel O'Rorke, sporting his familiar mutton-chop beard, riding at the head of his regiment, the 140th New York. *Thank you, God. Incredible.* He had found the brigade he had commanded before becoming chief engineer of the army. Now it was commanded by General Weed. It appeared O'Rorke's regiment was bringing up the rear of the brigade. And thankfully, the twenty-six-year-old O'Rorke was one of the best students he had taught at West Point.

While still some distance away, Warren started shouting, "Colonel O'Rorke! The Rebels are getting ready to breach the hill. I need your regiment on the crest to meet them. Colonel O'Rorke!"

The men of the regiment turned and a great cheer erupted for their former brigade commander, soldiers removing their hats, waving them above their heads. A rush of pride flushed his cheeks.

The cheering welcome continued as he shouted at O'Rorke like a wild banshee.

*4:25 p.m.*

O'Rorke turned in his saddle and eyed Warren, then turned and trotted toward him. The colonel was wearing a billowing blue military cape, soft felt hat, long white leather gloves. When he opened his mouth, his white teeth gleamed against his freckled face and raven hair.

Raising his voice to be heard, Warren said, "Paddy, where is General Weed?"

"General Weed has ridden ahead to locate Sickles and find out where he wants the brigade." O'Rorke said.

"Damn. I don't have time to find Weed. Without reinforcements, and soon, the growing Rebel swarms will overrun the crest of Little Round Top."

O'Rorke glared at Warren.

"Paddy, give me a regiment," Warren said. "Hood's division is hitting the southern crest, and the northern crest is being defended without any infantry support."

O'Rorke hedged a moment. "General Weed expects me to follow him."

Warren shouted, pointing to the hill, "Never mind that, bring your regiment up here, and I will take the responsibility. I'm giving you a direct order."

"Yes, sir," O'Rorke said.

O'Rorke turned astride on his horse, ordering the 140th New York to fall out from the road and march toward Little Round Top.

"Lieutenant Roebling will lead you up to the crest," Warren said. "I'll be right behind you." Roebling moved off with O'Rorke and his regiment following.

Warren had no way of knowing if O'Rorke's single regiment could hold off Hood's assault wave surging toward the crest of Little Round Top. But O'Rorke was one of the best regimental commanders in the Union army, destined to be a general. If there was only one regiment to send to the summit, his was the best choice.

---

*4:35 p.m.*

Warren spurred his horse forward, galloping until he located Sykes. Warren saluted and presented his case forcefully. "General Sykes. The northern slope of the hill is undefended, with Hood's division preparing to launch a full-on attack against it. I've ordered O'Rorke's regiment to the crest, but I need Weed's entire brigade to occupy the hill before the Texans arrive."

"Where is General Weed?" Sykes shouted. "His brigade should already be on the hill."

"Sir, I could not locate him," Warren replied. "I believe he is forward looking for Sickles."

Sykes swore, turned to a courier, and told him to find Weed and have his brigade march to the hilltop immediately. Sykes rode toward the wheat field.

Warren raced past O'Rorke's regiment heading toward Little Round Top and rode to the top of the hill.

---

## Meade

*4:28 p.m.*
*About ten minutes earlier*
*The Leister House*

Meade stood over the map table, studying the placement of Union defenses. What forces could he move to reinforce Sickles? When would the enemy attack Culp's Hill?

Captain Reese hurried into the small living room and said, "General Meade, I have an urgent message from General Warren."

"What is it?" Meade asked.

"There are no infantry troops on Little Round Top," Reese said.

Meade's mouth fell open. "Sickles did not place *any* of his soldiers on Little Round Top?"

"That's correct, sir. Sickles did not occupy the hill."

Meade slammed his fist on the map table. The wood crackled like a falling tree. "Son of a bitch! Has General Sykes's corps arrived on the battlefield?" Meade said.

"No, sir," Reese said.

Meade shook his head. *Forget an orderly reinforcement. Strip forces from lines not being attacked and throw them into Lee's meat grinder and hope for the best. Must hold Little Round Top at all cost.*

He turned to Major Benjamin Ludlow, one of his personal staff members. "Ride to General Humphreys and order him to occupy Little Round Top. Tell General Humphreys's division these orders come directly from General Meade and cannot be countermanded by General Sickles."

"Yes, sir!"

Meade turned to Captain Reese. "Tell General Warren I ordered General Humphreys to occupy Little Round Top."

Ludlow and Reese and departed the Leister House together.

## Ludlow
*4:45 p.m.*

Ludlow mounted his horse, paused, and watched Reese gallop down Taneytown Road. *Can't afford to take that longer route to Humphreys. Time is critical. Must take the shorter and riskier Emmitsburg route in full view of Rebel sharpshooters peppering Hancock's Second Corps.*

*Crap.*

He rode west from the Leister House, passing through Webb's brigade sitting unengaged on Cemetery Ridge, and turned south on Emmitsburg Road.

Ludlow raced along Hancock's corps, bullets whizzing past his head. *Lay low and ride fast.* He spurred his horse. After a few hundred yards, he spotted Humphreys's division, marching with colors flying in a line of battle toward the Emmitsburg Road. He turned off the road, galloped to Humphreys, and halted. "General Warren has informed General Meade that Little Round Top is unoccupied. General Meade requests you redirect your division and march it toward Little Round Top and defend the threatened position."

Humphreys swore loudly. "Please send my regards to General Meade and tell him I will execute his order immediately. But tell him the loss of my division along the Emmitsburg Road will create a large gap between General Graham's First Brigade, which is occupying the peach orchard, and the left flank of Second Corps on Cemetery Ridge."

"I acknowledge your message and will relay it to General Meade."

Ludlow watched as Humphreys turned his two brigades and reverse-marched them toward Little Round Top without missing a beat. Ludlow turned his horse and rode over Cemetery Ridge back toward the Leister House.

## Warren

*4:45 p.m.*
*Little Round Top*

Standing on top of the crest, Warren eyed Humphreys maneuvering his division toward Little Round Top while artillery shells whizzed by them, spattering the ground. Not a soldier so much as flinched. An amazing feat. Reese must have convinced Meade to order Humphreys's division to occupy Little Round Top. Warren walked over to the signalmen and scanned Cemetery Ridge with his field glasses. One of Hancock's brigades was force-marching down Cemetery Ridge, bayonets glinting in the glaring sun. More reinforcements were scurrying toward Sickles's Third Corps. *Good. If Meade can move enough reserves to Sickles's broken front, we might just survive this viper's pit.*

"Captain Hall," Warren said. "Have your signalmen ask army headquarters if the Rebels have attacked Culp's Hill."

Hall relayed the order to his signalmen, who began snapping their flags in short, sharp movements.

Warren gazed on Humphreys's division marching toward Little Round Top. He spotted an officer riding toward Emmitsburg Road with a soldier trailing, flying the division flag.

*Humphreys must be riding toward the Leister House. He probably wants to tell Meade about the monstrous gap in the Union line created by his division's departure from its assigned Emmitsburg Road position. But Little Round Top needs them more.*

---

## Mackenzie

*4:15 p.m.*
*Thirty minutes earlier*

Warren's second courier, Lieutenant Mackenzie, found Sickles and gave him the note.

Sickles read it, then waved his hands and shouted, "I can't spare any soldiers for Little Round Top. My whole command is necessary to defend this front. I'm the one who needs reinforcements, at least two divisions. Tell that to Warren."

---

*4:20 p.m.*

Mackenzie departed and galloped from the Trostle House through the wheat field toward Little Round Top. Devil's Den had erupted into a churning roar. Keening shells plunked in the middle of the field, erupting violently. The fighting descended on the wheat field like an avalanche. In the rear of the wheat field Mackenzie spotted Fifth Corps, its flag snapping defiantly, and General Sykes leading them into the knee-high wheat, heading for a thicket of iron, flames, and streaming smoke trails streaking through the sky.

Mackenzie rode to Sykes, saluted. "General Warren is on top of Little Round Top. It is unoccupied. I rode to Sickles and requested he man the hill, but he said he could not spare any troops. General Warren fears if the hill is not occupied in the next few moments the enemy will capture it and all will be lost on this battlefield."

Sykes swiveled in the saddle, squinting at Little Round Top. "I will send one of General Barnes's brigades to General Warren."

He turned to his aide, Captain Jay, and dispatched him to order Barnes, his First Division commander, to bring one of his brigades to Little Round Top.

Mackenzie wiped sweat from his brow. "General, thank you. I will ride to Little Round Top and report to General Warren that you are sending a brigade."

Mackenzie turned to one of Warren's aides accompanying him.

"Ride to army headquarters and tell General Meade that General Sykes is sending a brigade to occupy Little Round Top."

Warren's aide departed for the Leister House. Mackenzie galloped toward Little Round Top.

---

## Ludlow

*4:55 p.m.*

Several minutes later, Major Ludlow galloped down the Emmitsburg Road, spotting Humphreys's division flag moving toward him. Humphreys halted as Ludlow approached.

"General Meade orders you to return to your assigned position along the Emmitsburg Road," Ludlow said. "General Meade has learned that General Sykes's Fifth Corps is arriving on the battlefield, and General Meade has ordered him to occupy Little Round Top."

"Son of a bitch," Humphreys shouted. "My division had almost arrived on the Emmitsburg Road when you ordered me to countermarch toward Little Round Top. As soon as I had turned my two brigades around and starting marching, you rescind the damn order, telling me to march back to my position along Emmitsburg Road."

"Yes, sir," Ludlow said.

"Tell that flaming asshole Butterfield he should get his act together as chief of staff," Humphreys shouted.

---

*5:05 p.m.*

Humphreys turned and rode back to his division. Ludlow waited until Humphreys's division reversed itself with great precision. He then turned and rode toward headquarters.

---

## Warren

*5:00 p.m.*
*Five minutes earlier*
*The northern end of the crest of Little Round Top*

Warren stood near the signal station at the northern end of the crest. The Rebels had flowed through Devil's Den, splashing over the Union defenders like a fast-moving spring flood. *They'll be here shortly.* He looked back toward Big Round Top. Nothing. It was still quiet there and along the southern crest of Little Round Top. No enemy and no Federal reinforcements on the southern crest. He gritted his teeth. A sinister chill came over him like a shroud. *Damn.*

Captain Hall approached. "General Warren, two officers are riding up the hill."

Warren walked over to the northern crest and saw two officers riding over the crest. The officers halted, slid from their saddles, and saluted.

"General Warren, I'm Captain Augustus Martin, commander of General Sykes's Fifth Corps artillery brigade. This is Lieutenant Charles Hazlett, commander of Battery D. I've ordered Lieutenant Hazlett to place his battery on the top of this summit."

Warren exhaled, letting out a breath he didn't know he was holding.

"General Sykes ordered us to place the batteries to support Fifth Corps," Martin continued. "With General Sykes occupying the wheat field area, I believe placing artillery batteries on Little Round Top would provide excellent coverage for Fifth Corps."

"This is not your normal artillery placement," Warren said. "The summit is narrow, rocky, and uneven ground, making it nearly inaccessible to artillery pieces. If you could get them here, I'm not sure what they could do. You would not be able to depress the gun muzzles enough to thwart a frontal attack."

"Never mind that," Hazlett said. "The sound of the guns will be encouraging to our troops and disheartening to the enemy."

Warren humphed. A few heartbeats passed.

"My batteries are of no use in the valley if this hill is lost," Hazlett said.

"You're right about that," Warren said. These two junior officers understood the value of this hill. *Whether they can get their guns up here is a different story.*

A whip cracked down the hill. Warren cocked his head. Another whip cracked. What the hell? Warren raced to the northeastern slope. Hazlett's gun teams were slowly scaling the northern slope of Little Round Top. Horses and wagons lurched up the hill. Men standing uphill strained on ropes attached to the ten-pounder Parrott guns. *My God.* A lump rose in his throat.

What an extraordinary effort. One by one the tube and carriage of each gun, weighing 1,800 pounds, crested the summit.

Toward the bottom of the slope, Warren spotted a gun crew making little progress. *Crap*. He scrambled over the crest and slid down the hill toward the gun limber and jumped in alongside the struggling crew. Gripping the spokes of a wheel, he grunted and pushed with all his might, forcing the gun and limber slowly uphill. Sweat dripped off his brow into his eyes. Captain Hall jumped alongside Warren.

"Push, boys, push," Warren shouted.

Captain Hall shouted, "Well, I'll be damned. Never knew a general officer to pitch in like that. Come on boys, show the general what we got."

Warren was breathing hard. He had impressed Captain Hall, not that he cared much. The physical effort felt good; it freed chunks of anxiety like a dam bursting. Judging the distance to the crest, they were a stone's throw away.

"Push!" Warren shouted, his words falling sharp and harsh. A whip snapped. The horses strained against the leather harness; the gun crews grunted like galley slaves. Men rushed downhill, swarming around Warren and the gun limber. In an instant, they propelled the limber over the lip of the crest. Warren let go of the wheel and put his hands on his knees, gasping for air, his heart pounding in his ears. He sure as hell hoped the artillery pieces would make a difference.

"General Warren," Hazlett said, "only the guns will fit on the narrow hilltop. Ammunition will have to be run up the hill from the caissons parked down the slope."

"Very well," Warren replied, panting slightly as his breath came under control.

## Warren

*5:15 p.m.*
*Little Round Top*

Warren gripped his field glasses tightly as he scanned the battlefield. Standing next to him, Captain Hall was staring at the Leister House through his binoculars. "General Warren, I just received a signal from army headquarters. The enemy has not attacked Culp's Hill yet."

"Good," Warren said. He walked back to the high spot on the crest and peered through his field glasses again. *Oh, my God.* Humphreys's two brigades had abruptly reversed their march toward Little Round Top. "No! Turn around!"

His heart almost stopped. Why did Humphreys turn around? No other support was arriving to occupy Little Round Top. *My*

*God, this is going to be a horrific defeat and I'm powerless to stop the impending rout.*

Warren stood on the elevated knob, his field glasses fixed on the battlefield below. Battle smoke billowed upward as gray figures shrilled the high-pitched Rebel Yell, sounding like thousands of howling wolves.

Mackenzie arrived. "General Warren."

Warren lowered his field glasses. A lump formed in his throat.

Mackenzie continued, "I told General Sickles it was critical he occupy Little Round Top with one of his divisions, as it was the most important terrain to defend on the battlefield. But General Sickles refused to give up any of his soldiers. He asserted that his whole command is necessary to defend his front."

Warren swallowed hard. "While Sickles is defending undefendable ground, the enemy will find his way up here and the battle will be over."

Mackenzie added, "I found General Sykes, and he said he would send a brigade from Fifth Corps."

"Only a brigade?" Warren said. "We need more than a brigade!"

Warren walked over to the northern edge of the crest. No Union troops hurrying up the hill. *Damn. Where is Sykes's promised help?* He turned and gazed across the battlefield. Wailing screams sounding like screeching bobcats pierced the lingering white smoke. The Confederates were in full fury, bending around Sickles's exposed left flank, making steady gains against the retreating blue soldiers. Sickles's soldiers were fighting fiercely, giving ground reluctantly, the dead and wounded falling like sheared cornstalks.

Warren's jittery nerves stood on edge. The Rebels rushed forward like a great wall of gray water. Bullets started pitter-pattering on the summit like the beginning of a long, hard rain. White smoke was blowing up his way, masking the enemy's movements. He stood on the flat rock, presenting a perfect target but stubbornly refusing to move, refusing to be accused of not trying to muster the forces to defend it. Where were the blue soldiers coming his way? No reinforcements. Nothing.

## *Vincent*

*4:38 p.m.*
*Thirty-seven minutes earlier*

Colonel Strong Vincent sat on his horse at the head of his brigade in the rear of the wheat field near the George Weikert House. *Where are my orders?* One of Meade's favorite Fifth Corps officers and the youngest in the Army of the Potomac, the twenty-six-year-old Harvard lawyer commanded Third Brigade of Barnes's First Division in Sykes's Fifth Corp. Vincent fretted as a continuous stream of stragglers and wounded men rippled past him toward the rear. *Damn it.* He led attacks, he didn't observe them. Thick woods screened his brigade from the heavy fighting going on in Devil's Den, but the battle was thundering beyond the trees, rushing toward him like a wind-driven wildfire.

A shell exploded in front of him, showering dirt over Private Norton, the brigade's flag bearer. Crackling rifle fire broke out from the woods ahead of him. It was not aimed fire, but it would be in a few moments. Vincent grimaced and his pulse thudded in his ears; he was anxious to join in the fight. But without orders, his brigade sat out in the open, exposed. He stared through his field glasses, waiting for the enemy to emerge from the woods.

Vincent spied Sykes's courier, Captain Jay, galloping toward his brigade. Refusing to linger about any longer without orders, he spurred his horse forward toward the messenger. Sickles's soldiers were falling back, being pushed by a larger enemy force. His brigade could help shore up Sickles's defenses. The courier and Vincent reined in near each other. The messenger saluted, his face strained.

"Captain Jay, what are my orders?" Vincent said.

"Where is General Barnes?" Captain Jay said. "I have orders for him from General Sykes."

Vincent said, his voice cold and sharp, "I'm a colonel and I'm demanding to know your orders, *Captain!*"

Captain Jay paused, startled. "General Sykes told me to direct General Barnes to send one of his brigades to occupy that hill." He gestured toward Little Round Top.

Vincent's mind stirred with alarm. Barnes was in the rear of the division, near the Taneytown Road. By the time Jay located Barnes and Barnes ordered him to occupy Little Round Top, it would be too late. *Act now or all is lost.*

"I will assume the responsibility of taking my brigade there," Vincent said.

Jay's face paled. Vincent read his mind, knowing Jay's orders were explicit. He was to tell Barnes to place a brigade on the hill. He was a colonel. Barnes was a general and his superior. He could be court-martialed for interfering with the chain of command, intercepting orders, executing them without Barnes's knowledge or approval.

"Captain, I will execute Sykes's orders and place my brigade on that hill!" Vincent said. Jay paused as a tremor of misgiving covered his face. Then his eyes brightened.

"Yes, sir! I will ride to Barnes, telling him you're executing Sykes's order to him." Jay saluted smartly and rode off toward the Taneytown Road.

Vincent galloped back to the brigade. He rode to Colonel James Rice, commanding the Forty-fourth New York regiment. The thirty-five-year-old, full-bearded Yale graduate bore an uncanny resemblance to General John Reynolds. He saluted Colonel Vincent.

"Colonel Rice, your regiment will lead the brigade to Little Round Top. Get there as quickly as possible."

Rice nodded, ordering the New Yorkers to double-quick toward the base of Little Round Top.

Vincent galloped off toward Little Round Top. Private Norton trailed closely behind, holding the white brigade flag with its red border and blue Maltese cross. A roaring din thundered toward Little Round Top. Vincent spurred his horse, a lovely thrill surging through his chest. He risked court-martial by taking his brigade from the division without Barnes's permission. But something had to be done right away. *Stop worrying.* Barnes would approve of his actions, knowing he had to send one of his brigades, and Vincent's was the closest. If there was to be any reckoning, the risk was worth the punishment.

*4:45 p.m.*
*The southeast slope of Little Round Top*

As he neared the northeast slope of Little Round Top, Vincent grabbed his field glasses, examining the path upward. Too rocky for horses. He looked toward the hill's eastern slope, a gentler rise for horses to ascend. As he rode upward, following this path, Vincent arrived at a large rise, a spur twenty feet from the top of the southern crest of the main hill, extending southwest for a hundred yards. The spur acted like a lower rampart supporting the higher crest rampart. Vincent and Norton dismounted, holding the reins of their horses, working their way around the southern end of the lower rampart. A musket ball whistled by Vincent's left cheek, striking the rocks, fragments splattering about like a hard rain. He leaped forward instinctively, crouching, then kneeling on one leg, his heart beating rapidly in his ears.

A second ball zipped by, nearly hitting the flag.

"Down with that flag, Norton!" Vincent shouted. "Go behind the rocks with it."

Norton scampered to hide behind a large boulder, dragging his horse with him. A moment later, Vincent came tumbling after him with his horse in tow.

"That was a close call from expert sniper fire," Vincent said. "I didn't expect the Rebels to be hovering that close." He gave his reins to Norton. "Stay put while I scout Little Round Top."

Vincent crouched down and slithered clockwise along the base of the rock ledge, sitting snugly fifteen feet below the southern crest of the summit. He stopped when he arrived at the western slope of the hill facing Devil's Den. Below the Rebels were shellacking Sickles's soldiers, shoving the outnumbered bluecoats steadily toward Little Round Top. If Sickles's retreating troops continued to fall back on the western portion of the hill, they could ascend the hill and use its natural defensive terrain to protect themselves.

Vincent did not have enough men to cover both the western slope and the southern portions of the hill. He would leave the western part unoccupied since the southern section seemed more vulnerable to attack.

He duck-walked back to Norton and retrieved his field glasses, examining the saddle connecting Little Round Top with the long slope of Big Round Top, covered with dense woods. No way of knowing whether Sickles had any soldiers on Big Round Top, but he doubted it. Vincent's heart started pounding in his ears and his stomach rolled. The forbidding woods could easily conceal a large enemy force coming over Big Round Top and through the saddle. This was a dangerous area, making his brigade vulnerable to a surprise attack.

Vincent scurried to the left flank, stopping near the tip of the rocky spur. He crawled out onto a large flat boulder. He nodded. This marked the end of the line, the far left flank of the Union army. Returning quickly to where Norton was huddled, he watched his brigade scurrying up Little Round Top, stretched out over nearly a quarter of a mile, with Rice's Forty-fourth New York leading the way, followed by Woodward's Eighty-third Pennsylvania, Chamberlain's Twentieth Maine, and Welch's Sixteenth Michigan. As the brigade climbed the reverse slope of Little Round Top, shells began exploding over the trees, raking the treetops, showering the men with wood and shrapnel, killing and wounding several of them.

Vincent gripped his binoculars, scanning the rear of his brigade. A shell crashed near the Twentieth Maine, led by Colonel Chamberlain, an energetic officer and scholar. The earth quivered and dirt boiled up into the sky. A second shell whizzed toward Vincent, its demonic whistle making his scalp prickle.

A monstrous blast erupted. Flaring white light and burning heat hit him like a horse kick covering his entire body. He faltered to one knee, gasping for air. Using his gloved hand, he brushed off the blown dirt. *My God, that was close.* The shell had blown a horse from under its rider, the screeching rider landing on the top of the mangled animal. The rider crawled away, screaming like a banshee, blood dripping from his busted eardrums. A burly sergeant grabbed the screaming rider, pulling him from the logging trail.

Four other soldiers grabbed the wounded horse and dragged it squealing off to the side. Vincent gritted his teeth as Chamberlain and the Twentieth Maine walked by the carnage. As soon as the men passed the injured man and horse, they double-quicked the hill again, seemingly eager to escape the bloody scene.

Vincent greeted each regimental commander arriving on the lower crest. He walked them along the ground where he wanted them to form a line of battle. When Chamberlain arrived on the lower crest, he saluted Vincent.

"Colonel Vincent. Where would you like to post the Twentieth Maine?"

Vincent squinted. "Follow me. You're going to occupy the left flank of the brigade. In fact, you're going to anchor the left flank of the entire army."

Chamberlain stood up a little straighter. "Thank you, sir, for the honor!"

Vincent walked Chamberlain along the spur through the dark woods, stopping at a large flat boulder.

"Colonel Chamberlain, I place you here. This is the far left flank of the Union line." Vincent paused, eyeing Chamberlain staring at the terrain on either side of the flat boulder. "Do you understand you are to hold this ground at all costs?"

"Yes, sir!" Chamberlain said.

"Deploy your men and report when they are in position," Vincent said.

He stared at Chamberlain. Had he made the right choice placing the Twentieth Maine on the far left flank? Was ordering a professor of rhetoric to anchor and defend the entire left flank of the army as idiotic as Sickles moving his corps a half mile in front of the Union army? Colonel Welch's Sixteenth Michigan was his best fighting regiment. Welch would hold his position to the last man. But defending the area above Sickles's retreating soldiers on the extreme right of the brigade was the critical vulnerability. At the moment, the enemy on the far right continued to swarm *en masse* toward the hill. That's where he needed the Wolverines.

501

God, he hoped he had made the right decision.

*4:55 p.m.*

Vincent moved back to the center of the brigade and scanned the defensive line. Good. The brigade was in its defensive position before the enemy attacked. The bending battle line was shaped in a quarter-circle formation, with the right wrapping partially around the southwestern front of Little Round Top and the left fixed along the southeastern spur among thick trees. A sense of assurance took hold of him. The rocky shelf was a fortress, each boulder a rampart. The men were ready. They occupied the high ground. One thousand men waiting for the enemy to attack. Too bad another brigade wasn't occupying the Western slope.

Vincent eyed the woods in his front. What was lurking out there? Time to find out. He turned to Norton. "Have each of the regimental commanders deploy a company of skirmishers to the front."

Norton moved off. Within a few minutes, Vincent's eyes riveted on the skirmishers moving forward, disappearing in the dark woods. He waited, his chest tightened. The skirmishers returned. No shots fired. No enemy. This didn't make sense. He wandered the line, passed behind the Eighty-third. They had no word on the enemy, so he continued to walk down to the Forty-fourth New York, where he met with Rice.

"James, have you spotted the enemy?" Vincent said.

"No," Rice said.

"Let's walk over to the Sixteenth Michigan and see what's going on," Vincent said.

When they reached the Wolverines, they had a spectacular view of Devil's Den and the Plum Run Valley below. Looking down the hill, Vincent gasped, his breath catching in his chest. It looked as if a meteor had struck Devil's Den, creating a smoking crater. Masses of gray men were moving and firing as they charged through the smoking crater, pressing past the base of the two Round Tops. The enemy lines were rolling toward him in waves of plunging breakers.

"Get back to your regiment," Vincent said. "The Rebels will be here in a few minutes."

Rice nodded. They both quickly retraced their steps.

## O'Rorke

*5:16 p.m.*

O'Rorke reached the northeastern base of Little Round Top and halted. Lieutenant Roebling continued riding up the side, disappearing into a cloud of smoke. O'Rorke cocked his head. His regiment was moving toward him at double-quick in a column of fours, the regiment's five hundred men dressed in new Zouave uniforms of baggy blue trousers, red jackets, and fezzes. What a sight! He turned to Lieutenant Farley, riding next to him. "Order the men to scurry up the hillside."

Farley saluted, moved back to the soldiers in the lead column. O'Rorke spurred his horse up the hill, following Roebling. At the crest, his pulse quickened as he stepped into the feverish battle. He gagged, covering his nose with his gloved hand. Ugh! The rotten stench of decaying corpses. Sharp screams and rumbling moans echoed from the writhing wounded.

Hazlett's battery erupted with a blast of fire. O'Rorke's startled heart leaped into this throat. His ears buzzed with a high-pitched ringing. He turned and saw the enemy outflanking Vincent's brigade, running around to the right of the Wolverines. The lead Rebels rushed over the ledge of the summit, climbing up to the crest, focusing on Hazlett's battery.

"Damn," O'Rorke muttered.

He withdrew his pistol and scanned the summit ground. Too rough for horses. He dismounted, throwing his reins to the regiment's sergeant major. Turning around, he saw the first companies of his regiment cresting the hill, the men flying up the hillside, sprinting as fast as they could.

Across the summit, the Rebels had stopped momentarily, biting the paper cartridge, ramming home a ball, preparing to charge in one continuous wave. *Can't wait for the entire regiment. Will have to charge with what we have.* He raised his sword.

"Down this way, boys," he yelled. He sprinted forward, brandishing his sword. The lead companies of the regiment were running after him, bayonets fixed. O'Rorke sprinted toward the gap on the right side of the Wolverines. He ran down the slope toward the Rebels, pistol cocked, screaming. He turned his head. Good. The soldiers had followed, racing pell-mell down the western face of the hill. O'Rorke turned, glaring at the Rebels thirty feet below the summit. The blue soldiers slammed into the Confederate line like waves breaking over a jetty. Several of the Rebels returned a sheet of yellow fire; some threw down their muskets, raising their hands, surrendering; others turned, running back down the hill.

The New Yorkers had crashed headlong into the Rebels reloading their rifles. O'Rorke spotted a blurred figure in the smoke ahead. He paused, aimed his pistol, and fired. The gray devil screamed and fell to the ground. He then raced to the lower rock shelf recently vacated by the retreating Sixteenth Michigan. He began waving his arms and cheering his men to rush forward. The New Yorkers continued cascading down the hill, using their bayonets freely.

O'Rorke started to turn back down the slope. *Crack!* Blackness.

Dead before he hit the ground. A Minié ball had struck his neck, piercing his spine at the base of the brain.

---

## Warren

*5:18 p.m.*

Lieutenant Roebling arrived and shouted into Warren's ear. "A large enemy force is attacking below the southern crest of the hill."

"Who are they attacking?" Warren shouted.

Roebling said, pointing, "Vincent's brigade. General Sykes ordered him to defend the hill. We did not see him arrive because he came through the southern slope and deployed his brigade along the spur below the southern crest. He has repelled one assault, but the Rebels are getting ready to attack again."

Warren nodded. A thrill of delight mixed with alarm coursed through him. The southern slope was being defended, but Vincent's force was too small to repulse a large-scale attack.

"How big is the attacking force?" Warren asked.

"It's at least a couple of brigades from Hood's division."

"Texans and Alabamans from Longstreet's corps?"

"Yes."

Warren was grim-faced. Longstreet's men, especially Hood's boys, were Lee's best soldiers, on par with Reynolds's famous Iron Brigade. He needed more soldiers defending the hill.

---

## Vincent

*5:45 p.m.*

*The southern end of the crest of Little Round Top*

Vincent stood in the middle of the brigade's curved line, breathing hard. The hillside was blanketed in sheets of blue smoke hovering a few feet above the ground. There was a lull in the fighting. His brigade had pounded back two vicious enemy assaults over the past half hour, but the screaming Rebels would be back. He had sent a messenger to General Barnes requesting immediate reinforcements, but none had yet appeared. Vincent walked the line, encouraging his men. They stood shoulder to shoulder, eyes wide, muskets pointing forward, ready for the next onslaught. Their faces were blackened from biting cartridges, their bodies itchy from sweaty skin against coarse wool uniforms. He spotted Norton scooting toward him, his face smudged with black.

"How is Colonel Chamberlain holding the left flank?" Vincent asked.

"Very well. The Maine boys are tough," Norton said.

Vincent nodded. Maybe he had made the right choice placing the professor on the far left. "Take care of the wounded," Vincent said.

Terrible screeching pierced the air.

"Damn, the berserker devils are coming again," Vincent muttered.

Streaks of yellow flames crossed toward the blue line. Musketry rattled the blue line like pelting hail as the Wolverines

505

fired to their front. Without warning, the color bearer holding the Michigan's regimental colors skedaddled backward. The Wolverines on either side of the flag hightailed up the hill. The Rebels rushed to fill the gap in the line, firing point-blank at the blue boys.

Vincent's gut clenched. He rushed to the Wolverines. *Must shore up the broken line.* He started hitting the skedaddling soldiers with his riding crop, screaming at them to stand their ground. He ran to a rock and planted himself on top, brandishing his sword.

"Wolverines, charge," Vincent shouted. "Wolverines, charge!"

The retreating men stopped, turned about, and charged down the hill. The surprised Rebels halted, aimed, and fired as the two raging forces collided like dueling rams.

An ice pick pierced Vincent's left groin and pain seared down his leg. *Damn!* He crashed to the ground, clutching his inner left thigh. He lay motionless, momentarily unable to breathe. Warm blood pulsed over his hand. He glanced down to his leg. A bullet had ripped through his groin, lodging in his left thigh. Norton rushed to him.

Vincent whispered, "This is the fourth or fifth time they have shot at me. Now they have hit me at last." His blood-lust had drained, replaced by an icy coldness. He shivered.

A circle gathered. Norton placed his hand on the terrifying wound. "Carry him to the rear!" he screamed. Three men grabbed Vincent and carried him backward up the hill. The Michigan line continued to crumble, unable to halt the continuous enemy assault. The Rebels were mauling Vincent's brigade.

The three soldiers carried Vincent to the crest. Hazlett said, "Carry him to the Weikert Farm."

Vincent said, "No," but his voice would not work. He glanced at the gaping bullet wound oozing thick, dark blood. *God, what a mess.*

A distant voice said, "The wound is mortal." The words splintered inside Vincent's chest, stabbing his heart. He did not fear death, for he had done his duty, but he feared regret—dying far away from his precious wife, buried far away from the family plot, and always an absent, faraway father to his unborn child. His chest tightened and his breathing grew ragged and shallow. He fished into his pocket and gripped an ambrotype. He opened the cover and stared at his wife as the darkness slowly overcame him.

## Weed

*5:45 p.m.*

After receiving Sykes's order to occupy Little Round Top, Weed pushed his men forward at a running pace. His brigade arrived at the hill and scrambled to the top, witnessing helter-skelter. Weed dropped to his knee and gazed beneath the smoke. No blue soldiers were occupying the crest to the right of the Wolverines.

Weed stood and shouted, "Follow me! To the right of O'Rorke's regiment."

Weed's first regiment dashed forward, firing a blast of yellow flame, surprising the graybacks. With the arrival of the second regiment, Weed ordered its commander to continue to extend the defensive line to the right. After the second regiment was in line, Weed was satisfied with the defensive line protecting the western crest of the summit.

## Warren

*5:57 p.m.*

A deep pride swelled through Warren as he watched Hazlett, unflinching as the bullets showered past him. After the sixth gun was pulled onto the summit, Hazlett pointed his sword toward the valley in front of Devil's Den, telling his gun crews to load, take aim, and fire at will. Within seconds, a torrent of blinding fire belched from the barrels like jets of fountaining orange lava, shelling enemy targets below. The six-cannon blast cracked in Warren's ears like bursting, fiery clots. Smoke billowed upward around the gunners, masking them from Rebel sharpshooters.

Warren rode over to Hazlett. It was like riding through a hornet's nest as bullets from the unseen enemy flew thick and fast. Warren pointed to the southern crest. "Hood's boys are attacking Vincent's brigade. Hood will soon extend his attack to the Union center and northern part of Little Round. Your guns can't depress far enough to stop that attack. I'm going down the hill to get more units here."

A whistling hiss sliced his neck like a barber's straight razor. He froze, heart pounding. His neck throbbed as if branded by a hot poker. He grabbed his neck as a fresh surge of searing pain erupted. He held his breath. *Please, God, spare me from this wound. Damn!*

A warm wetness splashed his shirt collar. His heart sank.

Hazlett's eyes pinched with alarm. "How bad is it?"

"Not sure. Did it slice the jugular?" Warren whispered.

"Let me look," Hazlett said. He pressed two fingers over the wound and stared closely. "Nope, didn't hit the jugular. You'll live. But you're bleeding like a stuck pig."

"That's good. I'll live."

Warren wrapped a handkerchief around his neck, binding it tightly, like a tourniquet. He choked and a lightheaded wooziness filled his brain. Perhaps it was too tight. He loosened the cloth bandage slightly.

Warren waited to ensure he had stopped the bleeding. "I'm riding to get you more infantry here. Hang on."

Warren's neck wound was throbbing like a beating bass drum. He reached to touch it, his fingertips skimming lightly across the handkerchief, not feeling any wetness. *Yes.* Thankfully, the bleeding seemed to have slowed. That was sobering, missing death by an inch.

He guided his horse toward the steep descent down Little Round Top. "My job is almost done," Warren muttered. *Sykes is marshalling his forces to defend Little Round Top. I must update Meade.*

---

*6:17 p.m.*
*Meade's headquarters*

Warren rode to the Leister House, his neck throbbing with pain. In the small living room, Meade was talking to one of his aides. "Order Hancock to send Caldwell's division of the Second Corps to the far left to reinforce Third Corps."

The aide saluted and departed.

Meade eyed Warren. "Gouv, what have you been up to?"

"We've been busy trying to unscrew Sickles's mess," Warren said.

"How bad is the neck wound?" Meade said.

"A close call," Warren replied.

"Go see a surgeon after we finish," Meade said. "What's the status of Little Round Top?"

"We secured Little Round Top but at very high cost. Sykes provided the troops. When this is over, I'm recommending you court-martial Sickles's ass."

Meade looked at Warren. "Perhaps. But for now, let's focus on reinforcing Sickles's broken front. This day is far from over. I'm damn worried about the huge gaps in the line along Cemetery Ridge."

---

## Weed

*6:02 p.m.*
*Fifteen minutes earlier*

He looked toward the western sky. The Rebel yell erupted. Rebels were scrambling across the rocks, jumping from boulder to boulder, aiming and firing.

Weed gasped. A sharp, searing pain, like a hot knife, pierced his left shoulder. The bullet shattered his backbone, severing the spinal cord. Weed reeled, fell to the ground near Hazlett's guns. His legs were frozen. *I'm paralyzed.* He shouted to his aide. "I'm cut in two! Find Hazlett!"

The aide scurried toward Hazlett's belching guns, and a few minutes later Hazlett arrived and threw himself beside his friend.

Weed asked, "How bad is the wound?"

"Lots of bleeding," Hazlett said. "It appears to be mortal."

"Charles, I have some debts with some fellow officers I want to pay," Weed said.

Hazlett nodded, listened to Weed's instructions. Weed then pulled Hazlett closer. He whispered in his ear, "Charlie, please tell my fiancée…"

509

*Crunch.* Hazlett's body crumpled on top of Weed. He moved Hazlett's head to the side as blood poured from a Minié ball wound to the back of Hazlett's head. *My God. Hazlett is dead.*

Weed screamed. "Poor Hazlett! He has gone before I!"

Weed's adjutant reassured him. "You will be alright soon, General."

"By sundown, I will be as dead as Julius Caesar," Weed said. Weed's aides dragged the paralyzed general back to an aid station behind the crest..

Within a few hours, Weed was dead. The bodies of O'Rorke and Hazlett lay next to each other on the summit of Little Round Top, and Vincent's lay at the Weikert Farm, awaiting burial as the red sun dipped below South Mountain.

---

## Rice
*6:15 p.m.*

After Vincent fell, Colonel Rice had assumed command of his brigade. He had watched O'Rorke's red-jacketed 140th New York arrive in time to save Vincent's right flank, had witnessed Weed's brigade arrive, finishing shoring up the northern slope. His focus was now on his far left flank: Colonel Chamberlain and the Twentieth Maine.

Colonel Rice moved to the southern summit of Little Round Top. A tremendous musket fire erupted from the saddle between the two tops. His eyes shot down the southern slope and his skin pebbled as the Twentieth Maine barreled down between the two hills, screaming like banshees, rifles held at the hip, bayonets fixed, chasing a retreating Rebel brigade running at all speed toward Plum Run. It was pure mayhem. Chamberlain had swept the enemy away like a great wall of water rushing from a bursting dam.

Colonel Rice shouted to his adjutant, "Tell Chamberlain to stop the charge. The Rebels are going to run all the way to Richmond."

By the time Chamberlain stopped, he had swept the saddle clean of all Confederates. Rice's adjutant returned, reporting back, "Colonel Rice, you're not going to believe this. Colonel

Chamberlain made his charge after he had run out of ammunition. He didn't know what else to do but fix bayonets and charge."

"Amazing." Rice replied. "I want to write a note tonight to General Sykes and tell him about Chamberlain's bravery and how he saved the left side of the Union line."

Rice walked to the knob on top of Little Round Top. The Rebels had retreated down the hill, rushing for cover back toward Emmitsburg Road. Bodies littered Little Round Top. Hundreds and hundreds of shattered Union and Rebel bodies lay strewn about, bloating with the putrid stench of rotting meat.

He muttered, "The harvest of death is devilish."

## ✦ 34 ✦
# Sickles — Thursday, July 2

*4:33 p.m.*
*Two hours earlier*

Sickles chewed his cigar, sitting astride his white horse in the peach orchard. He cracked a grin as Meade's small bay bolted toward the rear. Meade's cavalcade raced pell-mell, trying to catch up to the commanding general.

Tremain said, "Looks as if Meade is going to ride that horse all the way to the White House."

"Damn, that coward loves to retreat," Sickles said. "Thank God he's gone."

"My guess is he's trying to find another safe location about thirteen miles away, like he did yesterday during the fighting," Tremain said.

Sickles smiled and wiped his wet brow with his white gloves. "I didn't bungle Meade's orders, Henry. By moving forward, I positioned the Army of the Potomac for victory, forcing Meade to fight at Gettysburg. If Meade gives me reinforcements, I'll crush Bobby Lee's army."

"You're really going to throw a twist on Old Bobby Lee today," Tremain said.

Sickles nodded. This was shaping up nicely. By day's end, he would be the beloved hero of Gettysburg. The savior of the Republic. And most likely the army's new commanding general.

The warble of blowing bugles reverberated over Third Corps. The convulsive booming of shells was marked by streaking smoke tendrils crisscrossing in the sky. The enemy artillery fire was blossoming into endless thundering, creating a murky fog, thickening like a visible doom.

"Time to ride back to the Trostle Farm," Sickles said. "The all-out battle will start soon."

Tremain turned and waved to the waiting cavalcade. "Let's move out!"

Sickles spurred his horse, galloping at full speed. Warmth radiated inside, and his skin prickled. No more snide scoldings for marching too slowly or sarcastic rebuffs for not wanting to occupy swampland far away from the action. He was the army's willing hero: a gallant corps commander risking it all to hold the high ground and turn back the enemy.

*4:45 p.m.*
*Trostle Farm*

Arriving at the farm, Sickles dismounted and lit his cigar. He sauntered to the south side, studying the terrain. The Trostle farm was in the middle of the battlefield, between the Emmitsburg Road and Cemetery Ridge. He gripped his binoculars and scanned the ground. Southeast was Devil's Den: massive stone blocks and boulders spilling down toward Little Round Top. Impossible terrain. The enemy would have great difficulty attacking through that interlocking rock formation. Westward was the peach orchard, the dominating ground. The orchard's trees were aligned in neat, open rows, providing an excellent field of fire for his four artillery batteries.

Deep satisfaction settled in his bones. *What a beautiful sight.* Twenty-four Parrott and Napoleon big guns in a line across the tip of this forward salient. With the artillery sitting on elevated ground, the enemy would not be able to penetrate it. Meade didn't grasp the importance of Third Corps holding the high ground. Southeast of the peach orchard was the large open wheat field—a good field of fire for artillery, but no protection.

"I may lack enough infantry to run a solid defensive line from the peach orchard to Devil's Den," Sickles remarked, "but I'll still make the enemy think twice when he sees those big guns in those gaps. This is going to work out just fine."

"We need Meade's reserves to fill in the wheat field," Tremain said.

"Sykes's boys should be arriving soon," Sickles said.

Sickles scanned the area north of the peach orchard where Humphreys had deployed his division along the Emmitsburg Road. Having Humphreys forward along the road created a half-mile gap eastward with Hancock's corps, back on Cemetery Ridge.

Sickles pointed. "I plan on plugging Humphreys's gap with artillery batteries. For God's sake. How could Meade not see the peach orchard is the critical ground to hold?"

"It's just like the Hazel Grove salient at Chancellorsville," Tremain said. "Holding Hazel Grove was the key to winning that battle."

"We're not retreating from the high ground again," Sickles said. "Damn, what a beautiful sight, seeing all these artillery batteries in the peach orchard."

Using his field glasses, Sickles scanned Seminary Ridge. His pulse rate climbed. The cannonading continued. Without question, the enemy would be coming soon. *When they do, they will be shocked to find I am holding the ground they covet.*

Sickles puffed on his cigar, drinking in the triumph of his achievement. "Thanks to me, we hold the high ground. I'm not giving it up, Meade, you ornery bastard."

He could see the newspaper headlines: *Sickles: Savior of Gettysburg.* He breathed in the sun-drenched warmth of a summer's day. He would live on forever in the history books, alongside other great generals. Hannibal. Napoleon. William the Conqueror. Sickles.

---

# Humphreys
*4:48 p.m.*

Humphreys rode to the Trostle Farm, dismounted, and saluted. His sharp tone left little doubt as to his frame of mind. "I spoke to General Caldwell about the gap between my forward line on Emmitsburg Road and his division on the ridge. Caldwell said he has no orders to advance."

"I just talked with General Meade, and I told him I could hold my advanced line," Sickles replied. "He was impressed that I was occupying the elevated ground in the peach orchard. He said he would send up Fifth Corps to support me on my lcft and tell Hancock to support my right. So Caldwell should be moving forward any time now to support your right flank."

Humphreys's brow creased. His eyes were fixed, as if he were perplexed.

"I also requested additional artillery support from Hunt's reserves, and Meade said he would send them immediately," Sickles said.

"Very well," Humphreys said. "The infantry and artillery reserves need to arrive soonest." Humphreys shook his head and departed.

---

## Sickles

Sickles smirked beneath his walrus mustache as Humphreys trotted to his division. Damn, he despised Meade's little butt boy. He had achieved his two goals: He had moved forward to occupy the high ground for his artillery, and he had prevented Meade from withdrawing. What he didn't expect was Meade agreeing to have all forces in the army supporting him. Hope resonated in his chest. This was going to be a grcat day.

Tremain joined him. "General Sicklcs, Third Corps is in position. Birney's division of five thousand men is anchoring your left flank near Devil's Den. He has deployed his division at an angle connecting to his infantry occupying the peach orchard, forming a *V*, with the tip at the peach orchard. On Birney's right flank is Humphreys's division of another five thousand men, whose line is holding the curve of the Emmitsburg Road. We have several artillery batteries located in the Devil's Den, peach orchard, and wheat field."

"Excellent," Sickles said.

"I want to congratulate you for following your instincts to occupy the high ground," Tremain said. "You have without doubt saved the day."

"Thank you, Henry," Sickles said. "Soon Lincoln also will be congratulating us for our deeds here today."

"I'm going to ride over to Devil's Den and see how Birney is doing," Tremain said.

"Good. I'm going to ride forward and take a look in the peach orchard," Sickles said.

⚬⚬⚬

*5:10 p.m.*
*The wheat field*

Sickles turned and headed across the wheat field. Hundreds of bright streaks of light flooded the sky like shooting stars as the cannons' thundering grew into earsplitting blasts. Thickening black clusters of exploding enemy shells were falling over the peach orchard. *Christ Almighty!* Was that enemy artillery? Where were the reinforcements Meade had promised? A small sliver of dread slid down his spine. He scanned Cemetery Ridge for infantry reinforcements and the promised artillery reserves. Nothing. No movement.

He glared across the battlefield. His stomach lurched and a sudden chill came over him. There were blue-uniformed corpses everywhere, flooding the ground, and the cries of the wounded filled the air. His breath rasped and his blood pounded in his ears. *What if the reinforcements don't arrive? What if Meade decided not to send support? Oh, my God.* His stomach recoiled as if he had swallowed lethal hemlock. There would be no rescue. He swallowed—or started to—but his mouth was bone dry. His chest tightened. *Damn you, Meade. You are going to get my entire corps massacred. What should I do?*

The cannonading paused. The enemy line exploded with massive flashes of yellow rifle fire as bullets whizzed overhead. His heart seized as if he were drowning. Artillery shells fired again, splitting the air like cracking whips and exploding with blinding flashes. The ground was rupturing like a massive earthquake. It was beginning. Any moment the wolf-howling Rebel Yell would erupt. *Where are Meade's reinforcements?*

A whistling, solid shot struck the center of a blue infantry line, cutting one boy in half before plowing a murderous path, killing a dozen more men. Through his binoculars he spied a young soldier sobbing over a dying man. Brothers, perhaps? The cannonballs continued to fly, reaping a harvest of death. My God, the deadly destruction the big enemy guns delivered at close range. He scoured the landscape for alternatives.

The Rebel guns fired nonstop, raking the Union line, decimating Sickles's isolated corps. The enemy guns then turned, delivering a deadly enfilade fire into the peach orchard salient. The air was filled with razor-sharp metal shrapnel. A shrieking scream, and Sickles jumped instinctively as shrapnel ripped through an orderly standing a few feet from him.

Sickles's stomach knotted. *Must get the Union batteries into position so they can conduct counter-battery fire.* Peering through the smoke, he spotted a Union battery departing the peach orchard. *Son of a bitch.* He spurred his horse, dashing to intercept the retreating battery. It was Captain Judson Clark's First New Jersey Light Artillery battery, which consisted of six 10-pounder Parrotts. If the artillery batteries departed, all would be lost.

Sickles shouted, "Captain Clark, turn around and place your guns to the left of the orchard! I will ride forward and show you where!"

"Yes, sir!" Clark said, with an ashen face. He turned and shouted to the artillery battery, "Right reverse trot! Follow me!"

*5:15 p.m.*
*The peach orchard*

Sickles dashed forward through the dense smoke toward the edge of the peach orchard. He cocked his head; Clark was trailing close behind. Arriving at the back edge of the orchard, Sickles stopped.

Enemy shells screamed toward Sickles as Clark rode beside him. Sickles leaned over, shouting into his ear, "Captain, your guns have to respond to the Rebel artillery fire! You will hold this position while you have a shot in your limbers or a man to work the guns! Do you understand?"

Clark locked eyes with Sickles and nodded. The battery of guns halted next to Clark. He shouted, "Action right!"

On a dime, the six large artillery guns turned instantly to the Confederate line. Clark dismounted and walked from gun to gun, yelling to the gun crews to use shell and case shot and ensure the fuses were cut properly. Clark moved behind the third gun and screamed, "Fire at will!"

The Union battery unleashed a terrifying broadside of deadly metal fragments toward the Rebel infantry lines. A short moment later, all the Union big guns of Third Corps opened up, nearly fifty weapons tearing, ripping, and shattering the enemy. The cracking booms rolling overhead were deafening. Sickles scanned the peach orchard, his ears ringing like a bell clapper clanging inside his head. Enemy artillery shells rained freely overhead like a summer storm. Union soldiers flew head over heels, horses cut in half, caissons and limbers blown to smithereens, wood splinters floating down from the sky like autumn leaves. The ground rocked beneath his horse as a nearby shell blast slapped his face.

Sickles paled. The acrid smoke was too thick to see whether the Union artillery was turning the tide. A sergeant carrying the corps' flag was visible, but little beyond that.

The thundering roar of a hundred dueling artillery pieces rotated around him. The whooshing of screaming shells, punctuated by the dreadful blasts of exploding caissons, propelled flying wooden splinters as lethal as metal shards. The rattle of musketry increased as hundreds of humming Minié balls flew by, some terrifyingly close to his ears.

The Union artillery gunners were answering the Rebels shell for shell, one after another, like lightning strikes. Grape shot shrieked overhead. Sickles gasped for air, his lungs suddenly paralyzed. Never had fire been this intense before. There was no protection. The shells were raining down everywhere, peppering the ground. *Give an order. Do something.*

"My God, perhaps there is nothing I can do," he muttered.

*Damn it, without reinforcements, Meade was right. We cannot hold the peach orchard. Hunt's cannons can't prevent the Union line from collapsing. I will die here.*

Far off, the warble of bugles echoed. With a thunderous crack, the Rebel Yell erupted, followed by an avalanche of Confederate soldiers bursting from the wall of trees and surging forward in a gray sheet over the blue line. There was a voice in his ear.

*5:25 p.m.*

Tremain shouted, "Enemy infantry are assaulting our far left flank. They are attacking in echelon from left to right across our front. Each brigade is waiting until the brigade on its right advances before launching."

Sickles nodded. "Holy shit."

He raised his field glasses to his eyes. The enemy lines studded with red battle flags were advancing, gaining speed. His heart filled with dread.

Enemy artillery shells exploded like flashing hellfire, spattering the soft ground skyward into a brimstone cloud. The ground was strewn with the dead, the dying, and the wailing wounded. The pell-mell slaughter was horrific. Sickles struggled to remain stoic. Reinforcements would not arrive in time to hold the Third Corps line.

The Rebels were attacking the peach orchard salient on two sides. Time to regroup Third Corps. He spurred his horse to the Trostle Farm, pulling up in the yard next to several of his aides.

He shouted to an aide in a shrill voice, "Ride to Sykes and tell him to order Fifth Corps to come forward."

Then he turned to another aide, shouting, "Ride to Hancock requesting Second Corps reinforcements."

The enemy shells screamed downward as if it was raining pitchforks, blanketing the Trostle farm with razor-sharp iron. The battlefield was the devil's cauldron, drowning the Union soldiers in sulfurous surface pools.

"Only atheists don't believe in hell, but here it is, right here on earth," Sickles muttered.

Smoke poured from the orchard as if from a wildfire. The Rebel Yell screeched again, a victory scream. The Third Corps' flimsy dike holding back the foul demons crumbled.

Several Union artillery batteries rushed toward him, heading for the rear. Close behind was Birney's brigade, fleeing pell-mell toward Cemetery Ridge. Sickles rode toward Birney's men. He drew his sword, pointed it toward the approaching red battle flags. He stopped, making a slashing gesture with his sword to halt a retreating colonel.

Sickles shouted, "Stop! Colonel, for God's sake, you must hold!"

Colonel Henry Madill, commander of the 141st Pennsylvania Regiment, stared at Sickles with a look of disbelief. With tears streaming from his eyes, Colonel Madill said, "Where are my men, General Sickles? Three quarters of my regiment are either dead, wounded, or captured."

Using his sword as a pointer, Sickles shouted, "Form a line here!"

Madill saluted and rode forward, shouting. Surprisingly, the fleeing men stopped, turned, and began forming a makeshift defensive line, which the Rebel line soon emerged from the smoke and decimated. Sickles's ears popped from a shell concussion. *My God, it's hopeless.*

But he would die a heroic death in the saddle rather than retreat.

"I'm no Meade!" Sickles shouted, as he brandished his sword. "I will not flee the battlefield."

Tremain rode up. "General Sickles," he yelled, "I suggest you move to put yourself out of range of heavy fire. The enemy is starting to concentrate on the brow of the hill where you are sitting."

Sickles shouted, "Hell, if there is a spot on this field where bullets are not falling thick, I would like to see it."

"I suggest you pass around the farmhouse to the back side, facing Cemetery Ridge," Tremain said. "There is an elevated ridge near the barn that will offer a better view of the fighting."

*6:00 p.m.*
*Trostle Farm*

Sickles followed Tremain through the low ground below the house toward the rear of the Trostle Farm. They emerged into dazzling daylight, a patch of battlefield empty of artillery and smoke. Sickles stopped on the knoll and fumbled for his binoculars. The elevated ridge offered an excellent view of the peach orchard. The sky was filled with a fury of hissing shells and trailing smoke streamers.

Scanning through his field glasses at the yellow rifle fire, something tugged above his right knee, like the hand of a small child wanting something. A wetness dripped down inside his pants leg. He leaned to his right in the saddle, reached down with his gloved hand, and ran it along his leg inside his boot. He pulled out his hand and stared. His glove dripped with dark red blood. No pain. Good. Maybe that was a sign it was not a serious wound. He tried to spur his horse. His right leg wouldn't move. He tried to remove his right foot from the stirrup. Nothing happened.

Seconds later, hell's black flames erupted below his right knee, as if his leg had been plunged into boiling oil. Someone shrieked, a blood-curdling scream. Then he realized that the voice was his own.

In a broken cry, he shrieked, "Captain Randolph. I have been hit."

Randolph turned to Sickles, staring into his eyes. "How bad is it, General?"

"Bad, I think."

Sickles took a deep breath, placed his right hand under the wounded leg, and slowly lifted it up over the horse's neck. He tumbled to the ground, striking the back of his head, momentarily seeing stars. Crumpled on the ground, he caught the first look at his shattered knee. *Oh, my God, I'm going to bleed out.*

"Your horse appears to be fine," Randolph said. "A Rebel shot must have bounced up and hit you."

"Bring me a strap from my saddle," Sickles gasped.

Randolph retrieved the strap and bent down next to the general. He grabbed Sickles under his arms and dragged him over to the barn, sitting him up with his back against the outer wall. Sickles snaked the saddle strap around the leg above the knee. Randolph grabbed the bitter end, pulled it tightly, and buckled it into place, creating a makeshift tourniquet to stem the bleeding.

Sickles screamed as darkness flooded his mind. His breathing sputtered like rattling hog snorts. A fresh surge of fiery pain like a branding iron coursed through his leg. Sweat poured down off his brow and down his face.

Randolph shook Sickles's shoulder. "Wake up, General."

Sickles opened his eyes. "Randolph. Please locate Dr. Calhoun."

Randolph stationed a guard of twenty men around Sickles, then he rode off in search of Third Corps' chief surgeon.

Sickles slumped against the barn, eyes closed, mouth open, breathing shallowly. Tremain's voice was shouting. He opened his eyes.

A high-pitched shriek and a thunderous explosion. The ground shuddered under the impact of a shell. The explosion rippled through Sickles's injured leg as if a sledge hammer slammed against his thigh bone, shattering it. A wave of wet nausea burped up his throat, coating his tongue with a sharp bitterness like burnt coffee.

"Tell General Birney he must take command," Sickles said.

Tremain nodded, motioning to a courier and relaying the order.

"General Sickles," Tremain said, "we have to move you. The Rebels are racing toward us."

"I'm waiting for Captain Randolph to return with the ambulance and surgeon," Sickles whispered. "But if they don't arrive in time, I want you to throw me over my horse and walk me to the rear. I refuse to be taken prisoner. I would rather die on the field of battle than be captured. Do you understand, Henry?"

"Yes."

*6:18 p.m.*

Expecting to see the enemy line at any moment, Sickles removed his revolver and rested it on his lap, waiting for the attack. After several minutes, Randolph and an ambulance approached, carrying Dr. Calhoun, and stopped next to Sickles. Dr. Calhoun jumped off and examined the mangled leg. "General, I need to get you back to the field hospital."

Calhoun, Tremain, and Randolph lifted Sickles into the ambulance. Tremain climbed in next to Sickles, and Dr. Calhoun hopped up next to the driver. The doctor turned around and said, "General Sickles, I am delighted to find you alive. A rumor had gone 'round that you were mortally wounded. Just in case you were not, I brought along a canteen of stimulants. If you need reviving, take a swig."

"Thank you, Doc." Sickles gripped the flask and took a swig, letting the whiskey burn his insides and numb his burning leg. He turned to Tremain. "Henry, would you grab a cigar from inside my jacket pocket and light it for me?" He took another swig.

Tremain found a big Havana, bit the end off, and lit it, placing it in Sickles's mouth. Sickles struggled to move more upright and started puffing, waving at the lines of men around the ambulance. "I'm alright and will be back on the battlefield shortly." he shouted. "You must hold your position. Don't waiver; stand firm, and we will surely win. I will be back soon."

The men of Third Corps cheered as the ambulance passed, waving their hats in the air. Sickles puffed a storm, waving. After a few moments, the show ended. As the ambulance moved toward the rear, Sickles threw out his cigar, covered his eyes with his cap, and folded his hands on his chest.

Rebel shot and shell exploded around the wagon as it trekked toward the rear. Sickles wanted to yell at Tremain to move faster, but his woozy mind was becoming fuzzy. He was slipping away. His stomach fluttered as they carried him from the ambulance into the field hospital.

He stared into Dr. Calhoun's face. "What are you going to do, Doc?" Sickles whispered.

Dr. Calhoun said, "I'm going to saw through the mangled tissue on your leg, severing the bone above the knee. I'm going to tie off the femoral artery using fine horsehair, then scrape the edges of the bone smooth to prevent them working back through the skin. I will pull the flap of skin over the bone, sew it closed, leaving a drainage hole."

"So you have some experience at amputating legs?" Sickles said, trying to crack a grin.

"Just a bit."

"Will…I survive?"

"Yes, but I'm not sure your corps will."

Dr. Calhoun placed an ether-soaked rag over his nose. Sickles closed his eyes. *I'm the wounded hero of Gettysburg.* He took one breath, then darkness.

## 35

# Meade — Thursday, July 2

*5:00 p.m.*
*About an hour and a half earlier*
*Leister House*

Meade stood in the small living room of the Leister House, staring down at a map. His eyes focused on the quarter-mile gap Sickles had created between Humphreys and Hancock's flanks. Thunderous cracking, rumbling, and hissing from areas surrounding the wheat field and Little Round Top blasted against the house, rattling the small-paned windows.

"God damn you, Sickles!" he shouted. "You don't have a lick of sense!"

Meade grimaced. The monstrous gaps had to be plugged. Unless he could shift reserve forces with the speed of a master chess player, he would have to retreat to the Pipe Creek line. He gritted his teeth, raised his right hand above his shoulder, and, with the arm speed of throwing a rock, drove his open palm onto the map table. "Son of a *bitch*!" he shouted at Biddle, standing across the map table. "Creating enough reserve forces means pulling front-line units from defending Cemetery Ridge and Culp's Hill."

Thunder belted the house, rocking it on its foundation. Meade's heart thumped in this throat. He darted out onto the porch and peered toward Little Round Top, its crest blossoming with flashing hellfire explosions and billowing black smoke. Jesus, the mound was erupting. In his mind's eye he saw Hell spewing from a fissure vent onto the demonic peak and pouring out its fiery death.

Biddle stepped onto the porch.

"I sure as hell hope Warren found enough troops to hold Little Round Top," Meade said.

Biddle blinked and remained tight-lipped.

"Let's examine the map." Meade sprang back into the house with Biddle hustling to keep up with him. Meade cast his gaze at the map, shaking his head as the battle-thunder continued to rattle the house. Where was he going to find several thousand more soldiers to send to the left flank? He wagged his head back and forth like a punch-drunk fist fighter.

"Damn it, James, all I'm doing is robbing Peter to pay Paul," Meade said.

He gritted his teeth and cringed. Unplugging more units just generated new horrific holes along the ridge like the one the First Minnesota regiment was trying to fill. One damn regiment trying to plug a gap previously held by a brigade. Impossible.

Meade closed his eyes and rubbed the back of his tightened neck. Today had turned into a high-stakes poker game, and he was playing against Bobby Lee, one of the masters of the game. Because of Sickles's idiocy, Lee's opening move had caught him with his pants down.

"James, fetch General Butterfield."

Biddle walked into the next room, returning with Butterfield.

Meade darted Butterfield a glaring glance. The chief of staff was holding a piece of paper.

"How do you think the battle is going?" Butterfield said.

"Not worth a damn," Meade said. "Lee is handing me my ass at the moment, thanks to your buddy Shit-for-Brains Sickles."

Butterfield shook his head and handed Meade the piece of paper.

"This is a telegram from General Halleck requesting to know your current situation. He said the president is very anxious," Butterfield said. "Do you want me to provide Halleck an update?"

"Sure," Meade said, his face flushing with fire. "Tell Halleck I'm in a fricking nutcracker and it's the president's fault. Tell Halleck it was Lincoln who promoted a corrupt congressman to corps commander. A man who claimed he had a bout of temporary insanity after murdering a man in cold blood."

Butterfield stared at Meade with a look of astonishment.

Meade's voice grew louder. "Tell Halleck that Sickles flagrantly failed to follow orders and now his eleven thousand men are being murdered in cold blood by the enemy. Tell Halleck that Sickles probably will claim temporary insanity again as his reason for disobeying orders."

"Is that what you want me to send to Halleck?" Butterfield said.

"Hell, no!" Meade stared until Butterfield sighed and glanced away.

"But here is what I want you to do. Start preparing withdrawal orders," Meade said. "Plan on using the Baltimore Pike as the avenue. If the Confederates penetrate the Cemetery Ridge line, they will control both the Taneytown and Emmitsburg Roads."

"Do you want me to issue retreat orders?" Butterfield asked.

"No, goddamn it," Meade shouted, his fiery temper unleashing like a whip. "We are still holding Cemetery Ridge by a thin thread. But I want you to be prepared to issue them, just in case. We may need to start moving our supply wagons and our wounded on the Pike Road toward the Pipe Creek defensive line."

"Yes, sir," Butterfield said. He paused as a deathlike silence erupted. After moment, he walked into the next room.

Meade frowned. Butterfield's face had flushed red and hot. He had that look of petrified fear. Pure panic. Dan was not a coward. *Damn it, George. Your flash temper frayed Butterfield's nerves and inflamed his fears. Duty demands you strive to curb your rage.* He glanced at the map again.

With his right index finger, Meade traced the path Slocum's Twelfth Corps would take if he ordered Slocum to reinforce Sickles's front. The route was almost a straight shot, like most interior lines of defense. *That's my advantage over Lee. But it's only an advantage if Slocum's reinforcements arrived in time to support Sickles.* Fifth Corps would have to fill the holes as best it could until then. *Sykes, you're going to have to prove yourself today as Fifth Corps commander. Let's see. Yes, you've had the job for only five days,*

527

*just as I have had this job for only five days.* After a long, frozen moment, he said, "Crap."

"General?"

"What?" Meade snapped. It was his intelligence officer. And Wiliams.

"General Meade," Sharpe said, "Ewell's corps has not formed to attack Culp's Hill. Ewell is waiting, I believe, for A.P. Hill's corps to first attack Cemetery Hill."

"When do you expect the Confederates to assault Cemetery Hill and Culp's Hill?" Meade said.

Sharpe pursed his lips and shook his head.

"Just give me your best guess," Meade said, with a throaty rumble.

"At the rate the Rebels are kicking off echelon attacks, I don't expect them to assault Cemetery Hill until early evening."

His heart rate quickened. Lee was making a mistake by waiting to launch an attack against Culp's Hill. "That's good news. Seth, order Slocum's corps to depart Culp's Hill and move to Sickles's left flank and assist him. As soon as I shore Sickles's busted left flank, I will move Slocum's corps back to Culp's Hill." Meade's voice hardened. "God help us, Sharpe, if Ewell attacks Greene's brigade before Slocum returns with his corps. The army could be destroyed." The throb in his head sharpened.

"Slocum's entire corps?" Williams asked.

"Yes, damn it!" Meade snapped.

He moved outside onto the porch and lit a cigar. The yellow sun had fallen halfway from its zenith toward South Mountain. The day remained blistering hot. Sweat stained his blue blouse. The deep booming of artillery fire from Sickles's left flank reverberated in the air.

Across the fields another high-pitched Rebel cry echoed, signaling another enemy brigade charging Sickles's left flank. Meade bit his lip and tightened his fingers around the porch column. He inhaled a shallow breath. The Rebel infantry would make quick work of Sickles's isolated soldiers. Meade pointed his binoculars in the direction of the shrill Rebel yell.

For the moment, Lee was attacking only the Union's left flank. Sharpe appeared to be correct. But he was seeing only Lee's opening moves. Perhaps Lee's main attack was against Culp's Hill, hoping Meade would abandon his right flank to support his threatened left flank. Lee was the master of exploiting an opponent's mistakes. Meade snorted, shaking his head. The Army of the Potomac was teetering on the brink of failure.

*5:15 p.m.*

Sharpe walked out onto the porch. "Lee's forces are laid out in a six-mile concave line around us," he said. "Longstreet's corps opened the attack on our far left flank. His three divisions are commanded by Generals McLaws, Pickett, and Hood. That's who Sickles is facing at the moment.

"Who is occupying the middle of Lee's forces along Seminary Ridge?" Meade said.

"A.P. Hill. His divisions are commanded by Generals Anderson, Heth, and Pender, and they are facing Hancock's corps nested along Cemetery Ridge."

"Whose enemy forces are facing Cemetery Hill?"

"General Ewell's corps is aligned across from Cemetery Hill and Culp's Hill. Ewell has two division commanders near us. General Early is facing Cemetery Hill, and General Johnson is facing Culp's Hill. We believe Rodes's division is sitting north of Gettysburg and acting as ready reserve for Ewell's corps. We believe Heth's division, which took a terrible beating from Reynolds's Iron Brigade yesterday, is sitting behind Seminary Ridge, acting as a ready reserve for A. P. Hill's corps."

"Where are Stuart's cavalry boys?" Meade said.

"We are still not sure."

"Are you suggesting we are facing a phantom cavalry? I can't believe Lee would not have Stuart playing a critical role today. Keep your intelligence boys active. I want to know where Stuart is before he hits us."

"Yes, sir."

"What's your best guess of Lee's attack plan against us?" Meade asked.

"It still appears to be an echelon attack, one brigade after another, directed at breaking Sickles's front. But at the rate they are going, Ewell's forces won't attack now until well after dark."

"So you think I'm still safe in moving Slocum's forces from Culp's Hill to reinforce our far left?"

"Yes, sir," Sharpe said. "As long as Lee keeps executing a deliberate echelon attack."

"Good. Keep your men patrolling Culp's Hill. I want to know as soon as possible when Ewell attacks it. We will have to send Slocum's forces back as soon as they are no longer needed on the far left flank."

Meade went back inside, walking over to the map table. Williams was staring at the map and looked up at him.

"Except for some artillery dueling going on at Culp's Hill between Slocum and Ewell, there appears to be little fighting on the right flank," Meade said.

Williams nodded in agreement.

━━━◆━━━ ◆ ━━━◆━━━

*5:30 p.m.*

Meade looked at his watch; it was half past five. He offered Williams a cigar and lit his own.

Slocum walked into the Leister House. "General Meade, it's Henry."

A blue haze of cigar smoke shrouded Meade's head. "Henry, you are responsible for the defensive line on Culp's Hill," Meade said. "But I need you to release all the troops you can spare to assist Sickles. They are required on the left flank to push back the Rebels."

"I have ordered General Williams's division to assist Sickles," Slocum said. "After they are on the move, most of Geary's division will follow, leaving General Green's brigade as the lone force on Culp's Hill. I strongly urge you to leave Greene's brigade occupying the breastworks he built."

"Thank you. That's a prudent move, leaving Greene's brigade in place. That will help immensely." Meade wiped his brow. "But be prepared to move your corps back to Culp's Hill if the enemy attacks it."

530

Meade and Slocum walked outside together. Meade's personal aide had Baldy saddled and ready to go. Meade grabbed the reins. He turned to Slocum. "Good luck, Henry! I'm going to ride over and see how Sickles is doing."

*5:50 p.m.*

Meade mounted Baldy and rode the Taneytown Road toward Little Round Top. Trailing Meade was a small cavalry squad of Lancers escorts and personal aides, working hard to keep up with the general.

Meade's neck stiffened as he flew down the road. Hopefully, Sykes was in position, providing a safe haven for Third Corps' retreating troops to reform and reconstitute. With any luck, Caldwell's division from Hancock's corps had arrived in the wheat field. But Sykes's corps was the key to avoiding a rout.

*6:10 p.m.*

He rode to the rear of the wheat field, stopping a couple hundred yards behind the Trostle farm house serving as Sickles's headquarters. Enemy cannons thundering beyond the peach orchard salient pounded the Trostle Farm with cannonballs. Stray bullets whined past, pelting the ground like lead raindrops.

Was this turning into a rout?

*If the Confederates gain possession of the two Round Tops on the left of the line, the enemy will have demolished the eye of my fishhook defense. Or if the enemy troops charge through the gap guarded by Thomas's battery and the Minnesotans and gain access to the east-west road, they will rush right to Cemetery Ridge, splitting the fishhook shank defenses, and take the Union forces from behind.*

Meade gestured for Biddle. "Order General Hancock to send another brigade to the assistance of Third Corps' General Birney. I'm not sure how long we can hold the left flank. I'm going to stay here, bringing up and placing reinforcements."

Biddle departed.

Meade sat motionless on Baldy as the dreadful scene unfolded in front of him. Sickles's spirited soldiers were falling in the wheat field as if the Grim Reaper's scythe were harvesting a crop of souls.

Soon the enemy would be rushing by Sickles's unprotected right flank held by Humphreys. *What a damn mess.*

───────◆───────

*6:25 p.m.*

Meade spurred Baldy to a gallop, riding forward a few hundred yards to scout the open space between the extreme right of Sickles's corps and Hancock's left. He stopped and gripped his field glasses, scanning the area. The gap actually was two smaller gaps, one created by Sickles ordering Humphreys's division to move forward, creating a 500-yard east-west hole between Humphreys's right flank and Hancock's left flank, occupied by Caldwell's division. The second gap was created by Caldwell's division departing Cemetery Ridge to reinforce Sickles's corps. The result was a treacherous point along the Federal defensive along Cemetery Ridge, a gap of more than 1,000 yards. It was a critical vulnerability guarded only by Thomas's battery and the First Minnesotans. Not nearly a large enough force to stop a Rebel assault.

Meade squinted toward Hancock's corps, looking for reinforcements. Nothing. He sucked in a sharp breath. If reinforcements did not arrive soon, it would be a catastrophic defeat. What else could he do? The only option left appeared to be for him to fill the gap himself. He turned and reached for his sword as he eyed Captain Carpenter and his escort Lancers.

## 36

# First Minnesota — Thursday, July 2

### *Colvill*

*4:45 p.m.*
*Not quite two hours earlier*

Colonel Colvill rode south along Cemetery Ridge, marching the Minnesotans at a double step. He resembled a menacing grizzly bear with his large lumberjack beard and his long legs dangling over his dark horse, feet outside the stirrups, nearly dragging on the ground. He pulled his hefty blue coat away from his itchy skin, riding through muggy clouds of soupy water droplets.

"Damn wool uniforms," he muttered.

Rolling, tearing, crackling volleys of rifle fire and the yells and screams of soldiers roared across the open fields like monster thunderstorms spawning tornados. Colvill scanned the whirling tempest of fire and smoke through his field glasses.

Silver-gray smoke poured from the peach orchard and the Emmitsburg Road in undulating sheets of lead toward Cemetery Ridge. During brief glimpses through the smoke, ghostly goliath figures crept about the battlefield. The eeriness taunted him. He blinked several times as sweat burned his eyes. He stared again through the fissures of thick battle smoke. The combatants seemed bafflingly tall, like giants. *Must be an optical illusion caused by the rifle and cannon firings, humid air, and light and shadows on this part of the battlefield. If not, this is turning into a real Black Flag.* He couldn't see any black flags through the heavy smoke, but there were certain Rebel units that were known to fly them, declaring that their unit would give no quarter—that this battle was to the death.

He cocked his head as the moving blue column tramped along the rolling slope, rifles resting on right shoulders, swaying back and forth like long wheat stalks in a light breeze. He smiled. The regiment was making good time, and he was back in command of the First Minnesota.

He gripped his field glasses and scanned Cemetery Ridge. Directly in front of the First Minnesota was a wide, empty stretch of grassland giving way to a distant thicket of trees. Beyond the curtain of trees in a wheat field rumbled a murderous den—shrieking missiles, whistling Minié balls, and shrill screams.

Off slightly to the left, two hundred yards ahead, he spotted six silent bronze cannons glinting on the westward crest of Cemetery Ridge. *Voilà.* Must be Captain Evan Thomas's battery. He turned his horse a bit to the left and aimed for the six cannons, spaced fifteen yards apart in a line, scanning for infantry units supporting the battery.

"My God," he muttered. The battery was isolated on the deserted Cemetery Ridge. His heart lurched as if he were freefalling. He slowed to a walk and glanced back at Cemetery Ridge. The closest supporting infantry was 350 yards north of the battery.

"That's one hell of a gap," he said, reining in his urge to curse. No wonder Gibbon ordered the First Minnesota to race down here. Without infantry support, the Rebels would spill across the open field like a breached dam and swamp the battery, rupturing the Union's defensive line. Stemming a dam burst with a makeshift levy required more than a regiment. Gibbon needed a division to plug the gap. He snapped the reins and started trotting toward Thomas's battery.

Captain Nathan Messick trotted next to Colvill and saluted.

"How is company G holding up?" Colvill semi-shouted.

"Just checking to see what's our marching objective?" Messick said. "Trotting at the double-quick, the boys are starting to pant pretty hard, like bushed hound dogs."

Colvill pointed. "That six-gun battery about one hundred yards over there."

Messick glanced toward the battery. "What infantry unit vacated this position?"

"Caldwell's. We are replacing his division. Hancock ordered Caldwell to support the fighting in the wheat field."

Messick's brows arched as he stared at Colvill.

"Holy shit, Colonel, one undersized regiment is supposed to the fill the gap left by a division?" Messick said.

"Yes, one artillery battery and the First Minnesota," Colvill said.

"We sure as hell could use Company C and Company L," Messick said.

"Damn Colonel Adams for volunteering Company C to act as a provost guard for Gibbon's division headquarters," Colvill said. "All he was trying to do was suck up to Gibbon."

Colvill slowed down to a walk, grinding his teeth.

"What really blisters my ass is that Adams volunteered the Minnesota Sharpshooters from Company L to support Woodruff's battery near Cemetery Hill," Colvill said. "Those sharpshooters with their carbine repeating rifles are the best marksmen in Hancock's corps."

"Those boys are deadly accurate at ranges up to 500 yards," Messick said. "At Antietam I witnessed a sharpshooter knock a Rebel officer off his horse at nearly 800 yards."

"Those Minnesota boys can shoot," Colvill said.

Messick turned and rode back to the column. As the regiment approached Thomas's battery, the shrieking thunder from the wheat field rose to a fever pitch. The Rebel assault was gaining momentum as the thin blue lines buckled. They would soon be eyeing Thomas's six Napoleon cannons as a strategic prize.

---

*5:00 p.m.*

Colvill marched the eight companies of the regiment behind Thomas's battery, stopping just past the six cannons on an open mound.

He turned to Sergeant Wright. "Order the men to form in two battle lines, lying down, their rifles loaded and ready." He pointed toward the wheat field. "The battle raging beyond the trees over there is racing toward us like a firestorm."

Wright saluted and shouted the order as he walked down the column. The regiment plopped down on their bellies, stretching out in their sweaty wool uniforms on the soft field grass, two long rows of hard-nosed faces, loaded rifles lying at their sides.

Colvill stood behind the two lines. An eerie quietness covered the prostrated regiment. Although the battery was sitting cold and silent, it felt like the deadly calm preceding a killer storm. A haunting breeze caressed his weathered face, teasing his tense jaw muscles.

With a heavy sigh, Colvill squinted, his eyes scanning for enemy activity westward across the open field with teeth clenched in edge-of-fear alarm. Rebels hiding in the white smoke occasionally showed their positions with a sprinkling of yellow rifle fire rattling overhead. An artillery shell crashed nearby Thomas's Battery C. The ground quivered. Several of the Minnesotans popped up their heads, watching the boiling black smoke.

The Rebels had discovered the isolated strategic target on this unoccupied stretch of Cemetery Ridge. A barrage of enemy artillery batteries erupted. Shells snaked over Battery C, exploding on the fringes of the First Minnesota.

He dismounted, walked his horse around the end of the regimental line. Shell craters dotted the ridge slope like gopher holes, some very near the boys.

"Sergeant Wright," Colvill shouted. "The boys are prime targets for enemy shells aimed at the Union battery.

Wright said, "The Rebel artillerymen always are overshooting."

"Got to move forward," Colvill said. "Redeploy the regiment partway down Cemetery Ridge, well in front of Thomas's battery."

Within moments, Wright had complied, stopping the men when they were to the left and several yards in front of Battery C. Without warning, a deafening blast erupted behind Colvill. He ducked, hunching his shoulders and covering his ears. His heart buckled into his stomach as he jerked around, spotting white smoke tendrils rising from the barrel of one of Thomas's cannons. "Damn it, that scared the crap out of me."

Moments later, Rebel gunners answered with an onslaught of shells that sailed over the Union battery and Cemetery Ridge.

Colvill sighed. The regiment was no longer in the overshot flight path.

Wright walked behind the two regimental lines and stopped next to Colvill, holding the reins of his horse.

"We are going to be here for a while," Colvill said. "Tell the men to keep their heads down and try to relax."

Wright saluted. "I'll emphasize the relaxing part. Snoring is authorized." He moved off.

---

*5:30 p.m.*

Colvill studied the men as Wright walked along the two lines. There was no chattering. Some of the men lay next to their rifles, letting the late afternoon sun bake them. Others propped up on haversacks, smoking pipes. The grinding cadence along Sickles's front was creeping closer. Growing smoke clouds drifted over the thicket, carrying a foul, sulfurous vapor. Colvill let out a breath. Death was approaching.

He scanned the two regimental lines. The great guns thundered incessantly, throwing hot iron both ways. No Minnesotan was skedaddling. A shell crashed near Thomas's battery, shaking the earth and rocking the men as if they were floating on a windswept lake. Colvill scanned the sky, letting his ears point his eyes in the direction of flying death. A second shell whistled with a sharp receding pitch like a teapot losing steam. His scalp prickled. A thunderous boom ripped the ground, opening it like a plow furrowing a field. He turned his head. The screaming shot bounced twice before piercing a tethered battery horse, then bounced once more before striking a second mare. Blood spattered skyward like fountaining lava. The other horses reacted frantically, neighing and squealing, pulling hard against their lines.

An undershot shell screamed over the heads of the First Minnesota, shattering the air twenty yards behind the regiment, throwing up sod and dirt on Colvill. A second undershot struck near Company K. Minnesota curses, cries of rage, and piercing screams echoed over the regiment. Behind Colvill, a chilling screech like an animal in distress erupted next to the tethered horses. Colvill cocked his head. A cannoneer writhed in agony, a gaping wound in his gut. The mortally wounded soldier cried out for a few torturous seconds before falling silent. Colvill stared—the soldier was a mere boy, looking no older than sixteen.

Shells continued to shriek toward Thomas's battery, some coming close, others closing on the First Minnesota. The shell bursts rained down searing hot shrapnel on the regiment. Most of the soldiers lay face down, curling their bodies into as small a space as possible.

Colvill glowered. Panic would be justified, as one stray shell was instant death. But the Minnesotans remained calm, each man possessing an abundance of physical courage. Conquering the desire to run was what distinguished the Minnesotans from many other units. They fought for one another. Abandoning your comrades was a disgrace, and they would choose death over disgrace. In the regiment's history, no Minnesotan had ever skedaddled. Not one.

Colville and Wright stood on the left flank of the First Minnesota, both scanning through binoculars toward the peach orchard. The regiment's location offered a panoramic view of the battle below. Sickles's two divisions formed on two sides of a square with the angle at the peach orchard. Artillery was on the high ground in the angle between Birney's and Humphreys's divisions.

"Sickles has created a dangerously exposed salient, whose right flank the First Minnesota is supporting. This is nearly an impossible task for an undersized regiment and one artillery battery," Colvill said.

"If the Rebels bust through, we are not going to stem them," Wright said. "All hell will break loose."

We need a division," Colvill said, "maybe two divisions to stop them."

Colvill kept his field glasses glued on the battlefield. Blue reinforcements plunged into the giant shadows, disappearing from sight. Colvill waited. After several moments, fragments of broken regiments stumbled out of the fearful fire, streams of bloody wounded chased by shrieking Rebels. His stomach spasmed.

Bloody bodies were strewn about like broken glass. Their contorted positions left no doubt about their horrific deaths. What a murderous bloodbath.

"Hell is real," Wright whispered.

---

*6:00 p.m.*

Colville listened as musket fire directed toward the First Minnesota increased. Two or three whickering bullets knocked the dirt in front of the regiment's defensive line. "That's small-arms fire," Colvill said, "and those are not stray shots."

A couple more bullets cracked close by. Colvill pointed. "Look down the slope over to the left front of the regiment. I think enemy fire is coming from a line of skirmishers or a squad of sharpshooters."

"I agree," Wright said.

"I need to talk with Captain Ball."

Wright departed and returned with Captain Ball, commanding Company F.

"Captain Ball. Take your company forward and flush out the enemy skirmishers on our left flank. Try and stop the enemy rifles from firing on the regiment."

---

## *Wright*

Ball saluted. He turned to Wright. "Have Company F stand and prepare to move out."

In few minutes, Company F stepped out smartly, led by Wright. They took a few paces forward toward the Emmitsburg Road, then turned and marched southwest toward Sickles's headquarters at the Trostle Farm. The enemy fire increased heavily as they moved, the musket fire peppering the ground, spitting up dirt clods.

Following Ball, Wright trotted Company F a few hundred yards from the regiments' position, stopping at the edge of the marshy ground of Plum Run Creek snaking across the front of the First Minnesota. Southwest was Sickles's headquarters, the

Trostle Farm, about 350 yards away. A scream lurched from behind. Wright turned; Private James Bachelor had fallen to the ground, wailing like a screeching cat, blood flowing over his boot.

Wright crawled over. "Let me take a look." He reached out and examined the wound. "You got a Minié ball hole about the size of a silver dollar that pierced through your right foot." He ripped off a piece of Bachelor's shirt and wrapped the foot tightly.

Bachelor continued to howl. Wright clamped his hand over his mouth, pushing hard.

"God damn it James, get control," Wright said.

Bachelor nodded, setting his jaw. The screeching stopped.

Wright reached for his canteen and held it to Bachelor's parched lips. Wright said, "Take a sip of the Devil's brew. It's some of that wretched Maryland whiskey."

Bachelor took a sip of whiskey and wiped his wet lips on his sleeve.

"That's some pretty potent fire water," Bachelor said.

"I'm leaving you the canteen and will come back to check on you in a bit."

Wright snaked back to the upper part of the line on the right flank, protected by sunken boulders and large stones. The sharp whistles of Rebel Minié balls zipped overhead, cutting through the bushes. The Rebels were coming…fast.

Wright said to Ball, "I'm not sure how much longer Company F can hold."

A blood-curdling Rebel Yell boomed across the battlefield. Hundreds of Sickles's bluecoats emerged in front of Company F, racing for their lives.

"Hold your fire!" Wright shouted. "Let Sickles's boys through."

The blue boys sprinted at top speed. To Wright's surprise, several of these soldiers stopped running when they reached Company F's position and joined them. As soon as the last retreating Union soldier joined Wright's men, he shouted, "Give it to them, boys!"

Company F's rifles cracked into a deadly fire, cutting down a wide swath of Rebels. Wright told them to fire at will, and the Minnesota boys poured a storm of lead into the enemy.

## *Colvill*

Colvill fixed his field glasses, straining to spot Wright and Company F a few hundred yards away, exchanging fire with the enemy. The work of the big guns was growing more furious. A rumbling thunder cracked overhead. The battle was blossoming in front of Company F. Colvill scowled.

The regiment remained hunkered at the ready. Colvill shook his head. With Company F detached and skirmishing forward, the First Minnesota had seven of its ten regular companies stretched along Cemetery Ridge. This left about 262 men in a battle line. Not very many men to cover a several-hundred-yard gap. One small regiment could not stop Longstreet's assault. If the Rebels charged, they were doomed.

The Confederates straddling the Emmitsburg Road blasted Humphreys's division holding Sickles's far right flank with a constant barrage of artillery broadsides. Then the Rebel Yell erupted. Colvill scanned Humphreys's division. After the opening collision, the forces tangled savagely. The Rebels pushed hard against Humphreys's soldiers, grinding them down like a rolling millstone with their massive numbers. They paused momentarily, letting their strength rise like a swelling river, then burst over the blue line, spilling over the sloping field toward Cemetery Ridge.

"My God," Colvill said, "how easily the enemy is swamping Sickles's corps."

*6:30 p.m.*

Colvill wiped the sweat from his eyes and brow. This was interesting. Sickles's forward salient was acting like a breakwater and had unintentionally disrupted the Confederate battle line. The Rebel brigades and regiments were ragged and intermixed, no longer attacking in straight lines. Sickles's caved lines were withdrawing but not just running pell-mell. The Union boys moved back rhythmically, hustling back twenty to thirty yards, halting in a loose line, tearing open the powder and ball pouch with their teeth, loading their rifles with a ramrod, aiming carefully, and firing at the advancing enemy. Then they would turn and sprint back another twenty to thirty yards and repeat, a tactical ploy making the Rebels bleed as they swept slowly forward.

Colvill struggled to take a breath. Was Gibbon going to send reinforcements? He spotted an orderly from Second Corps galloping toward him. The orderly pulled up and saluted.

"Colonel Colvill, General Sickles has been wounded and removed from the field of battle. General Meade has ordered General Hancock to assume command of Third Corps. General Gibbon is now acting commander of Second Corps."

"Do you know if either General Hancock or General Gibbon plans on reinforcing the First Minnesota?" Colvill asked. "My regiment is sitting out here alone. The Rebel artillery on both flanks have joined the battle, and the First Minnesota is receiving a constant pummeling."

"I will pass on your concerns to General Hancock," the orderly said. He gestured toward Cemetery Hill. "Hancock is now placing the Nineteenth Maine 250 yards north of you. I'm not positive, Colonel, but I don't think either General Hancock or General Gibbon has any troops to spare."

Colvill nodded, swearing silently.

*6:40 p.m.*

A major from Sharpe's intelligence unit arrived, saluted. "Colonel, the enemy to your left front sweeping northward into Humphreys's left flank is Barksdale's Mississippi Brigade. His 1,600 or so troops smashed Sickles's peach orchard salient. The brigade directly in front of you is Wilcox's Alabama Brigade. My guess is they number around 1,700 men. How many men do you have here, Colonel?"

"I have 262 men lying in a line of battle," Colvill said, his voice faltering.

The major said, "I will ride to Colonel Sharpe and tell him of your situation. But, Colonel, you have to hold at all cost. There is nothing between Wilcox's boys and the unoccupied Cemetery Ridge. If they get by you, the Rebels can ride all the way to Washington."

Colville shuddered. How could 262 men hold off Wilcox's 1,700 soldiers? The First Minnesota was terribly undersized, now minus three companies. He couldn't pull Wright's company back to the regiment, given the enemy hordes were less than fifty yards from Company F, firing and overrunning Sickles's retreating boys. The only hope was Company F standing firm like an iron wall, providing refuge.

Colvill drifted back along the regimental line, stopping at Company K. Lieutenant Lochren was standing, and he saluted.

"Lieutenant Lochren, the troops in front of us are from Wilcox's Alabama Brigade. We have to hold this position at all cost," Colvill said.

Raising his voice to be heard, Lochren answered, "Yes, sir!"

Colvill estimated the peach orchard was a half mile in front. Across the way, he spotted the Alabama Brigade, 1,700 strong, moving in long gray lines with a dozen red battle flags floating above them. *Holy Mother of Jesus.* His regiment was alone, expected to defend to the last man.

This was a death sentence.

## Hancock

*6:45 p.m.*

Hancock swore, watching Sickles's entire left flank disintegrating. He had just ordered Willard's brigade to charge toward Barksdale's attacking Mississippians. Hancock peered to the right of Willard's advancing brigade and through the smoke saw another Rebel line charging toward the Cemetery Ridge gap.

He shouted to Captain William Miller, his only remaining aide, "Jesus Christ, Billy. There is only a six-gun battery and small-sized regiment defending the gap."

Miller said, "Rebels are still on the west side of Plum Run. I think we still have time to find reinforcements for the gap."

"Well, let's find out," Hancock shouted.

He spurred his horse to a gallop, riding north past Humphreys's retreating men. Through the battlefield smoke he spotted shadowy, dark figures, lunging forward.

"I hope they are Federals that we can use to plug the gap," Hancock shouted.

As they galloped toward the soldiers, there was a rattle of rifles in front of him. Bullets whizzed by Hancock's head, one touching his left sleeve.

"Damn it, Billy. We've ridden into a swarm of Rebels."

His mind searched his body for pain. *None. Maybe I'm not hit.*

"Yelp," shouted Miller.

Hancock turned as Miller slumped in his saddle, his aide's face turning deadly pale. Miller's left forearm bone was shattered by a Minié ball, the bone fragments sticking through his coat sleeve.

Hancock yelled, "Get out of here, Billy! I'll be right behind you!"

Miller nodded, turned his horse, and galloped toward Cemetery Ridge.

Hancock glanced back into the hornets' nest, his muscles tensing against the flying Minié balls zipping past him. He was alone in the swirl of the smoky battle, with a limited view of what was happening around him. The brigade of screaming Rebels that had shot Billy was closing on him. A yellow flash erupted in the smoke like a lightning bolt and a bullet whickered past his head, making the hairs on his neck stand on end. "You cannot be captured," Hancock muttered.

He turned toward Cemetery Hill, spurred his horse. Bullets whizzed by him as he dashed away from the Rebels into an extended swale of low ground. The ravine shielded him for several hundred feet. He spotted Billy ahead, his horse walking slowly toward Cemetery Ridge, Billy listing to his left like a sinking ship, faltering from blood loss. Hancock pulled alongside, grabbed his reins, and towed Billy's horse behind.

Hancock shouted, "William, grip the saddle horn. I will get you to safety."

Miller nodded, groaning.

---

*6:55 p.m.*

Hancock stopped beside an isolated, undersized regiment of Union soldiers lying in two orderly lines on the ground. Miller said he could make it on his own and kept riding toward the crest of Cemetery Ridge.

Hancock dismounted and strode toward Colvill.

"Colonel, are these all the men we have here?" he said in disbelief.

"Yes, sir."

Hancock erupted with a string of profanities, his face grim. "What regiment is this?"

Colvill said with pride, "The First Minnesota, sir."

Hancock scowled. *At least it's the best regiment in Second Corps.* He remounted and rode back toward Lieutenant Thomas's battery. He estimated the attacking Alabamians to be the size of a brigade. The wall of gray soldiers was about four hundred yards wide. Hancock turned, sizing up the First Minnesota line. It was less than a hundred yards long. Scanning north through his binoculars, he spotted reinforcements from Gibbon's division, running along at best speed. "God damn you, Sickles. We should never be in this unholy mess." He frowned. The reinforcements would not arrive before the wave of Alabamians crested the ridge occupied by the First Minnesota.

Hancock paused, weighing his options. There was only one: Order the Minnesotans to charge the Rebel brigade. It would not bring victory. It would simply destroy the regiment, perhaps down to the last soldier. But he could not let the Rebels reach Cemetery Ridge. He began setting his mind to it, to order this regiment forward into the dark swirl.

He rode down the ridge slope to Colvill, standing twenty yards behind the center of the regimental line. Hancock remained mounted, his eyes glaring. He removed his sword, pointed it toward the advancing Rebels. It was decided. He would sacrifice an entire regiment, buying time to bring reinforcements to halt the Rebel brigade from marching into the gap, to prevent the enemy from splitting the Union line in two.

"Colonel Colvill," Hancock shouted, "charge forward and take those Rebel battle flags!"

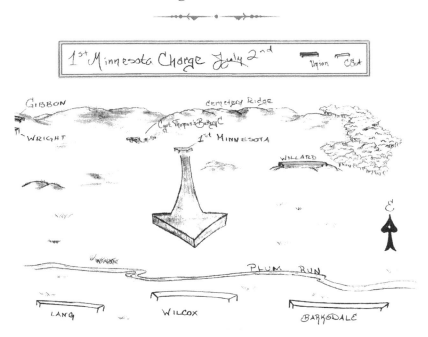

## Colvill

"Yes, sir!" Colvill said. Something in Hancock's voice. Colvill understood; it was a farewell. The First Minnesota had to be sacrificed. He clenched his huge fists.

Colvill walked toward Ellet Perkins, the regimental color sergeant, proudly flying Old Glory in the center of the battle line. He faced Perkins and the regiment. His heart raced.

Standing at attention, Colvill took a huge gulp of air, bellowed as loud as he could, "***Attention, regiment!***" A moment later a chorus of voices all uttering, "Attention, regiment!" The men sprang to their feet, aligning themselves to the directions of the company commanders, forming in a long line of double ranks.

In a carefully executed about-face, Colvill moved his right leg back about half the length of his boot and touched his right toe to the ground. Resting his weight on the heel of his left boot, he bent his right knee, and turned 180 degrees to the right on the left heel and on the ball of his right foot, resuming the position of attention.

Colvill and Perkins stood next to each other, staring at the brigade-sized Rebel force across the field moving toward them. For a moment, he stood stupefied, glaring silently across the field at the charging Confederates. A frightful sight, a swirl of red battle flags rushing forward. Colvill counted the regimental battle flags. *Five. Holy crap.* Hancock had ordered the First Minnesota to charge a force five times larger than their own. They were charging into a deadly, rushing whirlpool that threatened to swallow the regiment.

Colvill turned about face, looking at each of his boys, burning their faces into his memory. Sweat poured off his brow and his chin trembled as his fiery eyes said farewell to each of them. Each man stared back, giving a slight nod, acknowledging that few, if any, of the Minnesotans would survive the charge. No one ran. He sucked in a deep breath and held it, letting the warmth of the hot air fill his chest. Damn, he was proud of his boys. They were Minnesotans, the First Minnesota.

After a long moment, Colvill shouted, "First Minnesota, fix bayonets!"

The Rebel yelling cracked above the First Minnesota as the enemy drew closer. It was quiet along the Minnesota line, except the clinking of steel as the regiment fixed bayonets.

Colvill's heart was racing. This was it. Now it was his duty to lead his warriors. He looked at the line a final time. The regimental officers were dismounted, the orderlies holding their horses to the right of the First Minnesota.

Colvill shouted, "*Dress, **center, dress!***" The First Minnesota formed around the regimental colors. Every man immediately raised an arm parallel to the ground touching the shoulder of the man next to him. Then they all locked their heads toward the center.

Colvill shouted, "Ready, *front*. Shoulder arms!"

The men cocked their heads forward, lifted the rifle muzzles over their right shoulders, each gripping the buttstock in the palm of his right hand, staring directly forward at the oncoming Alabama Brigade. It was time to turn them loose.

He whirled toward Sergeant Perkins, holding the regimental colors high over the line. He nodded. "Here we go."

Colvill withdrew his sword, thundering, *"Charge, double-quick, Minnesota!"*

The men surged forward, charging savagely. They descended the slope, making no sounds. Colvill and Perkins ran side by side in the middle of the line, leading the charge a few steps ahead of the regiment. Perkins's flag was the only stars and stripes moving away from the Cemetery Ridge defensive line.

Colvill stared ahead at the charging Alabamians, coming in two parallel lines, firing as they charged. The last cluster of artillery shells had scarred the earth with deep cuts. The enemy bounced over the gullies, red battle flags rippling above them. They were three hundred yards away.

A blur in Colvill's peripheral vision caught his attention. He cocked his head slightly left and spotted a solid shot shell bounce twice and rip through Heffelfinger's company on the far left flank. Instantly, men rushed forward, filling the broken line. To his front, masses of gray coats filled his entire field of vision. *My God…* The charging Rebels were a terrible beauty, an overwhelming vision of red battle flags and hundreds and hundreds of bayonets glimmering brightly. *Pick a spot! Pick a spot!*

Colvill focused on the center red battle flag sailing toward him. The sight boiled his blood. Almost unconsciously, he picked up his pace like a bull rushing a matador's cape. Perkins kept pace alongside him. Colvill's feet seemed to fly over the terrain. He was breathing hard and his leg muscles started stinging, the burning choking out the seeds of panic. *Keep running hard.*

Without orders the double-quick changed into an all-out sprint, the soldiers running furiously downhill. Colvill started sprinting at full speed, his long strides outpacing Perkins. The high speed run was the only way they would pass through the storm of lead and strike the enemy.

Colvill focused on keeping a steady line, knowing his boys would fight desperately if they could survive the charge. He cocked his head, seeing the whole regiment running down the slope in two near perfect lines, swinging muskets, moving fiercely forward down the slope toward the dry creek bed like a small avalanche, determined to bury the enemy.

Colvill scowled, setting his jaw. This was the worst moment—just ahead, the waiting enemy, preparing to deliver the first salvo. Hundreds of yellow flashes streaked and rifles cracked across the Rebel line. A hail of bullets whistled around Colvill's head, thumping into soft flesh like smashing pumpkins, sending many Minnesotans crashing to the ground. The massive Rebel volley was followed by a heavy line of blue smoke that broke out along the forward Confederate line.

Colvill squinted as he peered through the smoke. The Rebels had to reload, giving the regiment a reprieve of about twenty seconds. Instincts took over, a cunning that had served the First Minnesota well in previous battles. The enemy was directly before them, reloading: slaughter them, and survive.

The Rebels were forty yards off, on an elevation on the other side of Plum Run, firing down the slope. The enemy was tending to overshoot, so Colvill crouched as low as his six-foot-five frame would allow as he sprinted toward the Rebels.

He narrowed his eyes, scanning the enemy line as the Rebels intertwined with smoke. The drifting clouds would help cloak the First Minnesota. Sputtering rifle fire sprayed from the gray shadows. Screams from behind bellowed over Colvill. His mind's eye saw his friends falling and their bodies crumpling to the ground. *Come on, let's close, kill them, and live!*

Colvill spotted Rebel cannons pointing at the regiment. His gut tightened, and he girded himself for the deadly fire. He cocked his head to the right and shouted, "Stay low! Cannons in our front!"

The cannons' yellow flames streaked toward Minnesotans with a volcanic roar. Grape and shrapnel whizzed through the air. One hot piece of metal breezed through Colvill's bushy sideburns, stinging his cheek. His eardrums shuddered at the sudden change of air pressure.

A scream down the line to Colvill's right. He turned and caught a glimpse of Private George Grady falling backwards. Several grape shots had ripped open his chest, bright red blood spurting out several inches. While the Rebel cannoneers reloaded, the Alabamians dropped a deadly fire by file, a long-ringing rattle of musketry. The infantry fire sliced through the First Minnesota. The pop and spit of bullets whizzed past Colvill, but none hit. He turned his head. No surviving Minnesotan waivered. Those behind the fallen closed the gaps. The enemy musket fire failed to stop the First Minnesota charge. A wild wolf howl rose in his heart.

Colvill straightened and screamed, *"**Charge!**"* A great roar erupted. The regiment dropped the muskets off their right shoulders and held them in bayonet position: waist high, the point leveled at the chests of the Rebels. The Norsemen rushed forward, fierce yells and screams breaking out from over two hundred throats, their gleaming bayonets approaching at break-neck speed.

Colvill gritted his teeth. The regiment had caught the Rebel line reloading, the gray-clad soldiers furiously tearing paper cartridges, pouring gunpowder, ramming balls down the muzzles. At a distance of less than ten yards, Colvill aimed his rifle at the chest of a tubby Rebel sergeant and fired. The man screamed, dropped his rifle and clutched his chest.

A thundering Minnesota barrage cracked like a lightning strike, sending sheets of bullets against the blazing enemy line. Colvill glanced left and right. Firing at point-blank range, the Minnesotan's ringing rattle of musketry had killed more than a hundred Confederates with a terrifying broadside of hissing bullets. The enormity of their momentum thrust Colvill and the regiment forward like a cattle stampede. He was flying over the ground with the ferocity of an attacking mountain lion. Colvill leveled his rifle at a Rebel officer with a long plume extending from his hat, stuck his bayonet into the enemy's gut, and lifted his rifle up as though skewering a piece of meat.

The Rebel officer's eyes bulged out and blood poured from his mouth as he writhed in agony.

Colvill pulled out the bayonet dripping with blood and searched for the next Rebel to kill. A demonic rage coursed through his veins. He was fearless, numb to danger and burning with battle fever. Another gray soldier swam into his vision and he lunged forward, stabbing him in the ribs. The man tumbled to the ground, quivering.

The enemy line broke, rushing back through the second Rebel line, halting the whole Alabama advance. Colvill drove forward, stopping in the dry creek bed and reloading his rifle. Through the hellfire smoke, he spied a dark shadow moving down the blazing slope toward the creek bed. He aimed, flicked the trigger, and the bullet exploded from the rifle with a sharp crack, followed by a scream from the cloud of smoke.

Colvill dropped to one knee in the dry ravine, holding his breath, his heart thumping in his throat. He removed his revolver and started firing at the long gray line. The regiment had sliced through the middle of the first Rebel line. At least several dozen Minnesotans had been killed or wounded. But the first enemy line had broken and was collapsing rapidly back through the Rebels' second and third lines.

Colvill's chest tightened, his throat parched. "Run, you devil bastards!" The outnumbered Minnesotans had shocked the Alabamians into a stunning halt.

Under an ashen sky flaring red from the setting sun, the First Minnesota held the ravine against the gray waves breaking around them. The regiment stood in close blue ranks, firing in a quick rhythm, bloodied but unbowed.

Colvill strained his eyes, trying to spot the Minnesotans' right flank, beginning to bend back as hundreds of Rebels swarmed. His men were firing, clubbing, bayoneting, and fighting hand-to-hand. The regimental colors fell, Perkins, shot in the thigh, trying to keep them upright as he tumbled to the ground. Seconds later, the colors defiantly rose again, a private grabbing them and running forward before he was gut-shot. Five times the Minnesota colors were struck, and five times the tattered flag bolted back, shredded by the firing into strings of red, white, and blue.

On his left flank, the Minnesota dead and wounded were sprawled over the dry ditch of Plum Run, forming the edge of the blue dead-line, the imaginary limit where no man advances but to fall. Three or four paces away, a well-defined rivulet of gray corpses marked the enemy dead-line. The soldiers at the edge of the dead-lines merely fired, without aiming and without cover, at the thickest mass in their front. Between the two dead-lines was a clear space of a few yards, for the living were unable to reach it to fall there.

Colvill stood behind the regimental colors as the regiment made its stand. Visibility came in intervals as the smoke ebbed and waned.

"I can't see to direct the fighting," he muttered. He crouched to look under haze. *Shit!* The Rebels were everywhere. The Minnesota color guard turned his head as he was raising his rifle to fire. He yelled, "Colonel, the boys are holding!"

Colvill started to say something but the words caught in his throat. A gleam of light burst on the smoldering slope on his left. A new wave of cracking rifle fire. Another jagged hole in the Union line. Scores of blue-clad Minnesotans were sprawled on the ground. He squinted. Some strove to rise to their feet. Some crept upon their bellies, using their hands, dragging their legs. Some lay dead, contorted like pretzels. Beyond the dead, a blast of yellow fire and puffs of smoke.

A bullet smashed between his shoulders like a sledge hammer, crashing him to the ground.

The hammer hit again, smashing his foot. He looked at his leg, grouted with red, with a plum-size bullet wound. He reached over his shoulder and his hand probed for the wound. He found it as his finger disappeared to its knuckle. Damn. A Minié ball had torn through his right shoulder.

He looked down at his mangled body, his face turning cold.

Captain Henry Coates of Company A knelt over Colvill's prostrate body.

Coates yelled in Colvill's ear, "Colonel, you are badly hurt!"

"Take care of the men, Henry."

Coates touched Colvill's head softly, "I'll be back for you." Coates stood and snaked toward the right.

Another enemy flank attack was rolling up, firing sheets of bullets overhead. Colvill glanced at his wound. White flecks of splintered bone covered his boot. He spotted a shallow gully a few feet wide and deep. He rolled forward, pitching into the small swale.

"Mother of Jesus," he screamed. He buried his face into grass as his breathing became shallow and the cracking rifles and despairing screams faded into the darkness.

## Coates

Coates's concern was the right flank as the Rebels extended their lines farther and farther around the regiment's right like a horseshoe. Heffelfinger's company was holding its own on the left flank. Corporal O'Brien and Company E were pushing the Rebel line back in the middle. A dense smoke curtain draped the right side of the line. *Good. The smoke will cloak my movements.* Shells burst and bullets whizzed. Coates could not spot the enemy. *Well, the Rebels can't see the Minnesotans, either. They don't know precious few Minnesotans remain.*

The sun was low in the west now, casting a long shadow. Coates found Lieutenant Colonel Adams on the ground, nearly unconscious from loss of blood. Coates stopped, bent over to Adams's ear. "How bad is it?"

Adams whispered, "Hit in the chest, hip, and leg."

"Hang on," Coates said. "We will come back and get you."

Coates moved on to the right flank. Lochren's Company K was acting as the far right point of the line. Captain Nathan Messick's Company G had refused his line, bending itself back at a right angle to Lochren's line. The Confederates had massed, enveloping the Minnesota right flank, pummeling the Norsemen with a sweeping point-blank fire. Messick's refused line shattered.

Coates withdrew his revolver and started firing into the gray swarm, the drifting smoke too dense for him to spot whether he had dropped any Rebels. The sun was sinking rapidly behind South Mountain. The First Minnesota had stalled the attacking Alabamians, but the regiment needed reinforcements immediately or the Rebels would sweep them away and race for the unprotected Cemetery Ridge. Coates grimaced. If they could hold until darkness fell, they had a chance.

---

*7:20 p.m.*

Beyond the right line, a tremendous collision of forces erupted with Union boys screaming like banshees. Coates moved to the far edge of the right flank. He shot a glance through the smoke. Holy God. It was Colonel Francis Heath and the Nineteenth Maine boys. They had rushed forward into the killing field, colliding with the Alabamians attacking the First Minnesota's right flank. The Maine boys poured volleys of musket fire into the Rebels. The enemy broke as Coates counted several red battle flags drifting back toward the Emmitsburg Road. The Alabama men on Minnesota's right flank dissolved into small pockets of resistance, some holding their arms up, surrendering. Those not surrendering kept up their deadly fire.

---

## Colvill

Colvill awoke to the whining of metal. His mind was fuzzy, and he was sweating profusely, weak and nauseous, covered from head to toe in his own blood. It was almost dark; it was time to get his boys back. Colvill clenched his jaw, sat upright. He spotted a few men of the regiment nearby, still fighting; the rest lying dead or wounded. No one would leave until ordered to do so, including his officers. He turned to a soldier a few feet away.

Colvill gestured for him to approach. Private Charles Muller of Company A crawled over.

Colvill whispered, "Find the senior ranking officer directing the fight and tell him to withdraw."

Muller saluted and moved off toward the left flank.

---

# Heffelfinger

*7:30 p.m.*
*(Sunset is 7:27 p.m.)*

Heffelfinger knelt in the ravine, firing his revolver. Then, as a cloaked figure approached to his right, he aimed his revolver at the phantom.

Muller shouted, "Don't shoot, Lieutenant. It's me, Private Muller."

As Heffelfinger lowered his pistol, a massive blow blasted his chest, throwing him. His lungs froze as he gasped for a breath. He reached inside his uniform coat, inspecting the wound.

Heffelfinger took a shallow breath. "I'll be damned." He pointed. "Look, Muller. A Minié ball penetrated my uniform and shattered my small wooden pencil. It smashed a leather memo book in my pocket, but it didn't penetrate any further."

"You're damn lucky, Lieutenant," Muller said.

"I'm not bleeding, but my chest feels like it's been hit by a freight train," Heffelfinger said.

"Colonel Colvill ordered me to tell the ranking officer to withdraw," Muller said. "Are you the ranking officer on the field?"

"No. I believe Captain Messick is the senior officer. He's on the far right flank."

Muller found Messick and passed on Colvill's order to withdraw. Messick gave the order and the companies on the far right began to move back.

Heffelfinger gave the order to his company to withdraw. He fretted. Disengaging and withdrawing under fire was a tricky task. Perhaps more dangerous than attacking. As they moved back, the soldiers helped as many of the wounded as they could move. The Rebels were laying down a deadly blanket of fire at the retreating Minnesotans. Heffelfinger spotted a narrow corridor, a space of about forty yards, for the regiment to retreat through. "Follow me," he shouted.

He raced back toward Cemetery Ridge as shells rained a fiery hell from the sky. Bullets zipped past him. He started running in a zigzag to evade the rifle fire. It was up to God if he got hit by exploding shell fragments. Heffelfinger was running near

Private Isaac Taylor of Company E. A terrible whining swirled over their heads. Cracking thunder. Iron fragments and flaming shards hurled through the smoke. The Rebels had lobbed an artillery shell over Taylor that burst above him, raining down knife-like shrapnel. Heffelfinger turned his head. Iron fragments cleaved Taylor nearly in half, pitching his mangled corpse forward, landing on half his face. Taylor's lower jaw was gone. From his upper teeth to his tonsils was a bloody gap of shredded flesh. Heffelfinger fell to his knees, retching as if he had food poisoning. He wiped his mouth with his sleeve, stood, and starting running again, panting like a dog. His blood beat in his ears.

Heffelfinger spotted Thomas's battery about a hundred yards ahead. He stopped to help the wounded, who were crying out. "Don't strand us!" "Don't let the Rebels capture us."

It was now dark.

---

*7:50 p.m.*

Many of the wounded were pulling themselves as best they could on elbows and knees. The surviving soldiers of the First Minnesota, bruised and bloodied, limped back again and again to help bring their brothers to safety under the regimental flag near Thomas's battery on Cemetery Ridge.

Heffelfinger stared at the survivors, covered in dirt, sweat, and blood, shaken by the horrific loss of life. Each glared back with glassy-eyed shock. Their clothes were riddled, looking like rags hanging on scarecrows. He walked up to Messick. "Have you taken a head count?"

"Yes. Twenty-five men."

"Twenty-five Minnesotans are not casualties?" Heffelfinger said. His gut heaved.

"I'll take another count in a moment," Messick said. "Many of the survivors were taking the wounded to the hospital, and some were working with the Nineteenth Maine capturing several hundred Confederates cut off from the retreating Alabama brigade."

Fifteen minutes later, Heffelfinger stood next to Messick as he took another head count.

556

"Forty-seven men. Forty-seven out of 262 came out of the assault without being killed or wounded."

"My God, what a brutal slaughter," Heffelfinger said. "Only forty-seven survivors."

"When the ambulance corps wagons roll out to the battle-field, I will send some of our survivors to assist bringing back our wounded. I hope to God Colonel Colvill is still alive."

Heffelfinger shook his head and stared at the regimental flag, carried back to Thomas's Battery C. He bowed his head, numb, tears running freely down his face. The fear of death was gone; the sorrow of surviving had begun. 215 Minnesotan casualties, many just youngsters.

The Rebels had nearly annihilated the Nordic regiment. But the Minnesotans had plugged the gap in the blue line. Despite their superior numbers, the Confederates had failed to push aside the First Minnesota.

## 37

# Meade — Thursday, July 2

*6:25 p.m.*
*Cemetery Ridge*
*An hour and a half earlier*

Meade sat astride Baldy on a grassy mound at the southern end of Cemetery Ridge, peering through his field glasses over the vast killing fields. Deafening thundering and sharp cracking belted his eardrums. Acrid smoke slithered through the evening air, singeing his nose hairs. He tensed, letting his gaze slide along the long gray lines racing toward Cemetery Ridge, cutting down swathes of blue defenders like a scythe slicing through tall young grasses. Thousands of flashing yellow streaks split the smoldering sky. *My God, Longstreet's corps is shellacking Sickles's boys.*

Meade turned to Biddle. "Ride to the Taneytown Road. Tell me if you see Slocum's reinforcements arriving from Culp's Hill."

Biddle raced off. Meade fretted and swiped at the fly looping around his slouch hat. *Damn it!* If Slocum's corps was not coming, he'd have to order a general retreat of the army.

After a few minutes, clattering hooves approached from behind.

"General Meade," Biddle shouted.

Meade cocked his head, letting his field glasses swing down from the neck strap, thumping his chest. Biddle's horse skidded to a stop. "Did you see any reinforcements coming?" Meade said.

"Yes!" Biddle pointed. "Lockwood's brigade from Twelfth Corps."

Meade craned his neck. He spotted Lockwood, sporting his mutton-chop side whiskers, riding at the head of his brigade. "Damn, that's great news!"

"Behind Lockwood is Williams's division. In total nearly 7,000 strong," Biddle said.

Lockwood was a West Pointer and a good officer. His huge brigade was easy to spot. Untested in battle, their new uniforms shimmered blue as a mountain lake and their bayonets glinted like crystal in the late-afternoon sun.

Biddle pointed again. "That's the First Maryland Potomac regiment in front, flashing nearly seven hundred bayonets, and behind them, marching four abreast, is the 150th New York regiment with another six hundred bayonets."

"Those bayonets are as useless as tits on a boar hog unless we get'em pointing at the attacking Rebels," Meade said.

Galloping hooves interrupted them. Hancock's senior aide, Major Mitchell, rode up, breathing heavily. He saluted, then pointed. "General Meade, General Hancock requests you send reinforcements to General Willard's right flank."

"Tell him I will send Lockwood's brigade," said Meade.

Mitchell saluted, wheeled to the copse of trees, and galloped off as quickly as he had come.

---

*6:30 p.m.*

Meade scanned the gap on the left side of Second Corps. Across the rolling field, he spotted a long gray line stepping off, bayonets fixed, moving toward the gap. "Son of a bitch." He could not delay any longer.

He turned to Biddle and shouted, "I will lead the way into the gap. Tell General Lockwood to have his two regiments follow!"

Meade drew his sword and swung the blade up into the air. His eyes locked with Biddle's, who was staring, mouth agape, plainly wanting to express his disbelief.

"General!" Biddle shouted. "I recommend not charging headlong into the Confederate line with just your escorts."

Meade scowled, his face flushed. "Damn it, James. I don't have time to wait. Now double-time those two regiments here."

Meade brandished his sword and spurred Baldy toward the gap. Cool air rushed past his face, fanning the fire in his eyes. He raced past the Union artillery guns, barrelling straight toward the middle of the advancing gray wave. He glanced back at the extended trail of Lancer escorts and orderlies racing after him. He turned resolutely forward and glared at a distant red battle flag, galloping hard for a hundred yards across an open field, outdistancing his escorts. He pulled back hard on the reins, sliding to a stop. He turned in his saddle; Lockwood's two regiments were still following at double-quick, rushing forward like a rampaging river. Good! Lockwood's regiments would arrive in time, plugging the gap.

Before Meade could charge again, Rush's Lancers arrived in a flying V formation and surrounded the commanding general. A rifle cracked and something plucked his trousers, thudding below his left thigh. Baldy snorted a throaty rumble, chomping at the bit. Meade patted Baldy's neck and the horse quieted. *Damn it. That thudding was a Minié ball hitting flesh. You're hit! No pain… yet. It must be bad—maybe even mortal.*

Meade reached down with his gloved left hand, feeling the hole in his pants leg. He pulled his hand back. Blood covered his white glove. *Devil be damned.* Either he or Baldy was wounded. Still no pain, and Baldy was calm. He reached down with his gloved hand again and blood flowed through his fingers, thick and strong, soaking his pants leg. He probed for a wound in his thigh. No hole and no pain. *Damn it! It must be Baldy.*

Lockwood rode up and saluted. Meade peered at Lockwood, the brigade commander's face turning pale staring at Meade's bloody trousers. "General Meade," Lockwood said, "Are you seriously wounded?"

Meade shook his head. "Baldy was shot by a Minié ball. I'm fine."

"That's a hell of a lot blood," Lockwood said. "Sorry about Old Baldy, but I'm glad you're not wounded. Where do you want me to place my brigade?"

Meade pointed toward the advancing Rebels. "I want you to hold this line as if it were the gates of heaven. Do you understand? The enemy can't be allowed to break through Cemetery Ridge."

"I understand." Lockwood saluted and galloped back to his two regiments, double-timing toward the gap.

<hr />

*6:40 p.m.*

Meade turned and started trotting toward Taneytown Road. Biddle rode up. "Good job in moving Lockwood's Brigade quickly to the gap," Meade said.

"How is Baldy doing?" Biddle pointed to Meade's blood-soaked leg.

"Poor Baldy. Wounded twice at the first battle of Bull Run. Once at the second battle of Bull Run, again at Antietam, once at Fredericksburg, and now at Gettysburg."

"I'll have the army's surgeon look at him when we arrive at headquarters," Biddle said.

Meade arrived at the Leister House, greeted by a groom and an orderly. Biddle told the orderly to find Meade a new horse and take care of Baldy's wound. The orderly walked Old Baldy around the side of the house.

A twinge of guilt came over him. "I sure hope to hell that Baldy forgives me and that his wound isn't mortal," he mused. "I've grown quite attached to that horse."

"I bet he pulls through just fine," Biddle reassured him.

Meade shook his head. Strange thing. He did not think about either George or himself during battles, but he always worried about Baldy.

Captain Bates handed him coffee, staring at Meade's pants leg, concern painted on his face. "General, do you want me to get another pair of pants for you?"

"Hell, no!" Meade glared, his face burning. "What idiot changes his clothes in the middle of a battle? Where is your common sense?"

Bates shook his head, kept his mouth shut, and retreated back into the Leister House.

Senior staff officers were gathering on the porch, waiting for him. Williams and Sharpe greeted him briskly.

"Lee has still not commenced an attack on Culp's Hill," Sharpe said. "And we still don't know where Stuart is."

561

Meade glared at Sharpe. The intelligence officer shrugged. "Damn it to hell," Meade said. "You can't find a cavalry force of 5,000 horsemen?"

"Stuart's force is not involved in the current battle," Sharpe said.

"That remains to be seen," Meade shouted.

Meade stormed into the Leister House, stopping at the map table. Sharpe followed and stood on the other side of the table, pointing out the enemy positions. Meade sipped his coffee, his eyes following Sharpe's index finger darting over the map.

"I still don't know what Stuart is up to," Meade said, "but Lee made a mistake in not attacking Culp's Hill earlier."

Sharpe nodded.

Captain John Tidball, commander of the Second Brigade, Horse Artillery, arrived, saluted. "General Meade, Confederates are preparing to attack Cemetery Ridge through the gap on Gibbon's left flank. I saw First Corps units sitting behind Cemetery Hill in reserve waiting to be called. They are desperately needed to fill the gap."

"Ride to General Newton and tell him to send Robinson and Doubleday's divisions to occupy the gap," Meade shouted.

Tidball saluted and headed for First Corps.

---

*7:00 p.m.*

Meade turned to Sharpe, directing the colonel to ride with him, grabbed his hat, rushed from the house, and mounted a new horse, a large black mare. He darted across the open field, riding toward Gibbon's line with Colonel Sharpe, a few aides, and orderlies in tow. Meade stopped to the left of Gibbon's line, in the gap along the ridge, about a hundred yards south of the copse of trees.

Through his binoculars he spotted a heavy Rebel force along the slope in the Union front, attacking ferociously. Shot and shell filled the air. Thousands of howling Rebels blanketed the battlefield. Smoke billowed upward in the dusking sky. *Will Newton's forces arrive in time?*

He pointed to a large attacking force of gray-clad soldiers surging for the gap. Sharpe rode close to Meade and yelled into the commander's ear. "Those are the Georgians and Floridians from General Wright's brigades."

Meade glanced toward Cemetery Hill. Help should be coming from that direction. But it would still be a disaster unless something slowed the Rebels soon, at least briefly. He must act. For the second time that afternoon, he straightened in his stirrups.

His aides and Rush's cavalry escorts closed ranks behind him, sensing he was going to throw himself into the breach once again. Without warning, Meade spurred the large black mare, lunging toward the Rebel line.

Biddle spurred his horse, riding alongside Meade. He screamed, pointing to his right, "There they come, General! There they come!"

Biddle's distant voice echoed in his ears. Meade reined up. To the right, he spotted Newton galloping in advance of Doubleday's division, followed close behind by Robinson's division. They were marching in close column by division, at a sharp double-quick, with muskets at a right shoulder, bayonets fixed. The two divisions raced southward down the Taneytown Road, swung to the right toward Meade, using him as a forward pivot point, and sprinted across the open field.

Meade beamed at the deft maneuver.

Newton halted next to him. "Sir, request orders."

Meade pointed with a gloved hand. "Plug that gap."

Newton turned to his aide and repeated the order. Then he turned to Meade and pulled out a flask, offered it to Meade. "Sir, I would be honored."

Meade took the flask, breathing in an aged fragrance achieved only after years in an oak barrel. He took a long swig, the bittersweet taste burning his throat.

A shell burst, cratering the ground, showering Meade and Newton with dirt. Meade smiled. "Good thing I put the lid back on," he said, brushing dirt off his blood-stained pants.

He handed back the flask. "Thank you, John." Meade spurred the mare, riding ahead of the skirmish line. Reinvigorated, hope renewed, he yelled to those near him. "Come on, gentlemen!"

*7:15 p.m.*

The Thirteenth Vermont was the lead regiment. Meade pulled out his sword, pointed it toward the Rebels. *"Charge!"*

The Thirteenth Vermont leaped forward, rushing past Meade into the Confederate line, firing a sharp fusillade and recapturing a Union artillery battery. The Georgians halted, apparently stunned by the massive attack by fresh Union soldiers, and scurried back across the Emmitsburg Road. Meade's breathing slowed. The immediate threat to the Union line had passed.

"It seemed desperate just a short time ago," Biddle marveled, wiping his brow.

"Yes," Meade said, "but it is all right for now; it is all right for now."

The Rebels had broken along Cemetery Ridge. *Damn, that was close. Too close.* Meade took a deep breath. The army had resisted Lee today along Cemetery Ridge. Despite Sickles's calamity, Meade had managed to get reinforcements into the fight in time to save the day. Now he had to reinforce Culp's Hill before Lee caught him with his pants down—again. God, what a day.

## 38

# First Minnesota — Thursday, July 2

## *Heffelfinger*

*8:00 p.m.*
*Near Thomas's artillery battery*

First Lieutenant Heffelfinger knelt near Thomas's six bronze Napoleons, glinting under the full moon. The other surviving forty-six Minnesotans were huddled nearby, most sitting or lying on the ground, gulping water from canteens, nursing small wounds, and washing blood from their faces, arms, and hands. He unbuttoned his blue jacket and rubbed his hand on his purpled chest, burning as if scorched by a white-hot iron poker. Strangely, his ribs hadn't hurt right after the Minié ball smashed his pencil and notepad and flung him on his back. Damn it, it sure hurt now. Maybe he had cracked a rib. *Will worry about that after we pick up our wounded.*

Heffelfinger stood and walked over to Captain Messick, a thirty-six-year-old cobbler from Faribault, Minnesota, the acting regimental commander. "Nathan, I want permission to take a detail and retrieve Colonel Colvill and the other wounded from the battlefield."

Messick nodded. "Permission granted. Take Sergeant Henry Taylor. His brother Isaac is missing. And get a few men from each company so they can scout the stops they occupied in Plum Run. Rescue the wounded and leave the dead."

---

*8:05 p.m.*

Heffelfinger nodded. He found Sergeant Taylor and several other men who eagerly volunteered for the assignment. Carrying loaded rifles, they crept out over the same ground that a few hours ago they had hallowed with Minnesota blood. When they arrived at Plum Run ravine, they fanned out. The full moon lit the battlefield, showing the gruesome aftermath of the charge, the Plum Run ravine strewn with the Minnesota dead. The mortally wounded were suffering, waiting alone to draw their last breaths, joining the dead unwitnessed and unattended.

The dreadful stench of death hovered over the creek bed, stinging Heffelfinger's nose. He draped his nose and mouth with a white bandana. The ravine was littered with coats and caps, some blue and some gray, muskets, bayonets and swords, scabbards and belts, some bent and cut by shot and shell. The boys of Minnesota and the boys of Alabama now lay quiet, side by side.

Heffelfinger found Colvill lying motionless, revolver in hand, eyes closed, his chest inching up and down. Heffelfinger shook his shoulder and whispered, "Colonel, it's Lieutenant Heffelfinger. We need to move you to the hospital."

Colvill opened his eyes, trying to focus. He whispered, "Christopher, thank you for coming back."

Heffelfinger gripped underneath Colvill's shoulders and Private Durfee grabbed his legs. Colvill's face contorted with pain, but he made no sound. They carried the giant Minnesotan to Thomas's battery, where Messick had arranged for ambulances to transport the wounded. They loaded Colvill into the ambulance wagon, covered him by a blanket to his shoulders. Messick crawled the two steps into the rear, knelt beside Colvill's head.

---

## Colvill
*8:20 p.m.*
*On the battlefield*

Someone's breath was pulsing against Colvill's ears. He opened his eyes and spotted Messick's face close to his ear.

Messick whispered, "How you doing, Colonel?"

"I'll live, I think," Colvill said. "Did we stop them?"

"Yes. We charged three times into their center, repulsing them each time. We were almost decimated. But Hancock ordered in Colonel Heath and the Nineteenth Maine boys just in time to repulse the attack against our right flank."

"How many men mustered after the fight?

"Forty-seven."

Colvill closed his eyes. "Dear God! Only 47 left with minor injuries out of 262 making the charge." Tears flowed down his cheeks. "Try to recover the boys," he whispered.

"We will," Messick said.

Colvill remembered Private William Bates from Company B fighting alongside him in Plum Run. Bates had groaned and pitched forward to the ground, shot in the chest, blood bursting out all over. A witty boy with a contagious smile. Colvill liked him. "Lieutenant Colonel Adams?" he whispered.

"He was shot in the chest, hip, and leg." Messick rubbed the side of his head. "He is being transported to the hospital."

Colvill nodded. "Take care of the boys for me."

Messick said he would and exited the ambulance. The ambulance took Colvill to the aid station on the Hummelbaugh Farm, a small two-story house, where he was triaged, the surgeons cutting off his uniform coat, shirt, and lower pants leg. They dressed the shoulder and foot wounds, then ordered Colvill be moved to Gibbon's division hospital.

Colvill's mind flickered, obsessing over the Minnesota dead. A picture popped into his head as he studied the two long lines before the charge. They were alive and limber, and he led them in their brilliant blues across the field. Now they were gone. So many boys dead all at once. His lips quivered as the ambulance bounced along. He struggled to breathe.

The First Minnesota had honored its country. The boys had rushed through hellfire toward an overwhelming force, with no hope for any success but to stall the enemy briefly, knowing most would die. For more than twenty minutes they held the Rebels at bay, giving Hancock time to plug the gap. Not a man wavered. History might not remember the First Minnesota, the regiment that willingly sacrificed itself to buy a little time for General Hancock. But Colvill would never forget.

In the dark and sweltering mugginess, he wept.

# Culp's Hill
## Evening, July 2, 1863

Gettysburg

Benner's Hill

Rock Creek

Transverse

Baltimore Pike

## 39

# Greene — Thursday, July 2

Greene straddled his mount, standing a short distance behind the middle of his brigade's defensive line. He plucked out his pocket watch. It was nearly six. Darkness would soon be creeping over the blue brigade, the sun sinking below the distant ridges of South Mountain. His soldiers huddled in the freshly dug trenches, the fortified rifle pits coiling along the heavily wooded crest of Culp's Hill, 180 feet above the enemy lines. He peered along Culp's Hill through his field glasses, locating the Rebels about 400 yards away on the eastern slope, just beyond Rock Creek. He lowered the field glasses onto his chest. Narrowing his eyes, he scanned the Union trenches.

Alert in the blackening shadows, the New York soldiers stood shoulder to shoulder behind brawny breastworks. They kept turning their heads like tracking hounds back toward the rumbling cannons roaring along Cemetery Ridge. An increasing nervousness crept across the brigade. The booming had started at four in the afternoon from the eye of the army's fishhook defense occupied by Sickles's left flank. The throbbing had pulsed slowly along the shank toward Cemetery Ridge and was edging toward the curved barb along Culp's Hill.

Greene peered through his field glasses, scanning Benner's Hill some thousand yards to the northwest, observing enemy cannon fire. A Rebel battery was exchanging fire with Union batteries ringing East Cemetery Hill. Greene exhaled. The Rebel cannoneers were increasing their rate of fire, apparently preparing the way for an infantry assault on Culp's Hill.

Greene shook his head. Big mistake, attacking these fortified breastworks. Johnson's Confederate infantry division of some 4,000 men was facing Slocum's entrenched corps numbering almost 10,000 men. Johnson's boys had been loitering behind Rock Creek all day. Greene was pretty sure the enemy could hear the chopping of trees, the sawing and hammering of logs, and the digging of trenches. The blue boys had worked relentlessly, damming the crest with logged breastworks like beavers on a river. If the Rebels assaulted the steep hill, it would be a Union turkey shoot.

Greene rode up and down the military crest, the brigade idling, resting in breastworks on the lovely high ground. The air was hot and sultry; the coarse fibers of his wool uniform scratched against his neck and thighs. Despite the itching, his tense shoulders started to relax. This was perfect. Slocum's entire Twelfth Corps entrenched behind skillfully constructed log breastworks, with most of the rifle pits constructed under Greene's engineering eye.

The steep slope down toward the enemy was heavily wooded but relatively free of underbrush and littered with boulders the size of haystacks. Beyond the hillside, tree-covered fields fell gently, flowing into Rock Creek. Greene's lips thinned in a moon smile. A night attack against the entrenched positions would be madness: Culp's Hill was a floating fortress in the sky, fortified by an entire corps.

Greene gripped his field glasses and scanned Benner's Hill again. The deadly dance between the artillery batteries seemed to be slowing, the sharp whir of shells from the Union batteries slackening, the Rebel battery having stopped firing altogether. He rode to the center of the brigade's defensive line.

When darkness fell, he would lose sight of the 60th New York, anchoring the left flank of the brigade. But the 60th held the strongest position, on the hill's highest crest. The terrain in front of the 60th was a steep walled hill, and the regiment's left flank was nestled against the dug-in Iron Brigade of Wadsworth's First Corp division. He inhaled sharply. Ireland's 137th regiment anchoring the brigade's far right flank was a concern. The regiment was 400 yards downslope to the south, occupying a connecting saddle of flat ground, positioned near Culp's Hill's second, smaller height. He rode that way, moving along the imposing wooden breastworks, admiring the skilled handiwork.

Greene spotted Ireland, dismounted, holding the reins of his horse on the flat saddle below. Greene halted next to him. They exchanged salutes.

"Based upon the approaching cannon sounds," Greene said, "I think Johnson will soon launch an attack against Culp's Hill."

"We are ready, General," Ireland said.

They stood tight-lipped on the belly of the saddle, the nadir between the upper and lower summits comprising Culp's Hill.

Greene studied the gentle slope beyond the breastworks of Ireland's regiment. How would the enemy assault these positions? Using his mind's eye, he placed himself at the bottom of the hill, crawling upward, probing his way toward the Union breastworks and beyond. A picture was beginning to form, the different possible course of enemy actions and tactics. He narrowed his eyes, squeezing them into slits. The flat saddle was his defensive lines' critical vulnerability. His heartbeat quickened.

"Colonel Ireland, if I were commanding the Rebels down there, I would focus my attack against your position." Greene pointed. "The narrow glen sloping upward through the wooded hills leads directly to your regiment's breastworks. An enemy advance from that direction would have the easiest climb to reach your front."

Ireland nodded. "You're right. The ravine acts like a funnel, channeling an attacking enemy into my regiment."

"Your regiment is sitting at the stem of the funnel," Greene said. "The enemy is going to attempt a breakthrough against you, using brute force. That's what I would do."

"We'll hold, General." Ireland waved his hand as if wiping a table. "Old Farmer Culp must have grazed his cattle on the hill in front of the 137th New York because it is scrubbed clean of undergrowth. The Rebs will have no cover, making for easy pickin's."

"Don't misunderstand," Greene said. "I feel relatively secure about your position, even though it sits in the critical vulnerability of the line. You also have Kane's brigade on your right."

Greene paused and wiped his brow with a handkerchief.

"Beyond Kane's brigade you have Slocum's First Division manning breastworks all the way down to the Baltimore Pike," Greene said. "You have 7,000 defenders protecting your right flank. You just have to hold this narrow point, the weakest link in the defensive lines."

"We will hold," Ireland said.

Greene turned around, pointing behind his New York brigade. "Candy's brigade is the reserve force behind your regiment."

"Good," Ireland said.

There was a momentary silence. Greene scratched his itching arms. Damn wool uniforms. He studied Ireland's face. Ireland's jaw was set as he gazed at the transverse breastworks. He was holding the brigade's critical right flank. The Scotsman was a superb officer, commanding a hard-fighting regiment. Greene mounted and rode up the hill toward the Sixtieth New York. A quiet confidence calmed his muscles; preparedness soothed his bones. He occupied a well-defended high ground. Fredericksburg in reverse. *We are ready.* God, he hoped the Rebels attacked soon.

---

## Ireland

*5:50 p.m.*

Ireland found Lieutenant Samuel Wheelock, his stocky, muscular adjutant, and summarized Greene's concerns. When he finished, Wheelock saluted and moved toward Company K, holding the line next to the 149th New York, filling in each company commander about Ireland's discussion with Greene.

Ireland spied Captain Frederick Stoddard, the Company A commander, and joined him. Ireland smiled, spotting many old-timers manning the breastworks. The young-looking, twenty-seven-year-old Stoddard commanded one of the regiment's four large companies, recruited along the back upriver of the Susquehanna in Broome County. Although the regiment had its fair share of boys between sixteen and eighteen, many of the men in Company A and the 137th New York were forty and fifty years old, making it one of the oldest in Greene's brigade.

The joke within Ireland's regiment was that General Greene, the oldest general in the army, favored the 137th New York because they made him feel young. Ireland liked them for a different reason—they were too old and ornery to run from a fight.

"Is Company A ready for the big attack?" Ireland said.

"We're ready," Stoddard said. "The breastworks are strong. But I'm not pleased we're sitting in this swale."

"I agree," Ireland said. "General Greene is worried that the easiest path up the hill is right through your front." Ireland's gut clenched. "The Rebels will most likely converge toward this saddle against our regiment."

Ireland glanced back over his shoulder at Cemetery Hill. In the distance a spattering of rifle volleys cracked over Culp's Hill. It was answered with several single shots, followed by a long silence. Just skirmishers harassing each other, probing for gaps in the forward lines. The attack would come soon, but it would not last long. The Rebels disliked fighting at night, and Slocum's corps was dug in, deeply.

"Freddie, walk with me," Ireland said. They walked toward the unoccupied transverse line jutting out ninety degrees from the main line. Arriving, they turned and walked behind the empty transverse breastwork, a makeshift, three-foot-high stone and wood wall.

"Greene's transverse wall is making a lot more sense now," Ireland said. "It's not as rugged as the main-line breastworks, but should serve the purpose if needed."

"The transverse line will hold one company," Stoddard said.

"If the enemy breaks through the saddle and threatens to attack the rear of the regiment, I'm going to order Company A to fall back and occupy the line," Ireland said.

Ireland pointed, scanning the main breastwork line and the transverse line. "How would you move your soldiers into the transverse while under enemy fire?"

"I'd probably pivot the company about a fixed point, like a gate swinging open," Stoddard said.

"Yes, that's good—the same way I'd do it," Ireland said. "Stay sharp. They'll be coming up this way if they attack and break through."

Ireland walked the regimental line. Stoddard was a top-notch officer. He would stubbornly defend the right flank of the regiment. A sharp hiss whickered overhead. Ireland ducked instinctively. After a moment, he popped up his head with a feral chuckle. The Rebels were reminding him they were lying in wait, ready to strike like a pit viper.

Ireland stopped behind Captain Gregg's Company I. The men of Company I were standing behind the breastworks, shoulder to shoulder, staring down the dark slope, rifles resting on the top logs. Some men had laid out extra rounds of ammunition in the nooks and crannies of the breastworks. Ireland spotted a tall, burly man, built like a big brown bear, with a V-shaped reddish beard, standing in the trenches, peering down the hill.

"Captain Gregg, your company looks sharp and ready," Ireland said.

"We're ready," Gregg said. He leaped out of the trench and saluted. "The men are stacked against each other as tight as I can get them. When the Rebels attack they will be facing a wall of fire."

Ireland nodded, eyeing the fearless look in Gregg's face, plainly itching for the enemy attack. George loved a good brawl, and the captain would surely get one soon.

Ireland checked with the other company commanders. Everything seemed to be in order. The 137th New York was ready. A cavalcade of pounding hooves clattered from behind. Ireland turned, spotting the Twelfth Corps flag and General Slocum, galloping toward General Greene a few hundred yards up the crest, sitting behind the 60th New York on the far left flank of the brigade.

## Greene

*5:52 p.m.*
*Culp's Hill*

Captain Charles Piltortan pointed. "General Greene. Look. It's General Slocum's flag."

Greene turned toward where his staff officer was pointing. "It's Slocum. I wonder what he wants?"

Slocum appeared agitated. Greene's gut clenched. Battle-thunder from Sickles's front grew closer. Whatever the news was, it probably wasn't good. A lump rose in his throat. He pulled out his pocket watch. It was 5:52.

Greene saluted. "Good evening, sir."

Slocum returned the salute, his dark eyes boring into Greene. "Good evening, George." Slocum cracked a half-smile in the way generals do when they're masking nervousness. "My compliments on the breastworks. I've never seen any finer. You've built a castle, which you may need if the Rebels attack."

Greene nodded, his gaze sharpening on Slocum's face. Something was up. Greene's heart raced, flopping about in his tightened chest. Slocum's entire corps was sitting behind impenetrable defenses on a steep, rocky hill facing one Rebel division. What could be the problem?

Slocum continued, hunching forward, his eyes darting, cloudy glass, like someone had just whipped him. "Meade is having a hell of time plugging the holes created by Sickles. Sickles's corps broke, and the survivors are falling back to the ridgeline. Meade has ordered me to send the entire Twelfth Corps to reinforce the left flank, but I convinced him to leave one brigade behind to guard Culp's Hill." Slocum paused. "That's going to be you, George. You are my best brigade commander."

Greene shuddered. His gut churned on the sharp edges of Slocum's stare. Slocum couldn't be serious.

"What?" Greene shouted. *My God, this is idiocy.* His pulse rate climbed as he hissed out a breath.

"George, after I pull out the corps, I want you to spread out your brigade and occupy as much of Kane's breastworks as you can."

Greene pursed his lips, bristling as if Slocum were a rodent that needed slaying. His eyes burned and sharp rage erupted. He clenched his fist and grumbled loud enough for everyone around to hear. "Ripping an entire corps away from entrenched defenses is absurd, sir."

Slocum remained silent, his eyes narrowing.

A moment of deadly clarity dawned. "General Slocum, sir. Johnson is sitting across from me with an entire infantry division. He has three times more infantry than I do, and he is commanding the Stonewall Division. Those boys can fight."

Slocum's face remained frozen like a marble statue.

Greene said, "Johnson can exploit any success he has in penetrating our lines with Early's division, which is sitting next to him facing East Cemetery Hill. And Early's infantry division is nearly 6,000 men. This move is dangerous."

Slocum raised his hand. "Good luck, George. We will return as soon as we can." He rode off, his cavalcade in trail.

Rage erupted inside Greene's chest, blocking his breathing. This was insanity. Why would Meade strip his right flank with the enemy poised to attack?

Greene screamed at Piltortan. "What use are the rifle pits if there are no damn soldiers to man them? Call in the regimental commanders. Hurry!"

Piltortan saluted and moved off.

Greene's insides curdled. Twelfth Corps men from Kane's brigade started pouring out of the trenches and dashing off like rats abandoning a sinking ship. A dark void consumed his soul, swallowing his hopes for enjoying an imminent attack.

A few moments earlier, his brigade had been part of Slocum's massive Twelfth Corps. In that state of connectedness, his brigade was indestructible. Now, they stood alone like prisoners before a firing squad, victims of Sickles's blunder. His isolated brigade protecting the far right flank of the army was outnumbered five to one by a fierce enemy waiting to attack. *Son of a bitch.*

A barrage of cannons started blasting in the direction of Cemetery Hill. The final blue wave of thousands of soldiers skedaddled out of the Culp's Hill trenches and sprinted toward the back side of Cemetery Hill.

Piltortan returned with the regimental commanders. Greene pointed to General Kane's empty trenches. "Slocum ordered us to defend the right flank of the army." He paused, his eyes glancing across the faces of his five regimental commanders. "Damn it, we are going to do it. Slocum said you are the best brigade in Twelfth Corps. That's true, but understated. You're also the best brigade in the army."

The regimental commanders stared, their eyes widened. It appeared the shock of the news had knocked every wisp of air from their deflated lungs.

"Here is what we are going to do," Greene said. He gripped Ireland's upper arm. "Colonel Ireland will move the 137th regiment down the defensive line, stretching out, occupying as much of Kane's brigade position as possible. Once Ireland's regiment is in place, I want the 149th to move down, then the 102nd, and then the 60th will spread out. I want the 78th regiment to move forward beyond the breastworks as skirmishers. Any questions?"

Goddard, commanding the Sixtieth regiment, piped up. "What about reinforcements? Can we expect any if attacked?"

"I will ask Wadsworth and Howard for reinforcements," Greene said. "One more thing. Keep all the colors concealed behind the breastworks."

"Both the national and regimental colors?" asked Lieutenant Colonel Charles Randall, commanding the 149th New York.

"Yes, I want both colors hidden behind the lines," Greene said. "I don't want the enemy to see how few regiments they are attacking." He paused. "Any questions?" Silence. "Let's move. And damn it, tell the men to keep their heads down."

Greene turned to Ireland. "Colonel Ireland, just a minute."

The others dispersed. Ireland stopped, took a step back toward Greene.

"David, you have the toughest assignment." Green said. "Our left will be the strongest defense because it sits on the crest of a steep rocky slope. But your defensive line has a much smaller elevation, making it harder to defend. If I were Johnson, I would focus my attack efforts against First Division's unoccupied breastworks on your right. Once Johnson realizes those breastworks are empty, he will flood them with all available men and try to overrun your position."

Ireland shook his head. "Damn."

"If the Rebels flank you or start to overwhelm your front, don't hesitate to fall back behind the ninety-degree transverse on your right. It's your safety net." Greene stiffened, staring at Ireland. The Scotsman seemed rattled. His breathing rasped and sweat dropped from his brow. "David, you are our last defense. If the enemy sweeps past you, they will be able to take Culp's Hill. You have to ensure that doesn't happen."

Ireland puffed out his chest and wiped his face. "We will hold to the last man, sir."

Greene nodded. Ireland would do exactly that. Greene remounted. "I will provide you with reinforcements as soon as they arrive." He trotted off toward the top crest of Culp's Hill, his heart stuttering.

Greene stopped at Redington's Seventy-eighth Regiment, occupying the middle of the brigade's defensive line. All but 30 men had sprung over the breastworks, forming into a 170-man skirmish line covering the front of the brigade's stretched front. When Redington shouted the order, the blue-clad skirmishers began trudging down the slope, disappearing from sight in a few minutes, hidden by the thick black woods.

---

## Ireland

*6:10 p.m.*

Ireland arrived back at his regiment, where his company commanders waited. They were gathered at the far end of the brigade line, standing in the flat saddle between the two large knolls of Culp's Hill. Ireland gestured toward the vacated breastworks. His skin prickled.

Stoddard said, "Where in the hell is the rest of Twelfth Corps? We've been abandoned, and the Rebels are getting ready to attack."

"Meade ordered Slocum's corps to move to the Union left flank to shore up the defenses behind Sickles's corps," Ireland said. "Slocum convinced Meade to leave one brigade behind to defend Culp's Hill. Slocum chose Greene's brigade."

"Son of a bitch," Stoddard shouted.

Ireland gritted his teeth, letting the news sink into his commanders.

The company commanders shook their heads, disbelief covering their faces. Ireland strode a few steps forward toward the breastworks. The sharp cracking of rifle fire erupted beyond the base of the hill where the Seventy-eighth New York skirmishers were pushing forward.

Stoddard said, "Colonel Ireland, we are grossly outnumbered and outgunned. How can a brigade hold off an entire enemy division, especially Stonewall Jackson's former division?"

"This is turning into quite a nutcracker," Ireland said. "But we are going to hold out to the last man. Slocum promised to return as soon as things started heating up over here."

Ireland pointed to the breastworks on the right of the regiment. "This is where Kane's brigade had thrown breastworks forward at a right angle to conform to the crest of the hill. I want the regiment to move down into Kane's breastworks."

Stoddard said, "We don't have enough men to occupy all of Kane's trenches."

"Spread out as far as you can, with at least the space of one man between you," Ireland said. "Captain Stoddard's Company A will move first, followed by the rest of the companies. After the 137th New York moves down as far as possible into Kane's breastworks, the 149th New York will move into our current position. Does everyone understand?"

The company commanders nodded.

"The 137th is now the extreme right of the Union line," Ireland said. "Company A is the far right company of the regiment. We must hold the line at all cost."

Ireland paused, looking each commander in the eye. "I expect the Rebels will focus the attack against our far right flank. If we can't hold, I want you to fall back on the transverse."

Ireland turned and pointed toward the trench built at a right angle at the intersection of Greene's and Kane's brigades, running across the swale between the upper and lower summits.

"I'm not sure we can get more than one or two companies behind the transverse," Ireland said. "Those who cannot get in line behind the trench's logs and rocks, fall in behind, acting as a reserve force. Follow me."

Ireland walked the length of the transverse as the company commanders followed. At the end of the line, Ireland stopped.

"We may have to execute that maneuver under fire. I've discussed with Captain Stoddard how I want Company A to execute. But if and when we do move back to the transverse breastwork, we will hold to the last man. If the enemy overruns the transverse line, they will have flanked our regiment and our army. Do you understand the importance of our position?"

The company commanders said in near unison, "Yes, sir!"

"Are there any questions?" Ireland asked.

The men shook their heads, remaining silent as if witnessing a funeral. Ireland gave the order to move into Kane's breastworks, and the commanders departed and moved the companies at a double-quick, stretching out down the slope of the hill. After the regiment spread as far as it could, the troops placed their rifles through the firing slits.

Ireland drifted to the center of the new breastwork position. The blue skirmishing fire at the bottom of the hill had trailed off to a spattering of cracking rifles. A quiet pall had descended over the trenches. Ireland dismounted, walked to the end of the line, the far right flank of the Union army. To the right of Stoddard's Company A, there was nothing but darkness and empty breastworks resembling medieval catacombs. Standing there was Sergeant Charles Fox, chewing on a small stick.

Ireland cracked a smile. He had guessed Fox would station himself as the last man in the line. The round-headed, square-shouldered Fox feared no one. A long, livid scar cut across his cheek and neck, marking the slicing stroke of a bayonet. Fox was comfortable flirting with the Devil, believing he would enjoy Hell, seeing all the Rebels he had put there.

Ireland adjusted the clasp of his sword-belt, touching the top of his holstered pistol. "Sergeant Fox. How are you doing?"

Fox blinked and scratched the side of his head. "I'm ready to send some more Rebels to meet their Maker."

"You're going to get your chance to play the Grim Reaper soon," Ireland said, careful not to let his voice rattle.

"From the front," Fox said, "the breastworks are impenetrable. But from the end, the Rebs could easily scamper in and move within the trenches up to our position." Wide-eyed, he took a deep breath and muttered a curse under his breath. "That wouldn't be good! Once the enemy gains access to the breastworks, we'd have a devil of a time."

Fox was right, but there was nothing more he could do. Ireland said, "Sergeant Fox, I can think of no other soldier I would rather have anchoring our flank. Greene has requested reinforcements from First and Eleventh Corps. As soon as they arrive, I will send them your way."

"Thank you, sir." Fox saluted.

Ireland moved off toward the middle of the regiment's line. A cold chill crawled through his chest. His big New York boys were tough, but they were dreadfully outnumbered. He shouted, "Aim low, boys, aim low. And keep your heads below the top of the breastworks."

Ireland sat on his horse, trying to pick up any sounds of enemy movements. It was dark in the thick woods, but his skin crawled.

⟶⟵ ∗ ⟶⟵

*7:40 p.m. (twilight)*
*(Sunset is 7:27)*

A wave of yellow flashes flickered in the woods below, then cracking musket fire.

Ireland shouted. "It's Greene's skirmishers." His heart started racing. The skirmishers were fighting valiantly, springing slowly backward from tree to tree, beginning to develop a rhythm of firing, retreating, covering, loading, and firing again. "Hold your fire until our boys get behind the trenches!"

His eyes strained, trying to pick out the blue phantoms as they retreated back up the hill. The air echoed with haunting Rebel yelping and howling. The blue soldiers stood in the trenches, waiting, trigger fingers twitching, as their skirmishers tumbled back toward the rifle pits.

"Hold your fire," Ireland shouted.

As the cracking noise approached, the soldiers gripped their rifles tighter. Ireland's heart leaped. *Don't shoot our skirmishers!* Before he could yell out, thin yellow ribbons shot out from the rifle pits and screams cracked the air. Bullets ripped through the chests of three New York skirmishers, corpses before they hit the ground, swallowed up by darkness.

Ireland's eyes widened. He sprang forward. "Don't shoot, damn it! Don't shoot!"

The firing from the rifle pits halted as other regimental commanders joined Ireland in shouting to cease firing. Ireland jumped down to the back edge of the breastworks. He spied several rifles tracking the blue skirmishers as if they were hunting deer.

He shouted, "Don't shoot until the skirmishers are back." He glanced down the dark hill. It was impossible to distinguish friend from foe coming toward them.

The retreating skirmishers stopped and knelt, screaming out, beseeching the breastworks defenders not to shoot. My God, they were caught between charging Rebels and panicky Union soldiers.

Ireland glanced around the rifle pits. Faces stared back grimly, hands clutching rifles. The regiment desperately wanted to fire. Ireland swore. "Damn it. Hold fire until the skirmishers are safely behind us."

From the dark shadows across Rock Creek, the Rebel Yell wailed. Masses of silhouettes bounded toward them like phantoms, hundreds of men in butternut uniforms.

Ireland shouted, "Hold your fire. Hold your fire."

For a breathless moment, the blue soldiers held fire, waiting for their skirmishers to scramble the final few yards. The final sprint was harrowing, the skirmishers barely pulling away from the Rebels, sweating, gasping, and baying like a pack of wolves. They arrived, leaping, tumbling, and flying head first through the air over the breastworks, thudding to the ground.

Ireland mounted his horse. His fingers fidgeted as he glared at the last man to dive over the rifle pit. Behind them the Rebel skirmishers advanced like a moving wall, stopping some fifteen yards away. They crouched, aimed, and fired at Ireland's regiment. Night momentarily became day, the enemy bullets thunking into the wooden breastworks like frozen rain slapping at a paned window. Ireland scanned the sweaty faces of the enemy, streaked with black gunpowder, looking like Indians wearing war paint.

Hellfire blasted from the breastworks near the top of Culp's Hill, probably the Sixtieth New York engaging the enemy. Ireland's men waited for the order to fire, sweat dripping down their faces. The Rebels had closed to only a few yards from the breastworks.

Ireland screamed, "Fire!"

The 137th unleashed a deathly volley, hundreds of rifles bursting forth yellow flames, leaping from the Union rifle barrels toward the enemy. The cracking thunder blasted his eardrums. The Minié balls ripped through the Rebels like a butcher cleaving pieces of meat.

Night again became day. The Confederate line fractured and halted. The air erupted with the metallic ringing of firing caps and the bursting of bullets. To the right and left of Ireland, musketry rattled. Smoke billowed up the steep slope and along the fortified crest, reducing visibility. The 137th had created a death arc, sweeping away the enemy wall. The whisper of aimed enemy bullets zipped by Ireland's head. He slouched in the saddle, trying to reduce his target angle.

Screams of wailing souls boiled from the front of the trenches. The 137th had aimed low, hitting most of the enemy in the legs, groin, and gut. The stunned Confederates faltered, staggered back a few yards, seeking cover behind large rocks and trees. They left the wounded where they fell. It appeared the Rebels had no idea they were attacking a fortified position.

Ireland wiped a hand across his face, swiping away the stinging sweat. The Rebels had not turned his army's right flank.

## Greene

*8:00 p.m.*

Greene sat on his horse behind the Sixtieth New York line. His eyes strained down the slope, scanning for enemy movement. The Rebels seemed to be backing off, but he knew a second attack was coming. There was not much time. The first volleys had staggered the Rebels, but Johnson's division still outnumbered him four to one. The brigade was spread too thin along the trenches to achieve the firepower required to halt three Rebel brigades.

Greene turned to his aide, Captain Charles Horton. "Tell the regimental commanders to hold this position at all cost. *All* cost, damn it. And tell them reinforcements are on the way."

"I understand." Horton said. He moved off toward Ireland's regiment.

## Ireland

*8:15 p.m.*

Ireland slumped on his horse, resting one hand on the pommel, the other holding his field glasses against his eyes. He peered at the field of fire. Minié balls zipped around him like buzzing wasps. A bullet's hot breath kissed his cheek. Before his hand could leave the pommel to probe his face, a sharp burning sliced across his left thigh. He glanced down at his trousers, a gaping hole and shredded cloth where a Minié ball had nicked him. He reached down to his thigh with his gloved hand, fingers finding a small hole. He pulled his hand out. Blood dripped from his glove.

Ireland tensed. Damn it…hopefully only a surface scrape. He crouched down lower on his mount's neck, seeking to reduce his target size even further. Edging toward the trenches, the New York sergeants screamed, "Reload!"

Ireland sat upright and looked into the trenches. Bright flashes and a storm of lead whooshed over his head. Ireland leaped off his horse and moved forward, kneeling just behind the breastworks. *Holy crap.* He might as well have a bulls-eye on his chest, sitting on his horse, giving the enemy a clean field of fire. Ireland turned to his adjutant, Lieutenant Wheelock.

"Sam, take my horse behind the 149th New York and tether it well behind the breastworks. And then hustle back down here."

Ireland handed Wheelock the reins, and Wheelock sprang up the hill with Ireland's horse in tow.

Captain Horton stopped beside Ireland and dismounted. Horton's eyes were wide. "Colonel Ireland. General Greene sends his respects and wishes to remind you to hold your position. He also says that reinforcements are on their way."

"God damn it," Ireland said. "I understand. We will hold."

"Fire!" a New Yorker yelled.

The trench line blasted a rain of bullets into the smoke-filled darkness. The lead storm was followed with the shrieks of the wounded and dying. The number of Rebel casualties was jarring. The enemy recoiled back down the hill. There was a pause in the firing as the regiment reloaded, waiting for the next assault.

Ireland drifted toward the center of the regiment's breastworks, behind Captain Joseph Gregg's Company I. The acrid odor of battle blanketing the breastworks singed his nostrils. The soldiers stood silently by one another, arm's length between, anticipating the next attack wave starting to form. Ireland prayed it would be a while before they charged again. Coordinating a night assault up a steep slope against an entrenched enemy was difficult.

Ireland's jaw clenched. West Point's vision of the grand infantry charge against entrenched troops was madness. Clapping hooves rippled down the hill. Greene halted.

"How is it going?" Greene shouted.

"We held off the first attack. It was an all-out charge," Ireland shouted.

"How's your ammunition?"

"We still have about forty rounds per man."

"I've ordered more ammunition brought to you," Greene said. "First Corps and Eleventh Corps are sending reinforcements from Cemetery Hill."

"We need them," Ireland said.

"Again, don't hesitate to use the transverse, drawing back your right flank," Greene said. "But once there, you must hold."

"We will hold. General, I must tell you, without the breastworks our line would have been swept away by the first swarm."

Greene nodded and extended his hand. Ireland gripped the hand and Greene shook it heartedly.

"Good luck, David," Greene said. "I'm depending on you, my fighting Scotsman. If anyone can hold them, you can."

Ireland basked in the rare moment of his senior officer's praise and confidence.

"I won't you let you down, sir," he said.

Greene nodded and turned his mount back up the hill.

Ireland glanced at the dark slope beyond the breastworks: nothing but emptiness peppered by the cries of the enemy wounded. Down the line toward the far right flank, he spotted the men at the end of the enemy line wedging closer together, creeping up the trench toward the crest and Sergeant Fox. He shook his head and wished Fox well.

---

*8:45 p.m.*

Ireland turned and spotted the advancing Confederates, coming again, three lines deep. More Rebels in this attack. Strangely, neither side was employing artillery, possibly because the slope was too steep. Bullets zipped thick and fast, crashing into the breastworks and flying overhead. Ireland crouched behind the trenches. He strained his eyes, looking for a clearer view of the assault.

"Here they come," Ireland shouted.

Rebels rushed forward, red battle flags floating above them, screaming the bloodcurdling Rebel Yell. His pulse quickened, banging in his ears, his skin hairs stood on end, and every muscle tensed. He held his breath. A multitude of dim phantoms started taking shape as they swarmed the slope. The enemy line of battle was forty yards away. The first Rebel line clambered toward the breastworks, slipping and sliding over large boulders and around thick trees.

The sharp metallic snap of cocking rifles echoed over the breastworks. Someone screamed from the trenches to take cover. Ireland dropped to the ground as the night exploded with a zig-zag line of fire toward the breastworks. And then the roar of rifles blasted from the trenches, swapping fire with the enemy. In this terrifying tempest of iron, the enemy struggled forward foot by foot, stepping over the dead and wounded, firing, kneeling, reloading, firing, and at last falling. The Confederates were pressing the line of breastworks relentlessly, but the regiment was holding, firing aimed volley after volley. With the machine-like precision of a Swiss watch, the New Yorkers poured a storm of lead into the advancing Rebels. The enemy returned aimed fire, hitting Ireland's New Yorkers.

In this dreadful moment, the New Yorkers were somehow winning the deadly battle. The killing field in front of the breastworks was filled with broken and twisted bodies. Ireland shuddered at the slaughter. What crazy Virginian kept ordering assaults against the breastworks?

Ireland turned his head and spotted Lieutenant Wheelock, crawling cat-like toward him. "We've learned from a couple wounded Rebels that Greene's brigade is facing Johnson's division, a Rebel force three times larger. Two of Johnson's brigades, Jones and Nicholl's brigades, are attacking Greene's center and far left. The third brigade is led by General George Steuart, who is attacking the 137th New York."

"Where is the Stonewall brigade?" Ireland said.

"We believe it's being held in reserve to exploit any success," Wheelock said.

"So our 400-man regiment is facing Steuart's brigade of six regiments numbering roughly two thousand veteran fighters?" Ireland said.

"That's about right," Wheelock said.

Ireland peered over the battlefield, the full moon just beginning to rise over Wolf's Hill.

"But we got the best of them in the first attack," Wheelock said. "A marksman from Company C, Corporal Stanton, is picking off a Rebel every time he fires. He has two other soldiers loading for him, and every time a Rebel fires from a belly position, Stanton returns fire, aiming at the enemy muzzle flash. So far Stanton counts he has shot thirteen Rebels."

Ireland nodded. He hoped the Rebels would call off the senseless assaults. A courier from Captain Stoddard arrived, saying breathlessly, "The Rebel left wing has crossed Rock Creek and is advancing up the south slope of the lower summit! They have discovered the vacant breastworks and are moving into them below our position."

*9:05 p.m.*

Ireland drew his eyes away from the Rebels trying to claw their way up the slope, and glanced toward the end of the trenches. Flashes of enemy fire were working their way around the far right flank. His stomach lurched. *Damn it!* The Rebels had entered Kane's empty breastworks beyond Ireland's line, enabling them to flow into the trenches. They were surging toward the summit like logs flowing in a water flume, driving the New Yorkers back onto themselves. Ireland's companies on the far right flank were streaming away from the Rebels. The Union trench system had been breached.

Ireland started to move toward the breach, stopping at the crack of musket fire to his left. A new wave of Confederate fire was pouring into the regiment's left flank. The fire was being returned by the New Yorkers from the center of the regiment's breastworks. The Rebels had not penetrated the trenches in the middle and far left flanks, but they were a few yards from the breastworks.

The enemy soldiers started firing behind hastily constructed breastworks built by stacking their dead. With each merciless Federal volley, waves of fire ripped into the stacked corpses. Ireland swallowed hard and his legs trembled as if he had sprinted a long way. The bloody battle was turning into a nauseating medieval ugliness.

Ireland moved toward the fractured right flank. Red battle flags bobbed from the trenches toward the 137th New York. Musketry cracked in spurts. Bullets zipped past him. He crouched into a duck walk.

*My God, we can't hold the Rebels. Have to bend the regimental line back into the transverse.*

He turned to Wheelock. "Tell General Greene the enemy has breached the breastworks below our lines. They are moving rapidly toward the 137th. I'm ordering Company A to refuse the line and bend it back parallel and in front of the transverse line."

Wheelock saluted, moving quickly on foot up the hill toward Greene's position.

Ireland stood and yelled, "Captain Stoddard. Refuse Company A's line! Bend back parallel to the transverse!"

## Stoddard

Stoddard shouted out the order, also yelling to keep firing. Led by Fox and Stoddard, Company A pivoted about the man on the far left of the company like a swinging gate. As they did so, they fired, checking the advancing enemy.

Stoddard pointed to a rock on the ground and yelled to Fox, "Hold this spot!"

Fox moved toward the boulder. Bullets were flying thick and fast. Company A swapped shots with the enemy, each volley from the combatants tearing through flesh. Wounded soldiers screeched and howled.

Fox screamed and pitched to the ground. Stoddard found the shattered sergeant on the ground, clutching his chest, blood spurting out thick and strong with each beat of Fox's heart. Stoddard placed his gloved hand on the ugly wound. It was mortal.

Fox grabbed the front of Stoddard's jacket and whispered, "Tell my parents I died doing my duty." He closed his eyes and fell still.

Stoddard's shivering hands laid Fox's head gently on the ground. His bottom lip quivered as he slid back toward the center of the line.

His company was formed at a right angle with the breastworks, holding a line across the saddle between upper and lower Culp's Hill. Stoddard turned around. They were still several yards in front of the transverse wall.

---

## Ireland

*9:15 p.m.*

Ireland hopped down to the transverse wall, spotting three Rebel regiments moving up the saddle, blasting Stoddard's company. He turned and scrambled toward the breastworks. He picked out Captain Henry Shipman, commanding Company F, holding his revolver, firing down the slope. Ireland moved behind, tapping him on the shoulder. Shipman whirled around, jamming his pistol into Ireland's chest.

"Henry. It's me!" Ireland said.

"Colonel, you startled me!" Shipman said.

"Apologies." Ireland pointed. "I want Company F to move out of the breastworks and to fall in beside Stoddard's Company A, extending his line across the saddle."

"Yes, sir! I understand." Shipman started shouting orders to Company F.

Ireland gripped his revolver. Shipman's company leaped out of the trenches and sprang alongside Stoddard's. Ireland blinked. Now he had two companies of some seventy men manning the bent right line, facing an attacking force of more than four hundred Rebels. It was pitch dark.

"Colonel Ireland. Colonel Ireland, it's Captain Horton," shouted Greene's adjutant.

"Here I am," shouted Ireland. He fell back a few paces behind the transverse.

"I'm bringing up the California Regiment led by Colonel Smith," Horton reported. "They are the first reinforcements to arrive from Second Corps."

"Good!" Ireland pointed. "Place them in the position just vacated by Company F in the rifle pits."

As the California Regiment took its place, the New Yorkers let out a cheer. Ireland muttered, "Thank you, General Greene."

The second Rebel assault against the breastworks had stopped. A pause loomed over the battlefield. Smith sent some skirmishers down the dark slope. Enemy fire erupted. The Californians rushed back up the hill and jumped into the breastworks.

Suddenly, Smith bellowed, "Abandon the breastworks!"

The California Regiment leaped out of the breastworks, retreating off Culp's Hill.

*What the hell?* Ireland rushed over to Smith.

"Sir, why are you retreating?" Ireland shouted.

"I will not have my men murdered," Smith replied. "I was told to report to a general. There are no generals here to report to. I'm marching my men back to Second Corps. I wish you luck." Smith spurred his horse away from the breastworks, leading the California Regiment out of harm's way.

Ireland stared. His heart stopped and his stomach lurched. *Son of a bitch.*

Horton rode up. "What is going on?"

Ireland said, "Colonel Smith did not expect to be engaged with the enemy. The damn coward claimed he could not find a general to report to so he ordered his regiment to retire."

"This is madness!" Horton fumed. "I will have General Greene deal with Colonel Smith later."

A new wave of howling. The Confederates had formed up and were charging again toward Company A, kneeling in front of the transverse. The enemy halted, fired a sheet of fire into the 137th, blasting the crest.

Ireland pushed Smith's treachery to the back of his mind. The Rebels were racing up the swale. The enemy seemed to sense that with one great effort, they could flank the Union defenders.

"Damn it, where is Wheeler?" Ireland shouted.

Bullets hummed past Ireland's head, ricocheting off the rocks on the upper hill. A sure sign the Rebels had shifted the direction of their attack to the abandoned breastworks. Ireland turned to his adjutant, crouched a few yards away, picking up his hat, plucked off with a Minié ball.

Ireland said, "Tell Captain Stoddard and Company A to fall back beyond the transverse breastwork immediately. Hurry!"

Wheeler raced down the slope. Ireland followed, heading toward the center of the transverse, the roar of musketry down the swale growing stronger. There was a mounting force behind this charge, gray masses of men moving forward unevenly. Ireland peered into the darkness. The Rebels were near the transverse, scurrying parallel to it, extending their lines toward the end of the transverse breastworks trying to bend around Ireland's far right flank. If successful, they would flood the empty ground behind Greene's brigade all the way to the top of the higher summit of Culp's Hill. They must be stopped.

Ireland swore. Stoddard's exposed company was scurrying back up the hill, falling in behind the transverse breastwork where Ireland stood. The men knelt, aimed their rifles, and began firing, delivering a wicked barrage. A thunderous cracking flooded the field, the blast mixed with screams of death and pain. The Rebels floundered, the broken bodies of the dead tumbling to the ground, the survivors wavering, staggering backward.

"Keep firing," Ireland shouted.

Ireland's boys reloaded rapidly, firing another point-blank broadside. More enemy screeching and yelling as the well-aimed New York shots thudded into the Rebels. Ireland knelt on one knee, firing his revolver. It was as though Ireland's boys had set fire to the night; smoke billowed from the transverse, obscuring the battlefield. The Rebels turned backward through the smoke, melting into the darkness.

For a few moments it was calm. Ireland reloaded his gun and thanked God for Greene's transverse breastwork. He was pretty pissed about building it that morning, but how could anyone have anticipated Meade would pull five of the six Twelfth Corps brigades away. Somehow, Greene had anticipated something like this. *Damn you, Meade.*

Ireland moved toward Stoddard. "Frederick, you did a great job wheeling into the transverse."

"Thank you, sir. But we are terribly low on ammunition," Stoddard reported. "We also are going to need reinforcements to extend the transverse. I'm worried the Rebs know our right flank is hanging out there in the air."

"I've sent a courier to General Greene requesting more ammunition," Ireland said. "I will speak with him about reinforcements. Again, great job, Frederick."

Ireland turned and headed back up the hill toward the Sixtieth New York to find Greene.

---

## Dawes

*9:20 p.m.*

Lieutenant Colonel Rufus Dawes, commanding the Sixth Wisconsin of the Iron Brigade, stood next to the Sixtieth New York, pacing back and forth, the blood-lust cries of the battle filling the air. Sitting on the Union's far left flank of Culp's Hill, holding the highest position on its summit, the Iron Brigade and Sixtieth New York had not seen much action. The steep slopes up to their breastworks made it almost impossible for the enemy to launch a viable attack.

Colonel Robinson, acting commander of the Iron Brigade, walked up to Dawes. "Rufus, I've received a note from General Greene requesting the Iron Brigade send a regiment, if at all possible, to reinforce Greene's brigade at the lower part of Culp's Hill. I think I can spare your regiment, as the Rebs are having a time climbing the steep slope in our front to engage."

Dawes grinned. "Will do, sir."

"Find General Greene and report to him for orders. Good luck," Robinson said.

Dawes saluted and moved off. He had been itching to get into the fight since the Rebels had attacked Culp's Hill. Now his boys had a chance to mix it up with the Rebels. He hustled back to his regiment, telling them they were departing immediately. After they formed up, Dawes aimed his Black Hats toward the hellish saddle.

The Black Hats raced down the hill as if sliding down a snowy slope. Dawes' mind was racing. *How do I find Greene?* He mused for a few seconds. He'd follow the sound of musketry; that's where Old Pop would be.

The musket fire cracking the loudest was near the saddle between the two summits of Culp's Hill. Dawes moved his regiment toward the firing, spotting a mounted officer just ahead through the smoke. Dawes made his way toward him. He grinned, recognizing the grizzled, grandfatherly figure.

Dawes saluted. "General Greene. I was ordered by Colonel Robinson to provide my regiment, the Sixth Wisconsin, to your command as reinforcements."

Greene smiled. "Damn glad to have the Black Hats supporting my brigade."

Greene reached into his jacket pocket and pulled out a card and a pencil. "I'm giving you a written order so if I'm killed, the card would prove that you carried out your orders to report to me."

Greene handed the note to Dawes. Dawes put the note inside his coat jacket.

Greene gestured toward the transverse and said, "Move your regiment down into the left flank of the transverse breastwork. Go as quickly as possible and hold the rifle pits at all cost."

Dawes saluted and moved back to his regiment. Standing in front of the regiment, he shouted, "Forward, run! March!"

Dawes led the charge, brandishing a sword in his right hand and revolver in his left hand. The Sixth Wisconsin lunged forward, bayonets fixed, rifles resting on their shoulders, jogging forward with the best speed possible in the darkness. The regiment ran a hundred yards downhill without receiving fire from the Rebels. As they neared the breastworks and the transverse, the enemy rose, firing wildly toward the Black Hats.

Dawes was stunned, his heart banging against his ribs. *Damn.* He had not expected the Rebels were occupying the breastworks. Dawes glanced left and right and yelled to fire. Before the Black Hats could return a volley, the Rebels jumped out of the breastworks and retreated down the hill. Dawes ordered the regiment to charge. The regiment leaped into the breastworks, recapturing them.

The Rebels had skedaddled without a fight.

Dawes shouted, "You cowardly bastards." He turned. "Down, men! Watch sharp, keep your eyes peeled! Shoot low, shoot low, the hill is steep. Quiet now; steady!"

Dawes peered into the dark woods ahead of them. His regiment had entered the breastworks on the right of the 149th New York. To the right at a ninety-degree angle was the 137th New York, occupying the transverse breastwork. After a few moments the Rebels attacked again. Ordered to hold fire, the regiment waited, coiled tight as a watch spring. The Rebel line was less than twenty yards from the breastworks.

Dawes yelled, "Fire!"

The Black Hats fired a blistering volley into the teeth of the Rebels, shredding the first attack line, knocking down most of the second attack line. Shrieking screams and squealing groans rang out. The Rebel attack collapsed. Loud cheers erupted from the Sixth Wisconsin.

Someone yelled, "Remember General Reynolds!" Some of the Black Hats scrambled over the breastworks, set on chasing the Rebels down the slope.

Dawes shouted, "Stay in the rifle pits! Damn it. We will extract our revenge by holding these lines."

The Black Hats stopped, slid back over into the trenches. Dawes asked for a casualty update. Two of his men had been killed by the surprise volley from the Rebels.

## *Ireland*

A jolt surged through Ireland. Thank God for the Sixth Wisconsin arriving on his left flank, delivering a devastating volley into the attacking Rebels. Greene's reinforcements were arriving just in time. With the Black Hat regiment occupying the left flank of the transverse, Ireland could reinforce Stoddard and Company A on the right flank.

Ireland found Captain Gregg commanding Company I. "We will be overrun if we don't shore up the right flank of the transverse defenses," Ireland said. "Take your company from the breastworks and place it on the far right edge of the transverse."

## *Gregg*
*9:40 p.m.*

Gregg's heart leapt. This might be a chance for hand-to-hand fighting. He quickly moved his company to the far right edge of the transverse. As soon as his men were in place, Gregg spotted the Rebels advancing alongside a stone wall approaching the transverse. He needed to attack first and throw them back before they could form a line to attack.

Gregg stood up. "Fix bayonets!" he yelled.

Metallic clicking rippled across Company I as the men snapped bayonets into place. Gregg waited a moment. Then he yelled, "Give them the cold steel, boys! Charge!"

Face burning, Gregg bolted forward, running with his saber in his right hand raised above his head, his pistol in his left hand pointing at the chest of the enemy. His men ran closely behind, shrieking like foul demons. His heart pounded. Screaming fiendishly, Gregg's boys crashed into the Rebels with a savage ferocity, gutting the Rebels with their bayonets.

Some of the Rebels froze, sheer fear on their faces.

"Kill them!" Gregg roared. "Kill them all."

The Rebels crumbled. Most turned and ran; others stayed to fire one last shot.

A flash of light burst in front of Gregg. His eyes bulged, nostrils flared, a low growl rumbling from his throat. A hot poker thumped squarely in his chest. He dropped to one knee, trying to suck in a breath. Another muzzle flash. His upper left arm shattered and burned. He screamed, but no sound came from his gaping mouth. Then he collapsed.

For several moments, he lay on his side, conscious but unable to move. Chattering voices rushed down the slope. He opened his eyes. The bright red Zouave pants of a Red-Legged Devil from the Fourteenth Brooklyn regiment stood over him.

"We've come to relieve Ireland's 137th New York," a deep-voiced Brooklyn accent shouted.

## Ireland

*9:50 p.m.*

Ireland knelt beside Gregg. "How are you doing, Joe?"

Gregg said painfully, "Shot up pretty good. Looks like I might lose my arm to the surgeons. How was the bayonet attack?"

"Savagely executed," Ireland said. "Just as your boys were running out of steam, the Fourteenth Brooklyn showed up, fixed bayonets, and charged forward. I think the Rebels are still running."

Gregg closed his eyes and grimaced.

"We will get you out of here and to the surgeon," Ireland whispered. "I will check on you later."

Ireland stood, yelling for his company commanders, "Fall out of the breastworks. We've been relieved by the Fourteenth Brooklyn."

Greene rode up to Ireland. "David, I'm damn proud of the 137th New York! You held the line and the right flank of the Union army. I have received word that Slocum is returning with the corps' other five brigades and should be here within twenty minutes."

"Good. That's good," Ireland breathed. His stomach rolled, and a knot loosened under his breastbone.

Greene and Ireland moved over to the breastworks of the 149th New York, looking down the hill's slope, a wasteland of shattered men.

The regiment had repulsed the enemy; the breastworks had held. Ireland walked down the swale, slipping on the bloody ground, looking for Captain Gregg. He learned Gregg had been carried unconscious to a field hospital, his left arm nearly shot off. They used his belt as a tourniquet, but the prognosis was grim. Joseph Gregg was twenty-six.

Ireland closed his eyes and eased a long exhale out through his nose. His thigh wound was throbbing. He peered at the gaping hole in his trousers. The bleeding had stopped. His brain twirled like a whirling dervish. Would General Meade ever know how desperate the fight was and how he had tempted fate by stripping most of Slocum's corps from Culp's Hill? Probably not. Thank God for General Greene and his breastworks that had saved the army's right flank. He had saved the day for the Union.

# 40
## Meade — Thursday, July 2

*7:30 p.m.*
*Almost two and a half hours earlier*
*Cemetery Ridge*

Meade sat on his horse on Cemetery Ridge, south of a copse of trees. He ran his tongue along his cracked lips and squinted as the fading daylight purpled the clouds over South Mountain. Along Cemetery Ridge the battle cries were grinding down, replaced by the protracted moans of the wounded and dying. Crickets chirruped by the thousands from the blood-drenched fields. Cannon fire had cratered the ground with hundreds of blackened cavities resembling cellar holes. A long breath slipped through his lips. *Look at those Rebel bastards run back across the Emmitsburg Road.*

Although rifle fire continued to crack over Culp's Hill, it appeared the army had held the fishhook line of defense by a mere hair's breadth. Sickles's catastrophic blunder had caused every conceivable and every unpredictable thing to go wrong. And it was the heartrending courage of the brave men of the Army of the Potomac that made the hair's breadth hold on Meade's defense possible. It was barely short of miraculous. Still, no matter Warren's heroic performance on Little Round Top, no matter the First Minnesota's unthinkable sacrifice, no matter Hancock's brilliant maneuvering of units to reinforce Sickles's mangled corps, no one believed the army had done any better than eke out a tenuous draw. He slapped a mosquito buzzing near his ear. Would Lee attack for the third straight day tomorrow?

Biddle rode up. "General Halleck is asking for an update."

Meade snarled and leveled a scorching glare at Biddle. *Christ Almighty.* Halleck would never understand what happened here today. How to explain such chaos and carnage? He slapped at another mosquito. What words could capture the jarring gruesomeness of blasting cannons shredding soldiers like cotton gins, and the slaughtering savagery of cracking rifle shots piercing soft flesh like flying shards of glass?

"I will send one shortly," Meade said, his voice shrill. He pursed his lips, refusing to let his volcanic rage erupt into a hellish tirade. *Give me a damn break, Halleck.* Biddle backed his horse a few yards.

Grabbing his field glasses, Meade scanned south along Cemetery Ridge. His skin prickled. Darkening shadows with sharp edges were slowly cutting across the battlefield, blanketing thousands of bodies. Many of the battlefield's grotesque figures were pinned to the ground with swords and bayonets like insects in display cases. Many of the wounded were creeping toward the safety of their lines. The hospital wagon lanterns flickered eerily like floating jack-o-lanterns as the ambulance-corps men made their ways to the wounded. He wiped his wet brow. The evening was dripping with humidity.

"God damn you to hell, Sickles." Anger and rage flowed through Meade's voice.

He stared at Seminary Ridge, occupied by Longstreet's corps and A.P. Hill's corps.

A shiver ran through him. *You can do this. You can defeat Lee.* He and Lee had both blundered two days in a row. Yesterday, Lee did not show his usual initiative and take Cemetery Hill when he had the chance. For some reason today, Lee's attack was piecemeal and uncoordinated. Meade extracted a cigar, rolling it slowly between his fingers. After a few moments, he lighted it, inhaled deeply as the soothing smoke worked its magic. He didn't have to worry about Sickles disobeying orders tomorrow and giving Lee the upper hand anymore. No more blunders for the Union army—well, at least not from Sickles's sorry ass. But if Lee blundered tomorrow... Meade set his jaw and slowly raised his chin. If Lee blundered tomorrow, he would make him pay dearly.

Almost unconsciously, his gloved hand swiped over his pants leg, hoping to erase Baldy's blood. Poor Baldy. Meade would change his trousers back at the Leister House and find out how Baldy was doing.

Meade spotted Colonel Randall riding toward him and was filled with sudden warmth and admiration. He had witnessed Randall's Thirteenth Vermont arriving on Cemetery Ridge and conducting a savage counterattack across the Emmitsburg Road.

Randall reported. "General Meade. The Rebels in my front are in full retreat back to Seminary Ridge."

"Colonel Randall," Meade said, pride pouring through his voice. "Damn great job stripping the Rebels of Lieutenant Weir's captured four Napoleons."

"Thank you, sir."

"I also want to congratulate you on leading the charge on foot after your horse was shot," Meade said grinning. "For a brief moment, I thought you may have been wounded."

Randall pointed back toward the regiment marching toward them. "Besides recapturing the cannons, we bagged more than eighty prisoners."

Meade spotted the Vermonters marching the prisoners toward Cemetery Ridge. "How many Vermont companies were involved in your regiment's attack?

"Five, sir!"

"It's a good thing General Stannard forced-marched the Vermont Brigade from the Washington defenses to Gettysburg," Meade said. "I'm impressed. Keep up the great work."

Randall saluted and departed.

Meade sucked in a rough-edged gasp. Tiredness soaked his muscles, his body spiraling into exhaustion. He reached his hand behind him and rubbed his lower back. It throbbed as if his saddle were a medieval torture device, inflicting hot, coal-like burning. He breathed deeply and held it for a few moments before exhaling forcefully. He clenched his hands and steeled himself for tonight's ordeal. What were today's losses, and how many men would muster for tomorrow's fight? Sickles's Third Corps had been practically destroyed.

A long, thunderous roar erupted from Culp's Hill. Meade turned his head toward his right flank, dread twitching throughout his tense muscles. The cracking rifle fires continued to grow. Sheets of yellow lightning erupted along the crest. *Crap.* The Confederates were assaulting Greene's lone brigade. Would today's fighting never end?

Meade motioned to his nephew, Captain Francis Bache, huddled with Biddle and George astride their horses a short distance away. "Ride to General Slocum and tell him he needs to reoccupy Culp's Hill. Immediately."

Bache departed. Meade pulled lightly on the reins and squeezed with his legs. The large black mare started to walk forward and Meade yanked hard on the reins, stopping her. *Damn it.* It was Slocum's duty to command Twelfth Corps. Riding over to Culp's Hill to support Greene was thinking like a corps commander. Twice today he had charged toward the enemy lines, brandishing a sword. That had to stop. His job was sitting in the center of the line at his headquarters, coordinating the army and the interior lines of support.

Sharpe rode up. "Johnson's division of Ewell's corps is assaulting Greene's brigade. So far, Greene has repulsed all attacks, but he will need reinforcements soon."

Meade scowled. "Will reinforcements arrive in time?"

"Yes. Greene has asked First and Second Corps for reinforcements. They should be there soon," Sharpe said.

Meade nodded. But what if they weren't?

Meade's large cavalcade of officers sat on horses a short distance away. Except for the two stars on each shoulder, most would not guess he was Commanding General of the army. Had Lee figured out yet that Fighting Joe Hooker was not commanding the army? Meade cracked a slight grin. No one would refer to him as Fighting George Meade. Maybe Cautious George Meade, or Tempestuous George, as was his style. But today, he had fought the Confederates head on, getting knocked down but getting right back up. Yes, he lacked the charisma of Robert E. Lee and George B. McClellan, but he had given Union soldiers something to cheer about today.

A few muskets cracked from the other side of the battlefield. Meade turned, spotting a twinkling of flashes like bright stars over Seminary Ridge. The firing stopped.

Beyond Cemetery Ridge, the enemy's dead and mortally wounded lay sprawled along the Union line. The Union dead and wounded were being removed, transported to hospitals and freshly dug graves. Responsibility for the dead typically fell to the victor, because they held the field. But after two days of fighting, there was no victor, leaving the battlefield a horror, filled with the corpses, the seriously wounded, and the dying, as well as the carcasses of horses and mules, also victims of the fighting.

Unlike past battles, this evening he did not mourn the Rebel dead. Perhaps because they had assaulted his home state of Pennsylvania? Whatever the reason, he wasn't racked with guilt. Every one of those sons of bitches deserved to die.

Was that how Lee felt about the Union dead lying on the fields of Virginia?

Meade rode south on Cemetery Ridge toward Little Round Top. Along the ridge, the moonlight bathed the killing fields in a haunting glow. The carnage was horrific. He stopped near Little Round Top. Strewn between the farm lanes were knapsacks, haversacks, and canteens, cast aside by soldiers during the fateful fighting. Intermingled were broken wagon wheels, exploded caissons, limberboxes, and demolished guns.

Meade sat for a long moment staring at Sickles's salient, the peach orchard. The terrain gained by the enemy today had been limited to that held by Sickles's advance line, thanks mostly to the brilliant efforts of Warren, Hancock, and Sykes, a corps commander for only five days. A great deal of the credit for these outcomes could be traced to Meade's decision to promote Sykes to corps commander and to send Warren to Little Round Top. *Thank God Lee conducted an echelon attack today.*

Meade turned, riding back up the ridge toward Cemetery Hill. As he puffed on his cigar, he took a moment and assessed his performance today. Maybe he had taken too great a risk shifting additional troops from other portions of the line to bolster Sickles's position. Leaving only one brigade on Culp's Hill was probably a mistake. But if the Rebels had broken through the center of Cemetery Ridge, Culp's Hill would not matter. The army would have had to retreat to the Pipe Creek line near Westminster. *You were damn lucky today, George. Damn lucky!*

He raised his eyes toward the sounds of fighting on Culp's Hill. The cracking rifles and earsplitting screams echoing over Cemetery Ridge indicated this was more than a scrap.

Meade summoned Biddle. "Captain Bache is delivering a message to General Slocum that I want him to occupy Culp's Hill immediately. Find General Slocum and have him provide an update to me on the fighting near Culp's Hill."

Biddle saluted and rode off.

Meade turned to George. "Perhaps I should have examined the left flank and ridden to the top of Little Round Top, pointing out to Sickles where I wanted him. But Sickles is a corps commander. I didn't have to check on the other commander's lines and positions."

"General, I gave Sickles a sketch showing where to place his troops," George said.

Meade nodded, petting his beard. "Also, I pointed to Little Round Top and told him to occupy it." Silently, he bore witness to the killing fields of Sickles's folly, then raised his eyes to Culp's Hill. "Sickles's disobedience nearly destroyed an entire corps. *Eleven thousand men.* I swear to God, if he survives, I will court-martial that blasphemous infidel."

Meade pulled on the reins, turned his horse through the lines, and trotted toward headquarters. He wiped the sweat from his face. It had been a frenetic day, frighteningly close to disaster. He had been out on the open fields for nearly four hours, under a broiling sun, without food. He had been on the front lines, been shot at, hastily shifting reserves and reinforcements to gravely threatened areas and unexpected threats. It was not perfect, but he had done his best. At least he hadn't lost the battle...yet.

*7:55 p.m.*
*Leister House*

He arrived at the small white farmhouse. Hundreds of lanterns glowed brightly, as if army headquarters was being lit by pitch-soaked torches.

Horses were tethered everywhere. Men hunkered around campfires, boiling coffee and cooking dinner. The odor of food made his stomach growl. He dismounted, walked through a crowd of officers, all saluting. Meade gave one quick salute. "Carry on!"

The small living room was filled with generals and aides and a haze of blue cigar smoke. Meade spotted Butterfield and Williams at a small pine table; a burning candle held upright by its own melted wax cast a feeble, flickering light.

Meade walked to the table and sat down. The room was stifling. Meade said, "Someone crack a window, but don't let the buzzing insects in."

An aide eased a window open a bit.

Meade studied Butterfield for a moment. "Well?"

Butterfield said, "I'm looking at the casualty reports. We took a huge licking today. I'm not sure Third Corps is a viable fighting unit; it may not be available for action tomorrow. In two days, we have lost two corps commanders: Reynolds and Sickles; a division commander—Barlow; and eleven brigade commanders, including Meredith of the Iron Brigade and Vincent on Little Round Top. These are heavy losses."

Meade drummed his sweaty fingers on the table. Butterfield was right about the casualties. More than Antietam. He shook his head. "There were times this afternoon when things looked bleak."

"No more than a guess," Butterfield said. "But I estimate the army at 58,000 infantry."

Meade winced. "Damn, we've lost about a third of our army."

"General, I was sorry to hear Baldy was shot today," Butterfield said. "One of the headquarters surgeons took a look at his wound and believes he will survive."

"I hope so." Meade's pulse throbbed in his neck. "That old warhorse has been wounded six times. How much can he take? Hell, how much more can the army take? Another day like today, and the Army of the Potomac will be under half strength—more than 50,000 casualties over three days."

Butterfield crossed his arms, his face a mask of skepticism.

*8:00 p.m.*

"Dan, summon all the corps commanders for a council meeting." Meade turned to Williams. "Seth, I need to send a message to General Halleck providing him a status report and my intentions for tomorrow."

"What are your intentions for tomorrow?" Williams asked.

"We are in possession of good ground. I'm committed to holding this fishhook line, maintaining the interior lines, a great tactical advantage. So we will remain in this present position. However, I am not sure if we will stay on the defense or attack."

An aide handed Meade paper and pen. Meade fished out his watch. It was 8:00 p.m. He wrote:

> *The enemy attacked about 4 p.m. After one of the severest contests of the war, was repulsed at all points. We have suffered considerably in killed and wounded. Have taken a large number of prisoners. I shall remain in my present position tomorrow, but am not prepared to say, until better advised of the condition of the Army, whether my operations will be of an offensive or defensive character.*

He reread the message. Maybe he should include a line about Sickles's incompetence. No. He would wait. Sickles had been severely wounded. Meade gave the message to Williams, who read it, nodded approvingly, and passed it to one of his aides to telegraph to Washington.

"General, why don't you lie down before the corps commanders arrive," Williams said, steepling his fingers. "You haven't slept in nearly two days. There also is a change of uniform upstairs. You need to change your bloody trousers. You look like the walking wounded."

Meade yawned, his throat was parched and his knees wobbly. Just the suggestion of sleeping made him bone tired. He turned to Biddle. "I'm going to take a quick nap. Wake me when Colonel Sharpe gets here."

Biddle said, "Please follow me, sir."

Meade followed Biddle upstairs.

Biddle pointed to the bed, "There's a clean pair of trousers. I will wake you when Sharpe arrives." He walked down the stairs.

Meade glanced around the small loft. A bed was snuggled near the wall. He sat on the bed, removed his boots, changed out of his bloody trousers, placed his glasses on a small table next to the bed, and laid his head on the pillow. Everything went dark as he fell into a dreamless sleep.

---

*8:30 p.m.*
*Sharpe visits Meade at the Leister House.*

A strong grip shook his shoulder, a voice telling him to wake up. He jerked like a cat thrown into ice water and opened his bleary eyes. "General Meade," Biddle said. "Colonel Sharpe is here."

For a fleeting moment, he was a young boy in Spain, and his dad was trying to wake him. The moment evaporated. As he roused from the heavy slumber, he muttered, "I'll be right down."

His heart pounded and his mind was spinning. Maybe he was still dreaming. He sat up, disoriented, his head throbbing, cracked his eyes open, and peered through the narrow slits. He pulled on his boots, grabbed his glasses, and hustled downstairs, his heavy boots creaking the floor boards.

He walked into the living room and glanced around. "James, where is Colonel Sharpe?"

"John Babcock asked Sharpe to join him nearby in the enemy interrogation tent."

"Hopefully our senior intelligence civilian can provide an updated enemy order of battle," Meade said. He stared out the window; moonlight was pushing out the fading twilight.

He yawned and sat down at the map table, resting his chin in his hand. Two candles flickered in the middle of the table. His eyes focused on the roads leading to Gettysburg from the

Union's logistics railhead at Winchester. The wooden floors creaked as someone approached.

"Good evening, General Meade," Sharpe said, saluting.

Meade, tight-lipped, returned the salute and glanced back down to the map. His empty stomach growled, and he covered it with his hand. After a moment, it rumbled again. When should he order the supply wagons from Winchester to Gettysburg? The army had only one more day's worth of supplies. All they had tonight for dinner was hardtack and little bit of bacon. Damn it. His hunger was punishment for leaving the supply trains at Winchester.

In a few minutes, the rest of his staff started trickling in. Biddle reported, "General, your headquarters staff is all here."

"Please sit around the map table," Meade said. They walked over and took their seats. Sharpe started slapping the dust off his jacket elbows and arms. Meade smiled. "My God, Colonel Sharpe, it looks as if you gave your face a mud bath. I think you got a little bit more handsome today."

Sharpe cracked a smile. "I need all the help I can get."

A servant came in and spread hardtack crackers and some pieces of bacon on the table. Meade glanced at each officer, bone tired and dirty as hell. He said, "Gentlemen, this is one of those occasions when I think a man is justified in taking a drink of whiskey." He turned to the servant. "Do we have any whiskey here?"

A moment later, the servant brought in a bottle of whiskey and three tumblers and set them on the table. Meade glanced at the bottle and smiled. "Colonel Sharpe," he said, "Won't you take a glass of whiskey? I think it will do you good."

Sharpe grabbed the bottle and a tumbler. He lifted the bottle up in the candle light and stared at it for a moment and then sat it back on the table without pouring any whiskey. He said, "General, I think you ought to take a drink. You need it more than any of us."

Meade stared at the bottle in the dim light of the candles. *Damn.* It was almost empty, perhaps enough for one moderate drink. He glanced into Sharpe's mud-caked face and then back at the bottle. *My staff deserves this drink more than I do. They did a hell of job today.* He said, "No, I don't think I care for any whiskey. I would like a cup of coffee."

Meade reached for the bottle, turned to Williams, and passed it. "Seth, please take a drink."

Williams looked at the bottle and shook his head and said, "I think I would also like coffee." Williams passed the bottle along, and each member of the staff in turn asked for coffee. The last man placed the bottle in the middle of the table, its scanty contents untouched while they drank coffee and ate hardtack and bacon.

Meade's chest swelled with gratitude and pride. Surviving today's merciless fight more than justified a sworn teetotaler breaking his abstinent ways. Damn, he was proud of these unselfish officers. They'd risked their lives today in the most harrowing battle of the war and would not take a sip of whiskey that they justly deserved because there was not enough for everyone.

After eating, the staff left, except Sharpe. Meade stood. "George, you can now take that drink."

"Only after you, General Meade," Sharpe said.

"I'm fine for now," Meade said. "Even though I think the Pipe Creek line is a better place to fight than Gettysburg, I'm committed to fighting here again tomorrow. I'm still not confident in the outcome of this battle. I must have more detailed information of the strength of the enemy. Can you get information of the number of Confederate troops that were engaged today and whether Lee has any fresh troops in reserve?

"I will confer with Babcock and provide you the enemy's order of battle in an hour," Sharpe said. He departed.

Meade walked back to the map table and sat down. He took off his glasses and started to clean them with a handkerchief. The door swung open and Hancock burst into the house, followed by Slocum. Hancock strode to Meade, extended his hand. "Congratulations, General! That's the best performance I've ever witnessed by a commanding general."

Meade swallowed hard, shook his hand, smiling sheepishly. Hancock's compliment was unexpected but welcome. His stomach began to untighten.

Hancock was in a spirited mood. His uniform was immaculate. Incredible. Meade glanced down at his ruffled blue jacket. *How does Hancock look so inspection-ready all the time? Hancock and Humphreys, two peas in a pod when it came to the best-dressed officers in the army.*

Meade turned, saw Slocum smiling, extending his hand. Slocum said, "We beat them back, General. But I think we cut it a bit close leaving only Greene's brigade on Culp's Hill. We have a nasty brawl raging there now. The rifle pits Greene built saved us from disaster. The rest of Twelfth Corps is moving back to their trenches now." Slocum yawned.

Meade nodded. His head was still fuzzy with cobwebs. Sleeping a half hour wasn't worth it. Slocum sat on a cot, laid his head back against the wall, and promptly fell sound asleep. Meade silently smiled. Let Slocum sleep until all the corps commanders arrived. Hancock and Meade sat at the table drinking coffee and discussing today's battle.

An hour later, Sharpe arrived back and joined Meade and Hancock at the map table with the two small candles burning.

Meade asked, "What Rebel units were we fighting today?"

Sharpe reached inside his jacket, removing a piece of paper. "According to Babcock's order-of-battle charts and updates from the Rebel prisoners, we've faced every division and brigade except one: Pickett's. Pickett's division of four brigades numbering 7,000 men has come up and is now in bivouac. It will be ready to go into action fresh tomorrow."

Hancock's face exploded into a devilish grin. "General, we have them licked!"

Meade shot Hancock a quizzical look. Slocum awoke, blinking his eyes.

Sharpe said, "All our corps and reserve units have come up and are now in bivouac and will be ready to go into action fresh tomorrow morning."

A dawning jolt shot through Meade and his skin prickled. The knot of doubt sitting in his gut loosened. Hancock was right. Lee had thrown everything he had at him over the past two days—except for one division. Meade still had his largest corps in reserve: Sedgwick's Sixth Corps, numbering almost 16,000 men.

"By God, I'll stay here," Meade said.

"Well, General Meade," Hancock said playfully, "don't you think Sharpe deserves a cracker and a drink?"

Meade eyed Sharpe, nodded approvingly. "Yes, indeed. Please, Colonel Sharpe, have something. In fact, I think I will join you."

They both began munching. Meade poured himself a glass of water and one for Sharpe. Hancock was right. Lee had been attacking with his entire army minus one division. Rebel casualties had been high. General Hood had been seriously wounded, and General Barksdale had been killed. Those were serious losses.

At Meade's shoulder, Biddle whispered, "General, the other corps commanders are arriving." Meade nodded but remained at the table, staring at a map.

Gibbon moved into the room, walked up to Williams, and said, "I don't think I'm supposed to be here. This is a corps commanders' meeting."

Meade looked up, caught Gibbon's eye, and winked.

Williams assured Gibbon, "General Meade specifically said he wanted you at the meeting."

———◦◦◦◦◆◦◦ ◦ ◦◦◆◦◦◦◦———

*9:00 p.m.*
*Leister House*

Generals Sykes, Howard, and Newton arrived next, followed by General Alpheus Williams. Williams was acting Twelfth Corps commander today, as Slocum was acting as the commander of the right wing, coordinating First, Eleventh, and Twelfth Corps. It was nearly 9:00 p.m. when Birney, now commanding Sickles's Third Corps, showed up, followed by Warren and Pleasonton, the cavalry commander.

"General," Biddle said to Meade, "everyone is here."

611

Meade nodded. "Please everyone, come around the map table." They moved in, some sitting, some standing, some leaning against walls, some sitting on a cot in the corner. Warren was the last to move into position, looking exhausted, a tight bandage wrapped around his neck. He walked to a corner of the room, sat down, closed his eyes, and almost fell asleep.

Meade stood at the head of the table and paused momentarily as his stomach twinged. Although he was in charge, a shiver darted down his spine. Unconsciously, he was waiting for the real commanding general to walk into the room, enabling him to take his place alongside the other corps commanders. His old Fifth Corps instincts tightened his chest, and his insides stopped free-falling.

"We had one hell of a fight today, gentlemen," Meade said. "But we are still holding our fishhook position."

He paused, watching the heads nod.

"This is the first opportunity we've had to all meet together since I took command five days ago. I want to hear about the battle and your casualties and supplies. And I want to thank everyone for the fine support you've provided for each other over the past two days."

Meade paused. His senior lieutenants were staring at him. Hancock was grinning.

"I want you to know, I did not ask for this command, nor did I campaign for it behind the scenes," Meade said. "But now that I have it, I will do my best."

"By God, your performance was brilliant today," Hancock shouted. He fished inside his jacket pocket and produced several cigars and passed them out. "Let's have a victory smoke to General Meade's great performance today."

"Hear, hear…" several voices shouted.

Meade lit his cigar. A glowing warmth flared inside as well as out. "I do request one change to how we operate. I would like more open discussion among us. In this way, you will know my plan for achieving victory and how you can best support it. As situations change, I want you to keep me informed about the enemy and whether a better opportunity for success exists, so I may redirect our efforts. At Chancellorsville, I felt strongly that we could have won with more open communications between Hooker and the corps commanders."

Meade paused; his generals shook their heads in agreement.

He continued. "I would like to hear about today's fighting from your perspectives."

There was a brief, awkward silence.

Hancock spoke first, describing the fight along Cemetery Ridge, singling out First Minnesota's bayonet attack against a much larger enemy force. When he finished, everyone joined in commenting on the fight, providing the condition of their corps, including supply and ammunition updates. Sykes mentioned Colonel Chamberlain's Twentieth Maine running out of ammunition and Chamberlain ordering a bayonet attack, repulsing the Rebels from Little Round Top.

"It was the damnedest thing," Sykes said. "Hundreds of graycoats tumbling down Little Round Top, chased by a regiment of bluecoats, bayonets fixed, screaming and yelling like banshees. Once the blue wave started to cross Plum Creek, I ordered the adjutant to stop the charge. I wasn't sure the Maine boys were going to stop."

Over the next hour the rhythms of their conversations were relaxed, informal, sometimes lively, as Hancock interjected with passionate updates. Meade's heart warmed, listening to the dialogue. Hancock was an easy conversationalist and mentally quick. No commander ever had a better lieutenant.

A courier pushed by the commanders, handing Meade a note. Meade read it, handed it to Butterfield, who passed it next to Slocum. It was from Greene, describing the fighting on Culp's Hill. Geary had just arrived, and it appeared they could hold Culp's Hill until morning. The Rebels were occupying some of the vacated Union trenches on the lower summit, with heavy firing on the right of the line.

The talking picked up again. After another half hour of discussion, Newton said, "This is no place to fight a battle." Quiet spread over the room.

Gibbon said, "What are your objections?"

Newton's face flushed a bright red. He glanced quickly around the room. Meade waited, enjoying the moment, as Newton's comment had generated sharp reactions. Newton was right. This was no place to fight. But he was pleased they were comfortable debating openly.

"I'm not pleased with the crooked line of defense," Newton said, a razor's edge to his voice. "It's shaped like a damn fishhook. If the Rebels get around the two Round Tops on our left flank or behind Culp's Hill on our right flank, as they are trying to do now, they will be in our rear and we will have to immediately retreat."

"I agree that we are defending a crooked line," Gibbon said. "But this place was in large measure selected for us. Here we are; now what's the best thing to do?"

Meade pursed his lips, letting the other corps commanders chime into the discussion. It quickly became apparent that everyone else was in favor of remaining where they were.

Newton peered at Meade. "I want to restate my concerns as minor. They most likely will be resolved after I consult with General Hunt and reposition the artillery supporting First Corps' front."

Meade's heart swelled and he nodded, suppressing a thankful sigh as he glanced around the table. Good. He didn't have to referee, and they had worked it out among them. An aide moved next to Meade, handing him a message. Meade read it. Nodded. The aide departed. Meade said nothing, glanced at Hancock.

Butterfield spoke. "Gentlemen, this may be a good time to ask two or three questions for the record."

Meade stared down at the map. He'd already told Halleck they were staying put. But he didn't want to override his chief of staff in front of the corps commanders.

Butterfield read the first question: "Should the army remain in its present position, or retire to another, nearer its base of supplies?"

Butterfield turned to Gibbon. "As the most junior commander, what is your thought?"

Gibbon looked at Newton and said, "Remain here and make such corrections in our position as may be deemed necessary, but take no step that even looks like retreat."

When it came Newton's turn, he said, "Remain in place but make some adjustments to the line and position of artillery."

Gibbon said, with a wry smile, "I am delighted you agree with my assessment, General Newton."

Newton smiled. "I was under the impression, General Gibbon, that I had convinced you of the necessity of minor adjustments."

Meade cracked a grin. A spark lightened the mood as the two generals sparred kiddingly, breaking the slight tension between the two.

Butterfield said, "Everyone desires to stay. Next question: Should the army attack or await an attack?" Everyone determined it best to wait for an attack.

Butterfield then asked, "How long should we wait?"

Meade studied each face as they answered in turn. The answers ranged from "one day" to "when the enemy moves."

Butterfield turned to Meade and said, "I've recorded all the answers, General, and I don't have any more questions, sir."

*11:50 p.m.*

It was nearly midnight when Meade finally said, "My intent is to remain on the defensive tomorrow and await Lee's attack. If the opportunity presents itself, I will take the offensive and counterattack Lee. Thank you, gentlemen. Please keep me posted on your situations tomorrow. Good luck."

The meeting broke; each of the commanders departed. Birney hung back and cornered Meade. "I object to General Hancock taking command of Third Corps today after Sickles was wounded. I should have assumed command of the corps."

A slow rage traveled up through Meade's throat as he studied Birney. What a son of a bitch. Like Sickles, he was always looking out for his own interests.

Meade said with a sharp tone, "General Hancock is your superior, and I claim the right to issue the order."

Birney stared at Meade for several seconds. Then he saluted and left.

Meade walked onto the porch, seeing Gibbon untethering his horse. "John," Meade called out.

Gibbon stopped and walked over. Apologetically, he said, "Sir, a staff officer summoned me to this meeting, although I had some doubts about being present."

"I wanted you here," said Meade. Gibbon shook his head. Meade continued, "You know, John, I'm not the ranking officer in the army I command. Both Reynolds and Sedgwick are my seniors. Reynolds is dead, but Sedgwick is still alive and kicking. But Congress has empowered President Lincoln to assign a junior to command. I received a telegram from Secretary Stanton that as commander of the Army of the Potomac I have the authority to place junior officers over senior officers as I see fit."

"General, I've never heard of juniors replacing seniors."

Meade paused. After a moment he said, "If Lee attacks tomorrow, it will be on your front."

"Why do you think so?"

Meade stared at Gibbon's unflinching face. He could almost see the wheels spinning in Gibbon's head. "Because he has made attacks on both our flanks and failed," Meade said firmly. "If he tries again, it will be on our center."

Gibbon said, with a wide grin, "I hope you are right. If Lee does attack our center, we will defeat him."

Meade gripped Gibbon's arm. "Good luck tomorrow, John."

Gibbon saluted and departed. Meade walked into the house and spotted Butterfield, Sharpe, and Captain Dahlgren, Sharpe's special operator, standing at the map table.

"Captain Dahlgren captured two important enemy dispatches today," Butterfield said. "One is from President Davis and the other is from General Cooper."

Meade reached out, took the dispatches, and said, "Captain Dahlgren, how did you intercept these dispatches?"

Dahlgren said, "Colonel Sharpe informed me that important dispatches from Richmond for Lee would be sent on July 2.

616

Colonel Sharpe knew the specified hour the courier was crossing the Potomac."

Sharpe spoke. "After crossing the Potomac, I knew the courier and his escorts would ride the Confederate supply route through Greencastle. I ordered Dahlgren to pick the best cavalrymen and horses and intercept the courier."

Dahlgren continued, "We crossed South Mountain using the Monterey Pass, avoiding Confederate patrols. We arrived in Greencastle and hid, waiting for the enemy courier and his escorts. When the courier's cavalcade arrived, we charged, using our sabers. The Rebels panicked and fled without a fight. We captured seventeen prisoners and intercepted two letters for Lee. One was from President Davis and one from General Samuel Cooper, adjutant general of the Confederate army. After reading the two letters, I rode alone back to headquarters to give the letters to you as soon as possible."

Sharpe said, "The letter from General Cooper denies reinforcements to Lee because Cooper fears General Butler's Army on the Peninsula is an imminent threat to Richmond. Davis's letter listed all of the remaining brigades in the eastern theater and why they needed to stay in their specific region."

Meade said, "This is incredible intelligence. I now know that General Pickett is Lee's entire uncommitted reserve and Lee will not receive any reinforcements. Damn! I have Lee by the balls." He turned to Butterfield and gave the letters to him. "Telegraph Halleck the two letters Dahlgren intercepted."

Butterfield departed. Meade turned to Sharpe and Dahlgren. "Great work, George and Ulrich. I'm looking forward to tomorrow if Lee attacks. If we don't have another Sickles-type screw-up, I think we can hand Lee his ass. Good evening, gentlemen."

Meade looked at his watch. A few minutes past midnight: July 3.

General George Greene

# ❧ Friday ❧

July 3, 1863

*General Robert E. Lee, Commander*
Army of Northern Virginia
Commanding for One Year

*General George G. Meade, Commander*
Army of the Potomac
Commanding for Six Days

*General George Sykes, Commander*
Fifth Corps
Commanding for Six Days

*General John Newton, Commander*
First Corps
Commanding for Two Days

*General David Birney, Commander*
Third Corps
Commanding for One Day

## 41

# Meade — Friday, July 3

*12:15 a.m.*
*Leister House*

Meade stood in the yard of the Leister House. Sharpe and Dahlgren mounted their horses and rode into the night toward the enemy interrogation tents. In the simmering July heat, Meade's face glistened with a thin sheen of sweat. He took off his slouch hat, pulled out a handkerchief, and wiped dry the thinning hair plastered to his scalp.

Hope welled in the hollow of his bones. It was a stroke of luck having Gibbon's division holding the center of the Union line. Based on Sharpe's intelligence report, Lee's main attack likely would be against Gibbon. As the former commander of the Iron Brigade, he was a fierce fighter. If fear had ever shadowed Gibbon's face, Meade had not seen it.

The noise from Culp's Hill had quieted. But danger slithered in the trenches on the lower summit. Lee was up to something. The Virginian liked to attack the Union's right flank. Now a strong Rebel force occupied a large section of abandoned Federal breastworks on the lower summit of Culp's Hill. At that critical moment yesterday, Meade had panicked. It was as if Lee had hit him with a right cross and he fell to the ground, stunned, struggling to do something. So in a fright he stripped almost all the forces from the right flank. What a dreadful decision, his worst one so far as the army's commander. He was damn lucky. How could he guess that Sykes's Fifth Corps and Hancock's reinforcements would hold back the Rebel tide?

He walked into the white house and told Biddle he needed to speak with Butterfield. In a few moments, Butterfield and Biddle entered the living room.

"Yes, General," Butterfield said.

"I want you to order Slocum to execute a daybreak assault and storm the Culp's Hill breastworks and drive out the Rebels."

"Do you want to wait until daybreak to strengthen the right flank?" Butterfield said.

"Yes. I'm against a nighttime attack. I sure as hell don't want a repeat of Sickles's idiot midnight attack at Chancellorsville."

Butterfield shook his head.

"I'm going to get up in time to watch Slocum's attack," Meade said.

Butterfield nodded and went into the next room.

Meade slumped down into his rocking chair.

Within moments, Williams delivered messages. Meade answered them, bleary-eyed. Afterwards, he stood shakily, his knees wobbling. He gripped the map table, steadying himself. It was like he was wearing a heavy jacket that had become rain-soaked, and now his bones had become heavy and brittle, ready to collapse under all the weight.

Meade turned to Biddle. "I'm going to try to get a few hours' sleep." He yawned for several seconds. "Wake me before Slocum's assault." Then he slowly climbed the stairs.

He sat on the bed, removed his jacket, boots, and glasses, then crashed onto the bed like a corpse—dead to the world before his head hit the pillow.

———————✦———————

*3:38 a.m.*
*(Sunrise is 4:48 a.m.)*

Thundering cannons rattled the house like a monstrous tornado. Meade opened his eyes and gripped the side of the bed, rolling like a boar in mud. He bolted out of bed, his heart pounding in his ears, his breathing ragged and raspy. He lurched to the small window. There was just enough light to distinguish the horizon. He put on his glasses and grabbed his watch. Almost four in the morning. He had slept a few hours in the sweltering loft.

Something was wrong. It was too early for Slocum's assault. Sunrise wasn't for more than another hour. A lump formed under his sternum. *Damn.* The rumbling was coming from Cemetery Ridge, near Gibbon's copse of trees. Was this Lee's final assault?

He pulled on his boots, scurried downstairs. He spotted Biddle at the map table, head lying on his crossed arms, snoring. He shook him by the shoulder.

"James. Wake up."

The aide-de-camp sat up. His mouth flopped open and he rubbed his eyes.

"The Rebels are attacking our center."

Meade and Biddle hurried outside. They mounted horses and galloped toward the sound of guns, stopping a short distance from the exploding artillery rounds. The rollicking shells were blasting the ground about two hundred yards south of the copse of trees. Meade clutched his field glasses, spotting a Union officer on horseback sitting calmly on a grassy rise in range of enemy batteries, shells spattering around him like popping corn.

"James, who is that officer on horseback?"

"Sir, I believe that's General George Stannard commanding the Second Vermont Brigade."

Meade squinted his eyes as the sky tinged with breaking sunlight. If Biddle was correct, the left center of the line was in good hands. Meade didn't know Stannard well, but he had spoken to him briefly the morning Captain Paine was sketching out the defensive lines. He liked his quiet and disciplined command style.

Meade yawned. "Wasn't it one of Stannard's regiments, I think the Thirteenth Vermont, that led the charge to retrieve Weir's captured batteries early evening yesterday?"

"Yes."

"Well, James. I've been impressed with Stannard and his Vermont boys so far. They are the right people to defend that spot," Meade said.

After a few more minutes, the shelling stopped.

Cracking thunder echoed from Culp's Hill. Meade turned. Biddle was staring at him. Meade's lungs seized, suddenly frozen as if paralyzed.

"Oh, my God," he said. "The firing must have been a diversion for a Rebel attack on our right flank. Let's ride over to Culp's Hill."

*4:00 a.m.*
*(Sunrise is 4:48 a.m.)*

They galloped around the back of Cemetery Hill. Was this Lee's main attack against his right flank? As they approached the summit of Culp's Hill he spotted Twelfth Corps rushing in long blue lines toward the occupied breastworks. The early stages of the attack appeared to be going well, Slocum assaulting with nearly 6,000 infantry. At several points the Union forces were closing rapidly with the enemy. Finally the Union troops bolted over the breastworks, flowing forward with a growing force, resorting to hand-to-hand fighting and slaughtering the Confederates unmercifully.

Meade rode to Slocum. "Good morning, General."

He was uncomfortable calling the thirty-six-year-old major general by his first name, Slocum being the ranking general on the field, senior to Meade. Although Meade was commander of the army, Slocum had an earlier promotion date. There had never been anything like this before: juniors taking command over seniors. Meade's mouth went dry as he studied Slocum's face, which showed no sign of being miffed by him being in command. Meade's muscles tensed as he shifted in his saddle.

Slocum saluted with a quick hand movement. Meade returned the salute. Slocum was the most cautious general in the army. He was reluctant to make waves, almost to a fault, and he never passed up an opportunity to avoid additional responsibility. Meade was still irked he had hung back on the first day of the battle.

"How is the attack going?" Meade asked.

"Twelfth Corps attacked the Rebels before they had a chance to attack," Slocum said. "We caught the enemy off guard."

"It looks as if you are routing them out of the trenches. Do you need reinforcements?" Meade said.

"Umm. I have two brigades from Twelfth Corps in reserve, as well as a couple regiments from First Corps and Eleventh Corps," Slocum said. Then he paused for a moment as a drop of

623

sweat appeared on his temple. "On second thought, reinforcements would be most helpful."

"I will have Sedgwick send General Shaler's brigade," Meade said.

"Thank you, sir," Slocum said. Then he saluted smartly.

Meade returned the salute, turned, and rode toward Cemetery Hill. He stopped and spoke for a few minutes with Howard, telling the Eleventh Corps commander to rouse his men and have them standing at ready arms, prepared to move to reinforce Slocum's attack on Culp's Hill. Then he rode along Howard's defensive position, paying particular attention to the posting of the artillery. He exhaled a long breath and cracked a smile. The big guns were well placed. He spurred his horse and galloped toward Second Corps, scanning the woods occupied by the Rebels on Seminary Ridge. It was quiet there. The Rebels apparently would not be attacking this morning along Cemetery Ridge. Thank God. He could focus on Culp's Hill, a battle he was winning.

There already had been a staggering number of Union casualties. If today's casualties were anything like yesterday's, the army would be at less than half strength. Even if they won, he was not sure how Lincoln would respond, perhaps with a visit from Colonel Hardie with Meade's relief in tow. His breathing quickened. Gloom draped his shoulders like an invisible cloak. There had never before been such death in this great Rebellion.

From afar, Meade spied a courier galloping across the field toward him. The young officer arrived, saluting. "General Slocum begs to report Twelfth Corps has reoccupied all the breastworks."

Meade nodded. "Very well. Thank you."

Time for a smoke. Meade reached into his jacket pocket, fetched a cigar, and lit it. Lee had failed to fracture the Union right flank. A good start to the third day of the battle. Meade puffed on his cigar. Could he actually hold his own with the indomitable Lee and defeat him? Sharpe's intelligence gathering said he would.

Meade rode south on Cemetery Ridge, with Biddle riding alongside. Meade cocked his head: riding twenty yards behind him were Rush's Lancers.

*4:30 a.m.*
*(Sunrise is 4:48 a.m.)*

They continued to the top of Little Round Top. It was swarming with hundreds of men, including Captain Hazlett's battery, now commanded by Lieutenant Benjamin Rittenhouse. General Hunt had worked through the night, placing and adjusting gun positions. The six rifled Parrott ten-pounders of Hazlett's battery anchored the left line atop Little Round Top. They could range most of the fields in front of Cemetery Ridge. A grin crossed Meade's face. Hunt continued to impress him. He seemingly was everywhere on the battlefield, checking the lines, adjusting artillery positions, ensuring his big guns had overlapping lines of fire. *If only Sickles had listened to Hunt yesterday. Hell, if he had just followed my orders when I pointed to Little Round Top and told him to occupy it! How many thousands of men would still be alive this morning if he had?*

Meade glanced down the hill toward Gettysburg. He had a clear view of the Union and Rebel lines. Union flags floated along the earthworks of Cemetery Ridge like a flotilla of ships marking the army's strong position. Hope rushed through his chest as he took a deep breath. The Union defenses were in good shape. The corps commanders were giving their all, supporting each other with guts and skill. It was good.

It *was* good, it dawned on him. And he had achieved it in six short days through open discussion of his intent and plans. Cohesiveness. It was what Hooker had failed to achieve at Chancellorsville.

But he'd done it. Without warning, without time, without preparation—and sure as hell without charisma. And, by God, that should count for something. But he doubted Halleck and Lincoln cared.

625

Meade turned his horse back down the hill toward his headquarters. *The hell with Halleck and Lincoln. And the hell with charisma.*

*We're going to win this thing.*

⚜

*4:48 a.m.*

*At the Leister House, just as the sun is rising*

When Meade arrived at the Leister House, signalmen were standing in a field beside headquarters, receiving updates from Culp's Hill. Sitting on his horse, he craned his neck back toward the copse of trees in Gibbon's front, still believing Lee would assault toward those trees, the central part of the Union line.

Meade dismounted and strolled slowly onto the porch, staring silently toward the Round Tops. He shook his head and stepped inside, telling Biddle he needed some quiet time. He sat alone at the small table as he visualized all the plays. Winning hinged on being decisive and opportunistic, like a bare-knuckled boxer feinting with one fist while striking a knockout blow with the other. The Union occupied a strong defensive line; Sixth Corps was rested, acting as a large ready reserve. *It's Lee's move, and he has two plays: attack our breastworks or retreat.*

Meade turned to Biddle. "We can wait all day in our defensive positions. Ammunition and supplies are continuing to roll in on the Taneytown Road in long wagon trains."

"How long can Lee wait for us to attack?" Biddle said.

"Lee can't wait. He is not being resupplied, and he is burning through the supplies he foraged in Pennsylvania before the Army of the Potomac arrived."

"Sir, if you don't mind my asking, what are your plans if Lee is repulsed today or if he retreats?" Biddle asked.

"If we repulse Lee again today, the Rebel army will have to fall back. After three days of fighting, Lee will be low on ammunition and most likely would depart for Maryland or Virginia to resupply. If that happens, I'm going to order General French and his several regiments bivouacking at Frederick to intercept the fleeing enemy and cut them off from home."

626

"French's forces are not large enough to tangle with Lee's army," Biddle said.

"I know. I'm going to order French's forces to move southwest toward the Potomac River and occupy the critical bridge-head at Harper's Ferry."

Meade pointed to the map table.

"The South Mountain range forms a natural screen to protect Lee's escaping army. Lee most likely will use Harper's Ferry as a crossing point. Sitting at Harper's Ferry, French's forces can harass Lee as he marches toward the Potomac River and Virginia."

Meade started scribbling on a piece of paper, writing a dispatch to General William French.

If Lee defeated him today, he would have to fall back to the Pipe Creek defensive line. If that happened, he wanted French to retreat to Washington. But no one needed to know his fall-back plan…yet.

"James, I feel good about the ground the army possesses. After riding to Little Round Top this morning, I'm certain the Rebels cannot turn our left flank," Meade said. He reread the French dispatch, giving it to Williams.

Meade's stomach started to unclench. What had changed? He now had a chance to plan. He loved planning, and finally there was an opportunity for some deliberate planning.

Sharpe walked in, saluting. "Stuart's cavalry rejoined Lee's army last night."

"Old J.E.B. is joining the party a little late," Meade said.

Sharpe nodded.

"I'm grateful, Colonel Sharpe, for the key information you provided on what units Lee has used and is planning to use today. This is the first time since taking command that I have a good feel for the enemy situation and what Lee might do."

"Thank you, sir," Sharpe said.

---

*8:00 a.m.*

*Leister House*

Meade reached into his pocket, retrieving his watch. Eight in the morning. Warren walked into the room.

"How is the neck?" Meade asked.

"Healing. I feel good…and refreshed," Warren said. "Sorry about almost sleeping through the council meeting last night."

Meade studied Warren. He was trying to give the impression the neck wound was trivial. But he was still struggling, a tightly wrapped bandage binding his neck.

"I'm pleased you're feeling better," Meade said, as he spied a red circle of blood the size of a half dollar spotting the white bandage. Meade grimaced. *Must watch him.* The wound looked more serious than Warren's self-assessment indicated.

"The Rebels are repositioning artillery and infantry to attack our center," Warren said.

"Interesting," Meade said. "Now that we have evidence of Lee's intent, we can respond. Gouv, ride to Sedgwick's headquarters. Tell him to move all his spare troops behind Gibbon's center position, massing them so they can rapidly plug holes in our line as they occur."

Warren saluted and departed.

Meade followed Warren outside. The sharp sun glared down, sizzling the grass. The sky was a brilliant blue. Meade paused for a moment, Biddle at his side. So Warren had observed the Rebels preparing to assault the center of the line. *Must talk with Hancock and Gibbon, telling them the Confederates are massing artillery to attack their lines.*

Meade mounted his horse and rode west toward Second Corps' lines, spotting Gibbon's Second Division flag, a white trefoil on a white rectangular field. He rode toward the flag, finding Hancock talking with Gibbon and Haskell. They were standing beside an old stone fence that stretched for a thousand yards on top of the crest. The wall was built knee high from small, rough stones piled on top of each other, making it wide at the bottom and narrow at the top. Soldiers were strengthening it using dirt and fence rails, creating a breastworks against musket fire and shell fragments. The men would have to kneel behind it to protect themselves.

Meade arrived and dismounted. "Good morning, gentlemen."

Hancock, in his booming voice, replied, "Good morning, General."

"Warren seems to believe the target of the Confederate assault is going to be Second Corps' front," Meade said. He turned to Gibbon. "Last night I said I thought they would assault your division's front. But after seeing your defenses behind the stone breastwork and the position of our artillery batteries and the excellent fields of fire, I would be surprised if Lee assaulted the center. It is not his favorite place to attack, knowing we can easily reinforce it. I'm more inclined now to think he will try assaulting our left flank again. Slocum defeated Lee's right flank attack this morning."

"Do you really think Lee will attack our left flank again?" Hancock said.

"Perhaps. But if he does, I feel confident about holding. Anchored by Little Round Top with Hunt's artillery and Sykes infantry on top, it is quite formidable."

"If Lee does decide to attack our center, Second Corps can handle it," Hancock said.

"If he does, I still will send you reinforcements," Meade said.

Meade mounted his horse and returned to headquarters. He sat down with Butterfield and Williams and did a map study of the logistics resupply challenges. They discussed the logistics issues they would face if they won today and Lee retreated toward the Potomac. They looked at different rail heads they could use to feed and refit the Union army as it pursued Lee. They also discussed the logistics challenges if Lee won and they had to retreat to Pipe Creek. They continued chatting after Gibbon joined them.

"General Meade," Gibbon finally said, "have you had any breakfast?"

"No."

<hr/>

*11:00 a.m.*
*Gibbon's headquarters*

"I would like to invite you to my headquarters. We are having an early lunch."

Meade's stomach growled. He was starving, but he should stay at the Leister House. "Thank you for the kind offer, John. But I should stay here to receive updates."

Gibbon countered. "General, my headquarters is in plain sight, and you would be absent only a few minutes. Sir, you really need to eat and keep up your strength. We don't know how long the fighting will last today once it starts."

"You're right," Meade conceded. "I will join you."

Meade departed with Gibbon. They rode together, chatting about yesterday's events. Biddle trailed. Gibbon's headquarters was a hundred yards east from the stone wall breastworks. Fleecy clouds floated over South Mountain; the scorching sun streamed down on the stacks of iron rifles and batteries of brass cannons. The gray lines along Seminary Ridge were quiet.

They arrived and dismounted. The aroma of stewed chicken filled the air. It was coming from a huge pan sitting on top of a mess chest.

"May I join you, gentlemen?" said Meade.

"Of course General Meade, please," said Hancock.

Hancock sat on one of the two stools at the makeshift table. Meade sat on an empty cracker box, and Gibbon took the other empty stool. The rest of the Second Corps staff sat cross-legged on the ground. A sergeant handed Meade a tin cup of hot coffee. Meade drank, savoring the hot bitterness burning his throat. Gibbon's aide served him a tin plate of stewed chicken, potatoes, and toast with butter. He ate it gratefully while listening to Hancock's endless stories. Newton and Pleasanton arrived, joining the feast.

Their lunch finished, Meade and the other generals walked over to a small tree providing some scant shade. Cigars were lit, and Meade pondered. If only he could be certain of Lee's plan for today. It seemed he had covered all options, but was his vision faulty? Was he seeing things as Lee saw them or as he wanted them to be? He remained silent, showing nothing of his disquiet as the generals talked, interested in hearing their recounting of yesterday's events and thoughts on what might happen today.

After several minutes Meade spoke up. "My guess is Lee will attack the center of our line late in the afternoon. But if he doesn't attack the center, he will attack our left flank."

Newton chimed in. "I don't think the Rebels will attack today. They had their fill yesterday. As soon as it gets dark they will be heading toward the Potomac."

"My guess is the Rebels will attack my front," said Hancock. "They will mass and attack our center line occupied by Second Corps, trying to sever our lines."

Gibbon added, "We may need more than two divisions of Second Corps defending the middle of Cemetery Ridge. If numbers determine strength, it's the weakest part of the blue line. If the enemy assaulted *en masse* with two or three heavy lines against Second Corps' 6,000 soldiers, the Rebels could sweep through my position."

Meade said, "I will reinforce your lines as soon as I'm convinced Lee is not attacking our left flank."

Gibbon nodded.

"Let's be ready for them wherever they hit us," Meade said. "Winfield, I want you to assume command of Second Corps today. John will return to commanding Second Division. Also, I think it's best to have the provost guards return to their assigned units. They are good men and I would rather have them fighting the enemy given our formidable position. We won't need them to stop stragglers and skulkers."

Meade turned to Gibbon. "Thank you, John, for the hot meal. You're right. I feel better."

---

*12:00 p.m.*
*Leister House*

Meade rode back to the Leister House. The oppressive weight of command pressed down on him as if he were lying on the ground, and heavier and heavier stones were being placed on his chest. Lee was getting ready to assault. All he could do was wait.

## 42

# First Minnesota — Friday, July 3

### *Wright*

*4:30 a.m.*
*Seven and a half hours earlier*
*(Sunrise is 4:48 a.m.)*

Sergeant Wright jolted awake out of a deep sleep and gripped his rifle, lying beside him. Sharp, cracking thunder echoed overhead. He rolled into a kneeling position and scanned the pre-dawn skies. No clouds. The thunderous rumbling split the air again. He jumped to his feet and the ground seemed to move in a slow spin beneath him. He stared northward. The darkened sky above Culp's Hill twinkled with tendrils of yellow light like a candelabra of flickering candles. *Damn.* It was a full-blown attack, happening two miles away on the Union's right flank.

He cocked his head westward toward Emmitsburg Road. No enemy fire from Seminary Ridge. He swallowed a thankful sigh. Good. He grabbed his canteen, draining the last of the tepid water. It was going to be a muggy one. He looked at his watch: Half past four in the morning.

Wright glanced toward Sickles's former headquarters, the Trostle House, checking for sounds of enemy activity. None. No immediate threat to Company F. He turned about and spotted Captain Ball standing a little behind where the boys slept. Ball was motionless, looking back toward Cemetery Ridge, where the remnants of the First Minnesota regiment should be located.

Wright made his way toward Ball, snaking around the scattered Rebel corpses. The flies were terrible. The suffocating stench of decaying bodies clung to his clothes and hair. At some point a "buzzard" detail would arrive, having the gruesome task of dealing with enemy corpses. The bodies would be buried in pits, and since the dead were Rebels, the mass graves would be unmarked. As he stepped over a bloated corpse, a sharp stab of Hell's fire singed his heart.

How would mass burials affect the soldiers in the afterlife? Without a proper Christian burial, would these souls forever be fated to a state of exile from God? His Methodist teachings didn't seem to make much sense in this war.

Wright walked up to Captain Ball and saluted. "Captain, did you get any rest last night?"

"My mind wouldn't let me sleep, thinking about the regiment," Ball said.

"Last night's orders said we could march at first light to join the regiment," Wright said. "It's plenty light for me."

"You're right. Call up the men and get them ready to move out."

---

*4:40 a.m.*

Wright saluted and darted about, waking the boys. In a few minutes the men were up and marching toward Thomas's battery. About 500 yards north along Cemetery Ridge they spotted Captain Nathan Messick and Corporal Newell Irvine standing together. Irvine was holding the tattered remains of the regiment's colors.

---

4:50 a.m.

Wright's breath rasped. They had found the regiment. Behind Messick and Irvine, the survivors of yesterday's charge were sleeping near stacked guns. Perhaps fifty or so men. *Christ Almighty.* That meant nearly two-thirds of those who charged lay on the battlefield or in nearby field hospitals. The survivors were all hugging the ground, sleeping, except those assigned as pickets, and Messick and Irvine.

Wright and Ball walked up to Messick. They both shook his hand.

"You're a sight for sore eyes, Nathan," Ball said.

"Great to see you, John and James," Messick said. "How did you fare yesterday?"

"Not bad," Ball said. "We had one hell of a scrap."

"But we suffered only three wounded," Wright said.

"Are you commanding the regiment?" Ball asked.

"I am the acting commander," Messick said, his red eyes filling with tears.

"I tried to get back to the regiment last night after we fell back to Cemetery Ridge, after you made the charge," Ball said, his voice filled with gloom. "But the brigade adjutant issued orders for the company to stay put until this morning. I was stewing all night." He paused. "What happened to the field and staff officers?"

Messick shook his head and glanced down to the ground. "Colonel Colvill was shot through the ankle and shoulder; Lieutenant Colonel Adams was hit three times—in the chest, groin, and leg; Major Mark Downie was shot in the foot and twice in the right arm; and Adjutant Lieutenant John Pellar was hit by an unexploded shell, breaking his left arm."

"And the company commanders?"

"Company commanders from B, E, I, and K all were casualties," Messick said. "Chris Heffelfinger was lucky. A Minié ball hit him in the chest but was stopped by a memo book in his breast pocket. He is bruised but will stay in command of the company."

"So we've lost Captains Sinclair, Muller, Boyd, and Periam?"

"Yes. But we might get George Boyd back today," Messick said, cracking a slight smile. "He went to the field hospital last night with a leg wound. I heard this morning that it may not be as bad as we first thought."

Messick pointed. "John, have your company linger here a little longer. I'm rousting the rest of the regiment. Once we are gathered we will march toward the copse of trees and rejoin Hawes's brigade."

Ball and Wright saluted and strode back to the company.

Wright glanced at Ball. "Under ordinary circumstances, a regiment suffering a loss greater than half would have been sent to the rear."

"But today is no ordinary circumstance," Ball said.

Wright found Sergeant Henry Taylor, staring down at the ground, distraught. "Henry, it's me, James."

Taylor leapt up and hugged Wright like a big brown bear and sobbed. Wright held him firmly. His heart was pounding and the fluttering in his stomach swirled downward like a dark whirlpool.

After a few moments Henry released his hold.

"Isaac is dead," Henry said. "My poor, poor mother."

"How did it happen?" Wright said.

"We made our charge and ended up in a ravine," Henry said. "We were a few feet from the Rebels and delivered a crushing volley, killing most of the Confederates in the front line. Then we dropped down behind rocks, firing as fast as we could. Then there was hand-to-hand fighting. We were getting the best of them, the regiment charging three times. But the Rebels held each time. There were just too many of them."

Henry stopped a moment, catching his breath, and wiping the tears from his cheeks.

"Then Colonel Colvill was hit. I couldn't see him after he fell, but he gave the order to withdraw. As we were falling back, an artillery shell exploded overhead." Henry's voice cracked. "A piece of hot shrapnel sliced into Isaac's head, cleaving him in two. He died instantly...and didn't suffer, thank God."

Wright said nothing. Isaac was gone.

After a pause to collect himself, Henry said, "I left Isaac where he fell, but I promised myself to return and fetch him. Then I fell back with the regiment. After we regrouped, I found I was the senior member of our company." He swallowed hard. "Our company of thirty-six officers and enlisted had been reduced to nine men."

"Did you look for Isaac last night?" Wright said.

Henry whispered, "Yes, a small group of us scoured the battlefield late last night. We found some wounded. But we did not find Isaac. I plan on going out again."

Wright thanked Henry for the update, a lump in his throat. He told Henry he would be back soon to check on him, then he moved back to his company. Just 47 of 262 men had not been wounded. And he bet some of the 47 were hit but stayed with the regiment. The First Minnesota had been torn to shreds like a tattered battle flag. Tears streamed down his face like hard rain. He inhaled a deep breath, letting it out slowly. But they had halted the Rebel charge and retired with their colors—and their honor.

*6:30 a.m.*

The sun was now well above the horizon. Messick called the company commanders and Wright together behind the regiment, telling them the First Minnesota was to join the rest of Harrow's brigade line a few hundred yards north. Gibbon's division was centered about a copse of trees. Webb's brigade was formed next to the copse; Hall's brigade was formed south of Webb's; and Harrow's was south of Hall's.

*8:00 a.m.*

Messick walked to the front of the regiment as the men fell into line. With Wright's Company F joining them, the regiment now numbered sixty-seven. Heavy infantry fire cracked in steady waves from Culp's Hill. It was quiet in front of Cemetery Ridge. Wright moved off to the side of the companies forming the skeleton regiment. What a pitiful picture; the boys' faces, hands, and clothing were stained with dirt, grime, and black powder. Their faces were haunted, their eyes hollow.

Wright yelled out, and the men began to move, slugging upward along the back side of the ridge. After a few hundred yards, the regiment passed Stannard's new brigade of Vermont boys taking position on the left flank of Gibbon's division.

Wright spotted the Vermonters, full regiments of newly minted troops. The thinned-out Minnesota regiment, in dusty, torn-up uniforms, was about the size of one of Stannard's companies.

*8:30 a.m.*
*Along Cemetery Ridge*

The Minnesotans halted just beyond the Eighty-second New York line anchoring Gibbon's left flank. Wright yelled to fall out, and the regiment moved toward Gibbon's division line. The First Minnesotans threaded themselves between the troops from New York on the left and the Fifteenth Massachusetts on the right, their sister regiment.

A chorus of whoops rang out. The Massachusetts boys had spotted the First Minnesotans arriving. Wright beamed. Word must have spread about Colonel Colvill's courageous charge yesterday. The regiment could use some cheering, and being recognized by the tough Boston boys was something special. Then the New Yorkers erupted with a thunderous yell, cheering the First Minnesota's remarkable feat. For a few moments, Wright's chest swelled with pride, buoyed by the cheering, as if they were marching in a victory parade.

Wright glanced ahead at the Boston and New York boys coiled behind a small makeshift breastwork, an extension of the small stone wall crossing in front of the copse of trees a few hundred yards to the north. The First Minnesota arrived along the defensive line. Wright ordered the boys to erect miniature breastworks, connecting with the Fifteenth Massachusetts and Eighty-second New York. They gathered cobblestones, sticks, brush, and fence rails, piling them into a barricade. Lacking entrenching tools, they used bayonets as pick axes, loosening the ground, and tin plates as shovels, scooping up dirt and sand to fill in the gaps in the wall. Then they filled knapsacks with dirt and piled them behind the wall like sandbags.

In a short time, each man had built three or four feet of barricade. The small breastwork was less than fifty yards long and two feet high, but the barricade would provide some shelter from the expected Rebel storm. The aroma of coffee drifted over from the Fifteenth Massachusetts. Wright's empty stomach rumbled. "Start fires and cook breakfast," he shouted.

Several small fires started behind the First Minnesotans. As they were cooking, Wright spotted Captain Farrell marching his company toward the First Minnesota. Company C had been performing guard duty for Gibbon's division. Farrell was a quiet man and a thorough soldier. Wright joined Messick as Farrell reported to him, saying Gibbon had ordered the division's provost guard back to the regiment.

"Do you think something is up?" Messick asked.

"Well, Meade does," Farrell said. "He wants the extra manpower on the battle line. Hancock believes the Rebels will attack our center position."

Messick nodded. "Sergeant Wright. Have the regiment bump up together along the line and squeeze in Company C between B and D companies."

Wright led Farrell's company toward the line. The day continued to heat up as Wright kept a close watch on the men. The morning passed with only scattered firing. Not enough to disrupt some of the sleeping Minnesotans slouched behind the small wall. Others passed the morning perched twenty yards behind the line on the gentle downward slope, sipping coffee, writing letters, enjoying the pause in the fighting. But the silence felt ominous, like a hovering shadow. Lee was up to something.

Wright cracked a smile. A rumor was floating about that if the Rebels hadn't attacked by noon, they were retreating back to Virginia. Maybe it was going to be a humdrum day. The First Minnesota deserved some quiet after yesterday.

## 43

# Meade — Friday, July 3

Meade stood alone in the shade of the Leister porch, having returned from visiting Little Round Top with Warren. The butterflies in his stomach were expecting the day's battle to erupt soon. What he expected didn't make complete sense. Lee's tactics were as clear as the driven slush.

He motioned toward Biddle. "I need a cup of water." Biddle disappeared inside the house.

Meade moved to the edge of the porch and, using his hand as a shade screen, glanced into the empty blue sky. High overhead, the blistering sun had started to fall from its noon zenith. He turned and stared at Little Round Top. The summit had provided a splendid view of Seminary Ridge, where the enemy was forming a long line of batteries and massing its troops.

"Here you go, General Meade." Biddle handed Meade a glass of water.

"Thank you, James." Meade's voice was raspy. He gripped the cup and gulped down water like a shot of whiskey. His throat cleared; he took another gulp and handed the glass back to Biddle. "Warren believes the Confederates are preparing to attack the center of the Union line, near the copse of trees," Meade said. "They are assembling what appears to be every available cannon and pointing them toward Gibbon's division."

"If Warren is correct, the Rebels will have to march across an open field over three-quarters of a mile long, exposed and vulnerable to Union artillery and rifle fire," Biddle said.

"Conducting a frontal attack across this long open ground is idiocy," Meade said. "As the enemy moves forward across the

639

open field, I can easily shift forces from the flanks, buttressing the middle of the line and repelling the enemy."

"The other possibility is that Lee's attack against our center is a diversion and the main attack will hit one of our flanks," Biddle said.

"That's a possibility," Meade said. "That's what I would do."

"I can't imagine Lee conducting a full-blown assault against the Union center," Biddle said.

"I agree." Lee had to be up to something, and Meade couldn't figure out what it was. "I'm not going to reinforce Gibbon until I'm sure Lee's main attack is against our center."

Meade suppressed a growing skepticism that all preparations for receiving an enemy attack had been made. Were they? What was he missing? Sickles's screw-up still troubled him.

Staff officers gathered in the yard, standing near tethered horses, chatting. The sharpshooters from both sides were quiet; their occasional musket fire had been missing this morning. Although the two great armies were locked against one another, they seemed to be taking a gentlemanly pause.

"Does the general desire anything?" asked Biddle, emerging from the front door.

"Damn it, James, if I want something I will ask for it." Meade's fiery face was as hot as wolf piss.

James struggled to mask his crestfallen face. Meade scowled. *Damn it, George, curb your rage.*

Meade walked off the porch and stood on the edge of Taneytown Road, staring northward. The blazing sun seared his flesh. He was still stewing over his Culp's Hill blunder. He would not move troops too soon today. He would wait until the enemy attack was in full motion.

Meade lit a cigar, taking several deep puffs, letting the hot smoke singe his fragile lungs.

Sharpe rode up and dismounted. "I just left the copse of trees. All indications are Lee is going to attack our center."

"Lee is trying to bait me, using his artillery against my center to cover his main attack, which will be another flanking attack," Meade said. "He wants me to move reinforcements to the middle of the line, so he can attack a weakened flank, skirt around the Round Tops, and rush his army toward Washington. I'm not going to fall for his deception. I'm going to keep my middle line thin, just 6,000 soldiers."

"That is not nearly enough to repel a massive enemy assault," Sharpe said.

"I'm rolling the dice again, counting on my ability to rush in reinforcements before the enemy breaks through." Meade smiled. Interior lines—a wonderful advantage.

---

*12:30 p.m.*

Meade walked around the house into the backyard. Standing in the crook of the fishhook battle line, he stared westward across the rising berm resembling the raised ledge of a beach. The tops of the copse of trees were visible. A few yards away, signalmen flapped their flags, slicing the thick air like knives. He peered at his watch; it was half past noon.

No couriers. No messengers. No news. His gut fluttered and his shoulders tensed. "Son of a bitch!" *Is Lee outplaying me? Am I stumbling into an enemy trap?*

A single rifle shot cracked and a bullet whizzed overhead. A few seconds later, a single rifle answered with a peppered bang.

"What the hell is going on?" Meade muttered.

He mounted a horse and galloped toward Gibbon's line with Biddle and three of Rush's Lancers following. The horse cut through the muggy air, creating a wind that hit his face like a blast furnace. Maybe Gibbon had some sign of Rebel activity. Ahead Meade spotted the blue figures huddled against the back of the small stone wall. As he approached, his horse lurched, stumbled into a shallow ditch, and halted on all fours. Meade slid forward into the horn of the saddle, crunching his crotch as if a sledge hammer had slammed into his stomach. Tasting the backwash of bitter bile, he let out a long, rasping groan. He leaned back, regaining his balance. He grabbed his chest.

"Damn it." He winced from the pinching sting of the old lung wound. He took small, quick breaths, the throbbing easing gradually, like a slow-moving iceberg.

641

Biddle reined up next to Meade. "General, are you alright?"

Meade nodded his head. "I need just a second." Meade continued to pant like a bushed bobcat. Without looking at Biddle, he spurred his horse toward the crest, riding to where the Confederate brigade had penetrated the Union line yesterday. He whiffed a rank and pungent odor. Putrefying enemy corpses oozed thick, brownish fluid from their mouths, noses, and bloated abdomens, marking yesterday's Rebel high-water mark. What a God-awful sight.

* * *

*12:35 p.m.*

Meade spotted Warren sitting astride his horse on the crest, looking through his field glasses toward Seminary Ridge. He rode over.

"Gouv, what will Lee do?" Meade rubbed his throbbing chest.

Warren pointed toward Seminary Ridge. "The Confederates are massing a long line of batteries. It looks like they plan on bombarding the center of our line. My guess is that after they soften our center, they will conduct an infantry attack."

Meade looked through his field glasses, guessing the Rebels already had well over a hundred batteries in a line and were adding more.

"You may be right," Meade muttered. "But it could be a diversion."

A courier from Howard delivered a message. "Confederate cavalry has been seen moving around the northern part of Gettysburg eastward toward Baltimore. General Howard believes it is General Stuart."

Meade turned to Biddle. "Where are General Gregg and General Kilpatrick's cavalry divisions?

"Both Gregg and Kilpatrick are by Rock Creek, near the Baltimore Turnpike, watering their horses," Biddle said.

"Good." Meade turned toward his nephew, Captain Francis Bache. "Ride to Rock Creek. Tell General Gregg that I order him to meet Stuart's cavalry."

Bache nodded, his face contorted, looking confused.

"Do you understand the order?" Meade said sharply.

Bache stammered, "Yes, sir, General Meade."

Meade stared at his nephew for a long moment. Biddle thought Bache was an empty-headed young man. But Bache had one attribute Meade valued more than any other: Loyalty.

Meade said. "Tell Kilpatrick I order his cavalry division to go south around Big Round Top and fall on the extreme right of Longstreet."

Bache saluted. "Yes, sir!" He rode off toward Culp's Hill.

Meade turned to Warren. "Well, Gouv. We've found Stuart's cavalry. Now what?"

Warren shook his head and furrowed his brow. "Lee has battered us for two days with piecemeal attacks. Today, his focus will be a single crushing blow. Looking at how he is massing his artillery, I believe he will first conduct a massive artillery barrage against a narrow part of the Union line. After the line has been shattered, he will hurl his infantry forward, trying to crack our defenses, split our line, and fold the two halves backward onto Culp's Hill and Little Round Top as one would swing open two double doors."

Meade nodded. "What about Stuart's cavalry?"

"Well." Warren said, rubbing his chin. "I believe Stuart's goal is to make the Rebel rout complete by attacking our rear defenses, destroying our logistics wagons, and capturing our retreating soldiers."

"Maybe you've figured out Lee's trap," Meade said.

Warren nodded, flashing a small smile.

"I want you to ride to Little Round Top," Meade said. "From there you can observe the barrage fire, warning me when and where the Rebels will assault our lines. If they do conduct an infantry assault against our center, I will reinforce it with infantry from our flanks. If they conduct an infantry assault against Little Round Top, you will be there, and I will send reinforcements."

Warren saluted and rode off toward Little Round Top. A clatter from behind. Meade cocked his head. One of Hunt's ammo wagons bounced toward the copse of trees, dipping with the rolling ground. A chill crackled inside him. Lee's attack was imminent. He galloped back toward the Leister House, finding Butterfield and Williams at the map table.

"Although I'm not convinced Lee will conduct an assault against our center with an infantry charge, he is giving the appearance he will do so," Meade said. "I want to move General Robinson's Second Division of First Corps from his reserve position on Culp's Hill to a reserve position in the rear of Cemetery Hill. From this position Robinson can reinforce Howard's forces on Cemetery Hill or Hancock's forces in the center of Cemetery Ridge."

*12:55 p.m.*

Meade strode back to the porch. He fished out his watch. Almost one o'clock. A messenger rode up, saluted. "General Meade, General Hancock sends his compliments and wishes to report the Confederate artillery batteries now stretch northeast from the peach orchard and north along Seminary Ridge. He estimates well more than 150 cannons. He believes they will commence firing very soon."

"Thank you for the report," Meade said. Although Warren's assessment seemed fitting, he was still uncertain. There were too many unknowns. Lee rarely acted in a predictable way. Why would he start now?

A courier rode up. The young lieutenant with a short, square face said, "General Slocum sends his respects and reports fighting has stopped on Culp's Hill. General Johnson's Rebel division has fallen back and Twelfth Corps has taken 500 prisoners."

Meade nodded. *Good.* The Union fishhook line was intact. Culp's Hill was the first clear Union victory in three days of battle. Lee had not expected him to attack this morning, nor had Lee expected him to win. Meade stood fidgeting, his hands clenching and unclenching.

He glanced past the aides standing in the yard in front of the Leister House. Several reporters, including Samuel Wilkeson of the *New York Tribune* and Whitelow Reid of the *Cincinnati Gazette*, hovered like vultures. Meade sneered. Whatever they reported, the news would take considerable time to reach the press. The battle was being fought in a region almost devoid of telegraph and railroad lines. He cracked a smile. Reporters without instant access to the telegraph. That seemed like poetic justice.

---

*1:06 p.m.*
*Rebel artillery barrage starts at 1:07 p.m.*

It was a few minutes past one o'clock.

Meade removed his glasses, wiped his face with his sleeve. A thunderous boom pierced the silence like a steam whistle. His stomach tightened as if in a vise.

His eyes jerked to the sky, spotting the dark gray smoke of a bursting shell directly above the crest of Cemetery Ridge, cracking like the first lightning of a thunderstorm. For a long moment an eerie stillness chilled the air. Perhaps a random firing. He peered through his field glasses. A plume of smoke was rising from the cratered field.

A second cannon blasted, its shell threading its way toward Meade's headquarters. Meade narrowed his eyes, spotting a wispy streamer like a comet's tail crossing toward him. The shell screamed downward, exploding near the Leister House, the earth vomiting clumps of turf, the impact leaving Meade and Biddle shaking in their saddles. A shell chunk ripped through a large chestnut horse hitched to a tree.

"Christ Almighty," Meade said, shaking his head. He surveyed the devastation around them. "I would have sworn this place was out of range for Rebel artillery," he muttered, as much to himself as to Biddle, "but here I am, four hundred yards behind Cemetery Ridge, where they *should* be firing, and *I'm* the damn targ—ahhhhh, *hell*," he exclaimed, glaring at Biddle. "They're not after my headquarters. The damn fool Rebels are cutting their fuses too long again, overshooting by a quarter of a God-damn mile!" He snorted. It was bad enough to be killed by the enemy because of their skill and cunning. But it was a damn disgrace to be killed by the enemy because of their infernal incompetence.

"Fine shooting," Meade said, staring at the unfortunate horse. *Poor creature.* He shook his head. *It could have been me instead of him.*

In an instant, sheets of yellow flames spewed out from a line of guns across Seminary Ridge, the blinding flashes followed by steel shards splattering the ground like rock-sized hailstones. A thunderous roar erupted, shaking the Leister House, ringing his ears.

Meade flinched. His face constricted; his throat dried up with dread. He turned to Biddle. "It's begun, the Rebel artillery attack. My guess is that the cannon firings can mean one of three things: the Rebel gunners are softening the Union lines for an infantry charge, covering a Rebel flanking attack, or covering a Rebel infantry retreat."

Biddle tremored, grim-faced. "My guess is that the Rebel infantry will attack after the cannonading."

"Perhaps," Meade said. "But if their gunners keep cutting their damn fuses too long, we will be hard pressed to witness an attack. Except on Leister House. They couldn't hit it more accurately if they tried." The exploding shells rained down, laying waste to vast parts of the Leister grounds, creating a thick, smoke-choked air.

Meade's staff sprang to their feet, scurrying for cover inside the headquarters house. Horses held loosely by orderlies bolted in fright, plunging riderless toward the ambulances loitering in the rear across Taneytown Road. Meade stood on the porch, gazing at the bombardment. Oddly, his fidgeting had stopped. It was as if ice coursed through his veins. His nerves were as calm as if he were sipping afternoon high tea.

It had been nerve-wracking, milling around all morning waiting for Lee to act. But now Lee had thrown the first punch. His next move would soon be revealed. Meade had prepared. Now he just had to wait. No more dwelling on what-ifs. Now he could focus on hitting back.

Meade glanced into the house. Many of the aides were inside, hunkered down. The ones in the yard were edging closer to the porch, situated on the leeward side of the bombardment.

Not wanting to miss any messages, Meade yelled for the signalmen to stay put. He narrowed his eyes, spotting the larger shells falling in arched curves toward the house. The smaller artillery shells were invisible and screamed like howling gray wolves as they streaked downward.

The minutes ticked by with no return Union artillery fire. Meade turned to Biddle. "How long is Hunt going to wait before returning fire?"

*1:16 p.m.*

Before Biddle could answer, Hunt's eighty Union guns thundered, joined seconds later by Hancock and Howard's fifty artillery guns. One hundred and thirty Union guns dueling with Lee's. Shells streaked across the sky, crisscrossing like enormous flocks of black birds. The earth shook beneath Meade's feet like an earthquake; the fields along Cemetery Ridge seemed to roll like gentle waves.

A courier rode up. "General Meade, sir. General Hancock reports the majority of the Rebel artillery rounds are flying over the crest, exploding several yards beyond the lines on the reverse slope. The men are hugging the ground along the crest but few are being harmed."

A Rebel shell shrieked toward Meade and Hancock's aide, exploding close by, hitting a driver and a wagon packed with ammunition.

The wide-eyed aide saluted, scrambled back toward the crest. Meade chuckled. He guessed the courier thought he had a better chance of surviving the artillery fire standing along the front lines. Meade continued standing on the side of the Leister House, watching the frightful explosions. He squinted toward Gibbon's line; visibility was becoming limited. The dimming sky darkened as if the roiling clouds of a thunderstorm approached.

Visibility had dwindled to fifty yards across the smoldering ground. No couriers were arriving with information. His mouth hardened, and he steadied his breathing. *Trust your corps commanders.*

"General Meade," Biddle said, "we have to relocate."

"No, I'm not going to relocate." Meade shook his head. "I need to stay at headquarters to command. If I move, messengers will not be able to find me."

"General, if you do not move there will be no commander to command," Biddle shouted.

Meade snarled and shook his head. "Damn it, Biddledee, we're not moving."

A clattering roar of Rebel shells sprinkled the ground in a steady stream, bringing continuous waves of death and destruction. Dead men and animals started piling up near the Leister House.

For the next half hour, the staff stayed put. The bombardment intensified; every few seconds a shell burst overhead or thundered on the ground. An eerie, high-pitched shell spiraled toward the Union headquarters. A thunderous explosion erupted about twenty yards away, the crater sucking the air into the ground. A metal shard whisked by his ear, sounding like a buzzing hornet. He staggered backward like a boxer hit with a right hook, eyes pulsating and skin contracting. The blast wave smashed his chest, and his paralyzed lungs gasped for breath.

The deadly shrapnel shredded a large oak and several small bushes. An orderly screamed, pitching forward while several metal shards ripped through his gut, as if he had been repeatedly stabbed.

"This is horrendous," Biddle said.

Meade cringed, shaking his head. He spotted a gunner running toward the Leister House, carrying a sponge bucket through the rain of shells and shrapnel. He stopped at a spring, filling the bucket with water to swab the hot gun tubes. As the soldier filled the bucket, a solid shot bounced near his legs, and he spilled the bucket of water. Scared but unhurt, the soldier refilled the bucket, running back to the Union batteries. *That was too close.*

"James," Meade shouted, "didn't any of those Confederate officers read Gibbon's *Artillery Manual?* Hell, if they had, they wouldn't be overshooting."

"General, we have to move, sir. I swear, your headquarters is the target of every Rebel gun."

"These Rebel gunners are pathetic," Meade yelled. "The Mexicans could at least cut an accurate fuse. I know because they were aiming at me during the war. And they got a hell of a lot closer to their target than this."

Meade gripped his field glasses, noting the artillery fire was literally riddling the tiny farmhouse. Over the next few moments, several shots tore up the front steps, crashed the porch supports, and ripped through the attic.

"James, shift the staff to the yard in the immediate rear of the house," Meade said.

Meade went over to General Williams. "I'm convinced Lee is going to assault the left center of our line. Warren is on Little Round Top and has not sent any information to the contrary. Send a staff officer to Slocum and tell him I don't believe the Rebels will assault Culp's Hill this afternoon. Direct him to make his line as thin as possible and to send all the troops he can spare to reinforce the line extending to the left of Cemetery Hill."

"Yes, sir," Williams said.

Meade added, "Also, have Sedgwick move Sherrill's brigade supporting Culp's Hill over into Hancock's Second Corps line."

Williams nodded and moved toward his staff riders. Meade paced along the little backyard between the house and the Taneytown Road. Rebel cannonading continued fiercely, the backyard a thundering den of whooshing shots and bursting shells. Meade saw some of his junior staff officers creeping toward the edge of the house. They were trying to slide around to the lee side, away from Rebel bombardment. He waved a hand. The four junior officers stopped, caught. Meade walked over, with Biddle trailing.

"Gentlemen," Meade said, "are you trying to find a safe place? You realize sitting on the open grass would provide you about the same protection as standing behind this farmhouse."

The junior officers listened, brows raised and mouths slightly opened. Skepticism flashed in their dark eyes. One of them groaned.

Meade said with a throaty rumble, "During the Mexican War, at the Battle of Palo Alto, one of our men attempted to protect himself from Mexican artillery. He was driving an ox team carrying ammunition. Finding himself within range of the Mexican guns, he tilted up his cart and got behind it. Just then General Zachary Taylor came along and shouted, 'You damned fool. Don't you know you are no safer there than anywhere else?' The driver replied, 'I don't suppose I am, general, but it kind o' feels so.'"

Meade chuckled at the punch line. After a pregnant pause, none of the anxious officers laughed or even cracked a smile. Meade studied their bewildered faces. Maybe he should explain the joke.

Biddle said, "General, the Leister House is 400 yards behind Hancock's line, and every damn Rebel cannon is overshooting."

A shot tore through the house, exploding near the circle of officers. A voice howled, "I'm hit."

Meade turned and spotted a visiting staff officer, Colonel Joseph Dickinson, clasping the ripped flesh of a slashed knee, the thick blood spurting from the open wound with each beat of the heart like a hand-cranked water pump. A couple of orderlies raced forward, fastening a tourniquet around the wounded leg.

"My God," Meade muttered. "Major Biddle, have some orderlies move Colonel Dickinson to Gibbon's division hospital behind us."

---

*1:30 p.m.*

Meade walked over to Butterfield. "Let's move headquarters down the Taneytown Road to see if we can escape some of this shelling. But I want to remain as close as we can to the Leister House so messengers can find us."

"Yes sir," Butterfield replied. "But it's going to be difficult for the entire staff to move. At least a third of the staff horses have been killed or wounded. This means quite a few of the staff are dismounted and will have to follow you on foot, performing messenger duties without horses until mounts can be located."

Meade nodded. "Leave the signalmen here. Make sure they have enough horses to ride between here and the new headquarters." He paused, looking for Biddle, surprisingly not close by. Meade shrugged, turning to his son George. "Let's ride."

Meade's small cavalcade rode south down the Taneytown road several hundred yards, halting at a barn, the first place along the road where the shells were not falling. The staff dismounted, tethering the horses in a grove of trees, and waited in the shadows. Meade stole an anxious glance at the Leister House, where shells were exploding in a steady downpour. His breath stilled in his chest, and a prickly sensation skittered down his back. My God, it was a torrential hailstorm of metal shards.

## Captain George Meade
*1:35 p.m.*

George turned to his cousin, Captain Bache. "Francis, where is Major Biddle?"

"Major Biddle and several of the junior staff members are still at the Leister House."

"What?"

"When the order came to move, there were not enough horses," Bache said. "To escape the shelling, Biddle and a few officers crawled into a small cellar under the house."

George peered anxiously across the fields at the Leister House, shells continuing to thunder down. "I hope Biddle and the aides survive," George muttered.

A shell burst overhead, marking Meade's new staff location with a white, round puff. A second shell whickered overhead, blowing up behind them, sending dirt clods into the air. George ducked as his heart clenched. How did the enemy find us? The rumbling sound of artillery grew louder, like an approaching thunderstorm. George looked toward Hancock's line. The area around the barn quaked as a heavy roll of enemy artillery fire blossomed overhead.

The wrenching power from the cannons was demonic, monstrous. George held fast, standing next to his horse. The tethered horses were skittish and neighing, looking to flee or rear. A bolt of uneasiness burst in his gut. His eyes narrowed, trying to pick up the flight of the incoming shells and predict where they would land. Several shells crashed near the barn, Meade's new headquarters.

But one shell was different, something terrible about its high whistling, its trajectory, prickling George's skin as he dove to earth. The shell hit a few yards away with a thundering explosion. The ground jumped up, hitting him in the stomach, knocking the wind out of him. He lay on the ground a few moments, gasping for air. After a few minutes, he pushed himself to his knees, taking quick, gagging breaths.

A second nearby shell burst above Butterfield and his staff officers, raining down steel fragments. One metal shard slapped Butterfield in the neck. He keeled over gracefully, as if performing in a tragic Shakespearian masterpiece.

George scrambled over to Butterfield. The chief of staff remained on the ground, moaning as if he were mortally wounded. George looked for blood, spotting nothing. Probably a bruise, at best.

Butterfield whispered, "I'm wounded; please get an ambulance."

One of his aides mounted a horse and rode swiftly to the rear of the lines to find an ambulance.

<hr />

*1:40 p.m.*

George made his way over to Meade. "George, how badly is Butterfield hurt?" Meade asked.

"Not bad," George said. I didn't see any visible wounds."

Meade cracked a smile. "With that performance, Butterfield might have a career on Broadway."

Meade turned to Williams. "You will be acting chief of staff until I can appoint one. I don't expect Butterfield to be returning."

Williams nodded. "Yes, sir." He paused. "General Meade, these are grim conditions for a headquarters. I suggest you move the headquarters back toward Power's Hill where Slocum has Twelfth Corps headquarters, using Slocum's signalman to communicate with the signalmen at the Leister House."

"I'm not so sure," Meade said. "I'm uneasy about commanding from the rear."

"General, dodging Rebel shells is ridiculous," Williams said. "You have to move."

Meade's breathing hitched, and his throat tightened. Messengers needed to arrive and depart freely at army headquarters. He didn't plan on issuing a stream of detailed orders, but it was critical to keep in contact with his corps commanders. He turned toward the Rebel fire. Massive waves of Rebel and Union cannonading cracked, hissed, and roared. No choice but to relocate to Power's Hill.

"You're right," he said reluctantly. He turned to the staff and yelled, "Let's move to Power's Hill."

Meade wheeled his horse and galloped that way, kicking up grass. He would let his personal staff catch up, but he needed to find out what was going on with the corps commanders. One mounted staffer, Captain Emlen Carpenter, and a few orderlies followed. Carpenter was riding nearly even with Meade as they crossed the fields, followed by several Lancer escort guards. Meade turned his head and glanced back. A few staff orderlies followed him, but most did not. No horses.

George had seen his father departing, and he hustled over to the tree where the horses had been tethered. His horse lay dead. He cursed and, having no other options, started running toward Power's Hill. Artillery fire pounded behind him as he ran.

*1:50 p.m.*
*Power's Hill*

Meade arrived on Power's Hill, leading the Lancers in a V-shaped formation. Slocum and his staff clustered around, the sight of the commanding general stirring up everyone. Slocum wore a surprised look, as it was relatively quiet on Power's Hill.

"Good afternoon, General Meade." Slocum saluted.

"General Slocum, with your permission," Meade said, "I will move my headquarters back here temporarily, using Power's Hill to communicate with the corps commanders. The Rebels have been furiously shelling the Leister farmhouse, but I've left a few signalmen there."

Slocum nodded approval. "We've had very little action on Culp's Hill since the Rebels retreated to Rock Creek around eleven this morning."

"Good." Meade turned to see where his staff and aides were, finding them absent. He was astounded, looking for George, finding it hard to believe his son had not been close behind. Where were they? Where in the hell was Biddle? Meade called over to Slocum's signal officer and ordered him to contact the signalmen at the Leister House.

Harsh swearing erupted behind Meade. He swiveled to see Slocum's aides restraining a large, stocky man. The local was pointing at Meade and bellowing; a slender infantry sergeant held his bayonet at the man's chest. Meade trotted over to the man. Carpenter and his mounted cavalrymen hovered close, pistols drawn and cocked.

Meade dismounted and addressed the man sharply. "What's the problem?"

The civilian said, "Are you in charge?"

"I am the commanding general of the Army of the Potomac."

Meade simmered as the civilian loudly presented his complaint. "My house is being used as a hospital. Union soldiers have been buried in my garden. And the grounds are littered with amputated limbs. I'm sure I have a claim upon the Federal government."

Meade's face flared fiery hot. "God damn you. Until this battle is decided, you do not know, and neither do I, whether you will have a government to apply to. If I hear any more from you, I will give you a gun and send you to the front line to defend your claim!"

The stunned man said nothing. He shook his head, moved on, muttering as he went.

"Disgruntled civilians! Almost as bad as reporters," Meade shouted.

He turned his attention back to the signalmen. They reported that General Warren had signaled from Little Round

Top, saying smoke from Union artillery was providing cover for a Rebel infantry attack. The Rebels did not appear to be hurt by the Union cannonading, so Warren suggested General Meade order the Union artillery to stop firing. In this way, they could conserve on ammunition, saving it for the Rebel infantry charge.

Meade concurred, ordering Carpenter to send a rider to General Hunt to tell him to stop firing. Within moments, a Lancer escort guard was streaking down Power's Hill toward Cemetery Ridge.

The signal corps officer reported they were getting no reply from the signalmen at the Leister House. "Damn it," Meade muttered. He could not remain on Power's Hill. He told Slocum he was returning to the Leister house and galloped back toward Cemetery Ridge, followed by a few orderlies and Rush's Lancers. The Union artillery fire was slackening. The rhythmic thundering of Rebel artillery fire was slowing as well. Was Lee really going to launch an infantry attack? If so, he was making an incredible mistake. Meade remembered the Union charge at Fredericksburg. A slaughter.

*Is it time to reinforce the middle of Gibbon's line? I swear by the fires of Hell, I'm not commanding anything sitting on Powers Hill.* "Carpenter, follow me. We're riding to Gibbon's front and finding out what the hell is going on."

# 44

# Haskell — Friday, July 3

*1:10 p.m.*
*Forty minutes earlier*
*In the heat of the battle*

Lieutenant Frank Haskell sat cross-legged on the rumbling ground behind the stone wall in the sweltering heat, his skin glistening on the nape of his neck. A few feet away, Gibbon sat, whittling on a small branch and smoking a pipe. He glanced back thirty yards at Lieutenant Cushing's six artillery cannons, thundering blasts above the wall. Haskell grimaced as he fished out his watch. Ten past one. The two-mile row of Rebel cannons had thundered in continuous broadsides for half an hour. Flashes streaked across the sky, hurling fragments of scorching lead. Haskell traced the flight of the shells, black smoky tendrils streaming from their conical centers. Upon impact, the ground shuddered, bursting open like Judas's bowels. His scalp hair prickled, and tremors rushed through his body. It was like a deadly, swirling thunderstorm hovering over army headquarters, unleashing Biblical devastation.

Haskell got to his feet. "Damn, when will it stop?" he muttered. His heart roared, pounding in his ears, as a creeping despair seeped through him. An eerie premonition came over him as his mind's eye recalled the thousands of grotesque corpses flooding the fields of Antietam. *Certain battles you can't survive, and this may be one of them.* After today's fighting, one of the armies would be ravaged—not dead, perhaps, but never as alive as it was before Gettysburg. The loser would be broken, and no one, neither Lee nor Meade, would be able to put it back together again.

An enemy shot whined overhead and fell short, erupting in the middle of Cushing's battery. Clapping thunder erupted as a limber chest exploded, spraying wooden splinters over the stone wall. A gun crew cartwheeled through the air, falling dead or maimed onto the weed-choked ground. Horses fell dead at their posts. Burnt flesh and smoke hung in a haze, obscuring the blood-red sun. Cushing shouted orders and within moments the remaining big guns were back in action.

Haskell spied Gibbon scurrying toward his horse and orderly. All down the stone wall it was chaos, servants bolting toward the rear, loosely tethered horses breaking free and plunging rider-less across the fields. Haskell shouted for his groom. No one responded. He dropped to one knee, peering under the billow-ing cloud of smoke, spotting several horses tethered nearby. He stood up, his left ankle throbbing like an abscessed tooth from the vicious horse kick last night. He lurched toward the horses, hobbling his way through the smoke, zigzagging to avoid bolting beasts and teamsters, leaping out of the way of supply wagons and ambulances scrambling to escape the hellish shelling. Damn, it looked like a routed army retreating.

The horses appeared in front of him. He edged slowly for-ward, reluctant to be kicked again. He found his horse tethered to a tree. The other horses pawed the ground, neighing loudly with fright, but his horse showed no fear.

Haskell shouted in an exasperated voice, "Sorry to interrupt, Blackie, but General Gibbon is waiting on us."

The horse ignored Haskell, refusing to budge. Haskell fum-bled about, trying to slip the bridle on as Blackie defiantly kept his head down, munching oats. A missile shrieked toward him, exploding close by. A horse pulling a mess wagon was struck by a piece of flying iron. The mortally wounded animal plunged forward into a tree, crashing the wagon and injuring the driver. Another thundering explosion burst overhead, shell fragments raining down on two mules packed with boxes of ammuni-tion. The man leading the mule train screamed in agony as shell fragments sliced his leg. Haskell nearly gagged, throttling the nauseous bile pumping up from his gut from the odor of burning flesh and the sight of bloody gore.

Raw terror set his nerves on edge, but he bottled it up like he had so many battles before. The volume of artillery fire was monstrous, the sound deafening, the ground a ring of fire. He gazed across the field toward the Union lines, witnessing the horrifying carnage.

Mounting his horse, he rode toward the Union batteries, the big guns blasting with a thundering roar. He spotted Gibbon dismounted near the guns, looking through field glasses at the firing line of enemy cannons positioned in front of Seminary Ridge. Haskell spurred his horse into a gallop and reined up next to Gibbon. As Gibbon's aide-de-camp, his job was to stay close to Gibbon. He cringed. Not a great performance so far.

*1:20 p.m.*

Gibbon stood waiting. With some relief in his voice, he shouted, "Good to see you. I thought something had happened."

"I'm a bit tardy," Haskell said. "It was hard bridling Blackie as he insisted on keeping his head down, eating his oats. The horse either has nerves of steel or he couldn't quite grasp the urgency of the situation."

Gibbon nodded. He turned away, pointing. "Let's walk up to the infantry line and check on the boys. They seem to have vanished in all this rolling smoke."

Gibbon and Haskell handed the reins to orderlies, leaving the horses behind on the sharp eastern slope of Cemetery Ridge. The two officers moved past the Union batteries, the big guns roaring continuously, creating an ear-splitting din. The cannoneers seemingly were oblivious to the noise, working hard to fire the guns as rapidly as possible, some swabbing, some ramming, some loading, and some cooling the iron barrels with water-soaked sponges.

Gibbon and Haskell groped forward at a snail's pace, looking for the infantry, hunkered down behind the stone wall. Twenty yards from the wall a hole appeared in the smoke, revealing the infantry armed with muskets, behind the breastworks, hugging the ground. Haskell peered up and down the stone wall. Amazingly, the men were not terrified, and many of them had chosen to lie flat, stretched out in the hot, baking sun, sleeping.

Lying down provided some relief from the dense, sulfurous artillery smoke, capable of searing the eyes and lungs.

Gibbon turned to Haskell. "The men are safer here than in the rear. The Rebs are shooting too high."

"One thing is for sure, Meade's headquarters must be taking a terrible thrashing," Haskell said. "The Rebel artillery is overshooting our lines by a good 200 to 300 yards."

"Let's hunker down and bide our time," Gibbon said. "There's nothing to do yet but observe."

Gibbon and Haskell sat down behind the crest, just south of Cushing's battery, watching the bombardment. The enemy artillery line was some two miles long, the range about a thousand yards. The Rebels were firing solid shot and spherical shells, focusing on Second Corps' position near the copse of trees.

Gibbon said, "Order the division colors unfurled and place them near me. It's critical couriers can find division headquarters. Plus, the Rebels couldn't see the flag through all the smoke."

Haskell shouted, "Unfurl the division colors." He motioned to the flag bearer to plant them by Gibbon.

Half past one in the afternoon.

Haskell shuddered. The hissing, screaming projectiles were striking some distance beyond the wall; the shelling continuing relentlessly. Every now and then a shell blossomed over the stone wall, showering the line with razor-sharp shrapnel, killing, slashing, mangling. The groaning cries of the wounded filled the air. His stomach writhed and his pulse raced. *Christ Almighty. When would the cannonading stop?*

There was a sharp, hissing sound. Haskell swiveled as a percussion shell struck nearby, scattering whistling fragments. A hot piece of metal kissed his cheek. His hand touched his face. *No blood. Thank God.*

Gibbon jumped up. "Let's move up to the front lines and see how the men are doing."

They headed to the stone wall, stopping to bolster the men. The soldiers were calm and relaxed. Gibbon turned to Haskell. "Let's move beyond the breastworks to get a better view of the Confederate infantry."

*1:35 p.m.*
*No man's land*

They hopped over the stone wall, moving down the western slope of the ridge a few hundred yards into the open fields between the two enemies' lines. Emerging from the smoke, they sat under some large elm trees, the drooping branches providing some welcome shade. From there they could see across the fields toward the opposite ridge, covered with low-hanging smoke from the enemy guns.

Rebel skirmishers were a few hundred yards in front of the Confederate artillery. The Rebels knelt on one knee, like a row of gray posts confronting a line of blue skirmishers, kneeling, equally silent and still. But no enemy infantry was in sight. Haskell turned back toward the stone wall covered by a blanket of white smoke. The booming cannons rattled his chest.

"I may not be a member of any church, but I've always had a strong religious feeling," Gibbon mused. "In all these battles I believe I'm in the hands of God, and it's according to his will if I'm harmed or not. That's why I'm ready to go where duty calls, no matter how great the danger."

Haskell nodded. It was a rare personal comment from the general. Haskell held a different belief: *Don't tempt God. If a shell is screaming toward you with your name on it, kiss the ground or run like hell.*

Haskell studied Gibbon for a moment. Some soldiers talked about mortality when they sensed death was near and going to pay a visit. Sometimes they would write a note or a poem, giving it to friend they thought would survive. Or they would forecast their own death, as Nelson had prior to the Battle of Trafalgar: *Tomorrow will be a fortunate day for you, young gentlemen, but I will not live to see it.* Haskell shuddered. Was Gibbon foreshadowing his Nelson-like day? The general had never spoken like that before.

A shell came screaming toward them. They flung themselves flat, hugging the ground tightly. A shell burst overhead, the flash a bright gleam of lightning radiating from a small cloudburst, fragments hissing in all directions, tearing and plowing the ground.

Haskell shouted something, words made incomprehensible by the howling of death come to call, falling from the sky all around them.

*1:50 p.m.*

Several moments later, the Union's heavy cannonading seemed to slacken a bit, the artillery firing rate slowing as the big guns silenced one by one.

Gibbon stood, pointed toward the stone wall. "Let's move back to the lines."

They walked toward the crest, crossed over the stone wall, and strode toward Cushing's battery, their guns momentarily quiet. Hazard's batteries continued to fire. In the rear of the ridge, stretching for a thousand yards, the field was filled with a shocking number of stricken horses and twisted corpses. They walked down off the slope, avoiding riderless horses galloping madly through the hail of slaughter. A sea of wounded soldiers whimpered for water.

Haskell stopped by an injured soldier and picked up a canteen. He held it to the man's cracked lips as the wounded soldier gulped. Haskell lingered for several moments among the critically injured men, collecting as many canteens of water as he could find, dropping them next to the wounded soldiers. He spotted Gibbon striding toward Webb's brigade, positioned in front of the copse of trees and the angle in the stone wall on Cemetery Ridge. Haskell sprinted and caught up with him, and the two continued toward Webb. The brigade commander was standing exposed in front of his line, just beyond the stone wall. As Haskell and Gibbon approached, soldiers shouted for Webb to take shelter. Webb ignored the calls.

Webb saluted Gibbon.

"What do you think this bombardment means?" Gibbon asked him.

"I think it is going to end soon, and then they will conduct a fierce infantry charge," Webb replied.

"It's beginning to look that way," Gibbon said. "They have shot a lot of ammunition. I'm not sure they have enough to begin softening another part of our battle line."

"It feels like a hundred Rebel guns are sighted on you, General Webb," Haskell said in a worried voice.

"I have lost about fifty men and officers, all lying down behind the stone wall," Webb said. "I have been struck three or four times with stones and dirt. But the brigade is still strong."

Gibbon nodded.

Webb was clearly irritated. "General Hays's Third Division is on my right flank. I think he's worried about my brigade holding, since I've been in command just three days. He sent over his staff officer, Lieutenant David Shields, to see how I was standing up. I was more than pissed, and I told Shields the men of the Philadelphia Brigade were in line and Goddamn ready."

"General Hays is probably just jesting with you because he's bored," Gibbon said, cracking a half smile. "But he is a tough fighter, so you won't have to worry about your right flank."

"Well, my Pennsylvania boys are tough fighters, too, and we will hold our own today," Webb said.

"I'm sure you will, Alexander."

## 45

# First Minnesota — Friday, July 3

### *Wright*

*1:53 p.m.*
*Next to the defensive wall*

Sergeant Wright lay flat on his belly alongside the sixty-seven surviving members of the First Minnesota. The regiment snuggled against the makeshift breastworks of rails, stones, sticks, brush, and dirt-filled knapsacks. The two-foot-high barricade was 120 yards south of the copse of trees. The cannonading pounded Wright's skull as if he had covered his ears with the palms of his hands and drummed his fingers on the back of his head.

Wright cautiously raised his head and glanced down the line, his saluting hand shading his eyes from the scorching sun. Sweat dripped from his brow, stinging his eyes. He wiped his face with his sleeve. The soldiers were taking it all with a peculiar casualness, many lying on their backs and sides, hats covering their faces, ignoring the hideous bombarding, the tons of exploding iron hitting a few hundred yards beyond the breastworks. Whistling its sinister warning, a shell hurtled through the air, aiming directly at Wright.

He wilted back into the ground, shoving his face into the dirt. His heart beat in his ears as if he had been sprinting up a hill. A crescendoing roar like a train in a tunnel thundered down on him. The shell exploded in front of the breastworks, creating a gale-force blast of flying shrapnel and rocks. His skin stretched; his eyes pulsed. His bones twisted into sponges. The blast sucked the air out of his lungs, and he fought for breath.

Wright popped up his head and breathed through his nose, filling his collapsed chest. He wiped the sweat from his face and glanced beyond the breastworks. Dark smoke tendrils rose from the ground like vents in the earth.

He craned his neck to see his pocket watch. His eyes grew wide. It was nearly two.

Enough was enough. A neverending hour of blistering artillery. It seemed as if Hell's gate had opened, spewing its fiery vengeance and black smoke. Then, as suddenly as they had begun, the Union cannons stopped firing. A few moments later, a Rebel shell fell short again, exploding in front of the breastworks, showering the First Minnesota with dirt and rocks. He buried his head deeper into the ground, gritting his teeth, expecting any minute to be blown to smithereens. Would the Rebel bombardment ever stop?

Through the blasting thunder and swirling smoke, several soldiers started hollering. The yelling was coming from his left and growing closer. Emerging from the smoke and moving slowly along the breastworks like a crusader on his mount was a tall officer on a large horse. Riding just behind was a color bearer streaming the large Second Corps headquarters flag.

*Damn.* It was Hancock...Hancock the Superb. Wright cracked a grin, hopped up from the ground, and saluted. Hancock smiled, doffing his hat, yelling out encouraging comments. Captain Messick, commanding the First Minnesota, walked up next to Wright.

Wright yelled into Messick's ear. "Hancock should get down and seek cover."

Messick shouted, "General Hancock, sir. Please consider dismounting. We've had several recent close calls along the line with Rebel artillery."

Hancock replied with a booming voice. "Well, gentlemen, there are times to take cover and times to stand tall. This is the time for the latter. So standing tall means a corps commander's life doesn't count. Let's lick those Rebs!"

Hancock moved forward along the line, riding north toward Webb's brigade and the copse of trees, indifferent to the shells flying overhead. Wright shook his head. It was true...Hancock was superb! What an inspiring leader! An eerie humming echoed across the battlefield, followed by a dead calm. The Confederate bombardment had stopped.

Wright glanced at his watch, his ears ringing like buzzing cicadas. *Damn, a one-hour artillery duel.*

Corporal Henry O'Brien of Company E stood up and yelled, "Here they come!"

*2:15 p.m.*

From afar, the long gray infantry lines seemed to be walking through a solid wall of smoke, giving them an eerie appearance. Wright's throat tightened.

The dull gray legions adorned with blood-red battle flags rolled toward them in perfect order, unfaltering and unwavering. It was a stunning burst of single-minded power, seemingly mythical and without limits, moving in unison to heavy-spirited drumrolls. Gooseflesh covered his arms. His heartbeat rocketed. The Rebel assault force was an army of death, casting a thick blanket of gloom as it spread out over the battlefield.

The Union artillery started firing, but it seemed to have little effect on the half-mile enemy front, a sloping forest of flashing barrels and glinting bayonets.

Wright turned to Captain Messick, staring pale-faced and breathing shallowly. "My God, we need more reinforcements in Union center, urgently."

# Pickett's Charge
## Afternoon, July 3, 1863

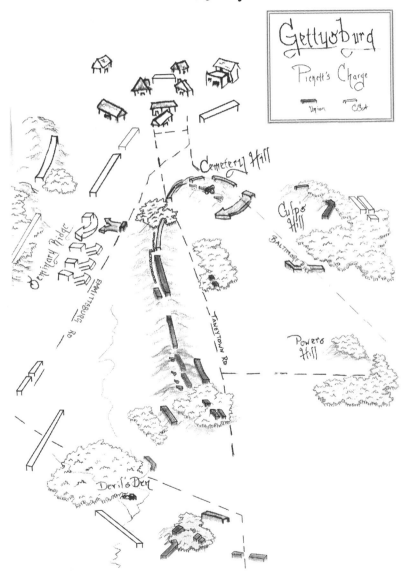

Gettysburg

Pickett's Charge

Union    CSA

Cemetery Hill

Gulps Hill

Baltimore

Seminary Ridge

Emmitsburg Rd

Taneytown Rd

Powers Hill

Devil's Den

## 46

# Haskell — Friday, July 3

*2:00 p.m.*
*Fifteen minutes earlier*

Haskell stood, blinking as if dazed, the lingering tang of Union artillery smoke stinging his eyes. He spotted a great red ball burning through the dense, yellowish clouds of smoke.

Two in the afternoon.

For one solid hour a monstrous storm had raged, far greater than a violent summer tempest of crashing thunder, glaring lightning, shrieking wind, and clattering hailstones. The earth had shuddered beneath his feet, and the hills and ridges had seemed to reel like a drunken man.

The horrific artillery duel had ebbed to stillness, the thick silence saturating the battlefield like a slow poison. He breathed out long and low, his gut unclenching momentarily. He stared across the valley of death, his eyes fixed on Seminary Ridge. Hundreds of silver-gray tendrils escaped the throats of muzzled Rebel cannons, curling and dancing skyward, darkening the sky like heavy smoke venting from chimneys.

Haskell sighed. "Hmm." No enemy infantry…yet. Was this firing pause the last drop of the curtain before the great final act of a Confederate retreat or attack? Or had it shown that, by all his bowling, the Rebel did not mean retreat? Surely the next fifteen minutes would provide the answer.

He turned and faced eastward, his narrowed eyes scanning across an open field sloping downward toward the Leister House. He shook his head and his throat constricted. A flood tide of mangled human corpses lay strewn across the field, resembling the gruesome remains of a Chicago slaughterhouse. Several dozen horses lay dead on their sides, their legs stiffened, their vitals and blood smearing the ground. It was heartrending. Haskell turned and walked toward the silent gun batteries, passing several stricken horses, killed and wounded around the batteries. Dozens of shattered men lay dead among destroyed caissons, limbers, and carriages, the surviving men shouting and scurrying to repair the torn-up batteries.

Haskell walked toward Cushing's battery, the exposed guns located behind and nearby the stone wall's ninety-degree angle. The batteries around the angle had suffered the greatest damage, serving as the bull's-eye for Confederate artillery fire. The enemy shells had plunked down constantly around Cushing's boys, his artillerymen suffering terribly.

Haskell stopped and knelt next to a private, writhing in agony, holding his gut. Haskell said, "What is your name, Private?"

"Arsenal Griffin, sir."

"How bad is the wound?" Haskell said.

"I think it's mortal, sir." Griffin moved his hands away from his stomach a bit and some of his entrails spilled out onto the ground.

"My God," Haskell whispered.

"A shell fragment tore away the flesh on my gut." The private turned his head and vomited up blood. "Lieutenant, please pull my revolver from my holster and shoot me. I can't take the pain."

"Private Griffin, I can't do that," Haskell said. "Let me get you a canteen, and I will get an orderly to take you back to General Gibbon's hospital. I will be right back."

A deep moan escaped the private's lips. "Don't leave me, sir! It hurts! Please shoot me," he said, with a pleading tone.

Haskell stood up and started jogging toward Cushing's battery.

"Lieutenant," yelled Griffin.

Haskell stopped and turned. Griffin had pulled out his revolver and put it to his head. "I won't be needing the canteen." He cocked the gun and shouted, "Good-bye, boys!" He pulled the trigger and blew his brains out of his skull.

Haskell's stomach lurched and lunchtime chicken chunks spewed out. He put his hands on his knees and puked again. He wiped his fouled hands on his trousers, stood up on his wobbly knees, and walked watery-eyed toward Lieutenant Cushing.

Webb reined up, his big brown horse skidding to a stop next to Cushing.

Haskell walked over to Cushing and Webb. Cushing's blouse was drenched with blood and his trousers were torn and blood-stained.

"My God, Alonzo!" Webb said woefully, "How badly are you wounded?"

"Shell fragments ripped into my right shoulder and abdomen and groin. The bastards got my balls!" Cushing grunted.

"Lieutenant!" Webb shouted. "Go to the division hospital in the rear and get those wounds treated."

Cushing shook his head, turned, and vomited.

"Alonzo," Haskell pleaded, "you have to get some medical attention. You're badly mangled and losing quite a bit of blood. Get some help… We still need you."

"Hell, Lon," Webb said, "you can barely stand on your feet and yell out commands."

Cushing shook his head. "No, I'm not going to the rear. I'm going to stay right here and fight it out or die in the attempt!" He paused and spit blood. "Sergeant Fuger will stand beside me and relay my orders to the artillerymen."

Webb said, "My guess is the Rebel infantry will charge our position."

Cushing paused as if he was trying to figure out a hard math problem. "Well," he said, "then I had better run my guns right up to the stone wall. Only two of my six artillery pieces are serviceable."

"Do so." Webb said. "I'm going to order Rorty's, Brown's, Arnold's, and Woodruff's batteries forward to the wall as well." He spurred his horse.

Cushing turned to Sergeant Fuger. "Order the cannons to the stone wall."

Cushing took a step forward and stopped, gasping.

Haskell's breathing hitched. "Alonzo?"

Cushing's face was ghostly white, his skin stretched thin like a blade of grass, his long brown hair straggling over his brow. He was holding his exposed intestines in place with his hand, blood oozing past his fingers.

"Looks worse than it is, Frank." Cushing spit out a gob of blood. "I'll go to the rear after the Rebel assault."

Haskell's stomach recoiled as if had swallowed a vial of hemlock. Cushing's dying blue eyes struggled to flicker. Alonzo would be dead in the next hour, one way or another.

Cushing turned, wobbled slowly toward the stone wall. His artillerymen were positioning the two guns about ten feet from the breastwork. Haskell judged the distance between the guns to be about eight or nine feet. The two-wheel caissons carrying the artillery ammunition were left behind, the men carrying all the remaining canisters forward, setting them next to the guns. Finishing, some of the men leaned against the wagon wheels, catching their breaths and wiping sweat from their sooty faces.

---

*2:15 p.m.*

General Hunt and his cavalcade rode up at a gallop. "Lieutenant Haskell, tell General Gibbon I just rode from Little Round Top," he bellowed. "The Confederate infantry is massing behind Seminary Ridge for an assault. I would estimate close to 15,000 Rebels."

Haskell glanced toward Seminary Ridge, the smoke clearing from the crests. His breath caught and his heart leaped.

Hunt shouted, "Also tell General Gibbon I've ordered battery replacements from the artillery reserve to take the places of the disabled ones."

Haskell scurried toward the southern side of the copse of trees, toward Gibbon's white trefoil flag. He stopped next to Gibbon, the general staring through his field glasses toward Seminary Ridge. An eerie silence fell over the Union lines. An ominous power was building behind Seminary Ridge, like flood-waters rising behind a large dike.

Gibbon said, "I'm inclined to believe the Confederates are falling back, the cannonading merely a deception to cover an infantry retreat."

Haskell shook his head, "I'm not sure about that, sir. General Hunt believes the massing graybacks are coming our way. Hunt estimates 15,000 Rebels. My guess is Lee will attack us. Either way, we will know in fifteen minutes."

Orderlies led two horses to Gibbon and Haskell. The officers mounted and rode toward Webb's brigade and Cushing's guns. As they were approaching Webb, several members of the Pennsylvania Brigade pointed, yelling, "There they are! The Rebel infantry is coming from the forest!"

Haskell and Gibbon halted and turned in their saddles. Legions of gray-clad soldiers were emerging from the woods on Seminary Ridge, three long lines separated by short intervals, the lines extending over half a mile in length. Haskell opened his mouth, but no words came out. The sun gleamed off thousands of enemy barrels and fixed bayonets. Hundreds of red flags waved along the line, marking the brigades and regiments. The gray masses deployed close together, man touching man, lines supporting lines. Confederate officers on horseback rode up and down, waving hands and hats, as though preparing for a pass and review.

Haskell glanced up and down the blue line of 6,000 soldiers. Some men paled, some tightened, some held their breath, and some showed slight grins. But no one talked as every eye watched the gray legions building, preparing to unleash a flash flood toward the Union ridge. It was a matchless sight, the Confederates preparing to make a rare offensive attack against fortified Union lines.

Finally, the Union boys could shoot back at an exposed enemy, the Rebels choosing to make themselves slow-moving targets. Like the Union boys at Fredericksburg, the Rebel boys would face massive waves of enemy artillery fire, the blue boys bombarding them violently with percussion shells, solid shot, and enfilading grapeshot. Waiting until the last moment, the Union men behind the stone walls would unleash a devastating blast of musketry.

Gibbon and Haskell rode down the lines, Gibbon telling his boys, "Don't rush, men. Let them come close before you fire, and then aim low and steady."

A soldier shouted, "We'll blast them, General, and then gut them."

Another soldier shouted, "This is revenge for Fredericksburg."

Haskell's face tingled. Gibbon remained calm, inspiring the rest of the men. Gibbon's greatest strength was his ability to motivate men. Men wanted to be led, not driven, and Gibbon was one of the best leaders in the Army of the Potomac.

A single voice called out: "Fix bayonets!" In moments, hollering spread up and down the blue line, sergeants repeating the command. In perfect order, every one of the 6,000 men gripped the handles of the double-edged blades sheathed at their waists, pulled them out, and snapped the wicked weapons into place. The sergeants bellowed, "Prepare to fire!"

Haskell sat transfixed on his horse like a marble statue. Through his field glasses he observed the Rebel assault. His legs cinched tightly around his horse's flanks. The click of the locks and the sharp tap of muskets hitting the top of the stone wall echoed along Cemetery Ridge.

Officers ordered the trefoil flags and colors of the brigades and divisions to the rear. Haskell smiled. Old Glory remained alone, waving along the lines as it first did in the Battle of Saratoga in 1777. On order, the color sergeants sloped the ensign's lances toward the enemy. Haskell's heart soared like an eagle, the Republic's icon standing proudly before the treasonous Rebel red flags.

*2:30 p.m.*

"The enemy is advancing!" someone yelled. Haskell gazed across the open field. Fifteen thousand Rebels were marching toward them, moving in perfect unison. Fearfully beautiful. And deadly.

Gibbon turned to him. "Ride to General Meade and tell him the Confederate infantry is advancing. The focus of the attack appears to be against Webb's brigade protecting the copse of trees.

Gibbon paused, scratching his neatly trimmed beard. "If the Rebels succeed in driving a wedge into our lines and piercing it, they will sever our army, and we will have to retreat. Tell him to send reinforcements immediately."

Haskell spurred his horse, racing toward Meade's headquarters. A thunderous explosion rocked the ground. He cocked his head. Smoke billowed along Cemetery Ridge. The Union batteries, including Cushing's, had opened up, shattering the air with steel and shrapnel, pummeling the advancing enemy. Haskell rode as fast as he could, arriving at the empty Leister House. A small group of signalmen told him Meade had departed for Power's Hill.

Haskell told the signalmen, "Send a message. The enemy is advancing his infantry in force upon Webb's front. Please send reinforcements."

Without waiting for a reply, Haskell rode back to the stone wall. He was unable to spot Gibbon, so he turned, riding south of the copse, stopping near Stannard's Vermont Brigade.

———————— • ————————

*3:00 p.m.*
*In the long grass*

As the gray line swept forward, Stannard's Thirteenth Vermont Regiment, hiding in the tall grass on the Rebels' right flank, suddenly stood and opened fire. Raking the enemy with devastating musket fire, they cut a fifty-yard swath through the gray line. The Rebels' mangled right flank recoiled back in haste, veered to the left, but not did not halt its movement forward toward the stone wall.

Haskell's breath stilled. With Union guns blazing point-blank, the Rebels continued to sweep forward across the open ground.

Haskell rode north along the stone wall, hunting for Gibbon, stopping at Cushing's battery. Cushing's smoke-blackened cannoneers had switched to double canister. A thunderous cracking greeted Haskell as the grapeshot sprayed the enemy with thousands of iron balls, shredding skin and shattering bones. Hordes of Rebels fell, screaming terribly, the fury of the Union cannon fire cutting vast swaths through the butternut ranks.

Haskell scanned the ridgeline. No mounted officers near the engaged lines. "Damn," he muttered.

Gibbon was not on the field. He was either killed or seriously wounded. A Lord Nelson prediction? Haskell's breath quickened. A torment of dread swept him over the field, and Haskell spurred his mount toward the copse, arriving as the Rebel brigades disappeared, dipping down into the swale west of the Emmitsburg Road.

---

*3:15 p.m.*

A Rebel officer shouted, "Left oblique!"

Moments later the graybacks emerged, the spear-point of the advancing wedge angling left directly toward the copse of trees and the zigzagged angle in the stone wall.

Webb was on the stone wall with the Sixty-ninth Pennsylvania, standing exposed, with an obvious contempt for the approaching danger, encouraging his Irish boys. Webb's brigade was the breakwater deployed at the angle to repulse the Rebel storm racing toward it.

"Remember yesterday!" Webb bellowed. "The Sixty-ninth halted Wright's brigade as it was topping Cemetery Ridge. So stand fast and give' em hell today, boys!"

The prospect of the Rebel hordes, three divisions of enemy infantry, piercing Webb's lone brigade was high. Webb would not retreat under any circumstances, holding to the last man, sacrificing his brigade and Cushing's battery. Hancock had to send reinforcements. Where was Gibbon?

The roaring din erupting from the angle was growing ever louder, the gray swarm whirling through the dense smoke, moving forward at a quickened pace toward the stone wall. Then it erupted—the terrible, wolf-like shrill of the Rebel Yell. Haskell removed his revolver as the Rebels halted before the wall, yelling, aiming, firing a yellow wall of leaping fire, scorching the sheltered Union soldiers with hot lead. Several Irishmen slumped to the ground, screaming.

The Union big guns continued to fire, sending enormous flashes of yellow flames over the Federal dead and wounded lying in front of the guns, the flames scorching them, igniting their clothes.

*3:25 p.m.*

Haskell spotted Cushing standing behind a cannon. Cushing's mouth opened and his jaw moved and the cannon fired a round of grapeshot. Abruptly, Cushing's head snapped back as a bullet pierced through his nose. Sergeant Fuger caught the mangled artillery commander as Cushing's knees buckled. The sergeant laid Cushing on the ground, where he died.

Haskell screamed. "*Son of a bitch!*"

3:30 p.m.

Haskell galloped along the ridge, the fighting along the wall growing fiercer. As he rode toward the angle, he counted a dozen red flags cresting the stone wall, defended by Webb's three flags. Webb's brigade was breaking.

"Oh, my God," Haskell shouted. The fate of the army hung upon a spider's single thread.

A fiery passion sharpened his rage like a chisel. The Rebel wall had to be stopped; the three-day battle boiled down to this moment.

He drew his sword, gleaming as a symbol of command, and galloped across the field, placing himself at the midpoint between the surging Rebels and the retreating Union soldiers. Haskell's face was fiery hot. Above the stone wall, the red flags of the Rebellion clustered. The Union wall, moments earlier proudly displaying Old Glory, was now missing its defiant banner.

Blue skedaddlers had bolted to the rear like a tide of rabbits, carrying the Republic's flag. A red flag waved over one of Cushing's guns, casting a dreary shadow over Cushing's corpse.

Haskell rode quickly back among the Pennsylvanians, bellowing harshly, "Halt! Face about and fire, damn it!"

Several stunned men stopped, startled by a single mounted officer, brandishing his sword, and screaming in a murderous rage. Haskell glanced back at the stone wall. Having stormed the wall, the Rebels reformed quickly, loading their rifles forty yards away, moving steadily toward them, bayonets gleaming.

Haskell screamed again, pointing to the enemy, "Aim and fire! And keep firing."

Several of the men obeyed Haskell's commands, taking quick aim, firing, loading, and firing again.

"Hold this line," Haskell shouted.

He spurred his horse and chased down those continuing to flee toward the rear, slapping them hard on the back with the flat side of his saber. Within a few moments, Haskell had rallied the men. They formed a ragged line, firing fiercely into the Rebel storm. Haskell's breath raced to keep up with his heart. Reinforcements were needed immediately if they were to hold this breach in the line.

Haskell looked toward the angle, but he could see very little, the defenders obscured by dust and smoke. Where was Hancock? Where was Gibbon? If reinforcements did not arrive soon, it would be a rout. His eyes searched for a general or anyone with the power to order reinforcements to the melting line. No officers were on horseback, including Webb. *Damn.* He must depart the fight and find reinforcements himself.

Haskell wheeled his horse and rode headlong toward Gibbon's left flank, aiming for the flags of Harrow's brigade.

Haskell pulled up next to Harrow, sitting on his horse. "General Harrow, Webb is hotly pressed and must have support, or he will be overpowered. Can you assist him?"

"Yes," Harrow said.

"You cannot be too quick," Haskell said.

Harrow turned and shouted, "Regimental commanders, follow Lieutenant Haskell at the double quick and reinforce Webb's front."

Haskell shouted, "Follow me, men!" Haskell started trotting toward the clump of trees, to be followed moments later by yells and hollers echoing from behind. He cocked his head and spied the First Minnesotans breaking ranks and racing pell-mell toward him.

# First Minnesota
## Pickett's Charge
## July 3, 1863

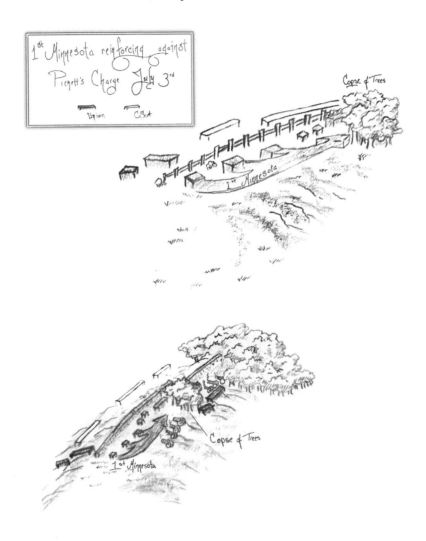

1st Minnesota reinforcing against Pickett's Charge July 3rd

Union    CSA

Copse of Trees

1st Minnesota

Copse of Trees

1st Minnesota

# First Minnesota — Friday, July 3

## *Wright*

*3:40 p.m.*
*At the copse of trees*

Wright sprinted northward along Cemetery Ridge, spearheading the First Minnesota's headlong dash toward the copse of trees. Ahead, the massive gray formation flowed toward the Union lines like cascading lava. *Christ Almighty.* Methodically, almost lazily, the Rebels' flying wedge was breaching the stone rampart at the angle and studding it with several red battle flags. A large portion of Webb's brigade was fractured and poured to the rear. The blue line was too thin. Wright lengthened his stride. *Must plug the holes in the line.*

Wright was puffing like a locomotive, his breaths short and fast, his heart pounding in his ears. He gripped his rifle across his chest with a two-handed carry, keeping his eyes locked on Haskell's horse galloping along the stone wall. Thundering Union artillery cracked and rumbled. Hissing bullets zipped and whickered along Cemetery Ridge.

Wright glanced to his left. Private Joe Richardson, a gangly older man in Company F, was running even with Wright with the soft, loping gait of a mountain lion. Each of his mighty strides was worth two of Wright's. Panting and mayhem aside, Wright found himself grinning. He liked fighting alongside Richardson. The private was a fierce fighter and a deadly shot, perhaps the best in the regiment.

Richardson cocked his head and yelled, "Th-th-they seem to b-b-be smashing Webb's b-b-brigade."

Wright yelled back. "Yes, I agree!" He chuckled. Richardson only stuttered when he was excited.

"W-w-we should m-m-move over th-th-there and help th-th-them." Richardson's leathery face was barely breaking a sweat.

Wright squinted, his eyes riveted on the copse of trees. The middle of the Union line was crumbling. He spotted a dozen red battle flags flapping near the stone wall and only three of Webb's Union flags defending against the enemy charge. The Rebels were howling as they sprayed bullets into the blue boys.

Wright glanced behind him. The First Minnesota regiment was not moving in formation but dashing wildly in a loose throng. He didn't give a hoot how they looked getting there. *Just get there and plug the line.*

Richardson started pulling away, muttering with great excitement as they sprinted toward the copse, combining his own unique phrases with Biblical quotes. "By the l-l-lovely l-l-little angels and th-the-the g-gr-great h-ho-horned s-s-serpent, we'll sh-sh-show them th-th-there is a God in Is-Is-Israel."

Wright flicked an awed gaze at Richardson. How in the hell could he run so fast and talk at the same time? And where in the hell did he pull that quote from?

Wright ran another ten yards before something hard and hot, burning like a sizzling cast-iron skillet, slapped his face and shoulder, knocking him sideways. Sparkling lights exploded in his skull and his heart kicked the bottom of his throat. He staggered to a stop and bent over, shaking his head and panting.

Richardson stopped and gripped the back of his jacket. He shouted, "Sergeant W-W-Wright. Are you h-h-hurt?"

Wright wiped his hand across his face; it was wet with blood. *Damn.* His mind raced as he waited for the scorching pain. None. Good. His left shoulder pulsed with a dull ache, but he could still swing his arm. Nothing serious.

"Let's go," he said.

He sprang ahead with Richardson keeping pace alongside. They fell in behind Captain Farrell, leading Company C into the melee. They did not have far to go until they reached the jagged line of Webb's men. Farrell surged forward of the regiment, Private Marshall Sherman on his heels. Ahead, a scream tore through the smoky air from Company C. Wright squinted.

Farrell had tumbled to the ground. The regiment continued forward at breakneck speed, swerving, veering, jumping around Farrell. Wright pushed along with a group to the left of Farrell's stricken body, lying face upward, breathing in rattling snorts. Gray brain matter swirling with crimson blood gushed from the bullet hole penetrating his brow. A swell of nausea lurched in Wright's throat. He slowed for a moment. Should he put a bayonet through him? *Damn it. Christians don't murder.* He clamped his lips, gulped down the puke, and kept running.

The First Minnesota arrived on the flank of Webb's brigade, joining a tattered regiment that had retreated from the wall. They formed a ragged line about twenty-five yards from Cushing's captured battery. Two enemy gray lines advanced at a trot, waving red flags, the lines bristling with point-blank rifle fire, bullets buzzing by like mad hornets. The Minnesotans stopped, aimed, and fired, delivering a rattling broadside. The enemy line halted momentarily, apparently stunned at the sudden appearance of the Minnesotans.

A little way in front of the regiment, Wright spotted a Rebel trying to shelter himself behind a broken artillery carriage. Wright raised his rifle. A bullet whistled past his head. He paused momentarily. Before he could fire, Richardson's musket cracked and the enemy soldier screamed and pitched to the ground. "I n-n-nailed that Reb r-r-real good."

Wright yelled, "Nice shot!"

Richardson apparently did not hear. Swearing and stuttering, he reloaded and fired again.

Somehow, without orders, the Minnesotans unleashed a crackling volley, pulverizing the front line of the Confederates. Wright cracked a half smile. Only a veteran outfit could coordinate such a devastating blow without a single command being uttered.

Wright spied Corporal John Dehn in the middle of the First Minnesota line, carrying the tattered regimental colors. Dehn screamed, dropping the flag. A Minié ball had shattered his hand.

Wright rushed toward the fallen flag.

"I got it!" shouted Corporal Henry O'Brien. O'Brien gripped the flag, holding it high, and sprinted forward fearlessly, bullets whizzing around his head.

A spontaneous Minnesota yell erupted along the line: "Charge…Charge!"

O'Brien bolted several yards ahead of the regiment, racing toward the enemy with the flag flapping majestically.

"Damn it, Henry!" Wright shouted. The idiot was imperiling the flag, sprinting ahead of the pack, alone and unprotected, outpacing all the other colors.

Wright and Richardson lunged forward, chasing after O'Brien. A rushing roar like a raging tornado billowed behind them as the First Minnesota and the supporting regiments of Harrow and Hall's brigades dashed forward to protect the flag.

With a jolt of pure clarity, Wright witnessed O'Brien's rashness become inspiration. It transformed the First Minnesotans' forward rush from a linear attack wave into the tip of a flying wedge of sprinting shock troops. It electrified Webb's broken, skedaddling brigade, which stopped running, turned about, and rushed to join the screaming flagbearer. It energized Wright, affirming his faith in his First Minnesota brothers, setting his blood burning hot with pride and purpose and speed.

The Rebels' faces froze, stunned at the sight of O'Brien screaming like a berserker, bent on penetrating the enemy lines alone, with the shock and awe of a hurled spear, without regard for the regiment's flanks, piercing as deep into the enemy hordes as his flying feet would take him.

"My God," Wright muttered. He kept breathless pace with a surging Union line, racing toward the stone wall like a demonic horde, focusing hellfire on the damned red flags.

---

## O'Brien

*3:43 p.m.*

O'Brien flashed a grin, his stomach tightened, and his pulse ratcheted up as he burst several yards ahead of the charging First Minnesotans and Gibbon's division. He loved raising hell, an addictive drug coursing through his veins like a lightning bolt. He glared at the frozen faces of the frontline Rebels. A grazing blow sliced the side of his head, burning like a branding iron.

"Crap, I've been hit."

His face tingled as blood poured down his cheek. He wiped the wound with his left hand; it came away dripping with blood. He shook his head, continuing to churn his feet, leading the regiment forward. His breath rattled. A few moments later, he whirled, a guttural growl rumbling in his throat. His right hand exploded like a smashed pumpkin. A bullet had pierced his wrist and sliced the flagstaff in half. O'Brien's knees buckled and his body crumpled backwards to the ground. Staring into the smoky sky, fear stabbed his heart, sharp as a bayonet. *Oh, my God. The regimental colors might fall into enemy hands.* None of the First Minnesotans would forgive him if the colors were captured, and he would never excuse himself.

Corporal Newell Irvine stopped next to O'Brien and reached to retrieve the flag. O'Brien gripped the half flagstaff firmly with his uninjured hand.

"Damn it, Henry, let go," Irvine urged. "I will take the colors forward."

O'Brien released his grip slowly. "Don't let the Rebs get it."

"I won't." Irvine took the flagstaff, sprinting forward toward the stone wall, screaming.

O'Brien stood up, wrapped his shattered hand with a handkerchief, and started chasing after Irvine.

## Sherman

Private Marshall Sherman spotted Irvine retrieving the fallen First Minnesota colors and racing toward the enemy. Irvine was too far forward, risking capture of the colors. Sherman darted toward the stone wall, teeth clenched. If his bare feet touched the ground, they sure didn't know it.

He stopped at the wall. A deafening roar thundered around him like Niagara Falls. He aimed and fired his rifle into a mass of graycoats. After volleying, he peered across the field beyond the wall, through the blue sheets of smoke. Sherman spied a Rebel lieutenant waving a red battle flag moving in a direct line toward him, racing alone in front of a gray swarm. A smile cracked across Sherman's face. Beyond the stone wall was his prize, vulnerable, waiting to be taken, the angry red flag shaking out its blazonry of stars and bars with a sort of fierce delight.

Sherman hopped the stone wall, dropped his rifle to his side, and fixed himself into the bayonet-charge position. The Rebel battle flag was forty yards off. Sherman screamed loudly inside his head, loping like a big cat, swift and silent toward its quarry. He focused on the lieutenant's face: mouth open wide, yelling, under the stiff brim of a gray Hardee hat with a plume stuck through the hatband. Sherman's heart pounded and his nostrils flared. He bolted the last ten yards like a crazed beast, rushing the Rebel in a wild fury.

Sherman skidded to a stop, pointing the bayonet at the lieutenant's heart. "Drop the flag and surrender!" He glared into the Rebel's eyes.

The officer stopped, surprise etched across his face. Wright pushed the bayonet until he hit flesh. The fateful moment had arrived, the Rebel officer standing motionless, with quivering lips. Sherman pressed the point of the bayonet, cocking the hammer of his empty rifle.

The officer's eyes widened. He glanced behind him, but only a few Rebels were there. He dropped the flag to the ground, surrendering with arms held high. Face burning, Sherman picked up the Rebel battle flag, screaming at the lieutenant to walk toward the stone wall. The enemy officer moved toward the Union line. Sherman followed with the point of his bayonet in the prisoner's back, muscling the captured Rebel quickly forward, dragging the red battle flag in the dust. A silent sigh escaped Sherman's lips. His breath rasped and blood pounded in his ears. *Thank you, God.*

The entire Federal line erupted in wild cheering as Sherman and his prisoner hopped the stone wall. The rush of emotion and adrenaline melted from his chest like thawing ice. His knees were wobbly and his head woozy. He shuddered. The Confederate assault had bogged down, many of the Rebels at the angle and along the stone wall throwing down weapons, surrendering. Those Rebels far enough from the stone wall started pouring back across the open fields toward Seminary Ridge. Sherman and his prisoner walked down the ridge's reverse slope and halted.

## *Wright*

Wright rushed up as Sherman stretched out the Rebel battle flag. "Damn," he said. "It's the colors of the Twenty-eighth Virginia." It was the regimental flag from Confederate General Richard Garnett's brigade.

*3:55 p.m.*

Wright ordered the First Minnesota to muster, circling around him for a head count. The men plopped down, exhausted. The adrenaline rush that had kept them fighting had worn off. With Captain Farrell's Company C, the regiment had charged the enemy with around 80 men. The First Minnesota had suffered 55 casualties in the past three hours, including 23 killed or mortally wounded. Yesterday, 262 from the First Minnesota had made the charge, with 215 casualties. It appeared 80 Minnesotans had been killed or mortally wounded in two days' fighting. What a horrendous sacrifice. Would anyone ever remember the accomplishments and sacrifices of the First Minnesota these past two days?

One of those killed at the stone wall was Sergeant Hamlin. Wright learned the news from Private Richardson. "I f-f-found Sergeant Hamlin's b-b-body. He had b-b-been shot in the leg, th-th-thigh, neck, and h-h-heart."

Wright's face grew cold, tears streaming down his face. With a choked voice, he said, "Please gather Hamlin's personal belongings, and we will bury him after we reform the line. See if you can find his Bible. I would like to send it back to his folks."

Richardson whispered, "Sergeant Hamlin d-d-died instantly."

Wright nodded as Richardson moved off. Wright turned away from the men, looking across the open field toward Seminary Ridge. He closed his eyes, remembering Hamlin, a twenty-three-year-old with a strong Methodist outlook on life, every day beginning and ending with a prayer and a reading from the Bible. He was the most universally respected man in the company, with an absolute trust in the Almighty. He hated war, prayed for peace, but was the most fearsome fighter in the regiment. Wright struggled to throttle his grief as tears flowed steadily down his frozen face. His gut clinched, and shivers traced down his shoulders and arms. He would dearly miss Hamlin.

A voice behind him said, "Sergeant Wright. Do you have the final muster report?" Wright turned around. It was Lieutenant Lochren. Wright handed him the report.

Corporal Newell walked up to him.

"Sergeant Wright," Newell said. "I can't find the lower piece of the severed flagstaff. It was lost in the fight."

"Here," Wright said. He grabbed the staff of Sherman's captured Confederate flag, snapping it in half. He gave one of the pieces to Newell. "Use this."

Newell shot Wright a surprised look. "Are you sure you want to use a Rebel flagstaff?"

"Yes," Wright said.

Newell used his pocketknife to shape the ends of the broken Minnesota and Rebel flagstaffs. He nailed the two ends together, reinforcing the joint with a leather strap.

Wright smiled as Newell spliced together the Rebel-and-Union flagstaff. "It's a symbol of what the First Minnesota accomplished at Gettysburg," Wright mused. "The Union and Confederates locked together in one of the most valorous battles in U.S. history. They're going to remember us, Newell. They'll never forget the First Minnesota." He studied the place where the two flagstaffs were joined together. He understood. Whatever had moved him to use both pieces had not been impulsive, but intentional. Prophetic. "The spliced flagstaff—it's foreshadowing the time when Union and Confederate unite. Upholding the colors of the old Union, together, forever."

## ✨ 48 ✨
# Meade — Friday, July 3

*2:30 p.m.*
*An hour and a half earlier*
*Power's Hill*

Meade mounted his horse. The sinking sun would hang for a few hours more above South Mountain, its bright threads stretching like tentacles across the smoky battlefield. Meade squinted and pulled his slouch hat down over his brow. He twisted in his saddle. His dark shadow blanketed Slocum, standing a few yards away. An emptiness filled him, the same frightening vacancy that had struck like an ambush when he relieved Hooker.

"The Republic is hanging in the balance," Meade seethed, "and I'm isolated on Power's Hill without my staff."

"Do you want any of my aides to ride with you?" Slocum said.

"No. I'll ride back to the Leister House and try to reestablish communications with my corps commanders. Keep me posted on enemy activity on your right flank."

Slocum saluted. Meade returned the salute and spurred his horse. He cocked his head momentarily. Carpenter was trailing a few yards behind, riding alongside Meade's shadow, which seemed to be growing like a ghostly vapor. Meade shivered. Was this a prophetic tremor, portending a disaster this afternoon? If the Devil was God's shadow, what about the shadow looming behind him? Was it the Devil, or was it his own fears?

Meade rode lickety-split down the steep slope of Power's Hill, swearing a blasphemous oath. Where was George? Where was Biddle? Where was his damn staff? Distant booming echoed from the battlefield. Great flaky streams of battery smoke spiraled upward along Cemetery Ridge. His skin pebbled as the howling winds trumpeted the Rebel storm surge. A rush of something resembling fear flooded his chest.

He bounced in his saddle as he galloped down the hill, his thoughts a skiff caught in a gale, turbulent and tumbling, his repeated mistakes consuming him. Twice he had purposely marooned himself behind the battle lines and failed to command the fight. The first day he had stayed twelve miles in the rear at Taneytown and that was nearly a disaster. Now, on the third day, he had chosen to ride nearly a mile in the rear to Power's Hill, leaving his staff behind. Hell, his performance today was no better than Hooker's poor showing at Chancellorsville. At least Hooker had the excuse of being knocked unconscious by a Rebel's solid shot slamming into the porch he was standing under. *What's your excuse?*

He peered ahead at the bright bursts of yellow flashing in the gray smoke. His mistakes beat inside him like twin pulses. He didn't fear Lee. But could his own style of command—a quiet leader governed by restraint and modesty—ultimately defeat a leader like Lee? Again Meade's mistakes rose up to accuse him. Was he fooling himself? Weren't the great military heroes they studied at West Point—Alexander the Great, Hannibal, Caesar, Napoleon—all exalted for their boldness, their undaunted courage, their charisma? Wasn't that why Lincoln had appointed four charismatic generals before him to command the Army of the Potomac?

Yes—and each of those bold, charismatic leaders had failed. None of Lincoln's chosen leaders had beaten Lee—until now.

For good or ill, this battle was his destiny. His calling. His duty. And if there was anything Meade understood, it was duty.

He whiffed, the odor of death assailing his nose. Duty demanded he lead from the front. He would correct the Power's Hill mistake—if there was still time.

"Damn it," he muttered. The battle was on, and he needed to command at the decisive point... but where was it? *If in doubt, ride to the sound of guns.*

Spotting a shortcut, Meade pulled hard on the left rein. His horse veered off the dirt road onto a path more suitable to a mountain goat. A moment later, the gelding lost its footing, skidding downward as Meade flew forward in the saddle, nearly tumbling over the horse's head. His stomach dropped a foot.

"Son—of a—biiiiiiitch!"

He rocked backward, tilting nearly parallel to the ground. The horse slid several yards, then regained its footing at the bottom of the hill.

Captain Carpenter rode up next to him. "Are you alright, General?"

"I will be when I get to the damn battlefield," Meade growled.

He spurred his horse and galloped at breakneck speed down into a dark hollow, then merged onto a crossroad toward the Leister House. Carpenter kept pace with him, gripping his revolver in his right hand, followed by several of his Lancers. Smoke poured down the road as from a great furnace. A lone rider raced toward his cavalcade—Captain Dewey, a thin young man serving on General Hays's staff. Dewey reined up, ashen-faced, and saluted as Meade halted.

"Sir," Dewey said in a high-pitched squeak, "General Hays sends his respects and states that the enemy infantry is advancing in great force against the copse of trees. Colonel Sharpe's aide believes that the assault is being led by General Pickett."

"Tell General Hays I will order General Sedgwick to send more reinforcements to him."

Dewey saluted and rode off.

*This is it. Do or die.* Meade turned to Carpenter, his pulse accelerating. "Send one of your staff officers to the left of the line to hurry Sedgwick's brigades reinforcing the center of the line. Tell the brigade commanders to double-time. Send a second staff officer to General Sedgwick and request he send all available troops to Gibbon's division at the copse of trees."

He turned and spied George running toward him. His son stopped next to him, gasping for air and sweating profusely.

"Where in the hell have you been? You're a sorry sight, George." He leaned closer. "Where is the rest of the headquarters staff?"

"My horse was killed during the shelling, so I ran behind you," George panted. "The rest of the staff is either rounding up horses or still at the Leister House."

Meade shook his head. "Captain Carpenter, have one of your men give Captain Meade a ride. George, ride to Power's Hill and find another horse. Then meet me at the Leister House."

*2:45 p.m.*

Meade spurred toward Leister House, arriving several moments later. The shelling had ceased. He scanned the grounds, cratered with large holes as if a giant had repeatedly dropped big boulders around the yard. Numerous round-shot shells had ripped through the house. None of his staff were there.

He scowled. "I can't command if I can't communicate." A rattling storm of fiery rifles cracked and popped from Cemetery Ridge. He nodded to Carpenter. "Captain, let's ride a ways toward the copse."

*3:05 p.m.*

Meade and Carpenter's Lancers rode a hundred yards toward the thundering cannonading and halted. The blue smoke on the ridge was too thick to see anything clearly. Meade shook his head. No way of knowing whether Sedgwick's reserves had arrived in time to bolster the Union center.

He sat motionless on his horse for a couple moments. Few knew where he was. The firing along the stone wall was growing into a continuous roar, dreadful volleys sweeping across the front line, the ground trembling beneath his horse's hooves. For a few shallow breaths, Meade's vision blurred.

"Most of Lee's infantry is attacking the Union center," he muttered. With Pickett leading the assault. A vague memory swam into his mind—something about the Mexican War and Pickett being the first to climb the parapet during the storming of the fortress at Chapultepec.

"General Meade?" Carpenter ventured. "Do you want to ride closer to the ridge?"

In his mind's eye, Meade saw Lincoln signing the order to sack yet another commander of the Army of the Potomac, and Colonel Hardie arriving in the middle of the night to relieve him. He read the order. *You are relieved for dereliction of duty for being absent for two-thirds of the battle.*

"Hell, yes!" Meade shouted. He spurred his horse to a gallop, straight toward Cemetery Ridge.

## 49

# Hancock — Friday, July 3

*3:15 p.m.*
*Near the copse of trees. Pickett's Charge is two hundred yards from the Union's stone wall*

Hancock sat astride his tall, light bay, thirty yards behind the copse of trees, swaying on the quaking ground. Union artillery guns thundered, belching long streams of fire. Hancock peered through his binoculars at the red flags flying over the legions of approaching graybacks. God, he loved the acrid stench of gunpowder loitering in the air. The Rebel onslaught drifted within musket range.

Blizzards of lead crackled along the hostile fronts like summer lightning. A bullet zipped by his face, creating a soft breeze.

As the screech of the Rebel yell erupted, Hancock spurred the bay, galloped northward several yards, and halted. He lifted his chin and grinned inside. The Union line above the copse of trees held, delivering withering volleys into the oncoming Confederate ranks.

He turned to Mitchell. "I've never seen such slaughter."

Mitchell pointed. "General, you need to ride back to the copse. The Rebels are massing to pierce our lines."

Hancock trotted down Cemetery Ridge, halting behind the copse. A gray wedge spiked with red battle flags thrashed over the stone wall. Pistols flashed with muskets.

"The Rebels are splitting our line," Hancock shouted. Unless Meade sent help from another corps, all would be lost. "Where in the hell are Meade's reinforcements?"

The rattling storm of blistering Union fire paused momentarily. The Rebel soldiers reloaded, restoring the storm's destructive power before erupting toward the Union cannons.

Hancock turned around toward the Leister house, spotting blue-clad soldiers racing toward the crest of Cemetery Ridge.

Hancock cocked his head toward Mitchell and shouted, "They'll stop the enemy breach. Let's ride to the Rebels' right flank."

Hancock wheeled his horse and galloped south along the crest of Cemetery Ridge. Two hundred fifty yards below the clump of trees, a colonel on horseback rode up and saluted.

"General Hancock! Colonel Arthur Devereux of the Nineteenth Massachusetts!" Devereux shouted over the din, pointing toward the trees. "The Rebels have broken through by the copse. The red colors are coming over the stone wall. Let me go in there!"

Hancock nodded. "Make it God-damn quick, Colonel!"

Devereux saluted and rode toward his regiment, shouting orders.

Hancock motioned to Mitchell to wait. Within moments, Colonel Devereux galloped toward the copse with the Nineteenth Massachusetts racing behind, screaming.

"Damn, that's the kind of tempered boldness we need," declared Hancock. "Not that loose-cannon crap we saw from Sickles yesterday."

Hancock observed the Nineteenth Massachusetts's attack long enough to see they were holding their own. As he rode down the ridge toward the Vermont Brigade, a Gibbon staff officer intercepted him.

"General Hancock, I regret to inform you that General Gibbon was wounded. He was rallying the Nineteenth Maine forward when he was hit."

"God Almighty! How bad is the wound?"

"The bullet penetrated his left arm and traversed the outside of his left shoulder blade."

"Is the wound serious?"

"He was carried from the field. It's an ugly wound. General Gibbon is in quite a bit of pain. But the division surgeon said he'll live."

"Who is commanding Second Division?"

"Gibbon turned his division command over to Harrow."

Hancock nodded. "Keep me updated on Gibbon's condition." He turned and rode toward Stannard's brigade, positioned along Cemetery Ridge. He spotted Stannard sitting on a horse in front of the Fourteenth Vermont. He rode up and halted.

Stannard saluted and pointed. "Look, General. Look at the Thirteenth and Sixteenth Vermont."

Hancock returned the salute and turned astride in his saddle. The two Vermont regiments were wheeling like a picket fence on the right flank of Pickett's division; they formed a perpendicular line to the enemy flank and knelt as one.

Hancock peered through his binoculars. "By God, General Stannard, the right flank of the Confederate assault is dangling by a thread."

Stannard nodded. "When the enemy comes within range the Vermonters will hit them with enfilading fire."

In short order, the concealed Vermonters stood and raked Pickett's right flank with a sheet of lead. Several hundred Confederates fell to the ground, screaming. Great masses of them seemed to disappear in a moment.

Stannard pointed again. "Several of the Rebels are throwing down their arms and surrendering."

Hancock said, "Well done, General Stannard."

"Thank you, sir."

As Hancock turned to acknowledge Stannard, a bullet hammered into his body, throwing him from his saddle. He tried to grip the pommel, but he slipped from his horse. Hands and arms caught him, laying him on the ground. He reached his gloved hand to his groin. Dark red blood.

"General Hancock. Are you okay? General Hancock!"

He opened his eyes and stared at Stannard's two aides on either side of him, kneeling on the ground. No air. He couldn't breathe. He pointed to his groin. *Am I bleeding to death?*

"Breathe, General! Breathe!"

Hancock sucked gently, gasping. A bit of air slipped past his lips. He sucked again. More air this time, and he breathed out. *Thank God, I can breathe.*

"God...Stannard...bastard Rebels...shot...crotch."

"Let me take a look." Stannard opened up Hancock's trousers. "Jesus."

Hancock bent forward. "Let me..." He was gushing blood from his groin. *Oh, Jesus, I'm dying.* The bullet had ripped through the upper part of the inside of his thigh, creating an ugly, jagged hole over an inch in diameter.

Hancock found his voice and gasped out an order. "Don't let me bleed to death. Get something around it quick."

Stannard yelled for a handkerchief. Grabbing the one his aide offered, he wrapped it around Hancock's thigh above the wound. "Hold tight, General Hancock." Stannard cinched the handkerchief tight.

Hancock gritted his teeth as Stannard pulled Hancock's pistol from the holster and used the barrel to twist the handkerchief into a tourniquet.

"General Hancock," the other aide reassured him, "this is not arterial blood. It's too dark, and it's not spurting out in jets. The artery hasn't been severed. You will not bleed to death."

Hancock nodded. "Thank God."

"General Hancock," Mitchell said, "I'm going to fetch Dr. Dougherty and an ambulance." He mounted his horse and galloped off.

Hancock struggled to prop himself on an elbow. "General Stannard," he rasped. "Leave one of your aides with me. Rejoin your brigade. If we repulse this charge, I suspect General Meade will order a countercharge. Let's be ready."

---

*3:45 p.m.*

Hancock's Second Corps surgeon, Alexander Dougherty, rode up in an ambulance with Mitchell.

Dougherty knelt beside Hancock. "Dammit, General. I've told you numerous times if you keep riding along the front lines you're going to get shot."

"You can't command from the rear, Doc," Hancock whispered.

"Let me take a look." Dougherty turned Hancock onto his back and removed the tourniquet, laying the pistol on the ground. The surgeon cleaned his glasses with his own handkerchief. "Now, General, this is going to hurt," he warned, lifting up Hancock's head and shoving a piece of leather between his teeth. "Bite on this."

Hancock bit down, rubbing his tongue over the slab. He shuddered, watching Dougherty wiping his forefinger with a handkerchief.

"Okay, General. Here we go. Bite down hard."

Hancock stared as Dougherty stuck his forefinger into the wound all way to the knuckle. It felt like a hot poker. Hancock shut his eyes, tears flowing down his cheek.

"Look at what I found," Dougherty said.

Hancock opened his eyes. Dougherty was holding a ten-pennyweight nail, double bent. "This is what hit you, General." Dougherty said. "You're not as badly hurt as you think."

"Damn, are the Rebels so low on bullets that they are shooting ten-penny nails?"

"Let's load the general into the ambulance," Dougherty called out.

A whip snapped and the ambulance jerked forward. Hancock gazed out the back of the ambulance. The Confederates were retreating, some running, some walking, and some crawling. When the ambulance was out of range of the enemy's parting shots, Hancock signaled a halt.

He turned to Dougherty. "Write this message down to send to General Meade."

Dougherty reached inside his jacket and retrieved a pencil and small book pad. "I'm ready, General Hancock."

"I have never seen a more formidable attack," Hancock dictated in short, grinding spurts, "and if the Sixth and Fifth Corps have pressed up, the enemy will be destroyed. The enemy must be short of ammunition, as I was shot with a ten-penny nail. I did not leave the field till the victory was entirely secured and the enemy no longer in sight. I am badly wounded, though I trust not seriously. I had to break the line to attack the enemy in flank on my right, where the enemy was most persistent after the front attack was repelled. Not a Rebel was in sight upright when I left.

The line should be immediately restored and perfected. General Caldwell is in command of the corps, and I have directed him to restore the line."

Hancock handed the message to Mitchell. "Take this dispatch to General Meade. Tell him…if we advance our lines and counterattack immediately, I believe we could win a great victory."

Mitchell jumped out of the ambulance, mounted his horse, and rode away.

Hancock turned to Dougherty. "By God," he rasped, his voice weakening with pain and shock, "I believe Meade has engineered one of the great victories in history…just as great as Wellington's defeat of Napoleon at Waterloo. God, I hope he orders the counterattack. In a few hours, the battle may well be over."

## ⟨⟨≈ 50 ≈⟩⟩
# Meade — Friday, July 3

A rumble like a stampede approached Meade through the haze. *Have the Rebels broken through?*

He stared into the thick smoke, seeing nothing. He reached for his sword, rattling in its scabbard.

He spotted a melee of Union soldiers fleeing the battle and racing toward him. Skedaddlers.

His drew his sword, pointing it forward, and spurred his horse toward the retreaters. Carpenter pulled up next to Meade as the Lancers fanned out behind them in a V shape, a moving restraining wall.

"Turn and fight!" Meade screamed. "Turn and fight, damn you!"

Several of the men wavered, stopping mid-stride. Meade's charging wedge apparently looked more threatening than the enemy. "Stop and form a line!" he bellowed.

The soldiers skidded to a stop, mouths agape, and turned about face. They formed into a makeshift line, trotting back toward the stone wall. They disappeared back into the smoke.

Meade halted, scanning the action. "I must find out what's happening," he muttered.

He galloped the long slope toward the copse, stopping thirty yards from the Union cannons. Through his field glasses he scanned the battlefield. A cannon shell burst in the air, shell fragments showering the stone angle. Smoke poured from the defensive line as if from a great forest fire, but the Rebels had not breached it. More men were needed at the angle, and quickly.

Meade tried to get a fix on the enemy lines. The Union cannons behind the stone wall were firing rapidly, double canister. Smoke hid the butchery beyond the wall.

"Damn it, how far away is the Confederate infantry?" Meade muttered. He rode among the cannons, yelling, "Keep it up, boys! Keep firing!"

Some of the artillerymen recognized the commanding general and cheered. Meade grinned.

Someone rode up and Meade turned, squinting through the smoke. "George, is that you?"

George saluted. "Yes, General!"

"Stay close."

Rifles fired at a blazing speed, yellow flames flickering out of their muzzle barrels. Meade yelled over the thundering cannons, "Let's head to the right and find out what's going on."

---

*3:20 p.m.*

They rode north toward Hays's Third Division of Second Corps, just beyond Webb's brigade. As they passed a section of Woodruff's battery, George hollered to his father. "General, that is Lieutenant Egan of the First United States Artillery."

Meade halted and shouted out, "Lieutenant Egan, do you know General Hays's whereabouts?"

Egan turned and pointed. "General Meade, just a few moments ago General Hays was on his horse, leading his troops over the wall. He charged the Rebels, and they faltered."

"Has the enemy turned back?" Meade shouted.

"Yes, the Rebels in our front have turned back."

Meade's heart stirred with hope. He spotted Hays dragging a captured Rebel flag behind his horse. Meade turned about and trotted south toward Webb's brigade and the angle, where the thundering roar of musketry continued unabated. Emerging unexpectedly from the wall of smoke were several small clusters of gray-clad men moving toward the rear of the Union lines with their hands above their heads. Further down the wall, several groups of blue-clad soldiers hugged the stone wall, firing toward clumps of Rebels, the enemy firing back. Some men were in hand-to-hand combat.

"George. Have the Rebels penetrated the Union line further down the stone wall?" Meade asked.

"I'm not certain, General."

Meade blinked and glanced around. He needed news, damn it! Were they winning or losing?

---

*3:25 p.m.*

Further south along the stone wall, massive cannon fire thundered, pouring hot iron into the Rebel line along the crest. A rustling pitter-patter echoed in the low-hanging smoke clouds. A group of Confederates materialized like phantoms over the ridge, the Rebel vanguard. Meade tensed, reaching for his revolver.

Then his tight lips twitched into a dumbfounded smile. *God almighty.* The Confederates were unarmed, exhausted, their gray shirts wet with sweat and blood. Those in the rear staggered along, bleeding badly from penetrating wounds, using torn shirts and pants as makeshift bandages.

They raised their hands and yelled frantically at Meade, "Where should we go? Where should we go?"

The Rebels were trying to surrender. He turned in his saddle, spying the provost guards in the rear, gathering prisoners. He turned back around to the Rebels, pointing.

"Go along that way, and you will be taken care of," Meade shouted.

Enemy shells began bursting around the ridge again.

"George, is the Rebel shelling covering an enemy retreat?" Meade said.

"My guess is yes," George said, barely audible over the exploding shells.

Meade peered across the field, but the dark smoke was too thick to see if the enemy was retreating. He rode down along the crest about fifty yards, spotting Haskell sitting on his horse, directing surrendering Rebels where to go.

"Where are Hancock and Gibbon?" Meade muttered. Shaking his head, he rode toward Haskell.

Haskell saluted, mopping his face with his tattered shirt sleeve.

"How is it going here?" Meade asked.

Haskell's reply was eager. "I believe, General, the enemy's attack is repulsed."

"The assault is already repulsed?" asked Meade, his tone betraying a lack of confidence in Haskell's news.

"It is, sir!" Haskell said, beaming.

That was what Meade wanted to hear, but first reports were often exaggerated or seriously mistaken. If Haskell was right, Meade had to worry about a follow-on enemy assault, perhaps on his flanks, and begin working a plan for a Union counterattack. "Follow me."

---

*3:45 p.m.*
*At the copse of trees*

Meade, Haskell, and George rode to the top of the crest near the copse of trees. A throaty roar erupted along the stone wall, the blue boys waving their muskets, yelling, "Fredericksburg! Fredericksburg!" Meade's heart soared as if it had grown wings. He swept the scene with his field glasses. *My God, Haskell is right.* The Rebel retreat was unfolding through the clearing smoke. *Thank you, God.*

His blue boys flaunted numerous captured red battle flags. Gibbon's victorious boys were shouting and yelling, pure joy bursting from their throats. The celebrating seemed more right than it was righteous—a fitting vindication for the Fredericksburg massacre.

Meade reached impulsively to doff his hat and cheer but stopped himself. *Remember, you are the commanding general.* Instead, he pumped his fist in the air and shouted, "Hooray!"

But George, filled with the spirit of a young warrior, ignored protocol and threw off his hat, yelling, "Three cheers for the Union!" The men surrounding him took up the cheer. "Hip hip hooray! Hip hip hooray! Hip hip hooray!"

701

Meade waited until the cheer died down. Then he turned to Haskell and asked worriedly, "Where are Generals Hancock and Gibbon?"

Haskell replied softly, "General Hancock was shot from his horse and severely wounded. He was carried from the field, bleeding badly from his thigh. General Gibbon was wounded in the left arm and left shoulder. He, too, was carried from the field."

Meade winced. "Who is in command of Second Corps and Second Division?"

"Sir, General Caldwell is the senior officer of Second Corps and General Harrow of the division."

"Where are they?"

Haskell started to answer, but before he could get a word out, Meade said, "No matter. I will give my orders to you and you will see them executed."

"Yes, sir!"

"Reform the troops as quickly as possible, keeping them in their places. The enemy might attack again. If the enemy does attack, charge him in the flank, sweeping him from the field."

Haskell nodded, his face glowing.

Meade looked toward Webb's shattered brigade. "Where is General Webb?"

"General Webb was wounded in the leg and thigh during the assault by Pickett's division. He was also carried from the field."

"Good Lord," Meade whispered. His four closest general officers had all been wounded in the past forty-eight hours. Only Warren and Humphreys were still standing, and Warren had suffered a neck wound. Hancock, Gibbon, and Webb had been carried from the field, and Reynolds killed on the opening day of the battle. These were horrific losses.

Meade turned to George. "Let's ride south along Cemetery Ridge."

---

*4:00 p.m.*

They rode along the breastworks, stopping frequently as Meade peered across the field toward the enemy defenses. Would the Rebels attack again? Was there an opportunity to conduct a counterattack? Meade searched through his field glasses, but there was no enemy activity at the peach orchard or around Little Round Top.

"It looks like the assault has been repulsed," Meade said. "Let's go see how General Howard is doing."

They turned north. On Cemetery Hill, Meade found Howard, Biddle, and the rest of his personal staff. From Howard, he learned that the Rebels' main attack had been south of Cemetery Hill. Both the right and left Union flanks were solidly anchored, with little damage.

Meade turned to Howard. "Perhaps we have an opportunity to launch a counterattack. I'm going to Little Round Top to meet with General Sedgwick and discuss the possibility of having Sedgwick's reserves attack."

Meade rode to Eleventh Corps' line with his personal staff and Carpenter's Lancers in tow, a growing cavalcade of more than thirty soldiers. The wounded were gashed and stabbed, moaning and screaming unholy laments. Some wounded were moving, creeping on hands and knees toward the breastworks, giving the field an odd crawling effect. One inched forward using only his hands, dragging his mangled legs. Another was missing his lower jaw. Meade steeled himself, shutting out the cries of the wailing souls.

As soon as he crossed over to the Second Corps lines, the soldiers and officers erupted into a thunderous cheer. Joy pounded in his ears. Again Meade was shocked but happy. The men welcomed him as a conquering hero, achieving what previously had been unthinkable: defeating Lee.

For many of the boys, it was their first glimpse of a fourth new commanding general in one year. Meade eyed his ragged and frumpy uniform, covered in dust and dirt. The soldiers probably expected something resembling the previous four commanders on their high-stepping horses. Meade chuckled. The Union army was back from the brink, barely escaping a terrible defeat, and remarkably, this frazzled-looking old man they were staring at had something to do with it. No longer was he both a novice player and a sacrificial pawn in a chess match with a grand master. By the grace of God he had sidestepped a crushing loss and emerged as a formidable victor.

Moving beyond the flanks of today's battle, Meade's joy evaporated as he struggled to absorb the bloodletting. The sweltering battlefield, bearing witness to the barbarity humans inflict on one another, murmured as the tangled wounded crawled and mewled across the bloodstained ground, like exhausted toddlers seeking their mother's breast. A vile breeze assaulted his nostrils, carrying the choking stench of death. He wiped his cheeks, burning with remorse. He let his gaze slide over the thousands of stiff, swollen bodies clothed in gray and blue littering the land. My God, the fields resembled a bivouac of the dead.

He cast his eyes down. *My God.* Two West Point classmates, he and Lee, both sworn to defend the Union, had issued the orders that had created this medieval hell. His fragile chest weakened; this moment had pulled a piece of broken heart away from him, an anguished piece that no one should ever be allowed to see.

General Pleasonton rode to Meade, headed toward Little Round Top. Meade stiffened his upper lip.

Pleasonton's face was beaming. "General Custer defeated Stuart's cavalry in a great battle a few miles northeast of here."

Meade's heart skipped a beat and rose in his chest.

"Thank God. That's good news. Where is Stuart's cavalry now?" Meade said.

"Stuart is riding north of us, circling back around to Lee's army."

Meade nodded.

"General, the enemy has been repulsed," Pleasonton said, in an impudent, cocky tone. "Order the army to advance while I take the cavalry and get to Lee's rear, and we will finish the campaign in a week."

Meade's face flamed. "I'm not ordering an advance against Lee's center that is defended by more than a hundred and forty guns. It would be a repeat of what happened here on Cemetery Ridge. Except this time it would be a Rebel victory."

Pleasonton frowned, saying nothing.

"General Pleasonton, take the cavalry behind the Rebels to find out whether they are really falling back. If there is an opportunity to assault Lee's right flank, I will do so. You're dismissed."

Pleasonton stared at Meade. He saluted and rode off.

Meade glanced toward Seminary Ridge, the Rebel cannons glinting in the western sun. His mind was racing. Pleasonton was right. The time to take advantage of the repulse was now. But the counterattack would have to be against Lee's right flank, vacant of Rebel artillery batteries. If the Union army could counterattack within an hour, it perhaps could turn its victory into a rout. The counterattacking force would have to come from Sykes's Fifth Corps and Sedgwick's Sixth Corps. *My God, Hancock, Gibbon, and Webb, all carried from the field.* His mind paused for a couple beats. *Who is capable of replacing them to conduct a coordinated counterattack?*

## 51

# Sickles — Friday, July 3

*11:00 a.m.*
*Seven hours earlier*
*A quarter mile away, departing from the Daniel Scheaffer House the*
*day after Sickles's leg amputation*

Sickles's stomach lurched and he snapped his head sideways off the pillow, letting his mouth droop over the right side of the hand stretcher. *Oh, God!* He squeezed his eyes shut and heaved, but nothing gurgled up from his empty gut. His spinning head pounded like a whiskey hangover. *Damn chloroform.* He puckered his fat lips like a soft kiss and spit the bitter bile coating his tongue, letting the yellow-green saliva drip down his chin.

"General, rest easy," Tremain cautioned.

Sickles opened his eyes and glanced at Tremain walking halfway between two of the four stretcher bearers. Tremain wiped his bushy mustache and chin gently with a handkerchief.

Sickles spit again. "I can't get this bitter taste out of my mouth. I need whiskey."

A hand gripped his left shoulder: Dr. Sim. "You can have a small swig of whiskey, but don't swallow. Gurgle it and then spit it out. Understand?"

"Yes," Sickles mewled. He turned his head back onto the pillow and peered left at Dr. Sim walking between the two stretcher bearers opposite Tremain.

"Stretcher bearers halt," Tremain ordered. "Place the stretcher on the ground."

Sickles's stretcher softly touched ground.

"Let's rotate stretcher bearers," Tremain said. "Here you go, General. Only a swig and don't swallow."

706

Tremain reached behind Sickles's neck, lifted his head, and placed the flask against his mouth. The smoky peat fragrance of rye whiskey wafted through his nostrils. *God, I love that smell.* Sickles took a swig, swirling the burning spirit about in his mouth, and then he spit it out.

"God, what a waste of good Maryland whiskey," Sickles bemoaned. "Can't we rest here for a while?"

"No, General," said Tremain. "General Pleasonton warned us that Confederate cavalry was roaming in this area. So we have to make the best time possible to Littlestown, where you will be placed in a railcar and transported to the nation's capital." Four new stretcher bearers arrived. "Pick up the general and let's move out."

The soldiers gripped the poles, picked up the stretcher, and started walking.

Sickles turned his head toward Sims. "Damn it, Doc. This constant jolting is killing me. Why can't I ride in an ambulance?"

"Because I won't let you," Sims said. "I'm afraid if you ride in a wagon, the jolting will cause your stump to hemorrhage and you would bleed to death."

"Jesus, Doc. I don't know if I can take much more of this."

"You lost quite a bit of blood when the twelve-pounder busted your leg into pieces, and more during the amputation. You can't afford to bleed a speckle more of blood."

"I swear. This jolting ride on the stretcher is going to break the sutures."

"No General, it won't," Sim smiled. "After I sawed off your leg, I scraped the end and edges of the bone smooth like polished marble. Then I cut your skin flaps like a fish mouth and sewed them to form a round stump. I used several extra sutures, knowing our gallant general would jump on his horse after the chloroform wore off and lead his men into battle again."

Sickles nodded with a tight-lipped grin.

"But if I let you ride in a bouncing wagon, you will hemorrhage and you will die. Even though I'm the best surgeon in the army, I couldn't bring you back to life even if your ghost ordered me to."

Sickles nodded. "Did you send my amputated leg to the new army medical museum?"

"Yes, I put your shattered tibia and fibula in a small coffin-shaped box."

"Good. I want the bones of America's hero displayed just like those Catholic Saints whose bones are exhibited in Europe's medieval castles. Hell, we should have my bones displayed at West Point. Maybe they could inspire the Pointers to fight."

Abruptly, the stretcher jolted and he floated momentarily like a feather in a light breeze. Then he crashed back down into the canvas, the stump on his amputated right leg scraping across the stretcher's coarse canvas like a red-hot claw.

"My God!" Sickles shrieked. "Stop." The stretcher bearers halted. "Damn it, Henry. This constant jolting is killing me. It might help if the stretcher bearers across from each other walked in an opposite step."

"Let's try," Tremain said. "Stretcher bearers on my side. Walk in an opposite step from your counterpart."

Sickles tightened his grip on the two canvas poles. The two soldiers on the right side did a half shuffle step and began walking in an opposite step. After a few minutes, Sickles piped up. "That's better. Much better. Thank you."

He licked his lips, craving another swig of rye. *This time I will swallow.* "Henry, I could use another swig of whiskey."

Tremain shot a glance at Sim, who shook his head. "Your surgeon says no," Tremain, said, "but I will light a cigar for you."

"Damn doctors!" Sickles muttered.

Tremain lit a cigar and placed it in the general's mouth. He started puffing; silver-gray smoke curled and danced above his head. Ah, the lovely taste of Havana tobacco. He flicked his gaze over his cavalcade. Forty soldiers carrying rifles over their right shoulders marched to the slow staccato beat of a single drummer. A squad of cavalrymen screened the escorts, who also rotated as stretcher bearers. Two wagons carried baggage and supplies. His heart roared, pounding in his ears. He was a wounded Anglo-Saxon lord returning to his kingdom's capital.

*5:00 p.m.*
*Five miles east of Daniel Scheaffer House, traveling to Littlestown, Pennsylvania*

The thundering of approaching hooves split the drummer's tat-tooing. Sickles's heart punched against the bottom of his throat. He drew a quivery breath. *Rebel cavalry?*

"It's a courier," Tremain assured him.

The messenger slid his horse to a stop a few yards from the stretcher bearers. His sweaty hair hung down to his shoulders like the strings of a wet mop. He caught his breath and called out, "General Sickles, the Army of the Potomac has repulsed a great assault by the enemy. The Rebels are retreating from the battlefield in full force. It's a great Union victory!"

Sickles removed his hat and waved it, shouting, "What a great day for the Republic!"

Tremain bawled, "Three cheers for the Republic."

A loud chorus burst forth from the cavalcade. "Hip hip hoo-ray! Hip hip hooray! Hip hip hooray!"

The cavalcade halted for several minutes as the messenger filled in the details of the Confederate repulse. Then it started again toward Littlestown. Sickles's body surged with excitement. His stump stopped burning. He was filled with an air of jaunty restlessness.

"Henry, let's pick up the pace! I can bear it. I need to visit with Lincoln before Meade sends his version of the battle."

Sim said, "No, General. You're too weak and feeble. Major Tremain, you will keep the same steady pace, but no faster. It's my job to get the general to Washington alive so he can recover and fight another day."

Sickles shook his head. "Christ almighty, Dr. Sim. You're worse than a mother hen." Sickles turned to Tremain, walking alongside the stretcher. "Henry, Meade never wanted to fight at Gettysburg. I received his Pipe Creek circular that said he wanted to retreat from Gettysburg and fight the battle in Maryland. If I hadn't moved Third Corps forward on my own initiative, Meade would have run like hell with his tail between his legs."

Sim interrupted. "General Sickles, it is time to rest, sir. Now drink this. It's a sedative that will reduce the pain and allow you to rest."

Sickles drank the laudanum. His body began to float. *By the grace of God, the nation's hero is being escorted like a wounded medieval lord and will soon arrive in the nation's capital. Thank you, God. I am redeemed.*

## 52

# Meade — Friday, July 3

Meade rode up Little Round Top and dismounted. He winced at the suffocating stench that smothered the summit like a brimstone cloud. He stepped toward the edge of the crest overlooking Devil's Den and the wheat field. He pinched the bridge of his nose. The slope reeked of putrid gases from the rotting flesh of hundreds of bloated enemy corpses lining the face of the hill.

Sykes darted forward and saluted. "General Crawford is advancing one brigade across the wheat field and into the woods southwest."

Meade removed his hand from his nose and returned the salute. "Is General Sedgwick supporting you?"

"Yes. He sent one brigade from Sixth Corps to form a second line behind Crawford's brigade."

Meade bobbed his head. "Good. Make preparations for an all-out assault." He grimaced. "What a God-awful stench."

"The locals gave us some bottles of peppermint oil midmorning."

"I hope to hell it's working because this hill needs to be defended as long as the army remains in Gettysburg."

Sykes cracked a slight grin. "No worries. The bitching has faded; the boys are all sporting peppermint smiles."

Meade stepped toward the north edge of the summit, scanning the battlefield with his binoculars. A menacing arc of roughly 150 artillery guns guarded the center of the Confederate line.

711

Meade shook his head. "Lee wants me to counterattack his middle. So do Hancock and Pleasonton. But that would be disastrous, just like Pickett's Charge was, assaulting our artillery guns."

Meade reached into his pocket, pulled out a piece of paper, and handed it to Sykes. "Read this. It's from Hancock. He wrote it when he was being transported from the battlefield."

Sykes fished for his glasses, read the note, and handed it back. "I agree with you about attacking those cannons," Sykes said. "Grape shot crushes bones like hailstones cracking glass. Our losses will be just as horrifying if you launch an attack against those Confederate cannons."

Meade stared down the slope, shaking his head.

"I'm baffled why Sickles didn't occupy it," Sykes said. "Forcing the enemy to charge uphill is both exhausting and deadly."

"By Sickles not following orders, we damn near lost this hill. The army would have had to retreat."

"Maybe Sickles doesn't have an eye for defensive terrain?" Sykes pondered. "Moving forward and occupying the elevated Emmitsburg road area is nothing like occupying the heights of Little Round Top."

Meade shook his head. "When I asked him yesterday why he was so far forward, he looked baffled and tilted his head like a puzzled dog."

"Fifth Corps lost a lot of men yesterday because of Sickles's blunder," Sykes said, "including Colonel Vincent, who was destined to become a general and division commander."

"I lost nearly all of Sickles's corps!" Meade exclaimed, his face contorting into a scowl. He held the gaze for a moment before looking away, his lips tightly pursed. He scanned the battlefield between Cemetery Ridge and Seminary Ridge. His stomach lurched. "By the love of God, I estimate five to six million pounds of human and animal carcasses are scattered across these fields."

"I've never seen such carnage," Sykes agreed.

Meade bristled. "This war has laid waste to a decent Christian burial." He paused, lowered his voice. "Without coffins, we bury the dead like animals."

Sykes said hollowly, "At least for the Union soldiers, the burial parties cover the bodies with knapsacks, shielding them from the dirt."

"I swear to God," Meade hissed. "If embalmers start circling the battlefield like vultures, I will embalm them using a bullet. I'm sick of those scavengers swindling grieving widows."

Meade mounted his horse. "Keep me posted on General Crawford's reconnaissance against Lee's right flank."

---

*5:20 p.m.*

Meade rode down the northern slope of Little Round Top. Biddle, Captain Carpenter, and his cavalry escort were waiting. Meade led the cavalcade for a few hundred yards and halted on a crossing road as a courier galloped toward him.

The messenger halted and saluted. "General Meade, General Sickles has departed the Gettysburg area and is being carried by stretcher to Littlestown. From there, he will be transported by train to the nation's capital."

"What's his condition?" Meade said.

"He is weak from loss of blood, but is calm and collected, lying on a stretcher, hat over his eyes, smoking cigars."

"Thank you for the report," Meade said. He peered at the blood-soaked wheat field, its stalks blown down and ripped from the ground. Meade lit a cigar and stared at the mangled corpses strewn about in this hellish place. *God damn you, Lincoln. Your favorite political general murdered nearly his entire corps.*

Meade flicked the reins and started riding slowly toward Taneytown Road. He turned to Biddle, riding alongside. "Well, that's the last we will hear from Sickles. Thank God, he can't do the army or me any more harm."

"You're not worried about him spreading rumors about you when he arrives in the capital?" Biddle asked. "Lincoln will visit with him as soon as he arrives, wanting a firsthand account of the battle. Sickles will immediately start his story-spinning."

"Hell no, I'm not worried," Meade barked. "How could Sickles possibly twist what happened in his favor? The son of a bitch disobeyed my orders to occupy Little Round Top. On four different occasions he was told. Hell, he was given a damn map marking his position. I even pointed at Little Round Top, telling him he had to occupy it."

"Sickles might argue you did not ride over and review his position."

"God damn it, James, I sent Hunt over to examine his front. Remember, I had just received a signal report from Little Round Top that a large enemy force was moving from my left flank to my right flank. At the same time, Slocum was reporting a large enemy force gathering on my right flank for an attack."

"I'm not as confident as you are, General, about what Sickles is capable of doing. If Sickles is willing to disobey orders and move his corps a half mile in front of the defensive line without regret, I believe he is quite capable of seeking to take all the glory for your victory at Gettysburg."

"Let me be clear, James," Meade blasted. "I don't give a damn about glory. So help me God, I'm not a hero. I protested like hell against taking command of the army. That's not heroic. As for the heroes," Meade pointed toward the burial parties working their way onto the battlefield, "we're getting ready to bury them."

Biddle was silent for a moment, acknowledging the fallen. "I hope you're right about Sickles, General. But that weasel could teach Machiavelli a few things. I truly believe, if given the chance, Sickles could convince the Pope that he was a Protestant."

"Enough!" Meade turned his horse away from the gruesome killing field. "That's the last we will hear from Sickles."

They rode north on the Taneytown Road. George rode up and saluted. "General Meade, the medical staff have turned the Leister House into a hospital. We've set a makeshift headquarters about a quarter-mile south of the house."

"I'm surprised," Meade said. "The Leister House was hit by a dozen or more shells, and the yard is filled with horse carcasses."

"The army engineers fixed the roof so it can provide shelter from the rain." George pointed toward the east. "We established your new headquarters in the shade of a patch of woods about two hundred yards over there."

Meade peered where George was pointing. His army commander's flag flew next to four large white tents pitched near the patch of woods. He turned his horse off Taneytown Road and followed George. The shadows of the trees dappled the rolling, grassy field. His horse cut a swath through the sweltering humidity; his skin glistened and the nape of his neck was damp. He removed his slouch hat and wiped his glove over his brow, his cheeks, his neck. He centered his hat on his head, removed his glasses, and wiped the beads of sweat from the lenses.

There was a beehive of activity ahead; a small town of white tents was popping up. Near the white tent sporting his command flag was a white-canvassed supply wagon. His cook was stirring a cauldron dangling from a tripod. His stomach growled. *Damn, I'm famished.*

---

*6:30 p.m.*
*Meade's new army headquarters along the Taneytown Road*

Meade, Biddle, and George dismounted at the new army headquarters and Meade handed his horse's reins to a groom. General Williams emerged from a tent on the edge of the patch of woods. He walked toward Meade with a big smile, sweat dripping from his face. "I've received a signal report from General Sykes. His brigade is engaging the enemy in the wheat field area and having good success."

"Excellent," Meade said. "So, this is army headquarters for this evening. How long have you been here?"

"I arrived about an hour ago. We've set up tables in your tent and mine. But it's almost impossible to work inside the tents. They're hotter than brick ovens." Williams pulled out a handkerchief and wiped his face. "So we've set up a map table outside your tent next to your rocking chair. My guess is that the staff will sleep on the ground outside the tents tonight. It's just too damn humid. It reminds me of those tropical Florida summers."

"What reserves can we give Sykes to reinforce his success?"

"We don't have many intact units near the left flank to support Sykes. The problem is that you moved roughly 13,000 soldiers to the center of the line and now many of the units are

715

not with their corps commanders. Sedgwick is reporting that five of his eight brigades are scattered about the battlefield, supporting other units."

"Damn. It was my hope that Sixth Corps would lead a counterattack with Fifth Corps in support. But it seems unlikely they'll be available."

"If you plan to use any of Slocum's Twelfth Corps for an attack, it would take them almost till dark before they were in position," Williams added.

Meade reached into his pocket and removed a folded message. "Listen to this. Hancock dictated this message while traveling in an ambulance to the hospital." Meade adjusted his thick glasses. "I will read you part of it. 'We have won a victory, and nothing is wanting to make it decisive but that you should carry your intention…'" Meade paused and wiped his brow. "Should we counterattack?"

"Yes, Hancock is right," Williams said. "There is a window of opportunity to achieve a total victory over Lee like Wellington did over Napoleon at Waterloo."

"Damn it, Seth. I'm well aware of the facts of Waterloo, including Wellington having a fresh army available under Prussian General Blucher to follow up the initial success. I don't have a fresh corps, unless you can crap a goddamn Prussian army on the battlefield in the next half hour."

Meade winced, grabbing his chest. The old lung wound flared. "The real question isn't whether to counterattack—it's whether we are in any condition to counterattack."

"General, I'm not making a case for a counterattack to achieve a total victory," Williams exclaimed. "When Hancock wrote the note he had no idea of the condition of the army and your ability to launch an attack. Winfield merely was pointing out an opportunity existed."

"Neither Sixth nor Fifth Corps are pressed up to launch a counterattack."

"They won't be before dark," Williams said.

"We've lost so many senior officers. Reynolds is gone. Hancock, Gibbon, Webb, and Sickles are wounded. We've lost several division and brigade commanders." Meade stared at his boots. "I'm not sure any of the new corps and division commanders I appoint this evening will be equal to the task."

"Sykes just replaced you as Fifth Corps commander; Newton replaced Reynolds as First Corps commander two days ago. Who will you appoint to command Sickles's Third Corps and Hancock's Second Corps? You will also have to find a replacement for Butterfield."

"Jesus," Meade muttered. He reached inside his coat and removed two cigars, handing one to Williams. They lit them and stood silent for a few moments. The sun was sinking lower over South Mountain, the amber light draining away with the heat of the day.

"Time is not on our side," Williams said. "The men are terribly fatigued and moving slowly. We've beat them today and our boys are bushed."

"I'm tired as well," Meade said. His knees wobbled and his muddled mind felt like he had been head-butted. He trundled over to his rocking chair, which had been placed outside his tent next to a table made from a flat piece of wood sitting on two barrels, and sat down. Williams walked over to speak with his staff.

Meade puffed on his cigar. *Don't come to a decision until you can be sure it is the correct one. An uncoordinated counterattack could be the ruin of everything.* He yawned. When was the last time he had slept more than a few hours? His stomach growled. He was starving. The army must be as well.

He turned to Biddle. "Check on the resupply effort. We need to get both food and ammunition moved to our men. And I'm starved. I saw my cook brewing something when I arrived. Is my dinner ready?"

Biddle departed.

Sharpe approached, carrying papers. "I have updates for you on Union and Confederate casualties."

Meade stared at him with eyes focused elsewhere, in a field of massacred soldiers, and gave an almost imperceptible nod.

Sharpe laid the papers on the table. "I estimate Union casualties around 23,000, and more than a fourth of the Army of

717

the Potomac. The Confederate casualties are 28,000, more than a third of Lee's army."

"Jesus, over 50,000 casualties in three days," Meade whispered. He drew a ragged breath. "Which Union corps suffered the highest casualties?"

"First Corps, 6,000 casualties: Reynolds was killed and five of his seven brigade commanders were wounded. Second Corps, 4,400 casualties, including the loss of Hancock, Gibbon, three brigade commanders killed, and three brigade commanders wounded, including Webb. Third Corps, 4,200 casualties: 17 out of 37 regimental commanders were casualties. Eleventh Corps suffered 3,800 casualties. The lowest casualties were in Sixth Corps, 240; Twelfth Corps, 1,000; and Fifth Corps, 2,100. Hunt's Artillery Reserve was 240 and the Cavalry Corps about 850," Sharpe said.

Meade swiped at an evening bug whining around his head just as his cook approached, carrying a plate. "General Meade, your dinner is ready."

"I'm starved, thank you. Please put the plate on the table. And bring another plate for Colonel Sharpe."

"Thank you, General Meade."

Meade pointed. "Grab that chair over there and please join me."

Sharpe grabbed the chair and sat opposite Meade at the table. The cook returned with a plate of food for Sharpe and quickly departed.

Sharpe smiled. "I guess you proved the Northern newspapers wrong by whipping the ravenous red-eyed beast running around Pennsylvania unopposed. You captured twenty-eight Rebel battle flags in today's fighting."

"It was too damn close," Meade said. "The Rebels breached the stone wall like a rogue wave. Just no supporting power behind it."

"This was a great victory," Sharpe said. "The Army of the Potomac's first one against Lee. Against all odds, General, you assumed command three days before the battle, and after three days of horrific fighting, you out-generaled Lee and handed him his first defeat."

"I sure moved around a hell of a number of reinforcements," Meade said.

"On July 2, you rushed 17,000 to the danger area, and today, you moved 13,000 to reinforce Gibbon's 6,000 troops against Pickett's 13,000 troops," Sharpe continued. "You gave the troops of the Army of the Potomac the leadership they have been waiting for and that they deserve."

"I was surprised how well the boys responded to me relieving the popular General Hooker," Meade said. "I believed that we needed a charismatic army commander to defeat Lee. I guess we proved that wrong over the last three days."

"Popularity is overrated," Sharpe said. "Men want a leader who has a strong character. It's character, not charisma, that forges camaraderie and combat effectiveness."

Meade raised his chin. His cook returned with two cups of coffee and removed their empty plates.

Meade sipped the coffee, letting the hot brew shock his nerves.

"I've observed you for the past six days, General Meade, under the most horrific conditions any new commander could face without warning. General, you have character, in spades, although I might add it's a bit salty."

"I'd like to think that my hot temper is like chili pepper. It adds a little spice." Meade smiled. "This army is loaded with men of character. There were lots of impressive performances out there. The Twentieth Maine on Little Round Top; the First Minnesota on Cemetery Ridge; the New York Brigade on Culp's Hill—heroes, all of them. And one of the keys to the victory was having you as my intelligence commander."

"The intelligence group performed well, especially Captain Dahlgren, capturing the secret documents from President Davis to General Lee," Sharpe said.

Meade furrowed his brow. "Warfare changed at Gettysburg. The Napoleonic frontal attacks we learned at West Point and used effectively in the Mexican War are becoming obsolete.

What is emerging is the beginning of the dominance of the tactical defense."

"I agree," said Sharpe. "Buford's brigade of outnumbered cavalry armed with repeating rifles was able to hold off Harry Heth's division for several hours, allowing Reynolds to arrive and provide support. Greene's brigade of outnumbered infantry, hunkered behind well-constructed trenches on Culp's Hill, enabled him to hold off Johnson's division until Slocum could reinforce him. Pickett's frontal bayonet charge failed miserably against our long-range artillery, short-range canister shot, and rifled weapons behind the stone wall.

"My guess is that Lee will start his retreat back to Virginia very soon."

Meade tapped his finger on his spectacles, pushing them up the damp bridge of his nose. "We'll see."

"Did you learn any lessons?" Sharpe asked.

"Hell, yes," Meade said. "Lincoln nearly lost this battle. The president should have never swapped out army commanders a few days before the battle. He should have fired Hooker right after Chancellorsville. The first damn time I met with all my corps commanders was the evening of the second day of the battle."

Sharpe put his hands behind his back.

"Appointing a political general who murdered his wife's lover in cold blood to lead Third Corps was beyond absurd. Damn politicians. What was Lincoln thinking? My mistake was putting unfounded trust in Sickles and believing he would follow orders. I won't make that mistake again. Sickles murdered nearly his entire corps."

"It's clear Lincoln favors politics over military skill in championing amateurs to command corps," Sharpe said.

"Gettysburg was a special place for us to fight," Meade mused. "We will never be in a place like this again. Halleck gave me the power to promote juniors over seniors in this battle. That's how I was able to send Hancock forward on the first day to take command of the fighting even though Howard was senior. That's also how I was able to promote Sykes to command Fifth Corps,

Newman to First Corps, and Gibbon to temporarily command Second Corps, even though they were junior in seniority."

"Perhaps one of your best junior officer promotions in the cavalry corps was Lieutenant Armstrong Custer to brigadier general," Sharpe said. "Custer delivered a licking of Stuart's cavalry in today's fighting."

Meade rubbed his neck. "Custer performed brilliantly. But I will never have this promotion power again."

"Why?" Sharpe said. "If it worked at Gettysburg, why can't you keep it for the next battle?"

"Halleck prefers short leashes on his army commanders. If he can't control promotions, what use is he to Lincoln?" Meade said.

"Maybe Halleck should learn to trust his new army commander," Sharpe said.

Meade cracked a smile. "Trust is not a strong suit of the White House boys."

Meade removed his slouch hat, wiped his hand over his scalp, and replaced the hat. "Gettysburg was special because the Army of the Potomac could stay on the defense for the entire battle. Logistics dictated that Lee had to attack us or retreat to Virginia. If Lee decides to retreat tonight or tomorrow, the Army of the Potomac will be back to its old game of chasing Lee and attacking him behind entrenched defenses."

"The Rebels showed utter contempt for the Army of the Potomac by attacking the middle of our lines," Sharpe said. "But we handed them their asses."

"Lee won't make that mistake again. I still wish we could have fought this battle at the Pipe Creek line. It was much stronger in its natural defenses and closer to our logistics heads and a much shorter distance to the Potomac to cut off Lee's retreat."

---

*7:44 p.m.*
*Sunset*

Meade and Sharpe lit cigars outside the general's tent. Meade glanced at the fiery red sky stretching over South Mountain. The rich reds were bleeding into the oranges; both would soon fade

721

into darkness. An uneasiness gnawed at him. As each minute ticked by, his reluctance to order an all-out assault was growing.

"Do you remember Sickles's fiasco, attacking at midnight during the Battle of Chancellorsville?" Meade asked.

"I do, and Sickles's men were rested," Sharpe said.

Meade shook his head and walked over to Williams. "I'm going to abandon Sykes's assault on Lee's right flank for tonight. The army is not in a position to support any success he may have. I'm also not sure what Lee is planning to do tomorrow. He might withdraw or stay and fight. Let's wait and see."

"I agree with your decision," Williams said. "This is the Union's first great win against Lee's army. With the battered condition the army is in and with the growing darkness, it's better to hold on to what we've achieved and not risk throwing it away."

"I'm determined not to allow the Confederates to slip away unmolested," Meade said. "But I'm no fool. I've learned a key fact about Lee. His great ability is defensive warfare. He loves watching us cross a field of fire as he sits behind breastworks and blasts the hell out of us. It's a great way to fight a battle. But Lee is not so great as an offensive general. Antietam and Gettysburg proved that."

Meade walked over to Sharpe, Biddle, and his personal aides. "I don't want to risk all we gained today. For three days the fight has been a tactical donnybrook, and we got the best of Lee. Now we are back to tracking, maneuvering, looking for opportunities to attack him. But we can begin that tomorrow."

---

*8:36 p.m.*

Meade met with Williams, fighting to keep his heavy eyes open. He wrote a dispatch to Halleck in Washington, telling him the army had repulsed the enemy today. As soon as he'd sent off the dispatch, he was flooded with self-doubt. Detailed planning was the way to reduce his doubts about pursuing Lee. Lee was a formidable opponent when maneuvering to gain the defensive advantage.

"I hear that Sickles is already spreading rumors that he is the willing hero of Gettysburg by virtue of moving his corps forward and forcing you to stay and fight after you told Butterfield to issue retreat orders," Williams remarked.

Meade stared. "Are you serious, Seth? Sickles is saying he is the hero of Gettysburg?"

Williams squared his shoulders. "General, with all due respect, you're the unwilling hero of Gettysburg. Sickles is already starting rumors that your orders were vague and he prevented you from retreating from Gettysburg."

"A blind idiot could see the strategic value of Little Round Top. In moving forward, Sickles isolated himself and jeopardized the entire Union line. That's my defense against Sickles."

"General, you must be more careful with reporters and politicians. Sickles will play dirty politics with both of them. They can hurt you by what they write and say behind your back. They can damage your reputation."

"Jesus Christ, Seth, I'm not fighting Lee in the court of public opinion. If that was the case, McClellan would be still commanding the army. Hell, his generals, soldiers, reporters, and politicians loved him. The crazy thing, Seth, is that the Confederates don't give a tinker's damn about the popularity of our generals." Meade paused. "Does Sickles care about the number of his soldiers who died unnecessarily today because he wanted to be a hero?"

"No. Sickles is the type of person who will not admit to making a mistake, let alone disobeying orders."

"Because he suffered a severe battlefield wound and his leg was amputated, he won't be rejoining this army," Meade said. "So I'm going to be generous and write in my official report that he misinterpreted my orders. I'm not going to openly impugn his judgment."

"Isn't General Ewell hobbling around and still one of Lee's corps commanders?"

"Yes," Meade said. "But Sickles will not be rejoining the Army of the Potomac."

*9:00 p.m.*

Meade turned just beyond his tent and walked toward a mound of boulders, the burdens of this day slowing him to little more than a crawl. He found a soft spot for his blanket on the ground under the open skies. He rubbed the back of his neck and felt his tense muscles begin to let go. He let his weary mind wander over this fateful week.

With the exception of Sickles, his lieutenants had accepted him as their commander, and he had led them to victory. He had done a good job in managing his corps commanders, giving them initiative to react to changing situations on the battlefield. He would never again place unfounded trust in lieutenants who lacked character.

He cracked a slight grin. Maybe the Greeks were right. The forthright hedgehog sometimes does beat the wily fox. But a quiet leader is a realist who expects unpleasant surprises. And Lee's army was still sitting across from the Army of the Potomac.

He removed his horn-rimmed spectacles, put them in his coat pocket, and closed his eyes tightly, savoring the wet blackness and the soft, splatting rain. He lay down and fell dead to the world, momentarily joining the still bodies scattering the fields.

————— • —————

*11:30 p.m.*

Raindrops pelted his face. He opened his eyes and squinted. A downpour had erupted. Sheets of rain fell straight down from the thick dome of darkness engulfing him. He rose to his feet and perched on a large, flat boulder, hatless, his back as stiff as a board. A wretched weariness gripped his body. He took a breath, coughed violently, his wounded lung wheezing with a tearing pain. *What's your plan tomorrow? Wait-and-see is no plan.* He had reached his limit. For six days and seven nights he had labored relentlessly, planning, moving, leading, fighting.

He needed more sleep. He lay back down on a flat rock and closed his eyes while his mind continued to fight. God, he wished he were falling asleep on the Pipe Creek Ridge. That was a great plan. *But between plans and execution rage the winds of war.* He had chosen to ride them, and they carried him to this place,

724

this day, this battle. A quiet, anything-but-charismatic leader of men who fought against his destiny with every ounce of his will, to no avail: despite his stubborn reluctance, he was doomed to play this hand on the roll of Lincoln's dice. Still, he alone had made the decision to fight at Gettysburg. And the cost of success was the lives of some 23,000 men entrusted to him, sacrificed so the Republic could live.

He shuddered at the memory, branded forever in his mind, of the carnage, the sheer, brutal butchery, of the last three days. Was this how the White House defined success? Or was Colonel Hardie riding a train to visit him again in the middle of this night, heralding a new commander of the army? Meade could hardly blame him. Losing a fourth of the Army of the Potomac could easily justify his immediate dismissal. Was this his ultimate failure?

Or was Gettysburg, for all its acts of courageous duty and shameful cowardice, noble sacrifice and selfish ambition, inspiring devotion and heartbreaking loss, the Republic's most important victory since the Battle of Yorktown?

Tomorrow was the fourth of July, and he would learn his fate soon enough.

Hancock, surrounded by three of his division commanders:
Francis C. Barlow, David B. Birney,
and John Gibbon during the Wilderness campaign

# ⚞⚞ Army Order of Battle ⚟⚟

## ———————— Army of the Potomac ————————

**Major General George Meade**

Chief of Staff: Maj. Gen. Daniel Butterfield
Adjutant General: Brig. Gen. Seth Williams
Chief Engineer: Brig. Gen. Gouverneur Warren
Provost Marshal: Brig. Gen. Marsena Patrick
Chief Quartermaster: Brig. Gen. Rufus Ingalls
Chief of Artillery: Brig. Gen. Henry Hunt
Bureau of Military Information: Col. George Sharpe

## ———————— First Corps ————————

**Maj. Gen. John Reynolds (killed July 1)**
**Maj. Gen. John Newton (assumed command July 2)**

### First Division: Brig. Gen. James Wadsworth
First Brigade: Brig. Gen. Solomon Meredith (wounded July 1)
   Col. William Roberston (assumed command Culp's Hill July 2)
   6th Wisconsin: Lt. Col. Rufus Dawes
Second Brigade: Brig. Gen. Lysander Cutler

### Second Division: Brig. Gen. John Robinson
First Brigade: Brig. Gen. Gabriel Paul
Second Brigade: Brig. Gen. Henry Baxter

### Third Division: Maj. Gen. Abner Doubleday
First Brigade: Brig. Gen. Thomas Rowley
Second Brigade: Col. Roy Stone
Third Brigade: Brig. Gen. George Stannard
   13th Vermont: Col. Francis Randall
   14th Vermont: Col. William Nichols
   16th Vermont: Col. Wheelock Veazey

### First Corps Artillery Brigade: Col. Charles Wainwright
Maine, 5th US Battery E: Capt. Greenleaf Stevens – 6 Napoleons

## ——————————— Second Corps ———————————

**Maj. Gen. Winfield Hancock**

### First Division: Brig. Gen. John Caldwell
First Brigade: Col. Edward Cross
Second Brigade: Col. Patrick Kelly
Third Brigade: Brig. Gen. Samuel Zook
Fourth Brigade: Col. John Brooke

### Second Division: Brig. Gen. John Gibbon
First Brigade: Brig. Gen. William Harrow
    19th Maine: Col. Francis Heath
    15th Massachusetts: Col. George Ward
    1st Minnesota: Col. William Colvill
    82nd New York: Lt. Col. James Huston
Second Brigade: Brig. Gen. Alexander Webb
Third Brigade: Col. Normal Hall

### Third Division: Brig. Gen. Alexander Hays
First Brigade: Col. Samuel Carroll
Second Brigade: Col. Thomas Smyth
Third Brigade: Col. George Willard

### Second Corps Artillery Brigade: Capt. John Hazard
4th US Battery A: Lt. Alonzo Cushing – six 3-inch ordnance rifles

## ——————————— Third Corps ———————————

**Maj. Gen. Daniel Sickles**

### First Division: Maj. Gen. David Birney
First Brigade: Brig. Gen. Charles Graham
Second Brigade: Brig. Gen. Hobart Ward
Third Brigade: Col. Regis de Trobriand

### Second Division: Brig. Gen. Andrew Humphreys
First Brigade: Brig. Gen. Joseph Carr
Second Brigade: Col. William Brewster
Third Brigade: Col. George Burling

### Third Corps Artillery Brigade: Capt. George Randolph

# Fifth Corps

## Maj. Gen. George Sykes

### First Division: Brig. Gen. James Barnes
First Brigade: Col. Williams Tilton
Second Brigade: Col. Jacob Sweitzer
Third Brigade: Col. Strong Vincent
  20th Maine: Col. Joshua Chamberlain
  16th Michigan: Lt. Col. Norval Welch
  44th New York: Col. James Rice
  83rd Pennsylvania: Capt. Orpheus Woodward

### Second Division: Brig. Gen. Romeyn Ayres
First Brigade: Col. Hannibal Day
Second Brigade: Col. Sidney Burbank
Third Brigade: Brig. Gen. Stephen Weed
  140th New York Col. Patrick O'Rorke

### Third Division: Brig. Gen. Samuel Crawford
First Brigade: Col. William McCandless
Third Brigade: Col. Joseph Fisher

### Fifth Corps Artillery Brigade: Capt. Augustus Martin
5th US Battery D: Lt. Charles Hazlett – six 10-pounder Parrotts

# Sixth Corps

## Maj. Gen. John Sedgwick

### First Division: Brig. Gen. Horatio Wright
First Brigade: Brig. Gen. Alfred Torbet
Second Brigade: Brig. Gen. Joseph Bartlett
Third Brigade: Brig. Gen. David Russell

### Second Division: Brig. Gen. Albion Howe
Second Brigade: Col. Lewis Grant
Third Brigade: Brig. Gen. Thomas Neill

### Third Division: Maj. Gen. John Newton (assumed command of First Corps July 2)
### Brig. Gen. Frank Wheaton (assumed command of Third Division after Newton departed.)
First Brigade: Brig. Gen. Alexander Shaler
Second Brigade: Col. Henry Eustis
Third Brigade: Col. David Nevin

### Sixth Corps Artillery Brigade: Col. Charles Tompkins

## Eleventh Corps

**Maj. Gen. Oliver Howard**

First Division: Brig. Gen. Francis Barlow
First Brigade: Col. Leopold von Gilsa
Second Brigade: Brig. Gen. Adelbert Ames

Second Division: Brig. Gen. Adolph von Steinwehr
First Brigade: Col. Charles Coster
Second Brigade: Col. Orland Smith

Third Division: Maj. Gen. Carl Schurz
First Brigade: Brig. Gen. Alexander Schimmelfennig
Second Brigade: Col. Wladimir Kryzanowski

Eleventh Corps Artillery Brigade: Maj. Thomas Osborn

## Twelfth Corps

Maj. Gen. Henry Slocum

First Division: Brig. Gen. Alpheus Williams
First Brigade: Col. Archibald McDougall
Second Brigade: Brig. Gen. Henry Lockwood
Third Brigade: Brig. Gen. Thomas Ruger

Second Division: Brig. Gen. John Geary
First Brigade: Col. Charles Candy
Second Brigade: Col. George Cobham, Jr.
Third Brigade: Brig. Gen. George Greene
60th New York: Col. Abel Godard
78th New York: Lt. Col. Herbert Von Hammerstein
102nd New York: Col. James Lane
137th New York: Col. David Ireland
149th New York: Lt. Col. Charles Randall

Twelfth Corps Artillery Brigade: Lt. Edward Muhlenberg

## Cavalry Corps

**Maj. Gen. Alfred Pleasonton**

First Division: Brig. Gen. John Buford
First Brigade: Col. William Gamble
Second Brigade: Col. Thomas Devin
Reserve Brigade: Brig. Gen. Wesley Merritt

## Second Division: Brig. Gen. David Gregg
First Brigade: Col. John McIntosh
Second Brigade: Col. Pennock Huey
Third Brigade: Col. Irvin Gregg

## Third Division: Brig. Gen. Judson Kilpatrick
First Brigade: Brig. Gen. Elon Farnsworth
Second Brigade: Brig. Gen. George Custer

## ——————— Artillery Commander ———————
**Brig. Gen. Henry Hunt**

## ——————— Artillery Reserve ———————
**Brig. Gen. Robert Tyler**

First Brigade (Regular): Capt. Dunbar Ransom
4th US Battery C: Lt. Evan Thomas – six 12-pounder Napoleons

# Army of Northern Virginia

**General Robert E. Lee**

## First Corps

**Lt. Gen. James Longstreet**

Maj. Gen. Lafayette McLaws' Division
Maj. Gen. John Hood's Division
Maj. Gen. George Pickett's Division

## Second Corps

**Lt. Gen. Richard Ewell**

Maj. Gen. Jubal Early's Division
Maj. Gen. Edward Johnson's Division
Maj. Gen. Robert Rodes' Division

## Third Corps

**Lt. Gen. Ambrose P. Hill**

Maj. Gen. Richard Anderson's Division
Brig. Gen. Cadmus Wilcox's Brigade
Brig. Gen. Ambrose Wright's Brigade

Maj. Gen. W. Dorsey Pender's Division
Maj. Gen. Henry Heth's Division

## Cavalry Division

**Maj. Gen. J.E.B. Stuart**

## Artillery Commander

**Brig. Gen. William Pendleton**

# Acknowledgments

With gratitude for the patience and encouragement of my brilliant critique group of friends and mentors who read the entire manuscript, I'm grateful to the following: Charles Coolidge, Peter Poulos, James Cutchin, Erv Rokke, Andrew Waskie, Christopher Miller, Paul Madera, Tom Anton, Buddhika "Jay" Jayamaha, Dennis and Debra Barbello, Paul Van Riper, and Lynne Pierce.

With special thanks to those who read the early chapters of the book and provided critiques and suggestions, I'm grateful to the following: Reg Riley, Sidney Chapin, Richard Sisk, John Fox, Anthony Tingle, Paul DeCarolis, Shawn Hartsfield, Andrew Pierce, Nathan Pierce, Hannah King, Albert Eaton, Keith Uebele, and Steve Stigall.

A huge, heartfelt thank-you to John Tim Lewis, whose personal counsel and direction have been indispensable. His insights were critical in understanding and developing General George Meade's character.

This book would not have been written without the help and support of some amazing people, including JoAnne Bishop, Ryan Burke, Guy Walsh, Larry Fiore, and Tim, Molly, and Kelly Lewis.

My profound gratitude to Fred Rainbow and Julie Olver, who provided unwavering support in this hugely ambitious project, and for providing invaluable developmental editing.

Thank you to Aaron Matney for his artistic drawings and to the gifted graphic designer Kim Murray. Thank you to Dale Gallon for permitting me to use his painting *Expecting a Battle* for the front cover.

Editor Peter Delaney masterfully brought his skills as eagle-eyed scrutineer to the text, offering his corrections, comments, and verdicts.

Heartfelt thanks to Lori Brown, the most gracious and capable editor an author could hope for. Your keen-eyed editing and tireless support through the whole writing process was magnificent. Thank you for crafting the superb back-cover copy. You're a true friend and champion.

A great debt of gratitude to my publisher, Lisa Norman, who had just returned from a visit to Gettysburg with her husband and saw the merit in Meade's story and its window into the hidden truth of the Union victors. Thank you so much for championing this story about one of America's greatest reluctant heroes. Without your support, Meade's revelatory story would still remain hidden.

Greg Bennett—friend, colleague, listener, and always a voice of encouragement. Thank you.

Dick McConn—a mentor, friend, and Air Force Academy Distinguished Graduate, who exemplifies General George Meade's quiet leadership of character, never seeking fame or glory in doing his duty to his family, his academy, and his nation.

Last, but by no means least, my largest thanks go to my wife, Lynne, always a voice of encouragement, who has been fighting alongside General Meade's side for the past several years.